The
Collected Papers
of
Sherlock
Holmes

Volume VII – Annals
(19 Holmes Adventures,
3 Scripts, and a Poem)

New Sherlock Holmes

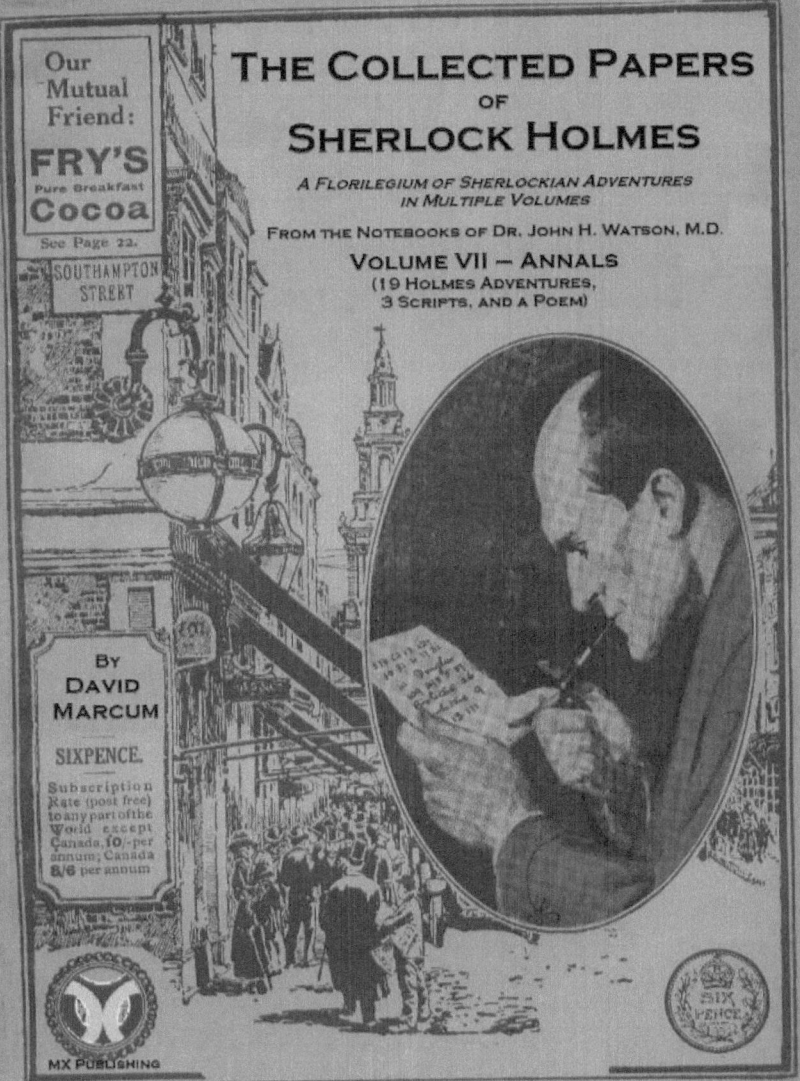

THE COLLECTED PAPERS
OF
SHERLOCK HOLMES

A Florilegium of Sherlockian Adventures in Multiple Volumes

FROM THE NOTEBOOKS OF DR. JOHN H. WATSON, M.D.

VOLUME VII — ANNALS
(19 HOLMES ADVENTURES, 3 SCRIPTS, AND A POEM)

By
DAVID MARCUM

MX PUBLISHING

SIX PENCE

Published by MX PUBLISHING, 335 PRINCESS PARK MANOR, London, England.

ISBN Hardback 978-1-80424-583-5
ISBN Paperback 978-1-80424-584-2
AUK ePub ISBN 978-1-80424-585-9
AUK PDF ISBN 978-1-80424-586-6

Published in the UK by
MX Publishing
335 Princess Park Manor, Royal Drive,
London, N11 3GX
www.mxpublishing.co.uk

David Marcum can be reached at:
thepapersofsherlockholmes@gmail.com

Cover design by Brian Belanger
www.belangerbooks.com and *www.redbubble.com/people/zhahadun*

Internal illustrations by Sidney Paget
Strand Title Page illustration by Frank wile
Various Photographs by David Marcum

CONTENTS

Forewords

Muniments

Three Sherlockian Scripts

Sources

☐ "It's Always Tme" (*A Poem*) *The MX Book of New Sherlock Holmes Stories – Part XII: Some Untold Cases (1894-1902)* (Originally published under the sobriquet *Anon.*)

☐ "The Abridge Disappearance" *The MX Book of New Sherlock Holmes Stories – Part XXXVII: 2023 Annual (1875-1889)*

☐ "The Intervention of the Dark" *No Holidays for Holmes*

☐ "The Peculiar Affair of the Three Owed Deaths" *Sherlock Holmes: Adventures in the Realms of H.P. Lovecraft*

☐ "Death at the Beadle's Store" *– Mr. Holmes' Neighborhood*

☐ "The Texas Legation Business" *The MX Book of New Sherlock Holmes Stories – Part XXXVIII: 2023 Annual (1889-1896)*

☐ "A Dreadful Record of Sin" *The MX Book of New Sherlock Holmes Stories – Part XLI: Further Untold Cases (1877-1892)*

☐ "The Exploited Assassins" *The MX Book of New Sherlock Holmes Stories – Part XLIII: 2024 Annual (1874-1888)*

☐ "The Dunfermline Tarriance" *Sherlock Holmes: A Year of Mystery 1883*

☐ "The Faulty Gallows" *Sherlock Holmes: A Year of Mystery 1885*

☐ "The Laodicean Letters" *The MX Book of New Sherlock Holmes Stories – Part XL: Further Untold Cases (1879-1886)*

☐ "The Jephson Affair" *Sherlock Holmes: A Year of Mystery 1884*

☐ "The Unintended Offenses" *– Steel True, Blade Straight – 2022 Annual*

☐ "Fate's Brushes" *– Steel True, Blade Straight – 2023 Annual*

☐ "The Tracking and Arrest of a Cold-Blooded Scoundrel" *The MX Book of New Sherlock Holmes Stories – Part XLII: Further Untold Cases (1894-1922)*

☐ "A Bucket's Worth of Help" *The MX Book of New Sherlock Holmes Stories – Part XLIV: 2024 Annual (1889-1897)*

☐ "A Meeting at the Lyons Café" *The Detective and the Clergyman: The Adventures of Sherlock Holmes and Father Brown*

☐ "The Curious Actions of Captain Graves" *Sherlock Holmes: A Year of Mystery 1886*

☐ "Gruner's Diary" *The MX Book of New Sherlock Holmes Stories – Part XLV: 2024 Annual (1898-1917)*

☐ "The Curious Circumstances of the Imitation Ripper" *The MX Book of New Sherlock Holmes Stories – Part XXXIX: 2023 Annual (189701923)*

☐ "The Terrible Tragedy of Litton House" Text version originally published as part of "The Haunting of Sutton House" in *The Papers of Sherlock Holmes* (2011, 2013), and as a script in *Sherlock Holmes Mystery Magazine*, No. 20 (July 2016). Performed on Imagination Theater November 24, 2013.

☐ "The Singular Affair at Sissinghurst Castle" Text version originally published in *The Papers of Sherlock Holmes* (2011, 2013), and as a script in *Sherlock Holmes Mystery Magazine*, No. 23 (November 2015). Performed on Imagination Theater November 23, 2014.

☐ "The London Wheel" Text version originally published in *The MX Book of New Sherlock Holmes Stories – Part IV: 2016 Annual*, and as a script performed live at the *Jubilee@221b* Conference, Toronto, Canada, September 25, 2022.

These additional adventures are contained in

The Collected Papers of Sherlock Holmes

Volume I – Tales
(9 Short Stories and a Novel)
The Papers of Sherlock Holmes (9 Short Stories)
The Adventure of the Least Winning Woman
The Adventure of the Treacherous Tea
The Singular Affair at Sissinghurst Castle
The Adventure of the Second Chance
The Haunting of Sutton House
The Adventure of the Missing Missing Link
The Affair of The Brother's Request
The Adventure of the Madman's Ceremony
The Adventure of the Other Brother
and
Sherlock Holmes and A Quantity of Debt (A Novel)

Volume II – Records
(5 Short Stories and a Novel)
Sherlock Holmes – Tangled Skeins
The Mystery at Kerrett's Rood
The Curious Incident of the Goat-Cart Man
The Matter of Boz's Last Letter
The Tangled Skein at Birling Gap
The Gower Street Murder
and
Sherlock Holmes and The Eye of Heka (A Novel)

Volume III – Accounts
(22 Holmes Adventures)
The Adventure of the Pawnbroker's Daughter
The Problem of the Holy Oil
The Trusted Advisor
An Actor and a Rare One
The Unnerved Estate Agent
The Cat's Meat Lady of Cavendish Square

(Continued on the next page . . . .)

Volume IV – Narratives
(19 Holmes Adventures)

(Continued on the next page . . . .)

Volume V – Chronicles
(20 Holmes Adventures)

The Stolen Relic
The Helverton Inheritance
The Carroun Document
The Reappearance of Mr. James Phillimore
The Keadby Cross
The Rhayader Affair
The Cliddesden Questions
The Affair of the Mother's Return
The Painting in the Parlour
The Two Bullets
The Coombs Contrivance
The True Account of the Bushell Street Killing
The Polmayne Puzzles
The Curious Cardboard Boxes
The Bizarre Affair of the Octagon House
The Peculiar Persecution of Mr. Druitt
The Service for the American Colonel
The Rescue at Ypres
The Problem of the Hindhead Minister
The Edinburgh Bankers

Volume VI – Muniments
(21 Holmes Adventures)

The Fashionably Dressed Girl
The Christmas Ghost of Crailloch Taigh
The Curious Affair of the Temporal Traveler
The Father Christmas Brigade
Some Additional Notes Regarding Mr. Melas
The Vodou Drum
The Tragic Affair at the Millennium Manor
The Canterbury Manifesto
The Noel Street Oracle
The Well-Lit Séance
The Templarian Tattoo
The Betrayer Moon
The Distasteful Affair of the Minatory Messages
The First Spivey Encounter

(Continued on the next page . . . .)

As always, this is for Rebecca and Dan, with all my love

"It's all one case."
by David Marcum

It's all about playing *The Game*.

That's the bottom-line reason behind these stories. And what is *The Game*? For those who don't know, it's reading the Sherlock Holmes stories with the firm belief that he and Watson were *real historical figures*. That Dr. Watson *wrote* the stories, and Sir Arthur Conan Doyle was his *Literary Agent*. That Our Heroes actually *lived* in Baker Street (for a couple of decades, off and on, and *not* forever) and solved real cases for real people, even if names and places and dates were changed and obfuscated to protect the innocent, or maybe because Watson's handwriting was bad, or because of some hidden agenda that the Literary Agent needed to fulfill.

By acknowledging that Holmes and Watson were real, living, breathing, functioning people, then it's a given that were born, lived, and died. (No magic immortal detectives need apply!) And if they were born and lived and died, then these lives occurred across a fixed period. These men aren't Time Lords who can be picked up and dropped into other eras, or supernaturally gifted monster hunters in a world where such things exist, and they cannot be remade into a plethora of completely different people to fit whatever agenda some current reader needs to project upon them.

No, the stories in these books are about the same Sherlock Holmes and Dr. Watson that one finds in the original Canon – those pitifully few sixty stories that were published from 1887 to 1927.

I've enjoyed the notion that Mr. Sherlock Holmes was real from nearly the same time that I discovered him – as a boy of ten in 1975. Before I'd even read many of the Canonical adventures, I found two other books that reinforced this idea: William S. Baring-Gould's biography *Sherlock Holmes of Baker Street* (1962), with its chronology of the events in Holmes's long and amazing life (1854-1957), and also Nicholas Meyer's *The Seven-Per-Cent Solution* (1974), in which Holmes meets historical figures such as Sigmund Freud. How could one read those books, especially at that age, and not be convinced that Holmes was real?

In the decades that have passed since then, my interest in Mr. Holmes has only grown. While I read and collect a great many volumes about my other "book friends", as my son called them when he was small – and there

1

are a great lot of them besides Holmes – I've always had a special interest in the consulting detective in Baker Street and his Boswell. Since obtaining my first Holmes book in 1975, I've managed to collect and read (and create a massively dense chronology for) literally thousands of traditional Canonical adventures. I've worn a deerstalker as my only hat, all year long and everywhere since age nineteen. I've been able to make four extensive Holmes Pilgrimages to England and Scotland (so far), wherein I pretty much visited only Holmes-related sites. So it was probably inevitable that, in 2008, I started writing Holmes adventures.

I'd always wanted to write, all the way back to when I was eight years old and intensely reading about The Three Investigators and The Hardy Boys. Not satisfied with just the official publications, I wanted more new stories too. I spent quite a few Saturdays of my young boyhood tapping away on my dad's typewriter to create new "books".

As I grew, I dabbled with writing little short pieces, mostly humorous, just intended to make family members laugh, because I loved to write, and it always came easily to me. By the late 1980's, I was a U.S. Federal Investigator employed by an obscure government agency, often sent away from home for long periods, conducting investigations that lasted anywhere from five weeks to three months. Once, when I was sent to Albuquerque for several months to conduct extensive field investigations, I impulsively stopped at a local Walmart and bought a hundred-dollar typewriter and a big pack of paper with some of my *per diem* money. (This was the early 1990's – a long time before personal computers or laptops.)

It was there that I sat down for my first real effort at being a writer – and before I departed I'd finished most of a 600-plus page Ludlumesque novel. (One can get a lot of writing done night after night in a bleak hotel room.) The book was coincidentally about a heroic federal investigator – not unlike myself – who stumbled into a vast Russian-led conspiracy in the American southeast where I'm from. I still have that book – *Civil Servants* – stored in my old federal investigator briefcase, pushed underneath my bed. Its plot is mired in the early 1990's when it was written, locked to the aftermath of the Cold War, but it isn't half bad, and it taught me the valuable lesson that other writers also know: *The secret to writing is to put your butt in the chair and do it.*

After that particular trip, I went back home, finished up what was left of my epic adventure novel, and then settled back into writing the occasional short piece for our private amusement – but it was inevitable that at some point I would write a Holmes adventure.

In the mid-1990's, the federal agency where I'd been employed was abruptly eliminated, a victim of the end of the Cold War and a move to reduce the size of government. (After all, the higher-up wise men thought, who needs security now? We won!) Over the next few years, I went back to school and obtained a second degree in Civil Engineering. Then, in 2008 at the start of the Great Recession, I was unexpectedly laid off from my engineering job. With time on my hands, and a desire to try my hand at Sherlockian pastichery, I began writing each morning after the daily job searching was finished.

I ended up with nine Holmes pastiches, written over several weeks, and then . . . I did nothing with them. That's right. Simply satisfied that I'd written them and that they existed, I put them in a binder labeled *The Papers of Sherlock Holmes* and shelved them with the rest of my Holmes Collection, happy with my secret collector's item.

But eventually I began to wish for other Sherlockians to see them. I shared one with a Sherlockian friend here and another one there, and the response was very positive. Finally I became bolder and wanted more people to see them, asking myself: *Why not put them in a real book of my own?*

I communicated about it with a Sherlockian publisher from whom I'd bought books in the past. He immediately offered to publish *The Papers*, and after a great deal of back-and-forth, my first book eventually appeared. For those who have had that experience – Opening the newly delivered carton to see *your book!* – there is nothing like it. It's a satisfaction that cannot easily be described.

That was in 2011. Over the next couple of years, I became aware of MX Publishing. I saw that an acquaintance of mine who'd also had his first book published with the same original publisher as mine had switched to MX, and I reached out to him. He informed me that he was happy to have switched to MX. With that in mind, I sent an email to Steve Emecz, Sherlockian Publisher Extraordinaire – and that was truly life-changing and improving decision.

In 2013, Steve republished my first book, *The Papers of Sherlock Holmes*, and he made the whole experience so painless that I set about writing a Holmes novel, *Sherlock Holmes and A Quantity of Debt*. That same fall, I was making my long-planned first Holmes Pilgrimage to London, and Steve arranged for me to have a book-signing in The Sherlock Holmes Hotel in Baker Street, where I was staying (when not traveling about to Dartmoor, the Sussex Coast, Edinburgh, and other locations). I was able to meet Steve for the first time on that trip, and found him to be one of the nicest, most supportive, and most thoughtful people around – and that hasn't changed a bit.

Jump ahead a little bit: In early 2015, I woke up early from a dream in which I'd edited a Holmes anthology. Instead of rolling over and forgetting the idea, I arose and started thinking about authors whom I admired and that I might want to invite to write stories. I ran the idea by Steve, and he was willing to publish it, so I began sending invitations. I hoped that I might get a dozen stories (at best) for a modest paperback volume. Fearing a lack of response, I kept sending invitations to everyone that I could think of – and then, amazingly, people started signing up. New Sherlock Holmes stories started to arrive in my email in-box – which quickly becomes addictive. More and more authors heard about it – some that I didn't even know about yet – and before we knew it, the little idea had grown into a three-volume hardcover behemoth of over 60 new Holmes stories – *Parts I, II*, and *III* of *The MX Book of New Sherlock Holmes Stories*, the largest collection of its kind ever produced to that point.

Early on, Steve and I had decided that the royalties from the project would go to support the Stepping Stones School for special needs children, located at Undershaw, one of Sir Arthur Conan Doyle's former homes. The books were a smashing success and received a lot of attention, and I was able to go to London in the fall of 2015 for the release party – what turned out to be Holmes Pilgrimage No. 2. There I was able to meet a number of the contributing authors in person – and to my everlasting regret, I was so thrilled that I barely remembered to take any photos!

After I returned home, I began to receive more emails, now asking when the next book was planned – *Good grief! A next book?!?* – and also stating that many authors (both returning and new) wanted to contribute.

I'd had no plans to do any more books, thinking that the first three were lightning in a bottle that couldn't be recaptured . . . but then I realized that the heavy-lifting in terms of decision-making and set-up and formatting and process-building had already occurred, so Steve and I decided to keep going. (I think I said to him "Let's do one more . . . .")

Part IV came out in the spring of 2016 – and after that, more people kept sending stories for *the next books* and wanting to join the party. We came up with the plan to have yearly books. But we received so many stories that it grew to twice a year. We now have an un-themed spring collection – the yearly *Annual* – and also a fall collection with a specific theme, such as Christmas adventures, seemingly impossible crimes, Untold Cases, etc. As more and more stories kept rolling in, it became necessary for each season's particular set to grow to multiple simultaneously published volumes. That's how, in just a few short years, we're now up to *Parts XLVI, XLVII*, and *XLVIII* (to be published in Fall 2024), and as I write this, I'm already receiving stories for *the final volumes* in the series, *Parts XLIX* and *L*. (After ten years, fifty volumes, and over 1,000 new Holmes stories, it seemed like a good place to draw a line under it.)

So far the books have raised over $125,000 for the school, now simply called *Undershaw*, and that will just keep going up!

As part of editing these books, I couldn't let them pass by without adding my own stories – editor's prerogative. Thus, that helped to motivate me to sit my butt in the chair and write more about Mr. Holmes. By way of these books, I've met some really incredible people, including the incomparable Belanger Brothers, Derrick and Brian. Derrick initially contributed short stories, while Brian – a truly gifted artist – became the MX cover artist after the original artist passed away.

At one point, the two Belangers wrote a series of Holmes books for children. Eventually they formed Belanger Books – another amazing Sherlockian publishing venture. Between MX and Belanger Books – both of which cooperate beautifully with one another – the Sherlockian publishing field is amazingly well covered, providing an opportunity for so many people to be Sherlockian pasticheurs when they would otherwise be excluded by those who happily and aggressively seek to squash that aspect of the Sherlockian experience.

In 2016, the Belangers asked me to assemble and edit a Holmes story collection for them. I did, and as it also consisted of traditional and Canonical adventures, and had many of the same authors as in the MX anthologies, I formatted it the same way. After that, I edited another one for them, and another, and those also grew to simultaneously published multiple volumes. This extra editing also served to motivate me to write more Holmes stories for each of those collections as well – because I didn't want those trains leaving without me being on them.

From there, I began to receive invitations to write still more stories for other editors' anthologies and magazines. Along the way I published a couple more of my own books – *Sherlock Holmes – Tangled Skeins* (2015) and *Sherlock Holmes and The Eye of Heka* (2021) – but most of my stories that I wrote over those years remained uncollected within the various anthologies and magazines in which they had originally appeared. All along, I stayed too busy with real life and family and my dream job (as a civil engineer working for my home town's public works department), along with writing more stories and editing various books, to take the time to properly collect them all into my own books.

At some point, I ended up writing my 100th pastiche, (along with 28 pastiches about Solar Pons, "The Sherlock Holmes of Baker Street" – but that's another story and another hero.) In 2021, I had the idea of collecting my uncollected Holmes stories.

The initial five books of *The Complete Papers*, published in 2021, contained 77 of those stories. Volume VI came out in 2021 with 21 more tales. This book contains 19 more – plus three Holmes scripts and a poem. Others are still in the pipeline to be published elsewhere. I have a number of other pastiches planned and promised for 2025, so Volume 8 of *The Complete Papers* will hopefully appear in the next year or so . . . *Fingers crossed!*

Many people have sports figures or musicians or actors or (curiously) politicians as heroes. My heroes have always been my book friends and authors – all the way back to when I was eight or nine and wondering about why I couldn't track down satisfying biographical information concerning the brilliant and prolific and mysterious author Franklin W. Dixon. I've always admired writers for what they accomplish and create while spending great chunks of their lives self-imposed isolation – something which I now understand. And at least if I had to set aside all that time to put my butt in the chair, I've been very fortunate that all of these stories almost told themselves. I almost never outline or plan. Instead, when I write – when I find that it's time for another story – I simply open a blank Word document on the computer and then wait for Watson to begin whispering to me. It's scary, but I trust the process now, and when it works – and it always has so far – there's no feeling quite like it.

Through these stories, I've achieved two important personal goals: In my own small way, I've become a writer, and I've also added to *The Great Holmes Tapestry*, a phrase I coined several years ago to describe the massive collection of narratives about the *true* Holmes and Watson – novels, short stories, radio and television episodes, movies and scripts, comics and fan-fiction, and unpublished manuscripts – that tell the complete and entire course of their lives from beginning to end. The Canon serves as the supporting structure – the wire core of the rope, the heavy steel girders of the skyscraper – but the thousands of traditional post-Canonical pastiches provide essential depth and color, filling in all the spaces around The Canon, and adding important information about The Whole Lives of Our Heroes.

I've long described myself as a missionary for The Church of the Traditional Canonical Holmes, preaching that the bigger picture of both Canon and the traditional pastiches should be seen and supported. This means giving respect and value to additional Holmes adventures, and not just those original sixty because they were the ones that came across the first Literary Agent's desk.

Ross MacDonald – (Real Name: Kenneth Millar, another of my authorial heroes because of his incredible private eye, Lew Archer) – said *"It's all one case."* In other words, a *Great Tapestry*. He meant that even though he'd written eighteen Archer novels and a number of short stories from the 1940's to the 1970's, they were never meant to stand alone. They were all part of one overall arching story – Lew Archer's story – spanning across multiple narratives.

It's the same with the Holmes adventures – *all* of them, Canon and traditional pastiche, mine and everyone else's. They fit together to tell the *entire* story of Sherlock Holmes, and with the stories in this collection, I'm incredibly proud to have added my own contribution.

* * * * *

"Of course, I could only stammer out my thanks."
– *The unhappy John Hector McFarlane,* "The Norwood Builder"

At some point during the foreword-writing for the various MX anthologies, I began to use the quote shown above from Mr. McFarlane in regard to *Thank You*'s. It's fitting – I can only stammer out thanks, and never adequately express how grateful I am for all the help and encouragement I've received over the years in all aspects of my life – not just the writing and editing of Sherlock Holmes stories.

First and foremost, I am always overwhelmed at how incredibly fortunate I am to have my wife and son in my life. In all aspects, my wife – over 36 years as I write this – is the kindest and wisest and most beautiful person inside and out I know, and she has been there throughout with complete support and encouragement when we went through such things as some terrible jobs and the grind of my returning to school to be an engineer. We have pushed through together, and anything that I can ever accomplish I owe to her. And equally amazing is our son, so incredibly funny and smart, and truly an amazing person in every way. I enjoy every minute spent with him, and it only gets better. I love you both, and you are everything to me!

Then there are my parents and sister, who put up with me during those first couple of decades – I probably don't even realize how bad that was for them. My parents did everything to encourage me – music lessons leading to a piano scholarship in college, providing all the books that I could read, and generally anything to help me grow as a person, so that it never occurred to me that I couldn't do whatever I wanted. And my sister was my best friend then, patiently listening as I rambled about whatever interested me. Even then, she probably heard more about Sherlock Holmes than she'd ever bargained for!

Next, I wish to send several huge *Thank You*'s to the following:

☐ *Steve Emecz* – When I first emailed Steve from out of the blue back in 2013, I was interested in MX re-publishing my first book. Even then, as a guy who works to accumulate *all* traditional Sherlockian pastiches, I could see that MX (under Steve's leadership) was *the* fast-rising superstar of the Sherlockian publishing world.

The re-publication of my first book with MX was an amazing life-changing event for me, leading to writing many more stories and then editing books, along with unexpected additional Holmes Pilgrimages to England. By way of that first email with Steve, I've had the chance to make some incredible Sherlockian friends and play in the Holmesian Sandbox in ways that I'd never before dreamed possible.

Through all of it, Steve has been one of the most positive and supportive people that I've ever known. He works far more than a full-time week at his day job, and he still finds time to take care of all aspects of MX Publishing, with the help of his wife Sharon Emecz, and cousin, Timi Emecz. (That's right – MX is just the three of them who get all of this done!)

Many who just buy books and have a vague idea of how the publishing industry works now might not realize that MX, a non-profit which supports several important charities, consists of simply these three people. Between them, they take care of running the entire business, including the production, marketing, and shipping – all in their precious spare time, in and around their real lives.

With incredible hard work, they have made MX into a world-wide Sherlockian publishing phenomenon, providing opportunities for authors who would never have them otherwise. There are some like me who return more than once to Watson's Tin Dispatch Box, and there are others who only find one or two stories there – but they get the chance to publish their books, and then they can point with pride at this accomplishment, and how they too have added to The Great Holmes Tapestry.

From the beginning, Steve has let me explore various Sherlockian projects and open up my own personal

8

possibilities in ways that otherwise would have never happened. Thank you, Steve, for every opportunity!

☐ *Derrick Belanger* and *Brian Belanger* – I first "met" Derrick Belanger when he graciously reviewed one of my early books, and we quickly became friends. Then he interviewed me several times for his online blog, and when I had the idea for the first MX Holmes anthology in 2015, he quickly joined the party and contributed a fine pastiche. From there he's written a number of others, and then he formed Belanger Books with his brother, Brian. It's turned into a Sherlockian powerhouse, working in tandem with MX Publishing, supporting each other to produce more and more wonderful Holmes adventures. I've very grateful to have had this additional opportunity to further contribute to The Great Holmes Tapestry by editing and writing stories for their different anthologies. Derrick continues to write, but he also stays quite busy as a noted aware-winning teacher, husband, and father, as well as running Belanger Books with Brian.

Over the last few years, my amazement at Brian Belanger's ever-increasing talent has only grown. I initially became acquainted with him when he took over the duties of creating the covers for MX Books following the untimely death of their previous graphic artist. I found Brian to be a great collaborator, very easy-going and stress-free in his approach and willingness to work with authors, and wonderfully creative and positive too. His skills became most apparent to me when he created the cover for my 2017 book, *The Papers of Solar Pons*, which was one of the most striking covers that I've ever seen. Later, when the Belangers and I began reissuing the original Pons books in new editions, and then new Pons anthologies, Brian's similarly themed covers continued to astound me. He truly deserves an award for these.

In the meantime, he has become busier and busier, continuing to provide covers for MX Books, and now for Belanger Books as well, along with editing and occasionally writing.

I finally met both Brian and Derrick in person in early (pre-pandemic) 2020 at the annual Sherlock Holmes Birthday Celebration in New York City, and they're just as great in person as they were by way of email. I immediately felt like I'd known them both forever. I cannot express to either one of you just how grateful I am.

☐ *Roger Johnson* – I had known of Roger for quite a while, having seen his name connected with the "District Messenger" newsletter of *The Sherlock Holmes Society of London Journal*. I could tell, even then, that he represented the finest kind of Sherlockian. When I wrote my first Holmes book, I sent him a copy – out of the blue, as he had no idea who I was – as a thank you, and with the timid and dim spark of a hope that he would review it, because having him do so would mean (to me) that what I had written was legitimized. He did write a great review, and we began to correspond. When I was able to get to England for my first Holmes Pilgrimage in 2013, I made arrangements to meet with Roger and his wonderful wife, Jean Upton, in person, and I discovered that what I'd already known by email was true: They are both the very best people!

Later, in 2015 on Holmes Pilgrimage No. 2, they invited me to stay with them for several days in their home, and that was one of the best parts of all the trips. They gave me tours, they showed me their incredible collection, they let me see life in a real British household and not just from a hotel room, and we had some wonderful conversations along the way. I was able to see them again in 2016, Holmes Pilgrimage No. 3, when we attended the Grand Opening of the Stepping Stones School at Undershaw, and again on Pilgrimage No. 4 in 2024.

I'm more grateful than I can say that I know Roger. His Sherlockian knowledge is exceptional, as is the work that he does to further the cause of The Master. But even more than that, both Roger and his wonderful wife, Jean, are simply the finest and best, and I'm very lucky to know both of them – even though I don't get to see them nearly as often as I'd like, and especially in these crazy days! In so many ways, Roger, I can't thank you enough, and I can't imagine these books without you.

☐ *Nicholas Meyer* – I started reading Nick Meyer's Holmes books before I'd even read all of The Canon, and for that

I'm eternally grateful. It was through his first two books, *The Seven-Per-Cent Solution* and *The West End Horror* (the latter of which is still one of my favorite pastiches to this very day) that I firmly understood that The Canon wasn't the be-all end-all of Sherlockian story-telling. I obtained Nick's first book as part of a free book give-away at school, and I found the second not long after when my mother took my sister and me to buy school clothes and I spotted it in the mall bookstore. (I sat cross-legged along an out-of-the-way wall in a Sears while my mother and sister shopped and started reading *The West End Horror* straight out of the bag.)

After those first two books, Nick went on to have a very successful career in film. (More about that in a minute.) But he has continued to dip in an out of Sherlockian pastichery with *The Canary Trainer* (1993), *The Adventure of the Peculiar Protocols* (2019), *The Return of the Pharaoh* (2021), and *Sherlock Holmes and the Telegram from Hell* (2024). He is a Sherlockian legend, and it's an indisputable fact that the publication in 1974 of *The Seven-Per-Cent Solution* – a *pastiche*, mind you! – was the beginning of the Sherlockian Golden Age when has grown and grown, and has never stopped, all the way to today.

If it was just that, Sherlockians – and especially pasticheurs – would owe him an unpayable debt. But then there's *Star Trek*, which he also saved. As mentioned above, I have lots of interests besides Mr. Holmes, although he does demand more and more attention as my years pass. But I've been a Trekkie (or Trekker, or whatever the correct term is) since I was a wee lad in the late 1960's, when my babysitter happened to watch one of the original prime-time episodes. After that, I grew up seeing the original series in re-reruns, and then I was among those who saw the first Star Trek film in 1979 (and truthfully felt mightily disappointed. I do like it better now.) But it was Nick Meyer's *Star Trek: The Wrath of Khan* (1982) which electrified the Trek Universe, jump-starting it into motion in a way that – like the Holmes Golden Age – has only grown. And how it's grown! Hundreds and hundreds of Star Trek novels and comic books, multiple films and television shows, with more in planning and production all the time, and fan interest around the world at an all-time high. As a nearly life-long Star Trek fan, who loves it nearly as much as The World of Sherlock Holmes, I credit the origin of this original escalation entirely to Nick Meyer.

I generally despise social media, but it's a very useful way for Sherlockians to connect. Imagine my thrill when I began to see occasional online posts from Nick Meyer – and when I dared to respond, sometimes he would respond back! I've learned that if you don't ask, you'll never know, so I connected with him a bit more often, and eventually I boldly asked him to write a foreword to one of the MX anthologies that I edit, and he most-generously agreed. After that, we've stayed in touch off-and-on, and that still never ceases to amaze me.

I met him in person at the 2011 *From Gillette to Brett* conference in Bloomington, Indiana, where he was the featured guest. I took my copies of his Holmes books, asked him to autograph them, and asked – like everyone does – when he'd write his next Holmes book. He certainly doesn't remember that, but he was the main reason I chose to attend that event.

One of my greatest regrets is that, while attending the 2020 Sherlock Holmes Birthday Celebration in New York, I was almost able to meet him in person again – and this time he'd know who I was – but I didn't get to speak with him, and it was my own fault. We had emailed ahead of time, planning to meet, and that day I entered the famed dealer's room and saw him seated at a table near the door, surrounded by many fans. I wandered away, intending to return in a just a very few minutes and dive into the crowd, hoping that it might have thinned a bit. But when I got back over there, he'd already left! Hopefully I'll get another chance, sooner rather than later, where I can thank him in person for so many things . . .

. . . including generously writing a foreword for this ongoing series of volumes. When I was considering who could write a foreword, I couldn't think of anyone more fitting. Through Nicholas Meyer I found pastiches, which have been so important to me over the years. Nick, thanks from the bottom of my heart for taking the time to be part of these books!

And finally, last but certainly *not* least, thanks to **Sir Arthur Conan Doyle**: Author, doctor, adventurer, and the Founder of the Sherlockian Feast. Honored, and present in spirit.

As I always note when putting together a collection of Holmes stories, the effort has been a labor of love. This time the labor and love have been mine. These adventures are more tiny threads woven into the ongoing *Great Holmes Tapestry*, continuing to grow and grow, for there can *never* be enough stories about the man whom Watson described as *"the best and wisest . . . whom I have ever known."*

David Marcum
Originally written September 8th, 2021
Revised February 11th, 2023
Revised September 21st, 2024

Questions, comments, or story submissions
may be addressed to David Marcum at

thepapersofsherlockholmes@gmail.com

Watson's Descendants
by Nicholas Meyer

It is generally felt that the short story was Sherlock Holmes's best venue. The novellas, by contrast, are judged to be . . . lesser. Even the fabled *The Hound of the Baskervilles* suffers from the detective's absence for many pages. Though *A Study in Scarlet*, *The Sign of the Four*, and *The Valley of Fear* remain deliciously absorbing, it is in the short stories that Holmes and Watson truly flourish.

As Michael Chabon has observed, all fiction is fan fiction. Almost from the beginning, Sherlock Holmes has prompted imitators of his creator's creation. Arthur Conan Doyle wrote sixty Holmes cases in all – fifty-six short stories and four novellas. When they ended, boys and girls, men and women of all ages mourned Watson's silence and the series' cessation. But it wasn't long before others took up – or attempted to take up – Sir Arthur's pen.

Writing a full-length Holmes novel has always posed a challenge, even for Doyle himself, to say nothing of generations of later writers and filmmakers. Short stories, on the other hand, pose problems of their own. A good short story must compress action and character. It must – obviously – be short. The gift of writing compelling short fiction remains in a class by itself. Poe, Doyle of course, Twain, Saki, and Hawthorne are among the masters of the form from the Victorian and Edwardian eras, but over the years, the short story has produced many masters.

I alas am not among them. Even as a kid in art class, my paintings were so huge the murals I attempted had to be unfurled in the hall, not the studio. And so it comes as no surprise that writing a short Holmes story does not come easily to me. In fact, it does not come at all.

I retain nothing but admiration for those writers who *can* create short fiction, and a special respect for those who can bring off simulacra of Doyle's charming and distinctive Holmes tales. There many practitioners, including some whose efforts, unfortunately, resemble nothing so much as taxidermy. But among the best I must number David Marcum, who, by this point has written more Holmes stories than Doyle himself. Characterized by unflagging imagination and ceaseless ingenuity, along with felicitous prose, these tales continue to provide what we all crave: More Sherlock.

All Sherlock Holmes stories, (except Doyle's), are of course forgeries. And it's the rare forger who can resist signing his own work. See if you can spot David Marcum's fine Italian hand.

Enjoy.

Nicholas Meyer
Los Angeles, 2021

A Note on the
Modern Publishing Paradigm

For the longest time, publishing something was mostly impossible for most people. The Great Publishing Houses – which sounds like something from *Dune* – are giant machines, with carefully calculated formulas to know just how many books they need to sell to make a profit. It's no different than selling cereal: Many of the boxes of cereal on grocery store shelves won't be sold, and they were never meant to be sold, and the manufacturers are okay with that, because they've calculated the amount that they do need to actually sell in order to stay profitable while figuring in just how much can be discarded.

It used to be the same with books. Publishers would create a print run of a certain number of copies, sending out so many of them to bookstores across the country. Some would be sold – enough, hopefully, to cover costs – while many copies would just sit there, unsold, forever. Then, after a certain amount of time, they would be removed – either destroyed, or "remaindered", to be sold at rock-bottom prices in bargain bins.

It's an investment by the publishers to go to the trouble and expense to create all of those physical books, hoping to make their money back on enough of them to justify the waste of the others. That's why they're so restrictive about what they publish: They must meet the razor-thin edge of profit. But that makes the path to being published a very narrow needle's eye.

Several years ago, the paradigm began to shift. Online sales began to disrupt the physical bookstore model. And as people ordered online, some publishers figured out that they didn't have to have back rooms and warehouses jammed full of physical books sitting around waiting for a physical customer to enter a store or a dealer's room, examine it, and possibly buy it. Instead, when an online order arrived, the manufacturing of the book could commence right then, only as needed, and not months or years earlier.

This print-on-demand idea had been around for a while. (When I was going back to school for my second degree in civil engineering, the campus print shop did the same thing for certain locally produced text-books, printing them as they were purchased on fancy copying machines.) Publishers and authors began to take advantage of technological advances to produce their own books – straight from author to reader, happily eliminating the giant publishing middlemen.

Steve Emecz of MX Publishing brilliantly took advantage of this, building his business and allowing authors who would have never had a chance otherwise – like me – to create and connect.

But there are certain legitimate complaints.

In the olden days, the giant publishers slow-walked books through the process, so that it sometimes took literally years for a book to actually be published. Authors could actually die before ever seeing their work excreted at the far end of the giant publisher's process. The print-on-demand process, by comparison, is nearly immediate. As part of the large publishers' slow walk, there were battalions of editors who went through books forwards, backwards, and upside down. With the new technology, where a file can be loaded with the book manufacturer with very little effort and time spent, there is clearly less editing . . . and mistakes slip through.

Some readers continue to expect flawless and perfect works, as if legions of editors were behind the curtain as in days of old, still involved in the process. For this type of reader/consumer, the new format of publishing will always be pain they just can't ease. That's why, with this set of my stories, I want to apologize up front to those who will find typos – *because in spite of every effort, there will be some typos.*

In my own case, I love to write and edit, and I spend a sizeable amount of time doing both, but I also have a very busy and rich life doing other things. I spend time with my family, and I work more-than-full time as a civil engineer, fitting in these Sherlockian writing and editing projects during lunch hours, evenings, and weekends. It's a high wire act with no safety net. I'm the writer and sole editor of the stories in this collection. My wife, with a Bachelor's Degree in Journalism and two Master's Degrees in English Literature and Library Science, and with a first job as a copy editor, used to go through my stories and catch what I missed – because you never *ever* see your own mistakes – but she has more than enough to fill her own time, and she just doesn't have any extra time to spare for playing uncredited editor on these projects. So they're all on me.

It's the same with the anthologies that I edit – any mistake that slips through in the end is my fault, because there are no other editors. When assembling a Holmes anthology, I receive the stories, format them to the "house style", print them on 8½ x 11-inch paper, edit and revise with a red pen, go back and forth with emails to the author – sometimes a lot of emails – and then plug them into a giant Word document for more editing and revision. But from the time I get the story until I send the final file to the publisher, there isn't anyone else to do additional editing or proofreading, and no time to work someone into the process. It's the new publishing paradigm.

As a print-on-demand publisher, MX does not have squadrons of editors. The business consists of three part-time people who also have busy lives elsewhere – so the editing effort largely falls on the contributors. Some readers and consumers out there in the world absolutely despise this – They foam at the mouth in rage, apparently forgetting about all those self-produced Holmes stories and volumes from decades ago with awkward self-published formatting and loads of errors that are now prized as collector's items.

These critics should recall that every one of these new volumes by various authors – even those that have typographic and formatting errors – are the very best efforts that can be produced by very sincere people who don't have professional full-time editors to help, and who would never ever have had the opportunity to publish otherwise, and because of these authors, there is thankfully more Sherlockian content in the world.

I'm personally mortified when errors slip through – ironically, there will probably be errors in this essay – and I apologize now, but without a regiment of editors looking over my shoulder, this is as good as it gets. Real life is more important than writing and editing, and only so much time can be spent preparing these books before they are released into the wild. I hope that you can look past any errors, small or huge, and simply enjoy these stories, and appreciate the effort involved, and the sincere desire to add to The Great Holmes Tapestry.

And in spite of any errors here, there are more Sherlock Holmes stories than there were before, and that's a good thing.

David Marcum

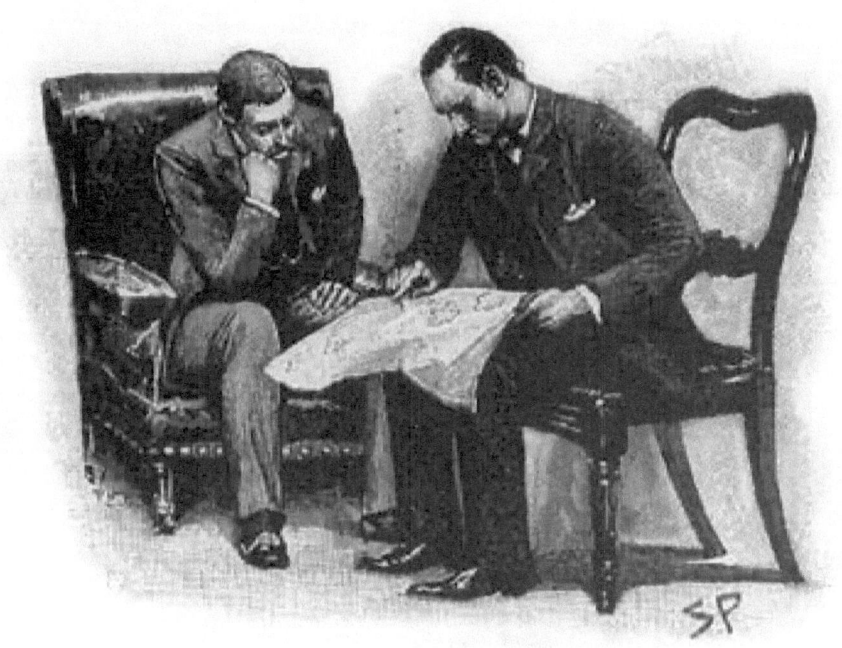

Sherlock Holmes (1854-1957) was born in Yorkshire, England, on 6 January, 1854. In the mid-1870's, he moved to 24 Montague Street, London, where he established himself as the world's first Consulting Detective. After meeting Dr. John H. Watson in early 1881, he and Watson moved to rooms at 221b Baker Street, where his reputation as the world's greatest detective grew for several decades. He was presumed to have died battling noted criminal Professor James Moriarty on 4 May, 1891, but he returned to London on 5 April, 1894, resuming his consulting practice in Baker Street. Retiring to the Sussex coast near Beachy Head in October 1903, he continued to be associated in various private and government investigations while giving the impression of being a reclusive apiarist. He was very involved in the events encompassing World War I, and to a lesser degree those of World War II. He passed away peacefully upon the cliffs above his Sussex home on his 103rd birthday, 6 January, 1957.

Dr. John Hamish Watson (1852-1929) was born in Stranraer, Scotland on 7 August, 1852. In 1878, he took his Doctor of Medicine Degree from the University of London, and later joined the army as a surgeon. Wounded at the Battle of Maiwand in Afghanistan (27 July, 1880), he returned to London late that same year. On New Year's Day, 1881, he was introduced to Sherlock Holmes in the chemical laboratory at Barts. Agreeing to share rooms with Holmes in Baker Street, Watson became invaluable to Holmes's consulting detective practice. Watson was married and widowed three times, and from the late 1880's onward, in addition to his participation in Holmes's investigations and his medical practice, he chronicled Holmes's adventures, with the assistance of his literary agent, Sir Arthur Conan Doyle, in a series of popular narratives, most of which were first published in *The Strand* magazine. Watson's later years were spent preparing a vast number of his notes of Holmes's cases for future publication. Following a final important investigation with Holmes, Watson contracted pneumonia and passed away on 24 July, 1929.

Photos of Sherlock Holmes and Dr. John H. Watson courtesy of Roger Johnson

The
Collected Papers
of
Sherlock
Holmes
Volume VII – Annals
(19 Holmes Adventures,
3 Scripts, and a Poem)

It's Always Time

When Sherlock Holmes needs to find a fact,
he has resources – of those there is no lack.
He steps across the sitting room to look
and pulls out a wonderful commonplace book.
Many a time was a cutting so there placed,
and with it, to a solution, Holmes has raced.
Or perhaps the help he needs instead has feet,
and he sends for The Irregulars of Baker Street,
with instructions to spread and scatter on the run –
to go everywhere, see everything, and overhear everyone.
While Watson has access to these resources, too,
there's something else he knows that *he* can do.
When tasked to learn more of Baron Gruner's hobby,
he traveled round to that quiet and solemn lobby
of the London Library there in St. James' Square
to seek a friend of his that functioned there.
In the stacks was that most useful Victorian,
Good old Watson's friend, Lomax the Sub-Librarian.
But all of these resources cannot aid
when a certain aspect of The Game is closely played.
One could ask for help from all these places,
but none will get you facts about the Unknown Cases.
For that you must seek a thing with clever locks,
known as Doctor Watson's *Tin Dispatch Box*.
It's full of adventures for which the world was not prepared,
but for those who've found it, these can now be shared.
So settle back – no matter how far one roams,
it's *always* time for more about Sherlock Holmes.

30

The Abridge Disappearance

"Mr. Holmes, they won't take me seriously! They're doing nothing!"

Lucas Harlaw was perched on the edge of his chair, and I expected that he would rise to his feet, the third time since his arrival, as his agitation and frustration grew.

Those feelings had not been caused by my friend, Sherlock Holmes, who had listened to the man's urgent appeal with sympathy and compassion. Rather, it was due to the fact that Harlaw's son had now been missing for three days, and he couldn't interest anyone into instituting a sincere search.

Holmes glanced my way, and I rose to pour a brandy for the unnerved father. He had refused the offer when first arriving, but this time I insisted. When I approached him with the glass outstretched in his direction, his head turned sharply, as if he were surprised. He had been gazing into the distance, and I could only imagine what tragedy he had been picturing.

While he took a drink, and then another, I recalled his unexpected entrance, not five minutes earlier.

I had come down late that morning, having been away the previous day to attend the funeral of a friend who, like me, had survived Maiwand three years before. For him, the thousand or so days since then had not been kind. Although I hadn't felt so at the time, with my initial wounds and subsequent wasting bout of enteric fever, I had been far luckier than Bob Chapleton – deprived of both legs, blinded in both eyes from wounds inflicted by the savage Ghazis who likely thought they were mutilating his corpse, and left without the use of his right arm. He'd been salvaged and treated and sent home to a horrified family who did the best that they could, but Bob had slowly retreated into himself until a rainy morning in late October when he mercifully slipped free of his bodily bonds.

It had been a grim gathering, not one of those funerals where people celebrate a long, well-lived, and happy life while carrying on a reunion with old friends and family. I was glad to be back in Baker Street. The rains that had followed me down from Weedon Bec in Northamptonshire were just as heavy that morning, and the hearty breakfast provided by Mrs. Hudson didn't lighten my mood. Holmes, sensing that I was feeling withdrawn when I made my appearance, simply said good morning and remained at his chemical bench, where he was examining some curious properties of a fungus he'd obtained on an ancient gravestone during our recent trip to Dunfermline.

31

The ring of the doorbell occurred just as I had poured my second cup of coffee and moved to my chair, carrying several of the morning's newspapers. Holmes glanced my way, and we both recognized that the insistent ringing that the caller was in some distress.

In a moment, quick steps on the stairs ended with a knock on the landing door. Holmes bade the caller to enter, and a tall man stepped in, looking from one to the other of us, wide-eyed and grim, before deciding that Holmes was who he needed to see.

"Mr. Holmes," he said, stepping across the short distance to where we sat. "My name is Lucas Harlaw. My son, Michael, has disappeared, and I can't convince anyone to help me!"

As I rose to direct Harlaw to the basket chair, Mrs. Hudson followed him in, asking if she should bring more coffee. Our visitor looked around at her, seemingly surprised that she was there. "None for me, thank you," he stammered.

"Something stronger, perhaps?" I asked. "A brandy? I know it's early, but – "

"No, nothing, Doctor . . . Watson, isn't it?"

I nodded.

"I've heard of you – both of you, actually. From Horace Wenlock, when you found his lost periapt last spring."

"A trivial affair," said Holmes, seating himself in his usual chair, his voice steady in order to bring some calm to the agitated man.

"Not so trivial to Horace," said Harlaw. "Finding it before the date named in the will meant nothing less than saving his inheritance and making sure there was enough money for his sister's surgery. He assured me that otherwise, she would be dead by now, so indirectly, you saved her life." He had settled into the basket chair, but immediately slid forward again so that he was perched upon the edge. "It was Horace who suggested that I seek your help, Mr. Holmes. My son – no one will listen."

"Calm yourself, sir, and tell us what has happened, and we'll see what we might be able to do for you. Please – explain fully, and leave nothing out."

Harlaw nodded and moved back into the chair, although he didn't relax, sitting perfectly upright as if stretched by a tight wire.

"I'm an attorney with chambers in Paddington," he began. "My work is often involved with legal documents related to construction. My wife and I have one child, a son. Michael is nineteen and attends The College of Mary, about five miles out of Abridge, in Essex. It's a Wesleyan school, built around fifty years ago by a minister named Anderson." As he related the story and set the scene, Harlaw calmed himself, but it was only temporary. "Abridge was on the coaching route from London to Chipping

Ongar, and Anderson initially ministered there. He started a preparatory school for the locals, and within a few years it had grown into the college. Since then, they've been rather successful. A number of wealthy alumni have provided for upkeep and modernizations.

"The campus is around two-hundred acres, but the major portion of that is forest, cut up with trails and paths. There are a dozen or so buildings for around two-hundred students, including four dormitories, a library, a science building, a gymnasium, a chapel, a dining hall, a music building with an auditorium, the steam plant, the college president's house, and the main building, Anderson Hall, which holds classrooms and administrative offices.

"Michael heard about the school through our church, and when it was time for him to go to college, this was really his only choice. He's studying music – not a career that I would recommend for a comfortable life, but it seems to call him. From all that I've heard, Michael is having a wonderful time – he has maintained a scholarship and a good group of friends. He's now in his sophomore year, and all has seemed well – until this weekend.

"Michael is a very conscientious young fellow. My wife and I have often joked that even as a child, he seemed to be like a thirty-year-old man, not taking foolish chances, making responsible choices, keeping us informed about anything we need to know. That's why this past weekend has been so upsetting – although we can't get anyone to take us serious!"

Suddenly Harlaw's emotions surged and he unexpectedly stood, his hands clenched. Clearly whatever had happened, even something that was being negated by others, was strongly upsetting the man.

"Please sit," said Holmes, "and continue your tale. The scene is set. Now – What has happened?"

Harlaw nodded and recomposed himself.

"Michael was due to come home on Friday evening. It isn't a far trip by train, and he usually stays with us in Paddington every weekend, unless he lets us know otherwise. His return this Friday was confirmed, because Saturday, the third, was his mother's birthday. It's only a journey of an hour or so, and he returns to school on Sunday afternoons. There's rarely anything happening at the school on the weekends – even the meals are rather scanty – so letting the students who are able to return home do so isn't discouraged by the administration.

"When Michael didn't arrive on time, we thought he'd missed his train – it has happened a few times – but then he didn't show up that night at all, and we received no word from him. By Saturday morning we were getting frantic. The school doesn't have a telephone, so I sent several wires, but apparently, since the offices were closed for the weekend, they went unanswered. I went down to Abridge on Saturday evening, but no one at the nearby Loughton Station, which is the closest terminus, remembered Michael boarding the train there on Friday, and at the college, none of his friends who were there remembered him leaving.

"I rousted several of the administrators, right up to the college president himself, but no one can offer any clue as to where he might be. I went to the police, but they had no inclination to take my fears seriously. They said that he hadn't been missing for very long, and that every spirited young man of nineteen sometimes slips the leash. Then he implied that my wife and I were being overprotective!"

He then stood up again, his body coiled with energy, as if he'd explained enough, and that we should join him in dashing to catch the next train. Holmes raised a calming hand, and after a moment and a couple of deep breaths, Harlaw again resettled into the chair.

"The attitude of the police wasn't entirely unreasonable," said Holmes. "At the time you spoke to them, your son had only been missing for twenty-four hours."

"Yes, but now it's Monday morning, and there's still no word. I returned to London Saturday night and waited for a while with my wife – she was becoming quite unwell – thinking that Michael might still arrive, but we heard nothing. Subsequent wires to the school went unanswered. Sunday we both went there, asking further questions of Michael's friends and at again the station. We spoke once more to the police as well, but their attitude is clearly that we are overreacting, and they have been much less than helpful. Finally, we recalled what you accomplished for Horace Wenlock, and I came back here to seek your help. My wife has remained at the school, trying to find some lead as to where Michael might be." His eyes shut and his fists clenched, and he cried, "Mr. Holmes, they won't take me seriously! They're doing nothing!"

I rose before he did and convinced him to have some brandy. Meanwhile, Holmes tapped his finger several times on the arm of his chair before nodding.

"I hope that this truly is nothing more than a young man thoughtlessly going about his own business, but it does sound out of character from the way that you've described your son. We can accomplish nothing here in London. Watson, will you accompany us to the school?"

I had no demands on my time that Monday morning, although venturing out into the rain was not very appealing. In minutes, bundled against the raw weather of early November, we joined Harlaw in the growler which he'd told to wait upon his arrival. On the drive across London, he clearly wanted to speculate regarding where his son might be, and what sort of trouble he might be in, but Holmes raised a hand to silence him.

34

"I need facts, Mr. Harlow – anything else at this point is a distraction." And he settled into a rumination, leaving the father and me in awkward silence – for in fact, there was nothing else that we could really discuss. I asked him once about his practice, but the answer was short, as if he too had no response for anything that was unrelated to his missing son. It was the same within the train from Liverpool Street Station, each of us weighted under our own thoughts, and only when we arrived at our destination did the sense of urgency reawaken.

We disembarked at the Loughton Station, a mile or so west of Abridge. Harlaw explained that the school was located north of Abridge, not far from the road leading to the upper reaches of Epping Forest. As he went to secure a cab, Holmes sought out the station master, who reacted a bit warily.

"I saw you with Mr. Harlaw," he said. "He's been in and out of here a half-dozen times in the last few days, along with his wife, asking questions, as if we'll suddenly remember something. I can tell you now, gentlemen, I don't remember his son. None of us do. Friday nights are especially crowded, and anyway, we wouldn't know the lad if we saw him."

"How did Mr. Harlaw describe his son?" Holmes asked.

The station master glanced at the returning father. "Tall and slim, like him. Said they look quite alike, and that the lad wears a long wool coat in cold weather – something like you're wearing, sir. An Inverness."

Harlaw joined us just then and confirmed his son's description. "I fear that if he wasn't noticed here at the station, it's because he never came here."

"It's very possible, sir," said the station master, "but then again, there's simply no way to tell. As I mentioned before, Friday evenings, with everyone getting away to London, are simply too busy to remember one lad among so many – and if you recall, Friday was dark and rainy and cold, like today. People were huddled up and moving quickly, and it wasn't too easy to see anything."

Holmes thanked the man, and when he'd stepped away, said, "I believe that he's right. If we don't find anything at the school, we can always return and do more excavating here – although that would be a tedious business that would require a lot of luck with very little chance of success."

Harlaw led us outside to the cab, and soon we were rattling east, out of Loughton and toward Abridge. Conversation was limited due to the rain thundering on the cab roof, and I very much pitied the poor driver and horse, and anyone else who had to be out working in the cold autumn torrent.

35

We passed through Abridge, and looking out through water-streaked windows, I could barely see the medieval buildings of the small town center. Then we turned north and, not long after, we were entering the grounds of the modest College of Mary which, Harlaw informed us, had recently celebrated its semi-centennial. All of the buildings seemed to be clustered together, and to the south, I could just make out the modest forest, in a low spot separated from the main campus by a series of athletic fields. As we traveled along the circular drive that ran by all of the buildings, I observed a number of people walking in the direction of the woods, most carrying umbrellas, and nearly all of them in waterproof coats. As we stopped at Anderson Hall, a large red-brick building surmounted by a high white tower, a man left the building to walk toward us. Harlaw reacted with surprise.

"Mr. Holmes, Doctor," explained Harlaw, "this is John Clark, the president of the college." He looked urgently toward the older man. "Dr. Clark, is there any news?"

Clark, who had an umbrella of his own, stepped forward to greet us. He was a heavy-set man in his fifties, dressed well against the weather. In the limited light, I could tell that he would normally be a good-natured fellow, but his expression that morning was grim.

Ignoring the anxious father's questions, Clark instead replied, "Mr. Harlaw. Gentlemen. Let us get inside."

He led us into the sudden warmth of the Hall, where we divested ourselves of our wet coats and hung them on a rack just inside the door. As we did so, a small woman came out of a side room to our right and ran up to Harlow, who turned and gave her a quick hug. She was followed by a small man in his thirties wearing *pince-nez*,

"Lydia!" cried Harlaw. "Any luck? What is happening?"

She shook her head, and Clark said, "Your wife has been very persuasive, Mr. Harlaw. She convinced us to conduct a more thorough search. You may have seen the people – students and staff – who are now heading toward the College Woods. We have suspended classes for the morning, and they intend to make a thorough sweep – not only the easy locations like the trails, the amphitheatre, the lodge, and the spring house, but also the areas below the ridge – along the stream, for instance, and the rough areas where someone might be if he . . . if he left the trails."

"Additionally," the man with *pince-nez* informed us, "they intend to search around the two sinkholes and the small cave."

Mrs. Harlaw gave a small gasp, and Clark frowned. "This is the Assistant Dean," he explained, "Martin Carlyle."

36

Mrs. Harlaw stepped away from her husband and grasped the smaller man's arm. "Sinkholes?" she said, a rawness suddenly in her tone. "A *cave*?" There was a rising note of panic in her voice.

Carlyle was suddenly speechless, as if he were a deer that had been surprised in the forest and was now unsure which way to bolt. "My wife," Harlaw explained, taking her gently by the shoulders and pulling her back to his side, "has a . . . *fear* of sinkholes. When she was a girl, one of the men who worked on her father's farm was fatally swallowed by one when it unexpectedly opened beneath him."

"They aren't unknown in this area," Clark explained. He lowered his voice and spoke to Mr. Harlaw, as if his wife wasn't also right there. "When speaking with your son's roommate, we found that he has had an interest in the sinkholes and the cave . . . and has been known to explore around them." He then glanced at Mrs. Harlaw, adding, "It would only be prudent to look there, considering the lad's fascination for such places."

Holmes said, "Would it be possible to speak to the roommate? Is he involved in the search?"

Clark shook his head. "No, he's resting in their room. He has a small touch of something and is running a slight fever, so it was thought best to excuse him. But wouldn't you like to visit the woods while the search is taking place?"

"Not yet," Holmes replied plainly. "I'm sure that your search will be most effective on its own, without our help. It looked as if you had more than a hundred people venturing forth. Our time will be better spent trying to determine where young Mr. Harlaw might have gone."

Mrs. Harlaw stepped forward. "You're Mr. Holmes," she said.

Holmes nodded, and Harlaw apologized. "I'm sorry, my dear – I should have introduced Mr. Holmes and Dr. Watson as soon as we arrived."

She ignored him, her gaze fixed firmly on my friend. "I've heard that you're a miracle worker, Mr. Holmes. I have a feeling – I sense that we'll need a miracle. Please – find my son."

Holmes started to reply, and knowing him so well by then, I knew that it would be something about probability and false hope, but then he caught himself and said simply, "We can but try, Mrs. Harlaw." Then he turned and reached for his coat, as did I.

Harlaw also started to put his on as well, but Holmes shook his head. "Stay here with your wife, Mr. Harlaw, and help coordinate the search. Watson and I can be more effective on our own."

Harlaw started to object, but Holmes added, cutting him off abruptly, "President Clark can show us the way, and introduce us when necessary."

He looked at Mrs. Harlaw, as if to seek her assistance in letting us work without her husband's presence. She nodded.

We stepped back into the driving rain, each taking a step apart from one another and pausing to raise our umbrellas. Then Clark led us to the right, around the building, and down a series of walkways through the center of the campus, pointing out features as we went, his voice raised to overcome the steady drumming of the rain. "There is the Center for Campus Ministry – our little chapel. It's one of the oldest buildings on campus. And over there is Pearson Hall, with the dining room and upper-class apartments." He gestured behind us and to the left. "Across from Anderson are the science and music buildings. We'll pass the library, and then we'll reach the dormitory where young Harlaw lives."

On the stretch between the chapel and the library, I noticed several round metal lids in the ground near the walkways, each about two feet across, rather like the covers to London's sewer manholes. There were strong jets of steam escaping from each one, and depending on the wind as we reached them, we had to detour to avoid walking right through the hot mist. When I asked the president about them, he proudly explained that they were access points to the buried steam pipes. "Our third president, Dr. Gambill, had the foresight to install steam heating in all of the buildings. The steam plant is at the far north side of the grounds, behind the music building, and the pipes run underground in every direction."

Holmes nodded, but he was looking left and right as he studied the layout of the various buildings. Then we reached a rather modern-looking structure of mud-yellow bricks, four stories, square and plain, without much character. "This dormitory, Copeland, along with the others of similar appearance, was constructed in the sixties," the president explained. Then, rather apologetically, he added, "One of the alumni provided the funds. His son was the architect – and his vision was, um, rather . . . uninspired. I'm afraid that explains the somewhat . . . ugly presentation, as compared to our other older buildings."

Clark held the door for us, allowing us to enter first. The lobby was plain, with a couple of unmarked wooden doors and an unmanned desk opposite the entry. Clark led us through a doorway on the right which opened into a narrow and dark stairwell. We went up one flight and then through a heavy door into a short hallway, where we were met by five closed doors. I knew in relation to where we had entered that we were in the corner located at the front right of the building. Clark passed two doors and then, at the center door, he knocked, and a weak voice inside bade us to enter.

It was the corner room, not very large. It had two windows, one looking back toward the central part of the college from whence we had just walked, and the other, on the adjacent wall, facing the nearby gymnasium. The walls were painted a dull bluish-gray, only adding to the cold damp feeling of that November day. There was a built-in closet with two doors, and there were also two desks, two small bookshelves, and two narrow beds. Nearer the front wall was the empty one, and the shelves and desk nearby were stacked with books and papers, displaying the same untidiness that I lived with every day in Baker Street. Clearly, Michael Harlaw had Holmes's same enthusiasm, and also his haphazard filing system.

In addition to textbooks, there were sliding mounds of sheet music, leaning towers of popular novels, and also several larger and heavier textbooks poking out from underneath scattered papers. Grouped together on the top shelf of the bookcase was a handsome set of the works of Edgar Allan Poe, as well as a number of novels by Collins and Dickens.

The bed across the room held a young man of nineteen or twenty, covered to the chin with a couple of blankets. There was much less clutter on his side, but one also had the impression that he had much less in his life that interested him. There was a cricket bat propped against one wall, and several textbooks stacked upon the desk. There was nothing on the bookshelf except a pair of dirty spiked shoes on the bottom shelf, almost certainly used when playing sports. There was also a half-filled bottle of clear liquid and a glass on the table beside the bed.

Clark introduced us. "Mr. Sykes, this is Sherlock Holmes and Dr. Watson. Mr. Holmes is a detective who was asked to come up from London by Mr. and Mrs. Harlaw to look for Michael." Then he looked at us. "This is Simon Sykes. He has been Michael's roommate since they began attending the college. They are in the same year." Returning his attention to Sykes, he said, "Please answer their questions." Then he stepped back, as if to cede the floor to Holmes.

"How are you feeling?" asked Holmes. I could see why he was concerned, as the young fellow didn't look too well at all. He was quite pale, with damp-looking skin and hair lying in lanky locks across his brow. There were red spots on both cheeks the size of shillings. Without waiting for an answer, I stepped forward for a closer look, touching his forehead with the back of my hand while explaining that I was a doctor. His fever was present, but fortunately very slight. However, I knew that it might rise as the day progressed, as was typical.

"How long have you felt this way?"

"Almost a week," he explained. "Since waking up on Tuesday morning. I've been to the infirmary twice – it's located over the library – and they've given me a tonic." He indicated the bottle. I picked it up, seeing that it was a willow bark concoction containing salicylic acid.

"Any signs of cough or wheezing when you breathe?" I asked, and he shook his head. "Does your fever climb at night?"

"It does, but not too badly. I just take another spoonful of the tonic prescribed by the nurse and then sleep straight through."

I nodded. "You should be fine if you don't stress yourself, or become too active before the fever breaks. Make sure to drink plenty of liquids." I looked around. "You have nothing here but the tonic. You need water."

"It's available down hallway," said the boy.

"You should keep some here. Drink it regularly – as much as you can take."

"I'll make sure of it, Doctor," said Clark. I nodded, stepped back, and deferred to Holmes.

"I'm sure you've been asked this before," he said, "but did Michael Harlaw give any indication that his plans last Friday had changed? That he wouldn't be returning to London at the normal time?"

"Not at all – but I actually didn't see him on Friday. He didn't sleep here on Thursday night, and our paths never crossed on either of those days." He pointed toward the shared closet. "His bag and clothes are still there – he didn't pack to take anything with him."

"Not since Thursday night?" asked Clark, frowning. "That's even longer than we believed. Why didn't you tell us?"

Sykes' eyes widened, and the accusatory tone in the president's voice made him suddenly look much younger than his years. "No one asked me specifically, sir. I just thought that since Michael was missing, everyone knew *when* he went missing."

Clark nodded and waved a hand, as if there was no blame attached.

"And you have no idea where he would have gone?" continued Holmes. "Does he have any friends with whom he might have impulsively traveled?"

Sykes shook his head to both questions, and he had no additional information to offer as Holmes continued to question him about Harlaw's activities and habits. Then he queried about the College Woods, and specifically Michael's interest in sinkholes and the cave.

"He's interested in everything around here, sir – the woods, the buildings, the secret history." He looked at Clark as if debating whether to continue, and then added, "He has keys to all the different buildings – so that he can explore after hours. He sometimes goes up onto the rooftops as well."

"What?" Clark asked, as if suddenly picturing Michael Harlaw in a new light – more than just a good student who had so far avoided attention. "*How* does he have keys?"

"From the older students," explained Sykes, now possibly regretting his frankness, perhaps due to his illness lowering his guard. "The graduates. There are lots of sets of keys to be found. The older students have them, and when they graduate, they pass them on to certain of the younger students. It's something of a tradition. But they never cause any problems!" Sykes hastened to add. "To do anything destructive would ruin it for everyone else. It's just that sometimes the students who have keys like to visit the secret parts of the campus – the tower in Anderson Hall, for instance, or into the basement of the dining hall, where one of the school's ghosts can be found."

"Ghosts?" I asked, wanting to know more before Holmes, for whom such aspects were irrelevant, could change the subject.

Sykes nodded, while Clark puffed in disgust. "There are several of them," the lad added. I wondered if he would have been so forthcoming had he not been ill. His eyes brightened as his enthusiasm for the topic made him sit a little straighter. "There's the ghost in the music building, who puts out lights in the auditorium. He died from too much opium. And the dining hall ghost – a student who hanged himself a generation ago." He became more energetic as each one was recalled. "Then there's the old lady who died in the lodge down in the woods – they say she doesn't know she's dead, and if the lights are put out in the house, she relights them as soon as you leave the building. And there's the 'Good Evening' ghost – a dead policeman who will speak on certain nights from a tree above the fountain where he was once killed.

"There's the one-legged ghost," the lad continued, further warming to the subject, "who was ambushed back during the Civil War on the spot where Anderson Hall was built. After he lost his leg, the doctors tried to save him, but he died there, and has been looking for his leg ever since. At night, you can hear him hopping around in Anderson, moaning and calling for his missing limb. And there is the couple that wasn't allowed to marry – a local girl and a boy from the college. They killed themselves, and they can be seen in the summer moonlight on the old stone steps, on the town side."

Clark was suddenly irritated. "This is all humbug!" he cried – quite possibly the first time I'd heard that phrase used aloud and outside a book. "I assure you, gentlemen – I've heard none of these stories, and none of this is true! Mrs. Walker was a fine lady – she does not haunt the lodge house! A young man did die of an opium overdose, but it was while he was at home, recovering from an unexpected surgery. Why would he haunt the auditorium? And a boy and girl killing themselves and then lurking around the stone steps after death – ? Impossible! Such a story would be well-known everywhere, and this is the first I've heard of it!"

41

Holmes continued to look at Simon Sykes. "You indicated that Mr. Harlaw has an interest in 'secret' aspects of the college's history. What form does this take?"

"What?" asked Sykes, still looking at the college president and realizing that he'd perhaps been indiscreet. "Hmm, it's nothing bad. He does research." He nodded toward Harlaw's desk and the teetering piles of books and papers. "He's read both of the college histories written by past professors, and he spends a lot of his spare time at the local newspaper office, looking at the old issues for any news about the college from years ago. It fascinates him. He's always trying to tell the rest of us about it – when this or that happened, or when someone famous visited – and he arranges tours for those that he can get interested."

"Tours? Tell us more about that."

"He . . . Michael finds out the history of the college, and then plans nighttime walks. He keeps them secret and mysterious. It's more fun that way. He only invites a few people at a time. I've been on several of them. We . . . ." He looked at Clark, who was looking ever more intently back at him. "We go into the woods and the basements, and sometimes onto the roofs. There's a secret room in the chapel – stairs that go up to a room in the wall – and we've sat on the Anderson tower at night underneath the flagpole, watching people walk below who have no idea we're up there."

"When was Michael's most recent tour?" Holmes asked.

Sykes pointed to the desk. "I'm not sure. I know that he had found something new he wanted to share, but he wasn't finished doing his research . . . ."

He trailed off as Holmes had already pivoted to the desk, pulled out the chair, sat down, and started sorting through the stacked papers. It didn't take long until he found a sheet near the top that interested him.

He quickly scanned it, read it again more carefully, and then turned to Clark, a hint of urgency now in his voice. "Does Guy Fawkes have any association with this area?"

The college president was obviously puzzled – as was I. "Why, not that I've ever heard," he said. "I believe that Fawkes was originally from York before he ended up in London. I've never heard that he was in this part of Essex. Why"

Holmes vaguely waved the sheet back and forth and then continued to search the missing boy's desk. He finished shifting through the remaining papers and books without finding anything else of apparent interest. Then he systematically went through the drawers, pausing only once to hold up a ring of a dozen or so old-looking keys. "I suspect these fit all the doors of the various college buildings," he said. "It's of interest that Master Harlaw didn't take them with him when he went missing."

"Of interest how?" demanded Clark, whose previous basic good nature, though worried, was now becoming impatient.

"Because where he was going this time, he didn't need them." Holmes then countered with another cryptic question. "Do you have a man who oversees the campus – someone in charge of the grounds and the buildings?"

"That would be Fielding. He'll most likely be at the steam plant."

"Take us there." Holmes's tone was suddenly urgent. "Immediately." He folded the sheet that he'd found and shoved it into his pocket. Then, with a look toward Sykes, a short thank you, and a curt wish that he feel better soon, Holmes was quickly out the door, suddenly hard upon a scent that none of the rest of us could even perceive.

"We'll speak later," said Clark grimly to the sick young man. I simply nodded in his direction. Outside, as Clark and I hurried downstairs to meet the now-fretful Holmes waiting in the lobby, the president asked softly, "Guy Fawkes?"

I shook my head. "Have patience. We'll know soon enough."

Outside, the rain had markedly diminished, which was a fortunate thing, but there was still a cold damp wind blowing from the north, causing a man to put a hurry in his step. Holmes was ahead of us by five or ten feet, walking north and going back the way we had come just a quarter-hour earlier. As we passed the library, Clark increased his pace to catch up. As they walked together, the president made comments that I couldn't hear while pointing straight ahead, indicating that we should continue in that direction to reach the steam plant. Holmes nodded, still deep in thought, but looking from here to there all around is in every direction. As we progressed, the walkway back to Anderson Hall veered away to our left and we approached what had been identified as the dining hall immediately on the right. Then just past it, with Anderson now far to our left across an open field and the science building now at our right, Holmes stopped, asking, "What is that?"

He was pointing to the field, and more specifically, to a set of stone and brick steps that stood in the middle, apparently rising to nowhere.

"Those are the old stairs to Memorial Hall. It was one of the original dormitories, before it was torn down twenty years ago. The building was constructed of wood, but the stairs were more permanent. While also originally scheduled for removal, they were left in place long enough that they became something of a permanent feature of the college landscape. Now we use them. Sometimes the choir will stand on them to give a concert, and in the spring, we have each class stand on them to record their photograph."

Holmes continued looking at the steps and Anderson Hall beyond them, and then he looked back toward the dormitory we'd just visited, and in several other directions as well. He nodded to himself and resumed walking briskly toward the steam plant, now obvious to us, at possibly at a faster pace than before.

We came to the proper edge of main campus and crossed a narrow paved access road. Beyond was a solid red-brick building, dwarfed by a pair of high smokestacks, constructed of the same material. They must have each reached a hundred feet or more in the air, and I could see that near their top, just before visibility was lost in the mist, that a pair of decorative letters had been worked into each structure using contrasting yellow brick. As seen from the campus, the left stack had the letter *C*, while the right had an *M*: *College of Mary*. Smoke was coming from each, both stacks high enough for the soot to be carried away by the winds without settling on the college below.

We walked carefully down a muddy gravel drive and around to the opposite side of the building, where Clark led us through a heavy door and into the clattering plant. The abrupt change from the dreary wet November day to the hot steamy room was jarring. One had the sense of overall hidden heights and depths inside, but views in every direction were occluded by a mass of criss-crossing pipes, partial walls ending at eye or knee level, and areas of dark shadows.

The noise wasn't deafening in the short term, but it would cause permanent damage after just a short while. I had treated men who had worked in the bowels of steamships for detrimental hearing loss, and I knew that whomever spent much time in this place would suffer the same disabilities. There was a constant roar of a flame somewhere out of sight, and a regular clanking within the pipes all around us. These ran along the floors and hung all around at differing heights, supported by heavy metal straps attached to the ceiling. They constantly shook and knocked, and there were numerous shrill hisses and whistles as steam was vented regularly all around us, without any set pattern. The air inside the building was wet, and my face was already damp. I wiped it with my handkerchief, thinking that if any of us had worn glasses, we wouldn't have been able to see past the sudden condensation – the same running dripping film that coated the interiors of all the windows.

Clark called for Fielding several times with no response, his voice lost in the din, and then with a shrug, he led us deeper into the hellish maze. Or so it seemed, but in less than fifty feet, with several turns that made me doubt that I could easily find my way back out, we were at the doorway of a snug little office, built against one corner of the building. Why it was so far from the outer door, I didn't know. It had a pair of internal windows

44

looking out upon the plant and the door had a window as well. These showed that the office was lit, but the accumulating water running across the glass meant that nothing inside could be seen.

The door was apparently warped, but Clark gave it a hard pull on his initial attempt – he seemed to know that would be necessary – and let us go in first. He followed and pulled the door shut, and I felt as if the noise level had been drastically muffled and the temperature dropped by twenty degrees.

Fielding was hunched over his desk, copying entries from one sheet to another. He looked up without surprise, recognized Clark, and then pulled a couple of twists of cloth out of each ear. "Mr. Clark," he said, glancing questioningly at Holmes and me. "What can I do for you?"

Clark started to explain about the missing young man, and who we were, but Holmes interrupted him. "Do you have a map of the campus?" he asked, the exigency quite apparent in his voice.

Fielding rose and looked curiously at Holmes. Then he glanced at the college president and, apparently deciding that authority to Holmes had been granted and that the matter was urgent, he turned to a cabinet, pulling open the top drawer and withdrawing a yellowed and folded sheet. He laid it on the desk and then flipped it open to reveal a map about two-feet-square, with the major points roughly reproduced here:

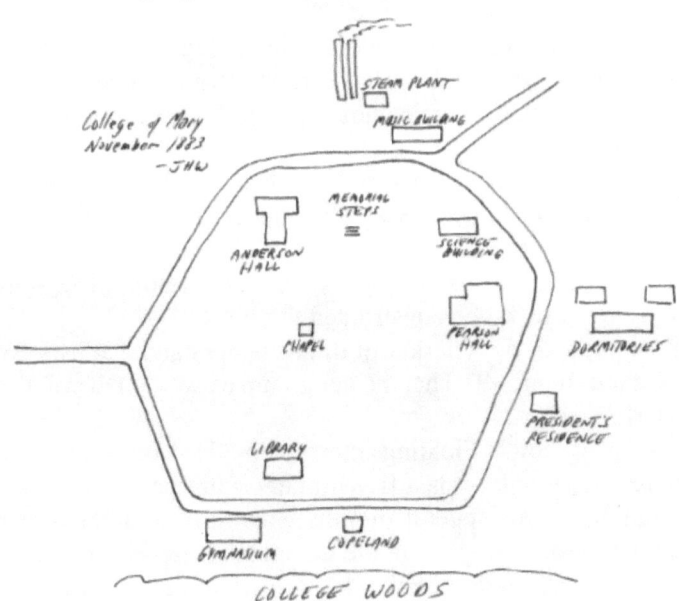

Without comment, Holmes leaned over, tracing his finger along lines from building to building, outlining a network of steam that ran underground to each building's heating system. I could imagine the larger pipes running up to smaller pipes inside walls and floors, and thence to metal radiators, where the heat would spread into the rooms. Meanwhile, as the heat was lost to the buildings, the steam inside the radiators would cool and condense back into water, running down through a series of return lines, carrying it again to the steam plant to be reheated and recirculated once again – something like a circulatory system, wherein the water was the blood, receiving heat energy in the same way that the lungs provided oxygen.

"Here," said Holmes, pointing on the map where Memorial Hall had once stood. "Would this building have been connected to the steam plant?"

Fielding nodded. "It would have." He was clearly curious as to what was going on, but he could tell that Holmes had no time for extraneous questions.

Holmes glanced at Clark. "The venting steam – I saw it coming from the access points in all directions as we walked here from the dormitory."

"That's right. There is an ingress point to the pipes – and sometimes two or three – at some point near every building."

"And at these points – Are the pipes simply buried in the ground, or can they be reached by way of *tunnels*?"

He looked at Fielding then, who nodded, beginning to comprehend Holmes's theory – as was I. "That's right. Brick tunnels, constructed underneath the grounds. There's enough space for men to enter and make repairs as needed."

"And there would have once been such a tunnel to Memorial Hall as well. Would it have been destroyed when the building was torn down? Or simply abandoned in place?"

Fielding rubbed his unshaven jaw. "Probably left in place – in case a new building was ever to be constructed there."

Holmes nodded, but Clark still didn't understand. "Why – Why are you asking about tunnels?" Then he caught up as well. "Do you think that Michael Harlaw – ?"

"The missing boy?" Fielding interrupted. "Do you think he's in one of the tunnels? He wouldn't last five minutes with the steam on – and it's been on continuous for several months, since the weather turned cold. There are big pipes running along the tunnel bottoms – iron pipes, some a foot or more across! – and they would burn whatever touched them. And the steam you see venting from the access points fills the tunnels as well – it leaks from the pipes. Anyone in there would be boiled alive."

Holmes looked grim. "But what about in an abandoned tunnel – the one that runs from Anderson Hall to where Memorial used to stand?"

Fielding nodded. "It might be safe – at least from steam. The live steam pipe running into Anderson enters on the other side of the building, and it would have been cut off from the one abandoned on the old Memorial side."

"Which is why," Holmes added, "there was no steam venting from the old access point in the field near the Memorial steps – as I observed when we walked by, and as shown here on the map."

"But Mr. Holmes," said Clark, raising his hands, "clearly you think that Michael is in a steam pipe tunnel – and if he is, pray God it's the one that doesn't have any steam. But what led you to this conclusion?"

"This paper from his desk," Holmes said, fishing it from his pocket and unfolding it upon the desk:

Guy Fawkes Tour!
Join the Latest Secret Tour of
The College of Mary and
Celebrate the 278th Anniversary
of The Gunpowder Plot!

"That anniversary," said Holmes, "is today – November 5th. In 1605, Fawkes and his friends were caught after trying to put explosives in tunnels underneath Parliament. *Tunnels*," he emphasized.

"But there was no evidence that tunnels were actually used in the Gunpowder Plot," protested Clark.

"It doesn't matter," said Holmes. "It's the popular perception. And the idea of tunnels – supposedly under Parliament and also on this campus – combined with today's date and Michael's fascination with history and the college's secret sites, suggest that he has been exploring the tunnels – and that he might still be down there."

"But sir – !" protested Fielding.

"Yes," said Holmes, raising a hand, "I know. He would be dead – cooked alive. But it was also cold last week when he went missing – when he likely decided to explore the tunnels on his own before leading a group on his 'official tour'. The steam would have been up then as now, and the pipes hot then too, so if he found a way in, he would have used the only tunnel that was cool enough to enter – the one between Memorial Hall and Anderson. Or so I've reasoned." He squared his shoulders. "And there's only one way to find out." He reached and folded the map. "Can you show us where the old tunnel terminates in Anderson's basement? I assume that there is a basement of some sort – I noticed small ventilation openings in the ground-level bricks as we walked by."

Holmes jammed the map into his pocket. Then we went back outside into the frigid cold, Fielding with us, and settled into a near-run across the narrow road and back onto the campus proper. We were motivated by our desire to locate the missing boy, and also due to the terrible bodily shock we'd taken when we stepped from the humid steam plant, which felt much like a tropical greenhouse, and into the bitter November midday. As we passed the field where Memorial Hall had stood, now marked only by its old stone staircase, I looked for some sign that the young man might be out there, just feet away, but of course there was nothing. Upon reaching Anderson, Clark led us to a side door of the old brick building, and I was glad to see that it was on the opposite side of building and the hallway where we had recently left Mr. and Mrs. Harlaw.

Just inside, we came upon a steep stairway leading up to the first floor. Clark veered left around it, and then just behind to a nondescript white-painted door leading back underneath the stairs. He pulled a key from his pocket and unlocked the door.

"Wait," said Holmes. "Is this door always kept locked?"

Clark affirmed it. Holmes frowned.

"Michael may have brought the specific keys with him to this building and this door, and left the rest of his key collection behind, and then someone could have found this door unlocked and relocked it on Friday or today, but I fear that since this door *was* locked just now, it means that he didn't come this way to enter the tunnel." He looked around. "Is there any way to verify if this door was found unlocked after Thursday night?"

Clark nodded and pointed to a doorway just across the narrow hall. "Mrs. Jenks would know."

He ushered us into her office, a tiny room littered with all sorts of knitted decorations, many involving cats in various ridiculous poses, and an overwhelming smell of cinnamon. The room was already crowded with just the lady, and Clark, Holmes, and I completely finished filling it. Fielding remained in the hallway, but he listened through the open door.

Clark explained to the fragile elderly lady behind a small desk that we were going to the basement, and he wondered if that door had been found unlocked since Thursday. "The basement – and the records we keep down there – falls under Mrs. Jenks' purview," he explained to us.

She was a short and thin little woman who had to be at least seventy, and she seemed as if she must be a permanent feature of the college – as if she had been seventy when the school opened, and she'd still be there, seventy years old, a hundred or more years in the future. She nodded sagely and said, "That door has *not* been left unlocked." She said it firmly, as if quoting one of the inviolable Biblical Commandments, her mouth tight. "I've had to go down there two times since Thursday – once on Friday morning, and again today. It was securely locked both times, and I relocked when I was finished. Had it been found unlocked, I would have reported it!"

Then she leaned forward and lowered her voice, her grim mien suddenly bright with curiosity as she looked from Holmes to me and back again. "Are you the men here to certify our ghost? I've written to London three times, in order to get on the Registry."

"Ghost?" asked Clark, a bit shocked. "What ghost? Surely you don't mean – ?"

"The one-legged ghost," she said knowingly, leaning back with a satisfied sigh, as if she'd been holding her breath about it for years and could now relax. "The records say that his name was Litton. Oh, I know that you don't *believe* in him, President, but he's *real*! Those of us who have spent any time here in Anderson Hall know it. We hear him hopping around, and crying out from the pain of his wound. Sometimes, if it's a very *still* day, and the sunlight isn't too *bright* – like today – we *see* him. I've been here since the building was built, and he never stops, year-in, year-out. His *pain* never stops, you see. Why, just this morning, I've heard him, again crying and knocking. I – "

"You *heard* him?" asked Holmes, speaking to the old woman for the first time. "Here – in your office?"

"No, just an hour ago, when I had to return some records to the basement. I wasn't scared, you know. I have no reason to fear *him* – or *any* of the dead who wander the College. We have a small vault downstairs where we keep the more important – "

"And did you hear him any last week?" Holmes pressed. "When you also went to the basement on Friday as well?"

She pursed her lips, and then smiled and nodded. "I *did*! He seemed especially active then. I didn't know what might be agitating him. Perhaps it was the anniversary of the day he *died*. I have often thought – "

But we didn't wait to hear what she thought. I don't know if Clark thanked her or not, but Holmes was already through the basement door and starting down the stairs into the darkness, with Fielding and me following, and Clark right behind.

At the bottom, Holmes lit a match, and for a moment I wondered if Clark would protest in fear that the place might accidentally catch fire. But Holmes quickly located where a lantern stood on a side table, and in seconds it was lit. He picked it up and stepped into the wider basement.

49

It was low, with even lower beams that made us duck our heads. It was clean enough, as clean as it could be, with no hanging cobwebs or piles of trash, often found in claggy basements where objects are hidden away because there is nowhere else to put them. There were shelves around the walls piled with documents, but I could only wonder how they hadn't already been ruined by the dampness down here. In the flickering light, the spaces behind the papers seemed to move, and I wasn't sure if it was just shifting shadows, or some sort of dank-dwelling insects or secretive rodents.

There was a terrible smell of rot and mildew, and cold was seeping up through the floor, which seemed to be a mixture of old broken cement, interspersed with numerous spots of bare soil. Some sort of room with a heavy open door was to our right – perhaps the vault which had been mentioned by Mrs. Jenks. Just past it, coming in low to the floor, was a big iron pipe, six inches in diameter. Just after it entered the exterior wall, it turned up and branched into a pair of smaller pipes, half the diameter of the larger, that went up through the basement ceiling. From where I stood, I could feel the heat emanating from the main pipe. This, then, was the incoming pipe from the steam plant. Beside it, returning through the ceiling and then out through the same wall near the floor, was a smaller pipe, which was likely the cold-water return.

Seeing it, Holmes turned the other way, where a similar set of pipes ran out through the basement wall in the direction of the old Memorial Hall. He walked up to them and then placed his hand upon the bigger one. He didn't flinch – for there was no steam in that pipe.

He knelt on the ground where the pipes entered, and I could see that there were several small ventilation holes set in the brickwork – holes opening to somewhere else: The abandoned steam tunnel. He leaned closer and called urgently, "Michael! Michael Harlaw! Can you hear me?"

There was no response.

He tried it again, and then another time. We all yelled together, and then we were silent, listening intently.

Nothing.

Holmes cursed. "She said she heard him just this morning! Just an hour or so ago!" He looked at Fielding. "Can you break down this wall to access the tunnel?"

"I can, but that wall is three feet thick. I'll have to go get some tools and some men."

"Stay with us instead. This isn't how Michael got into the tunnel. The door upstairs was locked, and there's no way through here. He entered from outside – by way of the Memorial Hall access point. Where is it?"

Fielding shook his head, looking abashed. "I don't know. Somewhere in the field between here and the science building, but I've never seen it. They tore down Memorial before my time, and must have covered it over."

"Then somehow Michael found it," said Holmes, "and he's left it disguised so that it wouldn't be easily noticed, giving him sole access. Let us pray that he didn't hide it too well!"

Holmes then repeated that Fielding would be more useful helping us search the field than trying to break through the wall – "At least for now," he added. In just a moment we were back upstairs and then outside, and this time the wet cold didn't seem to matter at all. Holmes paced off the approximate direction from where the pipe left the building, and we fanned out about twenty feet on either side of it. I saw our goal first – a spot about three-feet square, two-thirds of the way across the field to the science building, where the grass appeared to be more dead than that around it.

Holmes nodded. "That fits with where the access is sketched on the old map."

On approaching it, we found that it was a big piece of iron plating, covered with a thin layer of root-bound soil in which grass managed to grow. The grass and dirt along three edges showed where the lid had been pried up and lifted, with the fourth edge, its grass undamaged, serving as something of a hinge. Together, Fielding and I heaved and threw the entire thing back. I wondered that a single young man could have lifted and then replaced it so carefully, and I half-expected that we would find him immediately inside the access point, having been trapped at that spot because he couldn't lift the lid to effect his escape.

But he wasn't there.

We had exposed a square well about four feet deep, with walls constructed of what looked like rotting brick. Even as we were peering down and Clark was fruitlessly calling Michael's name, the door to Anderson Hall opened, and Mr. and Mrs. Harlaw, accompanied by the Assistant Dean, Martin Carlyle, came running our way.

"Oh my God!" cried Michael's mother. "Have you found him? Is he in that hole?"

"We suspect so," said Holmes, tearing off his Inverness and tossing it onto the wet ground. Then he pulled me aside, instructing me to send Fielding for seek additional help, and to bring back digging tools. Then he added in a low voice, "If the rest of the brick is in as bad shape as this access passage, there could very well be a cave-in. I'll work my way along the tunnel and see if I can find Michael – or," he said, lowering his voice even more, "determine where we need to dig down to make a recovery." Then, while he dropped to his knees and crawled over backward across the

51

lip of the hole, I turned and immediately sent Fielding on his grim errand. He headed toward the steam plant at a run.

I stepped back to the brick box's edge and peered down. Holmes was kneeling at the bottom and looking along a second tunnel which ran away from Anderson, toward the science building. "This one is caved in after only a few feet," he said. "Just past the opening to this box – just a couple of feet across – the tunnel opens up. It's a brick arch, about three feet high. The cave-in on this side looks to be old – not from the last few days." He shifted and looked back in the tunnel running to Anderson, which we had just crossed during our search. "This tunnel is clear – as far as I can see, anyway. I'm going to make my way."

"Holmes," I called. "Wait – I'll go back to the basement and fetch the lantern."

"No time," he said, and then he was gone.

I suppose that he'd been crawling for about half-a-minute when I wondered why I was still up there, simply waiting. Fielding had his instructions, and I could do nothing for the terrified couple or the fretting college representatives trying to comfort them. Meanwhile, employees and students who hadn't joined the ongoing search in the woods were starting to drift our way from adjacent buildings, but hanging back, as if sensing a tragedy in the offing. Soon I would be surrounded by a few dozen men and women who would be as useless as I felt.

I turned and clambered down backwards into the pit.

Kneeling on the muddy soil, I looked down the tunnel and saw a flicker of light somewhere in the narrow distance. Just how far was impossible to tell. "Holmes!" I called. "Can you see him?"

There was some response – possibly he said, "A moment, Watson!" but I wasn't sure. Then I heard him exclaim. I couldn't understand the words and whether they promised good or ill, but the served as the impetus to move me forward. I began to crawl into the hole, worming my way through the small opening into the larger passage and wishing that I'd had the sense to leave my coat behind as well.

The light quickly faded, blocked as it was by my body. What little of it that there was where Holmes had reached was likely considerably diminished by my added presence, but I kept going nonetheless. I knew from walking the distance above that it was just a few hundred feet, but here, crawling every brutal inch, it seemed as if it might go on forever.

As Holmes had said, the tunnel itself was constructed of brick, arched above with enough room for my back to move without scraping. But the cement between the bricks was rotten, crumbling and protruding in spots, and completely missing in others. Often the bricks were sagging or pushing into the tunnel, and in places they had fallen out entirely, leaving bare soil or ominous black voids behind them. Several times I leaned into the wall, or just barely brushed against it, and felt the brick-work move, as if I were pushing against a hanging drape. I gently moved back, hoping that my movement wouldn't bring down hundreds of pounds of brick and dirt onto my back. At other times, my passage seemed to cause crumbles of masonry to shower around me, without me having made any actual contact with the walls at all. I was terrified that I would cause it to collapse around me, leading to a substantial cave-in stretching far in both directions. I was no more than four or five feet below the surface, but soil is heavy, and wet soil heavier, and what was contained in that depth was more than enough to crush and suffocate me – as well as block the passage for Holmes's return.

Hanging from the roof of the tunnel were countless roots of varying thickness, grown deep from the grass above. Some were as thick as my wrist, but others were like threads, brushing along my face like wet spider webs. All of them were dripping with water that had saturated the ground above from the steady rains. While I mourned my ruined coat and suit, I was glad for my hat, which kept the wet twisted tendrils from dragging through my hair.

Perhaps worst of all was the constant and ever-seething population of *rhaphidophoridae*, popularly known as *cave crickets* or *spider crickets*. Bigger and lighter than the small, black, and friendly crickets one found in civilized places, these creatures were substantial. *Meaty*. It may have been my imagination, but I felt that they were radiating a vinegary odor which made my eyes burn. There were thousands of them, and as I approached and my eyes adjusted to the dim light, I could see that even as I watched them, they were watching me.

These creatures were possibly what I had seen behind the shelves in the Anderson basement, but then they were at a distance. Now they were all around me. Waves of them rolled away from me as I crawled, moving down the tunnel toward Holmes as my movements herded them forward, jumping frantically about with their thick grass-hopper legs as they were disturbed, sometimes hitting my face, and on several occasions landing on my bare neck. In a couple of cases, I felt them creeping further beneath my collar, pulled back by my movements, and underneath my shirt. Once one landed in my open panting mouth. I gave a grunt of disgust and spit the thing out, but I kept going. They were only crickets, and I would be able to rid myself of them later. For now, my help was needed.

The floor of the tunnel was plain soil – mud actually, as there was quite a bit of standing water. It was hard to find traction to push forward. Several times my hand slipped and I cried out. Traversing the tunnel was made worse by the presence of the old iron steam pipe, left abandoned in place. As I crawled I had to straddle it, at least eight inches in diameter, and I regularly barked my hands and wrists against the widened bell joints where the pieces of pipe had been pushed together. I began to worry about picking up some dread disease by way of muddy wounds that I might open on the ragged rusty pipe.

There was nowhere to go but forward, and I awkwardly thrust one knee ahead and then the other, matching the abbreviated stride with similar arm motions. I found that I was looking down, my breathing heavy, simply forcing myself to move, inch after inch, knowing that there was a finality in front of me, one way or another. Then, to my surprise, I heard a voice directly in in my path.

"Watson," said Sherlock Holmes softly. "He's alive – but we have to dig."

I looked up then and saw that Holmes had lit a match to let me see what he'd found – a young man, so similar in visage to his father, unconscious but breathing, his right leg buried under a cave-in of brick and stone and mud. Beside it was a mound of material that the young man must have previously removed, but without any measurable success. Apparently, the more he'd shifted, the more fresh material he'd loosened.

"Should I go back for help?" I said. "We can measure off the distance, and then excavate from above."

"I don't think that we can wait for that," he said softly. "In any case, it would probably bring down the entire ceiling onto us. With your help, I believe I can free him – but for God's sake be careful, or the whole structure will fall and engulf us!"

I have no sense if it was ten minutes or an hour. Time ceased to having meaning as we slowly freed Michael Harlaw from what would have been his unknown tomb. One brick at a time, one stone, pulled gingerly loose by Holmes and handed to me. One scoop of viscous soil after another, drawn away and collected behind me so as to not block our way when we eventually departed. I would turn and place it carefully along the tunnel wall. I didn't want to simply toss it, possibly dislodging more of the brickwork, and I also didn't want to inadvertently build a second randomly constructed wall behind us that we'd have to force across when bringing out the injured boy.

And boy he was, despite his age. He seemed too young for the situation in which he'd found himself – but then again, that had been true of so many tragedies that I'd witnessed, even before a similarly aged army had been slaughtered at Maiwand. So different had that day been – hellish heat, choking dust, and blinding sunlight that made seeing impossible, aching thirst beyond comprehension, and the sounds of killing artillery and dying screams. Here was cold and wet and dark, with the only noises coming from the scraping of stone and mud, and the dripping of water into what might be our graves, and the small grunts of effort, more and more frequent, as the next brick was pulled loose and moved aside, and the next and the next . . . .

But every task is completed one small piece at a time, and I was in the act of moving yet another brick, the last one it turned out, when Holmes murmured, "I have him. He's free. Let is bring him out of this Hell-hole."

It wasn't that simple. First, I carefully fought my way out of my overcoat, and then we wrapped it around the young man's lower body so that any injury to his legs wouldn't be worsened as we pulled him out. After tying the sleeves in place, we commenced our return.

The journey back to the daylight and the grass above was in some ways much worse than the trip in, but in the same way we had un-buried the boy, we accomplished it in small stages, crawling one foot or just one inch after another. When we were near the entryway, I saw that two men were down in the brick access hole – Clark and the boy's father. They had been calling to us the entire time, but Holmes and I had no awareness of it. Above us stood Fielding with a crew of men, all carrying shovels, picks, and long iron bars to use as leverage – now thankfully unnecessary. When we were out and the boy had been lifted into the dim rainy daylight, what there was of it, Clark ordered them to weld up the lid for good.

Meanwhile, Mrs. Harlaw had fallen to her knees beside her son, and it was her sobs that seemed to rouse him. With a feeble smile, he reached for her hand before again lapsing back into unconsciousness. It would be the next day, in the small facility that served as Abridge's only hospital, that he would awaken completely. With the strength of youth, he would quickly recover – and his parents wisely waited several days before sharing with him all the concern and anguish that he had inadvertently caused. It was a lesson he would long remember.

It was toward the end of November when the Harlaws visited us in Baker Street. The boy seemed to have no lasting ill effects – just a limp, which I recognized would vanish in time. He gladly accepted our offer of tea and biscuits. His parents were less relaxed, both of them sitting with a tense awareness of their son, as if he were still in danger, even in our safe sitting room. I knew that it would be a long time before they would be able to forget what had happened, or to allow themselves to trust their son as they had before. Although the young man didn't seem to have been greatly affected, a lesson about life's fragility had left his parents both shaken and nervous.

After a moment of enjoying his refreshments, Michael confirmed what Holmes had been able to piece together.

"I've learned quite a bit about the school," he said without any false modesty. His father watched him with a studied frown, but with something like pride showing far back in his eyes. "That kind of thing has always interested me – doing research about places where others don't know to look. Learning forgotten facts. Putting together the pieces. I believe that I know more about the College of Mary than most of the professors.

"Every few years, the graduating students bestow on a lucky few the keys that they've accumulated. An even greater secret – known to just a few students – has been the existence of the old tunnels. Last year, one of the senior fellows showed me how to find the tunnel between Anderson Hall and the old Memorial dormitory. I learned where all the other entrances are as well – quite a few besides the obvious places where the steam vents – but the rest of them are impassible once the heating system is activated each fall.

"I'd waited too late to explore the other tunnels – I planned to get into them in the spring – but I knew how to enter the one where you found me. I'd originally planned a tunnel tour for my friends on Guy Fawkes Day, in honor of his use of tunnels. I decided to examine its condition beforehand, so I entered on Thursday night. I believe that the rain weakened the brickwork. Before I knew it, there was a cave-in. I turned to jump back the way I'd just crawled, but my leg was trapped.

"I did my best to work myself loose, but it was impossible, and I was afraid that too much digging would finish burying me. My lantern had been buried under the mud and bricks. I yelled over and over, but no one heard me, and I lost track of how long I was down there. I thought . . . I thought . . . ."

He didn't weep, but he was clearly shaken then with emotion at the realization of how close he'd come to death. I hoped – as I'm sure his parents did as well – that he'd learned a lesson. But that day I suspected that he would continue exploring his fascination with uncovering unknown knowledge and finding out things that others didn't, even when it meant disregarding his own safety.

I was right. Soon after our meeting, Michael Harlaw decided that his study of music wasn't how he wanted to spend his time and energy. He transferred to the University of London to pursue a career in archaeology – a field in which he's now quite well known.

On that November day in 1883, before Michael had found his true path, I glanced from the young man of nineteen to Sherlock Holmes, himself just twenty-nine. I knew where I'd previously seen Michael's disregard for personal safety when weighed against *finding out*. I recognized the trait in the young man because I'd come to know it so well in Sherlock Holmes. My friend was just such a person. I could imagine Holmes at that age, deciding to explore a lost tunnel on his own, regardless of the consequences. On that day in 1883, when Holmes was just weeks from turning thirty, he still had the same quality. It was part of what made him so tenacious at determining the truth and serving as an advocate for those who weren't able to solve their own mysteries.

And even as Holmes would continue to push to understand and to know, and edge himself into danger, because it was what he did best, I would balance out these tendencies and ward him when I could.

For that was what I did best.

NOTE

Curiously, the college where I received my first degree in the 1980's had similar haunted buildings with ghosts very much like the ones described here. I also inherited keys to most of the buildings from former students, and wearing my deerstalker (which has been my only hat, all year long, since I was nineteen years old to the present), I would often visit these buildings by night, exploring roofs and basements, towers and attics and forgotten chambers, either giving guiding tours or on solo expeditions.

This campus also had old steam tunnels, just as described here, some still very much active, and others abandoned. (I live less than a mile from that school, taking walks there on a regular basis, and the tunnels are still there, as are the secret openings – if one knows where to look.) As a student, I would visit these tunnels, leading secret expeditions with other students or alone. Often, one could crawl through the crickets for quite a distance along the brick-arched tunnels, only to encounter a complete cave-in, with no visible signs on the surface to indicate where it had occurred, as the old rotten bricks had given away at some point long past.

It only occurred to me in later years how such a cave-in might trap or kill unwary visitors, and how it might be years – or never – before what happened was discovered and the bodies finally found.

I was really stupid back then.

– DM

My deerstalker and my dog, on a walk through the college,
at the partially buried entrance plate to tunnel that's very very similar to
the one that trapped Michael Harlaw. It's still there, if you know what it is . . . .
(Photograph – October 18th, 2024)

The Intervention
of the Dark Stranger

I – The Amateur Blackmailer

Sherlock Holmes did not willingly tolerate fools, and therefore I watched with some interest as he continued his discussion with Mr. Lloyd Cresswell. Even after two days, I was still trying to decide if there was some reason that Holmes would spending the evening in deep conversation with the apparent blowhard, or if Cresswell was, in fact, not the fool that he appeared.

"Even then," Cresswell was saying, trying to finish his story while laughing, "Stueckle insisted that he'd been attacked by a giant insect, and he was ready to move back home that night! *Haw haw!*" he guffawed – and then he started coughing.

He'd been telling a story from when he and Holmes were at university, and Cresswell had led a group of like-minded students – Holmes apparently not among them – to play a prank on a generally disliked fellow classmate. Stueckle, the young man in question, had terribly poor vision. On one occasion when he was bathing, *sans* glasses, Cresswell, who had somehow obtained a live lobster, tied it to a thin rope suspended from a long stick, and then approached Stueckle unseen, slowly lowering the writhing creature from above. The unsuspecting young man, in his desperate scramble to escape what he believed to be a massive and multi-pound spider descending upon him, had embarrassed himself, and nearly done an injury in the process. Further, having never seen a real lobster before, Stueckle refused to believe that the creature wasn't some insect that had been trapped in their joint lodgings.

"Even when he had his glasses on and could see that it wasn't a spider," continued Cresswell, once he could speak again, "he kept trying to count the legs!" He laughed again and looked my way, quite graciously including me in the conversation. "And when we cooked the thing, he refused to help eat it – and Stueckle would eat nearly anything! Quite the poor sport, I should say!" And he laughed once more.

I wasn't sure if Holmes had previously heard the story before or not. On several earlier occasions, even when Holmes had indicated that he'd been aware of this or that reminiscence, Cresswell had barreled forward anyway and finished telling what he'd started. Just then, after hearing of poor Stueckle, Holmes kept his eyes fixed on Cresswell as if he were watching for something indicative to happen in a scientific experiment. "Many people," he said evenly when our host was finished, "believe that lobsters are in the same family as spiders, but in fact the former are not *arachnids* but *malacostracans*. One wonders if lobsters had happened to be land creatures, would they still be considered a delicacy, or would we instead view them as large and repellent insects, disgustingly skittering about and no more to be eaten than cockroaches or scorpions?"

Cresswell's eyes widened at the thought, but instead of continuing along Holmes's line, he was instead reminded of another anecdote related to the recent discovery of a peculiar insect in his own basement. While that conversation continued, my mind drifted.

I was most surprised to be awake and alert just then, considering that we were sitting before a warm fire in Cresswell's study after a strenuous morning in the bitter cold, followed by a hot and hearty lunch when our task was complete. The satisfaction of a job well done, simple though it had been, should have meant that I was free to relax, dozing in my chair. But we had returned to the house to find that the cook had made a great urn of strong black coffee, and the three cups I had downed in quick succession to warm my inner man were still serving to keep me alert and curious. I knew that it would be some time before the coffee's hold relinquished. With nothing better to do, I remained seated near Holmes and Cresswell, on the periphery of their recollections.

In those early days of my friendship with Holmes, there was still much that I did not know about him. From the time we'd first met nearly a year before, my opinions had veered wildly from indifferent tolerance to fierce curiosity, from amusement to anger, and from impulses to quickly find new rooms where I could recover in peace from my war wounds to deep gratitude for being included in some of my friend's most-intriguing investigations. As he and I had traveled the day before to the very north of England, not far from the Liddel Water along the Scottish border, I'd felt all of those things during the long and cold journey, but the greater proportion of my thoughts were curiosity at the opportunity to meet one of Holmes's old school friends who now needed our help.

I'd found Lloyd Cresswell to be a big hearty fellow in his late twenties, the same age as Holmes, and just a year or so younger than myself. But Holmes and Cresswell were nothing alike. In addition to the physical dissimilarities, Cresswell was loud and boisterous. He had a large square head and rather small eyes, like a bull terrier. His full mustache was rather ridiculously waxed out to sharp horizontal points on either side of his face, and he spoke with hints of a Scottish burr – as did I to a lesser degree, having also grown up not far from the border between England

and Scotland, although I had been reared about one-hundred miles straight to the west, on the Scottish side.

For all the inconvenience of getting there, the matter itself turned out to be rather negligible. Cresswell, who had inherited a fine house and working farm a couple of miles northwest of Blackpool Gate, had recently received several blackmail letters, crudely written and spelled, alleging that he had promised marriage to a local girl, and demanding a cash payment, lest the matter be revealed in the public press. According to Cresswell, the assertions held no truth and, not wishing to have the matter handled locally, he had summoned Holmes, who he recalled from their school days had "worked out those little methods of thought which might see a way around this."

We arrived the day before, on the thirtieth of December, after a long train journey to Carlisle, followed by a shorter trip on the local line to Gretna, and then east by way of Cresswell's frigid carriage. He had met us at the station, shaking hands and then hastening us along. The ride to Cresswell's manor was all of fifteen miles, and too unpleasant to share much conversation. I spent much of it looking out the streaked carriage window as we passed bleak winter fields and tiny wide spots and localized gatherings that could barely be called villages. Then we arrived at Cresswell's home – ostensibly to celebrate the New Year, but in truth to sort out the little matter of the squire's extortion.

By way of examination of receipts kept in the household files, Holmes quickly confirmed that the handwriting on the blackmail notes was that of the girl's brother, a ne'er-do-well fellow named Andrew Wallace who had struggled to keep his farm afloat after the death of the pair's parents two years before. Andrew and his sister, Olivia, lived on the nearby smallholding and provided eggs to the Cresswell manor. Our host informed us that he had suspected Andrew from the start. I suppose my face had showed some surprise – a trait which I would have to control – for Cresswell noticed and said, "You wonder why I dragged you up here, Watson. *Who* did it was just part of the affair. I could have handled it myself, but I wanted Holmes to confirm my suspicions, and also I don't want anyone else here to know what Andrew has been up to. I don't think that I should involve myself – it might whirl into something worse, and the locals don't need to know what the poor lad has contrived. He's had some bad luck, and did something desperate. No need to break him for it, or ruin his reputation."

That was the first indication that I had of Cresswell's contradictory nature. He could be loud and rude, but he also seemed to care about those around him, and more evidence presented itself as our time there passed.

Yet this was the same man who had once terrorized a half-blind friend with a snapping suspended lobster. He was a contradiction.

Once the amateur blackmailer's identity was confirmed, Cresswell was all for having Holmes go back out that very evening to confront the young man, but my friend convinced our host to instead follow the blackmail instructions as described and leave the payment atop a well-known landmark four miles to the north, a large and notable flat stone just at the Scottish border along the Kershope Burn, not far from where the stream flowed into the Liddell Water. "That way," Holmes added, "we'll catch him in the act, and the shock will serve to rehabilitate more than if we showed up tonight, accusing him of a crime which he's only half-committed."

Privately I agreed with Cresswell about confronting Wallace quickly and immediately, as one would lance a boil now instead of waiting until the morrow, and I felt that way even more the next day, New Year's Eve, a cold but clear Saturday morning when Holmes and I settled into hiding a couple of hours before Cresswell was to deliver the payment. As instructed, he had wrapped it in a hessian sack. He'd insisted on sending the full amount requested, and then some, in spite of Holmes's initial abjurations to the contrary. Then Cresswell explained his thinking, and we had no choice but to accede to his wishes.

It wasn't as cold as the day before, but no less unpleasant. With the eastern sun at our backs, we watched from our blind, a stand of holly that had retained a full growth of concealing leaves into the winter. As the cold seeped into me, I churlishly half-suspected that Holmes had talked Cresswell into following through with the blackmailer's arrangement because he wanted to practice concealed observation and use the opportunity to follow someone in the countryside, especially in winter when there was very little cover to be found among the barren trees and bushes.

After a long period of simply shifting from one numb foot to the other, I was greatly of a mind to slip away and return alone to Cresswell's house by a different route, and to hunt up a good book and a glass of whisky, but in the end, I held to my post – and luckily young Wallace wasn't tardy. He must have also been in place early and watching when the delivery was finally made, for Cresswell had no sooner vanished over a hill to the south, back toward his manor house, when a tall thin fellow, his hair dark and rather long and unkempt, arose from a thicket near the stream and quickly retrieved the bag. A quick look inside confirmed to him that the payment he'd demanded was indeed included, and so he set off, also to the south, but along a different vector from that of Cresswell.

We knew from Holmes's questions the previous night as to where Wallace lived, and that he must be returning to his own home.

We caught up with him just before he reached the house, confronting him outside and in private, per Cresswell's instructions. Wallace was wary, but Holmes's concise and surgically precise description of the situation and how Wallace's involvement had been determined prevented any pretense of innocence from wasting more of our time. After just one half-hearted denial, Wallace admitted his crime. I could see that he was realizing just how much his foolish act was about to cost him when Holmes continued with the rest of Cresswell's instructions: To inform Wallace that not only was he to keep the demanded payment that was in the bag, but also the additional funds that had been added, rounding the amount up to a most tidy sum that would go a long way toward helping the brother and sister get back on their feet. We left Wallace there, trying not to weep until we were gone. As we passed around a grove of trees and out of sight, I heard the poor fellow, not that much younger than Holmes or me, give way to sobs.

"I don't necessarily agree with rewarding an attempted blackmailer," I said as Holmes and I walked away, my satisfaction at having helped with a good deed somewhat negated by my quarrelsome mood.

Holmes tilted his head in something like a shrug. "This is Cresswell's demesne – it was his decision. I'm aware that you don't see the reason for us to have made such a journey this far north, simply to carry out so small a task, but I believe that it was obvious, in addition to the reason given – not wanting anyone who lives around here to know the level to which Wallace has debased himself – Cresswell wasn't comfortable providing the additional charity in person." He glanced at me and continued. "I've also perceived that you think Cresswell is something of an empty shell, but I assure you – the man has hidden depths. We were once good friends, despite his apparent flaws, and that friendship has only dimmed by time and distance, not poor regard. You know, Watson, that I do not willingly tolerate fools."

When we returned to the manor, we found Cresswell standing twenty feet or so outside the front door, an expectant smile on his face. "Success?" he asked succinctly. I wondered how long he'd been waiting there for our return.

Holmes nodded. "I think that Wallace owes you a great deal." He and I then made to continue inside when Cresswell raised a hand. "Wait! Stop!"

We paused and looked at him. "Tradition, you know. It must be honored – for the luck of the house." And he glanced toward the front door. I saw now that it was partly open, and just inside stood the cook, Mrs.

Thealby, to whom we had been introduced the night before. She was looking out expectantly, while Holmes appeared to be puzzled. Then I had an inkling of what Cresswell was about.

"Ah," I said. "The Tall Dark Stranger."

Cresswell nodded and beamed, and the front door opened further. Mrs. Thealby, a thin woman in her early forties, stepped out toward us, smiling as well and nodding silently.

Holmes glanced from the two of them to me, his eyebrows raised questioningly. "Hogmanay," I explained. "It's today – the last day of the year. A Scottish holiday."

"*The* Scottish holiday," corrected Cresswell.

An enlightened look crossed Holmes's face. "Indeed." He turned his gaze upon Cresswell. "And the Dark Stranger – the 'First Footing', as I believe it's called."

Cresswell nodded. "That's right. To set the luck of the house for the coming year, the first person to cross the threshold after the midnight bell rings on Hogmanay should be a stranger – preferably a tall dark-haired young man. That's you down to the ground, Holmes! If you would care to be the first to enter, we'll have good luck all year long!"

Holmes shook his head. "It's already mid-morning. Surely someone has entered before now."

"Not so," Cresswell countered. "The men caring for the animals had no reason to come inside, and I haven't been back inside since. D-----d cold it's been too! Did you meander over half of creation on your way back?" His words were gruff, but he had a twinkle in his eye. "We – that is, Mrs. Thealby and I – believe that you'll be the first inside, in spite of the late hour. And that fits the spirit of the thing." He glanced my way. "No offense, Doctor, but clearly Holmes is the dark young stranger that fits the bill."

"As you've noted," I said, "the dark young man should be a stranger. Holmes and I have already spent a number of hours under your roof."

Cresswell flipped a hand, as if that were a mere technicality to be waved away. "We'll do the best that we can," he answered. "After all, most years on Hogmanay we have no strangers here at all. This will set us upon the right path for sure." He bowed toward Holmes and swept his arm toward the house. "After you, good sir."

Holmes, looking bemused, fulfilled his required role – although I half-expected that he would balk with a number of choice words regarding the foolishness of superstition. But perhaps, like me, he simply wanted to get this over with and return inside to the warmth, and whatever comforting refreshments that we might find therein.

64

"There," said Cresswell, once we had shut the door behind us and hung up our coats and hats. "The Dark Stranger has crossed the threshold, and we'll have good luck the whole year through! That reminds me of Davy Ingleby – do you remember him, Holmes? He had that coin that he insisted was lucky – meant the world to him. We swapped it one night, and he spotted it right off. Didn't expect that. Cried like a baby, he did. Like a baby . . . ."

As he spoke, Mrs. Thealby softly informed us that strong hot coffee was waiting in the kitchen, and I gratefully followed her, not deigning to hear the conclusion of Cresswell's account. I went through three cups before I began to feel warm again, having more than enough to remain alert throughout the afternoon.

And so after lunch we were sitting in Cresswell's study as I politely listened to more of his and Holmes's discussions of the former days of nearly a decade before, and I indifferently watched for signs that the man was not a fool.

II – The Hogmanay Dinner

I learned of another aspect of Cresswell's charitable nature that night at dinner. To celebrate New Year's Eve, and also to honor our visit, Cresswell had thrown something of a small dinner party, inviting a few locals, among them the vicar, a stooped widower named Tannen. He was a frowning and grim fellow, escorting a tall heavy-set woman of similar age, Miss Sipe, spinster. Cresswell had earlier informed us that he wouldn't be surprised if there wasn't some sort of announcement from them in the near future about tying up their separate lives. I didn't see it, as after their joint arrival, they generally ignored one another. But possibly at their ages, that might be the best sort of marriage they could devise.

The party also included a young man named Douglas Thealby, a thin lad of eighteen or so, several inches over six feet, and a lady of the same age named Elizabeth Selkie, both of whom were due to be married the next day, following the Sunday service at the nearby chapel. Thealby was a curious fellow, and the youngest son of Cresswell's cook. She and her husband had worked for the Cresswell family for decades, initially serving Cresswell's father. By the time the elder Mr. Thealby passed away a decade earlier, his two older sons had already also gone to work for Cresswell. As he grew, young Douglas had done what he could, but his forte was not physical strength or working outdoors. Rather, his gifts lay along the lines of theoretical mathematics. Cresswell had recognized this talent early on and had paid for the lad's education and additional tutoring. As I learned from conversation around the table, Douglas was also going to be financially supported when he went off to Cambridge in early 1882, accompanied by his new bride. Great things were expected of him, and Cresswell noted that some of the lad's notions were making people notice him as the new Newton.

This caused me to look at the quiet young man in a new light. When we'd been introduced, I'd thought him simply shy and awkward. He kept his eyes down much of the time, only looking up at odd times to glance around the room, mumbling responses when required, and probably not even a dozen of those passed his lips. He was a sharp contrast to his fiancé, Elizabeth, a rather stout and talkative young woman with pink skin, bowed red lips, and tight butter-blonde curls that spilled and bounced around her shoulders, as such a mane would never be tamed. She stayed beside her fiancé at all times, reaching out to regularly touch his shoulder when not holding his arm and pulling him close. Her gown was white with decorations and stitching in the colors of spring, and that, with her blonde hair, was a sharp contrast to the dark-haired and darkly clothed young man beside her.

"We'll marry tomorrow," she was explaining to Holmes and me as the dinner progressed, "and we'll go up to Cambridge just a few days later." She paused to poke around on her plate and, finding that she had eaten all of her own serving of beef, she reached across to her fiancé's plate, forking over some of his. "Jack Sprat and his wife," I thought to myself, unsure whether to be amused or to pity the poor young man. I decided that someone as quiet and shy as he, with his head likely in mathematical clouds far above the rest of us, was fortunate to have someone to look after him.

"Thanks to Mr. Cresswell," Elizabeth continued, "the house is already arranged. Douglas will begin attending classes in a couple of weeks, and he's marked down for great things! He's enrolled in a number of advanced sessions with some of the more famous professors. Of course, I'll manage things for him at home – our social life, you know, and making the right friends to advance Douglas' career."

Elizabeth's father, Calvin Selkie, was also in attendance at the gathering. His wife had died when Elizabeth was quite small, and fortunately, as he explained, he had enough money to hire a governess to raise his daughter to be a lady. He also praised Cresswell, more vociferously as his consumption of Cresswell's spirits continued throughout the evening. "D-----d generous of him!" he growled, glancing across the table to where Cresswell was talking with the vicar. "A boy like Douglas comes along but once in a generation. To be given this opportunity – Well, he's just lucky, that's all, that Cresswell could support him." He lowered his voice. "And I couldn't be happier that he and my

Elizabeth are going to marry," he confided. "When she set her sights on Douglas last fall, I had my doubts. The lad was spooked at first, I can tell you, like a forest creature, but in the end she wore him down. Other than going to Cambridge, she'll be the best thing that ever happens to him. He may learn a lot from those professors, but she'll be the true making of him. You'll see."

The food wasn't fancy fare, but it was warm and tasty and wholesome – what one would expect to find in this rural setting. Cresswell called Mrs. Thealby in from the kitchen so that we could all sing her praises. She was tall like her sons, rather thin like Douglas, careworn and aged beyond her years, but happy-looking nonetheless, and she couldn't keep from looking at her youngest son with beaming pride. As she departed, leaving a couple of girls behind to help with the serving, I asked Cresswell if setting such a fine table so close to the other upcoming events would cause the poor woman extra stress.

"Not this year, Doctor," he replied. "Since her son's wedding is tomorrow, on New Year's Day, she will not be cooking. I've hired someone to come over from Gretna and provide for the reception. Tonight is a substitute for our New Year's festivities this year.

"As you've seen," he continued, his voice rather loud, encompassing those around the two of us, "we don't have a large staff – just the Thealby boys working outside, along with two other men, and here in the house we have Mrs. Thealby, Porter serving as my major-domo, and a couple of girls – Sarah, the one there pouring for Douglas, and Emma, carrying the soup bowls back to the kitchen. While they'll both be fine cooks someday, they aren't ready quite to contrive a New Year's Dinner or prepare a wedding reception. Isn't that right, Sarah?"

His question startled the small dark-haired young lady who, like Emma, a tall blonde with a smiling rosy expression, had been working in the background while we ate, bringing in the food, refilling drinks, and generally doing what was requested or required for the guests. Sarah finished refilling Douglas Thealby's glass and then, with a glance toward him, stepped away quickly, nodding to Cresswell. She was a small girl, probably no more than eighteen, with dark hair and eyes. She kept them lowered, as servants often do, but once when thanking her for refilling my own glass, our eyes had met, and I was rewarded with a look of sharp intelligence, though perhaps mixed with a bit of sadness. It flashed across my mind what it must mean for someone with native intellect to be kept in a low position due to circumstances and gender. Douglas Thealby was fortunate indeed to have a patron willing to rescue him from such a life. Sarah, while probably not the next Newton, had potential as well – or so I had judged based on one quick glance. However, she would not be sent to

Cambridge. Fortunately she had a safe and steady place in the world, and the opportunity to rise, as Cresswell indicated, to be a cook in her own right some day.

During the meal, the conversation turned to what it was like to live so near the division between Scotland and England. "The border has wandered over the centuries," the vicar explained, "but generally in this area, it's always been understood that Scotland is north of Kershope Burn and Liddell Water."

"Of course," Miss Sipe interjected, interest on her wide face, "there was a great deal of Roman influence here, long before the arbitrary borders were set."

Holmes glanced up with interest. "I understand that not far away, at Gwenddolau's Fort near the old Roman Road, the Battle of Arfderydd occurred in 573 – with some interpreting *Arfderydd* as *Arthur*. The area is also known for a meeting between St. Kentigern and Lailoken – one of the original names of Merlin."

I was surprised to hear Holmes recounting such specific but esoteric facts, still under the impression then that he'd been serious when explaining nearly a year before that he limited what he put into his brain-attic. It would be several more years, specifically after the events at Mediobogdum, * before I understood the nature and depth of his interest in the Arthurian legends.

"Ah," countered the vicar, "there is some thought that the location was nearer Carwinley, south of the river . . . ." From there, the conversation ran for quite a while along local folklore, and I noticed several times how Cresswell seemed to simply sit back and enjoy the spirited byplay from everyone at the table – everyone, that is, except Douglas Thealby, who kept his head down and his gaze upon his half-emptied plate, except for when he'd unexpectedly look up, glancing around the room for a moment before returning to his own thoughts.

About nine o'clock, the meal seemed to wind down, and by unspoken mutual accord, we withdrew to the parlour, where spirits were passed around. By then, I was becoming rather weary as the day caught up with me. The effects of the black coffee following our return to the house had finally worn off, and taking on the heavy celebratory meal, followed by some particularly fine Scottish whisky, was threatening to do me in entirely. It was all I could to stay awake, and I began to realize with dismay that the evening was far from over: The guests were staying to midnight, to see in the New Year.

It was a small party, but it didn't ever settle into a lull as different groups formed, broke apart, and re-formed to converse. At one point I found myself speaking with Douglas who, free for once from the grip of his fiancée, became a bit more talkative. He was nearly enthusiastic about one of the Cambridge professors with whom he hoped to study when his conversation broke off abruptly. His gaze had shifted over my shoulder, and I turned to look, seeing that Sarah was carrying in more refreshments. He fell silent has he watched her serve them to the other members of the party, leaving me somewhat amused that someone so thin, who had already completed such a thorough meal, might still be hungry, coveting the food that was given to others.

Nearing a quarter-past-eleven, I saw that Elizabeth Selkie had pulled Holmes aside. He was paying her far more attention than I would have expected, considering her rather unpleasant personality. Curiously, she was speaking softly, in contrast to her more typical ebullience. I was surprised as Holmes caught my eye and nodded toward the hall. Then he said something quietly to Cresswell, while Elizabeth retrieved Douglas from where he stood alone on one wall. In a moment, they, along with Holmes and myself, had relocated to Cresswell's much-quieter study.

"Cresswell gave us permission to meet here," said Holmes as we settled ourselves. Then to the young lady he added, "You wished to speak with us?"

She glanced my way, and I understood that she had asked to consult with Holmes and not me, but now my presence was apparently to be tolerated.

"We have something of a mystery," replied Elizabeth, "Douglas and I, and tonight I asked myself: How often do I get the chance to speak with a real detective?"

"Indeed," said Holmes with gravitas, giving her his full attention, but with perhaps just a bit of a twinkle in his eye that only I among those there would recognize. Douglas was glancing up at Elizabeth with great discomfort, as if he greatly wished to be elsewhere. The uncharitable thought flashed across my mind that their marriage would give him many opportunities to feel that way, and then I was immediately sorry to have allowed such a surly idea to form.

"What seems to be the problem?" asked Holmes.

"Douglas is being harassed. Threatened. Terrorized."

The young man then turned toward Holmes, and then me, giving a little shake of his head. "It's nothing like that," he murmured. "Not really. Elizabeth, can't we just – ?"

"No, we cannot!" she replied firmly, her mouth tightening, even as her tone rose slightly in pitch. I noticed there were already well-grooved lines running down from each side of her mouth, indicating that this was a rather frequent reaction. "May I explain?" she asked Holmes.

He nodded for her to continue.

"It started a few days ago," Elizabeth Selkie explained. "The threats. I know that it bothers Douglas, even if he won't say anything. He's been even more nervous than usual ever since. He simply cannot settle when we discuss the wedding arrangements, or our move to Cambridge."

"Elizabeth – " Douglas Thealby's soft voice took on an edge, surprising me that he had it in him, but the effort collapsed abruptly when she lightly slapped his hand. He sagged back, ceding the battle before it began.

"Douglas has his own small cottage," explained Elizabeth. "It's nearby, nicely provided for him by Mr. Cresswell. Douglas' mother has her own house, also owned by Mr. Cresswell, where she lived with her husband, and then their three sons. Burl and Ian still live there with her, but when it became apparent that Douglas was marked for better things, and needed a place to carry out his studies – Did you know he's already written a paper that was read last year to the Royal Society? – Mr. Cresswell made the cottage available to him. Of course, he often eats here in the kitchen with his mother when he remembers – Douglas would never last a day by himself! – but the rest of his time is spent there, in the cottage, working out his little ways of thought: Formulas and theories and monographs." She glanced at him, not with pride, bit rather with a whiff of peevishness, as if his priorities were misplaced – or so I perceived.

"When I set my sights on Douglas and we became betrothed last fall, I began to visit the cottage, doing what I could to fix it up and make it more livable. In truth, I've come to know the place quite well, and I know when something isn't right."

Throughout her narrative, Douglas Thealby seemed to withdraw further upon himself. Elizabeth retained her firm grip upon his hand, but otherwise he was focused inward, his long legs crossed, his back bowed forward and head down, and his free arm wrapped around his torso as if he were in pain.

"And the threats?" Holmes prompted. I could see that he was attentive, which made me more curious, as the reasons Holmes might or might not be interested in some affair or intrigue were his own. I was never sure what might arouse his fascination.

"On Thursday," said Elizabeth, "I arrived in the morning to find the remains of a burned barrel standing in front of the cottage, still smoking. It must have been set alight the night before, but the fire had gone out before it was completely consumed. It had been filled with tar and pieces of wood, and the stench was awful, although the breeze was fortunately blowing it away from the houses." She glanced at her future husband.

"Douglas didn't even know that it was there. He had worked through much of the night, and had fallen asleep near dawn. Isn't that right?" she asked him, giving a shake to his hand, as if to wake him up. He nodded once without looking up.

"Was anyone able to explain it?" asked Holmes.

Elizabeth gave a toss to her blonde curls. "I didn't ask. Growing up here, Douglas was sometimes picked on for being quiet." She reached across and patted his captive hand, which he'd apparently permanently surrendered to her custody. "I thought it was something inexplicably done by one of the village boys to tease him."

"Yet you've described it as a 'threat'."

"It didn't seem so at first. But yesterday morning – Friday – I found something else when I arrived for my morning visit: A broken cake lying just outside the front door."

Holmes leaned forward, now more interested. "Outside? How close to the door?"

"Just outside. Some of it was *on* the door, as if it was thrown against it and then fell to the ground. Douglas would have stepped in it, should he have gone outside. He never looks where's he's going. He might have slipped."

Holmes nodded at something. "Was it iced? Round or square? Tall or flat?"

Elizabeth frowned. "What does that matter? There was no icing that I recall. And I suppose it might have been round, before it broke apart, and not too thick."

"And you're sure it wasn't bread."

"No. I did take the trouble to bend and touch it. It wasn't bread."

"Thank you. That is also interesting, though it doesn't sound like much of a threat either. Did you ask anyone in the house about it?"

"That I did, for I couldn't convince Douglas to say anything. Neither his mother nor the servant girls knew anything about it. No one had made a cake. Douglas' brothers were in the kitchen as well, but they took it to be a joke, insisting that Douglas had raided the kitchen for a snack and carelessly dropped it on the way back – in spite of their mother's insistence that she had made no cake for him to steal."

"And today?" asked Holmes. "There must be a third incident for you to be concerned as you are."

"That's correct. This time, someone has been *inside the cottage*."

Now I leaned forward as well. The girl's tone had changed, and this suddenly seemed a bit more interesting – and threatening after all.

"How do you know?" Holmes asked.

71

"This morning, I arrived as usual to find that Douglas had stayed up quite late and was still asleep. He doesn't lock his outer door – no one here does – so I walked in to find that the fire had gone out. That too is typical. As I stepped across to get it lit for the morning, I nearly slipped – the stone floor was covered with ashes and dead embers, evenly spread."

"Evenly? So there was no chance that a wind from down the chimney had blown it there?"

Elizabeth frowned. "Do I seem like a fool, Mr. Holmes?" She spoke as if she thought Holmes to be one. "The ashes were laid out in a rectangular shape, about three-feet-by-five, and a couple of feet from the fireplace. And besides – last night there was no wind to blow the ashes about."

"But what purpose would such an act serve?" I asked.

"That isn't the whole of it," the girl replied. "*There were footprints in the ashes!*"

Holmes raised a hand and gestured for her to continue. "A man's or a woman's?"

"They were a man's – about one foot in length." She smiled at the thought and patted Thealby's hand once more. She turned his way. "A footprint that's a foot long. Interesting, isn't it, Douglas?"

The young man remained focused upon his own thoughts, now no more engaged in what was going on than if he was asleep. Getting no response, the smile slid from the blonde girl's face and she returned her attention to Holmes.

He nodded to himself as if something made sense. "Which way were they pointed?" he asked.

"Pointed?"

"Yes. To some inner location in the cottage – Perhaps the bedroom? – or instead toward the front door?"

"Why, toward the front." She gave a twist to her head as she considered. "Do you know what it might mean?"

Holmes ignored the question. "Anything else?" he asked, and Elizabeth Selkie frowned.

"Isn't that enough?" she asked, apparently offended that the matter didn't generate the concern that she expected. "When he was younger, a great many people teased Douglas, but now that he's older – and has much larger brothers to take his part – he's left alone. That's why something like this seems so unusual. I don't know who could be playing these silly tricks, but possibly someone is jealous or our upcoming prosperity, and that very soon Douglas and I will shake the dust of this barren place from our shoes. The sooner we're away from here, the better." She stood up then, abruptly, and pulled Douglas Thealby up with her. "I thought that you might be able to offer some kind of advice," she huffed, "but I see that you don't give what's happened the importance that I do."

Holmes stood as well. "You're mistaken, Miss Selkie. I believe that these incidents have the possibility of great significance – to both you and your fiancé. I sincerely hope that an explanation will be revealed before Dr. Watson and I return to London."

"Really?" She seemed surprised, taken aback. "Then – Then I apologize, Mr. Holmes. I do. I thought – that is, I felt that you didn't give the matter any credence. But you'd best hurry if you're going to provide an explanation to us in person, for Douglas and I will be married tomorrow morning following the service, and we leave immediately for our honeymoon. Other than to return in a week and supervise our move to Cambridge, we'll be done with this part of the world – forever, I expect. In any case," she added, "I don't feel that any of this will matter once we leave here – hopefully for good!"

And with that, she turned and drew Douglas Thealby after her.

IV – Hogmanay

After they left, Holmes walked to the door, looked both ways, and then shut it. "What could it mean?" I asked. "Is Douglas in some sort of danger? Do you think this is related to Andrew Wallace's aborted blackmail scheme? Is he directing some new attempt toward the house from an unexpected direction?"

Holmes shook his head. "Not at all. I believe that, with Cresswell's charitable intervention, Mr. Wallace is on his way to an unexpected redemption." He stepped closer, lowering his voice. "What is your impression of Miss Selkie's story?"

I shook my head. "Many odd things end up having commonplace explanations, and even though I can't imagine the reasons for the burned barrel or the thrown cake, they don't appear to be very serious. The intrusion into the cottage, however, and the footprints in the ashes – "

"Yes, the sooty footprints," he interrupted. "That lifts this from the unremarkable to the *outrè*. I wonder . . . ."

He turned his attention to the very-full bookshelves that ran around three sides of the room, with Cresswell's desk centered amongst them. After a moment, his keen eyesight spotted the volume he sought, but as he reached for it, he suddenly stopped himself with a small surprised cry, dropped to his knees in front of the shelf, and then laughed. Then, without explanation, he stood, turned, spotted a small four-legged step-ladder nearby, and retrieved it. Carefully placing it before the shelf in question, he climbed to where he had a better vantage, peering closely for a moment before uttering another gleeful expression.

"Sometimes, Watson," he said, returning to the floor, "luck presents itself in the most unexpected ways. It's fortunate indeed that I was the tall dark stranger that crossed Cresswell's doorway this Hogmany – though more fortunate for some than others, I'll be bound!"

"What on earth are you talking about?" I asked with some growing irritation.

He smiled. "Have I not labored this past year to teach you the importance of observation? I already had some sense of what was happening as the evening progressed, but it was none of my affair, and I chose not to interfere. Now the rather unpleasant Miss Selkie has made the effort to involve me, likely to her regret, and I don't see how I can let things progress as previously ordered." He looked around the room. "Tell me – What do you notice about Cresswell's office?"

I looked here and there, seeing that it was quite filled with items that interested the man: Various objects on the desk, stacks of documents leaning this way and that, and many books of the sort that Cresswell would read, rather than simply place on his shelves for decoration. It rather reminded me in some ways of how Holmes loaded any flat surface in our sitting room with similar detritus. That, in turn, caused another association to form. "The dust," I said. "There's quite a bit of it."

"Exactly. Like myself, Cresswell apparently doesn't allow any housekeeping to be done around his important documents and possessions. Fortunately, dust forms a valuable record of what has occurred. Please observe . . . ." And he pointed to a spot on the floor by the feet of the ladder.

I bent to look but, finding that I didn't quite see what Holmes indicated, I dropped awkwardly to one knee. There, now quite clear, were four marks indicating where the ladder had previously been placed, quite close to its current location. Of more interest was a small and narrow boot-print, aligned in the direction of the shelves.

I frowned as I regained my feet. "But the boot print in the ashes was that of a man – a foot long, as we were told. This is much smaller, and clearly that of a woman."

"Indeed. Now, climb the ladder and look at the shelf in front of *A History of British Holidays* – the narrow green volume there, about six feet or so from the floor."

I followed his instructions, although I was unsure why, as the book was within easy reach and the ladder was unnecessary. However, upon climbing to eye-level with the shelf, I immediately noticed that a strip of unbroken dust lay upon each shelf in front of most of the books, although

74

there were some exceptions here and there. When I reached the shelf in question, I saw that a broken path from the green book to shelf's edge marked that particular volume. "The dust is disturbed," I said, rather needlessly. "Someone has pulled this book out already. Rather recently."

"Exactly. And now, since you're there, would you mind retrieving it for me? I don't think Cresswell will mind if I do a bit more research."

I pulled it down and returned to the floor, where I opened the book for a moment, flipping through the pages. It was densely written, with a publication date noted in the front of 1844, a decade or so before Holmes and I were born.

"About the same time that Dickens wrote *A Christmas Carol*," I noted. "That was in 1843."

"And that is relevant how?" asked Holmes, taking the book from me and tucking it under his arm.

"No reason, I suppose."

"Precisely. And now I'll take this up to my room for a few minutes of further reading while you return to the gathering."

He opened the door, turning right to the rear of the house, while I made my way back to the parlour.

Opening the door, I was quite surprised to find that the temperature of the room had dropped a good thirty degrees, and there was a strong pungent odor of something burning. I looked around with confusion and alarm, but Cresswell noticed my return and stepped forward, pushing what appeared to be a glass of plain water into my hands.

It's the *saining*, Doctor. You know – for Hogmanay."

I shook my head, and heard Holmes's voice behind me as he joined us. His study of the book must have been quick.

"Watson was raised in a household where his father, following the strict Scottish traditions, didn't celebrate many holidays – Christmas for instance – while his Church of England mother didn't hold with any of the Scottish substitutions like Hogmanay."

I looked at him with muted shock – for it was true, though we'd never discussed it. How, then had he deduced as much about me? My father's people never had any use for the Popish-sounding *Christ's Mass*, and my mother longed for her own family traditions, thinking Hogmanay to be just one step above human sacrifice. Thus, we hadn't celebrated much of anything – and somehow Holmes had deduced it. For it had to be deduction, as I knew he was too honorable to have gone through whatever personal papers I might have still kept which might have hinted at such facts. It was a discussion for another time, and I looked back at Cresswell.

"Holmes is correct. While I had heard of the tall dark stranger and first footing, both so desired at Hogmanay, I'm afraid that much of the holiday is a mystery to me." I waved a hand. "Such as the open windows, and the smoke, and this glass of – " I raised and sniffed it, and then took a drink. "Cold water."

"It's the *saining*," Cresswell repeated.

"I know the word," I replied. "Scottish for something like '*saint*' or '*sign*', I think."

Cresswell shook his head. "In this case, it refers to blessing, or protecting or consecrating. It's a Highlands custom, in which water is taken from a river – in this case the nearby Black Lyne – and then blessed. The river, of course, has to be crossed by both the living and the dead – but this close to Scottish border, there's no doubt of that!

"The smoke is from burning juniper branches – it's to cleanse us, and ward off evil spirits. The windows are opened to let in the fresh air and start the year anew. Sarah!" He raised his voice, looking left and right for the slight dark girl. "A glass of the blessed water for Mr. Holmes! Good, good. Now drink up, both of you. The New Year is in just a few minutes. Finished? Excellent. Now, it's customary to follow that with a wee dram of whisky."

After that had also been attended to, and we drank, Holmes remarked wryly to Cresswell, "It's a good thing that you apparently don't follow some of the other superstitious traditions for this time of year, including not taking anything out of your house without bringing something in, or requiring that the first man to enter the house after noon open the Bible on a random page and read a passage to predict the coming year." He cocked an eyebrow. "You don't require that, do you, Cresswell?"

Our host laughed at the thought. "No – at least not yet. But if you're volunteering . . . ?"

After that, we gathered with the rest of the group around the fireplace, our eyes on the mantel clock as it wound inexorably toward midnight and 1882. I glanced at our group as a whole, and yet even then it was broken into smaller subsets: Vicar Tannen was huddled with Miss Sipe, their gaze finally affectionate after several hours of indifference. I could only agree that they would soon solemnize their union. Cresswell stood near us, ready to toast with Calvin Selkie beside him. Despite their age difference, there was something similar about the two men. Douglas Thealby and Elizabeth Selkie were by the now-closed window, he looking at the floor, and she gripping his arm. Each had a glass in hand, as did Holmes and I. It had been provided by Sarah who, after passing our way and making sure that everyone was prepared for the New Year's Toast, had returned to stand with Mrs. Thealby and the other staff near the door to the kitchen. Curiously, as she crossed the room, she slowed, stopped, and then twirled in place once before ending beside Emma, the other serving girl.

An odd action, I thought, but no one seemed to notice. Except Holmes, that is, who had a small smile turning up the corner of his mouth.

And then, as the second hand neared midnight, we counted aloud each passing second until the clock began the new day. With cheers, we toasted one another, and then Cresswell, with a surprisingly fine baritone, began to sing:

> *Should auld acquaintance be forgot,*
> *and never brought to mind?*
> *Should auld acquaintance be forgot,*
> *and auld lang syne?*

> *For auld lang syne, my dear,*
> *For auld lang syne,*
> *We'll take a cup o' kindness yet*
> *For auld lang syne.*

We all joined in soon after he began. This song, in spite of my generally holiday-less upbringing, I knew. Yet I was most surprised when Cresswell continued alone, repeating the verse and chorus in Gaelic:

> *An còir seann luchd-eòlais dhol à beachd,*
> *'S gun chuimhn' orra bhith ann?*
> *An còir seann luchd-eòlis dhol à beachd,*
> *'S na làithean a bha ann?*

> *Air sgàth an tìm a bh' ann a rùin,*
> *Air sgàth an tìm a bh' ann,*
> *Gun gabh sinn fhathast cupan tlàth*
> *Air sgàth an tìm a bh' ann.*

I believe that there are several more verses of Robert Burns' original poem, written nearly a century before that night, all virtually unknown, but Cresswell ended the song after repeating the final line one last time.

"*For auld lang syne,*" I thought to myself. "*For old time's sake.*" New Year's was a time to reflect, and to resolve upon plans for the future. I looked at the people around me, all strangers except for Holmes, and wondered at the curious path that had brought me to this place. It was New Year's Day, 1882, and exactly one year since I had met Sherlock Holmes in one of the Barts laboratories. I had still been quite ill then, and living beyond my means, subsisting on my meagre wound pension in a Strand hotel whose rates were far more than I could afford. My New Year's celebration then, just months after being grievously wounded at Maiwand, had consisted of drinking too much the night before, alone, and then seeking some sort of distracting comfort the next day at the American Bar in the Criterion. A lucky encounter with a former acquaintance, followed by a too-expensive lunch at the Holborn – also more than I could legitimately afford – had led to my introduction to Holmes, and the notion that we could split the cost of rooms in Baker Street. What had followed, one slippery step to the next, was the most unusual year of my life – even more so than the time I'd spent in the Army and my near-death experience. And now I was toasting with strangers in a house near the Scottish border, and wondering about the curious events that had recently intruded into the life of young Douglas Thealby. If that was the way I finished 1881, I could only imagine with some trepidation (but assured anticipation) what 1882 might hold.

As I had ruminated, the group had devolved into general conversation, the guests mingling a bit more before departing for the night, and the household staff slipping away quietly to the kitchen.

Holmes and I stood with Cresswell as he said goodbye to his visitors. Calvin Selkie, slightly inebriated, made an effort to ascertain that Holmes and I would be at the wedding in the morning.

"We wouldn't miss it," said Holmes, and I could sense that there was some hidden meaning as he smiled and nodded to the young couple.

When they were gone, Holmes turned to Cresswell. "Might I assume that no one is typically allowed in your study without your permission?"

Cresswell seemed puzzled, but knowing Holmes from years past, he simply replied, "That is correct. It is my *sanctum sanctorum.*"

Holmes nodded. "Then I appreciate you letting us use it earlier this evening. I hope you don't mind that I've borrowed a book for a bit of bedtime reading – *British Holidays.*"

Cresswell shook his head. Clearly he wanted to ask why we had met with Douglas and Elizabeth, but instead he replied, "That's fine."

"Have you read it?" continued Holmes. "Perhaps to prepare for tonight's festivities?"

"No. I haven't touched that one in years. Why do you ask?"

"No reason. I simply thought tonight was very well done – quite respectful of the traditions."

"Thank you. We do try, you know."

With that, we said good night and went upstairs. As we paused before the door to my room, I said, "You have seen something that I've missed."

I could tell that Holmes was about to reply that such was often the case, or something along those lines, but instead he held his tongue, responding, "Possibly. Now I must think whether to interfere and let the

78

best laid schemes gang aft agley. It will be at least a two-pipe problem. Good night, Watson."

And then he turned and went to his own room.

V – New Year's Day

The next morning, the house was in an uproar.

Preparations for the wedding feast were underway when I came downstairs – which meant that a real functional breakfast was not to be provided, other than cold rolls and coffee, set to one side in the dining room. Mrs. Thealby was excused from work, but Sarah and Emma were busily helping the temporary cook and her staff that had been hired for the day by Cresswell. People moved about quickly, but gradually the chaos focused into order, and everyone met in the front hallway, dressed and prepared to travel to the nearby church for the Sunday morning service, and the wedding which was to follow.

As we stepped outside into the cold morning air, Holmes pulled me aside and said in a low voice, "There was a small bonfire lit last night outside Douglas' cottage, and around it were a number of burned sticks, wrapped in charred animal hides."

"Another threat?" I asked.

Holmes shrugged. "Rather some sort of reminder, I believe. I read more of the holiday book last night, and was expecting something, though I didn't know what form it would take. The smoking sticks and hides are actually called '*Hogmanay*' – the source of the word – and they, along with the bonfire, are a tradition to ward off evil spirits. Tossing them about the cottage does not seem to be malevolent in the same way as the 'Sooty and Weep'.

"'Sooty and Weep'?" I asked.

"The footprints in the ashes. That was one that I'd heard of before. If the footprints are turned inward, it means good luck, or perhaps a birth. If they're turned toward the outer door – as they were in this case – the meaning is death."

Suddenly the various incidents took on a much more sinister meaning.

"Is Douglas Thealby in danger, then?"

"I don't believe so – but as the time for his wedding approaches, things have become much more desperate. Ah, but we're ready to depart."

The church was less than a mile from the manor, and I was glad I'd worn my heaviest coat. The stone building was of typical Norman construction, a thousand years old if a day, its solid stones only intensifying the cold inside, as no fire had been built. The narrow windows failed to let in much of the weak January sunshine, and as there were no pews, only wooden chairs that could be moved from place to place as needed with terrible screeches on the stone floor, we didn't even have the comfort of warmth by sitting beside someone.

Vicar Tannen, dressed in black robes, stood with his face in shadow so that he appeared to be some hollowed-out bird of prey perched upon the altar. There was no joy in his sermon, no promise of hope for the New Year or the nuptials to follow. Instead, he chose as his topic a grim passage from *Deuteronomy* 28:15-22:

> *However, if you do not obey the Lord your God and do not carefully follow all his commands and decrees I am giving you today, all these curses will come on you and overtake you: You will be cursed in the city and cursed in the country. Your basket and your kneading trough will be cursed. The fruit of your womb will be cursed, and the crops of your land, and the calves of your herds and the lambs of your flocks. You will be cursed when you come in and cursed when you go out. The Lord will send on you curses, confusion and rebuke in everything you put your hand to, until you are destroyed and come to sudden ruin because of the evil you have done in forsaking him. The Lord will plague you with diseases until he has destroyed you from the land you are entering to possess. The Lord will strike you with wasting disease, with fever and inflammation, with scorching heat and drought, with blight and mildew, which will plague you until you perish.*

This reminded me of the religion of my father – and why I subsequently considered myself un-churched. Quite the inspirational text as a prelude to marriage, I scoffed to myself. And then, after letting my thoughts wander for longer than I could estimate, I was wrenched back as we had somehow transitioned into the initiation of the wedding, as non-family members departed, and the chairs were re-arranged for the ceremony.

Mrs. Thealby was placed upon the front row. Beside her were the two serving girls, allowed to come to the ceremony, and all three women were weeping. Why, I wondered, did women always seem to cry at weddings? Their apparent shared misery seemed to belie the shared convention that the day was a happy one.

I had some sense that Elizabeth Selkie and her father were moving around just outside the church doorway, as they hadn't been in attendance at the worship service – no doubt to preserve the superstition that the groom must not see the bride before the wedding. Meanwhile, Douglas Thealby stood at the front in a fine suit (no doubt provided by Cresswell, who I had decided was a generous fellow after all, fool though he might also be). He stared at the floor before him while his brothers stood beside him, chivying him into standing up straight to face his coming doom.

I was surprised then, just as the ceremony appeared to be ready to commence, that Holmes, seated beside me, muttered a curse under his breath, as if a disagreeable chore could no longer be avoided, and arose, walking briskly to the groom. The brothers watched with raised eyebrows as Holmes asked if he could speak with Douglas alone for just a moment. Then he drew him aside and whispered urgently to him.

I glanced around. Cresswell reflected the puzzlement that was upon everyone's face. It was a small group that was left after the majority of the congregation had departed, and every eye was upon Holmes and Douglas, who was now, for the first time since I'd met him, expressing an alert intensity as he stared unblinking into the older man's eyes and followed the conversation. At one point he nodded, and on another he raised a hand and squeezed Holmes's arm. Then he nodded again and returned to his brothers' sides.

Holmes rejoined me, settling into his chair and leaning over to say, "I had to do it, Watson. No one else was going to. Emotion should never be a factor. Logic is the key – but logically I had to interfere."

It was then that Elizabeth Selkie, in a frothy white gown, entered the church on the arm of her father. She had no veil, and her catlike smile was a testimony that she had almost achieved what she sought. From where I was seated, I saw that smile remain fixed as she walked the entire length of the cold dark room – and it was there until the vicar prepared to speak, only to be interrupted by Douglas Thealby.

"I believe," he said, his voice initially nervous, but gaining strength with each word, "that there is a place in the ceremony about whosoever objects should speak, or hold his peace thereafter?" He looked at the vicar, who simply gazed at him with confusion. "Isn't there?" asked Douglas again, his voice a little more urgent.

"Yes," replied Vicar Tannen. Then, clearing his throat, he added, "Yes, there is."

"Then I'm afraid that I must claim that privilege now." He looked at his intended bride. "Elizabeth, I cannot marry you – for long ago I promised to marry another."

There was a drawn silence for a long moment, broken only by the hideous screech of a chair leg on the stone floor as someone abruptly stood. I glanced to my left and saw that it was Sarah, the smaller dark servant girl. In spite of the darkened space, her face glowed, and her

81

clenched hands were pulled tight against her bosom. She appeared to be frozen, not even taking a breath.

Then Elizabeth Selkie took a step back, as if she'd been hit in the stomach, folding slightly and dropping the bouquet of hothouse flowers she'd carried to the altar. "You . . . you *what* . . . ?" she said, her voice turning ugly in just a few words.

Douglas nodded. "I grew up with Sarah – in the same house." He cleared his throat, as if he hadn't really spoken for a long time. "We . . . we made promises to one another, long ago. We share many interests, and she is so very smart, in spite of the limited opportunities that life has afforded her, while you . . . That is to say, we . . . we – Sarah and I – we always knew that we would be married. We'd discussed it. Planned it. It was even going to be on New Year's Day, because for us it symbolized a new beginning."

"But . . . but *why*?" croaked Elizabeth, straightening up and then glancing around toward Sarah, who had no eyes but for Douglas. "Why did you let things progress to this point?"

"Because you gave me no choice!" The words burst from Douglas' mouth, almost in a wail. "Last October, after paying me no mind for my entire life, and having been one of the many who were cruel to me, you decided that we should be married. I'm not a fool, Elizabeth, though you took me for one. I knew that when you realized I was leaving for Cambridge, and that I had prospects and support from Mr. Cresswell, you decided that I was your means of leaving as well." He gave a small glance toward Sarah, and then uttered a small sob. "I'm so sorry, Sarah! Sorry that I was weak, and that I let her bully all the will out of me. But Mr. Holmes understood." He nodded to my friend, who was now standing. I realized that I was standing as well. "He realized what all of your messages were, your New Year's messages, and he convinced me not to make a mistake – not to unhappily condemn myself to a life that I didn't want."

"Now see here – " rumbled Calvin Selkie, only to find that Cresswell's hand was firm upon his arm. He subsided, and let Douglas Thealby continue to speak.

"I knew all along what the messages meant, but I was too weak to acknowledge them."

"Messages?" asked Elizabeth. "What *messages*?"

"What you took as threats – the burned barrel, and the cake, and the footprints. The burned sticks this morning. All of those are traditions related to Hogmanay and New Year's. Sarah and I had read of them as we planned our wedding. Then, when you and I became engaged, I . . . I stopped speaking to her. I thought that it was the proper way to behave – to focus on my intended bride. But as time for the wedding approached, and I still wouldn't talk with her, she tried this – as a reminder that it was she and I who were supposed to be married today. Not the two of us, Elizabeth."

The slighted bride seemed to gather in upon herself, and as I wondered about her response, she suddenly flew into motion, her hands curved into vicious claws that swept toward Douglas Thealby's face. He simply stood there, and would have sustained terrible wounds, and perhaps have been blinded but for the dour vicar, who leaned into motion and stepped down between them, wrapping the furious hissing woman in a strong grip from behind until her father could come and calm her enough to lead her away.

The remaining group was silent for a few seconds, and then they began chattering excitedly to one another. Douglas was looking toward Sarah. I glanced that way too, to see Mrs. Thealby crying and smiling and hugging the girl closely, as if she had missed her for many years instead of working around her every day. Sarah had her arms wrapped around the older woman, but her face was turned toward the young man, her expression shiny with tears and quite the brightest spot in the room.

A beaming Cresswell stepped forward to ask Vicar Tannen if he could carry on with the wedding, substituting a different bride, but the grim old man flatly refused, indicating that there were licenses to obtain and that the banns had not been properly read. Not to be defeated, Cresswell then quickly arranged for transportation, loading everyone into carriages, and within minutes we were headed west to Gretna Green, just across the Scottish border, where immediate "irregular marriages" requiring only two witnesses had been the custom for many decades. We had more than enough witnesses, and soon the most-happy boy and girl were tied up right and proper, and as they should have been all along.

"*Le d'mhaitheas is le d'nì bhi fàs,*" said Cresswell when the service was concluded. Then he translated the Scottish wedding blessing: "'*A thousand welcomes to you with your marriage. May you be healthy all your days. May you be blessed with long life and peace, may you grow old with goodness, and with riches.*'"

The wedding feast that followed was perfect for a day to remember.

In a quiet moment later that afternoon, I had a chance to ask Holmes what had given him the first indications of what was going on.

"I saw how Sarah watched Douglas, who tried to ignore her, and how he would look her way when she wouldn't see. Not once did Douglas make an effort to see his intended's features.

"When the details of the various 'threats' were related, I recognized a few of them as being related to Hogmanay or New Year's – although why they would be directed toward Douglas made no sense. The sooty footprints are a tradition from the Isle of Man, while the thrown cake is from Ireland. However, there the cake is thrown *away* from the house to bring *good* luck. Why in this case was it apparently directed *toward* the house – except to be a *reversal* of good luck? To bring bad luck to the house. The same for the footprint facing the door – it was indicative of bad luck instead of good. Why would someone wish that for Douglas, and in ways connected to Hogmanay and New Year's traditions? Perhaps, I thought, it had something to do with the wedding to occur on New Year's Day.

"In Cresswell's study, we saw that the holiday book had been recently consulted – by someone who left a small footprint. You might have noticed that everyone here has rather large feet – except for Sarah. Additionally, everyone here is tall enough to reach the book upon the shelf, located as it was about six feet from the floor – again except for Sarah, who with her small stature needed the ladder. You saw where the ladder had been placed there previously.

"Back at the party, I watched Douglas and Sarah more closely, and it was quite apparent that they were very aware of one another, even if they never communicated. On several occasions, she would walk near him, stop, and spin around with her eyes closed before opening them in his direction and continuing about her business."

"Yes, I saw her do that once, just before midnight."

"I found an account of that action in the holiday book, described by a man named Fraser who later died at Culloden, wherein the single women will spin about on Hogmanay with their eyes closed, and then open their eyes to look upon the man they'll marry. On each occasion last night, Sarah would make certain that she did so with Douglas as her fixed aim. I feel sure that he saw it, and understood, even if he never raised his head to acknowledge it.

"The barrel filled with burned tar and wood, known as *clavie*, was also described in the book – another New Year's tradition unique to Burdhead, a small town in Moray. It's supposed to bring good luck – although I'm sure that Sarah included some variation to negate it that we either missed or didn't understand. Like all of her messages, it was clumsy and obscure and desperate, but she knew that Douglas would comprehend."

I thought back to the service, when Holmes had stood to speak to Douglas. "You waited until the very last minute, and then you interfered with what seemed to be marked reluctance."

He nodded. "In some ways it was not my business. Who is to say that Douglas Thealby might not have benefited from Elizabeth Selkie's strong-handed guidance?"

I held up a hand. "I think that I can safely say that."

He smiled. "Perhaps. But I try to hold myself aloof from such purely emotional matters. As a logician – "

I raised my hand again. "Stow that, Holmes. I've known you for a year, and I've started to figure out a few things. For instance, that statement about what you do and don't put in your 'brain attic' is just so much wind. Of course you stretch your mind with numerous facts that might be important at some point. How else would you have known about sooty footprints from the Isle of Man? And likewise, I've seen more than once how you are perfectly willing to interfere in people's lives if you think that they can be helped."

He started to protest, but I cut him off once again. "If you need some sort of justification to make things easier to digest, just think of yourself as the tall dark stranger who brought good luck to the house. Or simply tell yourself that Douglas Thealby, quite possibly the next Newton, has the potential to be of inestimable value to the British people across the coming decades, and isn't it better for him to be happy while he's doing so, instead of miserable?"

Holmes turned his head as he considered it. Then, he raised his glass. "An excellent rationalization, Doctor. I salute your good sense."

I nodded and returned the gesture, considering to myself how Sherlock Holmes himself was also likely to be of inestimable value in the coming years.

NOTE

*   See "The Mediobogdum Sword", *The Collected Papers of Sherlock Holmes – Volume VI: Muniments* and *The MX Book of New Sherlock Holmes Stories – Part XXXIV: "However Improbable . . . ." (1878-1888)*

The Peculiar Affair of the Three Owed Deaths

"What do you know of *Cthäat*?"

"Bless you," I responded to our visitor, Statton Baird. It was clear that he had a cold, and I was about to offer some unsolicited medical advice, but he shook his head.

"No, Doctor, I refer to *Cthäat*, the ancient god of water. I believe that it is trying to kill me."

I glanced at Holmes, expecting him to frown, or even terminate the interview, but instead he became a bit more alert. Typically Holmes had no use for such blather, and I had seen him rise and walk out when a client veered into superstitious beliefs. But not this time.

"I understood that the God of Water is Poseidon," I said.

"Or Neptune, as the Romans called him," added Holmes.

Baird shook his head. "No, gentlemen. I speak of something far older – older than mankind. A fundamental force far greater than the puny personifications created by the Greeks and Romans."

At that moment, as I wondered why an elemental and ancient god would seek the life of one small man, the wind shifted, causing the downpour outside to hit our windows even harder. Baird, startled, glanced that way with a hint of fear, as if the rain running down the glass was the Water God himself, trying to reach him at that very moment. It was a wonder that Baird had managed to make the journey through the driving rain to see us.

I had placed him close to the fire, hoping that his soaked clothing would dry quickly and prevent his cold from worsening. Now, having heard the root of his complaint, I found it ironic that a man so afraid of water appeared to be so damp.

Yet it wasn't the rain outside that had given Statton Baird that curious aspect. Rather, his whole bearing, from the way he carried himself to the bluish shine of his skin and fair hair, gave the impression that he was constructed of just a bit more water than the rest of us.

I was grateful, regardless of the impression he made, that he had knocked upon our door, for after three days near Barden, in the Yorkshire Dales, doing nothing but waiting, Sherlock Holmes was ready to abandon the whole reason for our journey. In truth, he was not always the best team player.

We had been asked – although that word is perhaps insufficient to describe the request from Holmes's brother, Mycroft – to make our way to Yorkshire, where we would be ready and in place if Miles Cosford bolted in that direction. Cosford was a spy for the Germans, not particularly adept in his craft, but he had been of some use to those in our own government whose business it was to play shadowy games with their counterparts in other countries. Cosford had been easily identified from his first efforts at espionage, and he was therefore cultivated, without his knowledge, by feeding him accurate but harmless morsels of intelligence in order to build his credibility and seeming effectiveness with his masters. It was not an unusual method of operation by spymasters on both sides, and this game required a great deal of finesse to sense when the other side figured out just what was going on, and then find a way to turn the poor pawn back the other direction.

In the midst of this dark gamesmanship, Miles Cosford had done something remarkable and unexpected: Quite on his own, he'd managed to steal a British secret of actual great importance, plans for a new nationwide harbor defense system, with a complex and encompassing system of powerful mines – and then he'd vanished.

As he'd already been used by the British Government, albeit unknowingly, for two years by then, there was absolutely nothing that wasn't known about him – his background and daily habits, and those little secrets that he believed were solely his own which could be used to bring pressure upon him when the time was right. In fact, the only thing that was not known about Miles Cosford was his location right then.

But there were fewer than half-a-dozen possibilities, and Mycroft Holmes's best agents were dispatched in that many directions, to be in place when Cosford appeared at one of them. Sherlock Holmes and I had been sent to Cosford's hometown, Barden, the thinking being that, despite the fact he'd departed from there years before, he might return to hide before attempting to take his prize to the Continent. It seemed to be a rather unlikely choice for him to make, when there were other areas much closer to the sea where he could disappear with greater success, but Mycroft had a hunch and wanted to place his brother there, just in case.

We had arrived after a hard day of traveling, and Holmes had immediately set out to speak to various locals and fix his nets in place. Now, after three days, there was nary a sign of the elusive agent, and my friend was becoming impatient. Then Statton Baird knocked upon the door of our shared sitting room on the first floor of the tidy Abbey Inn, and Holmes had – at least for a while – the possibility of distraction until something of greater importance occurred.

"You are both educated and knowledgeable gentlemen, I understand," Baird had stated, after asking for a bit our time, and full of apologies for bothering us without previously fixing an appointment. I had offered to request some tea from the landlord downstairs, but Baird asked for something stronger, so we were sipping whisky as he wiped his nose and began his narrative while the light from the wide west-facing window dimmed in the faltering January afternoon.

He was around forty, and small in stature – not more than a dozen stone. His skin, despite advancing into middle-age, was tight and fair, and had a cerulean shine to it. He wore no beard or mustache, and his light-colored hair was brushed back straight from his forehead, held in place with liberal amounts of Macassar oil. His suit was expensive and fit his thin frame well. It consisted of some material with a silky sheen, which caught the light as he moved. Overall, as mentioned, from oiled hair to the bright glow of his face to the shine of his shoes, he had a look about him of *dampness*.

"What do you know of *Cthäat*?" he had asked. After we had displayed our ignorance, Holmes indicated for him to continue.

"I've read your narratives, Doctor," Baird continued obliquely, nodding my way before looking back toward Holmes. "I'm aware of the wide-ranging knowledge that you've accumulated, Mr. Holmes, and I understand that you spent a great deal of your spare time when you first came up to London studying at the British Museum."

Holmes nodded. "In those days, when clients were thin on the ground, I devoted my empty hours to carefully accumulating data which I thought might someday be useful."

"I did the same at that age," replied Baird. "My father was still alive then, and he let me go off to London for a couple of years to gain some knowledge of the world. Theoretically I was a student, but I found the structured lessons of my teachers to be a bit dull and rote, so I ended up following my own line." He took a sip. "You and I are about the same age, Mr. Holmes – possibly you're a little younger – and we were probably at the Museum and Library around the same time. Mid- to late-1870's?"

Holmes nodded. "But I'm afraid that I don't recall seeing you there."

"And I don't remember you either, but we certainly must have passed one another unknowingly – either in the facilities, or in the street, or perhaps at the Alpha Inn."

I had lived in that area as well, for a short time in the late seventies, attempting to start a practice in Southampton Row during that period between when I took my degree in 1878 and then joined the army. I also had no recollection of Baird – but then again, I hadn't run into Holmes during those days either, and he'd lived just around the corner, in Montague Street.

"You say that you accumulated useful data," Baird continued. "Did that happen to include anything regarding old legends, perhaps?"

Holmes raised an eyebrow. "Some, but more in an academic sense – dry archaeological and anthropological facts – and certainly not any deep studies to memorize specifics. I was rather careful about what I put into my brain-attic, and much of that sort of thing, as you know, is superstitious clap-trap."

Baird started to reply, something sharp and sudden as if a challenge had been thrown down and accepted, but then he caught himself and took another sip of whisky. Then he set it deliberately upon the table beside him, as if deciding that he wanted no more of it just then.

"I agree," he stated, "that some beliefs are nothing more than nonsense – outgrowths from deep fears to explain incomprehensible events, or to be used by the strong to victimize the ignorant and the weak. But upon occasion, even if the descriptions are awkward or incomplete, there is deep truth in such things. Old, old truth."

A fresh and violent burst of rain upon the window seemed to emphasize the point. Holmes, however, was finally showing those first signs of losing patience, and clearly he was not in the mood for a spirited debate on the topic of the validity of superstitious beliefs, in spite of having nothing else on his docket for that day until word might come concerning the re-appearance of Miles Cosford.

Still, I thought that the distraction that our visitor had unexpectedly provided was important enough to encourage by way of buoying Holmes's mood.

"I fear we're wandering afield," I interrupted. "These legends – and this *Cthäat* – What do they have to do with the reason for your visit? You're in fear for your life?"

Baird nodded. "I've always had an interest in the mysterious," he answered, still circling the central point of his visit. "Ancient civilizations and kingdoms, lost inventions and processes, and legendary animals – such as the beast in Loch Ness, for instance, and the monster in the Humber. I recall reading in the paper that you both crossed paths with one of the black dogs of Dartmoor a few years ago. And then there is the Lumbering Man near York. Why, this area is awash in such stories, and surely some must have a basis in fact." He leaned forward. "I've heard that you're a Yorkshire man, Mr. Holmes."

"This is true," Holmes responded tentatively.

"Then I don't have to tell you that Rudston to the east is one of the most mystical locations in the country, as it is the end point for not one but *five* ley lines, including one of Britain's three Basic Alignments. And the Rudston Monolith is just a hop and skip – no more than a couple of miles as the crow flies – downstream along the Gypsey Race from Wold Newton. The stream often goes underground through the chalk aquifer before reappearing at Rudston. When it rises as far back as Wold Newton during flood conditions – or the Woe Waters, as they call it – ill fortune is at hand." His tone rose to match his enthusiasm. "It flooded the year before the great plague of 1664, and the restoration of Charles II, and the landing of William of Orange. And that area is included within the Wold Newton Triangle, whose point, as you know, is in the sea just past Flamborough Head, where many – "

Holmes finished his whisky in one final swallow, tightened his lips, and was preparing to rise, likely to show Baird to the door, when I interceded. "Mr. Baird, do you have something specific you wish to bring to our attention? I'm afraid that otherwise, we have pressing business."

"What? Oh, I do apologize. When I begin to discuss my passions, my thoughts go a hundred miles a minute in every direction. Yes. The British Museum – it was there as a student that I spent a great deal of time following my own interests in the various legends. One day, I came across references to a book that held specialized olden knowledge – *Al Azif.* It was written by Alhazred, an Arab who had obtained knowledge of ancient gods – entities who have existed long before the distant ancestors of man formed in the Stygian primordial seas. Some – just a few – translations have been made, but there are not more than half-a-dozen copies hidden around the world – the Bibliothèque Nationale in France has one, and so do the university libraries at Harvard and Miskatonic, both in Massachusetts. There is another at the University of Buenos Aires – and supposedly the British Museum itself has a copy, although when I requested to see it, I was told in no uncertain terms that I was certainly mistaken.

"What I've read implies that study of this document – *Al Azif* – and its translations is dangerous."

"Yet it interested you," interrupted Holmes.

Baird nodded. "The book contains ideas and knowledge that are far too minacious to be examined, but I dearly wanted to study it nonetheless. Some years after I was a student, I was able to travel to Paris, but my visit to the Bibliothèque Nationale was fruitless, as they too denied the existence of the book – the title of the translation being *The Necronomicon.* As I've grown older and the demands of life have absorbed my time, I've been unable to travel to Massachusetts or South America, so I've had to make do with the vague references that I'd found in the peripheral materials in the British Library.

"While my interest in the book and its subject matter has remained, it has also cooled when I had no way of furthering my research, as all doors seemed to shut. But recently the idea of these ancient gods – or rather one in particular – has reoccurred to me . . . *and I have become convinced that Cthäat is now reciprocally aware of my interest, and that it wishes for my death!*"

I glanced toward Holmes, even as the phrase "*Ineffable twaddle!*" nearly passed my lips. I was sorry that I'd delayed Holmes from seeing Baird out, as I now knew that his belief in some deadly supernatural entity would only generate Holmes's contempt. But I was surprised to see that, where he'd evinced growing irritation to that point, Holmes now showed a spark of interest.

"And why would this . . . this ancient god be interested in you particularly, Mr. Baird?"

"Because I cheated it – I lived when I should have died, and then I did so twice more!"

Holmes settled back. I could follow his thinking: *Now* we would hear something specific, as compared to ramblings about ley lines and sea monsters and deadly books.

"Last fall," Baird explained, "we were hiking – "

"We?" interrupted Holmes.

"Yes, my brother, Wyatt, and me. Three months ago, we were proceeding north through the Valley of Desolation, a rugged local area not far to the east of our manor. We were on our way to Simon's Seat – named, as many think for the Simon *Magus*, the Samaritan magician who confronted Paul and tried to buy his way into the Apostles in the Book of Acts. There are some theories that – "

At this, Baird glanced at Holmes and realized that his thoughts had again wandered. He coughed and continued. "It was a warm day for October, and Wyatt and I had passed the waterfall when he suggested that we should take a swim. We were hot from our walk, and as there weren't any people around, I whimsically agreed. Soon we were paddling about like boys in a part of the Dicken Dike that I've swum in a hundred times before – a deep spot where the stream flows against a big rock before taking a slight turn. But it was somehow unexpectedly deeper than before, possibly from rains a few days earlier, and suddenly I found myself being pushed toward the rock by the current, even as I seemed to lose all buoyancy. No matter how much I kicked my legs, I was locked in a completely vertical position, my face barely above the water. As it happened, I never had time to get a good breath, so I worked my arms frantically, trying to keep my face above water, even as I felt myself being pulled deeper. My kicking had no effect whatsoever. Never have I felt so close to death, and never before have I felt that I was going to drown.

"Behind me, not ten feet away, I could hear Wyatt lazily swimming and making some of the meaningless commentary that he provides to all aspects of his life. Yet I couldn't even get enough breath to call for help, and I knew that I was going to die just a short distance from where my brother was obliviously floating.

"Finally, with the greatest of effort, I somehow succeeded in working myself backwards, away from the flow that was pulling me unrelentingly down alongside the rock, and onto a spot where the bottom was barely within reach. I managed to gain traction and walk myself backwards, collapsing on the gravels at the edge of the pool, where I coughed and tried to catch my breath.

"Wyatt watched curiously, but with no idea how close I'd come to my end. When I could finally speak, I tried to explain what had happened – to convey my terror, and how the black water seemed to have me with no intention of release. He was skeptical, and kept urging me back in, but I simply waited until I was dry enough to put on my clothes and then, the desire to visit Simon's Seat having firmly departed, I set out for home.

"I didn't give that much further thought to it until a couple of weeks later, when we – Wyatt and I – were again hiking – this time in a different direction. The weather had turned colder, and we were walking along the River Wharfe near The Strid, not half-a-mile west of my manor house. Have you heard of it?"

It sounded vaguely familiar to me, but Holmes had read of it before. "It is known as the 'Killer Stream', I believe."

Baird nodded. "It is. The river is wide, thirty feet or more, and placid both above and below The Strid. It passes the old Abbey not far upstream. But then, for only a couple-hundred feet or so, the channel narrows to just a few feet across – in places the sides are so close that one might jump across from rock to rock, but to do so is almost certain death.

"All of the water in the wide upstream segment flows into this narrowing channel, but there is no perceptible change in the current. One would expect that such a volume of water compressed into so small a space would cause a sudden surge in speed, or there to be added turbulence as the flow bursts and crashes into the rocks that line the stream there. Instead, however, The Strid remains calm and flat, completely masking its deadly danger.

"The water there is dark from the upstream peat, so there is no indication of what's going on below the surface. In fact, what happens is that the river, which has been wide until it reaches The Strid, turns from a *horizontal* width to a *vertical* depth, extending far into the earth through cracks, passages, and caverns carved in the subterranean rocks. All of that water which should be constricted violently across the narrow surface passage instead moves in a steady progression through what is possibly the deadliest distance on earth before the river again rights itself and turns back into a wide and bucolic tree-lined watercourse.

"The banks of The Strid are made up of rocks, but there is no riverbed just below the surface to stand upon. In actuality, these rocks simply overhang the great bottomless void – and the bottom depth there has never been determined. These great rocks along the banks gently slope toward the water, and are covered with slick moss. They are so close that, to the ignorant, they seem like an inviting and enjoyable place to hop back and forth across the ditch-like flow, but in truth, nearly everyone who goes in dies. There are records of deaths occurring there over a thousand years ago, including a prince who would have someday been the King of Scotland. None of the bodies are ever recovered, sucked into the depths where the currents hold them forever entrapped, and no doubt pulverized into something that is no longer recognizable as human."

"And you fell in?" I asked, certain as to the point of his story.

Baird shook his head. "No, but it was a near thing. Our walk took us just upstream of The Strid, but I knew better than to approach the water. Only a fool would do so. However, there was one spot back from the edge where Wyatt, who was in front, stopped, peering down. I joined him to see that he'd paused before a muddy patch which had been crossed by some animal tracks – deer, it seemed. We commented upon it for a minute, and then he resumed walking, crossing the mud and back into the grass. The area was only ten feet or so from one side to the other, but halfway along, my feet went out from under me, for there was just the slightest slope down to the stream, and my boots had suddenly lost all grip with the earth. I fell heavily on my left side, and as I did so, I started slipping down the mud toward the upstream end where the river enters The Strid.

"I cried to Wyatt while attempting to kick the toes of my boots into the mud and dig my fingers in as well. My feet were in the water when I managed to stop, and Wyatt crept closer to the point where he could kneel down and reach and grasp my hand. I feared that his feet would slip as well, and that we would both tumble in and be lost, but he kept his center of gravity quite low and labored his way backward, dragging me with him on my stomach across the mud." He shifted in his seat, looking pointedly at Holmes, as if to emphasize the importance of what he said and where the story was leading.

"You indicated that this incident occurred sometime after the first," asked Holmes. "Later in the fall. It's now January. You also said you've cheated death three times. There has been something else then – another occurrence more recent and also related to water that has convinced you to seek our counsel."

"There has. Just yesterday. Again, I only survived by the unlikeliest of luck, and it has further convinced me that I'm on borrowed time. That my life is owed after I cheated my first death, and attempts are being made by the ancient water god to collect upon the debt."

Holmes nodded for him to continue, and I found myself intrigued, while still wondering how long this talk of a vengeful god might continue, and what we were expected to do about it.

"Early yesterday morning, I was walking the estate," Baird explained, "as I often do. I find that the winter is a good time to see what needs to be addressed in warmer weather. The barren trees, for instance, allow for a clearer view of the house and grounds.

"We have a spot where a small but brisk stream rises from a substantial spring and flows across the property. It isn't very wide or deep, and there is a nice pathway alongside it, landscaped, and with benches and a gazebo. After several hundred feet, however, it abruptly flows noisily back into a hole in the ground – a cave which has never been explored. Even in times of drought, it's said that this spring has never dried up, and where the water goes has never been determined.

"We don't have the numerous sinkholes and the karst geology of Ripon to the east, but there are still a number of such places here. We've always known to be cautious around our deadly little cave, and I was doing so yesterday, staying at what I thought to be a safe distance from the water's edge. But I had no idea how much it wanted to claim me.

"It was early in the morning, and there was a frost on the ground. It was actually somewhat thicker along the streambank as the spray froze and settled upon the earth. There is also the slightest of slopes down to the water – on a normal day, it wouldn't even be noticed, but when the grass underneath is dead for the winter, and it's covered with a skin of ice . . . .

"Much as I'd done just above The Strid, my feet went out from underneath me before I was even aware of it, and I was sliding down toward the water, where I would enter the rushing flow just a man's length above where it went underground. This time I was on my back, so I instinctively raised my feet high and then crashed them down, in order to dig in my heels, while at the same time clawing my fingers into the gravel and icy mud, hoping that my weight would be enough to slow and stop me. All the while, the icy spray was hitting me in the face, and my vision had telescoped onto that gaping black hole – only four feet in diameter, but suddenly my entire future. Even as I felt the first jab of my heels slipping, it crossed my mind that the water god – *Cthäat* – was trying once again to take me. I sensed the evil hunger dragging me closer. It was much

94

like when I'd nearly drowned last October. My actions, which should have slowed me, seemed to have no effect. Finally, with a wild cry and nearly at the water's edge, I pulled back my feet once again, threw down my heels with all my strength, and clawed my fingers into the mud." He held up his hands. "As you can see, my nails are severely damaged by the effort."

"I was aware of it," replied Holmes.

"And it worked. My momentum was arrested, and – with that great black maw still gurgling hungrily just beside me, and aware that any wrong move could start me sliding once more into its grasp, this time with no more streambank before me to stop my progress – I began to crab my way backwards, slowly up the slope – which is nearly flat at any other time, but now feeling like an interminable vertical slide.

"Finally I was on flat ground, and I rolled myself ever further from the stream and the cave, covered in mud and melted frost, and making great whoops and sobs as I tried to regain my breath and settle my panic."

When it appeared that Baird had completed his tale, falling into a dark reverie, Holmes set about the business of lighting his pipe while he gathered his thoughts. I waited to see his response, since I was uncertain exactly what Baird wished for him to do.

"This *Cthäat* – " he said, to my surprise. "What can you tell me of . . . him? Her? *It*?"

"Unlike many of the ancient ones who are better known, if not understood, *Cthäat* is a mystery. So many of the Old Ones have a physical form, although it's said that the horror and immensity and despair of each is more than any human mind can bear – to see or encounter them is to be driven mad. Their physical bodies often have appendages or tentacles, or something resembling elephant trunks or serpents projecting from their terrible faces. *Cthäat*, however, is an elemental, a shapeless mass of water, possibly with no apparent consciousness or self-awareness, but still hungry – a hunger older than the stars themselves. Perhaps *Cthäat* makes up the soul of the water of our world – perhaps it *is* the water! – and if so, then we humans, each of us more than sixty-percent water, are split-off pieces of the Old God, and it wishes to gather us back."

"But why you specifically?" I had to ask. "If such a being exists, and if he or she or *it* is the ocean and the rivers and the rain, and if all living things that contain water as well are part of it, then why have we been allowed to walk about on dry land for so many eons? And why do *you* in particular now owe this creature a death?"

Perhaps my tone was a bit hot, but I had never tolerated this type of ideology much better than Holmes. That's why I was surprised to see that he seemed amused at my outburst.

"I don't know, Doctor," replied Baird. "Perhaps at some point in our lives, we all return to *Cthäat* at an appointed time – from a natural death where our waters are gradually released back to the world from whence we've taken and held them for a while, or for some others, possibly something more abrupt. A drowning, perhaps, where *Cthäat* personally catches the scent and tastes his prey. As I said, perhaps I was meant to die in that stream last fall, and in saving myself, I've left *Cthäat* unsatisfied . . . and vengeful."

"And what do you expect us to do about it?" asked Holmes, finally posing the question that I thought would have been his first.

"I . . . I don't know, honestly. I know that you don't hold these same convictions, and that my little explanation will have in no way convinced you. But I wanted to share it with someone – if for no other reason than my next encounter with *Cthäat* might prove to be the last, and I'd like someone to know, whether it's believed or not. My brother would not take me seriously, should I decide to tell him. I know that you don't either, but at least you'll both *know*."

Holmes drew on his pipe for several moments, his expression focused far away. Then he spoke.

"I assume that you have extensive notes on this matter? On *Cthäat*?"

Baird nodded. "I do. About *Cthäat*, and many of the other Old Gods as well: *Crom Cruach, Gol-goroth, Ghatanothoa, Xinlurgash, Cthulhu,* and *M'Nagalah*. There are many more of them than is generally thought. I – "

Holmes held up a hand. "I'd be interested in seeing what you've accumulated. Not – " he hastened to add when Baird's eyes lit up. "Not that I believe in any of this, but it is interesting to see just how much froth has been generated by our forebears to explain what they didn't understand, and to put faces and names onto the bogeys in the closet or under the bed."

Baird's expression tightened a bit as he saw himself lumped into this gullible class, but he hadn't truly expected anything different from Holmes, so he nodded. "Would you care to join me tonight for dinner? Then we can look over my collection."

Holmes shook his head and glanced at the window, where the rain was still quite profound. "If you don't mind, I think we'll wait until tomorrow. The glass is rising, and it promises to be a better day. I'd like to have a look at this cave you mentioned – and maybe The Strid too, before Watson and I return to London in a day or so."

Baird nodded. "Would you join me for breakfast then? Anyone here can tell you the way."

And so it was agreed, and Baird, who was still damp, pulled on his coat and hat and departed back into the storm where, if he was to be believed, tiny bits of *Cthäat* in the form of rain likely assaulted him all the way home.

After he left, I shut the door and turned back to Holmes with a raised eyebrow, my question unspoken. He nodded.

"No, I don't perceive a crime here. In each case, as described, there doesn't seem any way to have contrived the accidents – and Baird certainly never suspected a human hand was at work."

"I might have thought it was the brother, Wyatt," I said, "especially if there's an inheritance to be had. But how would he lure Baird into the deep water of the stream? His near-drowning sounds more like the effect of turbulence in the water as it rounded the curve by the rock, creating bubbles which reduced his buoyancy. That sort of thing has happened before, and even ships have suddenly sunk when unexpectedly surrounded by highly aerated water – as you'll recall back in '86 when we so nearly lost our lives in The Wash."

I sat and took a sip of my neglected whisky. "Granted," I continued, "Wyatt called Baird over to show him the deer tracks in the mud near The Strid, but according to Baird, he then simply slipped in the mud after Wyatt had walked away. He never indicated that he suspected his brother."

"Likewise," Holmes added, "if they were both alone at The Strid as stated, Wyatt could have simply let his brother slide into the water to his death, instead of risking himself to effect a rescue. And yesterday, Wyatt wasn't at the cave at all."

"Thus," I summarized, "in each case, the man simply had bad luck, or was careless." I gazed speculatively. "If there's no mystery here, what is your interest?"

He drew on his pipe in silence, for a few moments, his gaze again had that faraway look of a few moments before. Then he finally spoke.

"I'm not entirely unfamiliar with the book of which Baird spoke – *The Necronomicon*. Although I didn't feel the need to confirm it to him, I also did a bit of research along those specific lines in my student days – enough to be concerned when I hear that object being discussed elsewhere."

"And it is as he described? With information about these ridiculous 'Old Gods'?"

Holmes nodded. "Although they wouldn't confirm it to Baird, the British Museum does, in fact, hold a copy of the document. I once held it, and mistakenly read a portion when I recovered it from a bold thief. I was unsettled for a week. It describes . . . how shall I describe it? *Alternate existences*, in which these Old Gods somehow subsist outside of our own

97

earthly plane. They all have menacing names that, when pronounced aloud as Baird did, seem to invoke some primal and atavistic fear deep in one's hind-brain by their very combination of syllables. One has the feeling that the written version and phonetic pronunciations are but sad and pathetic mortal attempts to futilely convey something that is beyond the ability of the human throat to utter correctly."

"Holmes," I said, suddenly a bit chill, "you sound as if you give credence to this foolishness!"

"I do," he said, "but not in the way you think. I have no belief in 'Old Gods', slumbering for eons, only to be awakened hungry and vengeful. If they were of such power and age, why rest *here*, on this little speck of mud and rock, in such a wide universe? Why concern themselves with something so insignificant if they are so powerful? No, I worry because *The Necronomicon* is written so slyly and suggestively that it seems to have a hypnotic effect upon the reader. I felt it myself, and I consider that I'm typically above that sort of influence. Should such a document be widely disseminated, who knows what mischief it might cause? When I recovered it for the Museum, I advised that they protect it to a much greater degree than what they'd done before, but they did nothing to improve their security. Someday it's going to be stolen again – much like the Eye of Heka back in '88 * – and mark my words, it has the potential to cause just as much misery.

"There are people out there who know about this book, and they will someday take it and make use of it. The other copies around the world are much better protected, but the British Museum – ? Ah, they think they know better than anyone. The people who want this book, and who are so influenced by it, are a cult, and a dangerous one. They are primarily a cult of *Cthulhu*, one of the more notable 'Old Ones'. I sometimes fancy that I should write a monograph about them and their twisted devotion, but then I think that calling attention to them and *The Necronomicon* would be worse than letting the affair slumber. But what if, while I think that it's slumbering, the cult is actually making secret moves that will be harder to defend against in the future . . . ?"

He fell into silence, considering what he'd likely already considered before. Recognizing that he was finished speaking for now, and that I'd probably never hear the full details of his recovery of *The Necronomicon* when it was stolen from the Museum, I stood and went downstairs to see if there was any message regarding Miles Cosford (although any certainly would have been brought upstairs upon their arrival), and to have a glass or two with some of the men in the inn's small bar.

When I returned to our sitting room several hours later, Holmes had stepped out, and he didn't return before I closed the door to my bedroom and settled into sleep.

The next morning dawned cold and crisp, and promised to have clear blue skies. As Holmes had predicted, the weather had markedly improved, but he warned me that it was only temporary, for the rains would likely return later in the day.

Borrowing a trap and pony from the innkeeper, and with the simple directions provided, we set off for Baird's manor house. "I sent a few wires last night while you were in the bar," said Holmes. "Then I went out and explored the area." We were making good time on the road just north of the River Wharfe, headed east out of Barden. Holmes nodded to our right. "Just over there is The Strid. Baird is right – it looks to be quite deadly."

"Good Lord!" I responded. "You didn't go there at night, in a driving rainstorm? What if you'd fallen in?"

"I took great care to assure that it wouldn't happen," he replied. "But I can see that, if one were to approach it with no warning, it would seem quite harmless. The river narrows there as described, but even at high water last night, where it passes between the rocks in places no more than a foot or two wide, it wasn't turbulent at all. Nearly all of that upstream flow goes underground. I'll admit that, even knowing what I knew, it was tempting to step closer to have a look – and one false step on that sloping moss would have been my last."

I craned to see The Strid through the trees and brush which lined it, but I could only gain a glimpse of the wider river through the trees. Giving up, I faced forward. "That way," said Holmes, gesturing ahead of us, "is the waterfall at the Valley of Desolation, and beyond it the stream – Dicken Dike. I saw no reason to venture that far last night, and Baird will show us the cave on his property this morning. His manor is just north of an imaginary east-west line running between The Strid and the waterfall."

But this plan was not to be, for when we arrived at the manor house, there were several vehicles already there, along with a number of uniformed constables, and a graying man in his sixties who introduced himself as Inspector Fetter.

"It's a pleasure to meet you, Mr. Holmes. Doctor." Fetter clearly wasn't one of those officious policemen who felt the need to exclude my friend in order to protect his own territory. "The dead man's brother, Wyatt Baird, said that you'd both be along this morning for breakfast. Apparently after Mr. Statton Baird visited you last night, he returned home and ordered that preparations be made for most honored guests." He glanced toward the door, where a pair of constables were standing on either side. "Pity it didn't work out as he planned."

Holmes frowned. "What has happened?"

"It looks to be a terrible accident. Baird – Statton Baird, that is – drowned this morning in his bath."

As Holmes glanced at me, and as I acknowledged the significance of a water-related death, the policeman continued. "There was one odd thing, however – he didn't actually die in the bathtub. Rather, he had somehow managed to pull himself out of the tub and across the floor before succumbing in the doorway between the bathroom and his bedroom. He was found this morning by the maid."

"What time?" asked Holmes. I glanced at my watch – just after eight-thirty.

"Seven o'clock. The maid always delivers a cup of coffee to his room at that time."

"And the bathwater?" I asked. "When was it brought?"

"No need," replied Fetter. "Baird made sure he had the best – including indoor plumbing and one of those water heaters. He ran his own bath every morning." He lowered his voice, although the nearest constable was twenty feet away. "Baird's brother told us about the visit to your inn last night, and that you'd be along this morning. Might I ask: Was there anything to it that might give a reason for suspicion? Because I must say, this death seems to be no more than an unfortunate accident."

"Mr. Baird had an interest in some old superstitions," Holmes replied. "Too much of an interest, it seems. He'd had a few other near-accidents of late, and he seemed to be obsessed that they might be related to these beliefs. There was nothing we could do about that, but I was interested in seeing some of the documents he collected about it."

Fetter nodded, appearing a bit relieved. "That's good to know – but I'd still be obliged if you'd have a look upstairs, since you're in the neighborhood. I've heard that you see things that the rest of us miss." There was no irony or masked bitterness to him, just good-natured admiration. Holmes readily agreed to join him inside. In truth, I'm sure he would have found a way to investigate the scene in any case.

Inside, the house was quite warm, and we hastened to remove our coats and hats. The inspector commented that Baird had also invested in centralized heating, making use of the same system that also warmed water throughout the house for baths and kitchen work. "Steam pipes," he explained. "Each room has its own radiator. I understand that after his father died, he returned from London and made a number of improvements."

100

We started toward the stairs, but then the inspector asked if we'd like to meet the brother, Wyatt Baird. Without waiting for an answer, he turned and led us into a room on the right.

There, seated alone in a chair at the far wall, was a man in his thirties, his eyes red-rimmed as he stared into space. To one side stood a constable, motionless and silent. The seated man, presumably the dead man's younger brother, seemed unaware of him.

Wyatt Baird was some years younger than his brother, and physically quite different. Where Statton Baird had been small-boned and pallid, Wyatt was tall, over six feet, and he had ruddy coloring. He carried the look of a man who spent much of his time outdoors. His hands were big and rough-knuckled, and with them he plucked nervously at the pleats of his trousers.

When the inspector had Wyatt's attention, he introduced us, but it seemed to make no impression on the younger brother. He didn't rise to greet us, nor did he speak whatsoever. When I murmured my sympathies, he nodded an acknowledgement, but didn't offer any other response. Holmes took a step closer and reintroduced himself, asking if his brother had shown any signs of being ill at ease the night before, but Wyatt Baird ignored him, returning to his own thoughts. After a moment, the inspector nodded for us to depart.

"Wyatt is a good sort, but clearly this has affected him. Statton was always the smart one, and Wyatt good-natured and popular, but never too bright. When I arrived, he broke down, not sure of what he's going to do now that his brother is gone. I don't know," Fetter concluded, "if you'll get anything useful out of him right now."

We then went upstairs to the first floor, and back along a wide hallway to a bedroom that looked out upon the rear of the house. Another constable was waiting outside the closed door. Fetter reached around us, turned the knob, and motioned us inside. There, without a word of warning, we found Statton Baird lying on the floor between the bathroom and bedroom, on his back, completely undressed, and surrounded by a large puddle of water that trailed from the body to the very-full tub. His eyes were open, marred by the glaze of death and staring with horror, upward into eternity.

The inspector started to speak but Holmes raised a hand, looking intently at the scene in front of us. Then he began to shift from side to side, a few steps this way and that to view the scene from different angles by way of the light from the north-facing windows.

"Were the curtains open when you found him?"

Fetter nodded. "The maid confirms that Baird always opened them himself when he rose each morning."

Holmes knelt by the body, concentrating on the dead man's head. After a moment he rose and gestured that way.

"Watson, if you would confirm my findings?"

I knew better than to ask what those were, and instead hoped that I would at least see what he had observed. Once I was able to examine the body, it was all too clear what he meant.

"This was murder," I said, rising to my feet.

The inspector was nonplussed, and looked from one to the other of us as if I'd spoken gibberish. "Murder? Impossible!"

"Watson?"

Assuming that I'd missed some of what Holmes saw, but that I'd seen enough, I responded, "This man was clearly dead before he ever left the tub. His lungs are full of water – so full that it can be seen where it still pools in his pharynx. If he'd been able to drag himself out of the tub, he'd have had enough life in him for at least some of that fluid to drain out. There are no signs of foam around the mouth or nostrils as one would expect if he were still alive and managed to crawl this far. More importantly, there are faint marks on his throat, symmetrical on either side of his hyoid bone, showing slight bruising made before death, where he was likely held under while he drowned. The bone itself," I concluded, "appears to be intact, indicating that he wasn't strangled."

"But how could someone have overpowered him like that?"

"Watson and I have seen this before," replied Holmes. "If a person is in a tub and his or her feet are suddenly jerked upward, by someone who is trusted enough to approach that closely, the upper torso is abruptly pulled under water, even as the victim reflexively and involuntarily inhales, instantly drawing a substantial amount of fluid into the lungs. If the feet remain raised, or if – as in this case – the body is held underwater by the throat, it's extremely difficult for the victim, even someone of greater size than Statton Baird, to gain enough purchase to rise out of the water. And in any event, so much water instantly entering the lungs serves to almost immediately stop the heart."

"But if the killer – whoever it was – had contrived to make it look like Statton died in the tub – perhaps falling asleep or passing out and sliding down and under – then why go to the trouble to remove him and then place him here in the doorway, along with so much other water?"

"Because it was supposed to look as if one of the supernatural entities that Statton Baird feared did the deed." Holmes explained, stepping to one side. "Look here – on the bathroom floor there, several feet beyond the body."

And there, with the sunshine through the window at the correct angle, Fetter and I both saw it, written in the dust on the floor by the far wall: The word *Cthäat*.

The letters were about six inches high and quite even. There were a few dried streaks in the dust, indicating that the author had likely dipped his finger into the spilled bathwater for use as his pen and ink.

"'*Cthäat*'?" repeated the inspector awkwardly. "What's that?"

"That is the name of one of the 'Old Ones', as Baird called them – and the particular one that he feared. It's a god of water. That was why he came to see us last night. He was worried that this supernatural being was seeking his death." And, in the face of Fetter's rising expression of disbelief, Holmes recounted the three previous occasions that Baird believed that his life had been sought by the ancient water god.

"Again I ask you," said the inspector, "why go to the trouble to kill a man in such a way that it might easily be dismissed as an unfortunate accident, and then deliberately re-set the stage so that it's revealed to be intentional murder – some kind of sacrifice to this heathen god?"

"I'm not sure that it would have been revealed as murder, Inspector," I said, "if Holmes hadn't noticed the word written in the dust." I didn't add that the inspector had been prepared to write it off as an accident when we arrived. "It isn't obviously located."

"Writing the word," explained Holmes, "was likely more for the killer's benefit – to privately fulfill some duty. This appears that Baird was put to death in connection with his fascination with *Cthäat*. If someone had simply wanted to confuse the issue by adding a superstitious element, then the word would have been placed in a more obvious location – perhaps left on a piece of paper, or possibly inscribed upon the body. No, there's a good chance that the word in the dust might never have been seen."

Fetter shook his head. "Ancient gods? It's a blathering ghost story."

"Not a ghost story, Inspector," corrected Holmes. "A story of a religion, although nothing like what you or I are used to. It's very real to some, no matter how ridiculous it might seem to those like us who are more rational-minded. Mr. Baird, here, believed it – although he certainly wasn't the one who dipped his finger into the spilled bathwater and wrote *Cthäat* in the dust alongside his own body. No, for that we'll need to seek someone else."

"The brother!" said Fetter, snapping his fingers. "With Statton's death, Wyatt becomes the new lord of the manor!"

"Actually," said Holmes with a shake of his head, "he does not." He glanced my way. "As I mentioned to Watson, last night I sent some wires. I never take a client's story at face value, and I wanted to know more about

Statton Baird. I confirmed that he was in London during the late 1870's, as he said, spending some of his time studying when he wasn't living the life of an entitled heir. I also asked some questions about Brother Wyatt. He's always been a good-natured lout, well-liked, but without much future. It has been rather expected that his older brother would care for him for the greater portion of their lives – for no one expected Statton Baird to die so early, or violently. In any case, the estate is entailed, and since Statton didn't marry and has no heirs, it does not pass to Wyatt Baird. Instead, the lands and the related fortune will go to a distant cousin in Berwick-upon-Tweed – an old bachelor parson who also has no heirs. After he shuffles off, it will pass even further away from Wyatt Baird. No, this death provides no financial benefit to the younger brother at all."

Holmes stepped toward the door. "I would like to see Baird's papers. And on the way, perhaps speak to the staff."

We left the little dead man where he lay, reposed in the water which had claimed his life.

Pulling the door shut and leaving the room guarded by the constable, we went back downstairs. On the way, Holmes explained that, except for the word written in the dust, the floor had been remarkably without clues. "No footprints, no streaks. Whoever reached the side of the tub and killed Baird took care during his or her approach, and even more so during the departure. One would expect to see signs of wet footprints walking away from all that spilled water, but there was nothing. Most curious . . . ."

The household staff, explained the inspector, was quite small, consisting of a butler, a combination cook-and-housekeeper, and a maid. The rest – a driver, a gardener, and a lady to clean several days a week – lived in Barden and were only on the property during the day, and had not yet arrived. The maid, a girl named Sarah Bell, was nearly cataleptic, having been quite shocked beyond her sensibilities upon discovering the dead body of her unclothed master. She was still in her teens and had only worked in the house since the summer. The housekeeper and cook, a heavy-set middle-aged woman named Mrs. Llewes, answered all of the questions for the both of them without providing any useful information. She confirmed that Baird always drew his own bath in the morning, around six a.m., and that Sarah always took up his first cup of coffee about an hour later. She related that the Master had been in something of a distressed mood of late – though she didn't know why – and that he was looking forward to Holmes's visit that morning.

"Poor man," Mrs. Llewes said. "He never had much blood in him. Always timid – unlike his brother, Mr. Wyatt. Both would have benefitted from having a little bit of the other – Mr. Statton a bit more brawn and health, and Mr. Wyatt some of the other's cleverness." She shook her head. "I don't know what will become of Mr. Wyatt. It's so very sad . . . ."

The butler, Creasy, was much more pragmatic when we interviewed him in the dining room after leaving the two women in the kitchen. He was in his fifties, built thin, and with a gray look about him that indicated heart problems. He shook his head.

"No, last night and this morning were no different than any other – except, I suppose, that the Master was looking forward to your visit this morning, Mr. Holmes. He instructed Merwin to have the papers you'd be reviewing laid out. I – "

"Merwin?" asked Holmes. "Who is he?"

"Mr. Statton's secretary," explained Creasy.

"Secretary?" exclaimed the inspector. "I've heard nothing of a secretary!"

"He's only worked here for a few weeks," explained the butler uneasily.

"Where is he?" countered the inspector. "In the study?"

Creasy frowned. "I couldn't say, sir. As a matter of fact, I haven't seen him this morning – rather unusual, I suppose, but then he sometimes leaves early to run an errand or two for the Master in Barden."

Holmes stood abruptly. "The study – show us the way!"

We were led through the winding ground floor, constructed without a sensible floorplan as was the case for so many ancient buildings that suffered awkward expansions through the centuries, until we reached a low-ceilinged room on the eastern side of the house, its handsome mullioned windows facing the weak winter sunrise. The room was very warm – and empty. At first I thought that it had a surfeit of heat from the steam radiators, but then I quickly perceived that something had been burned quite recently in the ancient fireplace along the northern wall.

Holmes dashed to the hearth and dropped to his knees. Fetter and I stepped closer, and we could see that the grate was mounded with ash, clearly a mass of burned documents. I could feel the warmth radiating from it, and I confirmed it by stretching a hand closer in that direction.

Holmes, meanwhile, was carefully sifting through the ash until he found some unburnt fragments of paper. Carefully lifting them out, he held them up for our inspection. I could see that they were handwritten lines with random meaningless phrases – "*it was only when the latter was understood*" for instance, and "*the thirteenth of his line, and sadly the last*". Others were of similar uselessness, but one held our attention: "*in the same way that* Cthäat *and* Ubbo-Sathla *will come forward to avenge, as prophesied in the* Cthäat Aquadingen.*"

105

Creasy had followed us in and was looking over our shoulders. "All of those are in the Master's hand – all that is, except for the last one. That looks to be one of the sheets that Merwin brought with him."

"It is far older than the others," added Holmes, "and it isn't written on any sort of paper that I've seen before." He looked up at Creasy. "Tell us about Merwin."

"He showed up nearly a month ago. He said to call him 'James', as his real first name was too difficult to pronounce. The Master was expecting him. They had been corresponding for several months about some of the papers that Master Statton collected and studied. Merwin is a little man – dark, quick, and clever in his ways. About thirty, I suppose. Welsh, I believe. He could be charming when he wanted to be. He teased young Sarah some, enough to quicken her heart a little, but nothing inappropriate. He initially simply came for a visit, but then the Master asked him to stay and help with researching his papers, so he took on the position of secretary. I gathered it was a temporary arrangement, and that when his work was done here, he'd move along."

Holmes tapped his lip and then asked for Creasy to show him Merwin's bedroom. Telling us to wait, he was gone for only a moment, leaving the inspector and me to puzzle over the various burned fragments of paper. As might be expected, we came to no useful conclusions.

When Holmes and the butler returned, Holmes stated curtly, "He's packed and gone. Nothing of any use whatsoever has been left in his room." He sat down at the dead man's desk and started methodically searching the drawers. Then, without finding anything, he rose and looked around on the crowded but well-organized book shelves. Finally he shook his head. "There's nothing here about *Cthäat* – or any of the Old Gods." He nodded toward the fireplace. "I fear that a great deal of it was burned from six and seven – between the time that Baird was killed and the body discovered." He looked at Creasy. "Would Merwin have been undisturbed in here during that period?"

The butler nodded. "This room is ignored until Master Baird comes in – *came in* – each day, usually sometime after eight, when he'd had his breakfast."

Holmes looked at Inspector Fetter. "We need to raise a hue-and-cry immediately. Unless he goes cross-country to the south, Merwin will have to pass through Barden to reach the rail line at Bolton Abbey Station."

Fetter looked stricken. "All my men are here – the two constables in the house, and the rest outside. I can disperse them quickly enough, but Merwin has a head start."

"Do so. In the meantime, I will alert my own forces to be prepared as well. We shall re-group at the Abbey Inn."

106

Clearly Fetter wanted to ask about Holmes's "own forces", but time was of the essence, and he followed us outside, where he gathered his constables and issued instructions while Holmes and I climbed into our trap and set off quickly back in the direction of the little inn at Barden.

"We're fortunate," he explained as we quickly returned along our path from earlier that morning. "Our agents in place to keep watch for Miles Cosford can easily be diverted to look for Merwin. With any luck, we'll find him before he's bolted."

It didn't take Holmes any time to locate one of his lieutenants, a thin lad in his twenties named Dean Aimes, brought down from London along with half-a-dozen others. They were all young men who had once been his Irregulars. They had since aged past their usefulness in that unofficial organization, and as they'd reached adulthood, Holmes had arranged for their education, training, and employment. However, they were always still available when needed for just such a mission as the search for Cosford, the spy.

The capture of Merwin was surprisingly simple. Another of the London lads, Sherman Ashe, had actually seen Merwin walking toward Skipton. With no time wasted, Holmes and I were back in our trap, racing to the southwest on the narrow road between two ancient stone walls. On either side of us, the fallow brownish land stretched under the January sky toward distant rising hills. From the west, clouds were beginning to pile in, and I realized that Holmes's prediction of returning rain was true.

The slope of the road increased, and Holmes lessened our pace to ease the strain on the poor pony. But the same rise had caused Merwin to slow as well, and we came upon him half-a-mile before Eastby. He heard us coming and, thinking we were simply a couple of local farmers heading into town, stepped to one side of the road in order that we might pass. As we came alongside, Holmes slowed down. "Need a ride?" he said, his normal tones layered in a thick Yorkshire accent.

Merwin shook his head and mumbled something that sounded like "No." Holmes nodded to me and then suddenly turned the pony across Merwin's path while I leapt down behind him. Holmes quickly followed. By the time he came around the trap, I had my service revolver against the little Welshman's skull, and Holmes was to one side, pulling the man's bag from his hand, tossing it aside, and then quickly checking to see if he was armed. He was not.

Cutting a piece from one of the pony's reins, Holmes tied the man's hands behind his back. All the while, Merwin didn't react as I would have expected. There were no angry protestations, or questions as to what was happening. Rather, he had a small sideways smile and, looking from one to the other of us, he simply remarked, "Mr. Holmes, I presume." That was all that he said, making no other comment as we loaded him in the trap and turned back toward The Abbey Inn.

There we found Fetter, who had set up something of a command post as he planned a district-wide search. He was somewhat unsettled to see that we'd already taken the prisoner. However, he set his feelings aside when we began questioning the man, who – despite being lawfully warned by the inspector that his words might be used as evidence – seemed most willing to talk.

"Of course I drowned him," Merwin said matter-of-factly. "He was delving into matters which should be left alone."

"Why kill the poor man?" asked Fetter, an angry tone in his voice. "He was doing nothing but sitting in his house, reading old papers. If it made him happy – ?"

"Happy?" asked Merwin, a tone of stridency entering his words. "His happiness earns him nothing. He was researching what should be left alone."

Holmes, who had searched Merwin's bag and found nothing but clothing, tossed it aside, stating, "I see that you took none of the documents with you."

When there was no response from the prisoner, he asked, "Whom do you represent? I suspect that you're part of an organization of some sort."

Merwin nodded. "Very perceptive, Mr. Holmes. I am a servant of a group that has taken on a responsibility that no one else wants. We watch. We educate when necessary – and we do surgery when required."

"Surgery?" I asked. "That's how you describe the murder of Statton Baird? Surgery?"

Merwin nodded. "Indeed. As a young man, he became *interested*. That in and of itself is not a bad thing. You, too, Mr. Holmes, were *interested* at that age." He placed a curious and serpent-like emphasis on the word. "Oh, we knew it even then. We watch and listen, observing who discovers hints of the truth. It is in that way that some of us are identified and recruited to carry on the work. Some others with a curious interest pick up the threads for a while and then drop them as their lives move on. You seemed to do that, Mr. Holmes, but we know that you've never entirely forgotten. You will bear further watching. But Mr. Baird . . . Ah, his interest was of a different sort. He was not one that we would recruit, and yet, left to his own devices, he delved deeper, seeking to know more and more without having the proper foundation of knowledge. A month ago, he wrote to the small library where I'm nominally employed. Somehow he'd found my name – which in and of itself was of great concern to us – and he was asking questions. I responded vaguely to judge how much he knew, and from his reply I learned that he knew too much.

108

When he invited me to visit this bleak place, I realized that events were working out as I'd hoped – he had willingly opened his door to me so that I wouldn't have to find my own way surreptitiously inside. Then, telling him just enough to set the hook, I contrived that he would then invite me to remain as his secretary. I revolved to stay until I'd learned what I needed – about what he knew, and about who he had told.

"It wasn't long before he shared with me the two incidents where his life was nearly claimed by the Water God. I was able to convey to him, in such a way that he believed to have originated the idea himself, that he owed a life. In truth, he'd cheated the Water God twice, so *two* lives were owed. I wondered who the second would be.

"Then, two days ago, a pair of linked events occurred. Statton Baird once again cheated the Water God, this time preventing himself from being pulled into the underground stream behind the manor. And he learned that you, Mr. Holmes, had come to Barden.

"He was quite excited to share with you his research, and that's when I knew this must end. Your curiosity so many years ago, Mr. Holmes, was of some concern to us then, but you had the sense to step back from the precipice. Statton Baird was about to pull you closer once more, and this time you might not be so lucky."

"You say 'of some concern *to us*'," said Holmes. "My interest in these matters occurred over a dozen years ago. You would have been barely out of childhood then. Who is this '*us*' to whom you refer?"

"I believe you already know," said Merwin. "You've spoken to several people over the years regarding writing a monograph about us."

Holmes nodded. "The *Cthulhu* cult."

"Oh, our concerns are greater than He, one of the greatest of the Old Entities. There are so many of the Elders, whom we both serve and oppose simultaneously. In the end, we will fail, and the universe will pull apart, fiber by fiber, atom by atom, until the last light winks out in the desperate dark void. But until then . . . Ah, until then, we will carry on as we are required."

"And you were 'required' to kill an innocent man?" I asked, routing us back to the main path.

Merwin nodded. "I was. The time had come. I could learn no more from him, and he was about to speak further in a manner that was proscribed. Therefore, I killed him by way of the water."

"And wrote '*Cthäat*' in the dust beside the body," added Holmes.

Merwin winced. "We do not speak the Elder Names."

"But you had no hesitation at writing it," interjected Inspector Fetter, declaring his presence for the first time since his outburst at the interview's commencement. I'd seen his expression react and change several times –

from anger to disbelief to astonishment and a bit of fear, and then back again.

"I burned the papers that Baird had accumulated," continued Merwin, "as there is no place for them, and then departed. Unfortunately, you have found me. In that aspect, I have failed. It is I who shall have to pay one of Statton's owed deaths."

"'Owed deaths'?" I asked. "You mentioned that before. What is 'owed'?"

"Statton Baird owed three deaths, one for each time he cheated the Water God – first when he was swimming in Dicken Dike, and next at The Strid, and then at the underground stream near the manor house. He has now paid the first with his own life. For my failure, I shall pay the second. The third will come about soon enough. They are *owed*!" His voice rose at the last word, but then settled back into the conversational manner he'd employed since the interrogation began.

"The third?" asked Holmes, his expression intent as he looked at the little killer. His brows were drawn, as if he were watching to see how a crucial chemical experiment played out. "Who will that be? Are there more of you out there?"

Merwin shook his head. "I do not know who of us walks in the world, and I do not know for certain, Mr. Holmes, who the third death will be." Then he leaned closer, his tone deadly serious. "But I have a sense that *you* will face the Water God, Mr. Holmes – and quite soon, certainly by spring. It seems that for your interference, *you* are destined to pay the Third Death."

Fetter sputtered, cursed under his breath, and leaned back, as if to get his face away from a foul stench. I looked at the little man in horror. He was clearly quite mad and most dangerous, and the way he made his pronouncement was most unsettling, despite the ridiculousness of the assertion. Holmes, however, continued to ponder him as if there were other secrets that might be unlocked, could only he could find the key. But then, seeming to realize that such a puzzle was beyond him, he straightened and indicated that he had no further questions.

That night, in the Skipton jail, Merwin – whose braces and even shoelaces were taken from him as a prevention against suicide after his statement that he would be the next to die – lowered himself to his knees on the floor of his cell, leaned forward over the provided water bucket, and carefully placed his head inside, whereupon he deliberately held himself in place while he inhaled a goodly portion of the contents, spilling not a drop and drowning himself.

A note found on his cot indicated that such was his intent, and that the Elder God *Cthäat* demanded it – the payment of the second owed death, charged to him because he had failed by being caught.

When word came the next morning of Merwin's suicide by way of Inspector Fetter, I was most unsettled. Try as I might, I couldn't comprehend how a man could end his own life in such a deliberate and coldly controlled way. Even after inhaling much of the bucket's water into his lungs, he'd held himself there, resisting the irresistible motions and reflexes that his body would have wanted to make to save itself. Something had given him the will to remain in that position, surrounded by the remaining water that hadn't entered his lungs.

The second owed death was paid.

Holmes hadn't responded when we'd heard the news about Merwin, and we didn't have long to ponder it. Just after Fetter told us, a message arrived for Holmes from one of his former Irregulars: Miles Cosford had been spotted, leaving a remote farmhouse (that we later learned belonged to a distant relative) and seemingly making his way in the direction of Bolton Abbey Station, opened just two years before. With a cry to follow him, Holmes leapt to his feet and ran downstairs and out, where a wagon had been kept waiting. Fetter joined us, and as we lurched into motion, Holmes and I explained our true purpose for being in Barden.

The rains had returned, and the day was dark and miserable. Our heavy coats offered some little protection, but enough, and as the rain dripped from the back of my hat and down into my collar, I again saw the sense of Holmes's deerstalker, which protected him both fore and aft.

We headed southwest along the River Wharfe, knowing that if the information we'd received was correct, we'd soon catch up with Cosford – and we did. He was alone in a small trap, traveling at a slow pace, likely to avoid attention. But he was vigilant, and it didn't take him long to see that we were coming up quickly behind him. He increased his speed, but his single horse was no match for our two, and we began to overtake him.

When it was clear that he wasn't going to outrun us, he tried a different strategy – to go cross-country. Instead of remaining on the road and going the long way around by Bolton Abbey, he jumped from the trap and, grabbing a carpetbag, set off straight south, making a beeline for the station. We pulled to a stop and followed him, and with a start, I recognized where we were.

"Holmes – if he makes it across, we cannot follow."

"He's right, Mr. Holmes," added Fetter. "The Strid is deadly at the best of times – and today it will be that much worse. With these rains, the slick rocks alongside will be treacherous. I don't care if Cosford is from around here and thinks he knows a way to make it across. We will not follow – even if your spy escapes!"

Holmes nodded. "Don't worry, Inspector. I would not be so foolish. But we will keep up with him to see if he instead turns aside and follows the river up or downstream."

The entire time, we had been headed south from the road toward the river, with Cosford never out of view. He would stop and look back, seeing the three of us – likely no more than dark silhouettes on that low day – inexorably dogging him. Each time he would speed up a bit before settling back into something between a walk and a lope. Finally he reached the river – and I saw The Strid for the first and only time.

Upstream, the rain-swollen river raged, and it did so off to our left as well, as it ran way into the gloom toward Bolton Abbey. But The Strid seemed to be nothing – except for a thin black line connecting the two turbulent watercourses, one wouldn't have recognized it from that distance as a stream.

Cosford reached the edge and then appeared to become indecisive. He looked left and right several times, and then back toward the three of us, always moving closer. He seemed to realize that he'd lost the advantage of distance, and if he turned up or down the river, we had but to alter our course and easily intercept him, the three of us separating and then catching him like a herd of wild hunting dogs.

He was a local man, though he'd been gone for years. He knew better. But he also must have felt that he had no other choice. He turned away from us, to the south again, and stepped onto a flat rock at the narrowest part of The Strid.

It happened so fast that I almost didn't see it. One minute he was there. The next, his feet appeared to slide rather than step, and though he remained upright as he raced forward, he dropped from our sight into the black water. Without thought, we turned and ran to the east, downstream, where in a moment the deep deadly waters reappeared as the churning river – but he did not surface. His body was never recovered – and Holmes was certain, by way of the fact that the stolen documents which were surely in the man's carpetbag never reappeared either – that the man had not somehow secretly survived and escaped to Germany.

No, the traitor was taken by the waters and never given back.

And while we were still standing around there, some time later, waiting to see if Cosford's battered body would return, Holmes said softly, out of Fetter's hearing, "Perhaps *Cthäat* has indeed claimed its third owed death."

112

I started to speak – to remind Holmes that he had no use for such superstitious foolishness. But standing there in the rain by the violent waters, so close to where so many had vanished and died over the millennia, more than we would ever know, I felt that there might be some truth to his words, and I shivered.

And I hoped that the third owed death had indeed been paid. But several months later, in mid-May as I was returning to London from the Reichenbach Falls where Holmes had fallen to his death while battling Professor Moriarty, I recalled that moment, and what Merwin had told us, and shivered again.

"But I have a sense that you *will face the Water God, Mr. Holmes,"* Merwin had said, *"and quite soon, certainly by spring. It seems that for your interference,* you *are destined to pay the Third Death."*

There was no reason that Holmes should have been required to pay any such debt. And yet, he was gone as well, his body claimed by the waters, and he too has never been recovered.

Such a loss was incomprehensible to me then, as it is now. How could a man of such value as Sherlock Holmes be taken? There was no fairness to it. No justice.

But from what I've been able to learn in my subsequent research, with nearly three years having now passed, delving into old documents at the British Museum, and by way of correspondence with learned men in England and upon the Continent, the Old Gods are beyond the puny concepts of "fair" and "justice". Such ancient and vast immensity and emptiness has no use for insignificant human ideas of fairness.

Or so one would think, if one believed in such ineffable twaddle.

JHW
10 January, 1894

113

NOTES

*   See *Sherlock Holmes and The Eye of Heka*, published in 2021, and included in Volume II of *The Collected Papers of Sherlock Holmes - Records*.

The Strid and the Valley of Desolation are located near Barden and Bolton Abbey, near the River Wharfe in Yorkshire. As described, The Strid is one of the most deadly watercourses in the world. More about it can be found at:

☐   *https://www.atlasobscura.com/places/bolton-strid*
☐   *https://www.snopes.com/fact-check/bolton-strid/*
☐   *https://www.youtube.com/watch?v=7ILpLoENZLE*

I personally understand Statton Baird's nervousness of water, as similar situations have occurred to me. In the summer of 2021, while swimming in a mountain river in the Great Smoky Mountains (not far from where I live, and where I've swam many times before), I entered an area where Little River, the main watercourse through the western side of the National Park, turns alongside a great black rock. The spot is very deep, but only ten feet from shallow shelving gravel. The water level was up that day just a bit from recent rains, and the churning turbulence from flowing over nearby upstream rocks was enough to aerate the water so that I suddenly lost all buoyancy. One minute I was floating, and the next, it was as if I was being pulled vertically straight down. It was all I could do to keep my face level with the surface, and kicking my legs did nothing whatsoever. Just a few feet behind me, as I faced the tall black rock, I could hear people laughing, completely unaware that I was about to drown. I couldn't even get enough breath to call for help. It was only by frantically pushing at the water with my arms that I was able to move backwards enough to get my toes on the sloping gravel bottom and inch up to safety.

In the fall of 2021, my son and I were walking on a trail along the shore of the wild Obed River. The river was high that day after recent rains, and churning and muddy brown as it flowed over the submerged rocks. We reached and crossed a wide muddy spot covered with animal tracks. It had a very slight slope toward the high brown water, and we paused to look at the tracks for a moment before my son went on ahead. I followed, and suddenly my feet went out from under me. I started sliding toward the swollen river. Luckily my son stepped back and grabbed my hand, and more luckily, we didn't both go in. Later that day, at a different spot on the river, we were both standing upright on another slightly sloping shelf when *he* suddenly started to slide toward the river, standing upright as if he were unwillingly skating across ice. This time I caught him. We decided then that it was time to leave.

Back in the early 2000's, when I was going back to school to be a civil engineer, I heard about a location nearby where a sizable stream, Ten Mile Creek, goes underground. While running errands one Saturday morning in January, I stopped to look at it. I walked back into the woods and saw it – a strongly running stream flowing into a black cave. The stream reappears several miles away and drains out of another cave into the Tennessee River– but as far as I know, the path between the two caves is unmapped. The ground at the entrance cave is slightly sloped, and that day it was covered by a skin of ice – over mud, as it turned out. I took a step, my feet went out from under me, and I started sliding on my back. It was smooth ground – no trees or rocks to grab. All I could do was try and kick my heels into the soil to stop my progression into the water. I was just feet away from entering the swift flow when I managed to brake to a stop – and then I had to work my way backwards and up to level ground without starting to slide again. No one knew where I was or had planned to stop there, and I suppose that when I'd been missing long enough and my car was eventually found, someone would have figured it out, but by then it would have been far too late.

I only learned about *Cthäat* when researching this story – but I'd already started to have the sense that I've tested my luck too many times against waters that want me – and have thus far been cheated.

I don't plan on giving them any more chances.

Death at the London Beadles Store

"**P**aul is dead."

I looked up in surprise, and Mrs. Hudson clarified. "Paul Beadle. He's dead.

She made the statement one late summer morning as she carried in my breakfast. I had only come down from my room a moment before and had remained standing by the landing door to assist when she arrived.

Taking the tray from her, I carried it to the dining table by the window, whereupon she took the plate with my bacon and eggs, along with a fresh pot of coffee, and set them at my usual seat. From across the room, where he sat by then fireplace tearing apart the morning newspapers, Sherlock Holmes said, "Surely not."

"Oh, it's true," confirmed our landlady – the finest of women, but sometimes a noted neighborhood gossip. "It was the storm last night. Surely you heard it! They say lightning struck the Beadles' house and ran in on the water pipes. Paul was at his sink and the electricity killed him. It must have stopped his heart, it did!"

I glanced at the clock on the mantel, confirming that it wasn't yet quite eight in the morning. "How did you hear about this so quickly?" I asked around my first sip of coffee.

"Well, isn't it obvious? When Clayton brought 'round the eggs, he told me that there was something doing three doors down. I could see nothing from the rear door, but there are still policemen going in and out of the front. I just spoke with Ada next door, and she told me about Paul Beadle. They say his brother is beside himself with grief."

That, I thought to myself, *seems unlikely.* John Beadle seemed a decent-enough chap, but he had never been one to express his emotions in an overt way. He would speak, but seemed to prefer quiet over conversation, and if one did manage to engage him in small talk, his negativity and sarcasm would soon give the whole encounter a rather unpleasant feeling – as if, when taking a drink of water, the faintest brown oily sheen was visible on the surface.

Hearing that the police were likely still on the scene, Holmes tossed aside one his newspapers and stood, a keen expression upon his face.

"I believe that I'll step over and see what's going on. Lightning killed him? My curiosity is aroused. Coming, Watson?"

I grunted that I would join him momentarily and began to eat more quickly. I glanced at Mrs. Hudson, who smiled sympathetically. When I finished, I was only a moment or two behind Holmes. I caught up with him on the pavement in front of the Beadles' front door, speaking with Inspector Lanner.

The Beadle brothers lived in a house just a few doors south of our own residence at 221 Baker Street, and on the same western side of the street. Their building was a duplicate of 221, one of the countless double-width mud-colored brick structures that filled London. For those who haven't visited London, these houses, a variation of the "two-up, two-down" terraced rowhouse design, are typically four floors (in addition to the basement level). Most were built near the beginning of the nineteenth century according to the same plan: Approximately twenty feet across with two street-facing windows, each floor has two rooms, a larger and a smaller, and a stairwell.

Mrs. Hudson's house has her quarters on the ground floor and in the cellar, while Holmes and I rent the first and part of the second floors – the *221b* upper-apartment address assigned to 221. The first floor front is our shared sitting room, and the back half of that floor is the stairway and landing on the southwest side, and Holmes's bedroom on the northwest, with doors opening from it into the sitting room and onto the landing. The second and third floors mirror this arrangement, and the second has my room at the rear, directly over Holmes's, with a view of our uninspiring rear yard, mostly empty except for access to the rear door by way of a mews, an always desperate-looking plane tree, and a small area where Mrs. Hudson – mostly without success – tries to grow herbs. (The yard never gets enough sunlight.)

The front of the second and third floors have servant quarters – generally used by the maid and the page, when one or the other or both are being employed, which is not always the case. (I suppose that Mrs. Hudson could have also rented these rooms to further lodgers, but she had enough on her hands with Sherlock Holmes.) The rear of the third floor has a box room that, while not technically part of our rent, is used by Holmes and me – and most particularly the former – for the retainage of old books and newspapers, case evidence and documents, and spare scientific equipment. At the top of the stairway passage on the third floor is a small walled-off area, separate from the attic, containing the building's bathroom.

This description is relevant, as it also applies to the layout of the Beadles' house, built to identical plans and specifications and with identical materials, but adapted much differently during the decades of their residence. One of these adaptations was the recent installation of a lightning rod, as Lanner was explaining to Holmes.

117

"He had it put in three weeks ago. It seems that in recent years, Paul Beadle had developed a morbid fear of lightning," Lanner stated. "According to his brother, it was becoming something of an *idea* . . . an *idea* . . . ."

As he struggled to recall the term, I interrupted. "An *idée fixe*. A notion that takes over one's thoughts to the point of distraction."

Lanner nodded. "That's it. Thank you, Doctor. This *idée fixe* of his was that the building would be struck and burned to the ground. Sometimes he worried about being trapped and dying in a lightning-generated fire, while on other occasions, he was simply concerned that everything they owned would be burned and gone – and that it was too late in their lives to be starting over with nothing."

"And yet," Holmes noted, "it appears that his fears were justified, in spite of his precautions. Lightning killed him."

"Just so."

Holmes turned to me. "Lanner says that, during last night's storm, lightning did strike the building, and somehow the massive electrical current electrocuted Paul Beadle. However, his brother John didn't discover the body until this morning, as they each have separate apartments upstairs, and they had already said goodnight and retreated to their own rooms."

He looked back at Lanner. "Is it known specifically how the lightning reached Paul Beadle without doing damage to the rest of the building?"

"It was apparently some cross-connection between the lightning rod and the plumbing," the inspector replied. "We have the lightning rod installer, Conway, inside now. Would you like to go in and hear his report?"

Holmes nodded with interest. "I would. We would. This is something new – beyond my experience."

"Mine as well," Lanner said, his eyes bright with enthusiasm. "I suspect that everyone at the Yard will be jealous that it was I who responded to this call. This is much more interesting and curious than wading around through some grimy East End cutting."

He led us through the front door, and into the Beadle's ground floor shop.

One aspect of that type of building's layout is that the ground floor can be residential or commercial. Mrs. Hudson used the ground floor at 221 as her primary living quarters, while the Beadles had converted theirs into a shop. It had been such when I first moved to Baker Street in early January 1881, over five years earlier, and I'd had the impression their little concern had been in existence since years before that.

I can only describe it as some sort of "Curiosity Shop". By definition, such a place stocks odd items and curios of all eras, usually with no particular emphasis. Some are no better than junk shops, but this one, at least, seemed to have a better class of random flotsam-and-jetsam. The blue sign over the door, with painted yellow letters spelling *London Beadles Store*, implied to the ignorant that it was a branch of some multi-city concern, when it was actually just the one location. I had only been inside a very few times – once when I moved to the neighborhood and spent most of my days walking to try and improve my health following my grievous war injuries, and then on two or three subsequent occasions when one or the other Beadle was ill and requested my services. Not that I was their regular doctor – for they had long been attended by Dr. Brady of Upper Wimpole Street – but sometimes I was the next best nearby substitute when he was busy elsewhere.

From my cursory examination during my rare visits, nothing ever seemed to change inside the small shop. And while I could not claim to have made a study of the matter, it seemed to me that no one ever brought in anything to sell, and more importantly, no great number of customers ever wandered in to buy. "I've heard that they have money," Mrs. Hudson had shared once, without being asked. "The shop is just something to keep them busy. Whether it's successful or not is of no account, as they're already taken care of – possibly by an inheritance."

She had offered this comment as a lure toward further conversation, but neither Holmes nor I were much interested then in discussing the Beadles, and the opportunity had passed.

Moving back through the shop, we found our way to the stairs leading upward. The stairway was in the same location as that of 221, but in this layout it was accessible by way of the large kitchen at the rear of the floor. We traipsed up the stairs, and I noticed a familiar smell in the air – not anything electrical, and not the odor of burned meat, as one might expect from the victim of an electrical discharge of massive voltage. Rather, it was simply the unfortunate and unpleasant smell that's often encountered when a human body passes suddenly.

The first floor consisted of a small sitting room overlooking the street, and a small office corresponding to what was Holmes's bedroom at 221. We continued onward to the second floor, and that's where we found John Beadle, sitting in his own little parlor in a chair near the front windows, staring stonily ahead in shock – but not to the point where he didn't glance up. After a moment, he seemed to recognize and then acknowledge both Holmes and me. We nodded back, and Lanner explained, "As you might expect, Mr. Holmes and Dr. Watson have a . . . professional interest in what occurred upstairs last night. Would you mind repeating what you've told me?"

John Beadle nodded and cleared his throat. He was a thin fellow, about halfway between five and six feet and perhaps ten stone. About sixty years of age, his hair was still brown and combed forward into bangs that were trimmed evenly across the midline of his forehead. It was not the best look that he could have chosen, but it had never changed since I'd known him.

His brother Paul had always maintained the same haircut – which might have been odd, or not, as they were identical twins. I'd never had difficulties telling them apart, however, because in other aspects they presented themselves quite differently. John always wore curious round *pince-nez*, and favored the loose-type clothing associated with an Indian influence, while Paul didn't wear glasses at all and was more likely to dress as a typical sensible Englishman.

John Beadle blinked a few times, cleared his throat again, and related the previous night's events, without his usual snide shadings.

"Paul became obsessed with worry about lightning strikes," he said, his voice sounding somewhat rough. "I went looking for him this morning when he didn't come downstairs as usual. I found him, on the floor of the bathroom . . . ." He shook his head. "He insisted that we install a lightning rod. He'd become terrified of lightning – I don't know why. I don't know anything about lightning, or how lightning rods work, but when I found him this morning, he was electrocuted on the floor of the bathroom. There was a burn mark on his hand. And the look upon his face . . . The installer is upstairs now. He looked horrified when the police brought him in, and said something about how possibly the rod had been accidentally grounded to the water pipe, so that when the lightning hit . . . ." His voice dropped away and he returned to staring forward, as if seeing again that moment when he discovered his brother's body.

Holmes glanced at Lanner, and then toward the doorway. Taking the hint, the inspector led us back out of the room and then up to the third floor, where two constables were on the landing, looking toward the narrow stairs that continued up to the bathroom, near the attic.

"The body was moved to his bedroom, just there," Lanner said, nodding behind him. Holmes pursed his lips, certainly because he would have liked to evaluate the scene *in situ* before it was disturbed. Instead of commenting, however, he moved past the constables and up the few short steps into the bathroom. I followed, remaining on the landing as there wasn't room in the small chamber for anyone else, and saw a thin workman in his fifties squatting on the floor, shaking his head.

I recognized him as Sam Conway of nearby Dorset Street. He worked as a handyman, staying busy doing all sorts of work – carpentry, plumbing, stone and brick work, and the occasional electrical job.

"I don't understand it, Mr. Holmes," Conway said, standing up and wiping dust from his hands. "The police came and got me first thing, saying that Mr. Paul had been killed – electrocuted to death by my lightning rod! It just isn't possible. I don't often get the call to install one, but I understand how to do it – running the rod from the roof to the ground, down through the building, mounted to the main beams and held in place by brackets and insulators so that the current can't jump anywhere else, nor touch anything that might catch fire when that great spark surges along the rod. I've been up and down the rod since I got here, examining every fitting, and it isn't anywhere near the water pipe, or any other metal that might transfer the charge. There's no sign of heat damage anywhere along the path, and besides that, the glass ball at the top of the rod, outside on the roof, is intact. So often when the rod is hit, the glass will explode. That's how you can tell if there's been a strike."

"I'd like to see for myself," replied Holmes. Lanner's eyes widened, surprised at this indication of Holmes's greater interest.

"Mr. Holmes," he began, "it's just a terrible accident. Lightning is such a mystery, after all. It can strike a hundred feet away from one man and kill him instantly, and hit another right on top of the head, passing all the way through him and setting fire to his clothes and knocking the shoes from his feet, and he'll have nothing more than a ringing headache and a scorch mark or two where it went in and out. The ways of God – "

"I'm starting to doubt whether God had anything to do with this," he said.

He turned back to Conway, asking specifically to see the lightning rod. Together, they climbed from the bathroom into the attic space. Conway had a lantern which he used to illuminate the tight area, pointing here and there while Holmes watched intently, sometimes asking a quiet question or two. Then they pushed back the leaded trap door that allowed access to the outer roof and climbed out together. In just two or three minutes they returned, and Holmes thanked Conway before joining the rest of us upon the landing. He then pointed back toward the bathroom.

"Where on the floor was the body?"

"Just there." Lanner pointed to just in front of the sink.

Holmes knelt down and examined the wooden boards. "No sign of splashed water. Was the faucet turned on when the body was found?"

"I don't know," replied Lanner. "Would it matter? If he touched it just as the lightning hit, no water was needed for the electricity to pass into his body – or so I understand. And if the water was still running, John

Beadle may have turned it off when he found Paul, just before he called us. Although that might be a bit unusual, people do the strangest things when discovering a body. I recall earlier this year when a wife discovered her husband, dead from a blow to the head by a fireplace poker. Without thinking, she reached out and picked up the poker, getting blood all over her hand and apron. She was that way when we found her. So often they seem to reach out and pick up the murder weapon. If I hadn't – "

But Holmes was already up and moving to the nearby bedroom, where the body was lying. The room, on the back and western side of the building, was quite dark despite the open drapes, and lit only by a single gas-lamp. It would be afternoon before the setting sun shown through the window. I knew this because my own bedroom's position corresponded to this one exactly.

Paul Beadle lay upon his bed, eyes closed, his arms beside his torso. Holmes picked up one hand, and then the other, leaning in to observe both closely, and poking and prodding the flesh of the fingers and palms.

"As you can see," Lanner said, "there is a burn on his right hand, consistent with an electrical discharge."

Holmes didn't reply, instead taking further time to closely look over the dead man from the crown of his head to the soles of his shoes. Then he proceeded to pull aside and rearrange the different garments upon Paul Beadle's body, looking at different spots – under his arms, at his waist, and so on. He took off the corpse's shoes and peered at his feet. After a few moments, he sat back on his heels, frowned as if ordering something in his mind, and then invited me to make my own investigation as well.

I looked at the burn mark, seeing that it did indeed look electrical in nature, the skin reddish around a black and charred spot. I then looked at the body's left hand. Further examination of the man's head revealed that there was damage to the rear of his skull, felt through the scalp around the upper portion of the occipital bone. It's possible, I thought, that the electrical shock didn't kill him, but was enough to render him unconscious. If he fell to the floor and hit his head . . . .

I looked inside his clothing, as Holmes had done, but saw nothing of significance – to me – and no other wounds. Then I looked more closely at the dead man's face – and what I observed caused me to take a small sudden shocked breath. Certain that Holmes had seen this as well, I was careful to give no other indication, as it was likely something he wished to keep to himself for a while, until questions could be asked and answered.

I looked again at the hands, and then the man's bare feet. There were no burns, but I did notice a number of unusual grooves on the sides and soles of the man's feet.

"Good, Watson," I heard Holmes murmur.

"No burns?" said Lanner, bending to look at the dead man's feet. "Well, they don't always show up, do they?"

As I stood, Lanner stepped further into the room, stopping beside Holmes and lowering his voice. "What did you see, Mr. Holmes? Is this death by lightning – An Act of God? – or is there something else going on."

Instead of answering directly, Holmes said, "Remove the body to the morgue for an autopsy. In the meantime, get John Beadle out of the house on some pretext. Tell him that he doesn't need to be alone right now. Only let him take a change of clothes – and make sure that he removes nothing else from the house. Get a warrant so that we can legally search it. And also . . . ."

With that, he drifted into silence while pulling out his small notebook, taking a moment to write a note that seemed to consist of a number of specific points, each highlighted by a small dash.

"Hand that to the police surgeon who does the autopsy – Questions to be answered."

Lanner looked at the list and frowned, but then nodded and stuck it in his waistcoat pocket.

"Come, Watson," Holmes said, turning abruptly and starting back downstairs. He passed by the second floor, where John Beadle was still sitting, and on downstairs to the shop, where he paused and looked from side to side for a moment before shaking his head. "We'll have to come back to do a proper search – when Beadle has been taken elsewhere." Then he led me into the street. I started to mention what I'd seen, but Holmes raised a finger to his lips. He was thinking, and didn't want to have a discussion.

The morning was warmer now, and I could tell that it would be another hot day. I wondered if the afternoon and evening would bring new thunder storms like those of the previous night. I glanced up toward the roofline, but saw nothing except the bright sky, which made me squint.

"You cannot see the lightning rod from here," said Holmes, reading my thoughts. "I examined it and verified that the glass insulating ball atop the rod has not been destroyed. Now: If you were the Beadles, who would you use as an attorney?"

The question surprised me, but the answer came easily. "Billings, in Marylebone Lane. I wouldn't know, except that I saw one of the Beadles – John, as I recall – coming out of there a few weeks ago while I was passing that way."

Holmes checked his watch. "Excellent. We should arrive about the time he opens his doors for the day." And he led me in that direction along the short march to south and east.

Silas Billings was a feeble man, grown ancient in service to the Law. An attorney of the old school, he was well known in that neighborhood for his good humor, patience, wisdom, and experience. Although not my usual lawyer, I'd had occasion to consult him before, and his path had also crossed ours once or twice in relation to Holmes's criminal investigations. He was a man who could be trusted, and he also knew the same of both of us. Hopefully he would have the answers that Holmes sought.

Billings' office was something from a Dickensian dream. The building itself seemed to lean in on itself from the left and right sides to the middle, as if the surrounding structures were resting wearily upon its shoulders, becoming more of a burden than could be endured over the passing decades. A narrow stairway, the risers of differing heights, felt more like climbing a rude homemade ladder than ascending typical steps. There was a strong scent of decay of the sort associated with very old books, which made sense, as Billings had filled the place from top to bottom with a truly astonishing number of ancient volumes. Should a stray spark ever find its way to any of them, the entire collection, and likely the adjacent buildings, would go up like a pyre doused in coal oil. One could only hope that nothing like this ever occurred.

We were met by Oliver St. Collins, Billings' skeletal and venerable clerk, who took us without question into his master's large chamber, on the first floor overlooking the street. Billings, then in his eighties, did not rise. He was a heavy-set man, rather collapsed in upon himself, and seated in a wide old chair behind a broad desk, his sunken head at nearly the desk's level surface. He coughed once or twice, raised a hand vaguely in greeting, and *Harrumphed!* explosively before asking, "Gentlemen – How may I be of assistance?"

"Have you heard of today's tragedy?" asked Holmes, leaping right to the topic at hand. One always felt so inclined to do so with Billings, for he wasn't much for idle conversation, and there was the sneaking awareness that he was running out of time, and one had best be about the business at hand straightaway and gone before the man's expiration occurred.

"Paul Beadle is dead," Holmes explained, "apparently by a lightning strike that ran in upon the water line, possibly from a cross-connection a lightning rod."

"'Apparently', you say." Billings further cleared his throat. "Sherlock Holmes doesn't say 'apparently' if he doesn't mean to imply some doubt. What is your doubt, sir?"

"First, let me ask if you are the Beadles' attorney. If not, then you understand that we have no business sharing any of our conclusions with you. Watson recalls seeing one of the Beadles departing from your office

124

a few weeks ago, but that doesn't necessarily mean you are either man's representative."

Billings weathered cheeks tightened in something of a canny grin. "I can confirm, gentlemen, that I have represented the Beadles in a recent matter. As you know, it is confidential – a privileged communication – but it may be that what you tell me might affect that privilege. Come, sir – no one knows better than me that time is short. Tell me why you're here."

"There has been a murder. Paul Beadle has killed his brother, John, assumed his identity, and has clumsily tried to pass it off with this farrago of a lightning strike and a mis-installed lightning rod. When last we saw Paul Beadle, sitting in his brother's Baker Street room, he was wearing Brother John's loose clothing and awkwardly sporting the dead-man's *pince-nez*." He glanced at me. "You will have noticed that they didn't fit, he had trouble seeing through them, and that he didn't have the characteristic long-term pinch-marks on either side of his nose." Back to Billings, he stated, "My question now is why did he do this, and go to such trouble, at this latter stage in their shared lives?"

Billings nodded. "I was wondering what might spin out from my recent service for the Beadles. This explains much – and yet, I don't know any details as to why." He then knocked sharply upon his desk, his big arthritic knuckles making a booming noise. I thought that it must have hurt him to do that – or instead, he no longer had any feeling left at all in those dark swollen knuckles.

Oliver St. Collins entered and Billings instructed him, "Give Mr. Holmes a shilling. I'm hiring him as my agent for a confidential matter." He turned back to Holmes. "There. As my agent, I can discuss a client's confidential affairs with you. And you, Doctor: It is my understanding that you are here acting as Mr. Holmes's agent – No, I don't need to know otherwise! – so to my best understanding, my arrangement with him also covers you. Unless you'd like a shilling as well?"

I smiled and shook my head and, after St. Collins had paid Holmes the coin and departed, Billings nodded. "Now – tell me what happened, and what you've figured out."

Holmes, smiling at the unexpected and rather neat arrangement, settled back. "I read it this way: Last night, Paul Beadle, for reasons yet unknown, killed his brother John by hitting him on the back of the head. It was certainly a pre-meditated plan, for a few weeks ago, Paul hired a workman to install a lightning rod in the house, having given the impression that he was suddenly fearful of lighting.

"After the rod was in place, Paul Beadle simply had to wait for a storm. One such occurred last night, and then he then killed his brother. The murder could have occurred anywhere in the house but, after changing

John's clothing, removing his usual loose Indian garments and replacing them with his own typical British togs, Paul took his brother upstairs and placed him in the bathroom.

"It was no great exercise to spot the substitution, as John Beadle always wore round *pince-nez*, while the body that was supposed to be Dead Paul had John's long-time *pince-nez* marks upon the bridge of the nose. Very clumsy, really, but Paul Beadle did the best that he could, I suppose, to make it seem as if it was him that had been killed. Not all murderers are clever."

Billings nodded. "This has been my experience as well."

"After the murder occurred and the scene was set, Paul then did something to create an electrical burn on the body. An autopsy will confirm it, but – and I'm sure Watson agrees – the wound had all the indications of a true electrical burn."

I nodded in agreement.

"I'm not sure yet what Paul used to create the burn," Holmes continued, "but a search of the premises later today will certainly find it. He likely thought that the unusual nature of the death would be enough to avoid deeper questions, but there's no evidence that a lightning strike actually occurred.

"Now," said Holmes, turning his hands up, "can you provide any information as to motive?"

"I believe that I can," said Billings. He knocked upon the desk once more, and his clerk returned. He received succinct instructions, returning in a moment with a file tied by a string. "The Beadles file," he confirmed, untying the string and pulling it open. Then he departed once more.

"Three weeks ago," Billings explained, pulling out several documents, "Paul Beadle came in to update his will. It seems that he and his brother had recently taken out very large life insurance policies on one another – something to do with arranging a survivorship to continue the business when one passed before the other. Paul wanted to make sure that this insurance policy was specifically covered within his will. He signed it, and a few days later, his brother John came in and did the same."

"And was it really John?" I asked.

Billings shrugged. "I supposed so at the time. I had no reason then to suspect otherwise – although I suppose it would have been prudent to have both of them come in together to take care of signing the papers. I put it down to one or the other of them had to stay behind to keep the shop open." Billings then pushed four folded documents across the desk toward Sherlock Holmes. "From what you tell me now, I'm not sure if I saw both Paul and John Beadle, or rather just one of them – Paul as himself, and the next time disguised as John."

126

Holmes smiled at the idea of the scheme and proceeded to examine the documents. As he finished the first, he offered it to me, but I shook my head. "Faster if you just share your conclusions," I said, "rather than making it a teaching opportunity."

With a barked "Ha!" he continued looking over the papers, and soon made his report.

"Both of these wills, and the also the insurance documents, were signed by the same man – someone who is right-handed. The dead man that we saw this morning – and I'm sure Watson can confirm this –was left-handed. [I nodded.] The evidence for this was clear – hand size, callosities, ink stains, and so on – which made the fact that the burn on his right hand – which he would not have used to turn on the water tap – all the more indicative that the dead man was not really Paul Beadle. Thus, John did not affix his signature to these sheets. The living twin that we saw this morning – the still-living Paul Beadle – was right-handed. As we spoke to him, he thrice scratched an itch upon his face, and he also reached for his tea-cup, with his right hand. It was Paul that obtained the insurance and changed both wills, and who killed his brother John, attempting to take his place."

"For the insurance," I said, somewhat unnecessarily.

Billings nodded. "I've known both of them for a long time, and they never got along. John was happy enough living in Baker Street to the end of his days – which as it turns out he did – but Paul hated it there. He has wanted to travel. And yet he was trapped there, as each of them was tied to the other by way of the conditions of their inheritance – a modest amount left in a complicated trust by their father, wherein they had to remain in one another's company, like an old married couple, 'til death do they part. The trust provided enough to live on and let them play at running the curio shop, but there wasn't enough to go elsewhere, should they be able to break away. Oh, Paul could have left at any time, but only if he'd been willing to step away from the small-but-steady income and find a real job – and that seemed to be beyond him.

"They couldn't get any meaningful income from the shop or the house – there's nothing in their shabby stock that would allow Paul to fund a new life, and the lease for the house was locked up tight, and has been for a generation – ever since their family first moved there in the forties, when Paul and John were boys. By coming up with this scheme, I would speculate that Paul thought of the insurance money as a new and separate source of funds that would allow him to walk away. He simply needed to obtain the insurance without his brother's knowledge, and then kill him for it."

"But why switch identities?" I asked. "This scheme would have worked just as well if John were found dead as himself, and not made up as his brother Paul."

"It's subtle," replied Holmes, "but possibly because by doing it this way, the idea of 'John', the survivor, leaving the shop, despite his known disinclination to do so, could be attributed to grief, as it was known that he wouldn't be likely to depart otherwise. As John was happy enough there otherwise, it would take something like his brother's death to shake him loose and make him leave. Paul, on the other hand, was anxious to get away – and if something like this occurred to John and then Paul departed as fast as he could, people might be more inclined to be suspicious that he'd arranged it."

"If so, it sounds as if he over-thought many aspects of his scheme," said Billings, "and yet, didn't think far enough to make the swap with his brother entirely credible."

"I suppose he counted on the fact that it would seem to be a most unusual way to die," said Holmes, "and he never thought that anyone would notice that there were long-term *pince-nez* marks on the dead man's nose, or see that Paul's tighter clothing, no matter the similarity between the twins, did not fit on John's corpse. The spots where Paul's clothes unnaturally constricted the body, as shown by the *post-mortem* lividity, were quite obvious."

He looked over at me. "I observed when you determined whether the body was right- or left-handed, and then, after some thought, examined the feet to see if there was any way to confirm the same thing from them too. People do have right or left feet – more often than not, you will step forward or recover from a stumble upon your dominant foot which matches your dominant hand – but I'm unaware of any signs upon the feet that can be revelatory in the same manner that handedness reveals itself. Perhaps that would be the subject of a future monograph. In any case," he added, "as you saw from looking over the feet, Paul's shoes did not fit John's feet, having left *post-mortem* indentations and wrinkles."

Holmes glanced at the documents on Billings' desk. "Those are evidence."

Billings nodded. "And even though the Beadles were both my clients, there is nothing that compels me to keep their affairs confidential when my services were a factor in a murder case." He cleared his throat once more. "What will you do now?"

"Find Inspector Lanner, explain the sequence of events, and return to the house to determine how the supposed electrical burn was applied."

And so we did. By then the remaining Beadle had been removed from the house for his own mental well-being – or so he was told – and Lanner

128

had obtained a warrant. A more-thorough investigation of the lightning rod confirmed that it had not been struck the previous night, and even if it had, there was no way that it could have transferred such a massive charge to the water lines, killing the unfortunate brother.

Holmes prowled through the different objects squirreled around the store until he found what he sought – a connected series of very old Leyden jars, suspiciously free of dust when everything around them was caked with it. Jars of that sort, coated inside and outside with metal foil, had been developed in the middle of the previous century during early experiments with electricity. The jars were able to store electrical charges, and then suddenly release them in the form of a strong and dangerous spark. They had likely been in the shop for years, and when Paul Beadle conceived the twisted plot to kill his brother, they served as the spark of an idea – so to speak.

Paul Beadle, who wanted so much to be able to get away from the house in Baker Street, got his wish and never returned there. After he was removed so that his house to be searched, he ended the day at Scotland Yard, in one of the interrogation rooms. Lanner deferred his questioning to Holmes, who laid out Paul's actions, one by one: Pretending to be his brother John to obtain life insurance and forge a will. Killing John with a blow to the head, and then discharging a sizeable spark onto the body to simulate an electrical death. Changing the dead man's clothes to swap places with him, whereupon he could then move away without exciting suspicion.

Initially, Paul denied the charges, but it wasn't long before his resistance collapsed.

"I hated him!" he hissed. "Our situation threw us together for life – from conception until death – but we were complete opposites, he with his snide Bohemian ways and lackadaisical manner. It maddened me! Then, I read an article about the jars that produce a massive electrical shock when properly charged, and I recalled that we had some in the shop. I learned how to work with them – more as a distraction then. But as some point, the thought entered my mind that John might have an 'accident' with them. But I couldn't figure out how to make that happen, and as I chewed on the matter, the idea of being killed by a lightning rod took hold. I made arrangements for its installation, letting Mr. Conway think that I now irrationally feared storms. The rod was installed within a day, and then I just had to wait for a storm. It would just be a terrible accident, and I could go away as John and not come back!"

He looked at us, the inspector and Holmes and me, as if seeking some understanding, some nod to acknowledge what he perceived as an intolerable situation. But I simply saw a scheming little man who, if not for Sherlock Holmes, would be sitting at that moment in the house he despised, wearing his dead brother's clothes and planning his imminent escape.

The jury saw him the same way and, six weeks later, he was hanged.

Not long after that, workmen took down the old blue-and-yellow sign proclaiming the London Beadles Store and tossed it into the back of a refuse cart. The house was cleaned out as well in preparation for new tenants, with most of the curios therein joining the sign, although some of the neighbors did pick through the lot before it was hauled away. I believe that some found a few items of interest from the Beadles' stock, but neither Holmes nor I made the effort to walk over and examine what was to be had. My first visit to the store, not long after I moved to the neighborhood, and my only visit as a potential customer, had convinced me there was nothing about the Beadles to catch my attention.

The Texas Legation Business

Chapter I

"It is," said Mycroft Holmes with a frown, "something of a pesterment."

"I didn't suppose," countered his brother, Sherlock, "that you invited us to catch up on the latest gossip from Baker Street, or to ask Watson his opinion about the Merseyside Derby."

Our conversation was interrupted by a soft knock at the door, followed by the entrance of one of the silent servants who roamed the halls of the Diogenes Club, slipping in and bearing a tray with tea and various comestibles that had been excellently prepared in the basement kitchen. Sherlock Holmes didn't appear interested, but due to an unexpected medical call I had missed my lunch, and was glad for the opportunity. It had been a number of years since I was in the Army, but I hadn't forgotten the basic maxim to eat when given the opportunity, as one never knew what might happen to prevent the next meal. Having known Sherlock Holmes for nearly as long as I'd been away from the military, I'd found this lesson to still be especially relevant.

Holmes took out his pipe, stating, "You needn't worry, Mycroft. The plans for the *Canopus* have been secured. Carpenter is buttoned up from every direction, and his meeting with Carrington on Sunday is a *fait accompli.*"

Mycroft held up a hand. "You make assumptions without facts, Sherlock. You should know better than that. I didn't call you here for an update on the missing clerk. Colonel Boothroyd has kept me informed of your progress. It has been satisfactory." His lips pursed. "No, there is another more-recent matter to which I'd like you to attend – and you, too, Doctor, if you don't mind."

I nodded my tentative willingness. I owed payment for the quantity of debt I was contracting, based on the amount of magnificent smoked salmon that I was greedily consuming.

"What," asked Mycroft, pinching the bridge of his nose, "do either of you know about the Texas Legation?"

I glanced toward Holmes, who for once didn't give any indication that he had some knowledge of the topic. I wiped my lips and cleared my throat. "I've heard of it," I said, almost timidly, as if I was an uncertain boy offering an answer in the classroom. "It was located somewhere near here, in the 1840's, before – " I did a quick calculation. Yes, I believed it was even before Mycroft was born in 1847. " – before any of us were born."

"That is correct," said Mycroft, nodding. "It was in Pickering Place, just around the corner in St. James's Street, from 1842 to 1845. Texas was still an independent nation then, and had similar legations in Paris and Washington, D.C."

Holmes was looking at me curiously.

"When I was recovering at Peshawar," I explained, "I got to know a fellow named Jefferson Brody. His mother was from Cornwall. She had moved to London in the early 1840's, and not long after met and married one of the Texans who was associated with the Legation. After the Legation closed and the other Texans returned to America, Brody's father remained here. Brody told me a little bit about it. I believe," I added, asking Mycroft to confirm, "that they established their little embassy in the years following their independence from Mexico, before obtaining American statehood. As I recall, it was set in place in order for them to have leverage as a way to negotiate favorably as an independent nation."

"Rather," explained Mycroft, "it was more of a ploy to maneuver for better terms when they finally became an American state. After they won their independence from Mexico in 1836 and formed a Republic, there was a great internal divide of opinion about whether to remain a separate country or immediately request American statehood. However, it didn't matter, as the United States wasn't immediately willing to accept Texas into the fold, as they would have entered as a slave-holding state, which upset the abolitionist-minded northern states, while also disrupting the delicate voting balance of free and slave states within the Congress.

"The Texas president, a fellow named Houston, argued for statehood, but he was also uncertain as to whether it would ever happen, so he initiated discussions with England regarding our support – financial and otherwise – should the new nation remain its own country. Britain very much wanted Texas to remain an independent country, and we offered to support them militarily by helping to defend their borders with Mexico *and* the United States. But it turned out that the Texans' overtures to Britain were less-than-sincere, and were instead used as a stick to goad the United States government into finally admitting them, rather than allow a further British influence to be established in their hemisphere – and in fact right at their back door. They didn't wish to be bracketed between British Texas and Canada – especially with their expansion to the Pacific already becoming a popular idea.

"With the election of James K. Polk as President in 1845, the path was finally clear for Texas to join the Union. Polk and Houston were both from Tennessee, and had served in the Congress together representing that

132

state in the 1820's – even sharing lodgings when they resided in Washington. Based on their arrangements, the Texans agreed to annexation in June of '45, and statehood was accomplished in December. Of course, this immediately set the country on a course toward war with Mexico the following year – the same war that became a training ground for all of the future American generals – Unionists and traitors – who served on each side of their Civil War."

Sherlock Holmes wasn't restless yet, but I knew – as his brother certainly did – that he wasn't concerned with the events of half-a-century earlier without knowing why they related to our summons to the Diogenes Club.

"Enough with the history lesson," he said. "What has happened *now*?"

"Indeed," agreed Mycroft. "But you know as well as I how history is always relevant. Here, then, is what has happened *now*: Late this morning, work was being done at the building which once housed the Legation. As I mentioned, it's within Pickering Place, a small square, but the address is No. 4, St. James's Street. There have been any number of residents – both business and domestic – within the location since the Legation departed in 1845. Workmen were pulling off the old wainscoting and found a small wall safe, about one cubic foot in volume, covered over and hidden. The safe's door was decorated with a flamboyant enameled painting of an American steamboat, and wording identifying the manufacturer as the '*Texas Lock and Vault Corporation*'. The workmen alerted their supervisor, Bessemer, who in turn notified the lease-holder of the building, one Amos Berry, whose father-in-law, Clive Loughborough, is the estate agent for Claude Jermyn. Loughborough then informed Jermyn – who was just up the street at Boodles.

"Jermyn walked down and was on site when the safe was broken open to reveal several bundles of Republic of Texas currency – a few thousand of their old money in packets of three, five, and fifty dollar bills – and a most-curious document. Jermyn, who as you know did a favor for us in '90 when his son's body was found in the wall of the Battersea Bridge, thought that the document might be something of interest to the Government. However, while walking around here to put it into my hands, he was followed and accosted in the street by one of the laborers who had been working on the building's renovation. The worker pushed Jermyn down and pulled the document from out of his coat pocket before the older man could defend himself. Passersby did nothing to help – apparently it happened too quickly – and the thief then dashed east toward Waterloo Place, where he vanished."

"Was Jermyn injured?" I asked. I recalled the man from when we'd initially encountered him, a little over four years earlier. He was a small fellow, in his mid-fifties, and very earnest and serious. From meeting with him then, one had the impression that he had no sense of humor at all. That was, however, possibly an unfair assessment, as we'd only had dealings with him in connection with the brutal murder of his son, and the revelation that it had been committed by his favored daughter.

"Not at all," replied Mycroft. "He was quite angry, actually, both at the assault and the perceived betrayal by one of his employees, and also the fact that he couldn't persuade anyone walking along the pavement to assist him. He gave chase, but it was futile."

Holmes then asked the obvious question. "And what was this document that generated such an unplanned and violent assault?"

Mycroft's quiet answer seemed to explode into the room: "For one-million pounds, to be paid to the government for the citizens living there at the time, Great Britain purchased The Republic of Texas."

We were quite silent for a moment as we examined that idea in our heads. Mycroft looked from one to the other of us as we pondered the implications, patiently sipping his port. Finally I was the first to speak.

"But surely that is impossible. It's been fifty years – and so much water under the bridge. Texas is no longer an independent country. The United States had their Civil War to preserve the Union. The idea that we could now show a document proving that one of their states was never legitimately a part of their country to begin with . . . ." I shifted my gaze back from the distant view I'd been imagining. "It *is* impossible, isn't it?"

Mycroft nodded. "Yes, Doctor, it is indeed impossible."

"I take it," interrupted Holmes, "that no record of payment has been discovered that would have solemnified the arrangement."

"That is correct. But that isn't the problem. The idea of pursuing such an agreement at this point in time is ludicrous. There is no legal enforceability. And in any case, the global disruptions that it would cause – even I find it difficult to see how such events would progress. The United States would not take it well, to say the least, if such a thing were to go forward. I'm certain that the Texans, despite being on the losing and traitorous side of the Civil War, would not react well to suddenly being told that they were now British citizens – and a million pounds wouldn't go nearly as far in the present day when spread among the current population, should payment be made. Mexico would certainly have something to say about it, and suddenly Canada would be at risk if the United States decided to reciprocate and annex parts of that country, based on old ties, treaties, claims, territory gained in battles, and varying and contested borderlines."

134

"Then I don't understand the difficulty," I said. "This is nothing more than a curious historical anomaly."

"I suspect," said Holmes, "that the issue isn't enforceability, but how such a document might be used to further some other agenda – either as a distraction, or perhaps to pour fuel on another fire that's already burning."

"Both," said Mycroft. "Our relations with the United States are generally cordial, but you may not realize that there is nevertheless some tension. After their Civil War, they rebounded into a great deal of wealth and influence – and with that has come a certain level of jealousy regarding our mastery of the seas. Oh, not to the level that the Germans have carried it. As you know, surpassing us in that sphere has become a rather dangerous *idée fixe* in the Kaiser's head. The Americans haven't carried things to that degree – but it is on their minds."

He shifted in his chair "I doubt if either of you are aware of the publication in America of *Influence of Sea Power Upon History.*" He looked from one to the other of us, and we both shook our heads.

"It was written 1890 by Alfred Thayer Mahan. It came about this way: Ten years or so ago, he was appointed a lecturer in naval history and tactics at the American's Naval War College. While there, he developed a series of lectures regarding the importance of powerful navies in world affairs – leading directly to the subject of his book. Around that same time, he was tasked with devising a war plan to match his strategic outline, and he determined that the American fleet was too weak and limited to be effective in a real war. Their navy had very few vessels that would be of any use at all. In order to demonstrate this, he devised a theoretical war between Britain and the United States – and he showed that we would win under current conditions, and what they would need to do to prevent that outcome.

"It was Mahan's belief that their insufficient navy wouldn't be able to cross the sea and attack us here at all, and that all of the battles would be fought alongside the American coast. We would be unable to land our forces, but instead we could bomb the harbors and shoreline, and blockade their ports – and particularly their economic centers.

"Mahan proposed that the American response would then be to overrun Nova Scotia by land and occupy our coalfield there – our only one on the Atlantic coast – thus denying a way to refuel our warships. He further advocated for a massive buildup of American naval ships – particularly battleships and torpedo vessels.

"Of course, this was all theoretical to some extent. Every nation has such contingency plans, but it's no surprise that Mahan's study received a good bit of attention, and in the four years since the book was published, their navy has since begun to modernize and expand in earnest. Not initially seeing it as a matter of security, Mahan freely shared his lectures with a good many other academics – including our own John Knox Laughton at King's College. Laughton in turn made our Government aware of the situation, and we've kept our eye on it ever since."

"And some in our Government," extrapolated Holmes, "see this as a legitimate threat – or at least they plan to present it that way as an excuse to escalate the situation into something more hostile."

"Indeed – or at least as something that they can use as a distraction while they further their own ambitions in the shadows. If the Texas document were to become public just now, on top of this recent American tension, it could be used to fan their flames."

"You wish us to retrieve the document," said Holmes. "It seems to me that you have a hundred foot-soldiers at your disposal already. Why us?"

"Because you are discreet, and so far this situation is known to just a very few. I have agents that I could redirect along these lines, but they are blunt instruments, and every one that learns the secret exponentially increases the risk of its being accidentally shared in the wrong place."

"Are you certain that the document is legitimate?" I asked. "Did Claude Jermyn have the chance to thoroughly examine it before it was stolen?"

Mycroft nodded. "Direct evidence is always best." He leaned toward the small table to his right and pressed a button, which I knew connected with a small and very discreet bell somewhere deeper in the building. In a moment, the door opened to reveal one of the Club's servants, a fellow named Jernigan. "Please bring Mr. Jermyn now," Mycroft instructed.

We hadn't seen Claude Jermyn since early July 1890, just before the opening of the Battersea Bridge. He had been on the Board of Directors for the Mowlem Company charged with constructing the bridge, and had been unaware – as was proven later at the trial – of his childrens' financial chicanery. The resulting murder of his son, and the bizarre way in which it was hidden in the final construction of the bridgeworks by Jermyn's daughter, would have been enough to break most men, but he was made of sterner stuff than that. Still, four years had aged him terribly. He had already been a fellow of small stature, but he'd since lost a great deal of weight, and his hair had thinned to a few wispy whitish fluffs.

The reserved and polite way in which he greeted us showed that we would always be associated in his mind with the great tragedy of his life, but he was still courteous as he took a seat and accepted a brandy from the servant. When the latter had departed, he began to speak.

"I knew as soon as I saw that document that it might be important. I said so to Loughborough, and this laborer must have overheard me. I learned later that the fellow had only worked there for a week – hired for the lifting and carrying. The last tenant was some sort of Italian hair stylist, and he did things with steam and oils that nearly ruined the walls. We have to get it repaired before the rooms can be re-rented. I generally let Loughborough take care of all that, but when the safe was found, he knew that it was beyond him."

Holmes leaned forward. "What can you tell us of the worker who assaulted you and stole the document?"

Jermyn shifted to face Holmes and pulled a sheet of paper from within his coat. "I understand from Mycroft that the less this is stirred up, the better. Here is the man's name – Stephen Newbold." He handed Holmes the sheet. "You can see that his address is in Limehouse."

"Hmm," responded Holmes, folding the sheet and putting it into his pocket. "Probably false, but we'll see."

"From what I could learn about him by asking questions of the other workers when I returned to the building," Jermyn continued, "he's something of a quiet one – didn't mix with the others very much, and I doubt that he would have lasted another week, even if he hadn't assaulted me or stolen the document. Clearly he had the idea he could get something for it."

"Describe him."

Jermyn closed his eyes, and after a moment he said, "He is his early forties, I suppose. Tall with broad shoulders, and oddly long arms with big hands. For his height, he has a longish torso with short legs, and blonde hair sitting on a rather flat head. Additionally, he had a reddish scar horizontally across his left cheek – it's quite curious, dropping from his left eye, and then making a sharp turn across his cheek toward his ear. I'm told that he'd said it was a badly healed wound received in a knife fight when he was young."

Holmes nodded. "For the short time you saw him, you have recalled a great deal."

Jermyn grimaced. "After . . . after the events of four years ago, when your observations and methods were so . . . so useful, I was impressed. I've since made an effort to notice more – details of my surroundings, and the people I encounter. Practice has only made it more effective."

"You have learned a lesson then that many will not undertake," Holmes replied. I was grateful that he had the courtesy not to pointedly look in my direction for emphasis.

"Do you think you can find the man?" asked Jermyn. "Track him down?"

"Your description is quite clear," responded Holmes. "In fact, I believe I already had an idea of his true identity and where to locate him."

137

"True identity?"

"Yes. The unique characteristics you've listed sound remarkably like a known thug-for-hire named Isa Ulford. I should be most surprised if he isn't the same man. I should have him by day's end."

Jermyn seemed quite impressed, but before he could comment, Holmes continued. "What can you tell us of the document itself?"

"It was parchment – about sixteen inches high and twelve wide. Folded in half each way – into quarters so that it was about eight-inches-by-six. The writing was faded but legible, and I got the gist of it right away – there wasn't any fancy legal *fol-de-rol* or Latin nonsense. Fortunately, none of the others in the room were close enough to see it – even Loughborough stepped back while I opened and read it to myself. The text was centered in the middle, with a few unmarked inches bordered on all sides. It was quite clear: For one-million pounds, Texas sold itself to England. It was all done up right and with a bow on it. There were two signatures. For the British was Richard Pakenham – "

"Envoy Extraordinary and Minister Plenipotentiary for Great Britain to the United States from 1843 to 1847," Mycroft interrupted. "He successfully carried our end during the Treaty of Oregon, but he was considered something of a failure in regard to the Texas question as the United States, despite our best efforts at the time, and with offers of financial aid and troops, nevertheless instead chose annexation to statehood in December 1845."

Jermyn nodded and continued. "For the Texans, the document was boldly signed by Sam Houston, their President."

He glanced at Mycroft, as if to see whether he should stop, but when he wasn't prevented, he continued. "There was a provision in the main text that seemed especially important – it was the last item before the signatures. In addition to defining the sale and describing the area to be purchased, there was a *caveat*, stating that the terms of the sale could be enforced for up to fifty years beyond the date of the signing."

"And that date being – ?" asked Holmes.

"The twenty-third of December, 1844."

"Good Lord," I said. "The fifty years is up in within days!"

"It doesn't matter, Doctor," assured Mycroft. "Fear not. As I've explained, the terms are unenforceable. For us to try and exercise the agreement now would cause worldwide turmoil."

"And yet," I said, "you indicated that there are those just now who *could* happily make use of such turmoil."

Mycroft didn't respond. Perhaps I was being indiscreet by discussing that aspect with Jermyn still present.

Jermyn cleared his throat and continued. "Beneath the formal signatures and dates was another smaller note, apparently added by President Houston as well. The faded ink had the same shade as his official signature, and it looked to be the same handwriting. It consisted of but a single word – maybe in Latin – and his signature again, this time dated the sixth of March, 1845."

"Do you recall the word?" asked Holmes, but Jermyn shook his head.

"Foreign languages were never my strong suit, and I didn't recognize this one."

"Presumably," Holmes continued, "there were two copies of the treaty – one for the Texans, and one for us. Apparently the Texans' copy was kept in the safe – and then left behind when the Legation closed in 1845, upon the acceptance of Texas into the Union, there being no further need for an embassy."

Mycroft nodded, and Jermyn added, "The story goes that when they packed up and departed, the Texans also neglected to pay £160 in overdue rent."

"What about the stacks of Texas currency?" I asked. "Were those taken from you as well?"

Jermyn reached into his pocket and pulled forth three packets, laying them on a small table. "He left it. Of course, anyone would realize that it's worthless now, except possibly to a collector."

Holmes picked up the old cash, looked it over, and then handed it to me. There were three bundles, each about an inch thick, with a paper band centered around the middle, labeled *National Bank of Texas.*

"It isn't much," said Jermyn. "Slightly more than eight-hundred of their dollars."

"Is there any sign of our copy of the treaty?" Holmes asked his brother, as if Jermyn hadn't spoken.

Mycroft shook his head. "As I said, there is no record of any payment being made."

Holmes raised an eyebrow, and said, "You've been busy, Mycroft. What time did the theft occur?"

"Around ten this morning," answered Jermyn.

"And it's two o'clock now."

"For whatever reason," Mycroft continued as if he hadn't been interrupted, "the arrangement was never consummated. It's likely that the Texans never truly wanted to be part of the Empire, and this was just a ploy to obtain some leverage in their quest to become a State. They fixed up the treaty to see which way the wind would blow. And as for our side of things? It would have been in accordance with our policy at that time to take ownership of Texas, which we didn't want to be part of the United

States, so I'm not sure what happened or why the payment wasn't made. Perhaps Pakenham muffed it somehow. His career, after all, wasn't noted for its brilliance."

We all fell silent, considering our own thoughts. Holmes's expression seemed the most distant as he was examining the problem. Finally, he seemed to reach a decision. "I don't suppose," he asked Jermyn, "that there would be any difficulty with Watson and me dropping by the old Legation office in Pickering Place."

Jermyn shook his head. "Not at all. I rather thought that you might. Shall I join you?"

"No need. I doubt that we'll be there long, or find anything of interest, but I would be remiss not to examine it, especially as it's so close."

With that, seemingly sensing that he had no more to contribute, Jermyn nodded and rose. Then he turned and departed. Sadly, it was the last we'd see of him. It will be recalled by many that he was found on Christmas morning, just a few days later, alone by the dying fire in his bedroom, the victim of a massive coronary failure that occurred sometime during the night. His loss to the country was tremendous, but I knew that he'd never been a happy man after the deaths of his son and daughter.

"Surely tracing this Isa Ulford should be your top priority," said Mycroft when Jermyn was gone.

"I'll set that in motion immediately," Holmes replied. "However, I should first like to examine the safe for myself."

Mycroft waved a hand. "Handle it as you see fit. In the meantime, I'll learn more about who would make use of such a distraction."

With that, Holmes and I departed. The convention that the two brothers might actually say goodbye to one another seemed to be, by common agreement, an unnecessary waste of time.

Chapter II

Outside, a cold wind blew along Pall Mall with just a few leaves from the previous autumn still skittering along the pavement. We stood just outside the door of No. 78 [1] to don our gloves, and I glanced across the street to No. 48, the building where Mycroft resided when he wasn't in the Diogenes Club behind us, or at his office in Whitehall. I could see that we'd been observed by Keeton, the longtime doorman of the residential building. He clearly recognized us, for Holmes was unmistakable in his Inverness and fore-and-aft cap, worn year-round, with indifference to whether he was in town or the country, and regardless of societal demands. It had only been a month since Keeton had been in our Baker Street sitting room, having worked up the courage to approach Holmes in the matter of his missing daughter. What was nearly a tragedy had been narrowly averted, and now the doorman was one of those countless grateful individuals who would do anything to repay Holmes for the salvation of his family's happiness.

I nodded, and Keeton returned it, and then we turned left and walked west into the wind.

As we passed the nearby Oxford and Cambridge Club, I commented, "It's difficult to comprehend the problems that the revelation of this document could cause. And yet, as Mycroft stated, the document itself isn't enforceable – and would not be enforced."

Holmes was silent for a moment, not speaking until we reached the corner, with St. James's Palace on our left. We turned right, up St. James's Street toward Piccadilly.

"There's obviously more to this than simply getting the document back before the instigator releases it," he finally said. "Wheels within wheels – that is the world in which Mycroft lives. In spite of his statement that he'll find out who is behind this, I'm sure that he already knows, and has probably taken steps to head off any revelations."

"Then why are we following along after Isa Ulford? Why weren't we sent directly to the document's final destination – the man who will use it?"

"We're here to obtain evidence – the links in the chain that Mycroft can use to maintain his omniscience when he confronts the master plotter. The facts that we gather now will be documentation and evidence later. But I wonder . . . ."

"What?" I asked as we neared our destination.

"Why did Ulford steal the document? How did he even know what it was, or that it was important? Jermyn pointed out that he alone looked at it. Even his man Loughborough stepped back. One would think that if Ulford were motivated to leave his job and follow Jermyn with theft in mind, he'd take the bundles of cash, not realizing they were worthless – Ah, but here we are."

The entrance to Pickering Place, No. 4 St. James's Street, [2] was a dark and narrow passage stretching back, tunnel-like, through the center of No 3, the long-standing and successful Berry Brothers and Rudd, Wine Merchants. It was only seventy or eighty feet up from the Pall Mall corner. The narrow pathway, just a couple-dozen darkened feet in length, brought us into the actual court, said to be the smallest in London. I'd heard that it was the site of the last duel fought in the capital, but the location seemed much too small. Perhaps with swords – ? But no – surely the last duel would have occurred long after firearms became the preferred weapon of choice.

141

The site of the former legation was easily determined, as there was a great deal of construction material – lumber, casks of nails, sacks of plaster, Portland cement, and such – stacked nearby. We wended our way up the narrow dark stairs and into a room where the sound of hammering let us know we'd accurately arrived. There we were met by a stout fellow in his fifties who introduced himself as Bessemer, the foreman.

He was the type who, after nearly every sentence spoken, touched two fingers to his brow, as if to tug at the spot where his forelock might have been a long quarter-century earlier. He knew that Jermyn had stepped around to seek help regarding the stolen document, so he'd been expecting someone to drop by. But he hadn't been expecting Sherlock Holmes.

"But I thought you were dead, sir," he added in a puzzled tone, as if inviting an explanation.

Those latter months of 1894 had been curiously strange. After May 1891, it had been widely believed that Holmes had died at the Reichenbach Falls. It was reported in the press at the time, although it turned out to be a less well-known fact than I'd initially thought. In mid-1891, I had set about recording and publishing a series of sketches of some of Holmes's cases – not necessarily the most exciting or important, but rather those which would illustrate both his methods and his personality. In late 1893, a combination of several events brought those recollections to a close. My poor wife, Mary, had passed away earlier that year, and my enthusiasm for the project – and indeed, life in general – had waned to a dramatic and grim degree. Next, the fellow who had served as my literary agent, arranging for placement of the narratives in a relatively new monthly periodical, had lost interest too, as he wanted to focus more on writing his own historical novels. [3] But most of all, the recent slanders in the press by Colonel Moriarty, the Professor's corrupt brother, had prompted me to write and reveal the true account of the events leading to Holmes's death – and after that was published in December 1893, it seemed rather anticlimactic to continue providing additional posthumous tales.

Holmes miraculously reappeared just months later, on the fifth of April, 1894, having spent three years wandering the world, carrying out various tasks for Mycroft in all corners of the Empire and beyond, and also tying up many of the loose ends related to the eradication of the Professor's criminal organization. Upon his public return to his old life, Holmes was rather amazed – and vexed – to discover that many didn't want to believe that he had ever actually been alive in the first place. In fact, much of the populace had fallen under the impression that the accounts I'd written were fiction, and as such, Holmes was merely a character in a recurring series of stories. When "The Final Problem" was published just a few months before Holmes reappeared in London, I had been amazed to see the public reaction upon learning of his "death". There was a period of great national mourning that had been completely absent when Holmes actually "died" in the spring of '91. Only when "The Final Problem" appeared in print did the great masses seem to acknowledge Holmes's supposed passing. That feeling and belief was still fresh in their minds when he returned, and many people initially seemed to think that he was merely an imposter, someone with the peculiar imitative mania to wear a deerstalker cap.

Holmes, who was already rather unhappy that two-dozen stories of his investigations had been published between 1891 and 1893, was further displeased at having to regularly verify his true identity on a number of occasions. On the other hand, he was often unwilling to admit that the publication of the stories had increased awareness of his abilities to a much greater degree than before his disappearance, leading to a regular surge of clients needing his help – much more than the old days when we'd first begun sharing rooms and had each commonly worried about making our shares of the rent.

Now, faced with someone he'd thought dead for over three years, Bessemer looked back and forth from one to the other of us, his unasked question about Holmes's reappearance remaining unanswered – for Holmes wasn't inclined to waste time explaining it, and it must be recalled that I wouldn't publish the account of how Holmes survived at Reichenbach for nearly another decade.

As Bessemer tried to form a query, Holmes looked around until he saw a noticeable hole in the wall. "The safe was there," he declared.

Bessemer swallowed and nodded. "Underneath that mildewy wainscoting we tossed over there. The Italian barber who was up here before had machines to make steam, and he'd mix it with olive oil and it has soaked the plaster something terrible – "

But Holmes had already walked over to the hole in the wall, where he was kneeling and feeling with his fingers, picking out crumbles of material where the safe had been located."

"This isn't plaster," he said. "It's cement."

"That's right," answered Bessemer. "The safe rested on a base of it, set just there onto that cross-brace, and then the cement had been slathered in around it."

"Did you have any trouble getting the safe loose?"

"Not particularly. It pulled right out."

Holmes broke off some of the cement and put it into one of the envelopes he always carried to retain bits of evidence. Then he obtained another piece and held it up. "See how it crumbles?" He proceeded to mash it until it disintegrated into bits that fell to the cluttered floor.

"Is that relevant?" I asked.

He nodded and stood. "The safe, please."

It was lying on a work-table near a window, a metal box, thick-walled, and about one-foot square. The front consisted of the open door, black iron with a colorful steamboat and logo brightly enameled above the combination dial. The other sides were dull and dusty metal with fragments of irregular cement clinging to them. Holmes pulled out his magnifying glass, using it to look at the object from all angles, including the scratch marks and distortions around the door. "You used a hammer and wedge to open it," he commented to Bessemer.

"We did. We thought about drilling, but that would take too long, and the wedge opened it fairly easy."

Holmes leaned forward and sniffed around the door. Then he pulled his handkerchief from his pocket and dabbed along the hinge. Then he held it up for us to see.

"Oil," I said. I looked at Bessemer. "Did you oil it before cracking it open?"

The foreman looked puzzled. "Not at all. It opened fairly easy," he repeated.

"Of course it did," Holmes said softly. Then he stood upright. "This renovation – when did it begin?"

"Two weeks ago, although we discussed it another week before that."

"Any particular reason that it began now?"

Bessemer nodded. "It seems that someone has expressed an interest in renting the place, quick-like."

"And the new tenants didn't like the previous arrangement."

"Well, as I said, that Italian barber had some strange ideas, and he'd done a lot of damage. If you'd seen – "

"Tell us about Stephen Newbold," Holmes directed, using Isa Ulford's false name.

Bessemer proceeded to give us a description that matched that provided by Jermyn. "He walked in nearly a week ago," he added, "seeking work. Quiet – kept to himself. Worked hard."

"We heard that he'd told how he received his scar," I said.

"That's right – in a fight when he was a lad. He offered the story one day as we ate our lunch. People were talking about their old injuries – construction can be a dangerous business. No one asked him about it beforehand, of course. It's a bad scar, and one doesn't just mention things that."

"Did he have any friends here?" asked Holmes. "Did anyone hire on at the same time?"

Bessemer shook his head. "No. He kept to himself, and he left alone at the end of the day. He didn't go to the pub with the rest of us when we left each evening. I had the sense that he wanted to get home."

"And the attack on Mr. Jermyn," Holmes continued. "Did he show any unusual interest in the document when it was first removed from the safe?"

"Not that I recall, but I wasn't watching him. I was the one who used the wedge and hammer, so my attention was on the safe. When it was open, we all backed away and let Mr. Jermyn look at what was inside – a bit piece of folded parchment, and some money. Later, after Mr. Jermyn left, I didn't notice that Newbold was missing. He could have been downstairs with the supplies, or smoking outside. It was only after Mr. Jermyn returned and told me what had happened that I realized that Newbold had left and followed him without any of us realizing it."

Holmes glanced around, and I saw that the other workers who happened to be in the room were surreptitiously watching and listening while half-heartedly pursuing their tasks. They seemed very still, wondering what would occur next. I thought that Holmes might question one or more of them, but instead he simply thanked the foreman and we departed, returning down to the small court, and thence out to the street. The afternoon was moving on, and clouds were beginning to drift in, giving the street a darkened feel.

"You saw the cement?" Holmes asked.

I nodded.

"Further tests on the sample I obtained would confirm it," he explained, "but it's fresh cement of modern origins – it's barely had time to cure, and certainly wasn't up to its full compressive strength."

I comprehended his thoughts. "So the safe was recently set into the wall – it hasn't been there for fifty years?"

"That's right. And for that matter, the Texas decoration upon the safe door, although somewhat scuffed and aged to appear otherwise, is of recent origin as well."

"Then the document is also forged!" I concluded. "This is all a tempest in a teapot."

Holmes didn't speak, although he shook his head slightly. I pulled my coat tighter, asking, "Is it time to find the Irregulars and have them locate Ulford?"

Holmes shook his head. "I fancy that I can lay my hands on him at any time. He isn't unknown to me. Rather than hie off in that direction, I'd first like to have a better understanding of the puppeteer who has set these events in motion. And if Mycroft isn't ready to reveal his name . . . ."

145

As I started to ask if this was drifting too far from Mycroft's request, Holmes glanced across the St. James's Street to No. 86, [4] where a bow window on the first floor, facing east, looked down upon us, and with a limited view back along Pall Mall as well. Suddenly I felt as if I were being spied upon, and I realized we'd likely been observed as we turned the corner a quarter-hour before and entered Pickering Place. Observed, and easily recognized. Unless he was in disguise, Holmes made himself known wherever he went.

Looking up at the first floor of the building across the street, I knew what the view upon where we were standing would look like, as I'd gazed down from that bow window on a number of previous occasions. I knew then who Holmes intended to consult in order to find more about the man behind these recent events.

Chapter III

In those days, I was quite disapproving of Holmes's friend, Langdale Pike, who then spent – and continues to do so as of this writing – his days sitting in that bow window of his St. James's Street club, a spider in the center of his own uniquely contrived web, and a great clearing-house of facts both important and subtle: Those that are immediately relevant, and others percolating for years until they might become significant. At that time, it was several years before I became aware of the infamous society blackmailer, Charles Augustus Milverton, but when I met the latter, who Holmes had described to me as being similar to the "slithery, gliding, venomous creatures, with their deadly eyes and wicked, flattened faces," I recalled my early impressions of Langdale Pike.

I had no use then for such parasites, trading on gossip and misery. It was only in later years that I became aware of the other hidden side of Pike's existence – how just as often he suppressed dangerous or damaging secrets instead of using them to expand his own income. How he manipulated events when possible to provide good outcomes for unfortunates that would have otherwise been impossible. And how he funded a number of charities and supported many a sad cause, all in the shadows without a single thought of receiving credit, privately storing up his treasures in Heaven rather than publicly here on earth. When I began to perceive the truth about him, I was ashamed. He was still a strange and languid creature, but not the vile reptile I had so long imagined.

At some later point, I asked Holmes why he hadn't corrected my earlier perception. "You knew what I was thinking," I said, the burden of my guilt heavy upon me.

"It wasn't my story to tell," he replied simply.

146

But upon that day in December 1894, I still thought of Pike as a distasteful sponge and acted accordingly, sitting aloof and judgmental while he and Holmes conversed.

After their usual greetings, sharing of news and recollections regarding those they had known many years before, and sly unspecific references to matters which were implied but not directly discussed, Holmes got down to business, frankly relating the events that had occurred just across the street in Pickering Place, and holding back nothing regarding the documented sale of the Texas Republic to England and its implications. I thought it quite indiscreet, but I also trusted Holmes.

Pike nodded. "It's almost certain to be Ronald Warrington, you know."

Holmes nodded grimly. "I must admit, he hadn't occurred to me."

"Wait," I added, speaking for the first time. "Ronald Warrington?"

Pike nodded. "His mother was a Knutsford," he added, as if that explained all, or at least that it was some kind of explanation – or excuse.

I turned my palms up and tilted my head, indicating that he'd told me nothing.

Holmes smiled grimly. "That possibility reveals a great deal, and why Mycroft chose not to tell us the other end of the story."

"Ronald Warrington?" I repeated, relaxing my upright posture to lean forward a bit.

"Indeed," confirmed Holmes. "The coal and steel magnate who has suddenly been teasing a business relationship with Alfred Krupp of Germany, at the expense of supplying our own naval shipbuilding efforts."

"But . . . I don't understand." Both Holmes and Pike stared at me as if I'd indicated that I didn't know how to add two plus two.

Then Pike explained. "It's rather simple. This document, outlining the sale of one of the American states to Britain, though unenforceable, would be a nine-days' wonder in the press. That would allow Warrington to complete whatever arrangement he has made with the Krupps while national attention is diverted elsewhere."

"The distraction could have been anything," said Holmes. "Any event would have served. We're lucky that he didn't arrange for the assassination of some minor nobleman to start a war on the Continent." He looked at Pike. "The old magician's trick: Do something flashy with one hand – in this case rile the Americans – while using the other to surreptitiously carry out the hidden agenda with the Germans. But where did he get the idea of involving the Texas Legation? That is truly obscure. Do you suppose that the treaty is real?"

"I expect that it is," responded Pike. "Warrington probably obtained is as a curiosity – Through some dealer, perhaps? – and then the idea suggested itself. A bit of research would probably show that the document has been floating around for years, although known only to collectors and historians."

"Possibly," said Holmes, pondering.

"Then," Pike continued to theorize, "with document in hand, Warrington could have learned where the former Legation was located and arranged to have it 'found' by workmen who were themselves likely set in motion by his own false intention to suddenly rent the place. But somehow – and this part doesn't sense – the document was stolen before it could be publicly revealed."

Holmes nodded in agreement, and I asked, "Then what should we do? Holmes, you've indicated that Mycroft likely already knows about all this – about Warrington. What is our purpose then? Do we continue chasing along the path of the stolen document?"

Holmes nodded. "I believe so. As I mentioned earlier, we are gathering a portion of whatever Mycroft requires for his overall plan – whatever that may be. He involved us for a reason. He knows that I will follow my own lines. Possibly along the way, we shall see something of additional value that we can provide that he doesn't expect."

I thought his use of "we" was generous, but I was happy to provide what help I could.

"There isn't much that Mycroft doesn't 'expect'," added Pike wryly – and it seemed to me how similar in some ways Pike was to Mycroft, each of them motionless in the center of their quivering webs, feeling every pull and vibration, and physically separated from one another by just a few hundred feet along Pall Mall. "I doubt if he thinks you'll limit yourself solely to pursuing this one low-level thief."

A question occurred to me, and I voiced it, despite my reluctance to appear ignorant: "If Warrington went to the trouble to fabricate a false Texans' safe, put the document in it, install it in the building, and then arrange for the rooms to be rented, requiring renovation leading to the discovery – I am understanding that correctly?"

Holmes and Pike nodded, and I continued. "He did all that so the document could be discovered there, in the old Texas Legation, giving it an extra legitimacy. Therefore, the document being stolen and removed by Ulford before it could be publicly revealed has seriously hampered his elaborate plans. Therefore, isn't Ulford, who probably still has the document, in serious danger, should Warrington find him?"

Both of them nodded again, and Holmes added as he stood, "That's why our next stop is Ulford's modest home in Lambeth, where we will find him first."

I thought then that Holmes should remind Pike to keep this confidential, but apparently he didn't see the need, instead thanking him for providing a short-cut to understanding. I stood and joined Holmes as we said goodbye, and Pike nodded in return, a wry smile upon his face as he read the judgment in my expression, before turning his gaze back toward the bow window and its view of the darkening December day, and the gaslights that were now lit along the bit of Pall Mall that we could see in front of the Palace.

Chapter IV

Holmes thought that it would be easier to find a cab in Piccadilly, so we walked north to the main thoroughfare and then east, finally intersecting with a hansom discharging its passengers outside Fortnum and Mason. My stomach rumbled with the thought of the various items for sale so close by, and I wished that I'd taken on a bit more at the Diogenes, but I'd be able to eat again soon enough.

Holmes gave the cabbie an address in Lambeth, and soon we were working our way east and south toward the Westminster Bridge. Throughout, Holmes was silent as he considered the problem at hand. Finally, however, I felt compelled to voice my uppermost thought.

"It seems to me that whoever came up with such an ambitious plot – a deal with the mightiest of the German munitions kings, to the cost of our own national interests – would have planned something a bit more effective than relying on an unenforceable fifty-year old treaty."

"Watson, you underestimate the ways in which the public and the press can be sent baying after a shiny object. Consider what's occurring as we speak to the unfortunate Captain Dreyfus in France. It's been less than two months since his arrest for high treason. I've heard strong indications that he is innocent, but you've seen how France has ignited since then. It fills their press. Their coffee shops and drinking spots and meeting places seethe with discussions and arguments and threats of violence. Dreyfus is likely to be convicted any day – and can you imagine what reaction that will cause? And I guarantee that in the shadows, there are those who are taking complete and orchestrated advantage of this chaos in very calculated ways – either those who are simply riding this wave for their own personal advantage, or others, more sinister, who are deliberately manipulating it and, most hidden of all, those who are responsible for it.

"No, something like the Texas purchase agreement, adroitly maneuvered and directed, could cover a multitude of sins. What's more worthy of consideration is the fact that this certainly isn't the only arrow in Warrington's quiver."

149

The idea left me aghast. "Surely – " I began, and then spoke again. "You mentioned assassination. Someone high in the Government? Or the Royal Family?"

"Not just our own," replied Holmes. "As I mentioned, Warrington, with the help of the Krupps, could have something planned on the Continent. Such an action elsewhere could serve to light the same fuse as here. But we are fortunate," he concluded before returning to his pondering, "that this affair has been discovered so early. Assembling the details will provide Mycroft a wedge to open this door, and knowing one plot will certainly lead to the exposure of the next, and the next after that."

As we crossed the bridge, a gust of wind rocked the hansom, and I pulled my coat closer. A glance at the sky showed the dark clouds were rolling constantly, and now there was a wet feeling in the air, as if rain was not far away. If the temperature continued to drop, there would be ice tonight instead of rain or snow.

Not long after leaving the river behind, we crossed under the tracks leading south out of Waterloo, near the Necropolis Station. Then we turned left onto Lower Marsh Street before making a sharp right. We were almost to Oakley Street, just past the school, when the cabbie stopped before a shabby little tailor's shop. Climbing down, Holmes paid and dismissed our driver. I expressed surprise, as we'd need a way back – particularly if the weather continued to turn bad.

"I expect," was Holmes's reply, "that we'll need something bigger than a hansom if we compel Ulford to depart with us."

Holmes led me along the front of the shop before turning through a narrow alley, arriving at a set of rear stairs that climbed to the second floor. There, upon a shaky landing with two adjacent doors, he firmly knocked upon the left. Then, after just a few seconds, he checked the knob. Finding it unlocked, he led me inside.

It was surprisingly tidy compared to what I'd expected for the residence of a man who was recently involved in assault and theft.

"Behold," said Holmes softly, gesturing to the snoring focus of our trip to the Surrey side: "Isa Ulford."

And indeed it was the curiously structured and scarred man described by Jermyn and Bessemer. But now there was no threat to him, for he'd been tamed by the contents of the nearly empty brandy bottle standing on the floor beside the sofa where he was sprawled.

He showed no reaction to our voices as we softly exclaimed upon observing, lying on a nearby table, a folded yellowed document, about eight-inches-by-six. A quick examination showed that it was the stolen purchase agreement.

Holmes turned up the overhead lamp, pulled out a chair, spread the document upon the table, and began a minute examination. From nearby, I could see that it was as described – a concisely structured agreement, with signatures of both the British Envoy and the Texan President. Below the main body of the text, in brownish and faded ink, was an additional notation – the curious word *asesvda*, followed by the Texan president's signature and a date, *March 6, 1845.*

Before I could ask what Holmes thought it meant, Isa Ulford stirred and sat up. "Here, what's this?" he mumbled, rubbing his face briskly and trying to focus. Then, as Holmes – who was still in his fore-and-aft cap – turned and stood, Ulford recognized him and sagged back onto the sofa.

Then he swallowed and his eyes dropped. "Ah, Mr. Holmes," he rumbled. "I shouldn't be surprised, should I?"

Holmes folded the document and slid it into his pocket. "There isn't be much time, Ulford," he said. "You are in danger. Tell us the truth, and we can help you."

"Danger? What danger?"

"The man who arranged for this document to be found in Pickering Place went to a lot of effort. You carried it off before it could be put to its intended use, and if I could find you so easy, it won't be any harder for him."

"No, Mr. Holmes, you don't understand. When it all went wrong, I helped salvage what I could."

"What? You knew about this document beforehand?"

Ulford nodded.

"Watson, watch the rear court. Someone could arrive at any moment."

I moved to the window, beginning to understand that there was more risk than I'd first perceived. The financial arrangement between the very-rich coal and steel owner and the Krupps would be massive, and a group that might consider assassination to further their plans wouldn't hesitate to remove a small-time criminal – or a detective and a doctor.

The rear court was empty, but it was also getting darker, and I tried to keep my focus there, instead of continually glancing back into the poorly lit room, thus ruining what limited night vision that I'd achieved. Behind me, I heard Holmes and Ulford converse.

"Who hired you? Ronald Warrington?"

"Who? No, Mr. Holmes, it was a fellow named Shields."

I could imagine Holmes nodding. "Roland Shields – Warrington's man of business," he said softly. "Much is suspected of him." Then, louder, he continued. "Tell us about the document, and the safe."

"I was hired a few weeks ago – by Mr. Shields. He said that they had an old agreement – the one that you put in your pocket – and that they wanted it found in such a way as to gain a great deal of attention, in order to help a business deal. It had been signed by the Texas Government years ago, and they wanted it discovered in the old Texas Embassy in Pickering Place. They found an old safe and fixed it up to look like something the Texans would have had. They put the sheet and some old Texas money inside and gave it to me. Then I got into the old Embassy at night – it was closed up and deserted after the last tenant had moved out – and found a place where the safe could be hidden. I took off the nasty old wainscoting, hollowed out a hole in the wall, and cemented in the safe. Then I fixed the wall so that the safe would be found later.

"Then I took a job there with the construction crew and helped out as needed, waiting until today, as arranged, to pull off the wainscoting and find the safe. Then, after it was pulled clear, I hinted to Bessemer how we could open it. But then it started to go wrong. There were people hired to wait outside. They were supposed to hear about the safe – to come in and make a big deal about finding it, so that it would be reported in the press. Instead, when Bessemer saw the safe, he sent for the rich man who has the lease, just up the street at his club. He came, looked at the sheet, and put it in his pocket to go and show someone else nearby. That's when I knew things were getting off-track – all that trouble to find and fix up the safe, and arrange for the sheet to be found, and now, before the news could be spread as planned, some other man was carrying it away, maybe never to be seen again.

"Without thinking about it, I took after him. It was easy to catch up and get the sheet back – it was just inside his coat pocket – and then I came here, to wait and find out what to do next."

"And of course, knowing the importance of the document, you ignored the old money."

He nodded. "It was worthless – Why grab it?"

"Did you notify Shields that you'd retrieved the document?"

"I did. I sent a message to him on my way back here."

I glanced around and Holmes was checking his watch. "Get your coat, Ulford. We have to leave – *Now!*"

The man may have settled down to get drunk upon his return, but it didn't affect his reflexes. He seemed to have some keen animal awareness of danger, for he was in his coat and with me by the time I was out the door. Holmes was right behind us, and we wasted no time reaching the ground. Instead of turning back toward the main street, Holmes led us deeper into the shadows, toward a rear alley – and not a moment too soon. Hearing steps coming down the passage from the street, we hid behind the

152

stairs to another building and watched as three men, all dressed in black and moving like quick-shifting shadows, crossed the distance to the bottom of the stairs leading up to Ulford's rooms.

Ulford watched, wide-eyed, while Holmes tugged at my sleeve. "This way," he murmured, barely heard. We slipped away into the darkness.

We emerged from the alleyways along Waterloo Road, where we had no trouble finding an empty growler to take us back across the river to Scotland Yard. Ulford seemed resigned to being carried to the police, but he was full of questions regarding who we'd seen climbing the stairs in such a silent and threatening manner. I didn't want to provide him any more knowledge than he already had – beyond suspecting that they were Warrington's men, I really knew nothing – and Holmes was silent, cogitating upon something with great intensity.

At the Yard, we had the cab wait while we went inside. Ulford was expecting to be arrested, and was surprised when Holmes instead summoned Inspector Stanley Hopkins, explaining that our companion was an important witness who needed protection before his testimony could be taken in full, no questions asked. Without comment, Hopkins understood and took Ulford in charge, leading him away to a hot meal.

Chapter V

Outside and back in the cab, Holmes directed that we should return the short distance to Pall Mall. "Mycroft will be pleased," I said. "In just a few hours, you're back with the lost document, the thief under lock and key, and his testimony as well."

"I'm not so sure," said Holmes cryptically. "And we have a stop to make before reporting to Mycroft." He pulled out his watch. "Is your friend Lomax still as diligent as always?"

"More so, I expect," I said. "As the years pass, he becomes ever-more serious about his work."

"Good. Then he'll still be there. It always saves time to have someone knowledgeable point the way and save a few steps."

Knowing that we were going to see my old friend, the librarian, I wasn't surprised when Holmes knocked the head of his stick upon the cab roof halfway down Pall Mall, a hundred feet or before we reached the Diogenes. Paying and dismissing the man, we crossed the street and entered the western side of St. James's Square, walking to the far northwestern corner and the London Library.

In spite of the early darkness outside and the imminent threat of bad weather, Lomax was where we expected to find him, at his desk deep within the surrounding protection of countless books. He was quite absorbed in some ancient text, taking the time finish what he was reading before looking up. Then he did so with a raised eyebrow, the closest he ever came to surprise.

"What?" he said. "Both here at the same time?" He smiled. "This is a rare treat indeed." He stood and offered his hand to each of us. "It's been too long. What can I do for you?"

Holmes pulled the document from his pocket, unfolded it, and laid it facing Lomax on the desk. "We are researching the background of this item."

Lomax adjusted his glasses, leaned forward, and gave it a short look before standing upright again, saying, "An agreement to sell Texas to the Empire." He displayed no shock. "It looks to be half-a-century old."

"I'm more interested in the later notation at the bottom," replied Holmes. "What can you tell us about how it came to be added?"

Lomax gave a half-smile. "Ah, Mr. Holmes – Librarians are like priests. We believe in confidentiality, and the right of our patrons to privacy, and to keep their secrets."

Holmes nodded and raised an eyebrow. "I understand – indicating that you're protecting a secret indicates that you have prior knowledge of that secret. But you'll notice a very slight indentation beside the second signature of the Texas president – as if a sharpened pencil point had rested there for just a moment. That mark led me to consider just how that signature came to be there, and just what that curious word – *asesvda* – might mean. From there, I determined that three people might be able to explain it to me. One is my brother, whom we will visit shortly. The second is the forger who most likely and so skillfully added the second signature, probably within the last month or so, despite the apparent age of the ink and the March 1845 date. That talented fellow lives in Islington – too far to travel tonight when there are better and quicker options. The third man – and this was a bit more of a long shot – is much closer: *You*, Mr. Lomax, who probably helped locate the word *asesvda* in the first place so that it could be added onto the original fifty-year-old document."

Now Lomax smiled fully and his face looked suddenly young, as if he were a boy seeing a magic trick performed. "Again, Mr. Holmes, confidentiality is our watch-word here. But perhaps I could direct you to a few specific volumes that might give you some insight?"

"That would be most acceptable," replied Holmes, picking up and refolding the agreement.

As Lomax led us away from his desk and into the ranges of shelves, I wanted to ask Holmes just what was going on, but I knew – or hoped, in any case – that enough of an explanation would follow that I'd be able to catch up soon enough.

A moment later, we were standing at a chest-high table while Lomax pulled a couple of old books from different but nearby shelves. He returned, placed them before us, and stepped back, as if willing to help if asked, but allowing Holmes to first find what he needed for himself.

The first book was a biography of the first Texas president, Sam Houston. [5] Holmes glanced through it quickly, and then more slowly, with purpose, as it seemed to provide some information that he needed. As he did so, I picked up the second, a smaller volume, and saw that it was a dictionary of the Cherokee language.

While I tried to recall the little I'd heard of the Cherokee: An American Indian tribe originally from the southeast who had been forced to migrate west in the late 1830's, resulting in massive deaths – almost an extermination. This had been done so that American settlers in that region could take possession of the Indian lands, regardless of the unimaginable pain and suffering that the relocation had caused.

As I considered what I remembered, Holmes was reading rapidly through a number of pages in the front of the first book. I opened the dictionary and quickly found the mysterious word: *asesvda*. There was a note that it this was the phonetic pronunciation, while the written form looked something like *D4RL*. It translated as "*cancelled*".

"Holmes," I said, holding the book out to him and pointing toward a small mark beside the word – as would have been left by the sharply pointed end of a pencil. It was the same sort of mark beside that word on the old document.

Holmes took the dictionary and handed me the biography in return, opened near the front to the early life of Sam Houston, former President of Texas. He was born in Virginia in 1793, and in 1806, moved with his family to Maryville, Tennessee, on the extreme eastern edge of the state, and at the western edge of the Smoky Mountains, a part of the greater Appalachian range, and not far over the border from North Carolina. There he led a rather carefree existence, refusing to help with his family's farm and store, and instead spending several years living with the nearby Cherokee Indians.

The biography went on to relate how he'd returned to Maryville in 1812 to open a school, and he later recalled that he had "*experienced a higher feeling of dignity and self-satisfaction than from any other office or honor which I have held.*" A year later, he joined the United States Army, fighting in the War of 1812 under the leadership of General Andrew Jackson, also a Tennessean (and the man later responsible for the Cherokee relocation, known as "The Trail of Tears".) After the war, Houston returned to Tennessee, becoming a lawyer, working with the Cherokee tribe, and also involving himself with the Jackson presidency.

155

In the early 1830's, he was convinced to settle in Texas, then a part of Mexico. He was subsequently involved in the struggle for Texas independence. The battle of the Alamo in February and March of 1836 served as a rallying cry for the Texans, and Houston was leading the Texas army that brilliantly defeated the Mexican president, Santa Anna, in April 1836 at San Jacinto. The Mexican president, captured as he fled while dressed as a woman, surrendered, and soon Texas became an independent nation, with Houston elected its first president. Later, when Texas became a state, he was one of its first two U.S. Senators. The city of Houston was named for him.

But what was important here was Houston's connection with the Cherokee, and the inclusion of the Cherokee word, along with his signature – apparently forged – upon the document.

Holmes and I closed the two books at the same time. "You may borrow those if necessary," said Lomax, still with a smile upon his face.

"Thank you, but no," replied Holmes. "We've seen what we needed. Your assistance was most useful."

"Simply doing my job, gentlemen." He replaced the books upon their shelves and led us back to the front of the building. Glancing through the door, we could see that a mixture of sleet and rain had begun to fall. "I wish you luck," he said as we departed. "Always a pleasure to assist the Holmes brothers in their work." Then he added, "And you too, Doctor."

It was a short but unpleasant walk to the Diogenes. We could have run, I suppose, but the street was already becoming slick.

Mycroft was waiting in the Stranger's Room by the time we'd removed our coats and were led through the building. Wasting no time, Holmes immediately handed his brother the half-century-old document, which Mycroft laid aside after a single glance.

"Ulford is in protective custody at the Yard," explained Holmes. "We spirited him away from his rooms just moments before three men in black arrived – presumably from Warrington, or the Krupps, or both of them."

Mycroft nodded, showing no surprise at Holmes's additional knowledge of the situation.

"I'm afraid," Holmes continued, "that it was Jermyn's involvement that derailed the plan. Of course you know that. Ulford indicated that there were men waiting nearby for the document to be discovered, so that it could be publicly paraded and generate attention, but before they could become involved, Jermyn was summoned and, recognizing the importance of what was found, he chose to leave and bring it to you. Ulford, mistakenly trying to help his employer, followed him and took it back."

Mycroft pursed his lips. "As I thought. Nevertheless, despite my plan being in disarray, it may be salvageable."

156

"*Your plan*?" I had to speak. "Excuse me, but I feel the need to understand. We have been to the London Library – " I realized then that Holmes might not want that aspect revealed, but he nodded, and I continued. "The meaning of the word written at the bottom – *asesvda* – is known – *canceled* – as well as its Cherokee origin. Apparently it was forged, as was the second signature of the Texas president, Sam Houston. But I don't understand why."

"Wheels within wheels, Watson," murmured Holmes.

Mycroft glanced at him with something like a smile, and then back toward me. "Doctor, when the Government – and by 'Government' I mean me – became aware of Warrington's inclinations to form an alliance with the Krupps at the expense of his own country, it was also soon apparent that to do so, he would need distractions. Not knowing what he intended, we – by which I mean I – devised a plan to provide him with another distraction, a tempting one which would be known to us, and which we could control to some extent."

"You already knew of the British copy of the document," said Holmes. "That's what you used – not the Texans' copy. You altered it, by way of the second forged signature and a later date, to make it seem as if it were the Texans' document, still in their possession a year after it was signed in 1844."

Mycroft nodded, and I said, "So the document itself was real – as was the sale."

"Apparently so – although no money was ever transferred. It seems that Houston never really planned for the sale to actually occur, but rather he did want a legal document to use as a cudgel, forcing the United States government to go ahead and annex Texas into Statehood. Somehow, Houston convinced Richard Pakenham, the British Envoy, that having such a document in existence would be effective if Texas ever needed to assert a rejection of attempts by the American government to take Texas under terms that they didn't like."

"And," I continued, "adding the world '*canceled*', written in Cherokee – a language with deep associations to Houston's background – gave both veracity to the document's authenticity, and also a legal method, as part of your plan, of proving the agreement was void if needed, but in a subtle way that wouldn't be easily or initially understood."

"That's correct," replied Mycroft. "It seemed unlikely that anyone would do the research necessary in the bowels of the London Library to find that the word *asesvda* was Cherokee." He looked at his brother. "That was an astute leap."

Holmes shook his head. "You were careless, Mycroft. I've seen how you rest your sharpened pencil beside what you're studying. You made such a mark on the document beside the second signature. I knew when I saw it that you were involved, and I'd already seen that the second signature was forged – the ink and the fading, while good, don't look as if it was written fifty years ago. Knowing that *asesvda* would have some obscure meaning, I pondered where to determine it – and where *you* would have determined it. Of course, it could have been something already in your brain attic, but I decided to see how it might relate specifically to Sam Houston. The London Library is nearby – right on your way to and from your office in Whitehall, as a matter of fact. Stopping there and seeking Lomax's help would have been very easy. And checking there was easier than tracking down the forger, Blaine, who added the second signature. Your additional pencil mark in the Cherokee dictionary was simply additional confirmation."

"So what happens now?" I asked. "All of your efforts to manipulate the events – finding and altering the document, getting it to Warrington's attention so that he'd be tempted to use it, and then waiting for him to find a clever way to do so just so you could pull the rug out from underneath him – it's all been for nothing."

"Fear not, Doctor. This wasn't the only plan afoot to outmaneuver and manipulate our straying industrialist. There are half-a-dozen other shiny objects in play to tempt him. While he flounders about, trying to salvage this scheme, the nets are tightening. There are several parallel stratagems in the works. He'll soon be brought to heel one way or another."

I wanted to know more. Why hadn't Mycroft just told us the whole story to begin with, instead of setting us along one strand, to find our own way to the center of the web. And if the plan that we knew about, concerning a lost and apparently real treaty to sell Texas to the British, was so curiously interesting, what else had Mycroft's agile mind conceived? But I knew that he wouldn't tell us, and Sherlock Holmes had known the same thing for much longer. Our work that night was done, and our parts played. Instead of pursuing it further, we said our goodbyes and departed with Mycroft's thanks. Finding a cab was more difficult as the weather worsened, but it wasn't too long before we were safely ensconced in our Baker Street rooms, and with a topic to spend the evening discussing.

Not too many weeks later, I was surprised to see a newspaper report that Ronald Warrington had negotiated a number of very lucrative arrangements with the Royal Navy, and that he would be on the Queen's next New Year's Honors list. I threw down the paper in disgust.

"They're rewarding that traitor with a knighthood!" I exclaimed.

Holmes simply shook his head, stating, "Mycroft did indicate that he had several other plans to bring Warrington back into the fold. I try not to worry too deeply about the machinations of Government. I fear that as the world becomes more tangled, we'll be drawn into them at some point, whether we want to be or not. For right now, let us leave it for another day."

And with that, he returned to the intense study of an old palimpsest, related to some ancient English Charter, that had absorbed him off-and-on for the past couple of months.

NOTES

1. The identification of No. 78 Pall Mall as the Diogenes Club, as well as No. 48 across the street as Mycroft Holmes's lodgings, is explained in *The Baker Street Journal*, (Vol. 67, No. 2, Summer 2017).

No. 78 Pall Mall (The Diogenes Club)
(Photo taken September 26, 2015)
Note the bow window in the Stranger's Room at the right:
"To anyone who wishes to study mankind this is the spot."
– Mycroft Holmes

My deerstalker and me at No. 78 Pall Mall (The Diogenes Club)
(Photo taken September 10, 2016)

*No. 48 Pall Mall
(Mycroft Holmes's Lodgings –
The building to the left,
as photographed from the front door
of The Diogenes Club, No. 78 Pall Mall –
Photo taken September 16, 2013)*

The lobby of The Diogenes Club, No. 78 Pall Mall,
(Photo taken September 12, 2016)

2.   Site of the Texas Legation, Pickering Place, St. James's Street:

(Photo taken May 31, 2024)

Although I can't find any documentation about it, on the day I visited the former legation in May 2024, there was a curious plaque standing in the center of the small court, seemingly removed from somewhere else, that looks to me like Sam Houston . . . .

More about the curious Texas Legation can be found at:

https://www.atlasobscura.com/places/the-embassy-of-the-republic-of-texas-london-england

3. For more about Sir Arthur Conan Doyle's decision not to be Watson's Literary Agent, see "Fate's Brushes" in this volume, and also in *Steel True, Blade Straight - 2023 Annual.*

4.

My deerstalker and me at No. 86 St. James's Street –
the site of Landale Pike's club and the window
where he sat and watched the world go by
(Photo taken May 31, 2024)

5   Sam Houston (1793-1863) was born in Virginia, but after the death of his father, the family moved to my hometown, Maryville, TN. Houston spent much of his early years living with the nearby Cherokee Indians, becoming known to them as "The Raven". Around age twenty, he taught school in a one-room cabin that still stands in Maryville. Not long after, he served in the War of 1812, and was elected to the U.S. House of Representatives in 1823. In 1827, he became Tennessee's sixth governor.

    In 1829 he moved to Arkansas to live again with the Cherokee, and in 1832, he traveled on to Texas, where he became involved in the struggle for Texas Independence. After winning the decisive Battle of San Jacinto in 1836, liberating Texas from Mexico, he held office as the first and third President of Texas, one of the first two Senators from Texas, and the seventh governor.

    A statue of Sam Houston is located beside the municipal building in downtown Maryville, TN, my hometown . . . .

*(Photo of Sam Houston Statue taken October 12, 2022 –
Maryville, TN – Note the Cherokee Seal on the statue's plinth)*

A Dreadful Record of Sin

When recording the investigations of my friend, Mr. Sherlock Holmes, I have attempted to strike a balance between those cases which best illustrated his unique and well-honed abilities and events that would capture the interest of the reader – even if, in some cases, they will never be seen by the public. Still, even when knowing that some cases cannot be publicly read, I've still made the attempt to transcribe them in an engaging manner.

As I've become more practiced and experienced over the passing years at which type of narratives generate the most reading interest, as well as the ways in which they can be constructed so as to tell a pleasing tale, I've also had to make certain that I didn't stray over several different well-defined lines and inadvertently provide too much information. Certain matters of State have needed to be disguised so that Holmes's methods could be displayed without giving away government secrets. Examples of this include the curse of the Burmese bicyclist, and also the affair of the Godolphin Street murder, and the secret document that was hidden at and then stolen from the premises. Had it not been recovered, then the country might have been plunged into war. But there was no need to name specific figures involved, when I could instead identify the principal actors by other designations and lose nothing in terms of showing how Holmes brilliantly handled the matter. Likewise, I have no qualms about adjusting other names, dates, and locations to protect those individuals who need not suffer from unnecessary public exposure while I describe the manner in which Holmes effectively finds his solutions.

The following adventure took place in the years just before Holmes was presumed dead, although neither the exact date, nor the specific identifies of those involved, need be related in order to describe Holmes's accomplishment. In this instance, hiding the identity of those involved will be additionally accomplished by consigning this document to my tin dispatch box, which holds so many of my other records of Holmes's cases, some simply because they are finished but have not been offered for publication, and others because they hold secrets, often dangerous or destructive, that have no business being held up for public scrutiny. It has been noted to me on more than one occasion, by more than just Sherlock Holmes, that making any kind of record at all of some of these cases is indiscreet at best, and that their very existence as a written record is a menace to the national interest should they be revealed. However, I insist that an accurate and complete record of Holmes's cases be recorded as best as possible, and therefore I'm including the affair of the Kilworth investigation.

But be warned: The matter was disturbing, greatly so, and this account shall remain locked away for at least a century.

– JHW

"It's my own fault," Mycroft stated, wiping his damp face with a handkerchief. "I decided to save time by visiting you directly, instead of asking you to join me at the Diogenes Club."

"You've just come from an important meeting," said Sherlock Holmes. "So important that you didn't want to wait to seek our help."

Mycroft barked a laugh. "Now I know how strangers at the receiving end feel when we seemingly read their minds." He glanced down at his stout frame. "No tell-tale papers protruding from my pockets. No ink stains of a unique hue on my fingers, indicating that I was recently writing with a leaky pen in a Cabinet member's office. No crumbs on my waistcoat from the unique refreshments served there. How did you know, Sherlock?"

"There were no physical clues. Only urgency could have diverted you in this heat from scurrying directly straight along to the club at this time of evening. What could be so serious?"

"Brian Kilworth's wife is missing – and with her, a number of most-secret state documents. Serious is far too insignificant a word for what might happen should their contents be revealed."

I may have given the impression that Mycroft Holmes ran entirely on fixed rails, as based upon Holmes's own description of him as related in the matter of Mr. Melas's encounter with the captive Greek. In that account, I have recorded, based on Sherlock Holmes's initial revelation of Mycroft's existence, that he was a man who went from his Pall Mall lodgings to his work in Whitehall, and from there to his Pall Mall club directly across the street from his rooms, and then back home again at the end of the day, and doing it all over again on the next. While this description certainly defines someone of eccentric behavior, in truth, Mycroft Holmes was not so rigid as all that. Many men at his level of responsibility had much the same pattern – home to work to club, and then repeating the following day. When someone asks me about it, I point out that in the same narrative describing Mr. Melas's unfortunate adventure, Mycroft departed from his club, the Diogenes, just after we left, and he beat us back to Baker Street, where he was waiting when we finally arrived, placidly smoking one of his brother's best cigars, apparently not put off at all by having to retrieve it from the coal scuttle.

In our dealings with Mycroft over the years, he was far more active than many would like to believe, and while not a frequent visitor to Baker Street, it wasn't entirely unusual for him to arrive, often unannounced, if some urgent and confidential matter needed Sherlock Holmes's efforts, and it needed to be discussed either in the greatest confidence, away from the Diogenes Club or Whitehall, or sooner than if Holmes went around to Mycroft's office during business hours.

This was just such a visit.

The specific date isn't important, but for clarity, I'll mention that the weather was hot, and when Mycroft finished climbing the steps to the sitting room, he was red-faced, winded, and damp. He wiped his scowling countenance with a handkerchief, asked for a tall glass of water, and then another, and then finally accepted some whisky. When he had found an acceptable level of comfort upon our settee, for the room was nearly as hot as the outdoors and there was no breeze from the open windows, he began to speak.

Holmes frowned in response. "Brian Kilworth? Isn't he the fellow who recently returned from Berlin with a trade agreement in his pocket – hailed in the press as an important step toward cementing further peaceful ties between Germany and Britain?"

"The same," agreed Mycroft. "He arranged it on his own. He's always been something of a rogue agent. He believes that he's allowed greater leeway because of his father, and he has no hesitation at taking it."

Holmes rose and circled around the settee to reach the shelf where his scrapbooks were kept, to the left of the mantel and behind my chair. He had first claimed that spot on the day he moved in, the third of January, 1881. I myself had brought my own things 'round from a Strand hotel the evening before, but hadn't had the foresight or the boldness to start marking territory, and therefore I lost any right to those shelves before I'd even given any thought about them. However, I had no objections to Holmes taking the space, as the door to his bedroom was just beside the shelves in question, while my own room had been located upstairs, and it seemed somehow appropriate for him to have those shelves because of that proximity. In any case, those early days were quite uncertain, as I'd only agreed to share the rooms because of the dangerous and poorly managed condition of my finances, and I had no set plans as to how long I'd stay. I certainly didn't do very much to make myself completely at home, at least not at first, in spite of the mothering I received from Mrs. Hudson as she took it upon herself to help accomplish my return to health.

In 1881, Holmes's scrapbooks were already formidable accomplishments, created over the previous years with notes and clippings related to countless individuals, events, and places. Holmes knew the contents of the multiple volumes forward and backward, and he spent a great deal of time keeping them caught up by regularly butchering our newspapers and then using the glue-pot to affix the clippings into the volumes, or making extensive notes in the margins. Many was the time he'd come in from some errand and, first thing, rush to one or another of the commonplace books to jot down some fact that he'd learned while out, unrelated to his current inquiry, before he lost track of it.

Now, almost a decade later, the shelves that we'd found mounted upon the wall when we'd moved in had been augmented by others, and there were many more books as well, all fat with data, and still referenced in Holmes's mind so that he could lay a hand on just what he needed at a moment's notice.

"'*Lord Benton Kilworth*'" read Holmes. "A bit before our time. Born in 1812 near High Roding." He looked up, his eyebrows raised curiously.

"A village and civil parish in the Uttlesford district of Essex," Mycroft explained.

Holmes shrugged. "I don't recall why I noted the fact. The ink is quite faded – apparently I wrote it down a long time ago, thinking there was something important about Lord Benton." He scanned the entry further. "Is he still alive?" he asked, glancing up.

Mycroft nodded. "He turns seventy-eight later this summer. Of course, he's been withdrawn from public life for quite a while, although he's still remembered with great fondness for his numerous accomplishments."

"Family made a fortune in shipping," Holmes continued to summarize. "Lord Benton made his name in politics, married late, had one son – Brian, in 1849. The lad's mother died when he was but two, and – Ah, this is why Lord Benton was of interest." He closed the book and replaced it on the shelf, saying, "He has had *four* other wives since the death of the first. Possibly more than that, since it's been a while since I first wrote this notation, over ten years ago. Possibly that's why I felt the need to make mention of him then. *Five wives?* That seems a bit excessive – and suspicious. And of those five wives, the first four all died before he married the fifth – there were no divorces, and each marriage only lasted for a few years before being . . . terminated." Holmes resumed his seat. "And Wife Number Five? Is she still alive?"

Mycroft shook his head. "Number Five passed nearly ten years ago – while you were jaunting across the ocean during your so-called career as an actor. Even if you had been here, however, it's unlikely that the fact would have made much of an impression. Lord Benton had long since retired from public life by then, returning to his reclusive estate near High Roding. His son, Brian, however, who is now in his early forties, has become the public figure, filling the role his father used to hold."

"And the wives?" Holmes pressed. "Did Lord Benton marry a sixth after the fifth – to make a round half-dozen?"

"He did not remarry. Five seems to have been enough. And his son, Brian, has made do with just the one wife for the past five years. He, too, married late, and has yet to produce an heir."

"And you say that Brian Kilworth's wife is missing?"

"She is. With important papers."

Holmes leaned back. "Tell us about it."

Mycroft never needed much time to collect his thoughts, and he continued immediately.

"Brian Benton's wife, Katherine, is now twenty-three years old. Her father was Simon Rackford, who made a fortune through property management in the East End. The girl's parents were both killed in a carriage accident when she was seventeen, and their affairs were managed by a cadre of lawyers. Katherine was the sole heir. A year after her parents died, she was married off to Brian Kilworth.

"I don't know the specific details, but I have the sense that the affair was managed with legal slickness by the attorneys – more like an arranged marriage of old than for love. However, that is no more than gossip upon my part as – contrary to what some would believe – I don't hold every thread in my hand, and the marriage of one girl to one older man more than twice her age does not often fall within my purview. The only reason I knew anything about it at all was because there was some discussion concerning the economic aspects of the absorption of the Rackford fortune into the Kilworth family. As is so often the case, the Kilworths are already quite wealthy, so it's no surprise that they have now become wealthier. Such is the way of things. Money begets more money."

"And Katherine Kilgore has disappeared," prompted Holmes. "What are the circumstances?"

"The Kilgores live in Mayfair, in the family home that initially belonged to Lord Benton, before he retired to Essex. It's where Brian grew up – him, his father, and his succession of short-lived step-mothers." Mycroft raised a hand. "No, I'm not adding emphasis to that fact, asking you to investigate the deaths of these women, or implying that there was some sort of nefarious plot by Lord Benton to remove them, one by one. I was just making note of the fact that the young man has lived in the house his whole life, and he remained there when his father left, and it's there that he took his new bride, Katherine.

"By all accounts, she has fulfilled her role adequately in all aspects, if without enthusiasm, except for producing an heir. Her duties have been slight, for the Kilgores do not entertain – at least not to the standard that many living in Mayfair expect. They do not participate in the general social cycle, instead having occasional visits and dinners with long-time family friends, many of whom have had connections with Lord Benton since his youth.

"Other than maintaining the household – duties that are apparently carried out in actuality by the long-time servants – Katherine Kilgore has led a rather typical tedious existence for the last five years, while her husband has risen from professional triumph to triumph. She doesn't appear to have any friends. She doesn't travel, and does not even leave the house very often – that according to her husband, who reluctantly sought help when she vanished.

"She disappeared exactly one week ago today, June 14th. It was another typical day at home, and according to the servants that Kilgore questioned, his wife had been seen reading in the morning room around ten o'clock. When a maid went to tell her that lunch was ready, she could not be found. The best guess was that she had simply slipped out of the house and vanished.

"The servants were initially uneasy, and grew more so, but no one sent word to the lady's husband, and he was told when he arrived home that night at six. Strangely, he didn't immediately notify the authorities, instead sending word to some of his friends, asking if Katherine was with them. When she couldn't be located, he widened his circle of inquiries, but still without positive results. It was only today that he felt moved to seek outside assistance – not from the police, but within the Government."

"Because of the important missing papers."

"Yes. Throughout his wife's absence, Kilgore has continued to come to work, while in the meantime leaving the search in the hands of the butler, Hollins. It was only this morning, as Kilgore prepared to leave for the day, that he went to his safe to retrieve one of the important documents related to his recent German work – only to find all of them missing, along with a number of other similarly confidential papers, and all of his cash reserves."

"Were there any signs that the safe had been tampered with?"

Mycroft shook his head. "None. It was at this point that Kilgore acknowledged that the situation was beyond the small efforts he and his staff had been making, and he realized it had crossed into the realm of national security. He sent word for one of my trusted agents, who went and made an examination. I don't say that you couldn't have found more than he, Sherlock, but he is thorough and skilled, and he saw no signs that the safe had been forced. It was locked when Kilgore went to open it, using the combination as he always does."

"Clearly, the wife has chosen to vanish on her own, and went to the safe to obtain funds to do so. Did she have the combination?"

"Kilgore says that she did not – but he admits that he had written it down and kept it in a box upon his dresser, and that she could have easily found it. 'She has all day to putter and prowl around the house!' he snarled when asked about it."

Holmes pinched his lower lip. "One can understand that she would take the money. But the documents? Of what use could those be?"

"None, if what we hear is true. According to the servants, who had her in sight every day – "

"Apparently not entirely," Sherlock Holmes interrupted.

Mycroft nodded. " – who *mostly* had her in sight every day, she had no friends or visitors. She made no calls upon people. When she shopped, it was always in the company of one or another of the servants, and they say she had no interactions of significance with anyone, other than when friends of her husband visited. She had no correspondence. Her only social life was with her husband's rare visitors, and they are all associated with him – people he grew up with, friends from Essex, and so on. He never invites anyone from work over for social gatherings."

"She sounds like a lonely princess locked in a tower," I said, offering my own small opinion. "Perhaps it's no wonder that she felt the need to escape."

"Possibly," said Mycroft. "Probably. But she seems to be helpless and without resources – other than the funds she took from her husband. He estimated it to be around two-thousand pounds."

Holmes whistled softly. "With that amount, she can purchase enough resources to get by for a while."

"If," I added, "someone doesn't take it away from her first."

Holmes nodded. "I suppose that you immediately checked the hospitals and morgues to see if such a woman has turned up."

Mycroft nodded. "That was my first thought – especially considering the nature of the documents that were taken. Some of them – Well, suffice it to say, Brian Kilgore had no business keeping that most-explosive material so carelessly in his home, but it's typical of how his arrogance and carelessness have increased over the years. At least if he didn't have sense enough to immediately seek help finding his wife, he knew to admit that the documents had been taken."

"I wonder," said Holmes. "You said that he opened the safe to retrieve one of the German-related documents – that he was taking it to work. Was it necessary that it be brought today?"

"It was. It needed to be reviewed by the Ministry."

"So, if he hadn't had to take it, then one would think that it might have been even longer still before he opened the safe and discovered the money and documents missing. But look at it a different way: Perhaps he

173

actually learned on the day that his wife left that she had opened the safe and took the contents. He waited a week to report that his wife was missing. Perhaps he would have waited indefinitely, if his hand hadn't been forced by needing the German document today. What is it about her disappearance that has caused him to make his own private investigation, without involving the authorities? There's something about this that doesn't smell right."

Mycroft agreed. "Thus my detour to see you immediately. I'm not sure what this is about, but I want you to act as an independent agent – and you as well, Doctor, if you're willing – to see what you can determine. Why is Brian Kilgore willing to let the disappearance of his wife continue for a full week, until he had no choice but to report it? You both know that in my work, there's a danger of seeing plots where none exist, and reacting to something that is merely unusual as if it has great weight and dangerous importance. I have a sense that there's something here, something that needs to be understood, but possibly it needs to remain unofficial."

"I suspect," added Sherlock Holmes, "that it would be best not to alert Brian Kilgore of our involvement – which is another reason that it was wise for you to stop here, Mycroft, instead of summoning us to the Diogenes. Silence is the watchword within its walls, but that doesn't stop gossip from occurring when visitors arrive or depart, and if news was spread to someone that knows of the missing Kilgore documents that Watson and I were summoned there just after you learned about it, the connection wouldn't be a difficult one to make."

He frowned and reached for his pipe. "Clearly, we'll need to locate the wife, without any help from Kilgore or the servants. It's quite a three-pipe problem, and I hope that you'll both excuse me while I ponder it." And he began to pack tobacco into the bowl, dismissing us as if we had both already departed.

Mycroft wasn't surprised, and with a nod in my direction, he rose and walked out. I heard him lumber down the stairs, pausing halfway at the landing to turn back toward the street door, which I heard open and close a moment later. I too departed upon my own business, and Holmes was still seated, considering his options.

I arose fairly early the next morning, as the temperature was already becoming too warm to stay abed. As I went upon my rounds, I stopped by Baker Street to see if Holmes had anything to share, but he had already departed. There was no note, either informing me where he'd gone, or of any task that I might carry out for him before he returned. Since I'd known him, he'd had many cases that might initially be classified the same as this one – to find a missing woman. But each had presented different challenges and, based on what Mycroft had told us, this one had more than most.

The woman had no friends, so there was no one of that class to question as to Katherine Kilgore's state of mind, or her intentions, or what plans she might have made. There was no one to whom she might have turned for assistance, or for a place to hide. Worse, it seemed as if her husband had some secrets of his own, for he had kept her disappearance concealed for a week, only prompted to seek help when it could no longer be hidden that she had taken an important document that he needed at work that day.

I had much to keep me busy, but as mid-day turned to afternoon, my calls were complete and, dulled by the heat, I wandered my way slowly north and west, working toward 221b by tarrying in a bookstore in Marylebone, and then taking a turn through the Paddington Street Gardens, considering as I always did that a substantial portion of the place had once been a cemetery. With the stones long-since removed before it was turned into a park, I had to wonder upon whose graves I was treading. Surely they knew that visitors there meant no disrespect – or so the small boy still in me sometimes hoped.

I hadn't been back in the Baker Street rooms for more than ten minutes before Holmes also returned, dressed as a rather shabby laborer, but not of the sort that accumulates deeply staining grime, and not carrying the telling odors of a groom or someone who works in an abattoir. He nodded and disappeared into his room. I noted that he carried a rather full carpet bag, and I knew what that was about.

Since long before I'd met him, Holmes had taken a great deal of time to create for himself a number of other identities. Over the years, I've never been quite certain just how many of them there were. Some he assumed as needed, building the character by way of clothing and theatrical makeup for a specific purpose – an urgently sincere clergyman, perhaps, or a drunken groom. But others were more artfully and deliberately contrived: Leonard Stoke, for instance, a shifty gambler with irritatingly nervous hand gestures (which served as a distraction for anyone speaking with him), or Hobbes Bates, a surly dock laborer who drank much and spoke very little – and who stood around various dives of terrible reputation, listening to conversations around him long after anyone who should have known better had stopped paying attention to him.

To help establish these and other invented personas, Holmes maintained rented rooms for them at different spots in London, making sure to keep the landlords paid, and stopping by to visit just enough, in character, to be certain that these created individuals' varied existences were re-confirmed. These rooms, barely furnished and less livable, were

175

not to be confused with those that he called his "hidey holes", also at a number of other locations across the capital. These, sometimes no larger than a big closet, were where Holmes kept disguises and changes of clothes so that he could drop in and hurriedly become someone else. He maintained all sorts of disguises, and also some his own "Holmes" clothing, so that he could instantly shed a disguise and re-emerge as himself, as needed. Sometimes, when he did too much visiting and identity-switching at any one place, the clothing of the different characters became unbalanced between different spots and had to be redistributed.

Holmes worked at maintaining these false identities and hiding places as hard as he did at keeping his scrapbooks caught up, and the re-balancing of clothing between them was something that he had to undertake on a semi-regular basis. Thus, him arriving that afternoon with a carpet bag, while in disguise, told me that he'd finished his day with some hidey-hole maintenance, and that he had returned home toting some of Sherlock Holmes's apparel. Soon he re-entered the sitting room as himself, pouring a drink at the sideboard, and then sinking into his chair across from me before the empty fireplace.

"Sometimes an ounce of luck is worth a pound of skill," he said, stretching out his feet before him on the worn bear-skin rug. I recalled when we had received the unwieldy thing, in lieu of a payment back in the early days when assistance toward accumulating that month's rent was much more important than having a rather inconvenient carpet. Now, a year after I had moved out, I found that I missed the thing.

"I take that to mean," I replied, "that in spite of the absolute lack of initial threads to pull, you reached forward and found one to pull anyway."

He nodded. "Years of throwing bread upon the water, so to speak, means that there are a number of individuals scattered about with whom I've had the opportunity to interact – some in positive ways, and just as many negatively. In nearly every case, I have some sort of leverage, where someone feels that they owe me for doing them a good turn, or conversely, that I have some influence because of knowledge of a past transgression."

I nodded. "And which type did you find with knowledge of the Kilgore situation?"

"No one within the Kilgore residence – but just one house away, as my disguised self sought any little job that might be tossed in my direction, I was happy to meet Emmy Hayes, now in her early twenties. Do you recall when we met her?"

I nodded. I did recall. The simple acknowledgement of that fact could not encompass all that was involved with her rescue from Dr. Ernest Hazelton's locked cellar in the house by Clapham Common, nor the horror when we discovered the two other girls also there who were beyond

176

saving. My attendance at Newgate on the morning of Hazelton's hanging was not required . . . but I attended nonetheless.

"When I recognized Emmy," continued Holmes, "I surreptitiously introduced myself. She was surprised, but not as much as one might expect. She has seen a great deal, as you know, and it has sadly hardened her. She made an excuse with the very-tolerant cook, introducing me as an old family friend, and we talked for several minutes in the rear garden.

"She told me that the Kilgore house is a strange one. The servants there are very withdrawn, all having been brought down from the family's Essex estate in High Roding. They're all country folk with little inclination to get to know anyone not of their circle. The Kilgore servants step out in twos or threes, never alone and, except for rare instances in passing, the neighbors know nothing about them.

"'I believe that they're very religious, though,' Emmy told me. 'Several times when I've passed them on their way to some errand, I've seen that they've been clutching Bibles, the way someone else might hold a knife as defense when walking down the worst street in London.'

"While this was interesting, it didn't help me toward discovering where Katherine Kilgore might be found. But then, Emmy continued, her expression wise and knowing.

"'You're fortunate that I'm curious, Mr. Holmes,' she said. 'They're just a little *too* secretive over there, and since I've seen things in my life, I wanted to know *why*. You know about what happened at Hazelton's – it was only someone becoming curious that led you to save me. One of the girls at the Kilgore house– her name is Lizzy Boles – hasn't been in London for very long, and one day when she was in the back of the garden, alone and depositing the refuse, I spoke to her from our side of the fence and said hello. She was surprised, but she didn't shy away – I guess there's still some of the country girl in her. I saw her again a day or so later, in the same place, and after a few weeks, we were making time to visit, even if just for a moment or two. She seemed to need a friend, for she's an uneasy sort of girl, and there's something about that house that unnerves her, although she doesn't want to say why.'

"I considered whether to visit the Kilgore house in my own clothes, by way of the front door, and to find an opportunity to question the servants in order to speak to Lizzy alone, but I decided that she would probably be too unnerved, realizing as she would that the members of the household would know that she had been questioned. Instead, I asked when Emmy might next expect to speak with Lizzy.

"'Why, later this afternoon – about two o'clock. Do you want to join us?'

"I did, and two o'clock found me waiting with Emmy in the mews by the refuse cans, out of sight of the Kilgore house. It was an unlikely opportunity, Watson: I had only minutes to not only meet the girl and gain her trust, but after doing so, to hear whatever she could tell me – all before she had to return to the house before suspicion was raised. It was seemingly impossible, and would have been, if not for the good will that Emmy had built up with Lizzy over the previous months. The poor girl's need for a friend is desperate, and thank Heavens she was willing to cooperate.

"Lizzy Boles is thin, with large dark eyes. She reminded me of a skittish fawn. When she saw me waiting with Emmy, I thought she'd turn and run, but Emmy called to her, and something in Emmy's tone calmed her. She stepped closer, looking back to make sure she was out of sight of the house, and then waited while Emmy introduced me under my true name. I knew that I only had a moment to make my case.

"'I don't know if you've heard of me,' I explained, 'but I'm a detective. I've helped Emmy in the past, and now I've been asked to look for Mrs. Kilgore after she disappeared last week. I've been asking around the neighborhood to see if anyone can tell me something that will help.'

"Emmy nodded encouragingly, and I saw that Lizzie paid close attention. I continued.

"'I had planned to visit the house next, fancied-up to call by way of the front door, but when I heard from Emmy that she could introduce us, I thought of speaking to you this way.' I took a step closer, lowering my voice even more from the soft tone I'd already been employing. 'I've heard that Mrs. Kilgore was unhappy. Did you see that? Do you have any idea where she might have gone?'

"My question about the lady's unhappiness presumed more than I specifically knew, but it became the new basis of investigation when the girl softly nodded her agreement. Then I struck gold when she began to speak, in a soft hurried rush, as if she could only say it once before time to turn and flee back to the house.'

"'She and I are distant cousins,' she said. 'Way back. My people served her people for ages. It shocked us where her parents died – and even more when she was suddenly married off to Mr. Kilgore.' Then she looked at Emmy. 'Are you sure that I can trust him?' she asked.

"Emmy nodded. 'He saved my life once. He'd do it again if I ever need it.' This was no time to show any false humility, so I simply nodded in agreement and did my best, disguised as I was, to look trustworthy. After the shortest bit of hesitation, Lizzy continued.

"'When I came here, Miss Katherine needed someone – anyone – that she could trust. She's . . . she's so alone, sir, and she doesn't know what

178

to do! She was in the house all day, and they watched her – all of the other servants. They came down from Essex, too, but they're people that have always worked for the Kilgores. They're all members of the True Ones. They think that I am too, but I'm not. When I came to London, I didn't come alone – My young man followed after me. I manage to see him sometimes, when I go with Mrs. Abrams, the cook, to market. I slipped him a note, and he found out what to do – who could help us. It was he who found a place for Miss Katherine to go when she left.'

"She looked again at Emmy, her gaze once again seeking reassurance, even if the words remained unuttered. Emmy nodded, and Lizzie spoke one final time before fleeing back to the house.

"'Michael Naughton,' she said. "That's him. He found a job working the stables near the Langham Hotel. If he trusts you, then he'll get a message to Miss Katherine. That's all I can tell you. I don't know where she went – only that Michael found a place for her that he felt would be safe, and that it was better if she went alone. That's why I'm still here – for now." She glanced over her shoulder toward the house. "I have to go! Don't make me regret this, Mister Detective!' And she turned and was away without another word.

"Emmy told me that she had no knowledge of Michael Naughton, so after thanking her, I immediately worked my way toward the Langham. I observe, Watson, that you had a call this morning in Queen Anne Street – no, the signs are numerous, and not worth recounting – but you had no idea that I probably passed not three-hundred feet from you as you unknowingly went about your business.

"Naughton was easily found in the stables just south of the hotel – a fellow of about Lizzie's age, strapping and straight-forward and capable-looking. Just the sort to entrust with a lady's rescue. I explained who I was and what I was about, and then emphasized that I had been given his name by Lizzie Boles. I was emphatic to establish that I was not involved in some mission to drag Mrs. Kilgore back to her husband – especially if there was a good reason for her to have left him. I dearly wanted to ask him about the members of 'the True Ones', as mentioned by Lizzie, but I felt that it was more important to simply stick to the point of finding the lady, as once I've done so, the details can then be painted in.

"Naughton weighed my request for some minutes, a stern expression on his face as he did so. Then, without explanation, he told me to wait there in the mews, leading to the hotel. He was back in less than ten minutes, with instructions: I'm to be at the corner of Goulston Street and Whitechapel High Street tomorrow morning at eight. If all appears above-board, I'll be taken to a spot where more information will be revealed. Are you free to accompany me?"

179

The question was unexpected, but I indicated my agreement.

"Excellent. Be here at seven."

"Do you fear some sort of trap?" I asked.

"I always expect a trap, even if I don't fear it, but in this case, I doubt it. Rather, they are being especially careful, and while I don't know why, I sense that they have reason to be." He glanced at the clock and stood up. "I'm going back out. It pays to have as many cards in one's hand as possible, and a bit of further research into the Kilgores, along with whatever I can find about these 'True Ones', may prove to be invaluable."

"Do you think that my presence will prove to be objectionable?" I asked, rising as well, but Holmes stated that after all these years, it would be expected to have me at his side.

"In any case," he added, "if the lady or her protectors are fearful, your participation might serve to calm their nerves and do something toward gaining their trust. You are a most dependable fellow, Watson."

The following morning was overcast, but the heat remained. The air felt charged, as if a storm was brewing. There was a smell to the air, some warning for the deep and primitive part of the brain, carrying a message to stay close to shelter, for danger was near.

If Holmes felt it, it made no difference. He hurried me into the third hansom we found – after first confirming that I had my service revolver. That was how I knew he wasn't as calm as he might seem, for he knew that I'd long-ago learned to keep my weapon close at hand when venturing out anywhere. After so many years, we both had enemies.

As we drove east, Holmes was mostly silent, but he did explain that he'd been unable to find much else about the Kilgores or the "True Ones" since the night before. "When people truly keep to themselves," he explained, "it's difficult to find a way to breach their defenses. Hopefully we'll learn more this morning."

We were at the corner in central Whitechapel ten minutes before the appointed time, and we were still standing there at ten minutes after the hour as well. Holmes had done nothing to disguise himself, and he was wearing his noted fore-and-aft cap, making identification a certainty. From the time I'd known him, and from what I'd learned about his days long before that, he wore that had at all times, except when in disguise. Some have argued over the years that it had no place in the city, being a country hunting cap, but such thoughts had no validity or importance for Sherlock Holmes. Social convention didn't matter to him whatsoever. This was the same man who had once shot the Queen's initials into the sitting room wall with a hair-trigger target pistol – to the high consternation of our landlady. That someone would forcefully state that he was improperly wearing a country hat and expect Holmes to care was ludicrous and meant nothing. For him it was functional, but I also believe that there was some memory associated with that type of hat which made him choose it. And most of all, he liked it, the way some chaps prefer a bowler.

Whatever the reason, wearing that hat made Holmes recognizable when he wished to be recognized. After another five minutes, when I was beginning to believe that we hadn't passed muster and that we would learn nothing new, a tall fellow in his early twenties approached by way of a nearby alley, bringing with him a short matronly woman closer to Holmes and my ages. She was dressed practically, nothing showy, but rather functional in a plain way. The young man, who I assumed to be Naughton from Holmes's description and recognition, spoke, saying, "This is Mrs. *Smith*."

He nodded toward the woman, with just enough emphasis on her name to indicate that it was likely false – and also that the young man was not given to comfortably uttering falsehoods. The woman glanced at both of us and said, "Mr. Holmes. And Dr. Watson, I take it?" Then she looked us up and down for another minute before glancing around.

"You both seem to be alone. We've been watching to verify it, but I still must ask upon your word of honor: *Are you? Are you both alone?* If we take you with us, can you guarantee, as gentlemen, that we will not be followed afterwards?" Then she awaited her answer.

"I promise this," said Holmes.

"I do as well," I said, adding, "Upon my honor."

She nodded, appeared to take one more instant to fully decide, and then said, "Very well. Come with me. Michael, you stay behind, to keep an eye out and make sure that no one comes along after us." Then she turned and walked toward the alley from which they'd initially appeared, moving without any hurry, apparently to avoid any increased attention.

Once she led us away, she moved with direct purpose, showing no inclination to look back to make sure we were keeping up. We turned this way and that, moving deeper into the warren of streets. I had no doubt that Holmes knew just where were at during any given moment, but I was thoroughly lost. If it had been a sunny day, I might have beheld some clue from the morning shadows to tell me our direction, but in the dim light, growing dimmer with every moment as some sort of atmospheric crisis approached, the inconclusive morning dusk was no help at all.

Finally, we stopped at a door in the rear of some anonymous and dilapidated two-story building. I had no doubt that if I followed the alley in which we found ourselves far enough to one side or the other, I'd discover a passage that would take me through to a street where I could determine our address, but that wasn't why we were here. Mrs. Smith seemed to read my thoughts.

"It will do you no good to remember where this building is located when we're done," she said. "This is just a place we've arranged for today's meeting. We'll never return here, and the people who run it know nothing." Then she opened the heavy metal door, which was unlocked, as if prepared for us. "Follow me." And she went inside.

As the door closed firmly behind us, she paused for a moment while our eyes adjusted. We were at the foot of a stairway leading up to an open doorway above us on the first floor. The light spilling down was just enough for us to see where to place our feet. There were no other doors at the foot of the stairs. The entrance through which we passed had only one terminal point: The room to which we were now climbing.

I was surprised when we entered it to see that it was mounded with all sorts of cloth. The air had the smell of fabric, blended together with many dyes into a strong scent that weighed heavily and tickled one's nose. There were bolts of all sizes and hues, piled and stacked everywhere. Across the opposite side of the room were a number of tall windows, high enough to see both the upper floors of the buildings across the street and the sky above them, now quite dark with an approaching storm. Even as I watched, the first heavy drops of rain hit the glass.

The room was lit by four equally spaced lanterns. I was glad to see that they were carefully arranged to stay away from both the bolts of cloth, and the many scraps and threads and pieces of fabric that littered every inch of the wooden floor, and most of the tops of the four large tables that were spaced around the room. On top of each table, beside the lanterns, were several large pairs of shears, all well-aged and missing paint from the handles. Beside them were a number of long straight-edges and wide-leaded pencils, apparently used for lining out and measuring and marking the cloth.

But all of that was seen in an instant and then ignored as Mrs. Smith crossed the room, leaving us facing her, another elderly lady, and between them one of the most beautiful women I have ever encountered.

Katherine Kilgore, for certainly it was she, was just a few inches over five feet. She was wearing a plain blue dress that only accentuated her female charms, and highlighted the lovely and healthy tone of her skin. Her face was round, and while her nose might not have been classically shaped, it fit perfectly with the arch of her dark brows, her wide-set and direct-gazing eyes, and the bow of her lips. All of this was framed by the richest and darkest red hair I've ever seen, worn loose and down to her shoulders. In that rough and unswept setting, the room seemed to rearrange itself around her, and her presence was made more dramatic by the high

182

windows which framed her, illuminating from the rear with the odd light of the coming storm.

My first impression was of the woman herself, and the striking beauty which had not been conveyed to us as a factor in the case. Then I saw two other things: One was that she had a terribly sad expression that, once noticed, could not be unseen, and which colored the perception of the rest of her. I was moved upon instinct alone to feel that she needed my help, and that I was the only one who could provide it. It was a unique effect, and I wondered if Holmes noticed it too.

The other thing that came to my attention, as my focus returned to the room around us, was that the elderly lady to Katherine Kilgore's right, opposite Mrs. Smtih, was someone that I recognized – a woman from one of Holmes's cases in the early 1880's who we had rescued from an abusive husband. She saw that I knew her, and she shared a small secret smile at my understanding, but then she shook her head, as if to say that I shouldn't acknowledge her previous troubles, or even speak to identify her. Somehow I knew from that look that she was telling me today's meeting should concern only the troubles of the younger woman at her side. I barely nodded that I understood as Holmes began to speak.

"Mrs. Kilgore," he began, and even from a distance of ten feet, it was obvious that the woman winced with discomfort upon hearing that name. "We appreciate that you have come from your place of hiding to speak with us. I want to assure you that Watson and I are not here to find you for your husband, or to drag you back. Neither of us have ever spoken with him, and he doesn't know that we're acting in the matter. Rather, we were asked by a representative of the Government to find where you were, so that the documents you removed from your husband's safe can be retrieved." He paused for a few seconds, and then continued. "However, whatever my original intention was in that direction, I perceive that you need my assistance – our assistance. Are you willing to share with us your story? So that we might understand, and see what can be done?"

Mrs. Kilgore looked at Mrs. Smith, and then the woman beside her, as if to see if they had any advice or opinion to offer, but all she received was a small nod from the latter. Then she looked back at us, weighing the decision as if she were considering the wisdom of taking a step off a cliff. Finally, with a sigh, she spoke, her voice rich and low and tinged with heavy weariness.

"May we sit?" she asked. "My story – what I have to tell you will take a few minutes."

We all moved to arrange some of the work stools, the two camps facing one another but still separated, as if attending a wary negotiation. I could see that even though we were trusted to a certain degree, it was not absolute, and that Mrs. Smith and the other woman, whom I shall call *Mrs. Jones*, were both tense and alert, as if they might need to spring into action at any signs of treachery in order to hustle Mrs. Kilgore away to safety, should Holmes and I prove untrustworthy after all.

It was only Holmes's reputation that had earned this meeting, but their well-earned distrust of men in general, as we were to find out, overwhelmed any other goodwill.

"You must understand," began Mrs. Kilgore, "that I knew very little about anything of the world when my parents died. I've had a good education. I'm curious and well-read and keep up with the news, but in terms of real life – ? I knew that my parents were wealthy, but I didn't know how wealthy. I still don't. Men that I didn't know managed their affairs before their deaths, lawyers and accountants and supervisors and foreman, and they continued to do so after. I meandered through my days in ignorant bliss, and when they died, I was told where to go and what to sign, and then I was told that I was to be married – a business arrangement to blend two fortunes.

"Brian – my husband . . . It was already arranged that I would marry him by the time I met him. I was . . . it was medieval – in so many ways. I know that now – " She turned to look at Mrs. Smith, who patted her hand. "But I knew no better, and I married him, and only after did I meet his family. Then I was swept to London and placed into a fine house with servants who did whatever I asked – as long as that was no more than choosing what I wanted to eat, or which dress to lay out for the day. But the servants had come down from Essex, and had been with the Kilgore family for their whole lives, as had their parents before them, and it didn't take long for me to realize that I was now part of something most peculiar, and far beyond my small experience."

She was silent for a moment, as if considering how to proceed. Both of the older women watched her intently, but she didn't glance at either of them, instead marshalling her thoughts to continue.

"Since you've found me," she finally said, "then you must know something about the Kilgores by now – the facts, the history. The fame of Lord Benton, and all that he accomplished so many years ago. He still gets by on the credit that he earned as a great man in past generations. I've learned all of this as the dutiful wife, educated about the family into which I was abruptly placed. Lord Benton, Brian's father, is a famed man – or so I've been told. I'd never heard of him until just before I was married. Have you met him? No? In person, he's terrifying. I found him so from the very beginning, and that was just a fraction of the terror I feel now . . . now that I know. He is nearly eighty years old, but he still has the size and vitality of a man half that age. He's tall and broad – much taller than Brian, his only child – and he has long white unkempt hair and a thick and tangled white beard. His fierce dark eyes are always angry, glaring out from under low and tangled white brows, and when he speaks, it's with the rumble of some dark raging Biblical patriarch bringing down God's curses from a mountaintop. His view of life . . . his view is one of rage and punishment and vengeance. I gather that he was once a person of great influence, but viewpoints changed and left him behind, and for that he's become much more bitter and hateful than when he was younger.

"He . . . Brian told me of his father's wives, how Lord Benton waited until middle-age to marry, and that his first wife was too weak to survive much past Brian's birth. Brian has always been a disappointment to his father. Smaller, less forceful. In spite of Brian's many successes, he has not impressed his father. And Brian . . . he might not have been a bad man, on his own, but he never had the spine to stand up to his father. Or the True Ones.

"Brian . . . Ah, Brian. He is so weak. In spite of our age difference, he and I have grown closer than I would have thought. We are confidantes in a way, but not like a true man and wife. He's never mistreated me, not once. No, it's his weakness that doesn't let him defend me."

She swallowed and took a deep breath, and I had an inkling that what was to follow would be even more disturbing than I'd expected.

"When I first met Brian, he was distant, awkward. I soon realized that he didn't want to marry me any more than I wanted to marry him. He was told to do so by his father, so he did it. I don't love him, and he doesn't love me, even now that we've known each other for five years, but he can talk with me, a luxury something that he never had before. After we married, he began to share things with me, gradually revealing the life in which I was now plunged. About the True Ones.

"That's what his father, Lord Benton, calls them – his followers. That's what they call themselves. I see that you've heard of them – or at least that you've heard that phrase. Does it mean anything to you? No? Then I must explain them, or the rest of the story – of why I had to escape – will have no meaning.

"Lord Benton . . . he is a deeply religious man, very knowledgeable of the Bible and other ancient texts after a lifetime of intense study. But what he believes, supposedly associated with the Christian God, has very little to do with Christianity. The only part of the New Testament that he favors are the times in Jesus' ministry where punishment was a factor – such as when Jesus took a whip and chased the moneychangers from the Temple. Lord Benton looks upon other aspects of Christ's teachings as degenerate puniness. Love for the hurt and injured is just weakness and moral failure. Compassion? He feels that the weak and downtrodden don't deserve it, and that Jesus was a fool to instruct us to care for the poor.

"He favors the Old Testament, and the God of bitter vengeance and harsh punishment, instead of forgiveness and tolerance. According to Brian, this was molded by events in his life. As Lord Benton's influence grew within the government, he seemed to be unable to find what he wanted in his personal life. His first wife produced Brian, who he has always considered unworthy. Then she died, and he remarried several other times – and these women died young as well, all too soon and before they could produce another heir. By then, Lord Benton had used his influence to set Brian up on a path to success, but already Lord Benton's own star was falling, and that only made him more bitter. He retreated to his estate in High Roding and began to brood – that, and to fall deeper and deeper into his twisted Biblical studies.

"He began to formulate his own interpretations, and to share them with those around him – preaching to the captive servants who had been in the family for generations, and who were beholden to him with nowhere else to go, and who were overwhelmed by his certainty and his forceful and dramatic presence. With no one to tell them different, Lord Benton's beliefs took root, reinforced with each succeeding generation. His estate became more and more isolated, as he convinced everyone within it that they were following the only path toward salvation, as interpreted by him, while the world outside was racing toward irredeemable sin and destruction. But inside the estate, under the guidance and teachings of Lord Benton, they would be safe, following the truth. His truth. They would be the *True Ones*.

"He allowed Brian to remain in public life, and to live in London, feeling that he would be Lord Benton's agent, fixed in a place to affect public policy in the directions Lord Benton wishes it to go. Brian is completely under his father's thumb, and any State secret to which Brian has access is immediately shared with his father. Heaven only knows what the old man does with them, but he has remained in contact with people that he knew during his own public career – foreign diplomats from countries who are no longer friendly to Britain, but who take the time to curry Lord Benton's good will so that he will gullibly share information. They recognize him for what he is, an old fool, but they tell him what he wants to hear.

"Brian knows all of this – he himself is no fool, and he's seen it time and time again. And he's told me, and it has frustrated him to no end, but there's nothing that he can do about it, nor is he willing to oppose it. I listened as Brian shared all of these things, dutiful as I supposed that I should be, but for the longest time none of it meant anything to me – none of it seemed real or important. But then . . . Lord Benton began to take an interest in *me*!"

She swallowed, and Mrs. Smith patted her hand once again. She then left her hand in place, squeezing lightly. Katherine Kilgore seemed to have reached the crux of her story – the turning point that I already dreaded without knowing any of the terrible details.

"Brian and I have been married for five years," she finally said, her voice even lower and strained, "and we have yet to produce an heir to what Lord Benton considers his *dynasty*." She said it with distaste. "It . . . it became more and more of an issue, to the point . . . to the point . . . ."

It was here that Katherine Kilgore fell completely silent, unable to relate what happened next. But she had already told Mrs. Smith, who took over, quietly filling in the next part of the story.

"Are you gentlemen aware of the ancient custom of *prima nocta*?"

Holmes and I were silent, both struck dumb with simple shock at the implications of what had just been introduced into the conversation. When we nodded, Mrs. Smith stated, "Lord Benton has exercised that right. Repeatedly, declaring his son to have failed him, and casting him aside. Lord Benton has inflicted himself upon Katherine, and now she is with child – Lord Benton's child. She is to be the mother of her own husband's half-brother. She did not reveal to her husband or her father-in-law that she has been impregnated. Instead, she chose to flee."

"They do not know," Katherine whispered. "If Lord Benton finds out, and he gains control of my baby . . . ."

This information was staggering. In just a few moments, we had gone from hearing how the innocent girl found herself literally sold into marriage with an older stranger, and how a respected elder statesman had transfigured himself into the leader of his own harsh cult while sharing State secrets with foreign powers, all with the collusion of his spineless but also well-respected son. But the implications of this outrage upon the gentle and helpless woman now before us was too harsh to imagine. I realized that my fists were clenched in rage, and forced myself to loosen them and breathe deeply, as that anger had no place in that current setting. But I could find it again when needed – and I would find a way to make use of it soon. This I promised to myself.

Glancing at Holmes, I found that his jaw was clenched, and his lips so tight that they had vanished, leaving a thin white line. He nodded, as if understanding.

"As you know," he said, his tone low and steady but vibrating still with a kind of electric menace, "I spoke with Lizzie Boles, who told me how she came to London to be with you, Mrs. Kilgore, and how she worked with Michael Naughton to arrange for your escape." He looked toward Mrs. Smith. "I assume that he asked around until he found you and your group. He knew enough to gain your interest, and you decided that you could trust him. Then you worked to make safe arrangements for when Mrs. Kilgore managed to leave."

Mrs. Smith nodded. "I and some other women operate an organization for abused women – helping to spirit them away, and hide them, and find new lives for them. There are a number of us, more than you know, with many well-placed to accomplish our work. We move in secrecy, and most of us have been abused ourselves, so we understand how a woman feels in that situation – the helplessness, and the anger, and the desperation most of all. We understand, and we have learned how to do what needs to be done. Working in the shadows as we do, we can bring pressure to bear. I'm not ashamed to say that we use blackmail and coercion and threates when necessary to force the abusive men – usually husbands – to provide funds, and to release their wives from their bondage.

"Michael Naughton had passed a message to Mrs. Kilgore, by way of Lizzy, to bring what she could to help with any coercion that might be necessary. When I saw what she'd carried away – government documents of the greatest importance – I'll confess that I was a bit intimidated. These weren't simply letters or diaries filled, as we usually receive, with embarrassing accounts of men's nasty secrets that can be used as leverage. No, we had something far more weighty in our hands – and dangerous. Far too much for us. Frankly, I wasn't sure what to do, and it was almost a relief to find that you were inquiring about the matter, Mr. Holmes, for we wish to put the documents into your hands and be done with them.

"But the question that still must be asked is: Will that be the end of your involvement? Will you return the documents to the proper authorities, and then step away? I know you are too honorable to try and drag Mrs. Kilgore back to her husband and that wicked family – more wicked still than you yet know – but will you do anything else to help? Will you stand up to this evil, and help put a stop to it?"

If Holmes hadn't replied immediately, I would have, but he spoke for both us by saying, quietly and decisively, "Of course we will put a stop to it."

Mrs. Smith nodded firmly. "Good. Good. Then there's more that you need to know." And then she proceeded to relate what else she had learned, both from Katherine Kilgore, and then by way of her own subsequent investigations, once she knew where to look and what questions to ask.

"Over the last twenty years or so, as Lord Benton Kilgore has entrenched himself deeper and deeper into his own self-based religion – for that's what it's become – he has apparently come to believe that he is something between an Old Testament Prophet and the Hand of God. His

188

bizarre sect consists of forty or fifty people, all living on his estate, and becoming more insular by the year. If he wasn't passing government secrets to foreign powers, he and those who follow him would probably only be hurting themselves, for they don't recruit, and they don't go forth and rain violence on their neighbors. Yet the harm he's doing to those who follow him is a just as much of a crime as if he has attacked his neighbors – a crime against society. Even if those in his cult are willing participants, it cannot be allowed to continue. You see . . . this is difficult to say and hear, gentlemen . . . Mrs. Kilgore is not the only victim of Lord Benton's exercise of *prima nocta*. Any woman on the estate, within the influence of his self-declared kingdom, is subject to the same violations. Women, teenage girls. Even . . . even children . . . ."

At that, Katherine Kilgore spoke, the last words I would hear her say: "I fear . . . I am afraid . . . that if I stay – that if he finds me – and if I have a daughter, that she too might be . . . She might be . . . That her own grandfather would . . . ."

More need not be related, although there was more, much worse, to be heard before we had finally seen the true portrait of Lord Benton Kilgore. When Mrs. Smith was finished relating all that she had learned, she looked at Katherine Kilgore, who simply nodded that it was all true. Meanwhile, Mrs. Jones quietly wept, overcome by the terrible visions that had been painted for us.

At the conclusion of our discussion, Katherine Kilgore handed us the missing government documents. Holmes promised that the situation would be "cleaned up" in a suitable fashion, and quickly.

"Best you don't worry about the details," he said. "It's time that a little Old Testament Justice be visited upon a certain blighted spot in Essex."

We thanked the three women, and they turned to leave, asking that we allow them some time to depart safely before we went back downstairs. As they walked past us to the door, Katherine Kilgore looked up and nodded toward us. Her eyes locked with mine, for only a second. It was a connection of some sort, one person to another, but if she was trying to convey a message, none that I could understand passed between us – nothing except, perhaps, an infinite sadness at what she had been forced to endure at such a young age. Then, with almost an imperceptible nod, she turned away and passed through the door.

I never saw her again, and can only hope she and her unborn child, with the aid of Mrs. Smith and Mrs. Jones and their able band of like-minded women, found the good life that they both deserved.

Holmes and I waited ten minutes before descending. No doubt the ladies had hurriedly vanished within seconds, but I think that both of us, so lost in our dark thoughts, were in no hurry to precipitously rush forth.

Perhaps if we had, we would have been able to be in a cab and on our way by the time the impending storm was fully unleashed. As it was, the rain was well and truly falling when we reached nearby Liverpool Street Station, where we were fortunately able to hail a hansom almost immediately.

"Whitehall," said Holmes in a clipped tone, providing the address of Mycroft's office.

We settled into motion, and I could only pity the poor driver and his beast as the torrent dropped upon them. I thought about discussing what we'd heard, but the rain was too loud, and in any case, I could see that Holmes was deep in thought, the recovered papers clutched protectively under his Inverness.

As quickly as the violence of the rains had started, it rolled away, and the heat of the late June day enveloped us again before we reached our destination. The pavement steamed, and suddenly I felt as if I were back in the tropics. I was glad to reach our destination, the massive governmental structure where Mycroft Holmes's office was located. Inside it was cool, and soon we were ushered in to Mycroft's sanctum.

If Holmes's brother was surprised at the quick return of the Kilgore documents, he didn't show it. He was quite matter-of-fact, and seemed ready to perfunctorily thank us and then return to whatever was occupying his time, showing no interest in how the pages had been recovered. But Sherlock Holmes was not ready to be dismissed, and proceeded to insist on relating what we had learned from Katherine Kilgore.

Mycroft listened without speaking, his level gaze devolving into a scowl.

"I won't ask if you're certain," he said, "for it's the unsubstantiated testimony of one woman who feels that she is wronged, supported by two anonymous ladies who run a shadowy organization ostensibly dedicated to taking the side of other wronged women."

I started to protest, but Mycroft raised his hand. "Hold, Doctor. I'm not saying that I don't believe you. This actually explains a good deal about how certain information has been leaking to both our enemies and our friends. This path has not been considered, and if it's true, it's easily verified – and fixed."

"But the women?" I said. "And the children! What of that crime?"

Mycroft's lips tightened. "You know the age of consent in this country, Doctor, and how hard it is to prove something when relying on testimony of people like Lord Benton's followers, who don't believe that

190

what he's doing is wrong, and wouldn't give him up to the law in any case."

Even as I started to cry out about the injustice, Mycroft and Sherlock Holmes both began speaking at the same time, each talking over the other.

"However," said Mycroft, "I hold a great deal of discretionary power to – "

"If you don't do something about this," growled Sherlock Holmes, "then I will be forced to – "

They stopped and looked at one another, their thoughts communicating back and forth faster than I could follow. Then Sherlock Holmes nodded. "How can we help?" he asked.

"Be at Liverpool Street Station at six o'clock. Armed, and in dark clothing. Sadly, daylight comes late this time of year, but my men will simply have to be more careful not to be seen while they fix the nets. You say there are fifty people at the Kilgore compound?"

"Approximately. So we were told."

"Then I'll have a special train made up accordingly to bring them all back to London for interrogation. Ostensibly, this is an espionage investigation directed toward Lord Benton, but our interrogators will certainly be on the lookout for other crimes."

I had more questions, and I'm sure that Holmes did as well, but we were dismissed, and so went to make preparations for our Essex campaign.

The special train from London to Chelmsford took seventy minutes. Mycroft had made sure that it had priority. There were five cars, but during the down trip, two were empty, to be used later when the entire population of Lord Benton Kilgore's estate, the "True Ones", were rounded up a brought back to London. The rest of the cars held a combination of Mycroft's agents and soldiers who would do what they were told, providing security while the agents sought evidence of Lord Benton's treachery and perversion. The interviews with the believers would scrape loose the additional charges.

Joining us was Michael Naughton, whom Holmes had gone out to find not long after we'd returned to Baker Street. The young man didn't say anything, other than to nod when he saw me, and none of Mycroft's men questioned Holmes about an addition to the troops.

At Chelmsford, we found dozens of cabs, wagons, carriages, and even vehicles borrowed from the nearby prison, all waiting to carry us swiftly north, the ten miles or so to High Roding, which straddled the road to Grand Dunmow. We never entered the village proper, however, before we veered east onto a narrow farm road, which the local driver on the lead cab assured us would run directly to the Kilgore lands. This was swiftly proven

191

correct as we approached a great wall which led off in each direction. The road took us to a closed gate, which seemed to be unguarded. On the wrought-iron archway which spanned it from side to side, worked into the design, was the word *Naqam.*

"'*Vengeance*' in Hebrew," whispered Holmes. He gave one of his silent laughs which always boded ill for someone. "A word he'll understand after tonight!"

All of the wagons pulled to a stop, dozens of them, lined up behind us. Except for the whickering of horses and the occasional small ring of metalwork upon the tackle, or the soft landing of many man climbing down and taking formation, there was no sound. Even when the lock on the gate was cut, I heard nothing. Then the men slid by us like dark ghosts, infiltrating the grounds and vanishing into the darkening gloom.

I realized that Michael Naughton was not with us. Apparently he had gone on ahead.

Over the next fifteen or twenty minutes, with occasional outbursts of yelling or indination, the occupants of the estate were rounded up – men, women, and children. All that we found were servants of all levels – farmers, grooms, household cooks and maids, footmen and a butler of sorts. As Holmes and I moved among the various searches that were occurring throughout the house, we saw that Mycroft's men were accumulating quite a haul of documents that had no business being there. They had been left unsecured on Lord Benton's desk, and his night table, and in less-likely spots throughout the house. This was an egregious violation of the Official Secrets Act of the previous year, and I couldn't help but wonder if the presence of so many secret documents at this location, without any sort of permission, wasn't a capital offense. It turned out that it was.

Our search found the other evidence we sought, and members of the True Ones as well – some of whom were already ranting about their religious mania as if it were a defense against their seizure. All that we couldn't find was Lord Benton Kilgore.

It wasn't until all of the discovered documents and the estate staff were being loaded for the return to Chelmsford, where further questioning would begin, that we saw Michael Naughton walking toward us from the darkness behind the great house. He had his hand on what appeared to be a tall woman, shuffling along in a long dress, a bonnet pulled up over her head and a scarf wrapped over her lower face. She would occasionally fight him or try and pull away, and Naughton would stop, cuffing her on the head with a riding crop until she resumed walking. As they approached, I could hear her deep voice cursing, an unceasing litany of offenses and promised punishments.

Holmes stepped forward and ripped off the bonnet and scarf, and when Lord Benton – for it was he – lurched forward as if he was going to attack, still spewing forth his venom, I stretched forth my arm, showing him my service revolver, aimed toward his head.

"Be quiet," I stated, carefully enunciating, but it only made the old man curse all the more. He was a curious specimen – tall and fat, probably close to three-hundred pounds, his eyes red and pig-like, his white hair long and unkempt, and his unnatural carrot-tinted skin reflective of a lifetime of bilious and wicked habits.

My command to silence himself only served to make the repulsive old man angrier, and he lurched toward me in a rage. I swung my pistol, ensuring that he went to the gallows without most of his teeth.

"You've killed him," breathed one of Mycroft's men, standing nearby, shocked and staring down at the fallen man. The others pretended to look elsewhere.

I bent to check, and Kilgore was still breathing. But not for too much longer.

The damage that Kilgore had already caused by his indiscreet dissemination of information was severe, but it would have been much worse had some of the documents provided by his son been given to agents of other countries. That was enough to bring about a quiet capital conviction of espionage and treason. His son received the same sentence, and I could feel no sorrow for him either, as he'd known what he was doing, even if he'd been too weak to resist his father's influence.

In consideration for his efforts, and how this successfully concluded investigation did so much to prevent any number of security disasters, Holmes was offered a knighthood – not for the first time. And like the other occasions when he'd had no use for it, he quickly turned it down. "Art for art's sake," he told Mycroft and me when the subject came up. "And in any case, should I ever choose to accept such an honor, I wouldn't want it to be in association with this seamy affair. I'd never be able to hear of it without being reminded of that vile old sinner's terrible crimes."

Of more importance – at least in my opinion – was that it didn't take very long for one member, and then another, of the evil man's congregation to turn and reveal the terrible activities that had been going on at the remote estate. I was reminded of Holmes's dictum from the previous year that the smiling and beautiful countryside had a much more dreadful record of sin than the vilest London alleys. "Look at these lonely houses," he'd told me as we passed through a remote area, watching the lovely scene outside our train window. "Each in its own fields, filled for the most part with poor ignorant folk who know little of the law. Think of the deeds of hellish cruelty, the hidden wickedness which may go on, year in, year out, in such places, and none the wiser."

And none had been the wiser – at least for the longest time – about what was occurring at that remote estate outside of High Roding. If not for the courage of Katherine Kilgore, finally forced to engineer her escape to protect an unborn child, how much more horror would have been visited upon those foolish people who had been convinced to submit to Kilgore's vile passions so that they could arrogantly and stupidly consider themselves the "True Ones"?

"Some of my most interesting cases have come to me in this way through Mycroft."

– Sherlock Holmes
"The Greek Interpreter"

"It is my belief, Watson, founded upon my experience, that the lowest and vilest alleys in London do not present a more dreadful record of sin than does the smiling and beautiful countryside."

"You horrify me!"

"But the reason is very obvious. The pressure of public opinion can do in the town what the law cannot accomplish. There is no lane so vile that the scream of a tortured child, or the thud of a drunkard's blow, does not beget sympathy and indignation among the neighbours, and then the whole machinery of justice is ever so close that a word of complaint can set it going, and there is but a step between the crime and the dock. But look at these lonely houses, each in its own fields, filled for the most part with poor ignorant folk who know little of the law. Think of the deeds of hellish cruelty, the hidden wickedness which may go on, year in, year out, in such places, and none the wiser."

– Sherlock Holmes and Dr. John H. Watson
"The Copper Beeches"

NOTES:

Droit du seigneur, also known as *prima noctis* or *ius primae noctis*, was a supposed legal right in medieval Europe wherein feudal lords were allowed to have sexual relations with subordinate women, in particular on the wedding nights of the women.

Of related interest: Back in the 1980's and 1990's, in my previous life as a U.S. Federal Investigator employed with a small little-known agency that's long since been closed, I investigated two cases that had some coincidental similarity to this matter. The first began as a routine background check to update the security clearance of a man whose wife had left him. Digging deeper, I found that he had some decidedly squirrelly and abusive habits, including cleanliness phobias carried to the extreme. When I finally tracked the man's wife down to interview her, it was on the condition that she be accompanied by two anonymous women who ran a local organization that was keeping her hidden, for fear of retribution from her husband. I was lucky to get permission to speak with her at all, and the interview was carried out in the neutral territory of the upstairs floor of a sewing company on a stormy day.

The other case involved renewing the security clearance of an old man who had worked in the nuclear defense industry since the days of the Manhattan Project. He was extremely religious, and considered himself to be an amateur preacher who lived with his massive extended family on a farm/compound in a highly rural area. Investigation revealed that he was a child molester of the absolute worst type, having convinced all of those who were under his cult-like sway that he had the right to rape any of the women that lived there, including his own daughters and granddaughters.

There is evil in the world. As Holmes knew, there is hellish cruelty and hidden wickedness all around us, year in, year out, and none the wiser.

195

The Exploited Assassins

"But Mr. Holmes," cried Dr. Clayton Walker-Baird, the noted physician, "what if he actually *did* kill the Queen?"

When the doctor arrived at our Baker Street rooms just fifteen minutes earlier, he'd been the same calm and steady man I'd known for over five years. Now, however, he had worked himself up into something of a frenzy – or as much as someone like him could ever become frenzied.

I was returning from Camberwell, where I'd gone to see my newly intended bride, Miss Mary Morstan, at the home where she was a governess for the Forresters. We had much to discuss regarding our planned marriage, and the time we'd shared had raced by. Mrs. Forrester, much in favor of the match, had made a merry lunch for us, and it had been a most enjoyable mid-day excursion. I have some recollection that the weather that day was actually dark and wet and chill, but after visiting with Mary, my heart was light and had no room for such perceptions. Thus, finding Dr. Walker-Baird on our doorstep had been rather jarring, pulling me back from my pleasant contemplations to that world where men and women of all walks found their way to Holmes's door, seeking solutions to their problems.

Walker-Baird had just arrived and was reaching for the bell, and his waiting carriage was standing nearby. He was a stocky man, around forty, with thinning sandy hair and a forward-pushing curvature at his middle. He had always been typically pleasant, and willing to tease in a friendly manner, yet one sensed he could turn offensive under certain circumstances. I had never seen him behave that way, or heard of it from anyone else, but it was still a feeling that I had about him. He seemed surprised to see me as I joined him at the door, and even more so when I explained that I shared lodgings with Holmes, with whom he was there to consult.

"Ha ha!" he said. "That should serve as a reminder that I ought to consider beyond the surface. After seeing you occasionally at Barts, I solely associate you with the hospital, without considering that you have a life elsewhere." He shook his head. "Ha ha! Education never ends."

He wasn't the first to say so.

As I unlocked the door, I reflected that Walker-Baird had always been a rather scattered fellow, although he was an excellent physician. His duties crossed all aspects of society, and when he was younger he could have locked himself into the finest Harley Street practice, but to his credit, he always made time for some of the hospitals where charitable efforts were most needed and appreciated.

Upstairs, I introduced Walker-Baird to Holmes and then made to excuse myself, but Holmes waved me toward my chair, explaining that, "Watson has been a most useful confidant in many of my cases." He made the statement as if there was no debate as to whether I would remain, and Dr. Walker-Baird nodded abstractedly as I handed him a whisky.

"Sir James Saunders said that I should speak with you," he began. Any calmness he'd carried in with him was starting to fray as the time approached to tell us why he was there.

Holmes nodded politely. "I've been of some assistance to Sir James once or twice in the past."

"So he told me, although he didn't provide any details . . . ." He left it hanging, apparently waiting for Holmes to happily babble forth just how he had been of service, as if he were interviewing for a job, but my friend simply maintained his sphinx-like expression, allowing the silence to uncomfortably grow. It was a technique of his that I've also used in my medical practice, wherein the other person feels compelled to fill the empty quiet. Walker-Baird frowned, shifted in the basket chair, took another sip, and then realized that it was his move.

"I was initially against involving outsiders," he continued, "but I didn't know who to approach. The two policemen acted most suspiciously in the matter, and Sir James – he convinced me that instead of first going to the authorities, you might provide some insight."

Holmes still didn't speak, but rather made a small motion with his fingers, similar to beckoning a wary dog to approach, indicating that the doctor should continue. I could see that he was becoming fractionally impatient with Walker-Baird's rather imprecise approach to the purpose of his visit.

"It's about a patient, you see," explained the doctor. He seemed to stop short, as if recalling something important he'd only now thought to consider. He leaned forward, his voice dropping. "Sir James assures me that your work is confidential," he said tentatively, as if wishing to avoid offense.

Holmes nodded. "You need have no fears on that account. This patient . . . ?"

"Yes, yes. At first, there was nothing special about him, but then – Ah, but there must be something special, or I wouldn't be here, now would I? He was brought in by the police – a pair of constables. He'd been captured by them and had sustained a few superficial injuries. Yet, for some reason, they landed him at Barts, when there were closer hospitals.

197

Then, when the patient finally spoke, and began to explain what had happened – what he said he'd done – "

Holmes raised a hand. "You're telling it out of all order, Doctor. What is the man's name?"

Walker-Baird nodded and cleared his throat, intending to concentrate. He sat upright and looked straight ahead, as if he were a student reciting his lesson. "Fowler. Boyd Fowler. He's a Scotsman – at least he seems to be, based on his accent and his address. He looked to be in his mid-thirties – about your age, I expect. Tall and thin – like you, Mr. Holmes, but with bigger hands, and his features show his Pictish heritage. A rough fellow – callosities upon his hands, very worn clothing, hair a bit ragged, but not too long past his most recent haircut. He seems to be a taciturn fellow – And truth-be-told, he didn't say anything at all when I first examined him, but as I questioned him while treating his wounds, he suddenly began to speak – and that's when he said he'd just killed the Queen."

When Walker-Baird finally got to the point of his visit, mentioned with no more initial emphasis than if had been another feature of Fowler's description, it surprised us both. Holmes and I glanced at one another, his gaze asking me if Walker-Baird might be delusional – an action that didn't go unobserved by the doctor. He nodded, as if he'd achieved the desired effect.

"Yes, that's what he said. It seems that he'd received his various injuries – a deep slice on his inner forearm, as well as other superficial cuts and bruises on his face, hands, and forearms, after shooting Her Majesty while she was on a carriage ride through one of the parks near the Palace earlier today." He stopped speaking, looking from one of us to the other as we considered the terrible news he'd just shared.

I couldn't believe it – that our Queen, who had been on the throne for over half-a-century, and who had celebrated her Golden Jubilee just the previous year, was *dead*! No, I thought. It was impossible. She couldn't be gone. It was too sudden. Too unthinkable.

Holmes was frowning, but he evidently didn't believe the story. Now sitting forward on his chair, looking intently at our visitor, he said, "Again, Doctor – I beg that you begin at the beginning."

Walker-Baird nodded, apparently realizing the shock of what he'd just told us.

"Sometime before lunch – around 11:30 – the patient was brought in for treatment, in the custody of a two constables. I was making rounds in the ward when I looked up and saw one of the nurses directing them and the patient to an empty bed. As I approached, I noticed that the prisoner was wearing manacles, and I asked that they be removed, but the officers refused. They both seemed rather agitated, but I assumed that it was related to the events of the arrest. I asked if the prisoner had been violent, or if I needed to summon a couple of orderlies, but the older constable shook his head. 'He's been quiet ever since we took him.'

"I nodded, uninterested in the details of the arrest. The younger officer took up station facing the greater room, his back to us, while the other, staying with the prisoner, pulled a curtain around the bed to prevent anyone from seeing what was happening during the examination. The ward was quite busy this morning, and I was working alone – which was unfortunate, considering what soon happened. I began to examine the patient, and as I mentioned, he had a deep cut on his forearm, a slice that had opened a small vein, making quite a bloody mess. Additionally, his clothing was torn, and his face, hands, and arms had fresh bruises, cuts, and abrasions."

"Of what sort?" asked Holmes. "As if he had been in a fight? Defending himself? Or possibly of the sort one might get when fleeing?"

"I see what you're saying," nodded Walker-Baird. "I would definitely say that they were of the latter nature, and that fits with his story. I was soon told that he'd run through brush while escaping, and the signs fit his wounds. General scrapes and cuts upon his face, and the front and backs of his hands. His clothing was somewhat torn and roughed as well, and in places his sleeves had apparently been pushed back, leading to additional similar cuts upon his wrist and forearms. Besides that, he winced sometimes as he moved, as if his body was sore as well, but upon examination, there were no wounds or bruises apart from those I've mentioned.

"The patient's name was Boyd Fowler, seemingly confirmed by a letter I found in his coat pocket, addressed to Boyd Fowler at Eunan Farm, in Aboyne. At that point in the examination, he was unaware of his surroundings, and didn't question me when I removed it. Almost immediately, it was snatched from my hand by the older constable."

I saw Holmes nod to himself, and asked why.

"Possibly no reason. But Aboyne is about fifteen or twenty miles east of Balmoral."

I nodded, trying not to show my surprise at this obscure fact stored in my friend's brain attic. I knew that he carried a well-earned and curated encyclopedic knowledge of the capital, but that he also knew a great deal of obscure British and Scottish villages, as well as their spatial location and distance from other sites, was yet another of his gifts that I often neglected to recall.

"You see a significance?" I asked. "You think that is the connection with the Queen?"

He shook his head. "It is simply a factor to keep in mind. Please continue, Doctor."

Walker-Baird nodded. "As I said, when I pulled out the letter, the constable snatched it from me, and he seemed most peeved when I tried using the man's name to get a reaction – without any initial success. He was nearly catatonic.

"Normally I don't see patients very much anymore. My duties have extended in an administrative direction. But I was taking a shift today – to keep my hand in, you understand," he added in an aside to me. I acknowledged it, and he continued. "It was a routine treatment, as I used to see when I was a young doctor working in the clinics and hospitals on Friday and Saturday nights. The cut on his arm had been rudely bandaged with a piece of tied cloth, clearly the missing piece torn from Fowler's shirt, and a tight splint in the form of a stick had been applied. The constable acknowledged that he'd had sense enough to do that. Although the rag was soaked with blood, the bleeding had essentially stopped. After disinfecting and numbing it, I started stitching him up. Fowler had no reaction – he simply faced forward as if nothing were happening, his eyes wide and gazing into the distance. I began to wonder if he'd been medicated before his arrival. I might have suspected that he was drunk, but there were no indications of alcohol use upon him, and he didn't seem as if he were sleepy or disoriented. He sat straight, his eyes focused on the curtain pulled round his bed.

"As I worked, I asked Fowler the typical chatter – questions like 'How did this happen?' and so on – but the patient made no response whatsoever. Then I repeated the same questions to the constable, who was nearly as unforthcoming as the patient.

"'He was fleeing from us,' was his limited response. 'Getting away from us, too, until he cut through a hedge. Got stuck – forced his way out the other side. That's where we were waiting. We got him, but he fought back. He has the cuts from the bushes – including that slice on his arm – and the bruises from where he resisted arrest.'

"'Where did this occur?' I asked, simply making vague conversation at that point while I worked, as the location of the arrest made no difference to the treatment.

"The constable stated, 'Hyde Park.' Then he seemed irritated, as if he'd said more than he meant to.

"I frowned. 'That's quite a distance from Barts. It seems like a bit of extra effort to bring a prisoner this far for such minor injuries. Didn't you consider a closer hospital – Charing Cross, perhaps?'

"The constable shook his head. 'We thought best to keep things discreet – so as not to attract too much interest.'

"'I wonder why,' I said, half to myself, for as yet there was nothing special about this patient or his injuries. 'Well, Barts is certainly out of the way,' I muttered, simply making another comment, but that seemed to finally raise Fowler's interest.

"'Barts?' he asked, his voice dry and raspy, as if he hadn't used it for quite a while. It was then that I heard his marked Scottish accent. 'I've been here before," he muttered, his eyes blinking and now looking around – at me, and the constable, and his surroundings. 'Just a month ago.' Then, after a pause and clearing his throat, he added, 'Late August.' He licked his lips. 'Was it August? What month is it now?'

"'September,' I replied, even as I pondered his words. That he had previously been to Barts interested me, but I also noticed that the constable frowned, significantly this time, his body tensing as if he were concerned. And that was a fact that he wished the prisoner hadn't mentioned. He shifted as if he were coiling in order to physically stop Fowler from speaking. Rather than comment upon it, however, and risking escalating the situation, I simply went about cleaning the patient's wounds for a couple more minutes, asking no questions, before abruptly rising and stepping out of the curtained area, stating that I needed some additional supplies. The nature of this whole encounter was making me more and more suspicious. The older constable squawked some protest, but I stepped past him and went about my business.

"I walked past the younger constable standing guard outside the curtain and on across the ward until I found a nurse helping another patient. I quietly asked that she locate any records from when Boyd Fowler had been treated in August, and to do so without attracting any attention. I'm not sure why, but something didn't feel right about this – the constables weren't acting like officers I've known before. I instructed her to hold onto the documents until I could check them privately – and that she should on no account bring them into the curtained area where the constables could see. Then I turned to a nearby supply drawer and found a roll of wider gauze – to fulfill my excuse for leaving the patient – and returned to finish treating him.

"Dr. Watson can tell you that keeping up a running prattle with a patient is one of the tools of the trade, and despite Fowler's lack of responses after his previous statement, I kept talking to him, even though he didn't answer. His eyes, however, were now more conscious of the treatment space, and he was also watching with interest as I bandaged his arm. My one-sided conversation, dull and innocuous, seemed to lull the constable, who had been so concerned a moment before when Barts was mentioned, and I felt safe to mention the hospital once again.

"'What brought you to Barts a month ago?' I asked, as if it were just more of the same clatter. Of course, the constable tensed, and I had to wonder what was so upsetting about Fowler's previous visit. Both the constable and I were surprised when Fowler actually replied.

"'To see the doctor,' he replied.

"'Here now – ' the constable grumbled.

"'Oh?' I asked, ignoring him. 'Which one?'

"'Crewe,' rumbled the patient.

At this point, Walker-Baird paused in his tale, looking at me to see if I caught the significance. I had, and nodded, and I noted that Holmes had seen my confirmation as well.

Walker-Baird continued with his narrative. "'Really?' I asked, aware that the constable was now even more alert, as if he were about to put a stop to all treatment and whisk Fowler back from whence he'd arrived. 'What for?'

"'Dreams. My dreams. Of killing her.'

"I lowered my hands, the bandage half-tied. 'Killing her?' Killing who?'

"'The Queen.' His focus had been upon his arm, but now he looked up, his eyes meeting mine. He seemed to be in terrible pain, and unshed tears were beginning to rim his eyelids. 'I dreamed it so many times, and today I did it. I killed her.' He gave a small shudder and sob. 'I killed her!' he repeated. '*I killed her!*'

"With that, the constable stood and rushed forward, pushing me roughly to one side and grabbing Fowler's shoulder as if he should shake the words back into him before they were spoken. But it was too late, and before I could be stopped, I hissed, 'You *killed* her? The *Queen*? How?'

"As you can imagine, I was stunned. Up to that moment, the patient had simply been another of many, more curious than some, but still just more wounds to be treated. They weren't serious, and although there was some mystery in the way he was being handled by the police, I've come across many stranger things. I was curious about his apparent catatonia, and that he'd been seen a month earlier by Dr. Crewe, but none of this was of more than passing interest – just another patient. But now – now this man had just quietly confessed that he'd murdered the Sovereign.

"I became aware that the ward around was still as noisy as before, nothing atypical or unusual. We'd been speaking so softly that nothing beyond the drawn curtain had been overheard. Even the younger constable standing just outside hadn't detected anything to spur him into motion in order to help his companion. But I sensed that some-such action was imminent.

"'She was riding this morning, as she always does,' Fowler said, his words coming more urgently as he seemed to be further waking up from whatever state he'd been in upon arrival. He was trying to talk around the older constable, urgently sharing his story with me while he could. 'I . . . I had dreamed it . . .," he said, quickly, looking into my eyes as if running out of time. "The plan . . . and I was waiting for her. *Them*. At the park – along Rotten Row. I had a pistol . . . I don't know where I found it. I had it, and when she drove by, I stepped forward and shot her. She . . . I *hit* her. She fell back. I *saw* it!'

"Tears were now running down his face. 'I thought she would cry out, but there was nothing – no sound at all . . . as if my ears were plugged. All I could hear was the roar of my own heartbeat. I dropped the gun. I turned and ran – never looked back. I don't know which way that I went, but then someone tried to grab me. I pushed into a hedge, to get away, but they were waiting. The police, on the other side. They arrested me, because I shot her. I shot her. I *killed* her . . . .' He gave a great sob, and then seemed to retreat back inside himself, his eyes losing focus once again.

"By now, the constable had allowed more than he'd ever intended, and he fully pushed me aside, taking custody of his prisoner while calling for his associate, who flung back the curtain and rushed in as if expecting to find that we'd both been overpowered. Instead, he was met with the prisoner being hustled out, and he shifted his emphasis to offering assistance.

"Ignoring the attention that they were receiving from the others in the ward, they hurried the Scotsman through the double doors to the hallway outside. After a few seconds, I regained my balance and followed, but they were already gone, and I couldn't find anyone to tell me in which direction they'd departed – although I'm not sure what my intention would have been had I caught up with them. The entire incident took no more than five minutes or so, and except for the prisoner's fantastic story, I don't know much of anything at all."

"You knew the name of the patient's doctor," corrected Holmes. "'*Crewe*.' You recognized him, Watson."

I nodded. "Dr. Patton Crewe is a specialist in the treatment of different sorts of mania." Then, unable to help myself, I added, "Some of his ideas are considered questionable – quite questionable, as a matter of fact. He dabbles in mesmerism and such."

Walker-Baird cut a glance my way, as if surprised that I was willing to be that candid with my criticism to someone outside the medical profession, but he added, "A minute or so after this all happened, another nurse came into the ward, looking for the two constables. Apparently they

203

had sent her to find Dr. Crewe when they first arrived, but she was there to report that he wasn't in the hospital."

Holmes nodded. "And what of the records that you sent the other nurse to fetch?"

Walker-Baird swallowed and pulled some folded sheets from his coat, handing them to Holmes. "Fowler has been seen at Barts on a number of occasions – not just a month ago, although that was his most recent visit. He first started seeking treatment a full year ago, when he moved to London. The forms showed that he came here from Scotland to '*find work*'. He was having headaches, and – according to the records – he believed that he was having '*bad thoughts*', although nothing about their nature was specified. He visited a dozen times in late 1887, and on each occasion, he was examined the physician-on-call. Then, early this year, he was first examined by Dr. Crewe, who happened to be responsible that day for walk-in patients. Although the records don't indicate way, Fowler was immediately sent down to the Somerset Asylum for three months. Afterwards, he obtained a release, and since then he's resumed making a nuisance of himself at the hospital – walking in at irregular times about his headaches – although never in the company or custody of the police. It was only chance that I happened to be there today. If I worked shifts more often, I might have recognized him."

Walker-Baird paused, and I rose to refill our glasses. Meanwhile, Holmes stood and walked to the open window, where the sounds of the street drifted in. They sounded no different than they had since I had arrived and met Walker-Baird at the front door. A moment passed, and then another, as Holmes looked through the medical notes.

As the silence continued, Walker-Baird seemed to become more worried, fidgeting and looking from my friend to me, and back again. Finally he could no longer keep it to himself. "But Mr. Holmes," he asked, "what if he actually *did* kill the Queen?"

For another moment, Holmes didn't replay. Then, turning back our way, he stated, "If the Queen has been killed, the news hasn't spread yet. No one in the street acts any differently, and the newsboy is still bellowing about the usual tripe. How long can they flog the story that Wilson took two-hundred-fifty wickets?" He took the glass I handed him and resumed his seat. "You mentioned that Sir James referred you to me. Did you discuss this with anyone besides him?"

Walker-Baird shook his head. "After the constables hurried away with the prisoner, I looked around, but everyone in the ward had already returned to their business. The hospital sees a lot of indigent care, particularly from Spitalfields and Whitechapel – people that don't go the London Hospital, for whatever reason – and they had already lost interest

204

in the abrupt departure of Fowler and the constables. Still very much concerned with what I'd just heard, I went looking for Sir James. We talked about it, and he started to seek out a telephone and ask a friend if the story could be true, but then he leaned toward discretion. Even though he was as rattled as I, he had no insight. The best he could do was to advise that I come see you immediately. He would have joined me, but he had a surgery that could not be rescheduled. He only hoped that, following this news, his nerves didn't cause him to botch it. I didn't even take the time to send a message for an appointment."

He turned his hands up. "Now, I don't know what else that I can do, or tell you. Sir James said you were the man for the job. It's far beyond anything of my experience. Can you look into this?"

Holmes rose. "I can – we can – and I'll report back to you and Sir James if it turns out to be anything that that I can share."

"Then that's all I can ask," replied the doctor, finishing the last of his whisky and rising to his feet. With a presentation of his card so that we had his home and office address, he departed.

Holmes and I resumed our seats, and he quickly re-read Fowler's medical reports before handing them to me. They appeared to be quite routine – typical physicians' scrawls, quickly written by busy doctors about a forgettable patient. There was nothing of value beyond what Walker-Baird had mentioned. Seeing that I was finished, Holmes asked, "What else can you tell me about this Dr. Crewe?"

I took a moment to gather my thoughts, giving Holmes the opportunity to rise, walk around me, and retrieve one of the scrapbooks kept on the shelves near the door to his bedroom. I heard him muttering as he looked here and there before saying something about "No help" as he returned to his seat, giving me an expectant look.

"I don't know much about him," I began. "He's been a presence at the hospital since not long after my return to England, and after first meeting him, and hearing of some of his ideas, I did a bit of research. He's had several papers published in lesser journals, and I was told by one or two people that his efforts were rejected by *The Lancet* and a few others of similar respectability."

"You mentioned mesmerism."

I nodded. "He advocates the use of such techniques towards pain management. I can't say that I entirely disagree with everything that he espouses. I saw many things in India demonstrating how the mind can fool itself, if only given the chance. And of course, every doctor is aware of the power of the *placebo*. But Crewe seems to be less of a *doctor* and more of a *sideshow attraction*."

"How so?"

"On occasion, he has been known to place a susceptible patient under his hypnotic influence and then make the fellow to appear ridiculous – imitating a chicken or a monkey or some such nonsense – for the simple amusement of the staff. I've never seen it happen myself, you understand, but I've heard about it afterwards. A man with such little regard for his patients and their ethical care has no business being a doctor."

The thought of Crewe's actions recalled the anger that I'd initially felt when I'd first heard of his antics. I pulled myself from that vision of mistreated patients to glance at Holmes, expecting to see him amused at my righteous indignation, but I found him nodding in agreement.

"When a doctor goes wrong . . ." he stated, and I was reminded of his long-standing (and well-proven) distrust of many in the medical profession. "One has to wonder," he continued, "what a doctor such as that could be doing with a man who he recommended be treated for three months in an asylum." He stood abruptly. "I believe that a visit to my brother is in order. Can you join me?"

During the hansom cab ride from Baker Street, Holmes related details of the investigations he'd undertaken for Sir James Saunders in the past. One sounded insignificant, while the other was apparently relevant to the nation's most urgent foreign policies – or so it seemed from the vague account that was given to me. I asked Holmes how he had come to Sir James's attention and assistance in the first place, and he indicated that other services he'd provided to different government departments had led to similar work, and so on, until a situation arose in Sir James's bailiwick that required Holmes's special skills. I wanted to ask more, but at that point our short journey was complete.

Normally I found myself quite interested when Holmes was relating his past cases, but on that day I was only partially paying attention as I tried to puzzle out how a visit to his brother might be relevant to what we'd just heard.

It must be remembered that at that moment in time, it had only been one week since I'd first met Mycroft Holmes, during the tragically failed attempt to save a poor Greek who had come to London seeking his sister, only to be murdered in an empty house down Beckenham way. In the days that had followed, I had thought of the elder Holmes in passing a few times, but not with any great interest – and when I did, it was mostly because I'd known Holmes for so long and never before learned that he had a brother – a fact that surprised me, although it shouldn't have. Meeting Mycroft Holmes had certainly been an interesting experience. Of course, the physical differences between the two Holmes brothers was a curiosity. Both were tall, with the same sharp all-seeing eyes and general facial features, but whereas Sherlock Holmes was slim, as if he used up every bit of fuel that he acquired by shoveling it immediately into a hot furnace, Mycroft Holmes was stout – somewhat corpulent really – and like a careful steward of his own resources, he seemed to be hoarding his fuel for burning at some later date that might never arrive.

I had expected that we would be traveling to Pall Mall, as we had just a week before, and to the odd club where Mycroft Holmes apparently held court, but instead we found ourselves in front of one of the many great buildings that line Whitehall, near the Horse Guards. Then I recalled being told that every day, Holmes's brother walked from his lodgings across from the Diogenes Club and around to his employment where he audited the books for some of the Government departments. As it was still mid-afternoon, I expected that was where we would seek him.

We stepped down from the hansom and crossed to the heavy double doors, opened by an expressionless fellow who kept his gaze outward. Holmes seemed to be recognized, for he led me inside with just a wave toward a man at a tall counter who nodded and made no attempt to question us. After passing down a number of interminably long hallways and up and down several flights of stairs, ever more toward the rear of the building to the point that I was thoroughly lost, we reached a plain brown door in a hallway of many similar entrances. Holmes knocked twice, then once more, opened it without response, and led me into a small, workmanlike, and rather dim room with a desk, a few chairs, and a small window looking west toward St. James's Park.

From behind the desk, Mycroft Holmes looked up without surprise. He rose and offered his hand to the two of us. "Sherlock, Doctor. You've come about the supposed assassination of the Queen."

I was taken aback as the elder Holmes waved us toward a pair of chairs, but also relieved at the word "supposed", implying that our fears were unnecessary. Holmes and I had both remarked during our cab ride that the city appeared to be rolling along as normal – a good indicator that Boyd Fowler's assertion had been the merest moonshine.

"Excuse the meagre accommodations, Doctor," Mycroft Holmes said. "I have a more formal office elsewhere, but I tend to avoid it if at all possible. I find that I can accomplish much more here, where I'm left alone." He glanced at his younger brother. "Not that your visit is an intrusion. You knew to seek me here instead of the other office because Preston fled west from Inverness?"

Sherlock Holmes nodded. "When I received word which way he'd bolted, I thought you'd be here, getting your pins lined up."

Mycroft looked back my way, as if measuring my trustworthiness, before returning his attention to his brother. "The situation in

Camastianavaig on the Isle of Skye is rapidly coming to a head, and unless we get things in hand quickly, it may catch fire like dry grass hit by lightning."

My confused expression must have been something to see, for Mycroft Holmes smiled with friendly amusement. "You appear to be all at sea, Doctor. I gather that my brother hasn't explained the full scope of my duties within the Government – at least, as he understands them. You could have, Sherlock. The Doctor has been cleared, as you know. Suffice it to say, I sit in an elevated position where I can see the *inter-relatedness* of things – including how today's event at Barts is part of a larger picture."

"So this Fowler fellow didn't kill the Queen," said Sherlock Holmes, pulling the conversation back to the reason for our visit.

Mycroft shook his head. "But the poor fellow is being used, nonetheless – shamefully manipulated – and we need to get an understanding of what is happening as soon as possible." He glanced my way. "Can I offer you something to drink, Doctor?"

I shook my head, rather dazed, as if I had abruptly fallen into very deep water. No doubt my eyes were wide as I struggled to catch up. Mycroft took a bit of pity on me, poured a generous brandy from a container on his desk, and pushed it in front of me, despite my refusal. Then, as I sipped, he explained.

"Soon after Dr. Walker-Baird went 'round to Baker Street, Sir James decided to postpone his surgical engagement. He thought about following Walker-Baird to your rooms, but instead decided that it would be better to drop in here and tell me what little he knew about this morning's event – not realizing that I already knew a great deal more about it than him. I estimated that you'd be arriving within the next hour or so – and here you are."

He looked back at his brother. "You know, Sherlock," he said, "that I have my fingers in many different pies. A lot of it is a complete waste of my time, but occasionally I'm pointed in a useful direction. Not long ago, word came that Donald Mirehouse, the cabinet minister, was behaving even more . . . *peculiar*, I suppose, is the way to put it. Even more peculiar than usual. His finances have become precarious, and he's been associating with some most-dodgy types – rather on the radical side of things.

"It might have gone unremarked, for he isn't the only one to get himself in that sort of trouble, except for the recent inheritance he received from his uncle, the textile industrialist. A routine – and discreet – evaluation revealed that instead of putting him on more solid ground as one would expect, the funds seemed to immediately be siphoned off . . .

somewhere. Furthermore, that curiosity led us to determine that the rest of his affairs are also in a perilous state of near-collapse.

"While we were trying to decide how to address the matter, other inquiries were set in motion – just to get our pins lined up, as you put it. It was then that we learned that Mirehouse has been in close contact with the German, Hans Andernach."

I cleared my throat. "I hate to interrupt," I said, "and I realize that I'm in far over my head, but I'm still trying to gather my wits about a possibly mesmerized man who says that he killed the Queen, and instead we're talking about a man from Inverness and a cabinet minister and the Isle of Skye. Would it be too much trouble to explain the connection?"

Holmes looked my way, his expression kindly rather than impatient. "I wasn't quite forthcoming last week when I brought you to the Diogenes Club," he explained. "Mycroft holds a unique position within the government – an *elevated* position, as he mentioned, where he can see how different events are connected and affect one another, and then he can set things in motion to nudge them in the way that most benefits England."

"It is also a *secret* position," added Mycroft, "although the Germans and the French each have a man who has somewhat similar gifts, attempting to carry out the same function. The Russians believe that they have someone as well, but he is a fool and will eventually lead them astray."

"A few weeks ago," continued Sherlock Holmes, "Mycroft had me do some preliminary investigation into Donald Mirehouse, as he was beginning to display signs that he's a weak link. It was then that I caught a whiff that there might be a plot to assassinate the Queen – but I was unable to find any other pieces of the puzzle."

"And the man in Inverness? And the Isle of Skye?"

"All part of the larger picture," answered Mycroft, "and unrelated to today's events – at least, it's nothing that need concern us right now."

"You mentioned a German," I said. "Are they behind this plot – whatever it may be?"

"It's possible," explained Holmes. "Hans Andernach, the man who has been in contact with Mirehouse, is a German agent."

"*The* German agent," amended Mycroft. "He was Bismarck's closest proxy when crafting their Triple Alliance Treaty six years ago. A German alliance with Austria-Hungary and Italy changed the balance of power – or at least forced us to respond. Together, those three countries are forming a virtual wall between us and Russia. But Andernach is also something of a rogue who sees the value of chaos to effect the changes he desires – even when the chaos is deadly."

"This is disturbing news," said Holmes. "So Mirehouse is in league with Andernach?"

"It seems more and more apparent," explained Mycroft gravely, "based on Mirehouse's finances, that he has been compromised by the Germans."

"What has been done?"

"Nothing overtly. Not yet. This has only come to our attention within the past couple of days. So far, we've made a further and deeper study of Mirehouse's records and his history. We've seen where he went wrong – a typical case of bad behaviour and blackmail – and how Andernach was able to gain influence over him. Fortunately it only occurred quite recently, so there's a good chance that very little damage has been done. At least, that's our fervent hope."

I looked from one of them to the other. "And you think that this mysterious damaged Scotsman at Barts has something to do with the plot against the Queen you sniffed out a few weeks ago?" I asked. "That he's connected to a compromised minister and a German agent?"

"It was when Dr. Walker-Baird mentioned a plot against the Queen," explained Holmes, "that I knew that we must confer with Mycroft."

"It's more than that," added Mycroft Holmes. "The fact that this Dr. Crewe is connected opens a completely new door."

"How so?"

"Do you both recall MacLean's attempt to kill the Queen in '82?"

We each nodded. In March of that year, Roderick MacLean, then in his late twenties, stood in the entrance of Windsor Station and fired a revolver at the Queen as she walked from her train to a waiting carriage. His shot missed – a nearby Eton schoolboy named Wilson used his umbrella to jostle MacLean's arm. Afterwards, it was learned that MacLean had been certified insane two years earlier, although he'd somehow been allowed to travel about freely and then obtain a gun. He was tried and found "Guilty, but Insane", and he'd spent the years since in Broadmoor.

Mycroft tapped a small stack of telegrams lying upon his desk. "After hearing Sir James's account, I requested some information. Fortunately I have the resources to obtain it quickly. I was interested to learn that MacLean, a Scotsman like Fowler, was also treated for headaches for two years before he was sent away – " He looked from one of us to the other to emphasize his next point. " – to the Somerset Lunatic Asylum."

I leaned forward. "The same hospital where Fowler was treated," I stated, unnecessarily, as both Holmes brothers already understood the significance.

"There's more," added Mycroft. "Do you know who treated MacLean while he was there? None other than Dr. Patton Crewe, our curious mesmerist. A quick review of both MacLean and Fowler's case files by the Somerset Asylum doctors revealed that Crewe's notes identified each as an '*ideal subject*' for his mesmerization studies."

"Good Lord!" I breathed. "Is it possible that MacLean was mesmerized and turned into some sort of sleepwalking weapon aimed at the Queen?"

Sherlock Holmes nodded. "We must re-evaluate what occurred six years ago – and consider today's events in that light as well."

"I already have men doing so," Mycroft stated.

"But Fowler is in custody," I said. "Surely he can explain what has happened. He simply needs to be properly interviewed by a medical professional with experience in this area."

"I suspect," interjected Sherlock Holmes, "that it won't be that easy. I believe that Mycroft is about to tell us that the two constables who brought Fowler to Barts are not legitimately employed policemen."

"That is correct," the elder Holmes confirmed. "Both the City of London and the Metropolitan Police have confirmed that neither organization has officers who took a supposed assassin into custody this morning along Rotten Row, and likewise neither has men who took a patient to Barts. Whoever these men were, they have gone into hiding with Boyd Fowler after he came to himself while being treated and spoke to the wrong person."

"We need to find out who they are," I said with enthusiasm, not realizing that both Holmes brothers already knew this. "And it's also of interest to know why they brought Fowler to Barts, as it sounds as if his wound wasn't too serious."

"Clearly," said Sherlock Holmes, "they brought him there to see Crewe, probably because he *didn't* actually shoot the Queen as he'd been trained to do while in a mesmerized state. He ended up being accidentally treated by Walker-Baird, and then, when he began to wake up and relate what he thought he'd done, they had to hurry him out without being able to consult with the mesmerist."

"It's a working hypothesis," agreed Mycroft. "As you will understand, this must remain most secret, and even many of my own agents aren't cleared to investigate it. I'll leave it to you, Sherlock, and you as well, Doctor, to see where the thread leads."

Sherlock Holmes stood. "Of course, Dr. Walker-Baird has been taken into protective custody," he said.

Mycroft nodded. "Not long after he left Baker Street."

"You don't think he's in danger?" I asked.

"It's possible," said Holmes. "He was unwittingly brought into this business when Fowler unexpectedly spoke with him. Whoever is responsible may try to keep these news from spreading – by whatever means necessary."

And with that, the meeting was abruptly complete. We had been dismissed, for there was nothing else to discuss. Mycroft stood as we departed, and it wasn't long before we were back outside, in front of the vast building.

Holmes preferred to walk for a bit, so we turned north toward Trafalgar Square before heading west along The Mall. As we progressed, I finally had no choice but to ask Holmes about his brother.

"You must forgive me for not immediately telling you of Mycroft's unique position," he replied. I held my tongue, suppressing the comment that he hadn't even told me of his brother's existence for nearly eight years. "It's something that he made for himself, unlike any other. He mentioned equivalent men on the Continent, but I don't believe it. No man alive has a more orderly brain than Mycroft. Every branch of Government funnels its questions through him and he sees their interconnections, and how one relates to the other. He specializes in *omniscience*. In this alone, he would be indispensable, but in fact he is also in charge the Government's various agents who work in secret, both at home and abroad. As their leader, and based on what they learn and also do at his bidding, many is the time that '*M*', as he's called, has decided national policy.

"But not a word of it must be hinted," Holmes added, glancing at me as we walked. The rains from earlier in the day had ceased, but there were puddles along the pavement which we dodged as necessary. "Should you ever publish anything else, as you did late last year when relating that little Mormon diversion, you must make no mention of Mycroft."

I nodded in agreement and we continued on for a good way, maintaining a companionable silence while Holmes was deep in thought. Finally, when we had circumnavigated around the Palace and then up Constitution Hill, I realized that he was heading for Rotten Row, where Boyd Fowler claimed to have shot the Queen. What we found were a vast number of our fellow Londoners, walking and standing and talking and living, all acting as if it were simply another normal day.

"It would appear," he said, "that that we might be tempted into overthinking this affair."

"How so?" I asked.

"Well, leaving compromised cabinet ministers and German agents to Mycroft's attention, we're left with Boyd Fowler and Dr. Crewe – the latter of which, I suspect, isn't too hard to locate. If I can get an idea of what he's up to, we can attack this tangled skein from his direction and let the rest sort itself out."

He turned my way. "If you don't mind, return to Baker Street and await developments. I have one or two lines to cast before I meet you there."

"Isn't there something that I can do?" I asked.

He thought and then nodded. "Yes. See what more you find out about Dr. Patton Crewe." He smiled. "With discretion, of course." Then he nodded and set off with typical briskness back in the direction from which we'd come. Within a moment, he was well out of site.

My own pace being less energetic and, already weary by our walk from Whitehall, I hailed a hansom and was soon deposited at our Baker Street doorstep. It was certain that Holmes had noticed my weary condition, leading him to suggest my more docile alternative service.

Upstairs, I divested myself of my overcoat and turned toward my armchair. However, instead of sitting down and likely falling asleep, I diverted myself to Holmes's scrapbooks, where – with a bit of luck and also some diligent searching using what little I had learned about his peculiar filing system – I confirmed that there was nothing there about Dr. Patton Crewe. I'm not sure why I had thought otherwise, but I had the nagging sense that I ought to check further. Then, I looked once again at the only Crewe that I'd run across – Pencombe Crewe, a fellow who had lost his place in society because of some gambling scandal. Thinking that there couldn't be all that many Crewes in the capital, and with a wistful glance toward my chair where the prospect of an afternoon nap awaited, I instead returned to my coat and hat and departed once again, on my way to several locations where I hoped to find further information.

My search was not without success. As the afternoon waned, I visited Barts, as well as a couple of other hospitals where I'd learned that Dr. Patton Crewe also attended patients. I also looked up his biographical information in the Barts Medical Library, with the aid of a most-helpful medical librarian, confirming that Crewe's father was indeed the ill-fated Pencombe Crewe briefly mentioned in Holmes's scrapbooks. I realized that while Holmes knew many things, he didn't know them all, and that it was possible, even likely, that he hadn't made this connection. Like Holmes, I have cultivated certain useful contacts over the years that seem to know a little bit of everything within their limited circles, and from one such, Dr. Johnny "One-Eye" Wingrave, I obtained the following story about Crewe's father.

There are those who somehow seem to be above the law, forever escaping whatever justice that is due to them, but Pencombe Crewe wasn't someone who was part of that lucky group. In the mid-1870's, he was a close pal of Bertie, the Queen's eldest son and heir to throne, and well-known for his notorious and scandalous behavior. Pencombe Crewe, a former soldier and sole heir to his late father's fortune, was often right there with him. In 1878, Crewe and the Prince had been gambling while on a trip to Paris, as was their wont, and heavy losses were incurred. There was some whiff of Royal cheating, and the Prince happily pinned the accusation on Crewe, whose reputation was not only destroyed immediately, but the shaken man was also left with an immense debt to repay – both his share and the Prince's. As if that weren't enough, over the previous few years he'd made enough enemies by way of the Prince's supposed friendship that is was easy for Bertie to go ahead and cut all ties, essentially ruining him and striking him from society, almost overnight.

Almost twelve months to the day after his association with the Prince ended, a year in which he became a pariah amongst the group that had formerly accepted him as one of their own, Pencombe Crewe hanged himself, leaving his motherless son, Patton, shamed and on the verge of destitution. Patton Crewe had been pursuing his medical degree at the time, and his studies had been nearly permanently derailed before he found a patron to support him. However, after receiving his degree (about the same time as me, and also from the University of London, although I had no recollection of him), he had started down the path to where he now professionally resided – a supporter of the dubious fringe treatments and benefits of mesmerism.

I returned to Baker Street about an hour before our evening meal, and Holmes joined me not long after. He was a good mood, standing before the fire and rubbing his hands energetically, and my report seemed to line up with whatever he had learned.

"Did your source of information indicate the name of the man who served as Dr. Patton Crewe's lifeline?" he asked.

I shook my head.

"It was Donald Mirehouse," Holmes said, now seated and smiling around his pipe.

"The compromised Cabinet Minister?" I asked.

Holmes nodded. "Mirehouse stepped forward and supplied the funds that Crewe needed to complete his studies, and then set him up in practice, in some ways similar to how Trevelyan was funded by Blessington in that Brook Street house back in '81. If he'd simply buckled down and gone to work, Crewe could have made a success of that life, but instead, he became rather vocal regarding the shabby way in which his father was treated by the Royals. He now has something of a reputation for expressing revolutionary thoughts, which can be verified with just the shallowest scratching of the surface."

"And he's tied up with this man Mirehouse, who is suspected of possible treason."

"And," added Holmes, "Crewe found a pair of 'ideal subjects', one of whom tried to kill the Queen six years ago – "

" – and the other who thinks that he did so today, even if it's all in his mind." When Holmes didn't immediately respond, I asked, "What are we going to do about it?"

"We are going to eat a bit of supper, and then join Gregson, Lestrade, and a few other policemen, along with the Irregulars, at Mirehouse's home in St. John's Wood."

He offered nothing further, and my anticipation of the coming confrontation didn't lessen my enjoyment of Mrs. Hudson's curried chicken.

Mirehouse lived in Eamont Street, just north of Regent's Park, and when we finished eating, Holmes suggested the idea of walking there before then shaking his head. "No, Lestrade and the rest are waiting for us. We shouldn't delay any longer." In any case, we ended up walking there anyway in a fruitless search for a cab, and in a short time we were at the Park end of the Eamont Street, where Gregson and Lestrade stepped out of the shadows.

"If your brother hadn't authorized this," began Gregson as they joined us, "I'm not sure that we'd be very comfortable serving a warrant to search a Cabinet Minister's house."

"Not to worry," said Holmes. "As my investigation progressed this afternoon, I put the Irregulars in place in several important locations. According to their reports, Crewe's home has been empty, while a man of his description was seen entering Mirehouse's residence late this afternoon, and he hasn't come out. However, a couple of men dressed as constables have been in and out several times. None of the lads recognize them – and you know that they have rather full knowledge of most of the London constables' identities. There is a window on the first floor front with closed drapes, but someone regularly pulls back the curtains, watching the street through a narrow gap. Likewise, there's a room at the rear of the second floor, overlooking the mews, that has closed drapes, but a light is lit there, and occasionally someone peeps from there as well. That will be where we'll find the prisoner."

"Prisoner?" asked Lestrade.

"Indeed. Boyd Fowler, the poor man who has been mesmerized in an attempt to turn him into an assassin. It was no fault of his that he was used in this way while simply seeking treatment for his headaches." He looked around and then waved his stick back and forth over his head. In just a moment, we were joined by Wiggins, the leader of his Irregulars, that band of lads and lasses who were able to go everywhere and see everything, remaining unnoticed while they gathered vital information. I hadn't encountered Wiggins for a few weeks, since he and his troops had been looking for Jonathan Small along the Thames.

"Any changes since your last report?" Holmes asked him.

"None at all," was Wiggins' confident reply. He had walked up and situated himself between the two inspectors, taking his place without any doubt that he deserved the spot. I was amused to see that he was now taller than Lestrade. Both men gave him rather sour looks, but neither could deny how useful he and the other Irregulars had been over the years.

"Excellent," said Holmes. "Then I see no reason to delay."

Though a police operation, Holmes was clearly in charge. There were no loud whistles or yelling. Rather, at a subtle gesture from Gregson, men slid from the shadows toward the house like darker shadows, and one would have been hard-pressed to hear even a brushed footstep. Gregson's work with the Special Branch, formed just five years earlier, had led to a number of useful advances, as these very effective agents demonstrated.

On the front step, Holmes quietly leaned forward to examine the lock. Then, as both inspectors pointedly looked elsewhere, he quickly pulled a wiry piece of metal from his pocket, made a quick manipulation with his hands, and softly unlocked the door. We could barely hear him as he counted to three before throwing open the door and stepping aside, allowing the various policemen to flood past him, suddenly moving from silence to deafening confusion and cacophony as their shouts and yelling filled the house.

A stunned butler appeared at the rear of the hall, and Lestrade tucked a folded warrant into his coat pocket without explanation before joining the sweep of men surging through the building. One of the officers had unlocked the back door, and more of them came in that way, adding to the number who had overwhelmed from the front. The surprise attack was complete and successful, and in less than three minutes, five men were assembled in the dining room, while the confused servants were being kept in the kitchen.

Donald Mirehouse was a blustering figure, wearing a much-too-tight smoking jacket belted across his barrel-like corporation. He had too-little hair on top, and what was on the back of his head was grown too long and combed forward over his fat orange face, held down with shiny Macassar oil across his too-great dome-of-a-forehead. Through his pursed mouth, he sang the old songs of "Do we know who I am?" and "I'll have you jailed!", with a chorus of "This will mean your jobs!" and all the other verses. The Yarders didn't care, instead focusing on Crewe, the two false constables, still in uniforms that were easily identifiable as rag-bag cast-offs from some old clothing shop, and the fifth man, sitting at the other end of the table, apparently trying to wake up and figure out just what was happening.

I stepped across to examine him and found that, except for having been drugged with some sort of sedative, he appeared to be in good physical condition. I reported that the wounds that Dr. Walker-Baird had treated that morning didn't require attention, and the bandages he'd applied, while needing changing soon, would do for the present.

Holmes took the lead in questioning the four others. Mirehouse tried to talk over him, but he soon shut up when one of the darkly clothed policemen took up station beside him in an intimidating way.

"There is much to be sorted over the coming days," Holmes began, "but suffice it to say, Mr. Mirehouse, you are going to be questioned at length by Government agents about this incident, and a number of others as well. What remains to be determined is if you will become the Government's tool – 'turned' as they say, to be useful in some way working against our enemies, particularly at feeding false information to Germany through your contact, Herr Andernach, or whether, if he doesn't take the bait, you finish your remaining days, however many or few there may be, in The Tower." He glanced toward Gregson. "He can be removed now. We don't need him for the rest of our discussion, and others are waiting to speak with him."

Mirehouse's face had been livid and angry when Holmes began, but within seconds it had blanched to a sickly dead orangish-white. As he was pulled upright and marched out of the room, he tried to turn and get Holmes's attention, whining of false accusataions and conspiracies and a mistake being made before finally raising his voice about working something out with money. When the door was shut behind him, Holmes turned to Crewe.

"You'll follow him in a moment," he said. "Over the next few days, we will uncover a great deal more than we already know about your involvement with MacLean's failed attempt to kill the Queen in 1882, but for now, I expect a few answers regarding Mr. Fowler."

Crewe was about my age, but he looked at least ten years older. He was a small and twitchy fellow, with the broken facial capillaries and the coloring of a drunkard. Unlike Mirehouse, who had started angry and then collapsed, Crewe was already broken, slumped in his chair, a shaking hand covering his eyes, and small sobs continually rolling forth while Holmes spoke.

For nearly ten minutes, Holmes questioned the little doctor, and gradually the story was pieced together. After MacLean was chosen in '82, trained for his task by way of mesmerization, and then arrested when the assassination failed, Crewe spent the following years in fear, aware that any moment MacLean's mind might clear long enough to implicate the doctor that had found and used him in such a terrible way. But that never happened, and gradually, and particularly after "Bloody Sunday" the previous November, Crewe's hatred of The Crown had reasserted itself, overwhelming any common sense that might have prevented him from taking another chance when he'd managed to avoid disaster the first time. When Fowler, having many of the same symptoms as MacLean, had presented himself for treatment, it had seemed like too good of an opportunity to miss, and Crewe had started laying the groundwork for Fowler to make his own attempt on the Queen's life.

That morning, feeling that the patient was nearly ready, two of Crewe's cohorts, the false constables later identified as Abraham Fields and Curtis Wigham, had taken him to Rotten Row for a rehearsal. It had not gone as expected. Instead of going through the motions in the way he'd been trained, Fowler had instead become agitated to the point where he attempted to flee, injuring himself in the process.

Mistakenly thinking that Crewe was working at Barts that day, the two false constables had carried him across town for treatment, and to discuss what went wrong, but when they arrived, a misunderstanding on the part of a staff member had ended up placing them directly into the ward for treatment of Fowler's injuries. This was all right, they thought, as he did need to be seen by a doctor, and afterwards they could still find and meet with Crewe. But then Fowler had started talking about how he believed he'd just killed the Queen in front of a stranger, the doctor who was binding his wounds, and they had panicked and chosen to depart immediately in order to seek Crewe elsewhere.

They found him at his home, and from there all four shifted to Mirehouse's residence, where they had waited through the day to see if Fowler's wild statement at the hospital had caused any problems.

Meanwhile, Fowler seemed to become more self-aware as Crewe spoke, and I noticed that he was nodding in agreement.

"That's right," he finally said, his Scottish accent strong and his voice raspy. He squeezed his eyes shut as if the light suddenly hurt his eyes "I remember . . . I remember some of it. What day is it?"

"September 19th," I replied.

"And the year?"

"1888."

"Thank goodness for that. I had no idea just how long these -------- have held me." He smiled then and shook his head, although that seemed to hurt him, and I thought of the problems he'd had with headaches. I would see about getting him some proper treatment.

Later, after Fowler was taken back to Barts, where I would examine him on the morrow, and Crewe and the false constables were removed to the Yard, Holmes had a word with Wiggins in order to dismiss him, and then we decided to walk back to Baker Street, this time through the Park. It was a pleasant evening, and not too late, the entire affair having been concluded in less than an hour.

"Do you suppose Andernach will be fooled into believing whatever Mirehouse is instructed to tell him?" I asked.

"I expect so. Mycroft is very capable at this sort of thing, and there are a number of similar fish already caught on his hook and dancing to his tune, if I mix a metaphor. I even know who some of them are." His voice saddened. "I suppose it's too soon to make a prognosis for Fowler's recovery," he added.

I nodded. "Until I've had a chance to speak with him, and for the specialists to have a look, it is. Crewe has been meddling with him for a year. Who knows how deeply his manipulations and suggestions have rooted themselves? But the fact that he was able to resist when taken for a practice run, and then to speak as himself tonight and have some understanding of his situation, is most promising."

We had entered the Park by way of the small bridge across the canal across from Charles Street, and were now walking south along the Outer Circle, in the stretch between St. Dunstan's Villa and North Villa. I could tell that Holmes, rather than being pleased at the outcome, was rather concerned and distracted.

"It's too easy," he finally said. "For men like Crewe to identify the weak links and turn them into weapons. How many others are out there, all of them living infernal devices, primed for explosion and waiting for the right opportunity? And all of them aren't all aimed at those in power, and they haven't been singled out by a mesmerist and turned into a weapon. Some are already madmen, all on their own, who could not care less who they hurt or kill – the powerful, or the weak and innocent and helpless. We've both seen that far too many times. The Irish dynamiters. Loudon, Baron Maupertuis' strong-arm man. That fellow who faked his death and then nearly made a pitchblende bomb."

Having observed the signs before, I could see that Holmes was on the way to working himself downward and into a brown study. "What you need," I said, "is a challenge." I should have remembered to be careful what you wish for. "Something that will keep you occupied. This was no more than a one-day distraction – moving about and asking some questions. Didn't you mention just this morning at breakfast that Abberline wants to further confer with you tomorrow about the Whitechapel killings?"

219

He nodded. "It's been eleven days since the last murder, and he has new information, based on what I told him that night. Apparently he's now seen as the lead man in the investigation."

"Well, then, that ought to keep you busy for a little while."

"I suppose, although I suspect it will turn out to be nothing more than some shabby little fellow with a grudge against street women. He's probably thrown himself into the Thames by now, never to be heard from again."

Sherlock Holmes was not often incorrect, but in this case, he could not have been more wrong. Those were still early days in our attempts to stop the Rippers and their Reign of Terror, and walking home that night, we had no idea of just what what was still to be faced, and almost immediately. I'd told Holmes that he needed a challenge. What foolishness, for he was about to face one of his most dangerous and taxing challenges of his life – and me along with him. * Never announce that you have plans, goes the old maxim, for the gods will disabuse you of that notion. Do you pray for patience? Beware, for you'll have the opportunity to learn patience. Do you think that life has never tested you? Be careful what you utter, for you *will* be tested.

Years after that night, I would remember our quiet walk home through the Park as one of the calm places before the mighty tempest, when preventing one man from killing the Queen amazingly seemed like a small case when compared to the evil we were about to face.

But on that night, I was pleased with what we had accomplished, and that was enough then to be going on with.

NOTE

For more about Holmes's activies during the inevestigation of The Rippers, see "November, 1888" in *The Collected Papers of Sherlock Holmes – Volume III: Accounts*. It was originally published in *The Watsonian* (*Fall 2015, Vol. 3, No.2*) and in my online blog, *A Seventeen Step Program* at:
https://17stepprogram.blogspot.com/2017/02/sherlock-holmes-versus-jack-ripper.html

The Dunfermline Tarriance

If truth be told, I have never cared for Dunfermline.

Such feelings initially derive from when I was a boy of six, and my parents chose to make the long and tedious journey there from Stranraer to attend a cousin's wedding. I have some memory that my father hoped to gain favor by our presence, as that branch of the family was enjoying a period of extended prosperity.

In the days of my youth, the word "unpleasant" was possibly the most polite way to describe extended travel. The railway system was not yet nearly as established or extensive, and most journeys across those distances were accomplished by way of massive horse-drawn coaches, with frequent stops to change animals or obtain victuals at notable coaching inns. At that young age, when time spent in unpleasant situations stretches to painful infinities, the trip was simply terrible – hour upon hour crammed into an overcrowded and odiferous box, squeezed between irritated adults in stifling heat and constricted within uncomfortably hot clothing, being rocked from side to side without any helpful view of the outside world which might provide the smallest bit of spatial awareness.

I remember that one fat man insisted on smoking within the coach's confines, while I was queasy in varying degrees all along the western coast up to Glasgow, and then on to Stirling before turning east beside the Firth of Forth and into Dunfermline. What followed were several days of confusion as we navigated through a few people that we knew amongst scores of strangers – all of whom were much taller than me.

In particular, I seemed to have been singled out by one middle-aged woman, a great-aunt I was told, who took it upon herself to terrorize me, illuminating every real or imagined fault of character that might manifest itself in a shy six-year-old boy over the course of a two-day encounter. Ironically, her name was Grace, and from what little I could observe at that diminished and intimidated age, I was the only one who received such her attentions, and also the only one who found her to be unpleasant. Was it possible that no one else saw just her true nature? By the end of the trip, I came to understand that it was she whom my parents had hoped to impress, gaining some sort of unspecified favor.

Eventually, we made the reverse journey toward home – with my parents in even worse moods than they had been on the outward-bound segment of our sojourn, as whatever they'd hoped to accomplish or gain at the wedding had most definitely not materialized. I had to wonder if it was due to Great-aunt Grace's unfavorable opinion of me – a question that

I wisely chose not to explore with my parents, as they didn't seem to realize it on their own.

Now, a quarter-century later, I was back in Dunfermline, a grown man recently turned thirty-one, and even though my older perspective revealed a town that was charming in a way that I could never have appreciated as a child, I had also just learned that it held horrors.

A day earlier, my friend Sherlock Holmes and I had made our way north with important new facts related to the sinking of the *Daphne* in Linthouse, just west of Glasgow. The tragedy had occurred just two months earlier, upon the ship's deep-water launch from the shipyard where she was being constructed. Nearly two-hundred workmen and boys were on board, prepared to continue their labors as soon as she was afloat – the typical procedure, as was later reported in the newspapers. However, the two anchored cables on either side of the ship failed, allowing the current to unexpectedly take the overloaded ship and heel her hard over onto her port side. She rolled and sank almost immediately, and one-hundred-twenty-four lives were lost.

The subsequent inquiry found the tragedy to be an unforeseen accident, apparently caused by instability of the failed cables combined with too many workers overcrowding the upper deck. Some alleged that there were other more deliberate causes for the sinking which were being hidden to protect the company, but that talk quickly faded away.

Then, while investigating a completely separate matter in London, Holmes came across sickening evidence that the sinking had been deliberate after all – over ten-dozen lives lost so that one man could be removed in order to accommodate another's insatiable greed. In Dunfermline, we – along with a representative of The Crown – had cornered the titled beast who had arranged such a terrible crime. It was not without cost – Holmes had taken a minor bullet wound across the shoulder, messy but fortunately superficial.

In spite of that, he had handily disarmed the man who we sought. His guilt revealed, the nobleman was unrepentant and arrogant. Knowing as he did how deeply rooted he was into the fabric of the Kingdom, he bragged that his exposure would do far greater damage than what he'd caused by taking the lives of those lost on the ship – "insignificants" he called them. He declared that his position was invulnerable, and that he was protected by a hundred other men of similar rank and title who had also benefited from his actions. "If I wasn't already knighted, Mr. Holmes . . ." he had sneered.

Hearing these vile pronouncements left me speechless, and I could see that Holmes was affected the same way. As I watched the exposed criminal – madman, really – smugly look from of us to the other, I felt a

222

rage growing inside that had only rarely known itself in the past. Yet before we could gather our wits, the Crown's man who had accompanied us from London spoke quietly, his tones level and his words measured. The nobleman's expression changed – he still projected arrogant confidence, but there was one flicker of doubt now weighing on his expression. He seemed as if he'd been listening to the perfect symphony before perceiving in the distance a sole dissonant note – an out-of-tune horn that was getting closer and louder with each heartbeat.

The agent from London then excused us both from the brightly lit room, so pleasant a place that it seemed as if nothing bad could ever occur there. It was more of an order than a suggestion or request, and knowing the man's authority, we did as he said, making no argument, confident that justice was about to be enacted while we silently made our way outside, and then back through the darkened and deserted streets to the inn where we had left our bags. The last we heard from the previously confident killer was a timid request for us to stay, his tone now tremulous and uncertain. We ignored him, pulled the door to his study shut, and departed.

It was no revelation the following morning to read in the early newspapers that the man we had exposed had been found in his study where we had left him. It seemed that he had, while carelessly cleaning his shotgun the night before, blown off his own head. His actions were inexplicable, as he had servants for such tedious work. As he had no heirs, the article tastelessly speculated as to the disposition of his sizable estate.

Holmes and I were at the small table in the sitting room adjoining our bedrooms, confronting a perfectly acceptable breakfast that we had no desire to eat, and with neither of us feeling the need for additional conversation or speculation. It was still some time before our London train would depart, and we had nothing better to do than wait. There was certainly nowhere that I wished to visit before we left, and any of those distant relatives that I met when I was a boy would have no memory of me, should they even still live there or be alive.

With a sigh, I glanced at the window and noticed it had begun to rain.

I have never cared for Dunfermline.

I was considering that it was time to check Holmes's wound when a strong knock sounded on the hallway door – surprising both of us, as we hadn't heard the approach of any footsteps.

I rose and crossed the short distance, opening it to find a staid middle-aged fellow, hat in hand, and another younger man, tall and well-dressed, his agitation obvious and immediate.

The older man nodded, his lips pursed in distaste, saying, "Dr. Watson? I'm Inspector McCrae. Might we speak with you and Mr. Holmes on a matter of some urgency?"

Considering that Holmes and I wished to shake the dust of this town from our feet as soon as possible, and worrying that we might be asked questions about the night before, I was tempted to tell him no and shut the door without explanation. And if it was already another case, Holmes was wounded, however slight, and he had no business overtaxing his recovery.

"Come in," said my friend from behind me, which was no surprise at all. I stepped aside and allowed the two men to enter. In the meantime, Holmes was moving from the table, his breakfast mostly untouched, to one of the two chairs facing a small sofa.

"Inspector McRae," repeated the older man, shaking Holmes's hand, and then turning to do the same with me. "This is Albert McCreevy. He's – "

The younger man stepped forward, offering his hand to me. "I'm Mr. Andrew Carnegie's personal assistant," he said in a curiously flat American accent. He pronounced his employer's name in the American fashion, with the syllables having equal emphasis, in contrast to the Scottish Car-*nay*-gie, with the weight on the middle syllable.

He was quite tall and thin, and there was something curiously reptilian about him, from the greenish tint of his foreign-looking and expensive suit to the way his forehead sloped back a little too steeply from his thin brows to his high thin hairline. What hair to be found there was combed straight back, and his skull was wide at the top, narrowing around his eyes, and then widening again where the mandible joined behind the zygomatic bones. He wore *pince-nez* over a flat nose, turned up so that one could see slightly into his pinkish nostrils. His mouth was a thin line over a minor bump of a chin – in fact, his Adam's apple peeking above his collar was more pronounced than the front of his jaw.

It was no surprise that his grip was cold and damp and limp.

McCrae was made of sterner stuff. He was at least fifty, solid and weathered, with short gray hair and matching military-trimmed mustache. His wool suit looked very much like one of my own favorites, and his handshake had been warm, dry, and firm.

"We're sorry to bother you," he began, his Scottish burr indicating that he was from further north, and not a native of Dunfermline. "When my superiors learned that you were here, Mr. Holmes, I was – "

"Mr. Carnegie has been kidnapped!" interrupted McCreevy, his voice on the edge of being shrill. Whereas McCrae had settled back into the sofa, the younger man remained perched on the edge, his feet pulled in, as if he intended to rise and flee at any moment, or perhaps punctuate a statement by jumping to his feet for dramatic effect.

"Andrew Carnegie the millionaire?" asked Holmes, his tone neutral, and giving no indication whether he was intrigued enough to commit his time or energies.

McCreevy nodded. "The same. We're here because of his new library – it opened last month. Mr. Carnegie has been making a quiet tour of Europe – meeting with investors, visiting his holdings – and he didn't want to miss the chance to revisit the town of his birth and see the library."

I knew that at times such as these, Holmes missed having access to his commonplace books, where he recorded any number of wide-ranging facts which might be of some use. Still, he appeared to recall more than I would have expected.

"A quiet tour, you say? Surely such a visit would have been reported in the newspapers."

McCreevy shook his head. "That's exactly what Mr. Carnegie didn't want. In spite of his wealth, he tries to live without seeking attention. I'm sure you're aware of his philanthropic endeavors?"

I nodded, saying, "Indeed. His charitable contributions over the last couple of years have been noteworthy."

"That's only the beginning. He intended to begin distributing his fortune much earlier, but life has a way of revising plans. However, now that he's started, he intends to spend the rest of his life giving away most of his wealth."

"But you're talking about millions of dollars," I said, trying to picture a rich man who would freely distribute his accumulated hoard. I would have bet that such a notion was impossible. Having already met a number of rich men by way of my association with Holmes, I couldn't imagine it. Even the best of them, when peeled down to their essential core, were greedy and felt that they deserved what they had.

"Mr. Carnegie is made of different stuff. He was born here in Dunfermline. His father was a weaver, and his family shared a main room with another family in a small house – he and I saw it just yesterday, not long after our arrival. After the family emigrated to Pennsylvania, he found employment as a messenger boy while only fourteen. Through canniness and hard work, he advanced to supervisory positions, making friends and investments where he could. By the time the Civil War started, he had founded his fortune and was appointed as the Superintendent of the Northern military's railways and telegraph lines. In the meantime, he invested in oil and bridges and steel, so that after the War – "

Holmes had heard enough. He raised a hand. "Are you here to convince us to buy shares in one of Carnegie's companies, or to seek assistance in the matter of his kidnapping?"

225

The reptilian man was caught up short, his enthusiastic spiel nipped just as it was gaining momentum. He looked at Holmes and me, and then to the inspector, as if seeking the help of an older adult to redress his perceived grievance.

McCrae cleared his throat. "Two days ago, we – the police – received a wire from London that Mr. Carnegie would be arriving to see his new library. You may have read of it. It's apparently his intention – as part of giving away his entire fortune – to build libraries all over the world. The first is here in Dunfermline. He and his mother visited here a couple of years ago, and attracting a great deal more attention then. He's provided money right along, and last month, it finally opened."

McCreevy nodded and started to speak, but McCrae continued first. "As stated, he wanted a quiet visit this time – no dinners or parades. He would just slip in and slip out for a couple of days – visiting the library, and a few other places that meant something to him when he was young, before leaving for America."

"This was to be his last European stop," interrupted McCreevy. "When we'd seen the library, and the old house on Moodie Street, we planned to travel on and sail for home."

"Mr. Carnegie and Mr. McCreevy presented themselves at the police station," continued McCrae, "and I was assigned to accompany them – more as a courtesy than due to any concerns. Yesterday we visited the library and the old house – without making announcements who he was – and also a few other spots which meant something to him."

"Who knew that he would be here?"

"No one," said McCreevy. "No one except the police, whom we notified before departing London." He looked at the inspector with an accusing expression.

McCrae shook his head. "Respecting Mr. Carnegie's wishes, we kept the information close. My superintendent knew, and a discreet sergeant that I'd trust with my life. In fact, we discussed the matter ahead of time upon receiving the notification that he was coming, and the three of us agreed to refer to our famed visitor as 'Mr. Smith'." He looked at the younger man. "We saw no need to call Mr. McCreevy by any other name."

"A pity," said Holmes, his eyes narrowing in something of a smile. "I believe that 'Mr. Jones' would suit him rather well."

McCreevy looked from Holmes to the policeman with confusion in his face, sensing that he was being ridiculed in some subtle way, but not quite understanding how.

"And the kidnapping?" asked Holmes. "How was that accomplished?"

McCrae nodded to the secretary. "We returned to our small hotel last night about seven and ordered dinner sent to our rooms. Mr. Carnegie ate alone, and at eight, I rejoined him as planned to go over some wires about ongoing business deals and to discuss our travel arrangements. Then, an hour or so later, I said good night and returned to my own room, with the understanding that I'd be joining him for breakfast at six this morning."

"That's quite early," I commented.

McCreevy nodded. "Mr. Carnegie sleeps very little and is an early riser. At the appointed time, I knocked on the door and entered. It was still a few minutes before breakfast was to be served, and I expected to find him waiting for me in his sitting room. He wasn't there. The door to his bedroom was open, and his bed hadn't been slept in. I thought that he'd gone out for some reason, although I couldn't imagine why he hadn't slept there. Then I saw the note on the table."

He looked to McCrae, who reached into his coat, pulling out a folded document. "No envelope." He handed it to Holmes, who studied it for a moment before passing it my way. It was a typical sheet of stationery, approximately twenty-four bond, with no markings or decorations. A message was centered on the page, written in black ink in block-capital letters:

We have Carnegie, and he will pay for his rich-man sins.

More information to follow.

I handed it back to Holmes, who – with McCrae's permission – retained it, slipping it into his own coat pocket.

"You then notified the police?" Holmes asked the secretary.

McCreevy nodded. "It didn't say not to. I didn't know where else to seek help. This needs to be kept secret – knowledge that Mr. Carnegie has been taken could rock the financial world! We must get him back as soon as possible!"

"Mr. McCreevy arrived at the station early this morning. I myself happened to be there, and he spotted me as soon as he entered. I could see that something had happened. When I saw what the letter said, I notified my superintendent, who had arrived shortly. He recalled that you were here, Mr. Holmes, and sent us to enlist your aid, while he takes the matter discreetly to his superior."

"Have you made any investigation at the hotel where he was taken?"

"Not yet, other than to send my sergeant, Dufrain, to keep watch. I was uncertain as to the best way to begin without letting on through my questioning that Carnegie is missing."

Holmes nodded and then stood. He winced, and I knew that his shoulder was in pain. "Until we receive a further communication, examining the hotel may prove useful."

I held up a hand. "First, I must change Mr. Holmes's bandages. He received an injury yesterday."

McCrae raised an eyebrow. "I'm sorry. I had no idea. Perhaps you should instead stay here and recuperate – "

Holmes shook his head impatiently. "This matter intrigues me, and there are certain points of interest about it. We will be ready soon." And he turned and walked into his bedroom. I retrieved my medical bag and followed.

When the door was shut, he took off his coat, partially unbuttoned his shirt, and pulled it back to reveal his bandaged shoulder. I was relieved to see that the wound was already starting to heal, and there were no signs of infection, drainage, or blood poisoning.

"Did you notice the ransom letter?" he asked in a low voice.

I nodded. "The ink?"

"Exactly. You've learned a great deal during our association."

I finished re-fixing the bandage. "What do you hope to find at the hotel?"

"I'm uncertain, although the next ransom note should prove to be quite interesting – and of course there will be one. It's rather fortunate that we happened to be Dunfermline."

"Hmmph," I grunted. "I suppose so – although I'd rather hoped to be on our way home soon."

"I suspect that our delay will be rather short," Holmes countered. "In the meantime, let's see how this affair plays out." He shrugged back into his shirt, rebuttoned it, and then got back into his coat, which I held for him. "Ready?"

We joined the inspector and the secretary, who were standing near the door, ready to depart. Holmes and I donned our coats and hats, because the September Scottish mornings were already cool. Then we went downstairs, where Holmes had a quick word with the landlord to inform him that we might not be leaving that day after all, and to hold our rooms just in case. Then we went outside and climbed into a four-wheeler.

It turned out that we didn't have far to travel. Our own temporary lodgings were in Canmore Street, and we traveled south and then east for ten minutes or so. At one point, McCreevy pointed vaguely west and said that Carnegie's birth place was not far in that direction, and that he'd chosen the inn where they were staying because it was near that old neighborhood. That seemed reasonable, until we arrived at The Whiteclaw

Inn – a most unlikely place for one of the world's richest men to tarry, even if he was traveling *in cognito.*

In fact, the lodgings where Holmes and I had spent the night, quite modest, were much nicer than the establishment which we now entered. It was an old building, with foundational cracks and moss-covered spots masking areas of damp and decay on the old stone walls. It was only two stories, and the slate of the low roof over the first floor was in terrible shape. In fact, there were several small trees growing up there in soil that had accumulated in valleys between the different peaks and gables. It exuded a certain shabby charm, which could also be said for the owner who met us as we stepped inside.

Mr. Ryan O'Connor introduced himself with a strong Irish accent. He was about forty with red hair and nose – the hair extending to his thick beard high on his cheeks, and even a few stray bristles growing from his bulbous nose. His thick brows lay across very blue eyes, bracketed by deeply grooved laugh lines which were now compressed with a wary expression. He recognized McCreevy and McCrae, as his wife, a short plump woman who joined her husband, asking, "What would the police be doing here, Inspector McCrae? The sergeant won't tell us a thing – he said you'd explain."

It was then that another man came down the creaking stairs and joined us. As there had been no noise prior to his appearance, he must have been sitting on the stairs just out of sight.

"This is Sergeant Dufrain," explained McCrae. "I sent him here after we were notified of the . . . incident."

"Incident?" asked O'Connor with surprise.

Holmes stepped forward. "It appears that Mr. *Smith* – " He glanced at McCrae to confirm that Carnegie had been known by that name here too. The inspector nodded. "It appears that he didn't sleep here last night."

"He's missing?" asked the women.

Holmes nodded, asking, "When was the last time that you saw him?"

The both started to speak at once, and then O'Connor gestured for his wife to continue. "It was last night, when I went up to retrieve their dishes after dinner," she said. "Mr. McCreevy's were in his room, as he'd already gone into Mr. Smith's sitting room. I went there next to gather those."

"That's right," agreed McCreevy. "I remember you coming in."

"And I last saw the two of them when they came back for the day," added the innkeeper. "About six, I expect."

The inspector nodded. "That's when the sergeant and I dropped the two of them off after their day of sightseeing."

"Who else is employed here?" asked Holmes.

"No one," responded O'Connor. "Not as employees – Rather, it's family-run. My wife and me, and our daughter Emily, and Amos, my orphaned nephew. He's fifteen, and totes things, makes up the fires, and so on. Emily acts as a maid and helps with the cooking."

"Do you have any idea how Mr. Smith might have left the inn?"

The couple looked at each other and then back at Holmes, each shaking their heads. "We do not. The doors – front and back – are locked each night, and that's how I found them this morning. We have the keys for the main doors – we don't provide them to our guests. If someone is going to be out late and wants to door left on the latch, we refuse and tell them to ring the bell. We'll get up to let them in. And no such request was made last night."

"Would your daughter and nephew have honored such a request without telling you?"

"Of course not. Emily!" he bellowed. "Amos!"

He needn't have yelled. Both had been listening just beyond a nearly closed door, and they entered when called. They were about the same age, he being a big handsome lad and she quite petite and pretty. I noted that as the entered the room, their hands seemed to be falling away from one another, as if they'd been holding them while surreptitiously listening. I deduced from that, and the way they stood close together, unconsciously touching shoulders, that these two cousins might someday be asking for permission to wed. I wondered if the O'Conners were already aware, or if the two young people weren't as discreet as they may have believed.

Holmes repeated his questions about whether or not anyone could have arrived or left by the front and back doors, and they confirmed that there had been no such activity during the night to their knowledge. The family slept in apartments at the back of the ground floor, and there were currently no other guests.

Holmes thanked them, and then asked if we could see "Smith's" room upstairs. The sergeant turned and led us into the darkened stairwell. It wasn't a great distance to the next level, as the ground floor had those low ceiling so common in old buildings.

The upper hallway was lit by a window that looked out over the front of the building. There was enough light to see that there were four rooms, two with open doors on the left – apparently those currently vacant – and two closed on the right. McCreevy stepped past the sergeant to the nearer door, pulling a key from his pocket. "Mr. Carnegie's," he explained unnecessarily as he unlocked it. Then, without stepping aside to allow us past him, he entered first before stopping with a startled noise, blocking the way.

The sergeant, next in line, moved forward and nudged the secretary out of the way. The rest of us followed. It was a modest sitting room, much like the one that we had left at our own inn not long before. This one was older though, with exposed beams running along the plastered ceiling, and much darker and heavier furniture anchoring the old rug which nearly covered the wooden floor. There was a double window on one side, which I soon learned looked out onto one of the sloping roofs at the side of the building, and a door which led into a darkened bedroom. This chamber had no window, as it appeared to be an interior room aligned in the same direction as the other closed door we'd seen in the hallway – where it was assumed that the secretary had slept.

At first I saw no reason for McCreevy's reaction upon entering. Then my focus narrowed to a round table near the center of the room, upon which a folded sheet of paper lay.

Everyone started in that direction, but at a sharp exclamation from Holmes, we stopped while he examined the rug, making his way carefully to the table. Only after he had looked at the paper from several angles did he reach and pick it up.

He examined it front and back, and his mouth pulled tighter on one side for just an instant. Then, he said, "Allow me to read this – the latest ransom note:

If you want to see Carnegie alive again, gather £50,000 by noon. Instructions will follow.

We are not afraid to kill him.

The inspector glanced at the sergeant, both with scowls of irritation. I took the note from Holmes and saw that it matched the previous message – same type of paper and ink, and the exact block-capital handwriting. As I handed it back, McCreevy wrung his hands.

"We must hurry!" he said. "They've barely left us any time at all. Inspector – Which way is he nearest telegraph office? I must wire Pittsburg immediately to arrange a transfer of cash."

"Wait a moment," responded the inspector. "Wouldn't it be best if we waited for Mr. Holmes to have a chance to complete his investigations? After all, there must be some clue as to how Mr. Carnegie was taken – and how this second note was left here in a locked room while the Sergeant guarded the stairs."

"I favor taking O'Connor and the lot of them to the station and finding out what they know," interjected Sergeant Dufrain, his voice a low and

231

intimidating rumble. "If there's a story to be told, he'd be the one to tell it."

Holmes shook his head. "No, Sergeant. Mr. McCreevy may be right – he needs to try and raise the money. There's no telling how long it might take to get to the bottom of this affair based on what clues there are here at the inn. In the meantime, these kidnappers seem to mean business. And I suspect that should word get out, as threatened, that Mr. Carnegie's life is in danger, financial markets on both sides of the Atlantic will be shaken."

The secretary nodded. "That's correct. Fortunes might be made and lost during the buying and selling that would occur if this news were to spread. Better that we pay them, get Mr. Carnegie back, and then see about catching and punishing them. Inspector, the nearest telegraph office."

"I can have Dufrain take you."

Holmes raised a hand. "I need the sergeant for a different chore. Mr. McCreevy can go alone."

McCrae was clearly nonplussed, but he nodded and gave McCreevy directions to an office several blocks away. Then, looking at each of us quickly, the thin man departed. We heard him noisily and hurriedly descend the stairs, and then came the sound of the front door opening and closing.

Holmes turned to the sergeant. "About that chore – "

"Yes, Mr. Holmes?"

"Leave by the back door and take a different route to the telegraph office. Take care not to be seen. Does the building have a rear entrance? Do you know the employees there?"

"Yes to both questions."

"Good. Slip in the back and confirm whether McCreevy actually sends a wire. If he does, it will be immediately. No need to wait around too long one way or another. Return here when you're satisfied."

The sergeant glanced at the inspector, the beginnings of a knowing smile forming on his face. Then he slipped out of the room and was gone.

"You suspect McCreevy then?" asked McCrae. "Can't say as I'm surprised. He's an odd one, and that's a fact."

"I do. Watson, explain the ink while I look through his and Carnegie's rooms." Then he turned and began the type of examination to which I'd become accustomed – crawling along the rug, taking measurements and looking all around from different angles, all-the-while making a series of mutters and clicks and other odd noises to himself. This was clearly a distraction to the inspector, as he kept turning his head to glance at my friend while I told him about the ink on the letters.

"Holmes has indoctrinated me with his methods, and although I'm not nearly as good as he, I can see a thing or two. The ink on the first letter was clearly written some time ago – and not recently. One would expect that it would be written much closer to when it was needed, at the time of the kidnapping. Likewise, the letter we just found on the table here was of the same age – quite dry, and possibly written weeks ago."

"And the stationery," added Holmes, returning to the sitting room from the darkened bedroom.

"What about it?" I asked. "I didn't notice anything about that."

"It wasn't new – rather there are minute age marks and discolorations in the paper where the acids from the initial manufacture have begun to break down. This in and of itself is meaningless, but the dimensions of the sheets are trimmed according to American size and custom, not British. This leads me to assume that the paper was purchased some time ago in the United States and brought here." He looked toward the door. "One moment . . . ." Then he walked out into the hall and in the direction of the secretary's room. McCrae and I looked at one another and then followed him.

The other room at the back of the building was entered by way of a narrow hall that ran from the door and into the actual bedchamber. This hall must have run along the back of the inner bedroom used by Carnegie, as accessed from the adjacent sitting room. It had apparently been constructed this way to allow the smaller room its own window on the back corner of the building. This bed had clearly been used the night before, with the sheets rumpled and the covers thrown back. A small trunk was sitting on a stand near the window, and Holmes was already searching through it by the time we joined him. Heedless of the fact that his efforts would be obvious when McCreevy returned, he tossed clothing aside as he delved deeper.

Eventually he gave a small cry of satisfaction and leaned back, pulling a leather folder from the depths. Opening it, he held it flat and turned so that we might see: It contained stationery of the same size and type as that upon which the two notes had been written.

He flipped through the papers with his fingers until he found an example. Then he pulled one loose that had a name and address inscribed at the top: *Albert McCreevy, Arbor Street, New York, NY, USA.* "There are also blank sheets, as we saw earlier – the ransom notes. Those are for additional pages, should they be needed in addition to the cover sheets."

He handed the leather folder to us. "You'll notice that the stains match those on the ransom letters." While the inspector and I examined the papers within the folder, Holmes continued looking through the trunk.

"At least then we can safely assume that this fellow really is Albert McCreevy from America, I suppose," said McCrae, folding one of the blank sheets and putting it into a pocket. "But what's his game with kidnapping Carnegie?"

Holmes looked up and shook his head. "Inspector, surely you don't think that man is actually Andrew Carnegie?"

McCrae frowned. "No, I suppose not. But he seemed legitimate enough yesterday – you can't fake a Scottish accent enough to fool a real Scotsman. And he looked enough like Mr. Carnegie from when he visited in '81. I didn't have any dealings with him then, but based on what I saw yesterday, I willingly accepted him. What makes you think that he's a fraud?"

Holmes looked at the piles of untrunked clothing and then seemed to decide that replacing them wasn't worth the effort. "Come with me," he said, leading us back to the larger rooms next door. Once there, he went into the bedroom and we followed. "Look at Carnegie's clothing."

There were a couple of suits hanging in the closet above a pair of worn shoes. Holmes picked up one of the shoes and began to examine it while McCrae extracted a suit, carrying closer to the gaslight on the wall to examine it. He then looked at Holmes and was about to shrug when he thought to take a second look. Whatever he saw interested him greatly.

"Would you care to see as well, Watson?" asked Holmes.

"The inspector can enlighten me."

McCrae looked up and gestured with the suit. "It's well-worn – not the suit of a wealthy man. And it has London labels – it was manufactured on this side of the Atlantic, and not in America."

"While it's possible that Carnegie bought some London suits when he was last over here, and while it's also possible that he's a frugal man who doesn't dress to fit his station in life, the odds are more certain that these items belong to a much poorer man – one who is originally from Scotland, and who looks enough like Andrew Carnegie that making this attempt was worth the effort."

"But what attempt?" I asked. "If this isn't Carnegie, then a wire to America asking for ransom will be worthless, as they'll know Carnegie is there – or somewhere else. Anywhere but here in Dunfermline."

"But what if Carnegie really is over here right now," offered the inspector, "touring about in much the same way that McCreevy described, and these two got wind of it and concocted this plan to get the Americans to pay?" Then he shook his head. "But they would be in communication with the real Carnegie, and could quickly verify that he hadn't been kidnapped at all."

Holmes smiled and rehung the suit. "If the sergeant's report goes the way I suspect, then we'll soon know the next part of what Mr. McCreevy intends. In the meantime, let me see if I can determine just how our *faux* Carnegie left last night while the front and back door were locked – since, in spite of the sergeant's suspicions, I'm not inclined to think that the O'Connor clan is involved."

With that, he moved to the sitting room window, overlooking the sloped roof across a portion of the first floor. He examined the window frame, and then unlatched it. "Notice," he said, "this window has been recently opened."

"The O'Connor's might have done that," said the inspector.

"True," responded Holmes, "but it's unlikely that they needed to go outside." The latch had turned easily enough, and without hesitation, Holmes then climbed out onto the gently sloping slates, moving immediately to one side and with great care, as they were mossy and slick from the recent rains.

"Look," he said. "There are smudges and portions of footprints leading from the window down to the edge." He crept lower and looked over. "It's just a five- or six-foot drop here – and there are marks in mud below where someone has jumped off."

Then he jumped off too.

McCrae and I looked at one another, and then I shut the window and we returned to the center of the room. In just a moment, we heard the front door open. There was muted conversation below, and then the sounds came of more than one person climbing the stairs.

Holmes entered, followed by Sergeant Dufrain. "The prints in the mud are the same size and width as the shoes in 'Carnegie's' closet," explained the former. Then he turned to the policeman. "Your report, Sergeant?"

"As expected, the secretary started in the direction of the telegraph office, but then went into a pub. Still there, I suppose. Should I have had someone stay with him?"

"Not necessary," said Holmes. "So far this is all meaningless – the ransom notes, the mysterious disappearance." He explained his theory about the false Carnegie. "McCreevy has to come back here to add the final piece."

"And what's that?" asked McCrae.

We heard the sound of the front door open and close. Then there were quick steps upon the stairs.

"Thus begins the last act," murmured Holmes softly and cryptically.

McCreevy entered through the sitting room's open door, flustered and obviously quite upset. It took him a moment to catch his breath, and he held up a hand indicating that he would respond soon to our implied questions. Then, with a deep final deep inhalation, he straightened, adjusted his coat, flattened his hair which had become rather untidy, and said, "They can't do it! The American bank! Not that quickly!"

Holmes stepped forward, his voice oozing worry and concern. "Can't do what? Pay the ransom?"

McCreevy shook his head, and there were tears starting to form along his lower lids. "That's right. They can send us the money by wire, but it will take time to arrange for such a notable sum. Verifications must be established on both sides. Before that can be done, the time limit will have passed! They'll kill him!"

"But surely," Holmes responded, "the kidnappers will understand. Perhaps if we leave them a note – "

"How? They've left no way for us to respond back to them. The communication have all been one way – notes left here on the table."

"An advertisement, then," said Holmes, energy in his voice. "We can place one in the newspaper, saying that we need more time. Will a day suffice, do you think?"

McCreevy shook his head, almost angrily. "We can't put anything in the newspaper that might give any hint that Mr. Carnegie has been kidnapped. The financial markets of several countries couldn't take the uncertainty that would cause."

"But if we phrase it so only the kidnappers understand?"

"No! Even if we could get it published *now*, what if they don't see it? What if they don't understand it? What if they simply don't believe it and kill Mr. Carnegie? No – we have to come up with the money *now* – Quickly! – and wait for their instructions on how to deliver it."

He fell into deep thought, pulling his lip and rocking a bit in place, casting his glance toward one of us and then the other. I was quite impressed with his performance, and would have believed that he was truly dreading the possible outcome of this terrible situation if Holmes hadn't alerted our suspicions. As yet, there was nothing illegal about this, other than wasting the policemen's time. I knew that the man's move must come soon. Finally he was ready and, with a seemingly genuine expression of beaming enlightenment, he looked at the inspector.

"Perhaps . . . perhaps some of the community leaders – the wealthy men of Dunfermline – can gather the ransom. Temporarily, so that it may be paid now, and then reimbursed tomorrow when the funds are transferred from America. If you can introduce me to them, Inspector, we may be in time to avert this tragedy before the next note arrives with the delivery instructions."

McCrae frowned and started to speak, but Holmes stepped forward first. "But Mr. McCreevy, the delivery instructions are already here," he said. "They were put into our hands while you were away, sending your wire to the United States."

It was fascinating to watch how quickly the man's appearance changed. When he was worked up with concern regarding the unavailability of the ransom money, and then suddenly enthused at his idea of raising the funds from the Dunfermline elite, there had been two spots of color the size of pennies on each of his otherwise pale cheeks. Now, he was suddenly and completely white, and his skin had taken on a sudden oily sheen.

Holmes withdrew from his coat pocket a sheet exactly matching the stationery from McCreevy's room. Unfolding it, he said, "We found this in your room this time. Clearly the kidnappers were free to come and go wherever they liked. Would you like to hear what it says?

> *Take the money to Pittencrieff House and leave it on the fairy statue at two o'clock today.*
>
> *No excuses or Mr. Carnegie will be mailed, a piece at a time, to every post office in Scotland.*

"Pittencrieff House?" Holmes asked, looking up.

Sergeant Dufrain nodded. "There's a fairy statue in one of the gardens on the south side."

Holmes looked back at McCreevy. "Is that where your confederate was to gather the loot once it was deposited there?" No response. Sergeant Dufrain had quietly moved between McCreevy and the door.

"You should know that your partner as already peached on you," Holmes prevaricated with absolute sincerity. "He was seen dropping off the roof last night while effecting his mysterious disappearance. The constable was suspicious and followed and arrested him. It didn't take long to get the truth out of him. Then we simply had to wait and see if you also took enough rope to tangle yourself."

This blatant fiction wouldn't have stood up to a rigorous examination, but McCreevy was in no position to make one. One could almost hear the roar of blood in his ears as his mind raced to catch up, while considering his best path forward. Finally, determining that surrender was the only option, he gave a weak smile and took a couple of steps to the table, where he sank into a chair.

"You have me then, that's for sure. But – " he added, looking cannily at the inspector, " – what's the charge?"

McCrae started to answer, then looked from the sergeant to Holmes to me, and then clapped his mouth shut. He rubbed his jaw. Holmes smiled and shook his head.

"The best you can do is escort them both out of town, Inspector. Other than wasting your time, no crime has been committed."

"But if you had let him carry through with his plan – with leaving that next ransom letter telling us where to deliver the money – we could have brought charges."

"I don't think so – for after all, the plot, as flimsy as it was, would never have progressed to the point where the locals actually put up the funds."

McCrae nodded. "I suppose that's correct."

"Isn't it better to have pinched this off early, and avoid the pesterment of arrest and a trial and even incarceration – all at the public cost and the peripheral embarrassment of Mr. Carnegie – for something so ridiculous?"

McCreevy seemed to bristle at hearing his plan so denigrated, but he didn't argue the point.

"Your compatriot," asked Holmes. "Do you know how to find him, or do we have to go through the rigmarole of making up a package and leaving it Pittencrieff House for him to recover?"

"But . . . but you said that you'd arrested him . . . ."

"I lied."

The thin American shook his head and explained in clipped tones that his partner, one Colin Dean, could be found at another inn not a dozen streets away.

And so he was – still asleep with a mostly empty bottle of whisky on the table beside him. It took quite a while for him to come to his senses and realize who we were, and I wondered if he would have been able to rouse himself and collect the ransom money, had the plan been a success. When he spotted McCreevy in our company, he initially thought that he'd been betrayed, and he awkwardly rose and lunged at his partner, but fell heavily when his feet became tangled in the bedclothes.

Holmes glanced at McCreevy. "You played a bold game with very poor cards," he said. "But choosing this thin limb to carry so much weight was a mistake."

"I know," said the false secretary, looking at his struggling associate with disgust. "I know."

Later, McCreevy explained to us, almost conversationally, that he (from Scranton, Pennsylvania, where he was aware of Andrew Carnegie from nearby Pittsburg) and Colin Dean (of Glasgow), had met a couple of years before in France and had fallen in with one another. It wasn't confirmed (but implied) that they had worked together to fleece the gullible wealthy whenever they had the chance, through a variety of ventures. A month earlier, they had seen in the paper an article where the Dunfermline library, as funded by Carnegie, was set to open. McCreevy had noted Dean's rather remarkable appearance to the wealthy benefactor, and the plan was born.

They had arrived unannounced, except for a vague wire to the police, with their story of visiting the new library and seeing the sites of some of Carnegie's boyhood memories without attracting any attention. They had boldly decided to notify the police for assistance, believing that officers in the smaller town wouldn't be sharp enough to see through their scheme, and that if they could rush the events forward quickly enough, there wouldn't be time to stop them. McCreevy had presented himself to the police that morning with the ransom note and his frantic worry, and it had meant nothing to him with the inspector suggested that they consult someone named Sherlock Holmes who happened to be in town just then.

Curiously, Holmes admired McCreevy's boldness, if not his execution, and nearly a decade later, the American confidence man was a useful recruit in one of the campaigns that Holmes contrived as part of his assault on Professor Moriarty's criminal web.

Some years later, we happened to be passing through Dunfermline once again and took the opportunity to visit with McCrae, now a retired Chief Inspector. We had stayed in touch over the years, seeing him occasionally, and he seemed glad to see us. He let us know that a year or so before, Andrew Carnegie had purchased Pittencrieff House, where the ransom was to have been deposited, and donated it to the city. Then, changing the subject, he said that he had something of a surprise for me, and made sure that we had time to accompany him.

Not knowing what to expect, we joined him in his automobile, whereupon he drove us through the city. As we neared Pittencrieff House, I expected that we would stop there, with our errand having something to do with Carnegie. Instead, we continued west, eventually arriving at a worn little cottage. With a smile, McCrae led us to the door while telling me, "I learned through a mutual acquaintance that you have family here, Doctor. I thought you might enjoy visiting with your Great-Aunt Grace."

Then the door opened, and I found myself face-to-face with the same terrible gargoyle of my long-ago youth. Despite her wizened condition and shrunken stature, she was still the shrew that I'd met so long ago, even as she now approached her century-mark.

And she remembered me, proudly recounting all the faults she recalled from our first and only meeting, and how it was obvious that none of them had been repaired or remediated in the decades since.

It was a terribly unpleasant hour, although Holmes and the inspector seemed to enjoy it. In fact, they appeared to find her quite pleasant company.

I have never cared for Dunfermline.

The Laodicean Letters

Chapter I

"I'll wager that you haven't seen one of these before!" crooned the hunchbacked man.

He had a beatific smile upon his wide face as he leaned upon the counter. From the other side, Sherlock Holmes stepped closer with enthusiasm, while I took a moment to study our surroundings.

The space was small – no more than a dozen square feet – and to call it a shop was charitable. Flaked paint on the front door spelled the words *Winslow – Antiquities*, but the room in which we stood had nothing more than an empty scarred counter, a shelf with a few collapsing old books that looked to be from the early sixties, and some forgettable trinkets in the window consisting of various nicked and dinged maritime devices – a brass telescope and astrolabe, for instance – and a grimy-looking gasogene of ancient manufacture.

The window was dirty and would need the better part of a day to clean, should one choose to do so, but judging from the equally dusty interior, such was not one of Mr. Winslow's higher priorities.

Holmes was leaning closer, shifting slightly to one side in order to catch what light he could from the front window. He was examining an ancient-looking document, curled and ragged at the edges. To assist, Winslow reached and shifted a lamp closer.

"The Laodicians?" asked Holmes, looking up.

"An early Christian church – from the Apostolic era. They were located in Laodicia, on the river Lycus, in Phrygia – now a part of Turkey. It was then one of the Asian areas under Roman control. The river itself is something of a curiosity. It flowed west from Mount Cadmus before vanishing into a chasm in the earth. However, after half-a-mile or so it reappeared. After flowing by Laodicia – "

Holmes tapped his finger on the counter beside the document, pulling Winslow back to the shop. "Thank you," he said. "My ancient Greek is quite rusty, and this isn't quite the modern incorrect version now taught in our universities." He straightened up. "Fifteen-hundred years?"

"If the text is to be believed, it should be two-thousand."

"Also years?" I interrupted. "That document is truly two-millennia old?"

Instead of receiving an answer, Holmes said, "I gather there's more to this than simply letting me read an ancient letter to a long-gone people."

"I thought you'd enjoy seeing it, Mr. Holmes," said Winslow. "And a few others like it as well."

Having been awakened early that February morning and urged into a cab before I'd had breakfast and coffee, I needed to know more.

The sun had not yet risen when Holmes knocked on my door. It had been a bitterly cold night, and I was still wrapped tightly in my blankets. I decided that continued sleep was my first priority and ignored Holmes's second knock. Then, as I should have expected, I heard the door open, and I sensed through my closed eyelids that a candle was being carried into the room. In seconds, I was awakened by a tugging at my shoulder.

"Arise, Watson!" Holmes cried. "The game is afoot – something a bit unusual. Not a word! Into your clothes and come!"

Five minutes later we were both in a cab and trundling through the silent streets on our way to the City – specifically, some unnamed lane that ran from north-to-south between Houndsditch and Leadenhall Street.

"Winslow's is a most peculiar place," Holmes was explaining while I struggled to follow. "I discovered it when I first came up to London. The shop itself isn't much to look at, but for those who know, it's a gateway to academic and historical treasures. He specializes in documents – the more ancient the better. Many is the time that the British Museum has decided they want this or that added to their collection, and they've recruited Winslow to their cause. He is a most effective agent.

"It was through the Museum that I first heard of him. In those early days when cases were few, I devoted a great deal of my time to study, attempting to gather all knowledge that I might need for my chosen profession. On one occasion, for instance, I was hired by a Manchester businessman with notions of social advancement to locate a rumored first draft of *Vortigern*. Have you heard of it? In 1796, it was touted as a lost Shakespeare play, before it was revealed to be a hoax, perpetrated by William Henry Ireland, the prominent forger. Jacob Sherwood, my client, had the notion that the forgery must have been copied from an original legitimate work, and based on a recommendation from a friend of his for whom I'd done a small service, he hired me to find it.

"The Museum scholars scoffed at the notion of a legitimate earlier version of *Vortigern*, but they pointed me toward Winslow, and it was fortunate that they did, for it was my introduction to a whole new area of study. After I had located the lost legitimate *Vortigern*, I did some further work for Winslow, helping him to authenticate that Shakespeare also actually wrote *The Birth of Merlin* and *Locrine*. From there – "

At this point, I had to interrupt. "Wait – Are you saying that there are other Shakespeare plays – *legitimate* plays – that are out there, unknown to the general public?"

Holmes nodded. "But like the suppressed books of the Bible, there are reasons for them to be hidden away."

This comment soon turned out to be of tangential relevance, although we didn't know why then. Before I could ask further questions about these earlier cases – for I knew that chances were high Holmes might never discuss them again – he raised a hand. "We're here."

Inside, we found the shop empty, but Holmes called out, and in seconds a door behind the counter opened to reveal Winslow. "Thank you for coming," he said in a high-pitched voice. "I knew that you wouldn't mind such an early summons."

With his twisted spine, he was no more than five-feet high. He had a long rectangular head, a full beard spilling over his chest, a little knuckle of a nose, and small round glasses over merry dancing eyes. He presented a warm dry handshake and seemed delighted to meet me.

"I'll wager, Doctor, that you were asleep not half-an-hour-ago." His eyes twinkled in the dim light.

Before I could affirm it, he continued, nodding. "Ha! Young Mr. Holmes isn't the only one who can observe and make a deduction! Never fear, Doctor! In a few moments, I'll have some breakfast for us and a bit of tea. Or perhaps coffee will be more to your liking? I see from your expression that is your preference. Coffee it shall be! But first – " He turned back toward the doorway. " – let me retrieve the reason that I've asked you here."

"An invitation to breakfast," Holmes said softly. "He already likes you."

Winslow was back in just a moment, placing the ancient-looking parchment on the counter.

After Holmes's examination and our discussion of the Laodiceans, I was still puzzled. "It's an ancient letter, then?" When they both nodded patiently, I added, "What is the significance?"

Winslow smiled, as if I were a bright pupil who had potential after all. "Let us adjourn to my parlor and we'll discuss it further."

"An honor, Watson," murmured Holmes as we rounded the counter. "You've passed a test. Distinct! Not everyone is invited into the inner sanctum."

Crossing through the doorway was as if we had entered another realm of existence. Whereas the front shop had been plain, bare, and dirty, Winslow's private quarters could only be described luxurious, although in a curious way. The furniture was old, but solid and beautiful. There were

243

fine rugs on the floor, and a number of lamps lit to make the room bright and cheerful. There didn't seem to be a speck of dust – which was surprising, as the vast majority of the space was given over to a truly impressive amount of old books and documents. Their familiar and peculiar and comforting smell was quite apparent.

The room had no windows, and every wall had built-in floor-to-ceiling shelves of some dark-stained wood. Tabletops and several desks all had books stacked on top, but neatly – very much unlike my friend's methods of filing, where leaning piles of papers were mounded against one another to form flying buttresses constructed of paper, with additional support from other sinister criminal souvenirs best left unnamed. Amassed dust was a constant source of disagreement in Baker Street, as Holmes wouldn't allow Mrs. Hudson to clean around his carefully hoarded documents, and therefore I was often set to sneezing or racing to open a window (when the weather allowed) when he went hunting for some hidden or misplaced sheet. No such dust was evident here.

Winslow rang a bell, and an elderly woman shuffled in from a door at the rear of the room. After inquiring our preference, our host told her, "Coffee please, Mrs. Harris. And perhaps a bit of breakfast as well?" She smiled, nodded, and withdrew.

We were directed toward a grouping of chairs surrounding a low wide table, upon which were three other documents, all somewhat similar to the one we'd just seen in the shop. Winslow had carried that one back with him, and laid it to one side of the others.

"Mrs. Harris and her husband run the house," Winslow explained to me as we were seating ourselves. He waved a hand toward the surrounding room. "The rest of the building is laid out along these same lines – each room filled with books and papers. I have more volumes arranged in the other rooms of this floor, and the same in all the rooms upstairs as well. A lifetime of scholarship and accumulation, you see. The Museum is drooling to have it all, you know, just waiting for me to slip from my mortal coil." He glanced at Holmes. "This is all willed to them, but there are others who covet what's here." He lowered his voice. "Should I one day end up deceased before my time and under suspicious circumstances, Mr. Holmes, you must be certain to check on Colonel Carruthers' alibi!" And then he laughed gleefully. Holmes smiled and nodded in return, but I could see that he was filing the thought away, should it ever be necessary for further consideration.

At that moment, Mrs. Harris returned from some other part of the house, skillfully carrying a large tray containing a coffee pot and cups, as well as dishes of eggs, bacon, and toast. She began to set them on a round dining table to one side of the room, the only such flat plane free of Winslow's accumulated detritus.

Winslow apologized for making us relocate so soon after we'd found our seats. We settled at the table in front of our plates and enjoyed the excellent breakfast. After we'd had a few moments to satisfy our initial hunger, our host resumed the conversation.

"What do you know of the Lost Books of the Bible?"

Holmes frowned, and I suppose I had the same expression on my face. While he ticked over the facts he'd stored in his brain attic, I spoke. "I've heard of a few – *The Gospel of Judas*, for instance, or *The Gospel of Thomas* – Doubting Thomas, I've always supposed."

Winslow shook his head. "No, those aren't 'Lost' Books. Rather, they were simply suppressed, or left out of the Canonical Bible for various reasons. *The Gospel of Judas* relates Jesus' story from Judas' perspective, while *The Gospel of Thomas* – and some do attribute it to the famed doubting disciple – is a collection of Jesus' sayings. There are dozens of such suppressed books – *The Book of Enoch, The Wisdom of Solomon, The Gospel of Nicodemus*. No, I refer to the *Lost Books* of the Bible."

"Such as the Laodicean document you just showed us."

Winslow nodded, pleased. "Exactly! Now drink up – No coffee around the texts, if you please! – and rejoin me across the room."

We did so, and in moments we were again seated at the small table which held four documents – the Laodicean letter we had seen before, and three others, all of similar appearance. Winslow leaned forward and picked up two of them, handing them carefully to Holmes. "This is the one you previously saw, and the second is something called *The Prophecies of Iddo.*"

"Shouldn't we be wearing gloves to touch them?" I asked, before realizing that I was second-guessing an expert who had spent his whole life around such items. If he wasn't being more cautious, who was I to question him?

Winslow smiled and shook his head. Holmes, meanwhile, had retrieved his glass from an inner pocket and was studying the documents with great interest. Then he looked up, asking Winslow, "May I see another?"

The crooked man leaned forward awkwardly and retrieved a third sheet, extending it to Holmes. "*The Annals of Jehu*," he said. The he explained to me, "Detailing the story of Jehoshaphat."

Holmes was looking intently at one document and then another. Then he said, "And the fourth?"

Winslow raised his hand. "A moment – First, what are your thoughts about what you've seen so far?"

"Clearly these purport to be some of the 'Lost Books' to which you referred – although as Watson pointed out, if they were truly the ancient texts, you would have been more careful, and you might not have let me handle them at all. That factor alone seems to call their authenticity into question. However, my quick study indicates that they would appear to be authentic. The parchment seems ancient, and without chemical tests, the ink also appears to be very old. But again, I say that your rather indifferent handling of the documents implies that they are forgeries."

"And here is another reason," said Winslow, leaning forward and handing Holmes the fourth and final document.

Holmes barely had it in his hand before he barked, "Ha!" and shuffled the sheets so that he could compare the new one with another already in his hands. After just a moment, he laid those two back on the table, facing my way, and handed me his magnifying glass. One look told showed even me enough to understand their thinking.

"They're identical!" I cried. "There are *two* of the Laodicean documents!" I looked closer. "I cannot believe just how similar they are – down to the irregular shapes and folds small tears at the edges, to the age spotting of the parchment in the exact same places, and to light and dark variations in the ink." I looked up at Winslow. "This is how you knew they were forgeries? Because of this duplication?"

He nodded. "But," I continued, "how do you know that one of these isn't the real thing? Or that the other two documents aren't real?"

"Because of the way I received them." He leaned back and re-settled himself in his chair, as if getting comfortable for a story, now that he didn't have to reach for any more sheets on the table.

"There are essentially nine 'Lost Books'," he explained. "These, as I mentioned, represent three of them: Paul's *Epistle to the Laodiceans, The Annals of Jehu,* and *The Prophecies of Iddo.* These 'Lost Books' are mentioned at different places in the Old and New Testaments, and Biblical scholars have worried about them for years. These aren't like the various books that were removed from the Bible entirely, or acknowledged by some and placed into the *Apocrypha – The Book of Tobit, The Book of Judith, Ecclesiasticus,* and so on. These untold tales, if you will, are referenced specifically within the Biblical texts, but they have never been found.

"Paul references his letter to the Laodiceans in *Colossians* 4:16. Jehu's narrative of Jehoshaphat is mentioned in *Second Chronicles* 20:34, and Iddo's prophecies are also discussed several places in *Second Chronicles* – 9:29, 12:15, and 13:22, I believe. These other untold narratives are – " Here Winslow raised a hand and counted on his fingers, repeating one when he reached the sixth and final entry. "*The Book of*

Jasher, The Acts of Solomon, The History of the Prophet Nathan, The Records of Gad the Seer, and two other letters from Paul to the Corinthians and the Ephesians.

"In addition to these books, there is another lost 'treasure', so to speak: *The Book of The Chronicles of the Kings of Israel.* The Hebrew Bible refers to some twenty of these works that no longer exist. These were apparently a very detailed history of that Iron Age period from which numerous other Biblical narratives may have been drawn. We're talking about a thousand years before Christ – kings you've heard of like Saul and David and Solomon, and others far more obscure: Zimri and Omri and Pekah and Ahaz."

Winslow smiled – I found that he smiled a great deal. He raised his hand again. "I can hear your thoughts, young Mr. Holmes: Enough with the history lesson. Why have I summoned you this morning – beyond giving you the opportunity to examine some interesting documents?" He glanced my way. "You are a very patient listener, Doctor." He then pulled a folded letter from his pocket – modern and rectangular shaped, I noted, and on paper and not parchment – and handed it to Holmes.

"Two days ago, I received this." Holmes took the letter, and then, after carefully studying it front and back, he handed it to me. It was handwritten in block letters on plain cheap paper.

"As you can see," continued Winslow, "the anonymous author says that he'll be in touch in one week. He is offering to sell me the entire recently discovered *Book of The Chronicles* – all twenty volumes – for the fee of fifty-thousand pounds. A paltry sum, considering their historical value – should they be legitimate. As evidence of the seller's good faith, and his '*respect*' for my '*professional integrity*', as he puts it, he included Paul's letter to the Laodiceans, Jehu's narrative, and Iddo's prophecies, with the idea that I would return them or buy them at additional cost when the negotiations for *The Chronicles* commences."

"Wait," I asked. "There are *two* copies of the Laodicean letter. Did the sender accidentally include both?"

"I like you, Doctor," said Winslow. "You ask the right questions. No, he did not. When I received the initial package, there were only the three separate different sheets. It was only yesterday, when I discussed the situation with another collector, that I learned that he too had been sent some of the 'Lost Books', along with the same offer to buy *The Chronicles.*"

Holmes looked up, surprised. "Another collector? I was under the impression that your collection was unique."

Winslow shook his head. "Oh, no, Mr. Holmes! Mine is only a patch on what my brother has accumulated."

247

It's a rare treat to see Sherlock Holmes surprised, and this was one of those instances. His eyebrows raised dramatically, and a boyish grin settled on his face. "You have a *brother*?" he exclaimed, almost happily.

Winslow grinned as well, nodding emphatically. "I *do*!" he cried. "Lord Carringer! I'd wager that you never suspected I could have so notable a sibling, did you, Mr. Holmes?"

And indeed, apparently Holmes had not suspected it, for his surprise from a moment before continued unchecked.

"And you say he also received an offer similar to the one sent to you?" I asked, rather needlessly.

Winslow nodded. "He did. It's not well known at all that we are related, so I suspect that the forger had no idea we'd compare notes. When I received my copies of the documents, I was skeptical, but they are really excellent and convincing. I was immediately curious about *The Chronicles* – but I don't have the funds to purchase them. I then set out for my brother's home in Mayfair, where I found that he'd also received three documents as offerings of the legitimacy of the entire offer: A copy of the Laodicean letter, as well as Paul's two lost letters to the Corinthians and Ephesians, also with perfectly ancient parchment and ink, and written in old-style Greek.

"My brother had been intrigued as well, and half-convinced of the legitimacy of the offer – for lost ancient documents *are* found every once in a while, you know, so it was possible. As you can see from the letter, the author was vague as to where he claimed to have obtained them, but that would have been established during negotiations."

Winslow lowered his voice. "My brother seemed somewhat surprised to see me, and I wonder if he would have shared his good news if I hadn't arrived on his doorstep when I did. However, it turned out to be of great value to both of us to compare what we'd received, as the duplicate Laodicean letters were enough to throw doubt on the whole offer."

"Why do you think the sender was so careless?" Holmes asked. "Surely if he's forged this many of the 'Lost Books', he could have forged one more, instead of repeating one of them."

"My brother, Edwin, and I discussed that. We feel that one of these copies of the Laodicean letter – either his or mine – was a first draft, and that it contains some flaw that we haven't yet seen. It's obvious to the forger, but not so much to anyone else. And given the circumstances – that both of us initially thought we were the only ones to receive an offer – we decided that he must have decided to use the flawed copy. He also likely made similar secret offers to other collectors as well, to generate a number of private sales, rather than start some sort of bidding war. There may very well be any number of these forgeries floating around. However he did it,

248

he certainly created something that would satisfy extensive examination. We wouldn't have known, had we not placed the duplicates side by side."

"Is that the nature of collectors at this level?" I asked. "Would you normally keep something like this to yourselves?"

"Secrecy is our way, Doctor," said Winslow, "and as I said, it isn't common knowledge that Edwin and I are brothers. We had something of a falling out when we were quite young – mostly repaired now, but I went my own way then and have lived my own life."

"What about the other collectors?" asked Holmes. "Those who might also have received an offer?"

"Really, there's only one other at our level: Colin Wright. His collection isn't as extensive as that of my brother and me, but its specialization, particularly in ancient Biblical texts, is second to none."

"And have you asked him about this?"

Winslow shook his head. "No. When Edwin and I discussed this late last night, we felt it was likely that Colin has also been approached, but then I suggested that we involve you, Mr. Holmes, and we decided that your investigations, and the impressions you receive directly from Colin, would be of more value than anything I could tell you second-hand."

Holmes nodded, and then held up the letter. "The Biblical letters aren't folded – they must have arrived in a flat box. May I examine it?"

"Certainly." And he pointed to a shelf near the door to the dingy front shop area, where a flat heavy-looking cardboard box, about sixteen-inches square, was resting on a shelf, atop a pile of much newer-looking documents, all with squared edges. "The string is inside it. I cut it instead of untying it."

"Excellent," murmured Holmes as he retrieved it. Then he returned to his seat and put it under intense scrutiny. After a moment, he set it aside, disappointed. "No return address. The label is written in block letters, using a moderately worn modern-day pen and typical blue ink. The wrapping paper and twine are available anywhere in London, and there's nothing special about the knot. There's nothing of interest in the box as well – no curious soil or seeds or scraps of anything that might give a clue to the sender's location." He looked toward Winslow. "The letter – was it originally folded, or flat like the sheets?"

"Folded as you see it – lying on top. And there was no packing material. The documents fit close to the walls of the box without being folded, and the box is so shallow that they would have essentially stayed in placed without the possibility of damage, unless the box itself was crushed."

"And the cardboard is heavy enough for that to be unlikely," added Holmes. "Besides, the British mail system is extraordinarily careful of its deliveries." He looked again at the outside of the box. "Typical postage, and mailed in Charing Cross. That, too, tells us nothing. It's nearly certain that questioning the clerks there would reveal that they have no memory of this anonymous-looking package." He shook his head. "This will need to be approached from a different angle – assuming," he added, "that is why you asked us here this morning? To determine who sent these documents to you and your brother."

Winslow nodded. "That's correct. If these are forgeries – and they appear to be – then they're the best that either Edwin or I have ever seen. Someone – Colin Wright, or another amateur collector that I don't know or recall – may buy a set, and they may then achieve some sort of legitimacy which they do not deserve, terribly confusing future scholarship." Winslow sat up straighter. "Can you see your way to looking into this?"

"Of course. First thing, Watson and I will need to visit your brother. Can you provide his address?"

Winslow shared a house number in Half Moon Street, and then Holmes abruptly stood, our business here apparently finished. He gestured toward the documents. "May I take these with me?"

Winslow frowned – the first time I'd seen him do so – but nodded, in spite of his seeming reluctance to let them get away, and Holmes put the four sheets into the cardboard box in which they'd arrived and wadded the string into his pocket. I stood, and then our host pulled himself upright and shook both of our hands. I thanked him for the breakfast, and he led us back through the shop and to the front door. "I look forward to your report, gentlemen," he said just before letting us out.

Chapter II

The sun had risen further as we walked south, although the light didn't penetrate very deeply into the narrow lane. Holmes was silent as we turned into Leadenhall Street, and still when it became Cornhill. He only spoke when we reached the Bank, and then just to say, "I thought that we would be able to find a cab easier here than if we'd turned toward Whitechapel or Spitalfields."

I agreed. The street there was full of them, hansoms and growlers discharging men in fine suits as they prepared to enter the massive buildings around us and carry out the Empire's tedious but demanding financial business. It always amazed me that this area, arguably the richest part of the richest country in the world, the center of so much of the world's monetary activity and accumulation and conservation of capital, was just a few hundred feet from possibly the poorest part of the metropolis, where people lived in filth and poverty and squalor, jammed dozens to a room (when they could find one at all and didn't live in the street) in conditions that should be unacceptable if anyone in these rich surroundings bothered to give any thought to it.

From just a few years of being associated with Holmes's cases, I'd already been educated enough as to what went on in much of the East End, and I was aware that it was only a matter of time until the accumulating pressure between these two vastly disparate but adjacent worlds, rubbing against each other with increasing friction, would ignite. But I kept such thoughts to myself, aware that it was all too easy to be accused of being a radical or a socialist or a revolutionary for taking too much of an interest in one's fellow man. Society would adjust, as it always did, and such suffering would be alleviated, but it would not be painless.

Only in the cab did Holmes share his thoughts with me as we traveled up Cheapside to the Holborn, and so on to the west. "I cannot profess to have the level of expertise attained by Winslow, but I'll confess that I would have been fooled, as he nearly was as well."

"I ask again," I said, "is it not possible that one of the Laodicean letters is the real thing? Why should they both be forgeries?"

He shook his head. "The odds are greatly against it. One of the two letters is certainly a forgery. If that forgery – either the one sent to Winslow or the other to his brother – is a fake, then it's very likely that the other two documents that were included with it are fakes as well. And if that set is fake, then why shouldn't the other Laodicean letter also be a hoax, contrived for the same purpose? It is unknown right now why a duplicate of the same letter was sent, but I favor the prosaic explanation – the sender didn't know that the two men were brothers, and thought that as rival collectors they wouldn't communicate or compare notes, so it wouldn't matter. Perhaps, as Winslow said, one has a flaw that we haven't spotted. Maybe the forger didn't have enough false documents prepared to make up a full package, so he used the flawed sheet, thinking that it wouldn't be noticed."

"It sounds as if this fellow is a master forger – it was only his careless use of a duplicated sheet that gave rise to any doubts. There doesn't seem to be any way to track him – certainly not by the package he sent. I suppose you don't want to wait until the next letter arrives, to arrange for the sale, with the hope that it will provide some way to locate him." I nodded to the box, sitting in Holmes's lap. "What will you do?"

He shook his head. "I know someone who can possibly help us. Perhaps we should have spoken to him first, but Winslow's brother seemed to be the next likely port of call. Hmm . . . ." Then he knocked on the roof of the cab with his cane, asking that the driver stop for a moment

251

at the next post office. By now we were well along Oxford Street, and it only took a moment for us to pull over. Holmes handed the box to me and jumped down. He was only inside for a moment before he returned, taking back the box as we lurched into motion, resuming our course to Mayfair. Seeing my unspoken question reflected on my face, he said, "I've sent a message to someone who owes me a few favors, arranging an appointment with an expert when we finish speaking with Lord Carringer."

I nodded as he fell silent once more, knowing that all would eventually be explained. Or so I assumed. It usually was, although there were occasions when I was still left a bit in the dark, and no amount of asking would reveal additional details if it was felt that they were not my business.

In those days, Half Moon Street, at the bottom edge of Mayfair, was not a place where I'd had much chance to visit, although that changed in later years. Number 13, on the east side of the street, was nearly identical on the outside to our rooms at 221 Baker Street, but it was a world away. It had the same number of floors as our lodgings, the same width, and the front door at ground level was also on the left side of the building. The bricks were the same dun color, and there was also wrought-iron metal-work outside the first-floor windows, though such was true for many homes in London. But the faint ring of the bell sounded with unmistakable *gravitas* when compared with the functional tone at our own door, and the austere butler who answered was nothing like our dear landlady, instead being cold and intimidating. When we presented our cards, he looked, sniffed, and announced that we were expected, and that he would inform the master to see if he was available. Then he invited us in, leaving us standing in an entryway of the same dimensions and layout as our own in Baker Street, but under a vastly contrasting froth of expensive decoration.

In a moment, the butler returned and then led us through to a room that was the located where Mrs. Hudson's parlor would be, but it was a very different place indeed. There, a tall handsome man in his fifties was standing to greet us, a peeved expression on his face. "Thank you, Cain," he said, and then nodded in our direction.

He was about the same age as his brother, but otherwise they couldn't have been more different. Winslow had been bent, clearly that way since birth, while his brother, Lord Carringer, had grown strong and tall. Both had the same thick gray hair, and they wore similar glasses, perched on similar noses, but whereas Winslow's eyes were friendly and amused by life, Lord Carringer's were pinched and squinted, surrounded by lines that did not come from laughter. He saw my examination, no doubt matched by Holmes's, and he spoke in response.

"Robert and I are twins," he said, as if he'd had to explain it before, "but our lives have taken far different paths, initially at Robert's insistence, but I soon understood his reasons – for taking a different last name, for instance – and eventually I came around to agreeing with his way of thinking. But that isn't why you're here," he added, gesturing to the box in Holmes's hand, and then to a similar one on a small side table. "I presume that you'd like to examine what I received."

Holmes agreed and stepped forward, pulling out his glass as he did so. It gave me a chance to look around the room. It wasn't very crowded, with just a few chairs that were more for decoration than comfort. I realized that Carringer hadn't invited us to sit, and perceived that he also didn't intend to offer us a great deal of time.

"Your brother has a vast collection," I said, feeling rather awkward. "He indicated that it fills most of his house – and he also implied that yours is greater. I take it that you don't keep it here in your home, as he does."

Carringer's mouth tightened, as he apparently didn't feel like discussing it with a stranger, but he replied, "I have some items here – upstairs – but the majority are in the building next door – Number 12, between this building and the hotel. I have opened doorways on each floor between this building and that one, allowing for access between them. It's there that my staff maintains the collection. Both buildings have been improved – together they are now like a fortress."

Then he glanced at Holmes, who had been looking at each document – both Carringer's and Winslow's – before laying them aside and studying the second box.

"These were likely mailed at the same time – they're virtually identical. Besides the duplicate Laodicean letter, there are two others, both different, and both seemingly authentic, although I suspect otherwise. Your brother said that these are supposed to be two of the letters written by Paul – one to the Corinthians, and the other the Ephesians."

"That is correct."

"And if they were authentic, is there anything about them that's surprising – and earth-shaking doctrinal assertions that would rock the Church?"

"Not at all. They are simply reiterations of various policies and beliefs that Paul shared in his other epistles. They have some of the same sniping and disagreements about procedural disagreements with Peter that the Biblical letters contain, but nothing that would need to be suppressed, or that might cause some kind of Holy War."

Holmes nodded. "So it's likely that the forger simply wants to collect some money for the supposed value of these documents, and isn't trying to spook anyone into buying and suppressing them so that a conflict can

253

be avoided – for religious folk are so easy to inflame about the least little things."

"That's correct. For instance, there was the incident at Antioch, as described in *Galatians* 2:11–13, wherein Peter described a confrontation he had with Peter over the fact that Peter, who used to eat with the Gentiles, stopped doing so after meeting with some men sent by James, Jesus's brother, because they weren't considered acceptable. Paul argued that *all* men were acceptable. To Paul's disgust, the people of Antioch, along with the disciple Barnabas, sided with Peter – which subsequently led to a falling-out between Paul and Barnabas as well."

"Even today," I noted, "such small things can cause wars. Are you sure there's nothing of this nature in any of these letters – even if they are forgeries?"

"No, nothing at all. Just references to Paul's past visits, and adjurations to stay strong and keep to the faith."

"Your brother mentioned Colin Wright," said Holmes. "That he would also be someone who would also likely receive an offer to purchase the lost *Chronicles* of the Israeli kings. Do you agree?"

Carringer nodded. "I expect so – but we decided not to approach him, once we agreed to seek your assistance in the matter. I would be curious," he added, "to know what documents *he* received – whether he has yet another copy of the Laodicean letter, or any of the others that Robert or I received, or if he was sent copies of the rest of the 'Lost Books'."

"Your brother told us of the others. Not counting these, I believe that the others so far unaccounted-for relate to Jasher, Solomon, Nathan, and Gad."

"That's correct."

"Are these all Old Testament documents, or further New Testament letters?"

"Old Testament. Jasher is mentioned in both *Joshua* and *Samuel*, Solomon in *First Kings*, and both Nathan and Gad in *First Chronicles*."

Holmes indicated Carringer's set of documents. "Do you mind if I take these with me? It may aid in tracking down their source."

Carringer appeared, like his brother, as if he would initially object, but then with a sigh he waved a hand. "Take them. I don't believe that they're legitimate, so do what you must."

"And Mr. Wright? Where can we find him?"

"That is both easy and difficult. Colin's home is nearby – No. 2 Tilney Street, just near the Park – but he's also out of the country right now. He has been for three months, at least. He's on a buying trip, I believe, seeking the journals of a brutal Wallachian ruler from the mid-1400's – some chap who massacred tens of thousands of Turks and Muslim Bulgarians four-hundred years ago. The last I heard, Colin is in Hungary, southeast of Sibiu, in the Carpathian Mountains. Some place called Poenari Castle – *Cetatea Poenari* as they say locally – near the Arges River. Much further than I would go . . . ." He pursed his lips. "But I can provide a letter of introduction. Perhaps his secretary, Roger Melrose, would be willing to confirm whether he's also received a box. He knows more about Wright's collection than Wright does – he's the real expert – and he'd also be interested and appreciative to know if the documents are fakes."

He moved to a small desk at one side of the room and composed a short note, which was then folded and provided to Holmes. Then, with our business at an end, he rang a small bell, and when the butler arrived, he instructed him to show us out. With no further words spoken, we found ourselves back on the quiet street. Holmes, shifting both cardboard boxes under his harm, led the way up to Curzon Street, and then west and north the short distance to Tilney. Pausing at the corner, he unfolded Carringer's note before passing it to me. It was addressed to Colin Wright or Roger Melrose, simply stating that Carringer had recommended that we speak with either one of them regarding a matter of some interest.

No. 2 was much nicer than the property we'd just left, with white stone at street level and red brick stretching three stories above. It was slightly wider as well, and its clean lines had a very solid elegance about it. Knowing something of Lord Edwin Carringer's rumored wealth, Colin Wright's finer house seemed rather indicative of his more-extensive resources.

His door was not, however, answered by a butler. Instead, it was opened by one of the two men we were seeking: Roger Melrose, a rather stout fellow in his early thirties. He was a smiling man, with his face having a natural turn to pleasant and open interest. We introduced ourselves, and he seemed to have heard of Holmes, for he ushered us in immediately without any request to first state our business. He glanced curiously at the two cardboard boxes in Holmes's arms, both of which were turned to hide the address labels, and asked that we step through to a well-appointed sitting room on our left as we passed through the immaculate entry hall.

Again looking toward the two boxes, Melrose motioned toward a small rectangular table, offering us seats which we accepted, and brandy which we declined. He sat down across from us, perched upon the front of his own chair and leaning forward. With his hands on the table, the fingertips pressed lightly upon the surface like two matching five-legged spiders, he asked, "What can I do for you, gentlemen?"

When Holmes didn't immediately answer, allowing the silence to build for an awkward moment, Melrose leaned back and clasped his hands.

He began to make unknowing washing gestures, squeezing and turning one hand within another, and then reversing himself. Was it a habit, or an expression of nervousness related to our unexpected visit? I looked at him again more closely.

He was well-dressed, with brown hair parted in the middle. He wore no wedding ring. His wrists were pale, as if he spent a great deal of time inside – something to be expected if his days passed working with rare documents – and his face was rather florid, possibly from enjoying the bounty of Colin Wright's table a bit too well. Other than a small cluster of three small *acrochordons* at the outer corner of his right eye, there was nothing unusual about him that I could see, although I had no doubt that Holmes had observed a great deal more – perhaps where Melrose had grown up from certain subtle aspects of his speech, or his daily activities as revealed by the callosities on his fingers.

Holmes, still without speaking, handed Melrose Lord Carringer's note and, while the secretary read through it once, and then again, Holmes opened one of the boxes, still obscuring the label, and pulled out the four documents that we had taken from Winslow's shop, saying without explanation, "We understand that you are Mr. Wright's 'expert'. What do you think of these?" I thought that his tone seemed a bit abrupt, but he surely had his reasons. He pushed the sheets across the table, but Melrose made no effort to reach for them. Holmes then took out the two sheets from Lord Carringer's box, laying them beside the others. It was then that Melrose spoke.

"May I ask who said so?" he countered, laying down the note and folding his hands back together.

"Certainly." Holmes reached a hand forward to tap the note, now lying on the table. "As you see, we have just come from Lord Edwin Carringer's residence in Half Moon Street. It was he who said so, and suggested that we speak with you. He's aware that Mr. Wright is out of the country, and he indicated that as you are knowledgeable in this area, we should seek your opinion." He glanced down toward the sheets, adding, "He received these various parchments as part of a negotiating tactic toward purchasing a larger item. These were sent as proof of the legitimacy of that item."

"And the larger item?"

"I would prefer to reserve that information at this time."

Melrose nodded, unclasped his hands, and pulled the sheets closer. The light was good in the room, and he had no apparent difficulty in making his examination. He looked at the first sheet, turning his head with interest and making a small humming noise to himself. Then he pulled over another sheet, and another. One of the letters to the Laodiceans was the second document he examined, and when he reached the second duplicate letter, which was the fourth in the stack, his eyebrows went up in surprise. He raised his head to look toward Holmes. My friend, however, made no explanation or comment, and Melrose returned to his intense studies.

Finally, after nine or ten silent minutes, Melrose pushed the papers back, gently gripped his hands once more, and said, "An initial examination would lead one to think that these are genuine – if there weren't two identical copies of the letter from Paul. After that, one would be inclined to think that forgery is involved. Of course, one of the two letters might still be the real thing, and there's nothing to say that the other documents aren't *bona fide*. Still, tests would need to be made, an evaluation to the most exact scientific standards . . . ."

Holmes raised a hand, his tone still surprisingly abrupt. "Did Mr. Wright also receive such a package?"

Melrose glanced at the two cardboard boxes, lying on the table. "It isn't my place to comment on Mr. Wright's affairs," he said, although there was some very slight hint of disingenuousness in his tone. Or perhaps it was my imagination. Holmes's manner throughout the interview had carried an equal hint of antagonism, and possibly Melrose was simply responding in kind.

"That's unfortunate," said Holmes. "I had hoped that you might be able to provide some information to that would make our task a bit easier."

"Is that so?" Melrose responded, now with something of a sneer in his tone. "Surely you understand my position, gentlemen. You both arrive with a note from Lord Carringer, seeking confidential information, although he has never been a great friend to my employer. At the same time, you don't seem willing to share very much information with me in return. There are *two* boxes there, but surely only one of them was mailed to Half Moon Street. Whose address is on the other? Why are you so careful to keep that information hidden? You indicate that these letters were sent in relation to an offer to purchase some larger item, but you refuse to say what that is. If my employer also received such letters and a similar offer – and I'm not confirming that he did – then it's my duty to protect his interests and not take a chance on spoiling his efforts to obtain the same item – should he choose to do so. I will say, however, that it is of interest that there was a duplicate of Paul's lost letter. That seems to be a rather careless mistake on someone's part, doesn't it?"

"I think that we can agree on that," said Holmes. He stood and retrieved the various documents from Melrose's side of the table. "I believe that our business is finished." As he spoke, he sorted the sheets, this time putting three in one box and three in another, as they would have

257

been originally received before one of the duplicate letters was left with Winslow by his brother. This did not go unnoticed by Melrose. Then, with a nod, he turned and left the room. I followed, with Melrose trailing behind. Holmes opened the front door, and we went outside. Without comment, Melrose closed the door behind us, while Holmes led the way to our right, where we soon reached Park Lane, just across from Stanhope Gate. There, Holmes pulled me to one side, a sudden urgency in his voice.

"Watson, make your way back and find someplace – a door or areaway – where you can keep an eye on Wright's house. If Melrose leaves, do your best to follow him, and when you get a chance, send word to Baker Street where you end up. Hopefully he won't depart through the back entrance until I have a chance to find help."

"What is going on?" I asked, surprised at the abrupt shift of tone. "What did you see?"

"I recognized him," said Holmes, "but I cannot recall exactly where. As soon as I find some assistance, we'll follow that thread. Now – take your post!" And with that, he turned and vanished to the north alongside the eastern edge of the park.

Chapter III

Without waiting to watch him out of sight, I slipped back into Tilney Street, being as cautious as I could. By then it was late morning, and the sun was bright that day and nearing its apogee. The street wasn't very long, just enough to hold half-a-dozen buildings on each side, and No. 2 was near the center, so there weren't a lot of choices in terms of places to hide. I was fortunate that nearly across the street was a building whose areaway gate was unlocked, allowing me to slip down and out of sight. I tried to prepare some sort of story in case my presence was questioned, but fortunately no one from inside the house ever seemed to notice me.

I was there for slightly over half-an-hour, and in that time, no one came out of No. 2, and there were no indications of activity. No one looked surreptitiously from a curtained window. There were no deliveries, and no servants departed on errands – suspicious or otherwise. I realized that we didn't even know if there were servants in the house, and I had no instructions about what to do if one of them left. At least, I hoped, I would recognize Melrose if he departed, even in disguise, as he would have trouble hiding his stocky shape.

I didn't know what Holmes expected: Would Melrose withdraw surreptitiously to pay a visit to some confederate in connection with the document scheme, or would he instead boldly surge forth with luggage, making a mad dash for the Continent? And what had Holmes seen that suddenly caused him to be so urgently and immediately suspicious?

I was still worrying about what to do if Melrose actually came outside, and how I would follow him down this quiet street without being seen, when a lad sidled into sight from the west. As he approached, I could see that he was rather disreputable, with an appearance that didn't fit with this neighborhood. However, as was usually the case, instead of being chased away, he would be ignored and left to carry out his business – which I was sure involved instructions from Sherlock Holmes.

In fact, when he approached, I recognized him as Tad Willocks, one of Holmes's regular Irregulars. I had first learned of these deputized agents a couple of years before, soon after finding out that Holmes was a "consulting detective", as he called his profession. Typically we dealt with an older boy named Wiggins, who served as the group's leader, but I often encountered many other members of the group as well.

Tad didn't appear to be doing anything but ambling down the street, without purpose, but I knew that he was looking sharply from side to side. That was how he spotted me, and soon he had joined me in the areaway.

"Mr. Holmes found me near Portman Square," he said. From that, I knew that Holmes had quickly walked north toward Baker Street until he located one of the Irregulars. "It only took a few minutes to round up more of us and send us back this way. Clive is behind the house, watching the mews. Has the man come out?"

"Not by way of the front. I haven't seen anything at all. I can't vouch for the back."

"Not to worry. Before walking up and finding us in the Square, Mr. Holmes paid a beggar, Blind Steve, to keep an eye on the entrance to the mews. He didn't see anyone come out."

"Blind Steve didn't see anyone?"

"He ain't blind." He didn't add any irony to his comment. In fact, he seemed almost irritated that I didn't already know about Blind Steve. "Mr. Holmes is waiting for you in a cab at the corner of Mount Street, across from the fountain."

I nodded and left Tad there, aware that he and the other Irregulars would do a better job than I could following Melrose if he decided to leave. Returning to Park Lane, I turned north, and in moments I'd spotted Holmes, standing impatiently beside the hansom. After we'd climbed in, the driver gigged the horse into motion, and Holmes began speaking immediately.

"After I left you, I engaged this cab and turned toward Baker Street. Along the way, I found the boys and sent them this way. Then I continued to our rooms, where I consulted my scrapbooks."

The cabbie had set a fast pace, and he barely slowed when we turned right into Oxford Street at the Marble Arch. "I knew that I'd made an entry about Melrose, but it was so long ago that the information initially eluded me. Thank Heaven for those books, Watson! Even a brain attic that is trained to hold many facts will only stretch so far."

"And who is this fellow?" I asked. "Apparently he must be fairly notable to generate such immediate urgency."

"He is – and he's kept a low profile for quite a while. I last heard of him in '77, when he peddled a supposed *fifth* copy of the Magna Carta, apparently found in a West Country manor that had been a monastery before their dissolution under Henry the Eighth. The British Museum was in a bidding war with Cornelius Vanderbilt. I was able to inform the Museum of the truth, but Vanderbilt went ahead and paid a fortune – three-quarters-of-a-million. This was just before his death, and in the confusion that followed, the lawyers decided it was easier to let the man go than try and recover the money. Can you imagine, Watson – being so rich that being bilked of that amount could simply be ignored?"

"And this forger? Did you hear nothing more from him until now? And if he made that much money from Vanderbilt six years ago, why does he need to carry out another scheme so soon?"

"An excellent question. I suspect that he enjoys the excitement more than the monetary reward. No, I've heard nothing more about him, although I've made periodic attempts to see if he's surfaced anywhere. Coming across him this morning was a complete shock."

"What was it? His appearance? The way he held and moved his hands, or perhaps the skin tags beside his right eye?"

"Very good. Yes, it was both of those things – plus his general description. Brown hair parted in the center, stocky build, traces of a Manchester accent. That, and the man's association with possible forged documents, made it highly likely that we'd unexpectedly run across Archie Stamford – for that is his true name."

"I wonder that he was able to obtain Colin Wright's confidence."

"Well, from what I've heard, Wright has more money than sense. He's spent the last twenty years buying whatever he could, outbidding private scholars and collectors and notable institutions. I'm sure that we'll find that Wright's past secretary left for some reason, and Stamford saw an opportunity to take his place."

By then, we had progressed some distance across central London, staying on Oxford and New Oxford Streets when practical, and taking side streets when the mid-day traffic became snarled. In Holborn, we turned north along Southampton Row toward Russell Square, and I thought to ask about our destination.

260

"You recall the telegram that I sent earlier? I was checking on the location of someone – another noted forger who I helped to corner back in my Montague Street days: Elliott Baines. I wired to someone that I know in Whitehall, asking permission to interview him."

"Interview him?" I asked. "Permission? Is he in prison? What prison will we find in this neighborhood?"

"Not prison. Rather, he's under semi-permanent house arrest, at the pleasure of Her Majesty's Government. There are times when having a forger comes in handy, you know, and at the end of the day, Baines was quite willing to trade some of his freedom for Government service instead of a lengthy stay in Newgate."

As I pondered this, we completed our journey, stopping in front of No. 48 Doughty Street. As we climbed down, Holmes must have noticed my expression. He smiled. "Yes, you're correct – this address does have some historical notability. Do you not recall who lived here?"

I shook my head, frowning – and then I remembered. "Dickens!" I cried. "In the early days – He wrote *The Pickwick Papers* and *Oliver Twist* and *Nicholas Nickleby* while living in this house!"

"That's correct," agreed Holmes, belying the idea he's once suggested that he only kept facts in his brain attic that might have relevance to his investigations. "Apparently the building was in some danger of being torn down, and the Government stepped in, secretly, to save it, while also making use of it as a facility to house the occasional favored miscreant. There's some talk of converting it into a museum, but not yet. For now, Baines is the grateful resident, and he's kept rather busy. But let us go inside – by now he should be expecting us."

As we approached, the door was opened by a slim man in his late thirties, in a dark suit and with a tidy military mustache. It was easy to understand that he was a government agent, set in place as a caretaker for both the house and the resident. He stepped aside to let us enter.

It was a lovely little building, three stories with dark brick, and I felt a small thrill as I crossed the threshold. Charles Dickens had long been a hero of mine, and I particularly enjoyed his first three works, composed in this building. But before I had a chance to consider looking around and taking a moment to appreciate the ambience of the author who had lived here and then moved away years before I was born, we heard quick footsteps from the back of the house. In seconds, we were confronted by curious scarecrow of a man – tall and disheveled, his gray hair and beard both long and wild, his clothing unkempt and shabby, and his manner frenetic and vaguely hostile.

"So, you've come to gloat!" he said upon facing Holmes, planting his feet abruptly.

My friend shook his head, looking faintly amused. "You know better than that, Elliott. When offered this opportunity, you leapt for it. It's more pleasant than prison, and you have your own chef. These are much finer rooms than where I found you, and you have important work that makes use of your skills in a positive way, rather than simply moving from one shady venture to another."

"Perhaps, perhaps. But it isn't just about the work. There's the thrill of the *game*, Mr. Sherlock Holmes. I think you, more than most, can understand that. Here I'm no more than a dull craftsman. I might as well be a cobbler making shoes. I should join a guild!"

Holmes laughed. "I should like to see such a guild, and who would be in it!" His expression sobered. "Elliott, we've run across someone who could be a member of that group alongside you."

"We?" asked Baines, looking my way. "This one?"

"Not him. This is Dr. John Watson, my associate."

"And are you a genius like Holmes here? A single-minded bloodhound?"

I shook my head. "No sir, not a genius. Instead, I have determination."

Holmes nodded. "That's it, indeed. Now, Elliott, we won't keep you long. Can you show us into your workshop? I want to ask your opinion about a few documents." And he lifted the cardboard boxes.

Baines nodded, his curiosity ending the cranky bantering. He took us deeper into the ground floor to a room in the back of the house, with a window looking out upon a small garden. I wondered if this was where Dickens had worked.

Holmes, again keeping the addresses on the box hidden, removed the sheets of parchment from each and handed the stack to Baines, who took them, adjusted the lamp on his desk, picked up a large magnifying glass, and began his examination. Meanwhile, I used the opportunity to look around the room. There were several high tables along the walls, each stacked with a number of sheets, some ancient looking, rather like what we had brought with us, and others along the lines of official government documents, both British and representing a number of other counties. The dates on these ranged from recent to several hundred years earlier. Many were in languages that I couldn't read, but I saw some that purported to be treaties, or grants of land transfers, or official-looking bonds and currency. Interspersed among all of them were a number of pens and brushes, bottles of ink, paints and dyes, rubberized erasers, balls of discolored putty, and knives that almost appeared surgical in nature. There were, however, no signs of the past presence of Mr. Dickens.

Baines immediately became deeply involved in the documents, studying both the front sides with the writing and the blank backs as well. Murmuring softly to himself, he often turned the sheets so that the writing upon them was upside down. He reached and grabbed a pad and pencil, making a series of neatly written notes. In fifteen minutes, he was ready to report.

"Forgeries, all of them," he said, "but all of them excellent. Although they purport to be from different Biblical eras, there are a few similarities – very few and very subtle – in the lettering that that show they were written by the same hand. I'm probably the only person on earth who could have seen it."

"And do you know who this person is?"

"What? Oh, of course. And I assumed that you did too. It's Stamford. He's made a specialty of this sort of thing. Haven't heard about him in several years – though in my current digs, I don't get out to gather news like I once did."

"He's surfaced," explained Holmes. "These were sent to two different collectors to give legitimacy to a bigger offer – he's offered to sell a larger work: *The Chronicles of the Kings of Israel.*"

Baines whistled. "Well, that's ambitious, isn't it? I wonder . . . ." He drifted off for a minute, and then looked at Holmes. "One thing you should know: These are all forgeries, but the text seems legitimate. What I mean is that they are *copies* of some original work. It seems as if Stamford has somehow acquired some of the *real* Lost Books of the Bible – and if he has these, he probably has others, maybe even the actual *Chronicles.* And that could be dangerous."

"How do you mean?" I asked, thinking that neither Winslow nor his brother, Lord Carringer, had intimated any indications of danger.

"What I mean is that many of the existing and accepted Biblical books aren't original – they're supposedly drawn from *The Chronicles*, in the same way that Shakespeare took some of his plots from previously published works. For example, *Romeo and Juliet* originally came from Arthur Brookes' 1562 poem *The Tragical History of Romeus and Juliet*, and *Hamlet* was first told as the story of *Amleth* in Saxo Grammaticus' *Gesta Danorum*, or *Deeds of the Danes*. You'll notice that *Amleth* is an anagram of *Hamlet.*

"*The Chronicles* may very well tell a different kind of story than what one finds in today's Holy Texts that were based upon it – to the point that they say something that might start a war! Oh, you think I exaggerate, Doctor, but surely you know enough about people to realize how passionately they feel about this kind of thing."

I nodded, knowing that he was correct. The masses did tend to cling to their religions, and they could become quite irate, and often violent, when this was challenged. And sadly, they chose to cling to their weapons as well.

"Fortunately," said Holmes, "we have a line on tracking down these items and keeping them from causing any problems." He began to collect the sheets back into the boxes. "Many thanks for your help, Elliott. I'll be sure and notify Whitehall of your cooperation."

"Yes, do that. For what it's worth." Then the prisoner, for I supposed that's what he was, waved a hand toward the stacked tables. "For every piece of work I finish, they send two more. I'm not sure that my debt will ever be paid, nor my sentence completed – but perhaps a miracle will occur. Good hunting, Mr. Holmes! Come back some time and tell me what happened – and if you can, bring the original documents with you when they're recovered. I'd enjoy seeing them."

Without committing himself, Holmes nodded and led me outside to our waiting cab. He instructed that we should next travel to Baker Street where, he told me, he'd see if there was any word on Stamford's latest activities. He was silent throughout the journey as he arranged his thoughts. I, too, considered what we had heard and learned.

When we arrived, Holmes told the driver to wait, as we might be leaving once again. He was correct. Upstairs was a small boy, Ike Denton, perched in Holmes's chair like a prince upon a throne, swinging his feet back and forth a foot above the floor. He had a message from Tad Willocks as to Archie Stamford's location. "The man you had us watching left not five minutes after Dr. Watson. We trailed him to Waterloo, where he caught the local to Farnham. And Mr. Holmes – he had several large trunks with him!"

I perceived that this was important, for a known forger fleeing the home of a notable collector with substantial baggage was highly suspicious, implying that Stamford had moved from creating documents to stealing them.

What follows next is quickly told, although there were still a few surprises before the tale was fully revealed. Our waiting cab briskly conveyed us to Waterloo, where we were in time to catch an express that bypassed all of the local stops to which Stamford would have been subjected. As such, we reached the Farnham station just ten minutes after Stamford disembarked. Before we'd left Baker Street, Holmes had written a pair of concise telegrams, sent by way of Mrs. Hudson, seeking official assistance, and we were met on the platform by Inspector Silas Beckett, who we had last seen the year before when Holmes solved the brutal murder of the divided linguist. Beckett had received word from Scotland

Yard to provide assistance as needed, and I quickly sketched the situation while Holmes ascertained from the nearby cabbies that Stamford had just hired one of their fellows to carry him and his trunks to a farm not far past Waverley Abbey. Beckett beckoned to one side, and three constables who had been standing there joined us. Hiring two cabs, we were soon on Stamford's trail.

We caught him as he was climbing down from his cab at a rundown farmhouse, talking with a little careworn woman who turned out to be his much put-upon old mother. As he had in the past, the man we had first met as "Melrose" had retreated here when things became too hot for him. He was quickly placed under arrest, causing a surprising torrent of vile cursing and spewing epithets to pour forth from the lady's wicked and filthy mouth. On principle, Beckett took her into custody as well, although it was later determined that she was likely innocent of any charges.

The trunks contained unexpected treasures: The cream of Wright's collection, as well as a vast amount of cash. It seemed that during the weeks when Wright was away from London, traveling in the dark places of the Continent, Stamford had been quite busy, dismissing the servants and quietly selling what he could of Wright's collection before moving most of the rest to rooms he had rented in another part of the city, leaving the house on Half Moon Street nothing but an empty shell. Using his exceptional skills, he had also forged documents to transfer the entirety of Wright's funds to himself. Most daring of all, he had created a new will, in which Wright apparently left everything to his secretary, Melrose. This took on additional significance when a telegram was found among Stamford's papers, notifying the perfidious secretary that Wright had been killed two months earlier while in the Carpathian Mountains, his body savagely assaulted near the *Cetatea Poenari*, apparently attacked by some kind of large animal which had torn out his throat and drained him of blood. Seeing a unique opportunity, Stamford had gone to work, day and night, to thoroughly loot his late employer's assets.

Ready to flee at any moment, but not yet finding it necessary, Stamford had come up with another plan: To forge a number of lost Biblical books and sell them to Wright's collector competitors. He was a master at quickly creating these documents, and when he had enough of them ready, he sent the boxes to Lord Carringer and Winslow. As suspected, he'd made two copies of the Laodicean letters, one with a small flaw, and rather than take time to create another, he'd simply included the flawed copy in the box to Winslow, not realizing that he and Lord Carringer were brothers and would compare the packages.

Of greatest interest were the originals from which Stamford had made his copies. Wright, whose money made him a very effective collector, had in fact been able to purchase all nine of the Lost Books, along with the fabled *Chronicles of the Israeli Kings*, from a source in Egypt. Where they had been located before that was never determined, as Stamford claimed not to know. The true and original stories upon which many of the Old Testament books were based were quickly found to be so shocking and divisive, and contrary to the established Biblical versions known so well by so many, that they were hidden away as soon as possible within the bowels of the British Museum, where a number of other similarly dangerous items were kept. * Holmes was briefed on the contents of the ancient writings, but he felt that I would be better off not knowing.

"It's for the best, Watson," he'd said. "They should never be read. The world is not yet prepared. In truth, I'm sorry that I saw them."

I resented this attitude, treating me like a child, but I also suspected that he was correct, and that once I had seen what the original versions related, I might never forget them, to my own dismay. In the end, I ceased my entreaties to learn the truth.

> *"Yes, sir; near Farnham, on the borders of Surrey."*
>
> *"A beautiful neighbourhood and full of the most interesting associations. You remember, Watson, that it was near there that we took Archie Stamford, the forger.*
>
> — Violet Smith and Sherlock Holmes
> "The Solitary Cyclist"

NOTES

*   For information about some of the other dangerous items kept within the British Museum, see:
  - ☐ *Sherlock Holmes and The Eye of Heka*, published separately in 2021, and included in *The Collected Papers of Sherlock Holmes – Volume II: Records*
  - ☐ "The Mediobogdum Sword" in Volume IV of *The Collected Papers of Sherlock Holmes – Volume VI: Muniments* and *The MX Book of New Sherlock Holmes Stories – Part XXXIV: "However Improbable . . . ." (1878-1888)*
  - ☐ "The Peculiar Affair of the Three Owed Deaths" in this volume
  - ☐ "The Man with the Writhing Skin" in *The Further Papers of Solar Pons* and *The Necronomicon of Solar Pons*

The Faulty Gallows

Chapter I

"No," said the Warden of Exeter Prison. "Sit over there."

Sherlock Holmes nodded and turned away from the chairs in front of the warden's unusually small desk, moving instead toward a grouping of more comfortable-looking seats before a south-facing window. The view would have been pleasant enough, I suppose, looking toward the Northernhay, had it not been broken into numerous vertical rectangles defined by black iron bars.

"I appreciate you detouring this way and interrupting your return to the capital in order to meet with me," Warden Hayes. "When I learned from our mutual acquaintance in Whitehall that you were holidaying in the West Country, I took it upon myself to have him send a message to you."

Several times before, I had heard references to this man in Whitehall – someone of mysterious influence who apparently sent cases Holmes's way, or provided occasional bits of obscure information. I was no closer to knowing who he was on that day in mid-1885 than I had been since Holmes and I first met.

Holmes smiled politely. "Did our friend specifically indicate that we were on holiday? More of a working sojourn, actually."

He didn't elaborate on our efforts of the last four days – or bother to explain that it hadn't been a holiday at all. Instead, we had traveled from London at the urgent request of Sir William Creighton, who required our presence in Glastonbury because ancient corpses were being looted from local church crypts. The thief had made no effort to hide his intrusions, and there was something of a public panic in the making. The locals had made much of the fact that one of the desecrated graves had Arthurian connections, and the tales were growing in the telling – including one purporting that relics belonging to Joseph of Arimathea had also been stolen which, while quickly disproven, still continued to spread.

Holmes, by examination of the four ransacked tombs, had decided that the vast differences in the dead bodies – social status, wide ranges of deaths, and so on – meant that there was no connection between them being chosen, other than the thief needed ancient dead bodies. Without this distraction, he was able to focus on the clues at hand, such as who had access and knowledge, and the physical evidence – specifically a notable and unusual footprint – to bring attention upon Abel Wills, a part-time verger at St. John's Church. Questioning the man had revealed the truth, but not before the final plan was put into place.

Wills was in truth a pagan, a part of a small sect with rather unusual beliefs. Apparently 1885 held some special significance to them. In order to celebrate *Litha*, one of their eight *Sabbats* during the year, and known to the common-folk as *Midsummer*, they had stolen the bodies to create what he called the "Glastonbury Zodiac", wherein each would be placed upon what he called "Ley Lines", or "Lines of Power", running in every direction from Glastonbury Tor.

It was dawn of the twenty-first of June when this was finally admitted, as Wills didn't part with the information quickly. With this revelation, we were able to race the short distance east to find that his co-celebrants were already laying out the ancient bodies on each side of the terraced hill leading down from St. Michael's Tower. These misguided zealots were quickly rounded up and the desiccated and fragile corpses removed before anyone from the public saw them – but one of the group, a wild-eyed young fanatic in his twenties, pulled out an ancient pistol and shot one of the police officers before fleeing.

While I cared for the officer, whose wound was serious but non-lethal, Holmes set off in pursuit of the young villain. Holmes trapped and subdued him and, after he was placed in the custody of the official force, Holmes was then able to deduce which ancient body was which, so that they were replaced within the correct vaults. What had threatened to escalate into a full-blown public panic was averted in the early morning hours before anyone was aware of what had happened. We were prepared to depart when a telegram from London had arrived, placed into Holmes's hand by the local chief inspector, requesting that we continue instead to Exeter.

Holmes didn't bother to show me the telegram, instead stuffing it into his waistcoat pocket. "When we return to London," he said, his tone short, "I must set aside an hour or so to re-establish that I am a free agent, and not an unchoosing blunt instrument of Her Majesty's Government." Nevertheless, however peeved as he was, we made our way to Exeter.

The train, by way of Bridgwater and Taunton, wasn't crowded, and we completed the journey in something just over two hours. St. David's Station was much as I remembered it from when I'd been there before, and a hansom covered the distance to the prison, less than a mile east, in just a few minutes. Recalling that the city's High Street was not far to the south, I was tempted to request that we take time to seek a late breakfast, perhaps a Cornish pasty from a shop that I once knew, as the quick bite we'd obtained at the Glastonbury Station had been insubstantial and unfulfilling. But Holmes, despite his initial apparent resentment at being directed to Exeter Prison, now had the bit in his teeth, and he was anxious to learn more about our summons.

Thus my request to detour for food went unuttered, knowing as I did that it was pointless. Instead, I asked about the telegram.

"You didn't want to speak on the train," I stated. "Perhaps before we arrive, you can relate why we've come here?"

Holmes waved a hand. "It was very vague and terse. Never mind that the Government can afford to spend a few more pence to add another twenty words. The message did include such terms as *'national security'* and *'public confidence'*."

"Who sent the message?" I ventured, unsure if I would be answered while really wondering who could influence Holmes to change his plans and begin a new investigation with just one telegram.

He shook his head and I was disappointed. "Someone to whom I owe a great deal. And I must admit, some of my most interesting cases have come to me through him."

Clearly he preferred to keep the identity of this individual secret, and I was no more informed when Warden Hayes referred to their "mutual acquaintance", with the apparent unspoken understanding between them that he be discreet.

The warden's aide finished pouring three cups of dark bitter coffee and withdrew. Then, after we had each sipped and made inane remarks about the value of a strong cup in the morning, the warden said, "I presume you heard about the botched execution of John Lee last February."

Holmes nodded, and I said, "'Babbacombe' Lee, as the papers are calling him – I presume because the murder took place at Babbacombe Bay."

The warden nodded. "Near Torquay. They're also calling him 'The Man They Could Not Hang'. Have you seen that?" He suddenly pounded the arm of his chair, surprising us both with his sudden vehemence.

Holmes nodded, setting down his cup on a nearby table. "I have. But surely it's a nine-day wonder. Just because the gallows failed to function – "

"Three times!" Hayes growled.

"Three times does not mean that Lee entirely escaped justice. After the failed execution attempts, the Home Secretary commuted his sentence to life imprisonment." He nodded his head toward the door and the greater portion of the prison. "I presume that he's still here?"

"Where he will stay if I have anything to say about it," replied the warden.

"I take it that there is some aspect of the failed execution that is troubling you," said Holmes, "since there can be no doubt of the man's guilt."

"That is correct – and he killed that woman. If you knew him as I did, you'd understand."

"You knew Lee?" I asked. "Before the crime?"

"I did. We did – here at the prison. He served time here – hard labor – for theft. Before his arrival here, he was known as a shiftless liar and ne'er-do-well, a young man destined for trouble. He was born just twenty miles southwest of here, in Abbotskerswell. A few years ago, he spent a bit of time in the Navy, serving as a cabin boy on the *Implacable*, moored at Devonport for training. After he injured his leg, he drifted, finding a job as a footman and ending up here in 1883 – accused and convicted of robbing his employer. I spotted him then for what he was – a liar and a bragger. The Americans have a phrase for such as he – a *confidence man*. But he never would have been very good at it, even if he hadn't committed murder and ended up here.

"As you'll have read, after his release, he obtained a job as a footman with a rich elderly spinster, Emma Keyse. Apparently he convinced her that he was something special, bloating and romanticizing all aspects of his short life. He's only twenty-one now, you know. At his trial, Lee's defense introduced letters to him from Emma Keyse implying that she loved him – either as a mother, or as a lover. It was hard to tell. In any case, he was in a good spot – which makes understanding why he murdered her unfathomable."

Holmes nodded. "It was mid-November of last year, wasn't it?" The warden nodded, and Holmes continued for my benefit. "Emma Keyse was found with her throat slit – by a kitchen knife later found beside Lee's bed, still covered with blood. She also had several gashes upon her head, and an attempt had been made to burn the body, supposedly to hide the crime."

"Not supposedly," countered the warden. "He was the only man in the house, and he had a wound upon his arm."

"That isn't definitive evidence," I interjected, recalling the incident. "A woman could have stabbed an elderly lady. And didn't Lee contend that he injured his arm breaking open a window after finding the fire consuming the body?"

Warden Hayes shook his head. "That is neither here nor there. The case has been tried, the evidence weighed, and the prisoner convicted. No, I didn't ask you here to reopen Lee's case. Instead, I need to see if you can reach a conclusion about why his execution failed – three times."

"The 'public confidence' mentioned in the telegram that sent us here," replied Holmes. "There is official concern that the public will believe that the official vengeance machine is untrustworthy if executions cannot be carried out to their ordained conclusion."

Hayes frowned. "Your tone, Mr. Holmes, has implications that you disagree with the notion of capital punishment."

"Not at all. The history of mankind is filled with recidivism, sometimes with great violence, and, when justified, removal of such violent undesirables has a very Darwinian aspect of improving the overall population."

The warden looked my way. "And you, Doctor?"

I took a sip of cooling coffee, an obvious ploy to arrange my thoughts. "As a doctor, I am oath-bound to protect life and do no harm. However, I have also been a soldier, and have been forced to take lives. The same is true since I've been involved with Holmes's investigations. And while I consider all life to be sacred, I understand that some individuals are truly evil, in the Biblical sense, and that capital punishment is a judgment by the community to remove those whose crimes have gone beyond what can be tolerated. As unpleasant as execution by the State is, these individuals have forfeit to right to further participation in society."

Hayes nodded. "'Unpleasant' is correct. No one looks forward to an execution, but sometimes it must be done, in the same way that a surgeon must cut out a disease or remove a gangrenous limb to save the body, or a mad dog must be put down to make the neighborhood a safer place. And when it is required, it must be done cleanly and humanely. In Lee's case, we failed."

"We only know what was reported in the London newspapers," said Holmes. "I docketed the facts in my scrapbooks, but they are two-hundred-and-fifty miles to the east. If you could refresh our memories of what happened that morning?"

"Certainly. It was the twenty-third of February, a cloudy day. There had been previous rain, but the gallows structure was dry – a fact that was ascertained later when rain-swollen wood was suggested as a reason the trap doors wouldn't function. James Berry was the executioner – rather new to the job, having taken over at the recommendation of Marwood, his friend who had recently retired. He had tested the workings several times the day before, and all was in order.

"That morning, Lee was led up to the trap door and the noose fixed 'round his neck. The various words were spoken according to law and tradition, and then Berry heaved upon the lever – but nothing happened. Lee was removed for a moment and Berry calmly made another inspection, in which everything worked fine. It was awkward, and unfortunate of course, but the procedure resumed after a moment – and again, the trap door didn't open!

"At this point, Berry became concerned, and not a little embarrassed. Remember, he'd only been the Chief Executioner for a few months, and he could see how this might reflect upon him. He and Garrison, the warder who assisted him, worked to widen the opening, and I verified that they had done so. Then Lee was once again set in place, visibly upset by this time – and understandably so. With grim certainty, Berry once again pulled the lever – and once again, Lee was left standing there, this time nearly collapsing with terror so that he might have strangled himself upon the closed trap door if he'd fainted and sagged to the platform while still in the noose.

"Dr. John Pitkin, the attending medical officer, then declared that he would no longer participate, as this had become 'cruel and unusual punishment'. I tended to agree and, even though I wanted the legal execution to be carried out according to the requirements of the law, I ordered that Lee be removed and returned to his cell. In any case, without Pitkin's participation, the affair could not continue until an acceptable replacement was found.

"Off and on for the next day or so, we spent the day examining the gallows, but couldn't find any reason that it failed to perform – and I refuse to believe that it was due to some divine intervention, as was suggested in some of the more scurrilous newspapers! If ever a man deserved to be hanged – ! In the meantime, the Home Office intervened, and Lee's sentence was commuted."

"And have there been any subsequent executions," I asked. "If so, have they been successful?"

"There have not," replied the warden. "It isn't as if we run capital prisoners through here like a slaughter house, Doctor. Many murderers receive life sentences. Others are excused from execution because of their mental condition. Since Roderick Maclean attempted to shoot the Queen at Windsor three years ago and got off with a 'Guilty but Insane' verdict, with the rest of his days to be spent in an asylum, quite a few killers have been given the same punishment."

As I noticed that the notion of an insanity verdict didn't sit well with him, he continued. "The last execution here was six years ago – Annie Tooke, who smothered and then dismembered an eight-month old child, hiding the torso at the Powhay Mill, the head behind the city brewery, and the limbs near the Shakespeare Inn. Marwood handled that one. She signed a confession a couple of days before the sentence was carried out." He raised his hand for emphasis. "If ever someone deserved execution, it was her."

"Do you trust James Berry?" asked Holmes, bringing the warden back to the topic.

"I do," said the warden. "He was recommended by Marwood – William Marwood, the official executioner – after his retirement in 1883, but he didn't immediately get the job. Over the course of his career, Marwood hanged one-hundred-and-seventy-six killers."

I nodded. "In the Army, I heard this bit of doggerel:

If Pa killed Ma,
Who'd kill Pa?
Marwood."

Hayes nodded. "I've heard that as well. During his time, he developed the 'long drop', which breaks the condemned's neck immediately, rather than letting him or her slowly strangle at the end of the rope from the 'short drop'. Much more humane, you see. It's only the families of the victims who want to watch the killers suffer – or so they would say until they actually watched it happen. Of course, we no longer allow the public to view the event. They would leave the prison afterwards much more grim than when they arrived. Marwood worked out something of system wherein he measures the length of the rope based on the weight of the man or woman to be executed. Too long, and the head is pulled off."

As this terrible image flashed across my eyes, the warden reached for a sheaf of papers on the table beside him.

"Marwood was friends with Berry and advised him to seek the job. I know that Berry wants to make a successful career of it, and this was a blot on his copybook, right out of the gate." He shook his head. "These executioners an odd bunch. Before Berry was appointed, Bartholomew Binns was given the job of official executioner. He only lasted a year. He was supposedly drunk at the time hanged Henry Dutton at Kirkdale – he miscalculated the weight, used an over-thick rope, and the man strangled. His last execution was a year ago at Kirkdale. He was drunk at that one too – Michael McLean –and it took thirteen minutes for the lad to die. He was just seventeen, and he strangled as well.

"After Binns was sacked, we learned that he spent the years before obtaining the job hanging dogs and cats. It makes one wonder what sort of fellow seeks this work, and what they've done to prepare for it. James Billington was hired last year as a secondary hangman to Berry, and I've heard that he's also had a lifelong fascination with the job – to the point that he made his own gallows and hanged various human figures he constructed of differing weights. There are rumors that he too has executed dogs and cats, although he denies it. From what I've heard and the little I saw last February during his job here, Berry shows no signs of such odd behavior, but still . . . ."

273

Then he seemed to remember the sheets he'd picked up.

"This is Berry's report from last March, which the Under-Sheriff requested that he prepare following Lee's muffed execution." He handed the sheets to Holmes. As he read them, Hayes rose and, unbidden, refilled our coffee cups.

When Holmes had finished, he handed the document to me. It was headed from the Executioner's Office in Bradford, Yorkshire, and dated on the fourth of March, 1885. The letter began by describing how he traveled from his home in Bradford to Bristol on 20 February, and thence to Exeter on the following day. After arriving and settling into the room provided for him at the prison, he made an inspection of "*the place of Execution*" – a coach-house in which the prison van was usually kept. He was accompanied by two warders.

The gallows was not the stand-alone wooden structure that I had pictured. Rather, Berry described it as a beam, four-inches thick, that had been placed at the top of the coach-house, presumably across the rafters. An iron bolt about two feet long ran through it, fixed on top with an iron nut, and with a loop at the bottom, through which the rope was attached. At the floor, a pit about six feet across and eleven feet deep had been dug into the earth and covered by a wooden platform containing two trap doors.

Berry wrote that the doors were only an inch thick, and that in his opinion they should have been thicker, three or four inches. The ironwork of the doors was "*of a frail kind, and much too weak for the purpose*." He tried the lever several times, testing the release of the doors and finding it satisfactory. I looked up.

"He says that you were watching him make the test through the window of your office."

"I was."

"Surely not this office," said Holmes, agreeing with my point. "This window looks out upon city – the Cathedral can't be more than a thousand feet that way."

"You're correct. I have a more-functional office at the rear of this building, with a view looking out upon the prison. Here is where I meet visitors. After Berry's test, he came up and explained that the doors were unsatisfactory. We agreed that they would have to do for Lee's execution, and the various repairs that he suggested would be made in the future."

I nodded and continued to read. At seven-thirty Monday morning, Berry was taken back to the place of execution by a warder and found everything just as he'd left it. He made no subsequent test of the trap door – to his regret. I would wager that he'd re-test the doors in the future for as long as he held the position of hangman.

274

Just before eight o'clock, he was conducted to John Lee's cell, where he proceeded to strap up the young man's arms. Then he joined the procession from the cell to the coach-house, where Lee was placed upon the trap door. Berry pinioned his legs, adjusted the noose and the white cap, and then drew the lever – but nothing happened. Lee was uncapped and un-noosed and taken into an adjoining room. Berry then tested the trap door, which fell easily. Lee was again placed in position, but Berry reported that "*when I again pulled the lever it did not act, and in trying to force it the lever was slightly strained.*"

Again, Lee was removed, and it was suggested that the woodwork didn't fit correctly. An axe and a plane were fetched, and a piece of wood was sawn off. This time, testing the lever didn't open the doors at all until the catches were knocked off with a crowbar.

"This says that Lee was led away after the door were trimmed, without mentioning that he was repositioned a third time. And yet it's generally understood that a third attempt was made. "

"That's correct, Doctor. I'm uncertain as to why Berry didn't mention the third attempt. He writes that the Under-Sheriff called off the execution after the trap doors were trimmed, but in fact a third attempt was made before Lee was finally led back to his cell."

"A curious discrepancy," remarked Holmes. "Has anyone asked why?"

"Not that I'm aware," replied Hayes. "The mood was becoming rather unsettled by that point. When recalling it for his report, I suspect that Berry simply wrote past that point without realizing he'd done so."

"It's a significant omission," replied Holmes. "It's unfortunate that Mr. Berry lives so far away. I would like to question him in more depth." He sat up straighter. "The letter mentions the warders who assisted him. Are they still employed here?"

"They are. Bradley Garrison is about thirty, and has worked here for five years. He's responsible for maintaining the gallows structure, among his other duties. Wiley Emerson is a young man, about eighteen or twenty, recently employed, who also was also present that morning. Would you like to speak with them?"

"Not just now. First, I'd prefer to examine the coach-house, and the gallows."

"Certainly, although it's been four months since the unfortunate event. What do you hope to find?"

"That is unknown until I see it." Holmes stood. "If you would show us the way?"

Chapter II

We went downstairs and out into the humid mid-day sunshine. The promise of early summer was in the air, almost contradicting the harsh and dour facility through which we walked. I could only imagine the place in winter, or on a cold and cloudy day in February when an execution would be taking place. It also crossed my mind that this was Midsummer, a day closely connected with the renewal and beauty of nature since ancient times, and that somewhere someone was enjoying it. But not here, in the bowels of the fierce stony institution.

"The current prison was built in in 1853," explained the warden proudly as we passed along the dark buildings. "It has four residential wings, laid out like a cross, and was based on the model prison design at Pentonville."

I had been to Pentonville, and found it hard to believe it should be a model for anything.

Holmes kept his own thoughts, and I made a polite noise of interest at the warden's comment. As we rounded a corner, Hayes asked, "Would you care to speak to Lee? He's in this building." He gestured to his right.

"Perhaps later – after we've seen the coach-house. Is this it?"

It was. It was a high-roofed building, made of solid granite blocks, and rising to cross-beams about fifteen feet above the ground. A pitched metal roof was centered over two heavy wooden doors facing into the yard which we'd crossed in order to reach it. They were closed, and Hayes called to a couple of warders standing some distance away, conversing alongside one of the grimy walls while they smoked. They dropped their cigarettes, stubbed them out with identical motions of their legs and feet, and then walked toward us. Hayes directed that they open the double doors and pull out the coach that was parked inside.

As the two men did so, Hayes gestured to the younger one, softly stating, "That is Wiley Emerson. He has only been here since last fall. He's the youngest son of a local squire who used his influence to obtain this position. Wiley is a good lad – hard-working, interested, sincere. But he isn't the sharpest fellow that's on our staff."

As he spoke, the doors were opened and coach removed, revealing that the wheels straddled the wooden trap doors set into the building's flagged floor. Holmes asked that everyone stay back, and then he began to approach the building slowly, shifting from one side to the other as he looked from several angles, both up at the rafters, and the structure on the floor. Then he spoke over his shoulder.

"Might you send for a couple of dark lanterns? I must admit, I'd pictured a more traditional gallows – an outdoor structure that I could inspect from underneath, or climb upon."

Hayes snapped to the warders, and the one who remained unidentified lurched into motion. Emerson remained in place, watching closely with wide eyes and an expression of almost childlike curiosity.

In the meantime, Holmes stepped to the coach, removing and laying his Inverness across the seat. Then he returned to his examination, this time entering the building, circling the trap doors and sometimes squatting to get a better look.

The warder returned with the lanterns, already lit, and carried them to Holmes, who took them with murmured thanks. Then he asked the warder to assist him in placing a tall ladder, leaning against the back wall of the shed, so that he could examine the rafter beam where the iron bolt and nut were centered. He climbed, both dark lanterns gripped in one hand, until he was even with the beam.

Hayes stepped closer, looking up. "There's no need to examine that, Mr. Holmes," he called. "The problem wasn't with the noose. It occurred when the trap door malfunctioned."

Holmes ignored him, placing one of the dark lanterns on the beam, directed toward the bolt. He held the other with his left hand closer to the nut's fitting, while he leaned in precariously to look through his magnifying glass, held in his right hand. I thought it was obvious that Holmes was inspecting the ironworks to see if they might have been tampered with, and said so to the warden. "If there was an effort to damage the trap door, something might also have been tried with the rope." Hayes did not appear to like being corrected, especially in front of the two warders, who were watching us with silent interest.

"Well," he grumbled, "I should think he'd find more on the ground than up there."

Holmes was climbing down at this point, and he turned to the warden, stating, "You're correct. I will. And in fact, there was no evidence of tampering up there. I presume that the rope is removed and stored elsewhere unless a hanging is scheduled."

"That's right. We go several years between executions. A noose left in place would simply rot."

Holmes nodded and then turned his attention to the trap doors. He walked to the lever, located off to the right side of the building where the coach wouldn't hit it. It was an iron bar, about four feet long, and sticking up from the floor at a forty-five-degree angle. It was connected to another thin bar, fastened to the floor near the lever. It ran across the floor, where it vanished underneath the wooden frame around the doors. Holmes looked it over with the aid of his glass and one of the lanterns. Then he gripped it and pulled back toward him. There was a metallic screech along the shed's floor, and the sound of something turning and grinding under one edge of the wooden trapdoors. Then, with a sudden motion and a loud bang that startled me, they dropped away, separating to reveal a black void in the ground.

The doors ratted for another few seconds, swinging back and forth and hitting the chamber wall a few more times until they settled into vertical stillness. "One of Berry's suggestions," said the warden softly, "was to have some kind of fixture installed underneath to catch the doors when they fall, so that they don't bounce back or swing once they open. We plan on making that improvement before the next execution."

Meanwhile, Holmes had asked for help to shift the ladder into the pit.

"No need, sir," offered Emerson. "There's already a short ladder down there, for when we do work on the doors."

"So there is. Thank you." And then he turned, climbed over the edge, and quickly vanished. The pit, however, was no longer dark, as Holmes shifted the two dark lanterns from one side to another. The warden and I stepped closer, and I could see that the pit was squared and ten or eleven feet deep. Holmes was standing on the ladder and he had partially closed one of the doors, intently examining its lower edges. After repeating the process on the other door, he looked up.

"I've seen what I can. Please have someone pull the doors up and re-lock them into place."

I looked around to see that several other warders had gathered to watch the proceedings. Hayes spoke to one of the new arrivals who had stepped a bit closer than the others, asking that he re-set the door. The fellow nodded and walked forward to pull at a couple of ropes that were affixed to the inner edges of the trap doors, each running through iron eye-bolts at one edge, allowing the doors to be drawn back into place. Meanwhile, Emerson had stepped forward and shifted the lever to reset the catch underneath that held the doors in place.

Hayes nodded toward the warder who had retrieved the doors. "Bradley Garrison, the other warder on duty the morning of the aborted hanging. He is responsible for maintenance of the apparatus – oiling the works regularly, checking for rust or wood rot, and so on."

I gave the fellow a closer look. He was physically much like Emerson – slim and wiry, quick in his movements, and not more than five-six in height. However, there the similarities ended, as Emerson's hair was sandy and thick on his square wide-eyed head, while Garrison's was dark and receding, and lay thin and close along his rather knobby dark-featured skull. In mood they also appeared to differ. Emerson had a childlike joy about him, even in such a terrible place, but Garrison was withdrawn and nervous, his gaze mostly lowered, but often glancing toward the warden and myself before quickly cutting his eyes away.

Through cracks at the edges and between the door, we again saw the shifting of the dark lanterns as Holmes looked here and there. "Was such an examination made when Berry was here?" I asked. "With lanterns from down in the pit."

Hayes shook his head. "Not to this degree. Of course, Berry and Garrison climbed in and out several times as they tried to determine what was wrong during the procedure, and when they shaved the doors, and once more when the execution was halted. What do you think that Mr. Holmes will find?"

"It could be anything – or nothing. He has his own methods, and they rarely fail him."

At that moment, Holmes's muffled voice called, "Release the trap doors!"

Garrison looked toward Hayes, who nodded. Garrison then stepped across while Emerson stepped back, and he pulled the lever. Again the doors dropped with a bang.

"Once more!" Holmes said, his voice more clear now.

The doors were re-locked and then dropped, and then two more times before the detective was satisfied. A moment later, his wool fore-and-aft cap rose into view, followed by the rest of him as he carefully climbed the ladder to its full length and found his footing on the lip of the pit.

"What did you discover?" asked Hayes, stepping forward, but Holmes simply shook his head, not ready to share his findings, whatever they might be. The warden's lips pursed in irritation, clearly vexed at the denial of immediate answers, but by that point in our friendship, having known Holmes for nearly four-and-a-half years, I was not surprised. It was his method to keep information to himself until he had verified it, or determined that its release would be useful in some way. Clearly he did not intend to immediately discuss what he had seen in the gallows pit.

Seeing that he would get no answers, Hayes gestured to the two nearby warders. "This is Garrison and Emerson, who assisted on the day of Lee's attempted execution. Which would you like to speak with first – or perhaps both of them together?"

Holmes turned to face the two men, Emerson with a friendly expression, and Garrison projecting a nervous wariness that would have been obvious to anyone. I was as surprised as the warden when Holmes said, "I'll need to speak with them later. For now, the investigation has taken another direction." He glanced back at Hayes. "I need to get up to London to verify a fact or two, but I hope to return by tomorrow, or the

279

next day at the latest. In the meantime, Watson will stay here in Exeter to act as my representative."

Hayes blustered, wondering at the abrupt swing in Holmes's plans, but my friend simply retrieved his coat from the coach while I watched Garrison and Emerson surreptitiously, noting that the former seemed to sag in relief that he wouldn't be immediately subjected to Holmes's questioning. I knew that Holmes also wouldn't have missed seeing it, and wondered why questioning of the man needed to be delayed, when he was clearly so brittle at that moment that a few pointed queries might have shattered him.

Having adjusted his Inverness, Holmes said to the warden, "Before we go, I would now like to meet John Lee, whose survival instigated this investigation."

Hayes's mood improved as he appeared to approve of this notion, and turned to lead us back the way we'd recently traveled. Entering one of the residential wings, as Hayes had called them earlier, we passed through a small guard office with two men on duty. Hayes tasked one to lead us to Lee's cell. It was a short walk, not forty feet down a low stone hall to an iron door on the right. Without any announcement, the guard inserted the key, turned it with well-oiled silence, and threw open the door.

A sour smell rolled forth, a dampness that caught in one's throat. It wasn't unfamiliar to me, but it was unpleasant nonetheless. By this point, our eyes had adjusted to the dim light from the gas lamps that lit the hallway. Light reached into the cell from a narrow opening high in the wall near one of the hall lamps, but there was no source of light within the cell, and no window, only a small metal ventilator opening above the cot where a man sat, facing us.

He leaned forward, his eyes blinking with lizard-like slowness and his face expressionless. I could see that he was rather small, and younger-looking that I had expected, in spite of knowing that he was just around twenty-one years of age. I suppose hearing that he was a murderer had led me to expect a more grizzled and rough specimen. John Lee, however, looked perfectly normal, although I expect that in full daylight, the conditions of his incarceration would be much more apparent.

"On your feet, Lee," said Hayes. "These men are investigating the circumstances of your execution."

The prisoner then rolled forward rather suddenly, with an unexpected bounce, and stood facing us, leaning forward a bit on his toes. Hayes appeared to be surprised, taking an involuntary step back, and the guard behind us who had opened the door growled a bit under his breath. I was glad that I hadn't reacted, and of course neither had Holmes, who peered at the young man closely, even as the prisoner returned his gaze, a slow smile straightening his tight lips.

"What is there to investigate?" he asked, his voice rough with disuse. "The Good God wouldn't allow an innocent man to hang, would he?" He glanced from Holmes to the warden. "Any word yet on my appeal to the Home Secretary?"

"Nothing," Hayes replied darkly, "and don't expect it. You're lucky to be here, now, and luckier that the Home Secretary commuted your sentence.

"He'll commute it further before he's done," Lee replied. Then he glanced at us. "Well? What's your game, gents? Here to look at the gallows, or to ask me questions about why I didn't kill that woman? I didn't, you know. God knows it. The real killer knows it. And more and more people are realizing it every day." He glanced back at Hayes. "Did you tell them? How I get letters from all over England, supporting my cause? Affirming my innocence." He smiled slyly. "Why, I'm even getting proposals of marriage. I'll have quite my pick of the fine ladies when I'm released." Then he jerked his thumb toward the warden and said in a confiding tone, "This one would drag me back out to the gallows this very afternoon if they'd let him. Oh, he hates me, he does! You can see it all over his face – Look at him! I'll make sure to shake your hand, Warden Sir, on the day that you're required to walk me out the front door."

"That's enough!" thundered Hayes, clearly having lost all patience with the artful little man. "Your sentence may be commuted to the rest of your life, but you will serve every day of it, to the letter of the law." He turned to Holmes. "Do you have any questions for this man?"

"Not yet. Maybe not ever. It depends on what I learn in London." He then faced Lee. "Understand this: I will know the truth of what happened here. Your false hope will do you no good."

Whatever that meant, it appeared to rattle the prisoner, for he blinked, and the crafty smile washed from his face. He certainly had no idea who Holmes was, for my friend's name hadn't been mentioned and his likeness wasn't so well known in those days. But Lee could clearly recognize that Holmes spoke with authority and knowledge, and as cryptic as his words were to the warden and me, they seemed to have some kind of weight with the convicted killer.

Having nothing more to say, and apparently nothing to ask, Holmes turned and walked out, leaving Hayes and me to follow. While the guard locked the door behind us, we walked silently out of the building, and to the wide graveled passage lying beside the building.

"As I mentioned," explained Holmes, "Watson will remain in Exeter until I return. I need to interview Berry. I hope that I don't have to go as

281

far as his home in Yorkshire, or that he isn't on business in the far north. What he tells me will have a bearing on the questions I ask when I return. Until then, Warden, thank you for your help."

Hayes nodded, clearly wishing to know more, but understanding that Holmes would not provide any information until he was ready. With nothing left to discuss, Hayes led us back to the front entrance and the street. The great door closed behind us, and we were left to return to our waiting carriage and the patient driver, still keeping watch over the bags we'd brought with us from Glastonbury. In five minutes we were dropped at a modest inn within sight of the great Cathedral, and ten minutes after that, I was alone in our shared upstairs sitting room, awaiting something to be brought up for a late lunch, while Holmes stepped down the road to send and receive some telegrams.

Chapter III

I had finished eating and was on my second cup of coffee when Holmes returned. "Good news," he said, making up a sandwich from the meat and bread our landlord had provided. "Berry is at Bodmin Prison, awaiting the chance to hang Alton, the Yeovil Strangler. There is some question as to whether he will be executed as scheduled or transferred to Broadmoor for the rest of his life. It's much easier to journey ninety miles west than go all the way to Bradford, in Yorkshire, or even somewhere farther away."

"And what you said to Hayes – Was that accurate? That you want me to stay here in the meantime?"

He nodded. "I hope that you don't mind that I said you'd stay. I assumed that you wouldn't want to chase Berry down, and that you'd prefer to be here at the finish."

"You're correct. But do you have any suggestions about how I might be of use while you're away?"

"Perhaps you can explore the local environs. Visit the Cathedral. Take a walk beside the Exe. Enjoy the Midsummer day. And, should you happen to find a spare moment or two, you might do some research on our two notable warders, Garrison and Emerson. Discreetly, of course."

He took a drink, wiped his mouth, stood, and dropped his napkin to the table. "Sooner started – " he said, retrieving his hat and coat. "I hope to return by the end of the day. Good luck!" And then he was gone, and I was left to consider how best to begin my task – for I knew that Holmes's references to wandering through the Cathedral or alongside the river were not how he actually wished for me to spend my time. Rising, I descended to the taproom, where the innkeeper informed me how to reach the local police station.

By those days, I was quite familiar with Holmes's methods, although I would never pretend to come close to mastering them. Still, over the course of several years at his side, I knew the sorts of questions to ask, and also how to communicate with the official force when seeking assistance or information. At the station, I identified myself to Inspector Watrose, asking that he seek confirmation of my identity with one of several inspectors at Scotland Yard. I waited patiently for just a few minutes – though I expected it to take much longer – until Watrose invited me back to his office.

"We're on the telephone," Watrose explained. "I reached an Inspector Gregson with the Yard. He speaks quite highly of you, Doctor." He looked like he meant to say something else, but he caught himself, instead asking warily, "And is Mr. Holmes with you?"

"Not at present. As I mentioned, we're looking into the botched execution at the prison earlier this year, and his trail led him west to visit James Berry, now at Bodmin. In the meantime, I've been tasked to find out what I can about two of the warders – those who assisted with the execution that day. Bradley Garrison and Wiley Emerson."

He nodded and leaned back, crossing his legs. "I can actually give you some information right now, as one of the conditions of their obtaining employment with the prison was a check of their police records – if any. Wiley Emerson is a fine young fellow. Strike any suspicion of him from your mind right now. He's from a good family, and has a generous heart – even if his head isn't all that it could be."

I nodded. "The warden implied something along the same lines. I take it, then, that Bradley Garrison's story has a different slant."

Watrose nodded. "Nothing criminal, you understand. But his people have always been rather shiftless, and he's no different. I suspect that he would have been in the prison as a resident if somehow Fate hadn't handed him the opportunity to find employment there. Five years back, Garrison happened to rescue the son of one of our councilmen from a burning building, and afterwards, the councilman rather took him under his wing, finding him the prison job and making it his mission to improve Garrison's opportunities. As far as I know, he's stayed on the narrow path since then – but as you know, Doctor, if such a one has a rotten spot in him, it will eventually show itself." He leaned forward, lowering his voice, in spite of the fact that we were alone and his office door was closed. "What does Mr. Holmes suspect? That Garrison took a bribe to somehow disrupt the hanging?"

I shook my head. "Holmes usually holds his notions and theories very close. I don't know if he attaches any real importance to the warders, or if he simply wants to make sure that he can eliminate them from his considerations. Do you have any other information about them?"

He sent for their folders from when they'd been investigated for the prison positions, and I was able to obtain their addresses. "Emerson still lives with his parents and siblings," Watrose said, "but Garrison has a small cottage near the bottom of St. David's Hill, not far from the station." He sketched how to locate it, and offered to have someone drive me there, but I declined with thanks, preferring instead to walk. I believed that Holmes would be gone long enough that I could examine Garrison's residence and still have time for a bit of exploring along the way.

It was quite a fine day, not too hot, and I walked along as the land gradually sloped up to the Cathedral. I approached from the south, pausing to catch my breath along the rather plain side – if any aspect of such a building could be described as "plain". I wiped my face and nodded to a young lady proceeding slowly across the lawn with a young child. Then I resumed around the building, now seeing it from the front. The great structure was breathtaking, and much finer in person than any illustrations could convey. There were many ornate stone carvings on the front – numerous historical figures and intricate geometric shapes wound in and through one another – that I felt it would take a lifetime to try and truly see all of them. I knew vaguely that work had begun eight-hundred or so years earlier, but I had no idea how long it had taken to complete, although I realized that multiple generations of workers and craftsmen had been involved, many spending their whole lives creating the masterwork before me, dying before they would ever see its completion.

Inside was even more overwhelming, and almost immediately as I entered, seeing the immense stained glass circular window above the main doors and the vast and intricate space rising out of site above me, I gave up trying to understand or comprehend any specifics, and instead let myself be overwhelmed with appreciation.

Later, when I'd left the Cathedral to wander along the High Street (where I did indeed obtain an afternoon pasty), and then down North Street and across the famed Iron Bridge, I came across St. David's Church, a much smaller building constructed in the Doric style and then about seventy years old. I wandered inside, finding it deserted, cool, and quiet. I sat to one side for a while, reflecting and appreciating the contrast with the vast Cathedral and reflecting upon the solitude before rising and continuing my mission.

Continuing downward along St. David's Hill, I located the small side street where Garrison's modest cottage stood, as indicated by Inspector

Watrose's map. It was a tidy affair on a minute lot, and the landscaping was well-tended and remarkably fresh looking. I also noticed that, despite the apparent age of the building, a number of recent improvements had been made – painted trim, new shutters, some patched stonework at the step to the front door, and most of all, an obviously new roof. Quite the investment, I thought, on a warder's pay.

Holmes might have been tempted to pick the lock and enter the building, all in the name of obtaining further information, but based on my own limited skills – and greater respect for the law, along with the certainty that I would certainly be caught – I decided to remain outside. In truth, I could think of nothing else to try, as I'd obtained a character sketch of sorts from the inspector, and I'd seen the house. I was considering the long climb back to the center of the city when a neighbor noticed my curiosity. I feared that I had tarried too long, but he was a gregarious fellow who seemed to accept my story about being interested in buying the place.

"Oh, I don't think he'd sell. He's lived there for five years at least – since he got the job at the prison, he once told me – and he's spent the last few months fixing it up proper. How long? Probably since February. That's right – it was late in the month, after the snow. The first clear day that the workmen could accomplish anything. You should have seen it before. Not that he didn't try to keep it up, but it was quite run-down, and too much for him, as he only makes so much working for the prison. I suppose that he got a raise in his wages. I know that he'd like to get married, but I don't see how he might afford it. Still, now that he's made improvements on the place – both what you see here, and quite a bit inside too – he might have a better chance at attracting a young lady's attention."

Our conversation wandered a bit from there, despite my attempts to nudge it back toward Garrison, and seeing that I'd learn nothing else, I extricated myself and worked my way in fits and starts up the steep hill to the Cathedral, and then around and back to the inn.

I was napping when Holmes returned. The sun was going down, and it was later than I'd thought. I was concerned that we might have already missed dinner, and in spite of Holmes's energetic wish to discuss the matter then and there, I insisted that we relocate ourselves downstairs, where we found a table in a quiet corner. There, over roasted pork and root vegetables, we could share the events of our separate inquiries without fear of being overheard.

I related my day, concerned that I hadn't determined enough to provide what Holmes had hoped to learn, but he appeared to be satisfied, and agreed with my conclusion that somehow Garrison had come into money at about the same time Lee's execution was interrupted.

"What did you see in the pit that alerted you?" I asked, recalling that he'd seemed to have a plan of action when he climbed back to the prison yard.

"Indentations upon the wood – where a wedge of some sort had been inserted between the doors and the lower frame. It was quite obvious under the bright lamps, and had made clear impressions upon the soft wood. It would have been impossible to miss – unless some was paid not to see it – or threatened."

I raised my eyebrows. "What did Berry tell you?"

Holmes smiled. "Ah, Watson, you've been involved in these affairs long enough to identify the important question. He told me everything – or at least all that he knew, for this is a bigger issue than sparing the life of one insignificant murderer.

"I found Berry alone in the small room set aside for him at Bodmin, reading his Bible and awaiting word on whether the contentious legal wranglings and appeals would allow him to complete his appointed task. He's in his early thirties, plain-spoken and solid. His eyes are rather heavy-lidded, giving him the impression of slowness, but his mind seems quick enough, and he puts his thoughts together well. He seemed thankful for the distraction – until I explained why I was there. His first reaction was to turn quiet, and then pivot to feigned anger. When he saw that neither would divert me, and when I explained what I already suspected and how I was prepared to share my conclusions with others, he finally began to speak. He asked for me to affirm that what he told me would remain secret, as his reputation and honor could be destroyed, but I provided no such assurances.

"It seemed as if he'd been longing to share his tale, but no one to whom he could tell it. He said that he arrived in Exeter in February and inspected the gallows apparatus as described in his report. All was typical – until the morning of the execution, when Garrison knocked softly upon his door at the room where he was staying within the prison.

"According to Berry, Garrison was quite nervous, and could barely explain what was expected. When Berry began to perceive that it was something underhanded and illegal, he was inclined to throw Garrison out and proceed directly to the warden. It was only when Garrison slowed down enough to nervously but clearly convey what he meant that Berry understood, with growing horror, just what was being asked of him – namely, to actively prevent Lee's execution. And to ensure the hangman's cooperation, Garrison then presented him with a small stuffed animal – a rabbit made from white-and-blue plaid gingham cloth. On the rabbit's leg were stitched two small initials: Those of Berry's youngest daughter. The rabbit had been removed, explained Garrison, from the Berry family home in Yorkshire the night before, at the same time his daughter was taken as well, to ensure the hangman's cooperation.

"Initially, Berry didn't believe the threat, stating that his wife would have notified him immediately that his daughter was missing. Garrison countered that this plan was more far-reaching than Berry realized, carried out by a person of great and dangerous influence, and that immediately upon kidnapping the daughter, the family had been warned to remain silent until James Berry could complete the task that was expected of him.

"When Berry demanded to know just what that might be, Garrison explained that he too had been recruited unwillingly. He didn't bother to explain how, or what leverage was held over him, although clearly he was an unwilling participant. He explained that several days before, he'd been given a small metal wedge, its dimensions previously calculated exactly to fit in the trapdoor's frame without looking too obvious, and painted with toughened yellow-brown enamel to match the surrounding wood. In the dark coach-house, it would be unnoticed, and it was up to Berry and Garrison to make sure that no one looked that way when the trap doors failed to open.

"Garrison didn't show Berry the wedge then, because it was already fixed in place in the trap doors. When the first attempt to open the door failed, and Lee was removed, both Berry and Garrison bent to get things in working order – they were the logical choices for such work, and no one present that morning realized that their efforts were combined to *prevent* any repairs from occurring. The door appeared to be fixed, and then, with Berry providing a distraction, Garrison re-inserted the wedge. Once again, the execution failed, and another seeming attempt at fixing the doors was made. As before, Berry and Garrison did this and that, looking quite busy but accomplishing nothing. They even suggested shaving the doors, but my examination showed that they trimmed wood from an area that would have no effect on how the doors operated – and in any case, fitting together the shavings at the bottom of the pit revealed that very little wood was actually removed. The wedge was again replaced, and for the third time, Lee did not hang."

"Berry's daughter?" I asked. "She is safe?"

Holmes nodded. "She was left at the family's front door later that morning, with a note pinned to her clothing requiring that Berry keep his mouth shut."

"And yet he spoke to you today. Why, if the implied threat against his family still stands?"

"Because it's been eating at him," said Holmes. "For all that his work is distasteful, it is necessary, and he fancies himself a professional. I believe him to be an honorable man. To have failed in his duty – to the

State and to himself – has been worrying him ever since. I think he was glad to be able to talk about it.

"Why," I then asked, "didn't Berry mention the third attempt to hang Lee in his report? He wrote it so as to suggest that after the third time supposedly repairing the doors, the prisoner was led away at once instead of again putting him again in the noose."

"Apparently he was concerned that all of his and Garrison's crambo around the trap door was becoming too obvious – by that time, the warden was watching them closely, and he was quite worried that the wedge would certainly be noticed. But it wasn't, and the third attempt failed as well. Berry was most relieved when the doctor finally put a stop to the proceedings. When he wrote his report, he left out the part of the third attempt, thinking that his 'official' version might be accepted as the true order of events, and that so many failed attempts wouldn't be recalled as time passed. He didn't realize that the whole fiasco would capture the public's imagination, giving so much attention to Lee cheating death three times."

"As simple as that," I said. "But why would someone want to save Lee? What value has one such as he to generate such a strategy?"

"Lee is no more than a pawn. Our next step is to ask Garrison what he knows."

Night had long fallen by the time we departed. The sky was clear, and the waxing moon was a week before being full. I feared that we might have to repeat my afternoon walk across central Exeter and then again down the long hill to Garrison's cottage, but a fortuitous hansom passed by, and we were delivered at our destination in less than ten minutes.

The temperature was mild, feeling like the low sixties, and just cool enough that I appreciated my coat. Around us was the soft constant hum of insects and night birds, but otherwise the night was quiet and still. Garrison's cottage was dark, except for a single lamp burning in the ground-floor window to the right of the door. When we knocked, shadows within the room shifted when someone abruptly stood, as shown by the movement in the light shining out on the small front lawn. The door opened and Garrison faced us, no surprise on his face. "Mr. Holmes," he said. "Doctor. Come in. I've been expecting you."

He directed us to the right, into the small parlor lit by the lamp, and made a perfunctory offer of something to drink, but we declined. "You know what this is about," stated Holmes. It was not a question.

"What else could it be? You've spoken to Berry?"

"I have. He told me how you coerced him into helping you. It's a nasty thing – to threaten a man's family. Why did you do it? How did they coerce you?"

"My sister," said Garrison. "They took her as well, several days before. She's safe now – it all worked according to their wishes."

"And the money?" Holmes pressed, gesturing around us. "The repairs you commenced at just that time. They did more than threaten you. They paid you."

"They did – but that was never mentioned at the time. I did what I did because they took my sister. The money arrived afterwards – with a note commanding my silence."

"Can I see it?"

"I burned it."

Holmes frowned by nodded. Then, "Berry didn't mention any payment."

Garrison looked surprised. "That's odd. If they paid me, then they certainly paid him as well. They didn't have to pay either one of us. We would have both kept quiet – if, that is, no one had come around asking questions." He lowered his gaze. "I've heard of you, Mr. Holmes. How you take hold of things and don't let go, and then you find out what others cannot. When I heard this morning that you were at the prison, and looking over the coach-house, I knew that it was all up with me." Then he looked up. "Will I be arrested? And lose my place at the prison?"

Holmes didn't answer immediately, instead looking around the room. It was a small place, quite modest, but clean and ordered, and maintained with an obvious sense of pride. One had the sense that Garrison was making an effort to be a good citizen with hopes for the future – not at all like the young man described by Inspector Watrose who would have been in prison by now if he wasn't working there. Holmes seemed to sense this as well, for he shook his head.

"These events are not your fault, and while you might have spoken up and allowed John Lee to be hanged, it's understandable why you didn't. Do you know who is behind this? Who initially approached you?"

"A stranger – a chap down from London named Paget. * It was he who gave me the wedge, explaining that it had already been specially made to fit the trap doors. They had planned it for a while. He told me what I needed to do, and how my sister had been . . . how she was taken."

"And is she well now?" I asked.

"Oh, yes. They treated her fine – except for terrifying her because the two men and woman who had her never took off their masks."

"Perhaps that's just as well," I said.

There was more we needed to know, but Garrison couldn't provide any further particulars. We rose, and he did the same. "My job?" Garrison asked. "Will you reveal me?"

Holmes shook his head. "No. But you have narrowly dodged a great hazard, Mr. Garrison. One doesn't usually get the opportunity to do that twice. From now on stay on the narrow path. And if you ever hear from Mr. Paget again – let me know immediately." And he handed the younger man his card.

"I will, Mr. Holmes. I will."

Outside, the door shut behind us, and we returned to the waiting cab. On the slow pull up St. David's Hill, I stated, "The name Paget – it's familiar to you."

"It is – the last piece of the puzzle."

"I'm glad," I replied, "because to me, there are quite a few major portions still unplaced."

"Let me explain. First, we weren't sent here by my acquaintance in Whitehall because the public's confidence in the execution system of punishment was shaken by these events – something I was able to clarify with an exchange of telegrams. Rather, we were to verify certain details regarding how Lee's execution was prevented. Lee, however, matters not at all. He was saved simply as an example of how one man – one powerful and corrupt man – can exert his influence wherever he chooses – even reaching into one of Her Majesty's Prisons to preserve the misbegotten life of a convicted murderer while he stands on the gallows."

"And this corrupt man is – ?"

"You've heard me speak of him before: Professor James Moriarty."

I could only nod in agreement. *It all becomes clear*, I thought, even if the edges of the picture remained out of focus. For some time, Holmes had been aware of some guiding figure influencing London's underworld, making deliberate moves to gain control of it – and of late he had perceived that this influence was expanding outside of the capital. By way of his many contacts in all levels of the London hierarchy – both those who knew Holmes in his own person, and others who interacted with him in a number of his other personas that he adopted to explore the city – he'd finally begun to learn the specifics of one specific man, a nondescript and obscure academic who draped himself in the mantle of respectability while building a web, strand by strand, into all levels of society. This man, Professor Moriarty, was constructing an organization unlike any seen before, wherein he depended on a few lieutenants who in turn commanded a larger number of commanders, with a widening pyramid of influence and authority extending from the Professor at the top, all the way down to a base consisting of every low-level cut-purse, pickpocket, and prostitute throughout London. And most didn't even know his name.

But Holmes did.

"Paget," I said, understanding now. "I recall him now. One of Moriarty's most-trusted lieutenants."

Holmes nodded. "And if this affair was managed at that level of the organization, then it was very close to the top indeed."

"If they didn't care about Lee, then what did this accomplish? You said it was to prove something – Moriarty's influence."

"Yes. After talking with Berry, and before returning from Bodmin Prison, I sent and received some wires to and from London. The man in Whitehall who asked us to become involved revealed that he'd already ferreted out that Moriarty has been courting Sir Malcolm Denbury – You recall Sir Malcolm, of the munitions family? – and that the old sinner had sought some sort of proof of the Professor's power. It's theorized that Sir Malcolm picked stopping Lee's execution at random – a test. We were to verify or disprove this notion."

"And so it has been verified. What happens now?"

"I'll have the cabbie stop so that I can send a confirmatory wire to Whitehall, and in the morning, Sir Malcolm will be confronted. This isn't a checkmate, but it does remove the possibility that our mysterious foe might have gained a valuable piece."

"And what about Garrison and Berry? It will likely become clear that they've both talked. Are they safe?"

"They will be. I'll make sure word reaches Paget that his specific involvement is known – and that if anything happens to either man down here, then there will be no place that Paget can hide. He'll see to their protection, with or without the Professor's knowledge."

"What about the warden? What will you tell him?"

"Why, nothing at all. Providing him with a report isn't part of our brief, whatever he might have assumed. Perhaps if nothing else, he'll be prompted to provide more trustworthy and humane methods of execution. After all, Lee's survival has shined a bright light on capital punishment – and that isn't a terrible thing."

"And the Professor . . . ?" I shifted around to see Holmes's face by way of the passing gaslights near the Cathedral. "Does this help your work? Do you progress in your efforts to outflank him?"

He shrugged and was silent for the longest time. Then, finally, he sighed. "I don't know. But you must give me time – you must give me time . . . ."

NOTES

* The chap down from London named Paget, mentioned by Garrison, is undoubtedly one of Professor Moriarty's high lieutenants, as described in *The Return of Moriarty* (1974) by John Gardner.

John "Babbacombe" Lee
(1864-1945)

John "Babbacombe" Lee was accused of murdering his employer, elderly spinster Emma Keyse, on 15 November, 1884. He was subsequently convicted and sentenced to die at Exeter Prison on 23 February, 1885, where he famously survived three attempts to hang him. His sentence was commuted to life imprisonment, and he was released in December 1907, by then famous as "The Man They Could Not Hang". He became something of a celebrity, meeting a number of important and famous people, although interest in him gradually faded.

In 1909, Lee married and fathered two children, but in 1911 he abandoned his wife before the second child was born, traveling with another woman to Wisconsin. He lived in the United States until his death in 1945.

Subsequent investigations have cast doubt on whether Lee actually killed Emma Keyse, with some suggesting that his initial lawyer at his murder trial, Reginald Gwynne Templer, a friend of Keyse, was the a true killer. Templer left Lee's trial midway due to health issues, and died in an asylum the following year.

James Berry
(1852-1913)

James Berry was England's official executioner from 1884 to 1891, carrying out 131 executions. He was known for his refinement of the "long drop method" developed by previous executioner William Marwood. In spite of this, one condemned prisoner was decapitated in late 1885, and another nearly so in late 1891, ending his tenure executioner. In later years, he toured as an evangelist and lecturing phrenologist.

Berry's report to the Under-Sheriff of Devon following John Lee's failed execution, including his curious omission of the third attempt to carry out the hanging, is reproduced below.

From James Berry's *My Life as Executioner*, Ch. 7: "Two Terrible Experiences" (Percy Lund & Co., London, 1892)

Executioner's Office
1, Bilton Place, City Road,
Bradford, Yorks.
4th March, 1885.

Re John Lee.

Sir,

In accordance with the request contained in your letter of the 30th inst., I beg to say that on the morning of Friday, the 20th ult., I travelled from Bradford to Exeter, arriving at Exeter at 11:50 a.m.,

293

when I walked direct to the County Gaol, signed my name in your Gaol Register Book at 12 o'clock exactly. I was shown to the governor's office, and arranged with him that I would go and dine and return to the Gaol at 2:00 p.m. I accordingly left the Gaol, partook of dinner, and returned at 1:50 p.m., when I was shown to the bedroom allotted to me which was an officer's room in the new Hospital Ward. Shortly afterwards I made an inspection of the place of Execution. The execution was to take place in a Coach-house in which the Prison Van was usually kept. Two Warders accompanied me on the inspection. In the Coach-house I found a Beam about four inches thick, and about a foot in depth, was placed across the top of the Coach-house. Through this beam an iron bolt was fastened with an iron-nut on the upper side, and to this bolt a wrought-iron rod was fixed, about three-quarters of a yard long with a hole at the lower end to which the rope was to be attached. Two Trap-doors were placed in the floor of the Coach-house, which is flagged with stone, and these doors cover a pit about 2 yards by 1½ yards across, and about 11 feet deep. On inspecting these doors I found they were only about an inch thick, but to have been constructed properly should have been three or four inches thick. The ironwork of the doors was of a frail kind, and much too weak for the purpose. There was a lever to these doors, and it was placed near the top of them. I pulled the lever and the doors dropped, the catches acting all right. I had the doors raised, and tried the lever a second time, when the catch again acted all right. The Governor was watching me through the window of his office and saw me try the doors. After the examination I went to him, explained how I found the doors, and suggested to him that for future executions new trap-doors should be made about three times as thick as those then fixed. I also suggested that a spring should be fixed in the Wall to hold the doors back when they fell, so that no rebounding occurred, and that the ironwork of the doors should be stronger. The Governor said he would see to these matters in future. I spent all the Sunday in the room allotted to me, and did not go outside the Gaol. I retired to bed about 9:45 that night. The execution was fixed to take place at eight o'clock on the morning of Monday the 23rd ultimo.

On the Monday morning I arose at 6:30, and was conducted from the Bedroom by a Warder, at 7:30, to the place of execution. Everything appeared to be as I had left it on the Saturday afternoon. I fixed the rope in my ordinary manner, and placed everything in readiness. I did not try the Trap-doors as they appeared to be just as I had left them. It had rained heavily during the nights of Saturday and Sunday. About four minutes to eight o'clock I was conducted by the Governor to the condemned Cell and introduced to John Lee. I proceeded at once to pinion him, which was done in the usual manner, and then gave a signal to the Governor that I was ready.

The procession was formed, headed by the Governor, the Chief Warder, and the Chaplain followed by Lee. I walked behind Lee and 6 or 8 warders came after me. On reaching the place of execution I found you were there along with the Prison Surgeon. Lee was at once placed upon the trap-doors. I pinioned his legs, pulled down the white cap, adjusted the Rope, stepped on one side, and drew he lever – but the trap door did not fall. I had previously stood upon the doors and thought they would fall quite easily. I unloosed the strap from his legs, took the rope from his neck, removed the White Cap, and took Lee away into an adjoining room until I made an examination of the doors. I worked the lever after Lee had been taken off, drew it, and the doors fell easily. With the assistance of the warders the doors were pulled up, and the lever was drawn a second time, when the doors again fell easily. Lee was then brought from the adjoining room, placed in position, the cap and rope adjusted, but when I again pulled the lever it did not act, and in trying to force it the lever was slightly strained. Lee was then taken off a second time and conducted to the adjoining room.

It was suggested to me that the woodwork fitted too tightly in the centre of the doors, and one of the warders fetched an axe and another a plane. I again tried the lever but it did not act. A piece of wood was then sawn off one of the doors close to where the iron catches were, and by aid of an iron crowbar the catches were knocked off, and the doors fell down. You then gave orders that the execution should not be proceeded with until you had communicated with the Home Secretary, and Lee was taken back to the Condemned Cell. I am of the opinion that the ironwork catches of the trap-doors were not strong enough for the purpose, that the woodwork of the doors should have been about three or four times as heavy, and with iron-work to correspond, so that when a man of Lee's weight was placed upon the doors the iron catches would not have become locked, as I feel sure they did on this occasions, but would respond readily. So far as I' am concerned, everything was performed in a careful manner, and had the iron and woodwork been sufficiently strong, the execution would have been satisfactorily accomplished.

I am, Sir,
Your obedient Servant,
James Berry

Henry M. James, Esq..,
Under-Sheriff of Devon,
The Close, Exeter

An Explanation: Three Stories with the First Literary Agent

A word about the next three stories in this collection, "The Jephson Affair", "The Unintended Offenses", and "Fate's Brushes" . . . .

As I've written elsewhere, after nearly a lifetime of reading and collecting Holmes adventures – not just the pitifully few Canonical Sixty, but thousands and thousands of other post-Canonical tales – I was finally motivated to try writing some when I suddenly had some free time after being laid off from my civil engineering job at the beginning of the Great Recession of 2008.

Each morning I'd do my usual job search activities, and then sit down and let Watson speak, while I tried to transcribe all that he said. I'd long had the idea for the Solar Pons origin story (which ended up being "The Adventure of the Other Brother"), but before I felt that ambitious, I wanted to practice, so I wrote several other Holmes adventures first. I never use an outline, so in each case, I just opened a blank Word document and started typing.

Over several weeks during the spring of 2008, I ended up writing nine Holmes stories – which eventually became *The Papers of Sherlock Holmes*. By writing without a plan, I never knew how the stories would start, progress, or end. Like Watson, I was always surprised as each new adventure unfolded. I was particularly surprised when, in "The Adventure of the Missing Missing Link", set in mid-1912, Holmes and Watson encountered Watson's famed First Literary Agent, Sir Arthur Conan Doyle.

He didn't have much to say in that one, and I didn't know that he would be back in future stories, because I never expected to write future stories. But then, over the course of the next 130-plus Holmes adventures that I've written (so far), he has unexpectedly made a few other appearances.

As of this writing, Doyle (as Holmes and Watson call him, regardless of his knighthood) has been in eight of the adventures that Watson has shared with me. At some point along the way, I decided that maybe I should try to get twelve of these Literary Agent tales, and then publish them in a separate volume. Hopefully 2025 will see that plan come to fruition.

Some of these stories have already been published, and then included in previous volumes of *The Collected Papers*, while others were ready to be included in this book, and as of this writing, three narratives with Doyle as a participant are awaiting imminent publication. I have my own ideas about Doyle – he isn't necessarily the sacrosanct figure beloved by so many Sherlockians. He brings a certain spin – sometimes comical, and sometimes explaining unresolved Canonical questions – to the stories in which he appears. Holmes doesn't much like him, while Watson – being the good person that he is – is tolerant, although he isn't fooled.

The Doyle stories that I've pulled from the Tin Dispatch Box so far are:

- ☐ "The Adventure of the Missing Missing Link" *The Papers of Sherlock Holmes* and *The Art of Holmes – USA Edition 1* and *The Collected Papers of Sherlock Holmes – Volume I:*

- "The Austrian Certificates" *After the East Wind – Part II: Aftermath (1919-1920)* and *The Collected Papers of Sherlock Holmes – Volume III: Accounts*
- "The Jephson Affair" *Sherlock Holmes: A Year of Mystery 1884* and *The Collected Papers of Sherlock Holmes – Volume VII: Annals*
- "The Unintentional Offenses" *Steel True, Blade Straight – 2022 Annual* and *The Collected Papers of Sherlock Holmes – Volume VII: Annals*
- "Fates Brushes" *Steel True, Blade Straight – 2023 Annual* and *The Collected Papers of Sherlock Holmes – Volume VII: Annals*
- "The Man With the Stolen Luck" *Steel True, Blade Straight – 2024 Annual* (Forthcoming)
- "The Body in Bishop's Crossing" *Sherlock Holmes: Into the Fire* (Forthcoming)
- "The Adventure of the Automatic Writer" *Silence: An Anthology of New Stories featuring Algernon Blackwood's "Psychic Doctor"* (Forthcoming)

I was very honored that two of these stories, "The Unintended Offenses" and "Fate's Brushes", received the Fiction Award for 2022 and 2023 respectively from The ACD Society.

The Jephson Affair

Sherlock Holmes was in a disputatious mood, made worse by the fact that he was away from our Baker Street rooms, and thus he didn't have the comfort of smoking his cherrywood pipe, which was his choice when in such a state. The long-stemmed pipe was not made for quick traveling, and he was making do with his sturdier black clay.

We had been summoned that morning to Portsmouth by a local inspector who believed that Holmes might be able to assist in the capture of Druland, the murderer. My friend had followed the case in the newspaper for several days as the killer ran circles around the local law enforcement, and his reactions had ranged from almost inappropriate laughter as the police were fooled once again to frustration at their mistakes and refusal to seek a consultant – namely Sherlock Holmes – who could do the job right.

Inspector Newley, who had worked with Holmes several years before on the matter of the Dalston reptile cages, had finally taken it upon himself to send a wire to Baker Street, and it was as if Holmes were a race horse poised at the gate. As a former soldier, I travel light and was ready to leave immediately, and of course Holmes was already packed. We were away from Waterloo Station almost before I had time to realize it, but even quicker still was Holmes's solution once we arrived. He had studied the letters reprinted in the newspapers, two of which had been shown as facsimiles, and with a cadre of policemen in support, he led us to the inn on western end of the old canal in Milton, where Druland, a surprisingly shabby little man, was holed up alone, gloating over the gruesome trophies he'd collected over the previous week.

In spite of his triumph, Holmes was disgusted – the chase had been too easy.

"But what a feather in your cap!" I reminded him. "This will go a long way toward building your reputation so that you will receive more and more calls from the professional force."

He shook his head and sank deeper into his chair. We were in a shared sitting room at the very inn where Druland had been arrested. In spite of the case being finished, Inspector Newley had asked that we stay over for an extra day, in case further statements were required. Thus, in spite of being close enough to be able to return to London by nightfall, we were figuratively treading water in Portsmouth.

Our inn was a decent-enough place, run by a widow who reminded me quite a bit of our own landlady back in London. When it was

300

determined that it was too late to return to the capital for the night, we had settled there. I must admit that when we left that morning, I had expected a trip of longer length. It seemed that we had only arrived to turn around and go back.

Attempting to change the direction of our conversation, I asked, "Do you think Druland will hang, or is he mad enough to spend the rest of his days in Broadmoor?"

Holmes frowned into the oily smoke drifting before his eyes. "What business is it of mine what happens to him now? The rope or the cell – what matters is that he's been stopped." His was in the mood for an argument and to be contrary, in the same way that he'd once claimed ignorance of the Copernican Theory, stating that it made no difference to his work and that if it took up valuable space in his mind that might be better used, he'd do his best to forget it.

I realized that, having been tossed into this brown study, he was likely to remain there until he found his own way out, regardless of whatever efforts I made. I was considering a ramble through the great port city before dark when there was a knock at the door.

We both looked at one another, and I asked, "Inspector Newley?" Holmes shrugged, and I rose to see who it was.

It was not the inspector. Instead, it was an acquaintance of ours whom we had met a couple of years before while attending the same lecture at Barts.

"Doyle?" I said, stepping aside and allowing the big fellow to enter.

He blinked, as the sitting room was quite a bit brighter than the darkened landing. He was a big fellow, about twenty-five then and just a few years younger than Holmes and me. He was clearly built for the rugby which he loved so much. After our initial meeting, we found that this pastime was an enthusiasm that we had in common.

He had a great square head cut across from side to side with a bushy mustache waxed out past his face on either side, a mouth that was pursed when he was quiet until it widened in a smile, and small eyes, almost resembling an English terrier. They looked even smaller when he laughed – which was a great deal of the time. But he wasn't in that sort of mood today.

Behind me, I heard Holmes rise, and he perceived that all wasn't normal, as his previous attitude seemed to drift away like the smoke from his pipe. "Doyle," he said. "You appear out of sorts."

Our visitor looked down and saw almost immediately that he'd misbuttoned his waistcoat. He started to fix it but was stopped by the folded newspaper in his left hand. Handing it to me, he proceeded to re-button the garment, and then he looked up at us, stating without preamble,

"You're mentioned in the newspaper. Late edition – for the capture of Druland. Inspector Newley told me where to find you."

I gestured to a seat and offered him a drink. He nodded, and I went out and downstairs to get whisky from the barkeep. When I returned, I found Holmes handing the newspaper back to Doyle, who set it aside and accepted his glass. He took a generous swallow and I said, in order to put him at ease, "We haven't heard from you in a while. Still making a go of the practice?"

He nodded. "It's doing well. Before I settled in, I looked around to see where the other doctors were located, and I found a good spot near the junction of Elm Grove and King's Road in Southsea – it's a residential area not far west of here. At first business was slow, but I realized that I had to do more than just put my plaque on the wall – I had to go out and meet the people. I advertised my services wherever I could, and made sure that my name was mentioned in the papers whenever I was involved in a meeting or attended an accident."

I could see that Holmes was impatient with this chit-chat, but he understood its usefulness.

"Still playing rugby?"

Doyle nodded. "But down here I'm spending more time playing for the local cricket and bowls teams." His eyes dropped, and then he looked back up. "And I'm still writing some."

I nodded. That was another thing that we'd had in common. I've long been a writer, keeping extensive journals of various day-to-day activities, but trying to present them in a more readable way than simple tedious notes on what I did on a certain day – I am no Pepys. My writing was especially useful during those long empty hours when I was recovering from my wounds at Maiwand, and I found that more and more, my time was turned toward recording those of Holmes's cases in which I participated.

Doyle, on the other hand, aspired to be a novelist, and I knew that he spent a great deal of his time between his patients' visits scribbling. He'd also once confided in me that, as a bachelor, writing helped to pass the lonely nights.

"It's because of my writing that I'm here," he added.

Holmes nodded, and I was surprised that he didn't add an "Ah!" now that the reason for his new client's visit was at last being revealed.

"Are you aware of the mystery of the *Mary Celeste*?"

I nodded, but Holmes waved the stem of his pipe, indicating that Doyle should relate it.

"She was a brigantine, about two-hundred tons, built in Canada in '61. She first sailed under the name *Amazon*, but later became the *Mary*

302

Celeste. In early November 1872, she set sail from New York. A month later, she was found abandoned, midway between the Azores and Portugal. One lifeboat was gone, and there was some dampness inside from open skylights, and a bit of water in the hold, but nothing disastrous. The glass on the binnacle was broken, but a vial of sewing oil was still standing upright, so it was difficult to tell if the ship had encountered rough conditions or not. The galley was neatly stowed, and it seemed as if there had been an orderly departure. The captain's papers and navigation instruments were missing, but the daily ship's log was found still on board. No reason for the abandonment was recorded, and the last entry, from nine days earlier, placed the ship almost four-hundred miles from where she was found.

"All sorts of theories arose as to why the entire crew would abandon ship. A sounding rod was found on deck, so it was thought that perhaps they feared running aground somewhere. Some proposed that they had been becalmed, but the fact that many sails were furled negated this idea. Others proposed that fumes from the cargo might have forced them to leave, but there was no clear evidence for that either."

"And how does this relate to your writing?" asked Holmes.

"Last year, I wrote a fictionalized version of the ship's abandonment. I changed some facts – I called her the *Marie Celeste*, and altered the date to 1873. I had her leave from Boston instead of New York, and I completely renamed the Captain and other crewman. I also added passengers in my version – including one named J. Habakuk Jephson, who is the narrator of the story. In my fictionalized account, I had a man named Septimius Goring suborn certain members of the crew to murder everyone else on board in order to take the ship to West Africa – but Goring lets Jephson live because the narrator carries a magic charm – or so Goring believes. It was nothing more than an amusing little exercise in fiction, and I was fortunate enough to have it published this past January in *Cornhill's* – which is nice enough, I suppose, although we all know that *Cornhill's* isn't what it used to be, and I knew that very few people would see the story."

"But someone did see it," I surmised, guessing the reason that Doyle had related this anecdote.

He nodded.

"It had more success than I would have thought, and some compared it to Poe's style, or even thought that it was by Robert Louis Stevenson. More amazing than that was when an American newspaper reprinted it as fact!

"I published it anonymously – as I said, it was an exercise, and I didn't want it to be associated with some of the more ambitious works I'm

303

attempting, should they ever be published. That's not the sort of tale I want associated with my name. I favor historical romances, you know, rather like Sir Walter's works – or so I hope. Yet somehow, my connection with the piece has been discovered.

"Six days ago – on Friday – I received a letter. This letter," he added, extracting several envelopes from his pocket and pulling one loose. He started to hand it to me, as he'd looked more my way than toward Holmes during his explanation, but then he put the letter into Holmes's outstretched hand.

I could see that the letter was yellowish paper, cheap and thin, and that the envelope matched. Similar stationery would be for sale in dozens of dock-side shops for those sailors who wished to post a quick note to a loved one, or perhaps to take care of a bit of business before leaving port. I had once sent such a last-minute note on that exact type of paper to a girl only minutes before shipping out to India – the result of uneasiness and doubts at my indefinite departure. Fortunately the letter never made a difference (assuming that it was actually delivered), as the girl married while I was away and molted into a quite unpleasant shrew. I was wounded at Maiwand, but I dodged the certain bullet that would have been marriage to Matilda Eaves.

Holmes finished looking at the sheet and envelope and passed them both to me. Having known him at that point for more than three years, and working with him on an ever-increasing number of investigations, it was natural that I would acquire some rudimentary skills – although never to Holmes's levels, and certainly not enough to avoid his impatience with me at the time. Still, I made a sincere effort to see what he had observed.

"It's curiously written in pencil," I noted, and Holmes nodded. "The lead is soft and the tip rounded – the pencil lines are wide, and there's no sign of a point digging into the paper, which might indicate hurrying or urgency. There are no misspelled words, and no attempts to mislead by intentionally making something incorrect. The lines are even across the page, with no up or downward slopes, and there's no crowding at the end of a line where word lengths were judged incorrectly. Whoever wrote this, while not having access to more-expensive paper or pen, put some time and thought into it."

I looked at the envelope. "It hasn't been stamped or franked – it was dropped directly into your post box."

Doyle nodded, and held up several other similar letters. "The same for these."

"There is a date lightly penciled on the top right corner of the rear of the envelope, and in the same place on the rear of each sheet. It's from a different pencil – sharper."

Doyle nodded. "I did that when the second letter arrived. I put the date that they were delivered on all of them."

Holmes nodded in appreciation, and then he asked me, "And the message? What's your opinion of that?"

I glanced at it again. "The name and address are on the front of the envelope – '*Dr. Doyle, No. 1 Bush Villas*' – but the letter doesn't duplicate that. There's no salutation at all, simply stating: '*Leave the* Mary Celeste *documents on the bench by your back door.*'" I gave the letter and envelope back to Holmes and asked Doyle, "Do the subsequent letters add anything?"

"Much the same." He handed the others to Holmes. "They're in the order by date."

"Hmm. All the same type of paper, and addressed the same." He counted. "One letter per day – including today I see." Doyle nodded. "Seven in all."

One at a time, he removed the sheets and read them aloud. "Saturday: '*Leave the documents on the bench. I will not be denied.*' Sunday: '*Leave the* Mary Celeste *documents on the bench*' – much the same as Friday's note. Monday. Ah, this is more interesting: '*You are in danger. Leave the documents tonight.*'" Holmes looked up. "And did you face any danger? Any attacks in the street, or were there any attempts from anyone to enter your home?"

Doyle shook his head. "Nothing. Of course, as this went along, I was more careful, and kept my eyes open. These documents – "

Holmes held up a hand. "We'll discuss that in a moment. To continue – Tuesday: '*You must leave the proof on the bench.*' The tone has shifted. He speaks of proof now, and not just documents, and the threat of danger has been dropped." He shuffled the papers. "Two more. Wednesday: '*Please provide the documents, and no harm will come to you.*' Ah, that is interesting. The tone has shifted to pleading. And finally today's message – much the same as the original, but again with a more polite approach: '*Please leave the* Mary Celeste *documents on the bench.*'" He set aside the letters beside his emptied whisky glass. "I would hope that you've kept watch to see when these were delivered?"

Doyle nodded. "As best as I could. Each has been dropped through the mail slot. The first was in the normal course of the day, and I have no idea when it arrived. Not knowing there would be a second, I paid no attention the next day, nor even on Sunday. By Monday I made a point of watching from my front window whenever I had a free moment between patients, but the layout of the building makes it a bit difficult, as the front window juts a little forward on the right side of the building, making it difficult to see if anyone approaches from the left. The door itself is set back in a little alcove between my building and the one next door, and even though there's a bit of brick arch and a gate to separate the door from the pavement, the gate is left open.

"On Tuesday I also tried watching from the first-floor window overlooking the front door, but somehow during one of the times when I'd stepped away, a letter was pushed through the slot. I don't know if I was seen watching from the windows, but yesterday morning the letter was waiting for me when I came down – delivered during the night. I resolved to wait inside the unlocked front door last night, and rush out as soon as a letter was delivered, but none came, and I thought that I might have outlasted this chap's patience. But then, when I opened up for the morning, the letter was outside, propped against the door. While I waited just inside, this person was just a foot away, having crept up to the house to carry out this curious mission."

"Based on your description of the story," Holmes said, "I would suspect that there are no documents."

"Correct. I made it up out of whole cloth, based on what I'd read in a reprinted newspaper account from last year."

"Yet it seems that something in your version has enough substance to attract attention, a dozen years after the incident occurred." Holmes set his pipe, now long since grown cold, on the side table. Then, tapping his lip with a finger, he asked, "Have you seen any signs of attempted entry?"

"I have not. I keep the house buttoned up tight. In fact, when I moved there, I made an effort to add extra locks – just a quirk of mine."

"So no one is likely there now, ransacking the place?"

The sudden image was clearly visible to Doyle, but after a small start and frown of concern, he shook his head. "No, I'm sure that it's locked up tight. And in any case, there's nothing for him to find."

"The bench where you're supposed to leave the documents? How would he know of that?"

"The rear of the house is open to a shared garden of sorts, accessed by several passages. He could have easily entered when doing his initial reconnaissance and picked it as a likely place. Passage in and out would be quite easy."

"It might have been easier to leave the notes there if it's so easily accessible," I theorized.

"Possibly," said Doyle, "but I rarely go out there, so I wouldn't necessarily have found them. And in any case, he's doing a fine job of delivering them to the front."

Holmes fell silent for some moments and Doyle, who had known him at that point for a couple of years, recognized that my friend was pondering the situation. Finally he looked up.

"I take it that this concerns you, since you took the trouble to seek our help."

"It does. If this person is willing to pester me for nearly a week, how much longer will he go, and to what level will it escalate?"

"Did you consult with the police?"

Doyle shook his head. "They are not the friendliest bunch here, and frankly I don't have much faith in them – including our mutual acquaintance, Inspector Newley. I've heard you go on about the failings of the London police, Holmes. Those of Portsmouth are sadly worse. No, when I read in this evening's paper that you were both in town, I realized that I had an opportunity to find out what might be happening here. I could have devoted more of my own time, of course, but when you know an expert and he's in town . . . Well, why keep a dog and then bark yourself?"

He finished with a smile, not quite realizing the implied insult in his words. That was Doyle – like a big happy dog himself, bounding through life with great enthusiasm, and often not realizing when he's knocked over a table and broken his master's favorite cup.

Doyle would have missed it, but I knew Holmes well enough by then to recognize the slight smile that narrowed his eyes – Doyle's comment had amused rather than insulted. With a sigh, he sat up straighter. "Assuming that tomorrow's letter hasn't already been delivered – unlikely – or that this man or woman hasn't gotten inside and is currently ransacking the house right now, despite your confidence to the contrary, and that he will continue with the same fruitless plan of attack, we have a chance to track him."

"What do you propose?"

"You will return home and have a routine night – reading or writing, or whatever you do. I have the impression you live alone?"

"I do. There is a daily staff for when the practice is open, but everyone leaves at the end of the day."

"Excellent. I'll follow along behind you shortly and keep watch. When the next letter is delivered – almost certainly deep in the night, if your visitor follows his recent pattern – I'll follow him and find out who he is. Then we can decide what to do next. Now, I'm somewhat familiar with Portsmouth. Give me directions to your home."

Doyle succinctly described the route from our inn to Bush Villas, a ten-minute walk west to an area near the intersections of Kings Road, Elm Grove, and Castle Road. Then we stood and, after shaking hands, our visitor departed, leaving Holmes in possession of the letters.

"What can I do?" I asked.

"Be prepared if I send word, I suppose. I intend to simply follow this fellow for now. It shouldn't present any difficulty – after all, if he remains true to form, he'll return to Doyle's front door at some point before morning. If I'm properly concealed, he should arrive and depart without ever knowing that I'm there."

With that, he adjourned to his room, where he set about preparing himself for his expedition. He returned in a quarter-hour looking like a sailor, and nothing like himself. I knew that he always tried to travel with a few basic garments that could be adapted into various disguises, but his true skill lay in the fact that he seemed to *become* a different person, carrying his entire body in a new way. With a nod he was gone, and I was left to my own devices.

Thinking that any possible summons for my assistance was unlikely during the next few hours, I set off to explore the nearby area, as had been my original plan, although I did limit myself from what I'd initially intended. The March weather had been mild earlier in the day, but it had turned cooler, and fortunately I had brought warmer clothing. Walking east along the canal, I took in the sights and smells of the famous port town, and it wasn't long before I was looking out over Langstone Harbor, breathing deeply the tang of the sea, along with the more subtle odors of manmade construction. After contemplating that for a while, I made my way south along the shore, stopping for an evening meal at a tidy little shop featuring fresh seafood. I had a friendly conversation with the owner, a one-legged old soldier who had returned after the Mutiny and settled there with his wife. He had one interesting story after another, and it was tempting to stay for the entire evening, but I finally excused myself and returned to our inn, to be ready should I receive a summons to Bush Villas. However, no messages arrived for me, and I was asleep rather early, awakening in the morning quite refreshed and curious to hear Holmes's report. It wasn't long in coming.

I had barely begun eating my breakfast when there was a knock at the sitting room door. I said to come in, and the door opened to reveal the landlord, gripping a small lad by the collar. "He says he's delivering a message from your friend."

I nodded that it was acceptable and the lad was released. "I'd be obliged if you'd walk him down and outside when you're finished," the man said before giving the boy a glare and then departing.

When the door was closed, the boy stepped forward. "Dr. Watson?" he said in a high voice. I nodded and he pulled a folded piece of paper from his pocket.

It was torn from Holmes's notebook, requesting my presence – and my revolver – at an inn near the Coast Guard docks, not far south from where I sat. While gathering my hat, coat, and gun, I asked the boy if he wanted to finish my breakfast, and without answering, he moved to the side of the table. Without bothering to sit, he began to eat, and he was done by the time I was ready to leave. As requested, I walked him down. When we were outside, he agreed to lead me to the specified inn.

As I arrived, Doyle was pulling up in a carriage, also accompanied by another boy who had clearly been sent to retrieve him as well. As he nodded and began to ask a question, I shook my head. Giving the two boys a few coins apiece, I watched for a moment as they vanished down the street. Then Doyle and I went inside.

The place was already surprisingly full for that time of morning, as many of the dock workers seemed to have stopped there for a bracer on their way to work. There was quite a bit of lively conversation all around us, and it was a bit overwhelming to step suddenly into the midst of it. Then, off to one side, we spotted Holmes, still in his disguise, at the bar. He saw us, stood, and led us to a rear table. He sat with his back to the wall where he could watch the bar, and he seemed to keep his eyes specifically on the stairway leading up.

"After I left our rooms last night," he began explaining without preamble, "I modified the plan. Rather than simply following our letter-leaver as intended after he made his delivery, I stopped at a small shop and bought some paper and an envelope – ironically of the same type used for Doyle's letters. I composed a note saying that I – speaking as you, Doyle – refused to relinquish the papers, as I understood what they represented and that I knew what to do with them. It was deliberately vague, but enough to provoke a reaction.

"After you were in for the night, and when I was certain that our prey wasn't yet in the street, I crept over and left the letter propped against the front door. It was labeled, '*Re: The* Mary Celeste.' Then I found an areaway across the street and hid in the increasing darkness.

"The hours passed slowly, in spite of being near a main thoroughfare. A constable walked by regularly, announcing his approach long before his appearance by his steady and noisy footsteps. It was just after one of these visits, sometime around five this morning, that I heard a scuff from several house-lengths away – unusual enough that I believed that it might be our visitor. I was correct – but he wasn't able to immediately complete his mission, and he gave me a shock in the meantime.

"As his shadowy figure was approaching from the west, another louder passer-by entered the area from the east, clearly inebriated and shuffling along on Doyle's side of the street. I was shocked to see that the first man from the west, upon hearing this noise, abruptly shifted his approach to my side of the street, whereupon he crept down into the very areaway in which I was hiding!

"I pressed myself further back into the darkness, barely breathing. Fortunately, the man paid no attention to anything but the street in front of him, where the drunkard was passing by, singing softly to himself. In a moment he was gone, and the first man crept out and crossed the street. I stepped forward to the spot he'd just occupied and watched through the rails as he arrived at Doyle's door. He moved with deliberation and caution, and in the dim light I could see that he'd pulled a letter from his coat and was leaning forward to replace it when he saw the one that I'd left there for him.

"He was frozen with apparent indecision for just an instant before leaning forward and snatching it. Then he pivoted and returned to the street, where he continued to the east, moving at a quick but silent trot. As he approached a streetlight, I could see then what hadn't been apparent when he was inches away in the darkened areaway – he was tall and broad-shouldered, and moved easily, coming to a sure-footed stop underneath the gaslight. There he read what I'd written. Even from a distance, I could hear him snarl as he rocked an involuntary step back. He turned, looked at Doyle's house if he were considering returning there, and then resumed his departure from the neighborhood – with me following behind.

"He walked steadily east until finding a wider road turning south toward the coast. We didn't travel very far – Southsea isn't an extensive place – and it became easier to stay with him as we progressed. The streets were steadily becoming busier and I could close up the distance. Finally he reached this inn and came inside. After determining that there was a small restaurant here, already serving to the public, I came in as well.

"He sat off to one side at the bar and, instead of ordering food, he was already drinking whisky, my letter and envelope lying before him, and another envelope, surely what he'd intended to deliver, beside them.

"I stepped to the bar nearby and ordered a whisky too, and when it arrived, I commented to him that we two appeared to be the only ones in need of a real drink that early in the morning. He glanced at me and then away, as if deciding to ignore me, but then he chose to speak.

"'Some mornings just require it, don't they?' he asked.

"Taking that as an invitation for further conversation, I took a step closer. 'They do indeed. I need something to prepare me for the upcoming day. And you?' I nodded toward the sheets on the bar. 'Have you had some bad news, perhaps?'

"'Rather, it's disappointing. A bit of business that needs winding up, but I can't convince the other party to see things my way.'

"His accent let me know that he was an American. While his appearance was rough, there was no sign that he was a sailor. His manner of speech indicated that his background was one of better breeding before he'd gone down whatever path that brought him to the bar this morning. As I mentioned, I'd seen that he was tall and broad-shouldered from when he stopped under the gaslight an hour or so earlier. Now, observing him in daylight, I found that he was probably in his mid-thirties, but he appeared older, as his skin was dark and weathered, and there was already gray in his recently trimmed hair. His hands were big and scarred, but he'd done some regular maintenance toward keeping his nails even and clean. His teeth appeared to be in good shape, and he had no obvious scars or marks of violence.

"I mentioned that I was new in town, and asked if he had any recommendations for a berth, as I implied that I'd rather leave sooner rather than later. He had no information to offer, saying that he'd only been there himself for little more than a week, and that the fine ship upon which he'd arrived, the *Savannah*, had already departed.

"I struggled for a way to make the conversation progress, and considered mentioning that my name was 'Jephson' to see if it provoked a reaction, but I couldn't see that anything would come of it, other than putting him on his guard. Finally, perceiving that he was apparently quite weary after his nocturnal outing, I insisted on buying him another whisky, and then another – both of which he gladly accepted. Then, refusing more and not noticing that I still hadn't finished my initial glass, he gathered the letters and stood, indicating that he needed some sleep. He nodded my way and weaved through the crowded room before climbing the stairs over there and out of sight.

"I spoke with the innkeeper tending bar, and he let me know that I'd been speaking with Mr. Guilford McReynolds of Tennessee – or so he identified himself when he arrived and took a room. I didn't want to ask too many questions, not wanting to raise the man's suspicions by being any more than casually curious, but I did learned that McReynolds – should that be his true name – has been staying here for a little more than a week, which coincided with his statement about arriving on the *Savannah*, and the approximate time when the letters began appearing at Doyle's door."

"What do we do now?" asked Doyle, leaning forward on his chair. "Summon the police?"

"For what?" countered Holmes. "He's done nothing actionable at this point. No, I think it would be best to simply go upstairs and confront him."

Clearly Doyle wanted some other action to occur, but Holmes's plan was the most sensible and direct. He stood, and we joined him.

We climbed the stairs and entered a dim hallway on the first floor, leading toward the back of the building. It was suddenly much quieter here than the already-raucous room below. Holmes led us directly to the third

311

door on the left, and I knew that he must have previously established where McReynolds was lodging. Reaching the door, he knocked softly, but there was no answer. A steady snoring could be heard beyond the door's thin panels.

The door was locked, but Holmes knelt and pulled out one of his lock-picks. It was open almost immediately, and he opened the door, allowing us to enter. Then he followed and pushed the door softly shut.

By the light coming through the thin curtains over the single window, we could see McReynolds sprawled upon the bed, on top of the covers. He was still dressed, although he'd managed to pull off his boots. Clearly the extra whisky foisted upon him by Holmes had affected him. The letters in question lay on a small table beside the bed.

At a motion from Holmes, Doyle pulled back the curtain while I lit a lantern. Then Holmes leaned forward and shook the sleeping man by the shoulder. "McReynolds! Wake up!"

With a groan, the man held an arm across his eyes and pulled a leg up. Then, realizing that he wasn't alone, he sat up suddenly, looking from one to the other of us as if he might jump to his feet and make for the door. Seeing that his path was blocked that way, and also toward the riskier exit from the window, he relaxed somewhat and said, "Who are you? What do you want?"

Doyle, who had been a dark silhouette against the window, stepped forward. "I want to know why you've been leaving letters at my surgery in Bush Villas!" His Scottish accent had a rather angry and righteous tone, and it filled the room, clearly intimidating the big man perched on the edge of the bed.

"Your surgery? You'd be Dr. Doyle, then. I . . . I meant no harm."

"If you meant no harm, why didn't you simply knock on the door and ask a question like an honest man?"

"Because . . . because I didn't know . . . ." He pulled his fingers through his tousled hair. Then, "It wasn't clear to me whether you published your story to set a trap – We're talking of crimes, after all! – or perhaps you intend to you use the information you've obtained for some even deeper and more devious purpose."

"Information? What information?"

"The truth about the *Mary Celeste*. Your story hinted that you clearly you knew what happened – and I didn't want make things worse. I thought that if I sounded mysterious and vaguely threatening, you might be inclined to turn loose of what you had. Then I could destroy it and be on my way."

Doyle took another step closer. "I have no idea what you're talking about."

McReynolds looked confused, glancing from Doyle to Holmes and me, and then back again.

"We're talking at cross-purposes," interjected Holmes. "Perhaps if we go back downstairs and discuss this, we can sort out what's going on."

McReynolds ran a hand over his face and nodded. "That would be best, I think." He reached forward and retrieved his boots. After they were on, he stood, taller than the rest of us. "Lead on."

Downstairs, the initial tide of dock workers gathering their morning courage had receded, and we returned to the same empty table we'd occupied a few minutes before. We all ordered breakfast from the innkeeper's wife, and then Holmes explained that he'd placed the reply against the door the previous night and then followed McReynolds back to the inn.

"Is your name Guilford McReynolds?" he asked.

The man nodded. "From America, and recently arrived on the *Savannah*. When I learned we'd be docking at Portsmouth, I signed off in order to find out more about that story from *Cornhill's* – about what truly happened on the *Mary Celeste*."

"But that isn't the truth," replied Doyle. "I had simply read about the ship and contrived my own fictional explanation – It was *fiction*! Surely you saw the various changes that I made – I altered the name of the ship, and the date, and the names of the crews. I added passengers when there were none, and even changed the point of departure."

"I understand that," said McReynolds, "but there was enough truth in what you wrote that I was concerned that the matter might be reopened – and I wondered where you had found out what happened."

"What truth was there?" I asked. "Was it about how the crew was murdered?"

McReynolds nodded. "It was. And clearly the man who murdered them in the story, Septimius Goring, was based on my half-brother."

Doyle shook his head. "I tell you, I didn't know about any truth of the matter. I simply wrote a fictional story."

McReynolds looked at him with a puzzled expression. "Then you have a gift of divination, sir."

At that moment our food arrived, and after we had it arranged and began to eat – everyone except Holmes that is, who ignored his plate while smoking his pipe and impatiently fixing his eyes on McReynolds – the American continued his story around mouthfuls of eggs and bacon.

"As I said, I have a half-brother whom I thought was represented in your story by Septimius Goring – "

"Goring was of mixed race," interrupted Doyle.

McReynolds nodded. "Yes sir. I'm from the American South, and before the War, my father had a . . . relationship with a freed black woman. It produced a son – my half-brother – Lucius. My mother was long dead by then, and I was their only child, so my father's adultery was no shame upon her at that point. Lucius and I grew up together in eastern Tennessee, which always leaned toward the abolitionist side of the slavery argument. When Tennessee seceded from the Union in June 1861, our county seceded from the State – which didn't amount to much, although the Confederacy never had much influence or support in that region. My father was dead by then, and Lucius and I journeyed north to fight for the Union.

"Something about the war changed Lucius – he became bitter and angry, and the killing seemed to become easy for him. And in spite of being on the side fighting to end slavery, he ended up hating the Union as much as he did the Confederacy.

"After the War, the two of us stuck together, working as laborers and eventually both going to sea. For a time he seemed to have mastered his rage, although it occasionally came out unexpectedly, getting us both into brawls and scrapes. What I didn't know was that he was becoming angrier and more bitter, and he'd conceived a consuming hatred of the white race. He had even come up with a plan – much like the one outlined in your story, sir. Unlike the character of Septimius Goring, who was merely a passenger on the boat, Lucius and I were serving on the crew. He had recruited several others of like mind who were in agreement with him, and they had decided to kill the crew and take the boat to Africa.

"He hadn't shared any of that with me, of course, and I had no idea what was planned until one dark night, when Lucius and the other crewman in his plan silently killed everyone else on board, moving like phantoms from place to place, slitting their throats and putting them quietly over the side, one by one. When I awoke in the morning to an emptied ship, the deed was done.

"When I arose, the sun was shining bright, but the sea was becalmed. My head hurt something fierce, and I later realized that Lucius must have given me something the night before to make me sleep – so that I wouldn't awaken and learn the truth of what was happening. In fact, he told me that some of his recruits had wanted to kill me as well, but he'd denied them the pleasure.

"It took a bit for it to dawn on me that the ship was far too still and quiet. Finally I saw a smear of blood upon the deck, which only added to my fears. I found Lucius on the bridge, and that's when he explained what had occurred. Needless to say, I was shocked and outraged, and we argued viciously, leaving me stunned at what he'd become, and also fearful when I understood that I was alone on a ship full of killers. And yet, he was my brother, and I somehow excused what he'd done, knowing what he'd seen and been forced to do during the War.

"I had made it clear that I wanted no part of this, and so they set me adrift in the lifeboat with a goodly amount of supplies – while making sure that the ship's name was eradicated from the lifeboat's hull. In spite of the calm waters and lack of wind, I drifted away, and that's the last of them that I ever saw.

"I was picked up nearly a week later, still in good shape from the supplies that I carried, and not too sun or wind-burned after seeking shelter under a tarp that I'd rigged. The boat that found me appeared to lean toward a philosophy of piracy, and they didn't ask too many questions or offer much information about themselves. I suppose that I was lucky not to end up cast overboard with a slit throat. I was set ashore in Lisbon and they kept the lifeboat.

"Several weeks later, I was shocked to read that the *Mary Celeste* had been found drifting and abandoned, with no indication of who or what might have happened. I was initially inclined to come forward and reveal what I knew, but something stopped me. Lucius and his crew might be dead from causes unknown – but they might also be alive, and I didn't want to bring attention to my brother, in spite of his terrible guilt. I held my tongue, and the mystery of the *Mary Celeste* became the stuff of great speculation and theory.

"Then, earlier this year, I happened across the issue of *Cornhill's* which told a thinly disguised version of what occurred. It seemed that after all these years, someone was hinting that the truth was known. I was quite concerned – My initial desire to protect Lucius was still within me, and I wondered why someone would write a story so close to the truth, and yet subtly altered. Was it to lure me – or someone else who knew the truth – into the open, and into the hands of the authorities? When I had the chance, I asked at the *Cornhill* offices about who had anonymously written the story, and they gave me your name, Doctor. I should have simply approached you, but instead, when we docked here in Portsmouth, I decided instead to see if I could get whatever information that you held – for I was certain that somehow you had documents that informed you of the story – without ever revealing my own connection. In this way, perhaps I might even get a line on how to find Lucius after all these years, for I've never ceased being concerned about his fate, or wondering what happened after I was put off the *Mary Celeste*."

After listening to McReynolds' curious story, I had the sense that there was possibly more that he wasn't telling, but what we'd heard was quite likely all he would reveal. Doyle spent several minutes explaining again that he'd simply fabricated a possible explanation for the mysterious

315

abandonment of the ship, and McReynolds seemed to accept that, simply commenting again that he'd hoped to learn more about his brother – although he'd admitted that it had puzzled him how such information might have come to be in the possession of a Southsea physician.

When the conversation had been becalmed and there was nothing left to say, McReynolds stood, thanked us – although I'm not entirely certain for what – and went back upstairs.

Doyle looked at each of us, back and forth, as if uncertain what to say. Finally he was moved to state, "A most curious story," he said. "I suppose there's a lesson there for me – as a writer of histories."

"What's that?" I asked, since I am something of a writer as well.

"Well, in the stories that I hope to tell – historical novels much in the manner of Sir Walter Scott – I'll be mixing my own fictional characters in with actual individuals. In doing so, I'll be creating conversations and motivations and actions for these real people that will likely be quite far from anything that they actually said or thought or did – for the purpose of allowing the story of my own characters to progress."

Holmes nodded. "It's taking on a great responsibility," he said. "Ascribing an action or a thought to a real person – something that they might never have considered, and would have found offensive – means that those who read your tales will come to believe that this is what the real person actually did or believed. Layer by layer, you will be defining that person and how they're perceived by history from that point on. Your story will be another thread in their tapestry – whether or not it's true."

As Doyle nodded, I also considered what Holmes had said. At that point in my life, I had been recording the details of Holmes's investigations in my own journals for several years – since not long after we met, and when I first became involved. I'd promised him long before that the truth should be told of at least one of his investigations – the Jefferson Hope murders – but I hadn't done anything toward actually polishing it for publication, and I had no real plans then – in 1884 – of doing so. Like Doyle, I suddenly considered the writer's responsibility when taking on the stewardship of someone else's reputation.

Just the year before, Holmes and I had encountered a wicked doctor who contrived a diabolical method of murdering his step-daughters for their inheritance. It seemed that it would be an easy story to tell – the man's evil nature was obvious from the scheme he enacted. But was there more to him – more that would never be known now that he was dead? What slippery path had led him from being a respected physician to that of an infamous murderer? It would be easy to record the facts, but what of the subtleties?

316

In the end, both Doyle and I found the same solution – telling the tales as best we could, with no intentional agendas or misstatement of facts. Doyle found fame with his historical novels, and I was able to fulfill my goal of sharing a number of Holmes's notable investigations with an enthusiastic public. In truth, Holmes never had much use for either of our efforts – but then being disputatious has always been a certain part of his nature, and as a writer, ascribing that aspect to him was no fictionalization at all.

Arthur Conan Doyle at No. 1 Bush Villas, Southsea
Mid-1880's

The Unintended Offenses
Winner – The ACD Society 2023 Fiction Award

As I recall, the sun was in my eyes that long-ago day as I approached Vicarage Gate from the east. My arrival was later than I had planned, but I had left too little time for my departure from Southsea that morning, and a series of meetings with some former colleagues had run longer than I'd expected. Then a stop in Salisbury Square that I'd thought would be quick and painless had devolved into a rather unpleasant row. Now, I had one last visit bit of business to attend to before my return home. Although I'd initially thought it would be an agreeable way to end my London visit, it had recently developed into something that I would have rather avoided if possible. I was thinking that had I but known, I would have rearranged my day to get this out of the way earlier – but that was when I still expected a satisfying outcome. As it turned out, Fate knew what she was about. I was supposed to be there in Kensington at that time on that day. In fact, had I not arrived when I did, it's doubtful that the business would have been satisfactorily sorted at all. It was only this morning's sad events that made me recollect it.

Leaving Salisbury Square, I had first strode into Fleet Street, thinking to take a cab and so cross to Kensington as soon as possible. But as a hansom wasn't immediately present, I turned west and started to walk, my steps purposeful as I dodged back and forth around those lesser-inclined for speed that day. I went over and over in my mind how such a misunderstanding could have occurred, and contrived one useless method after another to try and make things right. But it was set and done, and now all I could do was face the music.

Fleet Street became the Strand, and I was halfway 'round Trafalgar Square before my pace began to wear me down a bit. I was twenty-eight then, and in the full vigor of my youth – not as I find myself now, just a few months into my eighth decade. The events of this morning shook me rather more than I might have anticipated – which is why I want to record these long-ago events of late November 1887 now, while there is still time.

The light continued to fail as I eased my step and veered along the south side of the Square, making my way through narrow passages into St. James's Park. A slower pace did not make the news that I was delivering any easier, and my dread only increased as I passed along The Mall, through Green Park, and thus into Hyde Park. It was near the Serpentine that I considered simply abandoning my mission – trains for Portsmouth left regularly until the late evening – but that would be the cowardly way. I squared my shoulders and pressed onward.

The gaslights were being lit as I crossed the bridge and passed south of Kensington Palace, cutting through various paths and narrow streets until I was in Vicarage Gate. I hadn't been there too often – truth be told, I found the place a bit grim since Watson's wife had sickened even further. When she was at home, her illness lay over the place like a shroud, and when she was away, poor Watson – when he was there and not off gallivanting with Sherlock Holmes – was just the mere shell of the man I'd first met several years before.

No. 6 was a handsome building, identical to its immediate neighbors, with pleasant cream-colored bricks and matching bay windows on the ground and first floors. Watson had done well, and I'd never asked how he – a wounded veteran who'd made do for years on his Maiwand wound pension and part-time work at the hospital and as a *locum* – could afford it. I'd always assumed that he'd shared in some generous reward in connection with one of Holmes's cases. The white trim was tidy, and the iron-work protecting the area-way was freshly painted and rust-free.

In spite of the house's fine condition, I had told Watson when he bought the lease that it wasn't an ideal location for a medical practice, but he'd countered with the comment that the old physician who'd retired and sold it to him hadn't done too badly, and I realized that he was right – those in Kensington needed doctors close-by, without the need to travel to more expensive practices in Harley Street, Queen Anne Street, and even Brook Street. Clearly, in spite of the sadness in Watson's life, the practice was doing rather well. I wouldn't have expected otherwise from my hard-working friend. The brass plate with his name shined beneath the red lamp, and the pavement in front was well-swept, with no evidence there of the falling November leaves that cluttered the rest of the street.

I climbed the seven steps and stood for a moment to catch my breath. A dim light was shining in the entry hall, visible through the rectangular windows above and beside the door. The item I carried, buttoned in my left coat pocket, weighed heavily upon me, and I dreaded revealing it, but here I was. Still not too late, a part of me whispered. But that part had no business influencing the actions of a man of honor, which is what I have always striven to be. With a deep breath that released as a sigh, I rang the bell.

I heard nothing obvious, but still had the sense that there was movement in the house – the bell had set someone into motion. A moment later, the door opened and, framed in the hall light behind him was my friend, John Watson. I was surprised that he'd answered it himself, but his comments quickly explained.

"Doyle!" he cried, sincere pleasure in his voice. "This is unexpected! I had no idea that you were in town! Come in – come in!"

He stepped back and I crossed the threshold "My wife is traveling," he explained quickly, pushing the door shut behind me. "Her health, you now. A trip to France didn't work out right now, so she's down in your region – Bognor Regis actually. Best we could do, I'm afraid, and I hope that it will suffice. Had to get her out of the London fogs, you know – terrible this time of year. Her lungs, you see – they've never done well here."

He was babbling a bit, and I was rather shocked to find him so. Watson was always one of the steadiest fellows I've ever known – I suppose some of it was earned through experience, but I suspect that he was like that even as a lad. Some are. I believe that I'm made of much the same sort of stuff, and so I have always been one to recognize it in others. This rather nervous behavior – though I had only seen a moment of it – was uncharacteristic.

"Steady on," I said to him. "Has she been gone long?"

"Two weeks," he answered. He nodded over his shoulder toward the darkened hall behind him leading deeper into the house. "Makes the place rather lonely."

"But the staff . . . ?"

"Oh, they're here during the day," he answered. "When the practice is open. But when office hours have ended, I generally release them. The little bit of domestic work is finished early – I'm fairly tidy, you know – and there's no need for the page to remain if there are no patients."

"But surely you don't just sit here and brood every night after the office has closed?" I asked, concerned that he was sliding into some sort of melancholy which might require the evaluation of an alienist or the intervention of a friend.

"No, no," he replied – perhaps too quickly. "I keep myself occupied. I read and take walks, and drop around Baker Street rather regularly. In fact, I've taken to staying there as often as not. In fact, I was considering wandering that way tonight. It's where I recovered after Maiwand, you know. Back in '81. During those long months, Mrs. Hudson fed and fattened me, and joining Holmes on some of his cases got me up and moving about when I might have otherwise been tempted to sit by the fire and drink too much whisky."

I was relieved to note that he showed no signs of incipient alcoholism now, or even drug use.

"Holmes has had some interesting cases of late," he continued. "Just a few weeks ago, for instance, he set up an elaborate ruse to trap Culverton Smith. Did you read about it in the newspapers? I believe that *The Daily*

Telegraph made some mention of it. Do you remember Smith? He gave that lecture on the Black Formosa Corruption at Barts a couple of years ago – I think that you were there too."

He smiled and took a step back. "I'm glad that you stopped by. Come in, and we can visit for a while. The cook has gone, but we can wander over to the High Street if you'd like – there's a new vegetarian restaurant I've been meaning to try. Shaw says it's acceptable, which is high praise from him, for he rarely likes anything, you know. Here, let me take your coat."

He reached for it, and I was aware of the burden in the left pocket which I'd come to share with him. Now I regretted my visit even more. I must tell him the truth, but when I'd pictured doing so not so long before, I hadn't foreseen what an unhappy and lonely man I'd find.

Watson's wife, Constance, had never been suited for London. They had met several years earlier in San Francisco, when Watson was forced to travel to America to help sort and settle his drunkard brother's affairs. I myself has always wanted to visit there – I never had the chance when I sailed in my younger days – for it was always one of my dream cities. I can only imagine that Watson, himself a seasoned war veteran and man of countless adventures, found himself lonely as he opened a medical practice in Post Street, uncertain if he'd ever return to England. It was no wonder that Miss Constance Adams won his heart.

She was a bonny lass – before her health problems so overtook her. I was at the wedding in late 1886 – just a year before that night's visit to Kensington. Sherlock Holmes had stood up as the Best Man, and offered a toast that – while not as fine as what I might have done, given the chance – was adequate and sincere. That was possibly the last time that I saw the couple in a happy state.

While Constance Watson might have been acclimated to the cold damp fogs of San Francisco, she did not do well at all when the sulfurous poisons of London were stirred into the mix. Almost immediately upon her arrival, she began to have a series of respiratory problems that were only alleviated when she was able to leave the city. Her mother, having journeyed from America to be with her, became her nurse and traveling companion as they went here and there, trying to find a location that would allow the lady's injured lungs heal.

Meanwhile, Watson continued to work to build his practice, unable to join his wife while laboring to earn funds to pay for her health-restoring journeys, and trying to increase its value enough so that he could sell it and have enough to reestablish himself in healthier climes. It was a chase where he seemed to be gaining no ground, and based on what I saw in that initial greeting, it was wearing him down.

I was putting my hand toward my left coat pocket to retrieve the reason for my visit, before Watson could take my coat and settle me in his study by the fire with a generous serving of whisky, when through the closed door we both heard the approach of a fast-approaching growler.

Watson's mood changed immediately. The fellow who had greeted me in a mostly darkened house, glad to have a distraction, had vanished, replaced by someone alert and capable – a former soldier who hears gunfire, perhaps, or a physician who has heard an accident and is about to rush that way to offer assistance. It most reminded me of a hunting dog who senses the distant horns and is suddenly on point and tense for action.

Watson opened the door as the vehicle pulled to a stop and a figure jumped out to the street. Even in the dim gaslight from the streetlamps, I recognized that tall and thin figure hurrying up the walk.

"Watson!" called Sherlock Holmes. "Thank goodness you're here. We have need of your opinion." Then he glanced my way as he reached us. "Good evening, Doyle. Just arrived I see?"

"Yes," I replied, "but how did you – " I stopped myself, uninterested in hearing a recitation of the various clues that had provided the obvious answer. I had been trained to look for such things myself, so I knew quite well that there was no trick to it.

Holmes looked back at Watson. "MacDonald is in the carriage. He sought me out in Baker Street, and I maintained that we should recruit you if possible on our way to the Yard. There's a fellow there that you might be able to shed some light upon – at least that's my hope, although I'll concede that it's a bit farfetched."

Watson nodded. "I'll get my coat." And he turned back into the house, leaving me in the doorway with the new arrival.

Sherlock Holmes had never warmed up to me, and I must admit the feeling was mutual. I'd met both of them, Watson and Holmes, in early 1882 when we'd all attended a medical seminar. Watson was a decent fellow, and I found that we both had a passion for rugby – although Watson's playing days were definitely over by then, as his war injuries prevented him from pressing into the scrum. I had played since I was a lad, and I was on the team in medical school. Watson and I became friends when I'd get up to London to watch some games and he would accompany me, and a few times he came to cheer my team when I was able to play.

Holmes was always rather cold, and I felt as if he were constantly watching me, as if he might see something if he peered deep enough that would make him smile and nod to himself like he'd figured something out. I'd known a doctor in Edinburgh quite well with much the same manner, but he and I got along famously. Several times in the past I'd hoped that things might turn out differently – that Holmes and I might end up as friends, and that I'd occasionally be involved in his investigations. We had worked well together in '84 during the affair in Southsea, for instance, when I was being harassed by Guilford McReynolds. * But now, after all these decades have passed, I can confirm that a friendship between myself and Holmes was never in the cards.

Watson returned to the front door in a very short moment, wearing a coat and carrying his battered medical bag. He began to apologize as he was edging me outside, but I interrupted, surprised at my own boldness.

"I'd like to join you, if that's all right. I've done a bit of work with the police in the past – when I was in Scotland."

Watson glanced at Holmes, who gave a short nod. With that settled, Watson locked the door and I joined them in the growler.

Having been born and spending my formative years at the mouth of the River Forth, I recognized a fellow Caledonian when I saw him and, getting settled beside Watson, I offered a hand to the man across from me. "You must be MacDonald."

We shook, and his hand was large and warm and dry. He glanced at Watson with raised eyebrows.

"Inspector, this is my friend, Dr. Arthur Doyle – "

"Arthur *Conan* Doyle," I corrected.

Holmes's lips tightened but stopped short of rolling his eyes – often he can be a mannerless and offensive chap – and Watson revised his introduction. "Arthur Conan Doyle. He'd just arrived a moment ago, and wanted to come along with us. He's had some previous experience with investigations and police work – "

"In Edinburgh," I added. "I'm from there, you see. Born in Picardy Place, and I attended medical school at the University. Studied under Dr. Joseph Bell – perhaps you've heard of him? He was regularly consulted by the police, using methods rather like Holmes's here – " I glanced over at Holmes, who was looking fixedly at his folded hands on top of his stick. " – although Dr. Bell developed his quite a bit earlier."

"Nice to meet you, Dr. Doyle," replied the inspector.

"Conan Doyle," I corrected him. "It sounds as if you're also from Edinburgh. We seem to be about the same age. Perhaps we know someone in common?"

"Possibly. Is your father Charles Doyle, the artist?"

I nodded, suddenly a bit wary. "He is. You know him?"

"I know Dr. Bell, and recall your name being mentioned. And I have a cousin who is employed at Blairerno House, where your father resides."

He didn't add anything to his statement, but he had said it, as a policeman would, to establish a bit of ascendancy over me. Blairerno House was, to put it politely, a home for intemperate gentlemen. My father had long suffered from an artistic turn and, while his life was full of the tragedy of unfulfilled powers and of underdeveloped gifts, he also had his weaknesses – as everyone does – but he had also some very remarkable and outstanding virtues.

Watson was aware of this sad aspect of my familial history, and we had occasionally discussed our shared experiences – for his own brother had many of the same debilities of character as my father, without the benefit of my father's talents. I didn't know if Holmes had any notion about this, however, and I didn't intend to reveal anything further if he did not.

Watson, sensing my discomfort, intervened and changed the subject. "Why do you need my opinion?"

"It's about a man we found – rescued really – in Limehouse," explained MacDonald. "We've had our eye on a ship, *The Star of Surat*, for several years. She's out of western India. Smuggler, but always a little too slick for us. Finally, by way of a tangent investigation into the docks at the request of the Foreign Office, Mr. Holmes was able to gather the evidence we needed of just how they were unloading their cargo – by way of a secret hatch in the ship's hull, aligned with unknown below-ground structure built into the dock. This afternoon we carried out a raid from both the surface and along the smugglers' tunnels. All went according to plan – except we found a prisoner on the boat, and . . . ."

He looked at Holmes, as if to ask him to continue with the more complex part of the explanation.

"I was there when he was discovered," Holmes explained. "He was chained below-decks. Other than being quite weak and malnourished, he didn't appear to be otherwise mistreated, but he was clearly a prisoner. When he was freed, he insisted on leading us to the Captain's cabin, where he went directly to a cabinet and pulled out a set of papers. They appear to be hand-drawn military maps for the coast of Balochistan, with particular emphasis for the area north of Karachi, near Miani Hor."

Watson nodded, but I was confused. "Balochistan," he explained, "is the area directly between Afghanistan and the Arabian Sea. It's a hellish place, but it might be of strategic interest."

I started to recall it. "I read of it in the newspaper," I said. "We took control over it last month."

"Correct," said Holmes. "The maps were quite explicit in laying out routes to land and transport substantial amounts of supplies and troops to attack the British outposts, and the margins had a number of notes describing armament buildup – written in Russian, I might add."

"Russians," I said, nodding. Their treachery was never-ending.

"When confronted," Holmes continued, "the captain, officers, and crew refused to provide any information or explanation."

"They will," added MacDonald grimly. "But if we can get this prisoner to tell us about it sooner – "

"It's all very interesting," said Watson, "but I fail to see why I'm needed. You said the man isn't seriously injured."

"No, but he seems quite anxious to tell us something, and so far no one can understand his dialect. Knowing that you served in that part of the world, and that you likely had contact with a number of locals, I asked MacDonald if we could include you, in the hopes that you might be able to communicate with him before wasting time looking for someone else."

Watson relaxed a bit, a look of disappointment on his face. "The area is vast, Holmes, and I was never in Balochistan – never even near it. Anything is possible, I suppose, but the chances are slim to none that we can understand each other. Still – "

"We can but try," Holmes interrupted.

As the carriage rolled through the darkened streets, the four of us fell silent. We had covered in mere moments what it had taken me a good portion of the afternoon to traverse. Our driver was quite skilled, and we rounded Trafalgar Square and so into Whitehall as smoothly as I've ever traveled it.

Using the opportunity that the depleted conversation provided, I questioned MacDonald some about his Edinburgh connections, hoping to find that we might know others in common, but he was rather reticent in providing information, answering with clipped responses – usually simply the word "No." Sensing that he wished to maintain an objective distance, I eventually left him alone.

At No. 4 Whitehall Place – known colloquially as "Scotland Yard" before its move a couple of years later to the Embankment – we disembarked, and MacDonald led us briskly inside, moving with purpose through the confusing warren, along dim and crowded hallways. I saw a few familiar faces who I initially believed were raising their hands in greeting, but I gradually realized that their welcomes were for Watson and Holmes. "Quite right," I thought to myself. My days of working alongside Dr. Bell and the Edinburgh police were several years past and hundreds of miles north, whereas Watson and Holmes likely interacted with these men on a daily basis.

Eventually MacDonald stopped before a door marked *Infirmary*. Without knocking, he let himself in and we followed.

I was behind the other three as we crossed the well-lit room toward a dark-skinned man lying on a bed. He was the only patient there, although there were half-a-dozen beds lining either side of the room. An older

325

fellow in a white coat was standing nearby, holding a glass of water toward the man as if trying to get him to drink.

Moving closer, I was amazed to see that the fellow's forearms, sticking out from his patient's gown, were covered with black tattoos. The short sleeves of the white nightshirt that he wore instead of typical sailor's clothing did nothing to hide them. I glanced over and saw a pile of filthy-looking garments on a nearby table and understood that these were what he'd been wearing when he arrived.

The tattoos were highly complex, block lines both solid and broken, and rows of tightly grouped concentric circles that wrapped around his arms, progressing up from his wrists and underneath the gown's sleeves.

A step closer showed that his face was also covered with tattoos, though of much finer lines and less intricate detail. A series of thin parallel black lines ran down, side-by-side, from his lower lip and across his chin to his throat. Additionally, a *V*-shaped pattern was inked from underneath his black hair and across his forehead, ending at a point above his nose and between his heavy brows.

His skin was dark, so it was difficult to determine if he was pale from illness, but he exuded a weariness which could not be denied. In addition to the tattoo markings, his face was covered by a series of deep lines, connected by finer creases, giving it the appearance of deeply tanned and weathered leather. Some of the deepest lines radiated away from his eyes, but these were not from laughter. Yet I didn't think that they came from stress, either. Rather, they signified that he naturally observed the world with a squinted expression.

I started to make a comment, but Holmes raised a hand and spoke first. "Watson, see if you can speak with him while I look at the papers he was so interested in pointing out. MacDonald – "

He and the inspector moved to a side table, where they began to look through the sheets and maps while muttering softly. Watson pulled up a chair and began to speak to the man in some sort of mish-mash of hisses and glottal stops. The man in the bed made return noises of a completely different sort, but I knew that they weren't understanding one another, and both of their faces were showing more and more frustration. Finally, Watson leaned back and looked toward Holmes.

"It's no use. We cannot understand each other in the least. He's clearly Asian of some sort – "

"Not Asian," I interrupted, finally able to share what I'd recognized from the first. "Likely his ancestors came from Asia at some point in the very distant past, but that's not this man's immediate origin. I recognize those tattoos from when I was on a whaling ship to the Arctic back in '80. He's an Inuit from Greenland."

326

MacDonald looked surprised. "Greenland? What's an *esquimeaux* doing chained on an Indian smuggler's ship?"

I shook my head. "The term '*esquimeaux*' is offensive, Inspector. It means '*eaters of raw flesh*' – a term that the natives of the Arctic lands do not appreciate. Rather, they prefer to be called '*Inuit*' – that is, '*The People*'."

Then, without bothering to look at MacDonald's amazed expression, or to take too much satisfaction in seeing that I had bested Sherlock Holmes, I pulled up another chair and sat down across from Watson beside the man. Then, in spite of the fact that my use of the language was quite limited after so many years, we began to converse.

His name was Eeriuffi, meaning "*Warrior Wolf*", and he looked to be around forty – although he was so weathered and weary that he might have been younger. I had picked up some of their lingo during my time on the whaling ship when we'd gone ashore to the native Greenland villages. In spite of my lack of recent experience, and the fact that I had never known a great deal of their words to begin with, he was eventually able to convey his story to me, while the policeman, the detective, and the doctor watched and waited.

I reached forward and squeezed his arm. He nodded and smiled, and then lay back and settled into sleep.

"Several years ago, he was dissatisfied with his life and joined one of the whaling ships that docked at his village. He traveled about, moving from ship to ship, as he hungered to see more of the world. From whalers, he ended up on cargo vessels, going to both America and the west coast of Africa. Eventually he shipped through the Suez Canal and crewed in ships traveling back and forth along the subcontinent.

"Although he cannot yet speak English, he has learned some other languages – enough to understand when the officers of *The Star of Surat* were planning to deliver arms and supplies to the Russians as part of their anti-British campaign. He kept his mouth shut, as it wasn't any of his business.

"Two weeks ago, as the ship was returning to England, he inadvertently became involved in a shipboard brawl. Through no fault of his own – or so he says – two men were killed, and he was blamed." I glanced at the man, now snoring softly. "One has to wonder at his actual level of involvement, if he was kept chained. There's more to that story, I'm thinking, and it might bear further investigation, Inspector. In any case, the ship docked in Limehouse, but there was no indication that he was going to be freed, and he wondered what was to become of him. Then the ship was raided and the smugglers were arrested. When he was discovered, he was glad to point the way to the maps and papers as his own little revenge against the officers and their schemes, as well as thinking it might earn him some British gratitude."

MacDonald nodded, and he and Holmes stood to one side and conferred quietly. Meanwhile, Watson congratulated me on my successful assistance in clearing up the matter so neatly.

"Thank you, Doctor," said the inspector, turning back my way. "I'm not sure when we might have otherwise determined this man's origins, or understood why he wanted us to know about the papers. Of course, we would have come across them when searching the ship, but without his specifically calling our attention to them, they might not have received the attention they deserved. Now we'll let the Foreign Office figure out what to do next."

He led us back outside, where Holmes also thanked me for my assistance, and Watson shook my hand. Then, saying that he must be getting home, he turned and walked toward Trafalgar Square, declining Holmes's offer to share a cab.

As I stood there in the glow of my little triumph, Holmes spoke.

"You weren't able to complete your mission."

I glanced at him. "Hmm?"

He gestured toward my left coat pocket. "That object. The reason for your visit to Kensington tonight."

I felt a sinking feeling as I looked down the street and saw Watson turn the corner and vanish from sight. The success of a few moments before ran away as if I'd been drenched in cold water.

"You've tapped that pocket a number of times tonight," Holmes continued, "as if to remind yourself that the object is still there. While in and of itself it might have no connection to your visit to Watson, I suspect that its size – roughly eight-and-a-half inches by five-and-a-half – makes it a book. Or more specifically, some sort of periodical, since it seems to curve and flex with the movement of your coat."

He took a step so that he was now facing me.

"I know that you and Watson collaborated upon the narrative of the Jefferson Hope investigation – something that Watson threatened to see into print as soon as it concluded, mistakenly thinking that I'd be flattered, or that it would matter somehow if the truth of the affair was told. He had informed me how, after so many stops and starts, the project was moving forward, with him writing the bulk of the tale concerning the murders and subsequent investigation here in London, while you, with your desire to pivot from medicine to the career of historical novelist, would complete the fictionalized narrative of the killer's long-ago original days with the Utah Mormons."

I didn't quite know how to respond. From very little, Holmes had correctly pieced together the reason for my visit and what I carried. This was far more skillful than anything that Dr. Bell had ever demonstrated, either in the classroom, or when he and I had assisted the Edinburgh Police.

But there was more.

"Your visit tonight was to be something between a confession and an apology, was it not?" he asked.

I involuntarily tapped my pocket once again. "This is too much, Holmes!" I sputtered. "How do you know what was in my mind to do?"

"Because earlier today, as I passed the news stall at Baker Street Station, I saw the new *Beeton's Christmas Annual* for sale. My eye was initially drawn to it, knowing that you and Watson had contracted to publish the story there. Then I saw the title on the cover – words long ago from my own mouth – '*A Study in Scarlet*'. But of course you know what else I saw there on the cover as well."

My eyes dropped. I knew why the mistake had occurred, and it had truly been without any effort on my part. Nevertheless, I felt responsible. And ashamed.

I pulled the offensive volume from my pocket and studied it – seeing it there in the gaslight outside Scotland Yard as I had for the first time in the publisher's office earlier that day, and yet not seeing it at all.

At that point, *Beeton's Christmas Annual*, (created by Samuel Orchart Beeton, the founder of *Boys Own Magazine* and the husband of the estimable Mrs. Beeton), had been in existence for over twenty-five years. It was published in late November every year, containing a number of pieces in varying lengths and quality. By the time I'd approached the publisher, Ward, Lock and Company, over a year before, our manuscript had been rejected by what seemed to be nearly everyone else.

I'd been quite enthusiastic when telling Watson that it was finally placed, but his interest had been fleeting, as he was then involved with setting up a new medical practice and home with his bride. Then, not long after, her illness became the main focus of his thoughts. Meanwhile, I'd come to realize that I'd made an error, agreeing in my enthusiasm to receive a mere pittance for our work.

Not long after initially selling it – in November 1886 – I wrote to the publisher and asked if we might retain a percentage of the sales. I received a curt reply telling me, in short, that such a request was impossible, as the story had been bought outright for use in one of the Christmas Annuals – with the implication that an actual publication date was not yet even determined. It might be years until it appeared in print.

When I finally was notified that the tale would be included in the late 1887 edition, I was quite pleased, and dropped around to the publisher's office to obtain the contributor copy – only to see the horrible truth. It was a humble little volume, not very thick and manufactured on cheap paper – clearly meant to be read quickly and discarded. Across the top was *Beeton's Christmas Annual*, and – happily – in much bigger red letters was the title of our joint efforts, *A Study in Scarlet*. But then, tucked just below it, was that line which made my heart sink: *By A. Conan Doyle*. No mention of Watson at all.

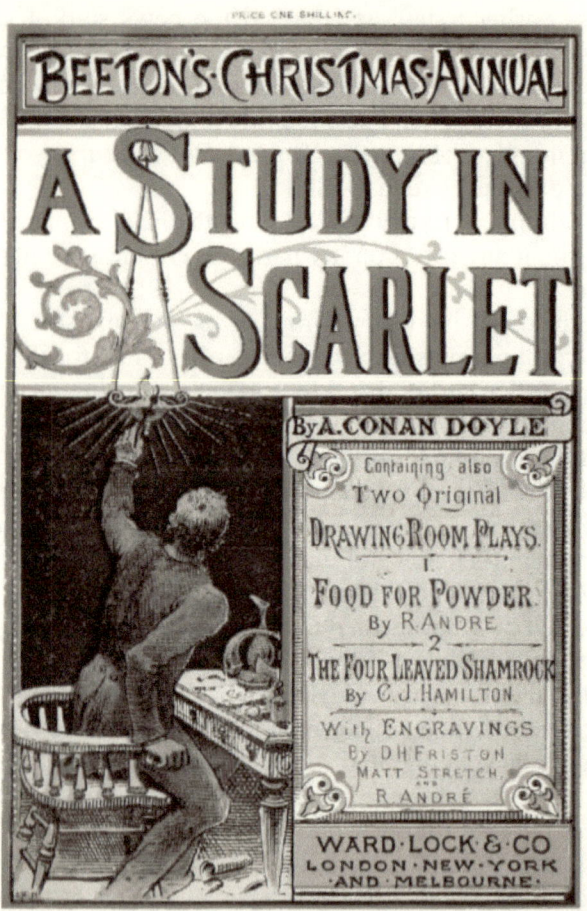

It was printed, and there was no fixing it – and in any case I had no leverage to do so. I had sold it, and it was the publisher's now, to present as they wished.

After the unpleasantness at the publisher's office, I'd stood outside in Salisbury Square and looked at the unassuming book further. A few other stories were listed on the right lower side of the yellowish cover, and the lower left was a curious illustration – a chap seated at a table, half-rising with his face turned away while he reached up with his left hand to light or adjust a lamp which was inexplicably hanging suspended from the *S* in the word *Study*. Perhaps this scene had something to do with one of the other stories – it certainly had no relevance or connection to what Watson and I had written.

At least, I considered to myself, my own name was correct.

I realized that I'd been lost in thought, once again sick that Watson's contribution was unacknowledged. "I didn't know," I said, looking up at Holmes's shadowed form, watching me like some raptor, his eyes barely visible beneath the brim of that fore-and-aft cap that he so favored. "They were supposed to use Watson's name too – before mine."

It was true. It should have read "*By Dr. John H. Watson and A. Conan Doyle*" – but Watson's name was missing.

"I made the arrangements with Ward, Lock in good faith. But there was a misunderstanding – the editor made a mistake. I had carried out all the business arrangements and answered their questions as they completed their paperwork regarding the sale of the work – the payment, and so-on. Watson and I were to be listed as co-authors – he for his part, and me for mine. But the editor, having only met me in my duties as literary agent, misunderstood. He thought that it was *fiction*. He knew that I wrote the middle part, and assumed that I wrote the rest as well."

"How much were you paid?" asked Holmes.

I lowered my gaze again. "Twenty-five pounds."

"For that amount of effort?" Holmes let anger creep into his voice. Then, after a pause, "At least the matter can be corrected when you reprint it elsewhere."

My silence went just a bit too long, and he suspected that there was something else wrong. "What is it, Doyle?"

I shook my head. "There won't be a reprint – at least not one that we have any say-so about. I . . . I sold all the rights."

"*All* of them? Watson's too?"

I simply nodded, and Holmes remained silent for a long moment. Still as well – he didn't tap a foot or finger, or even take a deep breath. Finally, his voice tight, he spoke.

"This is a disappointment – for Watson, of course, who doesn't need any further disappointments right now, and for me as well, as his friend, who was looking forward to something that might cheer him up. You understand his situation, of course."

"I do."

The silence fell between us again. I had spent my entire afternoon passage across London to Kensington trying to think of a way to make things right, and nothing had occurred to me. I sensed that Holmes was doing the same thing now – trying to think of any alternative – but apparently he was having as little luck as I'd had.

"I cannot recall any leverage that I might have with Ward, Lock," he finally said. "However, is it certain that the door is closed?"

"I'm afraid so. I stopped by earlier today there to pick up the contributor copy – this one. That's when I saw the cover. I was horrified – beyond horrified – and immediately demanded to speak to both the editor and the publisher. I'm afraid that it became rather heated. I . . . I said things that have irrevocably burned that bridge. I can think of no reason that they'll make any future corrections."

Holmes kept his gimlet eyes fixed upon me, but I'm not sure that he was seeing me. I realized that I was hoping for him to offer some solution – that I'd come to believe Watson's stories about him so much that I assumed the man would pull a miracle out of his pocket.

But then – he did nothing. Nothing, that is, except to murmur "Poor Watson!" – which was exactly what he would say to twist the knife a bit deeper in me.

Then he added, "I expect that you'll return to Kensington and inform him tonight – before he sees it on a newsstand as I did?"

I nodded my agreement, and he nodded approval in return. Then, with a curiously flat "Good night," he pivoted in the opposite direction and strode away into the darkness.

That was many years ago. After I caught up with Watson and told him the truth, he was most forgiving and understanding – no surprise to anyone who knew John Watson. I never heard what his wife thought about it. Perhaps she never knew, as she passed away less than a month later, leaving Watson even more despondent than before. I had thought to invite him to stay with me and my wife in Southsea, but instead he was immediately moved back into Baker Street, where Holmes and their landlady set about mending the poor broken man. In mid-1889, he married again, this time to the lovely Mary Morstan. They moved to a tidy little home and practice in Paddington, which was where they were living when

332

Watson received an invitation from an American publisher to dinner at the Langham.

He was ambivalent about attending, as having published one time, he felt no further need. I offered to take his place, where I was introduced to the charming Oscar Wilde (of later notorious fame) and publisher Joseph Marshall Stoddart of America's *Lippincott's Magazine.* Stoddart had no mistaken illusions about the author of the previously published Holmes narrative, and he was rather surprised when I showed up instead of Watson. Although I was no longer authorized to act as my friend's literary agent, I negotiated a deal wherein Watson would provide another story for publication – this one about the loss of the Agra treasure to the Thames and how he gained a wife.

Watson was always a writer – it was an inveterate aspect of his nature – and he always had a number of narratives nearly read for publication. I knew of the tale about how he met Mary, and convinced him to allow its appearance in *Lippincott's*. However, at that time he was more concerned with building his practice and being seen as a medical professional – unlike me, who would have traded teeth to be a professional writer instead of a doctor facing days of tedium and repetition. With the story of the Agra treasure, Watson was willing to take his majority share of the earnings, but he didn't want his name associated with the publication, so in a reversal of what had happened in *Beeton's*, where my name was solely on the cover by mistake, the February 1890 publication of *The Sign of the Four* was intentionally shown to be by *A. Conan Doyle*.

Curiously, this arrangement settled in and continued for the rest of our friendship. After Holmes's supposed death in May 1891, Watson felt called to inform the public of his "late" friend's gifts, and I arranged for these shorter narratives to appear in a new monthly periodical, *The Strand.* Since my name was already associated with the previous publications, it seemed natural to leave it in place going forward. (I must admit that Mary Watson was not pleased by this arrangement, and I became a rather unwelcome visitor at their home during the months leading up to her untimely death when I needed to stop by for publishing-related appointments.)

All told, I served as the agent to get sixty of Watson's writings before the public. I only co-wrote one other adventure, telling the portion of *The Valley of Fear* that related to the long-past events concerning the Pinkerton detective's Pennsylvania investigation.

The years flew by, as I was told would happen when I was a young man and didn't really believe it, and before I realized it, Watson and I – along with everyone that we had known that were still with us – looked up and found ourselves old. I turned seventy a couple of months ago and, while my mind feels like a young man of twenty-eight, my body wears every one of those adventurous and fulfilling years.

Still feeling mentally young as I do, it always comes as a shock when my compatriots fall victim to age. So it was last week when word came of Watson's unexpected death. Although he was just weeks away from turning seventy-seven, he still had the heart of a young warrior, and he was one of those who seemed as if he would go on forever.

His service this morning was well attended, as would be expected, and it was there, while conversing with Mycroft Holmes, that I learned the exact circumstances of how Watson had passed: He and Holmes had been to the Continent on a rescue mission of sorts, successfully bringing back the liberated individual to England. But Watson had caught pneumonia and had passed a few days later.

After the interment, I lingered in the cemetery, watching from a distance as Sherlock Holmes and a few of Watson's other close friends thanked the last well-wishers. Then the party dispersed, and I felt free to approach and also offer my own condolences. As usual, Holmes's manner to me was shielded and cold.

After the expected words had been exchanged, I should have left – turned and walked away – but I felt moved to continue. "You have never cared for me, Holmes. I wish that it might have been different."

His lips tightened, as if this were a conversation that he didn't wish to have. Then, with a sigh, he spoke.

"You're correct, I suppose, Sir Arthur," he said, using my more formal title, rather than calling me Doyle as he had for the first two decades of our occasional association. "It's curious – I always told Watson that modesty was no virtue, and yet in your manner, I always found that a bit more modesty would have made you easier to take."

I thought that was all he'd say, and as I tried to decide whether to respond – two old men by then, talking about something that really didn't matter anymore – he continued.

"Watson saw the film you made," he added. I raised my eyebrows curiously. "The ten-minute interview that was shown a couple of months ago." I then recalled what he meant. "The film where you referred to him – about four minutes along – as 'Holmes's rather stupid friend Watson'."

I blinked, my eyes suddenly hot. My vision fogged from the forming tears – which come all too easily as my age creeps closer to my own funeral. But where my emotions are often closer to the surface, it is usually for no reason at all. This was different. I was alongside the grave of one of my oldest friends, and between the time I'd last seen him and his death, he'd heard an offhand comment I'd made over a year before for a filmed interview in which I'd unintentionally maligned him – I had reduced one of the finest men I have ever known to being "rather stupid". My shame was monumental.

"Watson never said what that meant to him – how that hurt him – but I know that it did. And you know that it did too."

He was right. It has always been one of my failings to let my mouth run away from me when I think that I'm being clever. I had given no thought to what I was saying that day, simply speaking for ten minutes or so on a variety of topics, and covering my discomfort with a false and careless avuncular bonhomie. I hadn't given any further thought in the months since of what I'd said that day.

I looked up and saw Holmes's hawk-like gaze focused on me. He looked as if he meant to say something else, but then his lips tightened again and he shook his head, as if answering a question that he'd just silently put to himself. Instead of speaking, he fixed his constant deerstalker to his head, gave me a nod without meaning, turned, and walked toward the cemetery gate.

I was left standing beside my deceased and resting friend, weeping an old man's tears, praying that my silent entreaties for forgiveness might be heard. For decades I'd had no doubts about life after death. The thought had comforted me when my son was taken too early. But now, my spent and broken body propped alongside Watson's grave, I had doubts. I needed him to know that I was sorry – so very sorry. That I hadn't meant to disparage him so carelessly, or to damage our friendship at the very end.

I prayed that he would hear my apology, but no sign was forthcoming. He didn't let me know that he understood. There were no whispered words of comfort – simply the eternal wind sighing through the weary trees.

I remained there until the sun dropped behind the nearby buildings, and then later, even as the wind turned cold.

Sir A.C.D.
28 July, 1929

NOTE

*   See "The Jephson Affair" in this volume.

Fate's Brushes

Winner – The ACD Society 2024 Fiction Award

From the Diary of Dr. John H. Watson
17 August, 1893

"Damn you, Doyle!" I cried.

His nostrils flared. A low growl rumbled in his broad chest.

"Why are you denying the truth?" I asked, the frustration of many days of watching him do so pitching my voice higher than I wanted.

Then I saw his hands, already tightly clenched, clench tighter. I flashed upon the memory that this man boxed. When we'd talked about it in the past, Doyle had always referred to it as "the manly art", admiring the defined limits and proscriptions of the Queensbury System over the illegal bare-knuckle bouts – although he admitted he'd done both, and was proud of it.

"You can drive boxing underground," he told me a couple of years ago as we discussed and compared the formalized boxing contests versus the matches that occurred illicitly in East End warehouses and basements and pubs, or some distance from the city in remote pastures or barns, far from the gaze of official authority. "You can make it illegal, but you cannot stop it. Instead of having contests safely in the presence of the three *P*'s – the Public, the Press, and the Police – you will force it back into hiding. You can have boxing in the open, or in the back parlour of a public house, but you are going to have it somehow. It is better, surely, to have it in the daylight, where, if there has been any brutality or viciousness, there will at once be a shriek of 'Foul!' or 'Shame!'"

He'd gone on to describe for me the time in '80 when he'd served on a whaling vessel as ship's surgeon. When the steward noticed that Doyle's gear included a set of boxing gloves, an informal bout was immediately arranged, and when it was concluded, the steward grinned and said, "So help me, he's the best surgeon we've had! He's blackened my eye!"

Now this same man, so full of admiration for a formalized fight, was facing me across the small parlour, his eyes carrying a wicked glint, his burly form tense with rage, his knuckles white, and his terrier-like eyes squinting and red and focused somewhere beyond me, as if I were nothing more than an obstacle to be knocked aside before things could go back to normal once more. If he hit me now, no formal rules would govern his actions.

336

Should he rush me, or throw a punch, I had no chance against him. He was seven years my junior, and even though my war wounds were more than a dozen years in the past, they still left me vulnerable. And after the past two years, I had nothing left with which to defend myself, and in truth, very little will to do so.

I felt the weight of my service revolver, which I'd long ago learned to keep beside me at all times – Sherlock Holmes's death two years ago didn't eliminate the number of my enemies still remaining in the world – but under no circumstances would I withdraw it from my pocket, even to convey a warning. A firearm would only escalate the situation, and might unexpectedly lead to a terrible accident. Should Doyle attack, I would defend myself as best I could, but only with my own hands.

After a long moment, however, the need for such thoughts seemed to subside. I watched as the anger and rage drained away from his face, as waves from a receding tide will sink and vanish down through the shingle as it bleeds noisily back to the sea. Doyle no longer wanted to fight, but he was no less certain of his position, even if it was a complete denial of the truth.

"She's sick, Doyle!" I cried softly. "Everyone can see it but you! She knows it too, but you keep telling her it's nothing – that she'll be better soon. She wants to believe you – "

"You're wrong, Watson!" he said, his voice low and strained, his growling Scottish burr more obvious with the passion constricting his voice. "There's no way in the Devil's Hell . . . ."

He drifted to silence, as if he didn't believe his own words of disagreement, but couldn't take the next step to acknowledge that I was correct. Rather than discuss it further, he turned and walked out, surprisingly closing the door gently, and leaving me to consider yet again why I had agreed to join him on this this foolish journey.

I let out a long breath, really a sigh, unaware that I had been holding it. I realized that my stomach muscles had tensed without conscious decision, apparently preparing for a body blow that I'd instinctively expected. I couldn't recall a prior instance when I'd seen my friend so angry. But I understood how he felt. During those past times when I'd received similar news, I had also wanted to rage against the unfair injustice of the cold, dark, and indifferent universe, and to repeatedly deny the truth with the childlike belief that doing so would negate it. I also knew personally that, as a doctor, one initially and adamantly refused to believe or admit that a close loved one could be seriously ill. "How could I have missed the signs?" one asks. "Did I spend too much time focused on the health of others, while right beside me, growing beyond the point of

337

treatment, was an illness that was now beyond defeat? What could I have done?" The grief-filled irony is simply too much to bear. I know what is in store for Doyle, as I've already experienced too much similar to what he's going to face in my own sad and weary life.

I wandered across the crowded parlour to a stiff horsehair chair. It was a singularly uncomfortable place to sit, but it was the only piece of furniture that was located beside the parlor's open window, and the stifling August heat was rather unpleasant, even in Lucerne. The hotel manager informed us when we arrived that the City is having an atypical heat wave, and in spite of the cold glacier-fed waters of the adjacent lake, the humidity is most unpleasant, settling in the streets like a sunny fog, forcing me to pause far too often in order to wipe my face with a cloth and seek shade and refreshment.

The heat is different from a London summer, and also from that of India and Afghanistan. It feels intuitively wrong to sit by an open window within sight of snow. Not far away are the Alps, still covered in vast amounts high-elevation ice that won't entirely melt throughout the heat of the season. The mountains aren't far away, and it wouldn't take long to reach from our small hotel. I suddenly felt the urge to stand and walk out, leaving Doyle and his wife behind, and the rest of my empty life as well. Just then, I had the certain belief deep within me that if I stood and started walking right then, that exact moment, with no thought of gathering my things or even taking a sip of water, I would never stop. I would go and go and go, never running out of energy, and would keep going forever, stepping out of my life, and all that reminded me of what I'd lost. I gripped the arms of the chair, intending to rise and go forth with absolute faith that my instinct was correct. It felt real, this notion to simply move on, one of the most certain things that I have ever known.

I almost did it. I don't know what would have really happened if I had. But I had just the thinnest slice of a moment of second-guessing myself, and the feeling passed, a visceral experience as if I had been alive for the first time in so long, and now once again I was dead, without the good sense to lie down and stop fighting.

I frowned at the distant mountains, and then at the closed door, I could hear Louisa Doyle – "Touie" to her friends and family – begin coughing yet again in a room down the hall. I didn't have to see to visualize how her body was wracked with each effort. I saw it far too often when her symptoms began, in her and others as well.

Touie Doyle has consumption – tuberculosis – and her husband refuses to believe it.

338

This is my third time in Lucerne, but truth be told, I don't have much memory of the first two trips.

The initial visit was in May 1891, over two years ago, and then I only passed through on my way back to England, in a fog of equal parts grief and anger. Holmes and I had hurriedly left London a couple of weeks earlier, in late April, crossing by night into Brussels. As we'd set out upon our journey, I was puzzled, trying to determine just what my friend was thinking. His monumental efforts had just led to the arrest of the Moriarty gang, but the Professor had slipped out of the net, and Holmes suddenly felt the curious need to get out of the country.

Not entirely certain why, I accompanied him.

Moriarty had nearly caught up with us in Victoria Station – although I'm not sure what he would have actually done had he arrived just a minute earlier, before the train departed. Had the loss of his organization and livelihood and means to power driven him mad? Did he intend to confront us? To attack Holmes in front of a hundred or more witnesses? Would he have pulled a gun, or thrashed him with his cane, or charged him with his bare hands?

Clearly Holmes had been worried about something – much more so than I'd ever seen before. In the past, he'd had no hesitation at facing all sorts of criminals and madmen, and he'd bravely let himself be the bait in any number of traps. This time was different. Our train left London, and he seemed enthused with the idea that Moriarty would pursue us. I wondered then if he was setting a trap after all. It seemed likely.

A bit later, Holmes and I were passing an hour on the Canterbury platform, awaiting departure on the next leg of our journey, when he spotted Moriarty's special train approaching in the distance – following us as he'd predicted. We hid behind some luggage as the Professor passed, mistakenly thinking he was still on our trail to Paris. After he was out of sight, Holmes immediately decided to scoot in a different direction, with me trailing in his wake. Why, I wondered, were we fleeing to the Continent along an entirely different path, when we could now turn the tables and follow instead of being followed? Instead of a trap, were we trying to avoid the Professor? Then we could have just as easily stayed in England, for the villain was well on his way to leaving the country without us. We could have stayed behind and he wouldn't have known it – he had no organization left to send him word that we'd returned to London. We certainly weren't following him in order to effect an arrest, for we went a different way.

Holmes first mentioned that we would cross to Dieppe by way of Newcastle, but then he impulsively decided to make for the narrow piece of Belgian coast at Ostend, and then onward to Brussels, where we spent that night, and then two more days, doing . . . nothing. On the third day, in Strasbourg, Holmes received a wire from the Yard that Moriarty had officially escaped. While he cursed bitterly, I pondered at his apparent surprise, as we'd already seen the Professor pursuing us to Paris – and we hadn't followed, and we hadn't (to my knowledge) notified anyone to look for him when he arrived there.

I held my tongue. From there we meandered through the Rhone Valley, and then over the Gemmi Pass, down through Interlaken, and so to Meiringen . . . and the Reichenbach Falls.

It had been over two years since those events – since the Professor had caught up to Holmes, even as I was so stupidly lured away from him at the last. What had I been thinking? I suppose that, as I had so often in the past, I was trusting Holmes to have a plan that he was keeping to himself, but that he'd reveal when he was ready. How often had he told me that I lacked the gift of guile? As many times, probably, as he'd demonstrated an actor's flair for the dramatic. Nevertheless, my blind trust and the expectation of his omniscience failed me, and betrayed Holmes. I was a fool, responding to a false message from the nearby hotel, requesting an English doctor and leaving Holmes alone to face the Professor. When I realized what I'd done – !

I had climbed my way to the edge of the precipice that hung over the roaring Hellish cauldron and saw the two sets of footprints leading to the edge and none returning. The mud lying churned by the dangerous drop. Holmes's alpenstock and cigarette case and the sheets torn from his notebook, with a message of explanation to me, written in his neat handwriting . . . .

It took several days for me to be convinced that any attempt at recovering the bodies was absolutely hopeless. ("The bodies", as it was repeatedly phrased to me, were "lost", but I had no interest in whether Moriarty was ever found. I hoped that his evil carcass was trapped in rocks directly under the most punishing and destructive force of the roaring water, to be battered for eternity. But Sherlock Holmes deserved better.)

It was then, after the tragedy, that I saw Lucerne for the first time, simply passing through on my way back to London. Mary met me on the platform, her waif-like figure standing in the smoky choking darkness, surrounded by more inspectors and constables than I could count, all shielding her as best they could from the fumes and fog, turning outward to meet my arrival as a sign of respect for Mr. Holmes.

A year later, I returned to Reichenbach, this time by way of Lucerne, which was a much easier route than that first traveled cross country by Holmes and me in '91. Mary had accompanied me. That turned out to be

340

a mistake. For some time, I had been arguing that she and I needed to get away from London, as her health was worsening, and I would not make the terrible mistake of missing any time with her by sending her somewhere to recuperate without me. It was she who argued for a visit to Switzerland, with perhaps (she suggested tentatively) a stop in Meiringen, and then on to the Falls. She thought it would do me good to revisit the site of my sorrow, and possibly – so she gently hinted – to exercise a ghost.

The trip, of course, only weakened her further, and if I'd had any sense, I would have expected that from the beginning. Mary was already ill by then, but I denied it, every day foolishly convincing myself that I was seeing little signs of improvement. When we reached the Englischer Hof in Meiringen, and I renewed my acquaintance with Peter Steiler, the landlord, Mary took to her bed for three days to rest and renew her energy. With abject apologies, she told me that I should make the rigorous climb without her. Thus, I was left to make to trip back to the cursed ledge above the Falls alone.

Thankfully, I saw no one on the climb, and the end of the path, at the very edge of the chasm, was deserted. Unless some mountain spirit was hidden in the rocks above me, peering down from his concealment, there was no one to witness the renewal of my torment.

I ranted into the cacophony, venting a year's worth of suppressed rage – at the loss of my friend, and also cursing at what I'd been unable to admit before: The inevitable coming loss of my precious wife. For I could no longer deny it.

Now, I am back in Switzerland, and tomorrow Doyle wishes to see the Reichenbach Falls.

And he is denying his wife's illness as well.

When Doyle first approached me earlier this summer, proposing a trip to Switzerland, my immediate response was to decline – at first politely, if a bit abrupt, and then more forcefully. Mary had been gone by then for just two months, and I had no intention of taking a meaningless holiday. In fact, it was becoming clear, even to myself, that I had very little intention of doing anything whatsoever.

Doyle, as usual, was like a terrier with a rat. He shook and shook me. He was bound to the inexplicable notion that I would join him on the tour. He had been invited to give a series of lectures in Lucerne, and he was taking his family with him. I wondered at the wisdom of such a plan. Last November, Touie gave birth to their son, Kingsley, and I could see that she wasn't recovering well. Doyle clearly favors the newborn lad over his four-year-old daughter, Mary. (I can never hear her name casually mentioned without feeling a sudden lurch, as if the ground has dropped away beneath me.) The girl spends much of her time in the company of her mother, and the maid does much to assist them.

I finally relented. I don't seem to have much spine left in me anymore. Leaving my practice was no difficulty. Nor was the cost of the trip. To my surprise, I'm financially comfortable after participation in a number of Holmes's more remunerative cases, and when Mary passed, I sold my Paddington practice for a further tidy sum. (It has always been quite busy due to its location near the station.) With the notion that I should still stay in harness, I re-purchased my old Kensington practice from the doctor who took it off my hands several years ago. (In the five years and some months since then, he's suffered his own series of misfortunes, growing from his daughter's steep and steady mental decline.) Kensington has the advantage – from my perspective – of being much less bothered by patients, which suits me right down to the ground. When I moved back there, I told myself that doing so would allow me time to write, and I certainly accomplished some of that, but during my time living there, I have done very little living.

Touie Doyle is an enigma. I've known her since just before the wedding, eight years ago this month. Doyle had once told me the awkward way they met: She, then Louisa Hawkins, along with her mother and brother, were visiting Southsea (where Doyle had a practice), and the brother was struck with a sudden and violent attack of cerebral meningitis. Doyle, having an extra room in his house, offered to take the lad in for further treatment. Unfortunately, young Hawkins died a few days later. ("Such a death under my own roof naturally involved me in a good deal of anxiety and trouble," he'd told me. "Indeed, if I had not had the foresight to ask a medical friend to see him with me on the day before he passed away, I should have been in a difficult position.")

The funeral was carried out in Doyle's home, and grieving Mrs. Hawkins had been quite upset at the pesterment that they had caused him. From such a beginning, Doyle's path led to marrying the girl, Touie. "Gentle" was how he described her. "Amiable" as well. And once he stated, "She has a quiet philosophy."

Another time he told me of her own small income, brought with her to the marriage, which "enabled me to expand my simple housekeeping in a way which gave her from the first the decencies, if not the luxuries, of life."

This is the same quiet woman, two years older than Doyle, who is willing to believe his reassurances that she is going to be well, and that her illness is not serious. I have to convince him, so that he can be honest with her.

18 August, 1893

Meiringen is probably twenty miles from Lucerne by crow's flight, and more by carriage. After less than a quarter of that distance, I knew that Doyle's insistence that Touie and the children relocate from the city to the village was a mistake. The motion of the vehicle made her queasy, and her coughing has been steady, although Doyle tries to blame it on the various summer pollens in the air. It's true: One only has to look and see the haze of the infinite specks hanging and dancing in the morning sunshine, following the paths of some incomprehensible Brownian motion. But the pirouetting particles don't explain the minute blood stains that sometimes discolor poor Touie's handkerchief. That was happening before we ever left England.

When we arrived this morning at the Englischer Hof, Peter Steiler came outside with great enthusiastic bluster. He seemed to think for a moment that Touie was Mary, back once again to make another try for the Falls after she was unable to ascend last year. Then, when he saw that Touie was someone else, and that another man was attending to her, a shadow crossed his face. He examined me more closely, and I suppose my inherent bone-deep grief was apparent. He pulled me aside as Doyle helped his downtrodden spouse to the ground.

"Your wife, Doctor Watson?" he asked. "How is she?" He started to say something else – perhaps to tentatively query if was also in Switzerland, or perhaps back in London. Perhaps he considered confirming that she was dead as he suspected, but whatever it was that he'd started to say, he stopped himself.

I nodded. "She passed away last spring."

"I am so sorry." I could see that he meant it. Mary had charmed everyone who met her.

He glanced over his shoulder toward the Doyles, the big man supporting Touie as she coughed and coughed.

"She is sick, this one?" Steiler asked, identifying the obvious. He suddenly looked wary. "The consumption?"

I nodded once more. "But her husband refuses to believe it," I confirmed in a low voice. "He thinks that she's simply picked up some transitory illness and will be better, given time."

Steiler shook his head. "Two years ago, the Professor tricked you with a story that a woman, in the last stages of consumption, had stopped here on her way to Lucerne when a sudden hemorrhage overtook her. That she wanted an English doctor." He looked again at Touie. "And now a woman with the same disease is truly here." He glanced at me, I suppose to see if I appreciated the incredible way that Fate's brushes had managed

343

to paint such a picture – a dab here, and swirl there, and then, when one steps back, the vast pattern is revealed. But all that I heard in his words was the same accusation I'd held against myself since the fourth of May 1891: I had been tricked away from Holmes's side with the false story of a dying English lady, and from that moment onward, my life has been a declining waste of days.

Touie begged off seeing the Falls, and I could have willingly missed them as well. The heat was already unpleasant, and I knew that by this afternoon, when we reached our destination, we'd be most weary and unhappy. But Doyle was insistent. He generally is, no matter the topic or direction.

We walked in silence for quite a while, Doyle several feet behind me as I led the way, each lost in our own thoughts. I should have realized that Doyle couldn't normally be quiet for that long. As it turned out, he was planning a round-about way of broaching a topic heavy on his mind.

"My lectures," he began, innocently enough.

I made an indifferent querying noise.

"They went well," he said. "My preparations were more than adequate, and my presentation was quite good, if I do say so." A silence then, waiting for some response from me. I had none. It was difficult to generate false interest.

"When I was finished," he eventually continued, "and the host asked the crowd – And there were many of them! – if there were any questions, do you know what they wanted to know?" This time he didn't wait, and his voice darkened. "About *Sherlock Holmes!* I doubt if there was a single person there who gave a damn about my lectures!" He was suddenly talking faster. "They all waited politely through whatever I had to say in order to ask questions about *Holmes*! What was he like? Was he really as eccentric as portrayed in the stories? Am I ever going to write the true story of Holmes's death?"

He stopped suddenly, hearing what he'd said. It had been a point of contention once – that his name was on the stories instead of mine, giving readers the impression that he was the author – but that had long since ceased to matter to me. Still, he realized that he'd stepped close to the edge of something sore between us, and he pulled back.

I still said nothing, and after a few more minutes of steady climbing, we reached a flat portion of the path where we could make progress along the same contour of the mountain and still catch our breath. Then Doyle began to speak once again.

"Have you considered it?" he asked. "Writing about what happened here at the Falls? There's a lot of speculation about it, you know. The newspapers were vague, and a number of people know about Holmes only through the stories and don't even realize, to this day, that he's dead."

I was still silent, beginning to understand the direction of his clumsy effort, but I wanted to force him to carry it through to fruition.

"I spoke to Newnes," he continued. "He says that he'll pay extra to have the story of Holmes's death." He took a quicker step to get alongside me. "Have you thought about it?"

I considered my response. My first impulse was to snap, *Yes, I have thought of it. It haunts me to this day, and I wonder constantly if writing about it will exercise that particular ghost.* But other considerations stopped me. If I write that story, it will somehow feel like finally closing the lid to Holmes's coffin – something which I'm still not yet ready to do. During the long spell of Mary's final illness, and the worse months since she left me, writing has been the only thing that comes close to joy. Twenty-one of Holmes's cases have been published in *The Strand* so far, and I have another one ready for next month – this time telling about my first meeting with Mycroft Holmes, and the dead man we found at The Myrtles in Beckenham. But I've written up many more narratives as well during the lonely evenings, and see no end in sight. When I write them, it's as if Holmes is still alive – that I just have to go around to Baker Street and find him in the sitting room, with a new client seated alongside in the basket chair, or perhaps I arrive as the client is climbing the stairs. Or possibly I'll hear a knock on my own door as Holmes has stopped by to retrieve me on the way to some urgent matter, saying, "Bring your service revolver, Watson!"

To put down in words the details of his sorrowful death, and then to share it with strangers, is more than I want to consider right now.

But Doyle has always been persistent if he gets his teeth in an idea.

"Have you seen the letters in the press?" he asked, changing course. "From the Professor's brother, Colonel Moriarty? They're scurrilous, Watson. *Scurrilous!* It's libel, it is, and must be addressed! You should tell your side of the story – the *true* side! You *need* to tell it!"

It was not lost on me that his pivot to relating the details of Holmes's tragic passing was conversationally too close to Doyle's recounting of the reaction to his lectures. He isn't a subtle man, my friend Doyle, nor particularly clever, although he thinks that he is. I let him lapse into silence while I pondered my response. It was only when I heard the roar of the Falls in the distance, though still out of sight, that I paused, breathed deeply and regularly for a moment, and then spoke.

"Why do I need to relate the circumstances of Holmes's death?" I asked as he turned to face me, planting his feet in the tall grass. "I can write of a dozen other confrontations with Moriarty that define who he

345

was, and the criminal misery that he caused, and how Holmes defeated him every time. Why should I tell of Holmes's final encounter with him?" I nodded my head up the trail toward where it had occurred.

"But you'll have to address it!" he countered. "Colonel Moriarty is accusing Holmes of the Professor's *murder*! How can you let that go unchallenged?"

That did bring me up short – just a bit. But, knowing the Colonel, I shouldn't be surprised. In his own way, he is as crooked as his dead brother, and he certainly has his own agenda, far beyond protecting the deceased's reputation. But Doyle's insistence was puzzling.

I turned and walked on, and he followed, but he wasn't finished. He tried to encourage me from several other different directions – repeating references to the public's curiosity, and the publisher's willingness to pay extra. "Newnes gave me to understand that we can have just about whatever we ask for. After all, he knows that without us, *The Strand*'s subscriptions will drop almost overnight."

We were nearly to our goal. The Falls, sounding like the combined cries of a legion of damned souls, was just over the next rise. The air had become markedly colder as we neared the turbulent glacial runoff. We could both see the never-ceasing mist rising above the abyss.

"Tell me the truth," I said abruptly, stopping and turning toward Doyle. "Why do you want this particular story told more than another? Don't you understand that – " I started to say that telling it meant that I would have to release that much more of my friend, and that I'd already lost too much already. But instead I said, "Don't you understand that telling this story is likely to be the end of the stories being published? Doesn't Newnes understand that? You mentioned how much the magazine's subscriptions will decrease. I don't doubt it. The public – many of them anyway – still think that Holmes is alive. When they find out he's dead – that he's been dead for over two years – they'll lose interest. Is that what you want?"

He didn't reply, instead blowing out his mustache like an overgrown pouting child. It brought out something ugly in me. "Is that what you want?" I repeated. "You mentioned your lectures, and the questions they asked afterwards. Do you think you were invited here to discuss your *medical knowledge*? Your historical novels – *Micah Clark* or *The White Company*? Don't you realize," I said, swinging the final blow, "that this entire trip was funded what you've received as my *literary agent* for *my* Holmes stories?"

He took a step closer and his bulk and height, an inch over six feet, and the fact that he was uphill of me, was rather intimidating. I was reminded of yesterday, when I confronted him about Touie's health and he nearly lost his temper. Was this to be the new basis of our friendship: Always on the verge of incipient fisticuffs? I wouldn't last past the first occasion.

"Yes, I realize it!" he snarled. "It's obvious to me every day – even here in Switzerland! They don't care about *my* work – about what *I've* written or accomplished! They only want to hear more and more and still more about *Sherlock Bloody Holmes*!"

Then he turned, as if taking himself out of the temptation toward violence, and clambered hurriedly uphill and over the rise to the path terminating at the Falls.

I felt ashamed, as if I'd taken something he wanted to keep hidden and private and dragged it out into the sunlight and thrown it, writhing and secret, on the mist-covered grass.

After a moment I followed him, approaching slowly, with the half-thought that wouldn't it be ironic if I had to fight Doyle in the same spot where Holmes battled Moriarty. But he was well-back from the drop-off's edge, his gaze directed upon the ground at his feet rather than toward the terrifying torrent spilling down the sheer rocky mountainside into the foaming void far below.

I slowly placed myself beside him, silently, facing the Falls rather than my friend. I could tell that he'd regained control, but there were still things to be discussed between us.

"You must understand," I finally said, my voice loud to be heard above the roar. "These stories . . . this writing. It's all that I have now, and – " My voice nearly broke. "I fear that even the writing isn't enough. It isn't going to be enough . . . ."

He turned my way, almost a surprised look upon his face. "Enough for what? What about your work? Your practice . . . ?"

I shook my head. "I don't know, Doyle. I've changed. I'm more than a doctor now – or less, perhaps. After my return to England – after Maiwand – I believed that after I'd recovered enough, the Army would take me back. That's what I planned. Then, when they didn't, I had the distractions of Holmes's case to keep me busy. I worked some at Barts and the London, and as a *locum* when needed, but being part of Holmes's investigations . . . That became my *real* life.

"By way of that work, I saved enough to buy a practice. I had enough money put aside long before I actually did so. It was only when I married that I put myself into harness – and that was all right, because then *that* was my life, and it was wonderful, and what I wanted. But then . . . Holmes . . . ." I glanced toward the Falls. "And then Mary died too, and I found that I no longer have any interest in working at a practice – or anything else. If you hadn't made the arrangement with *The Strand*, and given me a reason to write, and to relive all of those adventures, I don't know what would have happened. At best, I'd probably have followed my father and brother into alcoholism. But now . . . now you want me to give that up, and write the story of Sherlock Holmes's final investigation."

He shook his head. "You can write whatever you want. I . . . somehow in my mind I've associated your writing with me. I suppose I thought the decision had to be mutual. But it doesn't. I know that. But I can't be a part of it for much longer. Every day that passes ties me tighter and tighter to Holmes. It's as if he is a great rock, chained to my ankle, and it's been tossed over that ledge. It outweighs me, and there's nothing I can do to stop myself from being pulled forward, sliding and scrabbling through this mud, and into the drop."

I contemplated what he'd said, and I understood his position. I wondered if I were truly correct – that writing down the narrative of Holmes's final encounter with the criminal professor would somehow spoil things for me. Whether it would make writing other adventures after that less real somehow, and therefore less therapeutic. As I started to say something about that, Doyle spoke again.

"If I don't do something now," he said, his voice lowering almost to the point where I couldn't hear it over the Falls, "I fear that it will be too late." He'd been looking around, never quite in my direction, but now he raised his eyes to mine, and I felt like he was sharing one of his fundamental fears. "I know you're right. About Touie, and her illness. I didn't want to admit it – that my wife could be sick on my watch. That she might . . . that she might die . . . ."

He stopped and swallowed. Then, "I feel like time is running away from me, Watson! That if I don't take the reins now – that if I don't make a name for myself while I still can . . . before my life changes, and before Touie is . . . ."

I laid a hand upon his arm. "I'll do anything that I can," I said. "If it means writing about what happened here . . . ."

He nodded, not looking my way. "She and I – we'll go home," he said, pulling back on the version of himself that he typically wore to face the world as one would a sweater. "We'll see specialists. You . . . we may both be wrong. It could be something else. Something treatable. I'll do whatever it takes. Whatever she needs . . . ." Then he began to sob, his arms hanging limply to his sides, overcome with wracking grief. Knowing that I could offer nothing more, I stood beside my friend at the edge of the great gulf as he acknowledged what was inexorable.

After a while, following a period when we'd both lapsed into a meditative silence, I took a few steps forward, as close as I wanted to be to the deadly waterfall.

When I'd finally reached here, alone, that dreadful day in May 1891, calling for Holmes again and again, even after reading the note he'd left behind, the writing of which he had credited to Moriarty's courtesy, I lost all sense of time. After moving aimlessly back and forth, side to side, up and down, indecisively for what must have been hours, calling and looking for any sign of hope, I'd finally gone back down the mountain to seek Steiler's help. I met him and a group of men on their way up, for he had finally decided on his own, based on my reaction when I'd raced away from the hotel hours before, that something must be terribly wrong.

When I returned again the next year, on the one-year anniversary of the terrible event, I'd been alone, as Mary was too weak to climb with me. That time there had been no frantic searching. For the most part I'd stood in one spot – where I stood today – staring but not seeing, as one does when planted before a gravestone while the sun shifts and the shadows lengthen. I recalled that on my second sojourn to that spot, I'd spent as much time grieving the inevitable upcoming loss of my Mary, not *if* but *when*, as I had honoring Holmes's death.

That memory, now over a year old, was still fresh. I looked over at Doyle, and I could read similar thoughts crossing his face as well. In this powerful and deadly place, he was looking elsewhere, seeing a future of misery. He had finally acknowledged that Touie has tuberculosis, and with that the understanding, if not yet the full acceptance, that sooner or later, it is terminal.

Doyle, who had been thinking to himself the whole time, seemed to become aware of my restiveness. He shook his head and looked around in more detail. "It was right here then?"

I nodded. "The two sets of footprints led to the edge. Neither returned. Holmes's stick and cigarette case and the note – you've seen it, framed in my study – were on that boulder."

He kept looking back and forth, as if getting a sense of the place – I suppose for when I wrote the story of what had happened here, as I inevitably would.

He glanced up at the mountain behind us, leading toward the highest reaches of the waterfall. "So steep," he said. "And slick, with nary a handhold or ledge." He looked back toward the edge. "You don't suppose that after he fell, he somehow grabbed onto something, beyond where you could see. He might have been hanging there, for the longest time, calling out unheard over this dreadful roar, until . . . . ." His voice trailed off, seeing as he did the look of horror on my face. It was, of course, just one of the many guilty things that had haunted me since that day, for I'd had no way to lean over and check to see if Holmes was gripping a root or protruding rock somewhere beneath the ledge. When men had eventually arrived and climbed to the other side, where they could see where most of us were standing, there was no one beneath us, hanging below the ledge. No one at all . . . .

A bit later, Doyle had another thought. "You've told me how it confused you – how Holmes's actions upon traveling to the Continent seemed without purpose." I nodded. "It's clear to me that he was protecting you . . . and Mary. That he had decided upon this method to eliminate Moriarty once and for all. After all, he wrote in his note that he suspected the summons calling you back to the inn was a hoax. He must have contrived to find a way for Moriarty to get on your trail, and when you were called back to Steiler's hotel, he realized that this was going to be the place of reckoning. He let you go. It was a truly noble thing that he did . . . ."

His voice faded. It wasn't a brilliant or original conclusion, but I knew that Doyle had presented it as something of a peace offering, an attempt to make amends and offer me an opportunity to feel better about something. It didn't help, but I appreciated the gesture.

We stood there for quite a while, long after I was ready to depart. I am certain that I will never pass this way again.

The first time I saw Eiffel's Tower, during the Paris Exposition, it was a wonder. The next time that Holmes and I were there, I made a point of walking out of my way to see it again. On a third visit, I did the same, and realized that it wasn't as inspiring to me anymore. Rather, I was simply making a detour to put my eyes on it, as if fulfilling an obligation or completing a chore. *When in Paris, see the Tower. Right. Done. Next.* It has become the same for this damned waterfall. Very tall and high. Very loud. Very dangerous. But I have seen it – three times now. It won't be any different should I see it another time . . . and Sherlock Holmes isn't here. He hasn't been here for a long time.

Eventually we turned away for the long descent, and the promise of something refreshing in the Englischer Hof's bar. As the comforting building finally came into sight, I said, after neither of us had spoken for the entire descent, "I can write up an account. Of Holmes's death. But surely Newnes realizes that this will change things – that the readers will drop away."

Doyle looked at me sheepishly. "It's already a *fait accompli*," he explained softly. "I've told him that we're ready to wind it up." He raised a hand. "He's going to pay very handsomely, and he understands the consequences, although he argued with me – quite strongly! This . . . this will free me to write, and to be known for my own works . . . and it will be good for you, too. Watson! It's time. Time to start living again! You hide in your house, writing all night. It's been that way for months! You're starting to drink too much. You . . . well, you need to live again, that's all!"

Throughout his speech, he looked rather like a boy confessing to spilling ink upon the rug. I suppose that I should have been angry, but I've had a difficult time generating any strong emotions of late. And in my heart, I know he is right, although I don't feel ready to make my way back to the living, and I don't remember how I should act when I get there.

In any event, it was a useful afternoon. Doyle has now acknowledged that Touie needs treatment, and he's done what a friend could to salvage me, even if just a little bit, and even if I don't want to be salvaged.

But regardless of what happens, I'll continue to write, even if another word is never published.

The Tracking and Arrest of
a Cold-Blooded Scoundrel

The year 1894 presented Sherlock Holmes with a wealth of investigations, the records of which were enough to fill three massive manuscript volumes which rested on my desk in our shared sitting room. This level of activity was even more impressive when considering the fact that Holmes was away from London for the entire first quarter of that year, spending the last days of his supposed death upon the Continent, involved in a number of investigations which still remain largely unrecorded, while awaiting indications that he could finally return to England.

After his unexpected reappearance on the fifth of April, and the subsequent arrest of Colonel Moran later that evening, he immediately resumed both his residence and professional practice in his old Baker Street rooms. The following weeks were spent routing out the pale phoenix that had attempted to rise from the charred bones of Professor Moriarty's wrecked organization, as both the Professor's wicked but more-inept brothers – the Colonel and the station master – had each made their own plays to become the new spider at the center of London's criminal web.

I had known the Colonel from long before I met Holmes – in both India and Afghanistan, as a matter of fact – and he had devoted a great deal of effort during the past three years when Holmes was believed to be dead harrying me personally, before I was able, with the much-appreciated help of a number of Scotland Yarders, to put an end to those schemes. Meanwhile, the youngest Moriarty, curiously named James like the other two, had concocted his own bizarre plan where he disguised himself as his dead academic brother using makeup and a false bald pate, and a truly peculiar structure of straps and harnesses buckled around his body to change how he carried himself, attempting to convince the Professor's former creatures that he was their vanished leader, risen from the dead and ready to take up the reins anew, his argument being that since a body had never been found downstream from the Reichenbach Falls, then he surely must be the real Professor. Within days of Holmes's return, the youngest James Moriarty ended up fleeing to the Continent in disgrace and defeat.

With that business sorted, Holmes settled down to the resumption of his consulting practice, although in many ways it was much different than that of the earlier days of the 1880's, before his "death". Then, he was still unknown to the greater portions of the capital, although the public and the professionals who needed his services managed to find their way to the upstairs sitting room to seek his aid. He regularly eschewed public praise, preferring to let the solution of the puzzle or the thrill of the chase serve as the source of his satisfaction – although fees to pay the rent were never unwelcome. But during those years when he was presumed dead, I had taken it upon myself to record and publish many of his adventures, revealing not necessarily the most complex or serious of cases, but instead providing a cross-sectional representation of both his abilities and his personality. A round two-dozen of these had appeared in a popular periodical before drawing to a close in late 1893, at which time the manner of Holmes's presumed death was revealed to the greater audience who had previously been unaware of it.

The general grief-filled reaction was overwhelming and surprising, and gratifying to me, as I was able to bring about a previously unimagined awareness and admiration for my friend. And then, just a few months after the details of Holmes's "death" were published, and when people were still greatly aware of the "fresh" news that he was dead, he returned to London and resumed his life.

He was not initially pleased to learn that he had become something of a legendary character in his absence, and people unnecessarily noticing him in public was distasteful, but he couldn't argue that his post-death fame did result in a noticeable increase in the number of visitors to his resumed practice. The spring and summer of '94 saw cases both large and small, such as the affair of the Borehamwood Typhon, an example of the former, and the peculiar matter of the red leech, the latter. Holmes did a most-workmanlike job organizing the facts in a succession case that had international implications (as the scion of the Smith and Mortimer union was the heir to a vast munitions fortune), and there were several matters related to discovery of hidden chambers in old houses used for nefarious purposes, such as the well-deserved ignominious end of Sean Harrison, the bulky abuser of women and children who hid in a defiled priest hole with his little white dog, and that of Jonas Oldacre, one of Moriarty's little fish who had escaped the net, and the shabby chamber he constructed as a hidey-hole in his Norwood residence. But one of the most important of the cases in that busy period, lasting as it did for much of the year, was that of the Huret assassins.

I had come down to breakfast on a rainy morning in early November to find that a visitor had just been admitted to the sitting room. The chances were almost certain that he was there to see Holmes, but it was just possible that he was seeking medical help, for sometimes patients still sought me. Several months earlier, I had sold my rather unfulfilling practice and returned to Baker Street, settling into the old routine rather

353

easily. I quickly determined, however, that the fellow was indeed there for Holmes.

He was still in his dressing gown, and his breakfast plate, pushed back on the table near one of the two tall windows, indicated that he'd been up for a while and had begun his day with an appetite – something that was not always the case. Before entering the sitting room, I'd called down to Mrs. Hudson from the landing that I was up and ready to eat, and I could already hear her starting up the steps as I opened the door to the sitting room and paused to examine the small man standing near the fireplace, rubbing his hands and seeming appreciative of the fire that was drying his damp clothing.

He was probably about thirty but looked quite a bit older. His features were pinched, and his careworn body was small, not much over five feet, and clearly a product of those regions of the capital where poor nutrition, meagre resources, and heredity combined to limit his opportunities for growth. The ideal British man is often presented as something resembling a tall, strong knight of old, but too often, what we produce, due to neglect and harsh circumstances, is something like this smaller specimen, held back from his or her full potential by hunger and ignorance, and the necessity of working in terribly unhealthy conditions while the country's industrialization requires more and more raw labor to grind forward yet another day. The city is always filled with men such as the one that stood before our fireplace that day, but there was something about his eyes that showed a shifty intelligence, as if he were cornered in an alley instead of a sitting room, considering which side he might run in order to have the better chance of escape. His eyes were dark and shadowed under a low brow, but a spark of interest was apparent when Mrs. Hudson came in with the breakfast tray.

"Would you care for something, sir?" I asked, moving to help Mrs. Hudson make room on the table. I saw that she'd brought more scrambled eggs than were typical for just my portion, and I understood that she had already taken the opportunity to prepare the fellow some food, should we choose to offer. I caught her eye, and she nodded with a small smile.

The man didn't answer, but I heard that he was already in motion toward the table. As Mrs. Hudson departed, pulling the door shut behind her, I did make sure to get my own portion first, before leaving our guest the remaning goodly amount.

"This is Simon Radlett," explained Holmes from behind us, sitting in his armchair and going through the complex operations of lighting his first morning pipe. From the time it was taking, the previous day's dottles weren't quite dry. "He has brought something of interest."

By this point I was seated at the table, eating my bacon, eggs, and toast a bit quicker than I would have preferred, but failing to match Radlett's speed. He'd claimed what food I hadn't, more than half of what Mrs. Hudson had carried up. For her to have had extra amounts ready so quickly, she had apparently begun preparing it while Radlett was first speaking with Holmes, and also while realizing that I would be down soon. Radlett finished quicker than I, with signs of satisfaction before my plate was halfway cleaned. Placing his own plate on the table – for he had never sat down – he wiped his mouth along his dark sleeve and turned back toward Holmes, "That's right. Ran across it this morning, and knew that it was important. Came right over." He lowered his voice and glanced back my way. "It's related to that *Hoo-ray* we've been hearing about."

He finished the statement by giving an exaggerated nod to punctuate its importance. I pondered his pronunciation of *Huret* – the name of the mysterious French assassin whose rumored deeds had been the subject of so much of Holmes's attention since his return to London in the spring. A terrible assassination had occurred at mid-year, and since then, there had been a number of other attempts, all prevented by Holmes, but some of them quite narrowly.

On the twenty-fifth of June, French President Sadi Carnot had been assassinated in Lyon, following a public speech. He'd entered his carriage and was getting seated when an Italian named Caserio, young and well-dressed, had rushed from the crowd, pulled a dagger from within a rolled newspaper, and plunged it into the President's back. Carnot collapsed, bleeding profusely, and he was driven away immediately to seek medical help. But there was no hope, as his liver had been pierced and the internal haemorrhage was too great.

Meanwhile, Caserio, just twenty-one years of age, had been immediately seized by French officers and rushed away to protect him from the crowd's vengeance. When their efforts to lynch the assassin failed, the angry citizens turned upon businesses and residences owned by Italians, and wreaked further vengeance on the Italian Consulate. It was later learned that Caserio had committed the crime in retaliation against the 1892 execution of the anarchist Ravachol. Initially there was no question that he had acted alone – but then, a few days later after the assassination, a letter had arrived, addressed to the editor of *The Times*, from a man identifying himself as *Huret*, mysteriously stating that he was behind the crime that had occurred in Rue du Pré Botté. There was no specific reference to Carnot, but a sharp reporter had quickly realized that this was the street in Lyons where the Palais du Commerce was located – the site of the Carnot's speech and subsequent murder.

The letter stated simply:

355

The death in Rue du Pré Botté was accomplished by another's hand, but it was my mind that controlled him – as I do a number of other hands, all in place at the sides of other notable men.

When I say so, these men will die. I ask for no payment of any sort to prevent this. It will happen.

You have been informed.

Huret

Inspector Gregson immediately consulted Holmes, who examined the letter, but he provided no specific assistance other than a brief analysis: The envelope had been mailed in Aldgate. The envelope was new and plain. The paper inside, upon which the message was written, was old and yellowed. It had likely been quarto-sized, but the top of the sheet had been trimmed away. Even I could see that had been done to remove the letterhead, done with two strokes of long-bladed shears.

The body of text and the signature were typewritten, and Holmes noted with interest that there were a number of distinctive characteristics that could be used to identify the machine when it was eventually located. Likewise, the typist also had distinctive traits, emphasizing his right hand, and certain letters as well, by the strength in which they had been imprinted upon the page.

Holmes was of the opinion that the letter was genuine, and not the attempt of some crank to generate panic. Likewise, he was certain that the reporter hadn't produced it for the purposes of creating a story, although he declined to explain the basis of his belief. He pointed out the trimmed-away letterhead, and the fact that a new envelope had likely been used because an envelope to match the stationery probably had the same identifying information that was on the letter. It was curious, he noted, that a letter relating to a French assassination was mailed in London. He indicated to Gregson that he had some thoughts about that, but that he would keep those to himself for now, and that he was available to assist them further, should additional information be discovered or letters be received, which pleased the inspector. Then he wanted to keep the letter, which did not. In the end, however, based on the vast number of services that he had provided to the police in the past, the document was left in his custody.

Soon after Gregson departed, Holmes began searching through his files, humming to himself. Clearly he wasn't frustrated at not immediately finding what he sought. Instead, he seemed certain that eventually it would be – and it was. He finally pulled a manila folder from beneath a stack of others just like it, opened it to reveal several documents (the contents of which were not shared with me), dropped in the Huret letter with them, and then turned toward the door. "As usual, Watson," he joked, "it was in the last place I looked!" Then he burst into one of his peculiar fits of laughter, the sort that always boded ill for someone.

"I'm off to see Mycroft," he added. "I have a little notion . . . ." And that was the last I heard of that letter for many months, although the rest of the year brought with it a number of encounters with the hands that Huret claimed to control.

When the police had left that day in late June, I had gathered that the official force expected a bit more from the famed resurrected consultant, but that was as far as he would commit publicly. However, I knew that Holmes continued to make inquiries. Unfortunately before the short note could be properly quashed by the authorities, it was mentioned in *The Times* – only once, but enough to generate a great deal of short-lived interest. The reporter irresponsibly referred to Huret as "*the Boulevard Assassin*", perhaps trying to provide something to fire the public's imagination in the same way that the Whitechapel murderers of 1888 had come to be lumped under the general *sobriquet* of *Jack the Ripper* after one of those myriad killers sent a letter to the press signed with that name.

The Government's quick suppression of the story only served to feed the public's curiosity, as evidenced by successive days filled with rising fear of conspiracies and the possibility of further imminent assassinations on a wide scale. Soon after being consulted by the police, Holmes was also approached by a *Times* reporter asking him his thoughts on the matter. Despite Holmes's own private inquiries, he publically scoffed, stating that, "There are a hundred other agents – A thousand! – all muddling about, crossing one another's paths, questioning their sources and secret contacts. They're probably all offering payments for bits of information, and before long, there will be a dozen different sightings of this 'Huret' – A dozen dozen! – based on whatever tale is bold enough to earn the price of a whisky. No, the field is too crowded for my talents."

Over the next several months, in between his many other investigations, Holmes was responsible for preventing nearly a dozen other assassination attempts, some in England, and others in Paris. All were carried out by men who initially called themselves *Huret*, but in the end, after substantial interrogation, were found to be someone else. They each had the same story: They were either members of various radical

357

groups, or lone wolves who had worked themselves into violent anarchistic frenzies. Each had been approached by a mysterious figure – identifying himself only as "Huret", who offered planning and the means to carry out different murders. They couldn't describe this figure, as their meetings were always in shadows. Huret spoke either French or English as needed, based on the killer he was grooming, and his appearance was always concealed by dark clothing, and a melodramatic hood that hid his features. He had the resources and information to place them in a position to commit murder, and all he asked was that they claim the name "Huret" when the crime was committed.

Holmes's successes in catching the various lesser Hurets had brought him the gratitude of two governments, but he seemed no closer to catching the elusive master. Then, in mid-October, he had, seemingly without reason, begun to spread the word that he was closing in on his prey. I'd seen no indications of it, but as always, there was much that Holmes didn't share with me.

And now a fellow had shown up speaking of *Hoo-ray.* I didn't yet know what information that Radlett had brought, but he'd already earned a free breakfast for his trouble.

I finished my own meal, refreshed my coffee, and moved to my chair by the fireplace. On the way, Holmes reached across to hand me a visiting card, the front of which stated:

Gerald Fenton Westhouse
Westhouse & Marbank
Wine and Spirits Merchants
Fenchurch Street

The card was stiff and thick, with a warm tan color and clearly containing a great deal of rag content. The text was embossed, with the name of the company darkened and thickened for emphasis. I had some vague memory of the place, perhaps from an advertisement, as I knew I'd never personally visited a spirit merchant in Fenchurch Street.

Turning the card over, I saw that there was a handwritten message. The black ink wasn't unusual, and the words had clearly written in ornate script by a right hand using a new pen with a wide nib: *Huret – 5 November, 11 a.m. Fenchurch office.* I looked up at Holmes with surprise. He gave a slight nod and said to Simon Radlett, "Sit down, there in the basket chair, and tell us how you came by this card."

Radlett, who had been standing halfway across the room, centered evenly between the chairs, the dining table, and the door, looked suspicious, as if he were a stray dog that was being enticed into a trap with bits of food and gentle voices that would all go away when the cage door slammed shut. And yet, despite his instinct to flee, he had willingly brought the card to Holmes, so in the end it was his decision to stay and explain, likely hoping for some sort of reward beyond a plate of bacon and eggs. He warily sidled to the chair, first standing behind it, and then slithering around to the front. He sat down on the front edge, his short legs resting on the floor as if he might still roll forward and bolt at any second.

His mouth tightened as if considering what to say. Then: "I'll admit it – I pulled it from a gentleman's pocket. A man has to eat, don't he? I spotted him this morning in Leadenhall Street as he ran some errands, and saw that he was careless with his wallet. I came up behind him to lift it, but it went wrong – he felt my hand – and the card was all I could grab before he turned and tried to stop me. He swung his stick, but I ran away. In a few minutes, when I was alone, I looked at what I had – that card and nothing else. I was about to toss it away when I saw what was written on the back. I've heard that you were asking questions about that *Hoo-ray* gent, so I came here, the very next thing." He leaned forward, pointing a finger to the card still in my hand. "You'll notice that the man works in Fenchurch Street – just around the corner from Leadenhall Street."

"That had not escaped my attention," said Holmes. "Although presuming that the card belongs to the man you robbed isn't certain. It could be his, with the appointment written on the back to remind him. He could be someone else, and the card was given to him by Westhouse – or he could have found it on the ground and picked it up out of curiosity." Holmes's words diminished the possible importance of the man, but at the same time, I could see that he was most interested.

Holmes was leaning forward now as well, looking toward our visitor. "Tell us more about this man you tried to rob," he said.

Radlett frowned. "I only took the card, Mr. Holmes. Nothing else. He wasn't *robbed*." He seemed offended as he rubbed a dirty hand across his whiskers. Then he looked into the fire, ruminating. "About fifty, I suppose. Dressed like a toff – expensive-looking clothes and hat. Shiny boots and shiny stick. And fat – he doesn't miss any meals."

"And he raised his stick to threaten you when he felt you reaching into his pocket?"

"That's right."

"Show me." Holmes abruptly stood. "Come up behind Watson and try to take something from his pocket. There – grab your stick, Watson. Now, stand there while Radlett robs you."

I rose more slowly, uncertain as to the purpose of this exercise. I retrieved my stick from the stand by the door and returned to the center of the room, awaiting further instructions.

"Now," said Holmes to Radlett, who had also risen, "was this man walking or paused?"

Radlett, confused, seemed to visualize the scene. "Umm, he was stopped – looking into a window."

"Was he holding the stick, or leaning upon it? And you approached him from behind? Good. Which direction? Show me."

I pantomimed a man looking into a shop window, holding the stick vertically and gripping it at the top as directed. I was aware of Radlett stealthily nearing my right side, where the stick rested, and then I felt his hand slipping around from behind and into my coat pocket. If he was demonstrating his typical pick-pocketing technique, it was no wonder that the man on the street had perceived his clumsy intrusion. Holmes hadn't given further instructions, but I played my part, turning toward Radlett, crying "*Stop!*" and raising the stick threateningly as I did so. The small man jumped backward, as if this were real and he was in actual danger. Then, after a few hurried steps, he stopped, recalling that this was simply a pantomime, and looked expectantly at Holmes. "It was just like that," he confirmed.

"Thank you. And after he raised his stick, you fled."

"I did. And then, when I was around the corner, I read what was written on the card and came here." He looked from one of us to the other. "Today is November 5th," he added, as if we didn't understand, "and it isn't that long until eleven o'clock, you know."

Holmes nodded. "Then it seems that the next logical step is that we should obtain a cab and visit Westhouse and Marbank in Fenchurch Street."

I saw that Radlett gave a small nod, almost involuntarily. But did I also see the merest shadow of a smile play upon his lips?

"Watson, will you go downstairs and summon a growler? And will you let Mrs. Hudson know that we'll need to miss our appointment with Desmond Wagenaar later this morning? Are you ready, Radlett?"

I nodded, now puzzled, but racing to catch up. Radlett seemed to be in a similar state.

"You don't need a growler, Mr. Holmes," he said. "I'm not going with you."

"Of course you are," replied Holmes, his tone tolerating no disagreement as he strode across the room to where his hat and coat were hanging. "How else will we identify the man from whom you lifted the card?"

"I described him for you."

360

"A fat man in his fifties, well dressed? Pshaw! I could put forth my hand and have five-dozen such as that here in Baker Street within an hour. No, your identification will be invaluable. Now Watson – about that cab?"

He looked directly at me to see if I understood, and I nodded, grabbed my coat and hat, and walked out to the landing, pulling the door shut behind me. But instead of immediately going downstairs and out to the street, I took the upper treads up one floor to my room, so recently vacated, in order to retrieve my service revolver – for surely this was what Holmes was indirectly reminding me to do. I knew that there was no other reason for him to tell anything about an appointment with Desmond Wagenaar, because the man had died five years earlier. I had killed him . . . .

Wagenaar was a good coiner and a bad man. His skills were of such quality that the security of the national currency was threatened. Mycroft Holmes had enlisted his brother to track Wagenaar to his lair and stop what he was doing. Extra caution was advised, as the coiner was also known to be a murderer many times over several decades.

At that time, I was newly married, living in Paddington with my bride and establishing a practice. Thus, while I had regular contact with Holmes and some knowledge of his activities, I was not fully informed of the current status of every case. I was making my rounds on that day when I received a terse message from Holmes seeking my help – or so I believed. I knew enough to be suspicious, for it was a single sheet thrust into my hand on the street by a boy I didn't know, simply stating, *Mr. Holmes needs your help – Baker Street. Urgent!* Before I could question the boy, he had run away. I responded to the summons by immediately changing direction and hurrying toward our old rooms, but it was one of the few times that I'd foolishly gone out without a weapon.

I knew better. I suppose that, in my newly married bliss, I'd foolishly forgotten that being associated with Holmes was a dangerous business. From the early days when Holmes had started inviting me to join him in his investigations, when my health permitted, I had seen that seemingly routine situations could unexpectedly pivot into danger with stunning immediacy. Additionally, Holmes's activities during the years before I met him had generated a truly impressive number of enemies who wished to do him all sorts of harm, from physical damage to taking his life. This had continued into the 1880's when I started working with him, and the longer our association continued, the more enemies that I made as well. Therefore, it had become my policy to go armed – but there were still times when circumstances prevented it, or I simply forgot or chose to do otherwise, and that morning was one of those, when leaving my service revolver behind was a serious mistake.

361

I hadn't walked far before I was taken from behind, pulled into the mews immediately past Dorset Square, just as one reaches Park Street. A bag was thrown over my head, and two men held me from either side as I was tossed into a carriage. Five minutes later, I was dragged into the back of an empty house north of Regent's Park and the bag was removed. I found myself facing Wagenaar – then simply a menacing stranger, completely unknown to me. He was standing alongside Holmes, who was bruised and bleeding, gagged and tied thoroughly to a chair.

Wagenaar had a gun, pointing it toward Holmes's head. "Doctor," he said, avoiding any delays, "tell me where Holmes keeps his important papers, or he dies now."

I had no knowledge of what was occurring, and no time consider. Without thinking, and with no cry of warning or signal of my intentions, I pulled loose from the two nonplussed and careless men who were holding my arms and rushed directly toward the man with the gun.

It was a distance of just ten feet, and even as I covered it, I could see Holmes's eyes widen in surprise. Wagenaar was caught unaware as well, having certainly pictured the events he'd orchestrated playing out in a much different manner.

It was over in seconds. I slammed into the man, outweighing him by twenty or thirty pounds, without mercy, as if I were still a young Rugby player. I violently raised my knee into his groin, even as I felt some of the ribs at his sternum snap underneath my driving shoulder – medical experience gives one a good sense of just where to aim. It was a matter of physics, with my mass and forward motion driving him backward into the unforgiving wall, even as my left hand reached for the wrist holding the gun, forcing it up and away.

Wagenaar was surprised, but only for a second or two, and then, despite his injuries, he began to fight back. His strength must have been immense, although he had seemed only average size. Perhaps he felt a desperation, aware that he was suddenly and unexpectedly in a life-and-death struggle. I got my other hand up and across his body, now using it to further grasp his wrist, attempting to make him drop the gun, or at least direct it away from me or Holmes. Meanwhile, he hit me in the back with his other hand, balled into a fist, but not very effective against the thickness of my wool coat. Then, he managed to pull the trigger. The gunshot sounded like an exploding naval shell in the small room, but thank Heavens the gun was aimed toward the ceiling.

Behind me, I could hear the two other men yelling, and I feared that at any moment they would come forward to assist their leader, possibly to put an effective bullet in my skull, but perhaps they were too fearful of where Wagenaar's gun might end up pointing when the next shot was fired. Meanwhile, Wagenaar was fighting to turn his hand and use the weapon upon me, and I could see that his finger had wound tightly around the trigger. He would fire as soon as he was able.

I gave no further thought to the men who had been holding me, for whatever happened now would be finshed soon. For an instant, my entire universe was reduced to Wagenaar's hand and that gun. And in spite of my advantages in weight and surprise, he was accomplishing his intention. The gun was turning, and he was ready to fire.

Then, at the very last, I shifted my right hand further up, grabbing the barrel and turning it away from me and toward him. I pulled the barrel up toward his head just as he fired, a deafening blast. Perhaps my tug on the gun contributed to his pull upon the trigger. Between me and the wall against which he was pressed, he spasmodically jerked, his sour breath making an involuntary groan as the air escaped his dying lungs past his vocal cords, already relaxing in death. He went limp. The tunneled vision I'd had of the gun shifted, widening, and I looked into his eyes, no more than inches from my own. Blood was already pouring down his brow around them, as he'd fired the gun straight up through his own head, tearing off the top of his skull and spattering the wall behind.

So much for my Hippocratic Oath.

But I had also been a soldier.

I watched as the hate-filled and awful awareness of what he'd done, boring into me, vanished as he focused on something else far away and eternal, and far more important. Then I released him and he slid down the wall, out of my view.

When he dropped, I turned. The two men were gone, having fled when death entered the room. I freed Holmes, who immediately and profusely apologized for my involvement, but I waved it away, instead asking, rather shakily, about the men who had brought me here. "Will they return?" I glanced at the gun, now on the ground, still in the dead man's hand, wondering if I ought to quickly retrieve it.

Holmes shook his head. "Griggs and Barton. I know them. Cowards – the both of them. They'll be easy to retrieve when I'm ready. First, let's check the house to make sure that everything has been recovered."

As we explored, he explained just who the dead man was, what he'd been doing, and how his death was not a tragedy in the least. I found, having just been responsible Wagenaar's demise, in spite of the fact that it occurred in a situation of his own making, that I didn't want to know too much about him. Holmes also told how his own carelessness had allowed for his capture not an hour earlier, and how, when he'd refused to reveal where he kept his accumulated evidence, the idea of finding out through me had surfaced, with a plan to collect me soon put into motion.

363

Holmes explained that we were in Wagenaar's own home, boldly used for his illicit activities, and we found all of the coiner's tools in the cellar, along with the wasted fruits of the dead man's labors. As we climbed back to the ground floor, Holmes thanked me again for my unexpected reaction, leading to his rescue. "I never get your limits, Watson," he said. "There is always something to be said for the direct and unexpected approach . . . ."

Years later, I could still only wonder at how such a spontaneous action on my part could have easily gone so very wrong. Rushing the man had been madness, I realized, and Holmes or I could have been killed during the wild events of the short struggle. As the passing minutes removed us from the event, I vowed that I'd never go out without being armed. Holmes knew that I had followed this rule ever since, but just now, as we prepared to depart with Radlett, he'd still felt the need to subtly remind me to bring my gun in a way that Radlett wouldn't understand. For some reason, there was danger associated with our upcoming journey. But in truth, it was rare that danger wasn't associated in some degree during any journey taken with Holmes.

Having retrieved my service revolver and stepped outside to hail a growler, I returned to the entryway, where Holmes and Radlett had just descended. Holmes knocked on the door to Mrs. Hudson's parlor, and when it opened, he handed her several telegram forms, asking that she have them dispatched immediately. Then he led us outside to the waiting cab, where Holmes murmured instructions the driver to head toward Fenchurch Street along a specific route. There was more, but his voice dropped too low to hear.

Radlett seemed nervous, much more so than when he had spoken to us upstairs. I had sensed that he was glad that we were taking action, as based on the card that he'd delivered, but that he'd expected nothing further afterwards, except perhaps some form of remuneration. Now he was being pulled further into the affair. I was also more nervous than I would have expected, stemming from Holmes's cryptic reminder to make sure that I was armed. I stayed alert to pick up on any other cues that he might direct my way.

We were moving west along Marylebone Street, each keeping to our own thoughts. It was only as we were turning into Tottenham Court Road that Holmes finally spoke.

"Did you know, Watson, that Simon here was once an Irregular? Just for a short time, in the late seventies, when I still resided in Montague Street. How old were you then, Simon? Not quite fifteen, I expect."

Radlett frowned. "That's right," he replied, his tone suddenly rather terse, I thought, for such a simple question.

"You were only involved in a few errands, as I recall," continued Holmes, seemingly oblivious to Radlett's change of mood. "Following a few people, or keeping watch on their houses. The last time was . . . Who was that? Whaley, I believe? Or was it Tibbles?"

"I don't really remember. As you said, it was a long time ago – half-a-lifetime for me." His tone was level. There was no enthusiasm for him about reminiscing.

Holmes nodded. "Indeed it was. Much has happened since then. Do you still keep up with any of the others from those days?"

Radlett shook his head. "That was too long ago. Everyone went their separate ways – those of us that survived, in any case."

Holmes started to say something else, but stopped himself. He then seemed to lose focus, his eyes drifting from inside the carriage to the passing street, as if he were tired of speaking about the past, and instead viewing something from those long-ago days. Radlett, meanwhile, seemed to pull inward, crossing his arms as if to ward off a blow and staring down toward his feet.

There was something happening here that I did not understand.

We had reached the intersection with New Oxford Street and turned east, following the thoroughfare toward our destination. The random changes in London street names were often a cause of consternation for visitors to the capital, with New Oxford turning into to High Holborn, Holborn, Newgate, and Cheapside, before finally becoming Fenchurch Street – each segment of the same thoroughfare lasting just a few hundred feet, or possibly just a thousand, before transitioning to the next. Our cab plodded steadily onward, and I wondered at Holmes's seeming indifference, headed as we were to follow up a clue to the mysterious assassin. He wasn't hunched forward, using every minute between now and the end of the journey to consider possibilities and plan strategies. Instead, he was idly watching the passing buildings with little interest. At one point, over the street noise, I heard that he was softly humming "*La Donna è Mobile*". I was certainly more tense than he was, having been forewarned to go armed, and Radlett was the most strained of all, the condition becoming more noted with each passing mile.

We weren't long past Lincoln's Inn Fields when Holmes stirred, now more alert, his eyes on Radlett. Something had changed. I sat up a bit straighter, aware of the weight of my revolver in my coat pocket.

The cabbie gently gigged the horse to the left, turning us smoothly toward Gray's Inn. Radlett was suddenly alert, as if sensing some sort of danger. Holmes raised a hand.

"I asked the cabbie to stop here, on our way to Fenchurch Street," he explained. "There is someone who I hope to question before we go further."

"Who?" Radlett asked, his voice a high tight whisper. He cleared his throat."It's getting on toward eleven."

Holmes didn't answer. The cab slipped to a halt and I recognized the doorway. We were at the offices of my attorney, Marchmont. What on earth could Huret have to do with the lawyer?

We stepped down, and I kept an eye on Radlett, should he choose to run. I think he considered it, looking speculatively at both Holmes and me. I'm sure that he realized he could outdistance me in a footrace, especially as he'd be able to dodge into the narrow alleys that formed the rabbit's warren of this neighborhood. But he certainly also understood that he'd have no such luck when testing himself against Holmes.

We entered the building to encounter Marchmont's taciturn secretary. I hadn't seen him or the lawyer for several months – since selling my Kensington practice, as a matter of fact. As expected, nothing had changed, for it never did in these quiet austere chambers.

The secretary seemed as if he'd expected us. He led us through a door into a short hallway, where we found Marchmont, a heavy-set middle-aged man, standing in a hallway. He greeted us all, shaking our hands, and then, without comment or questions, he directed us into the small conference room where in the past I'd conducted several bits of my own business, and where I'd also been either an observer or participant when Holmes cleared up one or the other of his cases. When we were in the room, Marchmont nodded and walked back out, and the secretary closed the door behind him, leaving the three of us alone to find seats around the long rectangular table.

Holmes removed his hat and coat, laying the former at the head of the table, and placing the folded coat on top of a nearby cabinet. Then he stood behind the chair usually reserved for Marchmont. Meanwhile, I also removed my hat and coat (for there was no coat stand, and in the hurry to get us placed in the conference room, the secretary had neglected to offer to take them) and laid them on the same cabinet. I then chose a chair near the door, pulled it back from the table, and sat, and leaving the other seats, those farther from the exit, for Radlett's choosing. He kept his coat and hat on, and seemed inclined to stand.

"What's going on here?" he growled, his short figure tense as he sensed the implied threat. He glanced from the closed door to the tall curtained window, as if considering which was a better chance for his escape: Getting past me or defenestrating himself. "I brought you the card. There ain't no need for you to force me to go to Fenchurch Street, let alone stopping here. What is this place?"

"Didn't you read the sign upon the door?" Holmes countered. "That should have answered your question."

"I can't – " Radlett stopped himself, his mouth popping shut before he could let anything slip. Holmes advised him to have a seat.

"I expect that our visitors will arrive soon," Holmes added, apparently ignoring Radlett's aborted comment, "but they may be delayed."

At first the little man ignored him, but finally he pulled out a chair, several down the table and across from where I sat, and perched himself on the front edge, much as he'd done not so long before in Baker Street.

"Visitors?" asked Radlett. "Who?" But again Holmes didn't answer.

There was a low shelf near where Holmes stood, containing a variety of volumes. Some appeared to be thick and ancient, bound in cracked black leather – surely legal tomes from bygone days, perhaps left over from when Marchmont had acquired the practice from the original founder, now long dead. There were other books there, too, including a copy of *Whitaker's Almanac*, easily recognizable by its green boards and red spine, which was marked with the curious circular symbol at the top and the trident at the base.

Holmes had been studying the book shelf, which caused me to notice it as well. Then he leaned down and retrieved the *Whitaker's* before placing it on the table by his fore-and-aft cap and taking a seat.

"Watson," he asked, his fingers resting lightly on the almanac. "Do you recall several years ago, when the cat-and-mouse game against the Professor was escalating? There was a fellow, one of Moriarty's mid-level agents, who sent me information as he was able."

I nodded. "Porlock – or so he called himself. He was able to let you know about the White Hart plot, in time to save Calvin Thurlow – the poor man who needed a job. There were other instances, as I recall. He sent the message about where the grape leaves were picked when we were tracking the Rippers, and he tried to prevent the murder of that rich American at the moated house in North Sussex. I'm sure that I have other instances recorded in my notes."

Holmes tapped the book, drawing attention to it. "Porlock was a very clever fellow. You'll recall that back in '88, he used the *Whitaker's* to send us a message warning us of the Birlstone murder. It wasn't something that he and I had worked out before. He came up with that method on his own for that particular event, although he and I used it afterwards."

He tapped the book again. "The *Almanac* was quite useful for that sort of thing – something that the original creators never envisioned." Suddenly he slid it across the table, where it came to rest across from Radlett. "Don't you agree, Simon?"

367

Radlett jumped as if Holmes had pushed a swamp adder toward him. Then he nodded, warily. "I suppose so."

"Do you make much use of the *Almanac*?" Holmes asked. Even as Radlett shook his head, Holmes added, "Open it up and tell us some of the most useful parts."

Radlett looked from him to the book, and then again, before reaching and pulling it closer. He flipped it open and turned a few pages, staring at it. From where I sat, I could see that it was upside down. Then he closed it and said, "All of it is important, I suppose."

Holmes nodded, and then looked at me. "Even in 1879, Simon couldn't read. And yet, somehow he read that card this morning and recognized the French name when he lifted it from the man in Leadenhall Street."

Radlett, who had never relaxed, seemed even more tense, but he didn't rise, nor did he say a word. Holmes continued speaking to me.

"You'll recall that Porlock was killed – tortured by Moriarty and then thrown into the Thames." * Simon Radlett gasped, and Holmes continued. "Just another of the many crimes that were draped like heavy chains to Moriarty's black soul." He glanced toward Radlett. "Of course, Porlock's death occurred many years after you and I parted ways, didn't it, Simon?"

The man didn't speak, his eyes fixed on upon my friend with seering intensity. Even more did he now appear to be a cornered animal.

Holmes looked back my way. "Porlock's murder was – I was outraged. But it only served to show just how malevolent Moriarty was. When he learned that Porlock was assisting me, he killed him – because of the betrayal, and also to send me a message, and as a lesson to his creatures. I was never able to determine just how he learned what Porlock was doing. But by then the specifics didn't matter. Events were crowding fast upon us, and he was one more casualty in the escalating war."

Then Holmes stopped for a moment, glanced over at the almanac, and then back up to Radlett. "You couldn't read fifteen years ago, Simon, and you can't read the book that Porlock used – can you?"

Radlett's suspicious mien was starting to crumble. He didn't look angry or trapped now. Instead, he began to chew at his lower lip, looking back and forth from Holmes to the book. Then he shifted in the chair and leaned forward, putting his head closer to the cover, staring intently. He raised his hand, apparently to once more touch the almanac, but then he dropped it back to his lap. Then with something between a sob and a sigh he leaned back, looking up toward Holmes. His face was now marked by grief.

"You're right!" he whispered. "I can't read it! What does it matter? Can you tell me what happened to my brother? To Alf? I was never able to find out."

Holmes nodded, his face marked by compassion.

"I can tell you, Simon. It's a terrible story, and your brother was very brave. But now is not the time. As you said, it's getting on toward eleven, and we have other matters to discuss – namely, the true reason that you brought that card to Baker Street."

Holmes stood and walked back around the table, retrieved the *Whitaker's*, replaced it on the low shelf, and then resumed his place at the head of the table.

"As you've perceived, Watson," he said, "Alfred Bassick, known to us as 'Porlock', was Simon's brother – actually half-brother, I believe. They were both Irregulars for a short period in the late seventies, but as often happened with many of them, they were seduced away by better pay, despite the fact that they migrated to the wrong side of the law. But while they were Irregulars, they had both been my responsibility for a while, and that did not end. I kept in touch with Alfred, the brother later known as 'Porlock', and at one point was able to do him a great favor – getting you, Simon, out of a hole in which you'd found yourself."

Radlett's eyes widened. Clearly, he'd been completely unaware of this.

"Your brother never wanted you to know what we'd done for you. Afterwards, he felt himself to be in my debt, and the best way that he could repay it was to provide information as he wormed deeper into Professor Moriarty's organization. I'll forever regret how he was eventually rewarded – with his own death."

Radlett cleared his throat. "But what about the book?" he asked. "Why did you trick me? Why are we here?"

Holmes shook his head. "I recalled that in the old days, you couldn't read, and I suspected that it was still true. I've followed your rather dubious 'career' over the years, and I've seen no signs that you have improved yourself. Certainly you weren't learning to read on your own, and no one was requiring it of you. Things might have changed in that regard during the three years I was away from London, but I doubted it. When you showed up this morning with that card, claiming to have read both the message, written in cursive, and the information on the front, I thought that you might be lying. Therefore, I contrived the little reading test just now with the almanac."

"But . . . but surely you didn't come here to this office just to trap me – to read a book?"

"No. I could have had you try to read while we were still in Baker Street, but I didn't want you suspicious any sooner than you had to be. After spotting the false note of your visit this morning, I contrived to take control of the situation. Apparently you wanted me – and Watson as well, I suppose – to race off to Fenchurch Street about Gerald Fenton Westhouse at eleven o'clock, which meant that we should *not* do that. Instead, as we left, I had our landlady send telegrams to Marchmont, asking if we could use his office as a wayside for a while, and also to the police, requesting, among other things, that they have Westhouse brought here to meet us, assuming that he's available. Based on what I've discovered over the last few months, and more through recent developments, I'm not surprised that he's been pulled into this, but I want to determine the full extent of his involvement – if any – with the so-called 'Boulevard Assassin'."

I tried to recall specifics regarding the little I knew about Holmes's recent inquiries. His association with the affair had begun with the arrival of Inspector Gregson to show him the letter, written by Huret and sent to *The Times*. He'd made some observations then but offered nothing of great value – or so I thought. He'd consulted with Mycroft, and he'd averted a number of other Huret-connected assassination attempts, but as far as I knew otherwise, he hadn't heard anything from the agents he'd set in to motion – certainly nothing that would cause him to leap up and rush forth upon the hue-and-cry in which we were now engaged.

"It had to be the original letter," I speculated softly, almost tentatively, thinking hard and trying to make a connection. "You saw something in the original letter that intrigued you – for I'm unaware that you've received further information since then."

Holmes nodded. "Good, Watson! And correct. There *was* something familiar about the letter, something that I chose for the moment to keep to myself, and a bit of focused research confirmed my conclusions well enough to proceed. From the beginning, I knew who wrote it, but Mycroft and I decided to set plans in motion to let events play out, and see where Huret led us – and he's revealed a lot since mid-year. You might be interested to know that soon after we began, your own writings – particularly an issue of *The Strand* from September 1891 – provided me with a most-important confirmatory clue."

"September – ?" I asked, trying to remember to which entry he was referencing. That fall had been a difficult period for me, just four months after Holmes's supposed death, and Mary's health sliding downward to a new level of seriousness and concern. I still had a medical practice for which I cared nothing, as my mood deteriorated and I recognized that my wife's condition was steadily and inevitably deteriorating. I found distraction and solace only by writing, and from my extensive notes and journals, maintained over many years, I had a plethora of Holmes's cases from which to choose.

Every night, I wrote ceaselessly after Mary had been put to bed, recording one account after another, in much the same way that I'd written with such focused dedication following my return to London after being injured in the Afghan War. As the months passed, I accumulated more and more completed records of Holmes's adventures, one after another piling up along one side of my desk, and I only managed to tear myself away from the writing long enough to evince a limited interest and involvement regarding which of those was chosen for publication. By the time one of the stories would appear in *The Strand*, I had already written many more, and was working on yet another. *What was significant about the story from September 1891?*

"I have no recollection of which particular narrative you mean," I finally said, my confusion apparent.

Holmes smiled. "No matter. All will be clear soon enough – for I believe that I hear the arrival of visitors, and Gregson's authoritative tones."

The door opened to reveal the secretary. He stepped back, allowing Inspector Gregson and a heavy-set man, about ten years older than Holmes and me, to enter the room. Holmes and I stood, and Holmes asked, "Is he under observation?"

Gregson nodded. "As he has been these last four months. He'll be ready when you are."

My immediate reaction was to ask who "*he*" was, but I knew that Holmes would reveal that fact only when he was ready.

"Excellent!" Holmes turned to the man, who was looking most confused and unsettled. "Mr. Gerald Fenton Westhouse?" he asked. The man nodded. "Thank you for coming. Please take a seat."

The man seemed to find a little fortitude. "You act as if I had a choice. This policeman – " He glanced sourly at Gregson. " – collected me at my workplace as if I were under arrest. *Am* I under arrest, Inspector?"

"No, sir. As I explained, we wanted to remove you to a place where we could speak in confidence."

"By making it appear as if I were being detained?"

"There was a purpose to that, as I'm sure Mr. Holmes will explain."

"I will," said Holmes. "Please, sit down. This won't take long."

When we had settled, Holmes pointed at Simon Radlett, asking, "Have you ever seen this man before?"

Westhouse glanced that way. "Never."

"He didn't try to rob you this morning in Leadenhall Street? You didn't raise your stick to him and chase him away?"

Westhouse reddened. "Of course not! What is this? What are you trying to involve me in?"

"Is this your card?" Holmes pushed the one given to him by Radlett across the table. Westhouse took it and read the front. "It is."

"And the back? Did you write that? Or was it written by someone else and provided to you?"

The wine merchant turned the card over and glanced at the inscribed words. "Never seen it before," He said, tossing it back toward Holmes. He seemed to have no recognition of the assassin's name.

I glanced at Radlett. His face was pale, and he seemed to quiver with tension.

"Gentlemen," said Holmes, "please note that Mr. Westhouse picked up the card with his *left* – and dominant – hand. Earlier today, Mr. Radlett here demonstrated to Dr. Watson and me earlier this morning that when he robbed you, sir – when he *said* that he robbed you – you defended yourself by holding your cane in your *right* hand, and that when he approached you from your right, he found that card in your right coat pocket, where a right-handed man would have placed it."

"Ridiculous!" Westhouse snarled. He hit the table with his fist – his left fist – for emphasis. "What is this nonsense? I've never seen this man before, or you either, sir! No one tried to rob me, and I've never before seen what was written on that card!"

Holmes nodded. "So I thought, and as I'm sure Mr. Radlett would have admitted the same to us soon enough. And I already knew that you were left handed, for you and I met once before, seven years ago. In October 1887, as a matter of fact, although you wouldn't recognize me now. I was in disguise."

Westhouse frowned. "Disguise? What nonsense is that? Why would anyone want to visit me in disguise?"

"So that I could get a look at one of your employees while I asked you a few general questions, and so that he wouldn't recognize me when he came to visit my rooms a few days later."

"Employee? Which one? What is this about?"

"I manufactured an excuse to meet with you so that I could get a look at one of your salesmen – Mr. James Windibank."

Suddenly, as if bright sunlight blew away the fog of my confusion, I recalled the case to which Holmes had earlier referred, the story that had appeared in the September 1891 edition of *The Strand*. I had happened to visiting Baker Street that day in October 1887, discussing with Holmes a wide variety of topics, when a new client had arrived – Miss Mary Sutherland, whose fiancé, one curiously named *Hosmer Angel*, had vanished.

Holmes had recognized the similarity between those circumstances and several other cases, leading him to the suspicion that Angel was actually someone else in disguise, disingenuously courting the girl as a way to her money. She had provided Holmes with a number of typewritten letters from Angel, all of which had given him a number of clues as to the specific machine upon which they'd been written. He'd also noted that the girl's stepfather, James Windibank, a claret salesman for Westhouse and Marbank, conveniently took business trips to France and was gone whenever Hosmer walked out with the girl.

He'd immediately suspected that Windibank was posing as Angel. He'd corresponded with Windibank, and the return letter, typewritten on Westhouse and Marbank's stationery, had shown the same wearing and defects as those on the letters to the unfortunate girl from Hosmer Angel. Holmes was then able to confront the man, exposing that Windibank, by promising the girl marriage and disappearing before the ceremony, hoped to be able to keep her at home as a sad lonely spinster, forever bound to the mysteriously vanished Hosmer, while he remained in control of her substantial inheritance. It was a diabolical plot, and Windibank had proved himself to be a true villain.

I looked up to see that Holmes was watching me, smiling. He knew that I was now caught up.

"Windibank?" asked Westhouse. "What about him?"

"Has his work been satisfactory of late?"

"Why – No, it has not. His sales have dropped, and his traveling expenses have increased with very little return. He's been put on notice that he'll need to do better, or be sacked. He isn't happy with me right now, but I'm running a business."

"Interesting. And when did this trend begin?"

"What? Oh, I suppose in the spring sometime. He became rather insolent as well. Something the matter at home, I suppose. I'd heard that there was trouble – that his wife had left him."

Holmes glanced toward Radlett. "Simon – How did you become involved in this?"

The little man lowered his eyes. "I was introduced to a man," he mumbled.

"Who? Windibank?"

"I don't know that name."

"No, I don't suppose so. Was he about thirty-seven? Five-feet-seven inches in height? Strongly built, sallow complexion? Black hair, a little bald in the centre?"

I recognized that description of Windibank that I'd recorded in my original narrative, adjusted forward seven years from his then-age of thirty or so. Westhouse confirmed it. "That's him – that's Windibank!"

Radlett nodded. "That's right. They – this man knew that I . . . that I have no use for you, Mr. Holmes. After Alf died while working for you. I've done some things for him before – for Windibank – and a few days ago, he approached me with a simple task: He knew that you've been looking for this *Hoo-ray*, and that the word is going around that you're getting close to finding him. He said for me to take that card to Baker Street and get you interested in this man here – to tell you that I'd found the card in his pocket. You were supposed to charge off to the office in Fenchurch Street and then arrest him . . . but I have the idea that something else is supposed to happen when you get there."

Holmes looked toward Gregson. "*Did* anything happen when you arrived?"

"Not a thing."

"Hmm. Then perhaps whatever happens requires my presence." He looked back to Radlett. "When were you introduced to this man?"

"Last spring."

"You started to mention 'they'," asked Holmes. "Who might 'they' be?"

Radlett's eyes widened, and he involuntarily shook his head.

"It was in the spring. Might I theorize that it was in that same period when there were some thwarted attempts to restart the Professor's broken organization?"

I wondered if Radlett would be able to follow Holmes's thought, using words like "thwarted", but Holmes had more faith in him. Radlett knew what he meant, and he gave a small nod, without offering any explanation.

Holmes continued.

"This man you met – who we have identified now as Windibank – was he working with Colonel Moriarty, or the other one – the youngest brother who oddly disguised himself as the dead Professor?"

"Him," said Radlett softly. "The younger one. I don't know who he thought he was fooling with the bald wig and never falling into the waterfall. Everyone knew that he wasn't the Professor – but it didn't matter, for we were all still afraid of him. He's a little crazy, he is. He had come from France last spring to try and take over, and that's where he met the other man – this Windibank – who was over in France a lot as well. They were working together, and had big plans. But then you came back to London, Mr. Holmes, and the two Moriarty brothers ran away – but

374

Windibank was still here, and he went ahead with whatever he was doing. I've run errands for him ever since."

"And it didn't bother you to work for the youngest Moriarty, even though the Professor murdered your half-brother."

"He wasn't the Professor," Radlett countered with a shrug, "and he was working against you, which suited me."

"I see. And what do you know about Windibank's plans?"

"Nothing. He was gone to France a great deal, but he paid me to run his errands when he was here. I suppose he trusted me as much as anyone."

"Do you know anything about a letter he wrote to the newspapers last summer?"

"Not much – just that he did it, and then right after, he said he'd made a mistake, and that he wouldn't do anything like that again."

Holmes nodded and spoke to Gregson. "That fits with our assumption that he realized that I might recognize the Huret letter came from the same typewriter as Windibank's, and he refrained from providing any further emphasis to it, hoping it would be forgotten." He included me in the thought, looking my way. "And that's what we let him think, giving him more and more rope while we learned about the organization he and the younger Moriarty have constructed, while preventing additional murders that they arranged.

"And Mr. Westhouse?" Holmes looked back at the now-much-puzzled merchant. "Do you know anything about Mr. Windibank's plan?"

Westhouse had gone pale as he realized that something was going on, involving him, beyond what was easily understood. "Plan? I do not. I . . . I'm just a businessman, a wine and spirits importer. Windibank has worked for us for a number of years. His performance has fallen off, but he's been a trusted employee for a long time. He would have to be, wouldn't he? He travels for us, making regular trips over to France. Even though his sales have declined, he's never given us a reason to distrust him. I just thought . . . thought that he was going through a low spot. I didn't – Just what has he gotten us into?"

Holmes didn't answer him, instead turning to Gregson.

"Well," he asked, "have we allowed this to go on just about long enough?"

Gregson nodded. "I was in a meeting with your brother this morning, Mr. Holmes, and now that Windibank seems to be spooked, it's probably time to shut him down. We don't think we'll get anything else useful by letting him run loose."

"I agree. Where is he now?"

"Still at the spirits office in Fenchurch Street. I observed him there when we picked up Mr. Westhouse an hour ago, sitting at his desk off to one side. If it surprised him that you weren't with us as intended when we staged the arrest, he might have bolted, but even so, he's being watched from a half-dozen directions – some of my best men who've had experience tracking the Dynamiters, as well as your brother's agents, and even those slippery children you employ. He won't get far."

"Then let's go retrieve him." Holmes stood. "Can you have your men keep Misters Westhouse and Radlett in isolation for another hour or so?"

"I can," replied the inspector. "Here?"

"I think not. We've intruded on Mr. Marchbank too much already. Take them to Baker Street. Watson and I will explain to them later what has happened. We owe them that much."

Westhouse sputtered, especially as Holmes had talked about him as if he wasn't there, but Simon Radlett simply hung his head. I could only wonder at what thoughts were crossing his mind.

Gregson opened the door and murmured a few words to a waiting constable. Then the officer, with four more of them, came in and took custody of the merchant and thief.

Not long after, we were back in our cab, this time with Gregson instead of Radlett. Another group of constables were following behind us. Holmes looked at me. "What needs to be explained?"

I ordered my thoughts. "I believe that I generally understand. When you saw the Huret letter, something about it reminded you of the letters Windibank had typed to his step-daughter, back in 1887. You recognized the defects in the typeface, and possibly the you saw a similarity in the paper." Holmes nodded. "You still had the old letters – I remember you searching for and finding some documents in a folder – and a comparison showed they'd been written by the same man."

"Remarkable," Gregson murmured.

"From there," I continued, "you worked out a long-range plan with Mycroft and the police to keep Windibank under observation – to see about his involvement, if any, with Carnot's assassination."

Holmes nodded. "The operation has grown over the last months as more aspects were discovered. After the youngest James Moriarty fled last spring to the Continent, still strapped into his outlandish Professor costume, we kept an eye on him. When Windibank tied himself to the Carnot assassination with his careless Huret letter, and drew our gaze in his direction as well, it wasn't long before we saw the two of them associating. Neither is a master criminal, although both are consumed with ambition and pleased with their own cleverness.

"It wasn't difficult to scotch their various planned assassinations as the year has progressed. But as their activities have flattened, it was decided that enough is enough, so we intentninally spooked Windibank by putting out word that I was getting close to identifying Huret. He knew that he'd made a mistake sending the letter, so he's likely been anxious ever since. His response, apparently, was to frame Westhouse, or at least involve him, and draw me in at the same time – two birds with one stone, as they say, since Westhouse was apparently going to sack him any day now. Soon we'll know specifically what he intended."

Westhouse's establishment was near the eastern end of Fenchurch Street, where it joins with Leadenhall Street to become the short stretch of Aldgate High Street, which in turn becomes the Whitechapel High Street. It's a narrow but bustling road, and the wine and spirit merchant's building was rather more prosperous-looking that its neighbors. Holmes informed me that the partner, Marbank, had died years earlier, so we didn't have to worry about any interruption by a second irate owner.

We had stopped just up the street, and once we'd alighted, Gregson raised a hand and waved twice. Without any hint as to what was coming, a dozen men, both in and out uniform, bled from nearby buildings, all armed and moving with the air of silent danger hanging about them. These weren't plodding constables, their Size Twelves broken down from endless repetitive rounds. Instead, we saw highly skilled and trained agents of various government branches, and it was good to know that they existed.

A few terse words from Gregson sent two of his men around behind the building, where they would give instructions to the others already waiting there. Then, without any drama at all, we walked quickly into the building.

It was one large room, with a pair of offices at the back, their doors closed. The entire front space was filled with desks, most with a number of men that were either bent over their work or engaged in conversations. To the right, a couple of desks back from the center aisle, was one man who stared straight toward us, even as we approached him at great speed. The initial conversation that was chattering throughout as we entered quickly died, shock filliling the room upon seeing so many grim men, all charging in one direction, with weapons pulled and aiming directly at James Windibank.

The object of our interest was glaring, singularly focused, upon Sherlock Holmes, instantly recognizable in his fore-and-aft cap and Inverness. Then, with a snarling curse, Windibank tried to pull open his desk drawer and reach a hand inside, but Holmes increased his speed and with a single graceful sweep, laid his weighted stick alongside Windibank's jaw, snapping the man's head back and causing his chair to flip over, throwing him to the floor alongside the next desk.

There is always something to be said for the direct and unexpected approach.

Holmes's motion carried forward, and he had Windibank jerked upright and in a wrestling hold before the evil little man could gather his wits. His face was swelling, and the skin had split, letting blood run onto his collar. No one made a move to aid him, in the way that a mad dog is to be avoided. Instead, half-a-dozen constables took him from Holmes and confined him immediately in wrist and ankle shackles. Then he was tossed onto the center aisle floor, surrounded by men who either faced him, weapons drawn, or faced outward, similarly armed and holding back any others who might choose to become involved. No one did.

Windibank's thin hair fell over his eyes and stuck to his sweaty face. He fought his bonds while shrieking like a hopeless Bedlam maniac, bloodying his wrists. It became apparent that he was crawling across the floor, bucking up and down like a land-trapped shark, trying to get to Holmes. One of Gregson's men grabbed him by the feet and yanked him back. Windibank suddenly bent double, trying to sink his teeth into the man's hands. After that, he was given a wide berth.

Inside the top drawer of Windibank's desk, we found a button, with wires leading down and under the floor, thence over to Westhouse's office, where an electrically devised dynamite bomb had been cleverly concealed in the man's desk.

Presumably when Holmes came to see Westhouse at eleven, based on the card that Radlett had brought to Baker Street just an hour or so before, Windibank would have detonated the device, killing both the man who was likely going to fire him, as well as the detective who had long served as his nemesis. It didn't matter that many others would have died as well. Windibank, knowing that he was setting off the explosion, had planned to duck and take cover behind his own desk and protect himself. Possibly afterwards, he could have even helped the wounded, presenting himself as a hero.

A handwritten note was found in his desk, implicating Westhouse as the master assassin. It seemed that he planned to toss it somewhere in the rubble just after the explosion.

Windibank twisted around on the floor, always so that he could see Holmes, cursing and promising my friend a painful death for crossing him – or so we assumed, because no one could truly understand his raging bleats by way of his shattered jaw.

"*Holmessss!*" he hissed. "*Holmesessssss . . . .*"

After Windibank was brought to Scotland Yard, he was treated and questioned thoroughly. Like so many men of his wicked ilk, he couldn't help but brag after enough pressure was brought to bear. It always seemed as if that type believed that their clever and boastful explanations would sway the authorities into somehow agreeing with them – as if we would all lean back, once we'd heard it all explained in the *correct* way, and look at one another, nodding at the previously unrealized wisdom and cleverness, and then laughingly step forward and unlock the handcuffs, and possibly shake his hand and apologize.

After hearing James Windibank, no one was laughing.

He boasted of crimes that none of us, even Sherlock Holmes, had suspected, from even before Holmes aided the evil man's step-daughter. He explained how he had become more and more bold with his own plans, using the cover of his traveling job to commit a number of crimes in multiple countries, accumulating funds as he did so, but finding that simple riches were not enough. He liked the challenge of operating in the shadows, and he liked bragging about it.

He'd met the youngest James Moriarty in Paris, and they'd found ways in which they might benefit one another. Moriarty had a venture wherein he could make investments based on periods when the markets were destabilized – especially after the shattering events of a string of assassinations. Carnot was a trial run, from which both Moriarty and Windibank made a small fortune.

Afterwards, it was Windibank's idea to propose that the assassinations were being carried out by one man, the fictional Huret, when in fact he would recruit a number of other killers working under that name to confuse the issue – an entire *nest of Hurets*. He'd set this in motion by writing to *The Times*, using old Westfield and Marbank stationery – and only afterwards realizing that the newly returned Holmes, whom he hadn't previously considered, might somehow recall the typewritten letters he'd sent to his step-daughter years before. He knew that Holmes had originally found him then based on the fact that the girl's letters had been written on the wine merchant's typewriter, so he sent no more of them. But he'd been correct in his fears: Though he hadn't known it, and after he finally came to believe that it hadn't been noticed, Holmes was indeed on his scent, and he stayed that way throughout the subsequent months.

When it seemed that Holmes suddenly might be getting closer, according to the recent stories spreading through the underworld, Windibank had the idea to throw Westhouse, whom he greatly disliked, into the fire, using him as lure to kill Holmes, and also chalk up another killing by Huret. He boasted that he had tied some of the false Huret's activities to when Westhouse was visiting the Continent, in the hope of lending further confusion that the business owner might be involved.

Once the affair was completed, and the prevention of a number of crimes throughout the latter half of 1894 could be acknowledged, thanks for Holmes poured in from all quarters. Our sitting room was nearly as deep in congratulatory telegrams as had been Holmes's hotel room in Lyons following the defeat of Baron Maupertuis, also back in '87. After Windibank was hanged, following the much-argued decision of whether he would die in England or France, Holmes even received the French Order of the Legion of Honour, as well as an autographed letter of thanks from the new French President. As was typical of him, they were tossed into a drawer in his desk.

Back in Baker Street on that eventful Guy Fawkes Day, Holmes explained to Westhouse and Simon Radlett just what had happened. Westhouse, suddenly drawn into the affair, cared about nothing besides returning to his business in order to set things right. As quickly as he was involved, he departed. But Radlett seemed to have no interest in leaving, instead remaining seated with his head down.

Holmes retreated to his room for a moment, returning with a bottle. "I bought this last spring, intending to drink it to celebrate when the matter was concluded." He handed it to me. It was a labeled *Champagne Huret*.

"Imported by Westhouse and Marbank," he explained. "Windibank really is a rather arrogant and careless fellow. It didn't initially occur to him that writing Huret's letter on his firm's typewriter might be a poor idea. And he apparently took the assassin's name from one of the primary wines that they sell."

He shook his head and asked if I wanted a glass, but I declined. He then nodded in agreement. "I find that I'm also rather not in the mood myself just now."

Putting it aside, he and I instead settled back with lit pipes, whereupon Holmes asked, "Is there something else, Simon?"

He looked up. "Why am I not under arrest?"

Holmes didn't immediately answer, instead taking several draws upon his pipe.

"I suppose," he finally said, "that I owe a debt – to your half-brother, Alfred. But since he isn't here, I can repay you – and offer you a different path now, if you want it. Alfred was very brave, and did a great deal to help defeat Professor Moriarty, and after all that, I wasn't able to protect him when he . . . when the Professor killed him."

Radlett had been looking at Holmes, perhaps hoping for more, but my friend fell silent once again, lost in his own memories. Those months leading up to Reichenbach had been terrible, the worst that Holmes and I had faced since the battle against the Rippers in the Autumn of Terror.

He'd grasped so many ropes during that time, each with its own special aspects and dangers, and no one could fault him when his grip had slipped on a few and something had gone wrong. The matter was so complex, and he'd sacrificed so much to wrest a victory. During his struggle with the Professor, he'd nearly died a dozen times over, but when someone else had perished as part of the struggle, he'd punished himself terribly. I knew that the death of Porlock, and the guilt he carried because of it, would always haunt him.

And perhaps Simon Radlett now realized it too.

"Tell me," said Radlett, his voice little more than a rough whisper. "About what Alf did, and how he helped. And what made it so important for him to choose to be on *your* side."

And Holmes did tell him, including many things that I had not heard before. I tried to listen well, because it wouldn't have been suitable just then for me to take notes, and I wanted to remember all of it for when I had the chance later that night to record yet another chapter in the great ongoing battle when Sherlock Holmes had vanquished the dragon of our age.

When I look at the three massive manuscript volumes which contain our work for the year 1894, I confess that it is very difficult for me, out of such a wealth of material, to select the cases which are most interesting in themselves, and at the same time most conducive to a display of those peculiar powers for which my friend was famous. As I turn over the pages, I see . . . the tracking and arrest of Huret, the Boulevard assassin – an exploit which won for Holmes an autograph letter of thanks from the French President and the Order of the Legion of Honour.

– Dr. John H. Watson
"The Golden *Pince-Nez*"

"There's a cold-blooded scoundrel!" said Holmes, laughing, as he threw himself down into his chair once more. "That fellow will rise from crime to crime until he does something very bad, and ends on a gallows.

– Sherlock Holmes
"A Case of Identity"

NOTES

Bassick

*   Alfred Bassick was initially introduced in William Gillette's play *Sherlock Holmes* (1899), and later portrayed the Basil Rathbone film *The Adventures of Sherlock Holmes* (1939). He can also be found in "Enquiry in Conduit Street" in *The Collected Papers of Sherlock Holmes – Volume VI: Muniments* and also *The Nefarious Villains of Sherlock Holmes – Volume II*

The Other Moriartys

Colonel Moriarty's vicious attacks on Watson during Holmes's supposed death were brilliantly retrieved from the Tin Dispatch Box by Marcia Wilson and presented as five novel-length adventures: *The MoonCursers*, *A Sword for Defense*, *The Narrow Path*, *The End of All Things*, and *A Fanged and Bitter Thing*.

The narratives describing the youngest Moriarty, who oddly tried to fool everyone into thinking he was his older brother by way of an elaborate disguise and harnesses and straps, were edited by John Gardner: *Moriarty's Return*, *Moriarty's Revenge*, and *Moriarty*.

The Other Hurets

Some of the cases in the latter half of 1894 in which Holmes defeated the other Hurets include:

- ☐ "The Adventure of the Boulevard Assassin" *1894: Some Cases of Mr. Sherlock Holmes* – Hugh Ashton
- ☐ "The Boulevard Assassin", *The Confidential Casebook of Sherlock Holmes* – Kathleen Brady
- ☐ "The Adventure of the Boulevard Assassin", [Internet Fan Fiction] – Sarah G. Hadley
- ☐ *Sherlock Holmes and the Boulevard Assassin* – John Hall
- ☐ "Huret, the Boulevard Assassin", *My Dear Holmes* – David Hammer
- ☐ "The Case of the Unseen Assassin", *Sherlock Holmes & Mr. Mac* – Gary Lovisi
- ☐ "The Boulevard Assassin", *The Continued Casebook of Sherlock Holmes* – J.A. Roberts
- ☐ "The Boulevard Assassin", *The Secret Documents of Sherlock Holmes* – June Thomson
- ☐ "The Adventure of the Parisian Gentleman", *The Mammoth Book of New Sherlock Holmes Stories* – Robert Weinberg and Lois H. Gresh

The following adventure, while not specifically about the Boulevard Assassin, provides peripheral details about one of the other Hurets:

☐ "The Adventure of the Red Barrow Horror", *Sherlock Holmes: The Impossible Cases* – Daniel McGachey

Champagne Huret

Holmes's bottle of *Champagne Huret* should not be confused with the current company manufacturing *Champagne Huret Colas*, as the latter apparently went into business in 1960. Their association with the name *Huret* is unknown.

https://www.champagne-huret-colas.com/la-maison

A Bucket's Worth of Help

Chapter I

At that time of night, Fleet Street, with its various legitimate commercial interests paused until daylight, was mostly deserted. But not entirely, for that thoroughfare, like every street in London, was never truly still, even at three o'clock in the morning, and there were those afoot whose tasks were best completed in darkness.

As Sherlock Holmes and I walked westward through the autumn fog that had settled in from the nearby river like a slow but inexorable overland flood, an ephemeral tide that rose almost before one was aware of it, our footsteps echoed from the pavement and walls of the surrounding buildings in a lonely way that would have never been perceived during the tumultuous daylight hours.

Thankfully the claggy mist was not the choking and acidic sort, or one of the thick and impenetrable white banks of dense oily vapor piled higher than a man's head that left the throat raw while burning the lungs, forcing one to progress forward only inches at a time, one hand held outward so as not to walk into a building or lamppost. Heaven help someone who had to move at speed through such a *ceò* as that. I'd once come upon a man who had been running through such a fog, in terror for his life, and hit a common lamppost straight on. His end was mercifully quick, but the instant of his death must have been terrible. Thankfully on this night, we trod through a mere swirling vapor lying just two or three feet above the ground, giving the setting a dreamlike feeling – but also a sense of heightened awareness, as if one were being hunted.

If Sherlock Holmes's plan had worked, we were.

Ahead of us, under distant gaslights, we saw occasional movement as solitary figures appeared, walking in front of us in the same direction for a moment, or crossing a street from one side to the other, or perhaps tarrying under a lamp to light a cigarette or consider which direction to take. They were but passing shadows, dark shapes that one could only assume held some spark of eternity within them, identifiable as human beings only by their upright carriage. Seen in a different place on such a night – a distant village cemetery during the witching hour, perhaps – they might have been liches or wraiths.

But our prey this night was not any supernatural creature, and whoever was stalking us from ahead and behind was under the mistaken impression that we would soon be victims. As usual, Sherlock Holmes was three steps ahead, and when Richard Magellan made his play, the trap snapped upon him before he quite knew what had occurred.

We paused under the dim gaslight at Chancery Lane, on the northern side of the street. Holmes, as was typical of him, made no sudden move when we heard steady and intentional footsteps approaching us, louder as the distance decreased. There was no need for reaction, as he was already prepared. He had been since our walk had begun just five minutes earlier, when we'd stepped out of Silas Haynor's hovel in Tudor Street, having made our visit quite obvious, and then started walking north to Fleet Street. From there we'd turned west, knowing that we would be accosted long before reaching the Strand. Our pace along the north side of the street had been slow but unremarkable, as befit the conditions. We passed the Mitre Court passage on our left, leading down into King's Bench Walk, and my thoughts imagined the opening as it must have been just a month earlier, jammed with red-headed men, spilling back into Fleet Street. I considered, when writing the matter up, whether I ought to change to name of the location to spare the residents any bother. [1] This thought led me to recall our old friend, Kirbishaw, the attorney who lived at 5A King's Bench Walk. [2] He would be fast asleep now, and I wondered if he'd be surprised at knowing the drama transpiring just a few hundred feet north of his front door.

But those thoughts were chased away when we heard the purposeful and distinctive strides of someone getting closer. Richard Magellan's limp was unmistakable from the echoing footsteps, but such a large and vigorous man as he wasn't slowed by it.

He was tall and broad, by then just forty years of age (although he'd never see forty-one, as he would be predictably murdered in his cell on the night before his trial), with thick black hair and a matching beard, long and lying tangled down his chest. He maintained a fierce scowl under twisted wiry black brows, and one expected that every word from his mouth would be expressed as a towering roar of rage – but in fact, his tone never rose above a low purr, a sly and insinuating voice that demonstrated both his intelligence and his bitter malevolence.

He was from a fine family, with ancestors and brothers who had all served the Realm with distinction for generations. But as Holmes often had occasion to note, sometimes an otherwise healthy tree will form a branch that, for no apparent reason, twists and deforms. Such was the life of Richard Magellan, matriculating at both Oxford and Cambridge (while graduating from neither) and then, by way of dark connections and owed favors and a fair amount of blackmail, establishing himself a successful attorney before a series of scandals inevitably left his career in ruins. And yet, having lost his wife and children – she returned with the boy and girl to her family, who were powerful enough to protect them – and his apparent source of legitimate income, he demonstrated no diminishment of financial resources, continuing to reside in a comfortable home in Bruton Street, on the Conduit Street end, not far from a certain Colonel's house that was located there.

None of Magellan's background seemed immediately relevant, however, when the man himself appeared out of the darkness, his black suit the same color as the night behind him, his legs invisible in the swirling mist. He seemed to glide toward us, and I pondered how such a big man with a limp could move so oddly, his upper body showing no motion as if he were rolling forward on wheels like some levitating *nosferatu*. His angry face appeared to float a fathom above the ground, equivalent to the same distance in the opposite direction that a man at death is supposed to be buried in the earth. The expression on Magellan's bitter face just then put one in mind of death. He had ours fixed in his mind, but Holmes's plans were otherwise.

"Did you think you could just stroll down here and then walk away?" Magellan asked in his low cunning voice as he stopped before us. He waved a massive hand. "As soon as he received your wire, Haynor told me you were coming to see him. Surely you didn't think that he would simply answer your inquiries."

He said it as a statement rather than a question. Holmes nodded, his eyes deeply shadowed from the lamplight by the bill of his fore-and-aft. "Of course not. But apparently you did believe that we were that foolish – else, you wouldn't have broken cover just now to accost us."

Magellan laughed, but there was no joy in it. He suddenly seemed a bit more tense, as if dimly starting to become cognizant that he'd made a mistake by approaching Holmes in such a way. Still, thinking he had the advantage, he pressed on, waving a hand once more, this time, indicating that those unseen should join him.

And they did – six or seven shadowed brutes who appeared from various nearby alleys and narrow passages. They converged slowly, in a tightening circle on all sides. Some carried cudgels or life-preservers, while a few just clenched their fists. It was with effort that I didn't draw my service revolver then, knowing that there were other factors at play here.

"We were waiting," said Magellan, becoming confident once again as his troops assembled. Above the greasy smell of the fog I grasped a new sour smell – the promise of violence wafting off the barely restrained pack surrounding us. And yet, Holmes showed nothing but polite amusement. Still, knowing him as I did, I could see that he was as tense as a tightly stretched wire, the stored and restrained potential energy there ready to snap loose at the slightest instant.

"We followed you right along from Haynor's," Magellan continued. "It wouldn't do to take you there – the old man has been too loyal for your killing to happen upon his own doorstep, within hearing of the neighbors. But the river is close enough from here. You can both toss a prayer toward Temple Church as we pass by." His voice lowered even more as the intensity increased. "Take them, boys!"

And his trained beasts began to move.

But their motion was short-lived as Holmes raised a hand and said, his voice sharper and commanding, "The Professor won't be very happy with you this night, Magellan."

We were outmatched and outnumbered and hadn't made any defense, nor pulled any weapon, and yet mention of James Moriarty stopped the looming thugs in their tracks. To a man, they looked toward Magellan, seeing how he would react.

He didn't change his stance, and yet he was suddenly taut, in that way a hunted animal will freeze with all senses alert for the direction of the fast-approaching threat, ready to jump and flee, but uncertain of his direction. Then he swallowed and asked, his voice softer now, and undoubtedly uncertain, "What do you mean?"

Mention of the Professor in this way, aloud and unexpected, had served to shake our foes on previous occasions. Fear of Moriarty, a name that that those in the shadows dreaded to hear or mention, was a powerful tool.

"You made a mistake this night," replied Holmes. "The mistake of allowing yourself to be removed from the board. The Professor will miss his Bishop – able until now to cut diagonally through any number of difficulties."

"You have nothing," was Magellan's low reply.

"I have everything," countered Holmes. "All three of the railway employees have provided sworn statements. But that isn't all. I also have the evidence in hand of your complicity in the Lyles forgery, the Umbershot explosion, the Connaught Street blackmail affair, and the murder of Jenny Elnathan twenty-one years ago behind the Bodleian Library. Ah, I see that that one stings. You didn't think anyone would ever connect you with poor Jenny, but there's really no escape."

Magellan's face had raced through a plethora expressions before settling on rage, and he was starting to step toward Holmes, his great hand folded in a fist and any fear of the Professor forgotten, when Holmes raised his voice and cried, "*Now, Patterson!*"

And from the same alleyways and passages and nearby streets that Magellan's men had just vacated boiled two-dozen policemen of all ranks, surrounding us in a matter of heartbeats.

With a roar, Magellan reached into his coat, certainly attempting to retrieve a gun. I moved at the same moment, finally pulling forth my own revolver, but neither of our efforts mattered, for Holmes was quicker. With a one-footed pivot and lift, he whipped his own lead-loaded stick savagely across Magellan's raging face, laying out the devil with a flat smack upon the stones, his now-unconscious form licked and tasted by the delicately curious tendrils of fog while the blood from his laid-open face pooled beneath his shaggy head.

We had been uncertain as to how many men Magellan might bring with him. It seemed that he'd felt he could finish us with seven, besides himself, and now it looked as if there were far more policemen than necessary to load them all into the Black Marias which soon joined us, harshly disturbing the silence. But there was a method to bringing so many officers. In those exponentially escalating days of Holmes's struggle against Professor Moriarty, it was sadly uncertain exactly who could be trusted, so extra officers were on hand to keep any that might be on Moriarty's payroll from doing something against our interests – such as stealthily unlocking Magellan's cuffs when no one was looking and letting him scurry away into a nearby alley. With so many officers present, no mischief was possible. And in any case, Magellan was going nowhere fast on his own.

Magellan was roughly placed into a separate Black Maria by himself, slid unconscious along the floor at the feet of four policemen. The seven hoodlums were to be questioned at the Yard, but their leader was set for a more demanding performance. He would be taken to the Woolwich Arsenal, where, upon receiving medical treatment, the Government was most interested in questioning him regarding the recent theft of the prototype for the Caiden-Keller naval gun, a bold and audacious act which would have certainly compromised the national safety and interest in countless spots around the globe had the theft been successful.

Holmes had been recruited by his brother Mycroft when the gun went missing, instructed to work separately from the official Government investigation, as it was uncertain whose loyalties could be trusted. The gun, so far the only one built, had vanished while being shipped from the Arsenal to Portsmouth. The special train upon which it was loaded had passed through the Three Bridges Station without incident or question, but when the train arrived in Crawley [3] just a few moments later, the car with the gun was missing, with the two cars that had been on either side of it now joined to one another. The method used to steal it had been fast and clever, as the train had arrived in Crawley within a minute of being on time.

It had taken very little for Holmes to determine that the gun and its car had been shunted onto a hastily constructed temporary siding when the train was stopped, broken apart, and reassembled. He saw no need for false modesty, pointing out that the signs he observed would have been initially missed by most involved, though seen eventually, and the gun would have been completely removed from its hiding place before the scheme of misdirection was fully comprehended and investigated.

Of greater interest and effort was how a squad of a dozen soldiers and the train's crew could, to a man, have been suborned into being complicit with the theft – for they must have been in order for the train to have been so efficiently stopped and the car with the gun moved along the abandoned siding where it was found. Holmes, recognizing in the plan Professor Moriarty's arrogant and ambitious signature, had quickly nudged the investigation into verifying that every one of the men set to guard the gun, as well has the crew of the train, had been mercilessly pressured into cooperation by vicious threats to their families, as well as the selective taking of hostages. As the truth was uncovered, with one man and then another breaking down and confessing his unwilling involvement, it became apparent that no direct connection could be made with Moriarty. With the great naval gun recovered and the hostages already freed following the theft, Holmes recommended leniency toward all those involved.

Holmes recognized from questioning the train's engineer that the man he described, waiting in a carriage and watching while the engineer's part in the plot was explained and proof provided that his daughter had been taken, was unmistakably Robert Magellan. Holmes had long known that the great bearded villain was one of the Professor's trusted lieutenants, and it was then that he decided to make use of a long-withheld resource of his own: Silas Haynor, a man who had spent his life dabbling poorly in many criminal activities, and who had some connections to Magellan. But older than those were Holmes's own connections with Haynor, whom he had met and aided years before, when living in Montague Street.

In those days, Holmes had been attempting to commence his career as a consulting detective, but with cases quite thin on the ground, he'd devoted a great deal of time in study, pursuing topics that he felt might be of use as his profession became more successful. Much effort was spent pursuing mastery of various subjects in the British Museum, located adjacent to his Montague Street rooms, but he also managed to make connections and associations with individuals of varying degrees of wickedness within London's criminal community, convincing them to teach him a surfeit of useful skills. Silas Haynor was one of these, and during the course of their association, Holmes had found opportunity to rescue Haynor's wayward daughter from a particularly verminous master in the East End – earning Haynor's eternal, if secret, gratitude.

Knowing that Haynor was associated with Magellan, it was easy for Holmes to make himself seen when asking Haynor for information. It could only help Haynor to shore up his own reputation within the criminal community when he, as a good soldier, immediately reported this to Magellan, who lost no time in arranging his aborted trap for Sherlock Holmes – and me as well, the satellite of little interest to Magellan who happened to be carried along to the meeting.

Inspector Patterson, the Scotland Yard inspector who was so deeply involved in building the case against Professor James Moriarty, was speaking with Holmes, arranging that he and I would be at Magellan's questioning in Woolwich in the morning – now just a few short hours away – when Holmes glanced over at the men being loaded into the Black Marias. He held up a hand to pause Patterson's comment and then stepped that way, apparently recognizing one of the seemingly anonymous fellows.

"McMurdo?" Holmes asked, surprised. "What in Heaven's name are you doing mixed in with this lot?"

He stepped over and pulled the shackled man to one side. I joined them. Patterson looked as if he would as well, but then he turned a different direction and began giving instructions to a sergeant.

The deep-chested man, who I recognized as one who had brought no weapon, choosing instead to rely on his fists, was somewhat shorter than his compatriots. He had been facing in the direction of the carriage in which he was to climb. He seemed at first as if he didn't hear Holmes's question. Then it became apparent that he did, but instead wanted to ignore it. He paused, and his great shoulders heaved with a deep sigh. He turned to face my friend, his protruding and heavy-set features carrying an expression of shame.

"Hello, Mr. Holmes," he rumbled, his broad shoulders slumped in defeat. "I'm sorry."

"Sorry?"

"For being part o' this – for being here tonight to attack you. I should ha' known you'd be out in front of us. I . . . I hoped you wouldn't recognize me when we . . . when we walked you down to the river . . . ." His voice faded.

"Why are you here, McMurdo?" Holmes asked, his voice dropping significantly. "You don't have any association with these people – or you shouldn't. What happened?"

390

The big man closed his eyes, and then squeezed them tight. A teardrop formed at the corner of one eye, just visible in the nearly useless lamplight. "What does it matter, Mr. Holmes? I'm fair caught."

Rarely had I seen someone appear to be so defeated. McMurdo was much changed from when I first met him a couple of years before, when he'd answered the door of Pondicherry Lodge in Upper Norwood. [4] On that night, the big man had looked at us with distrustful yet twinkling eyes, reflecting in the light of the lantern he held to investigate the unexpected visitors. That day had been a dreary one, with a dense and drizzly yellow fog lying low upon the great city, and mud-coloured clouds drooping sadly over the damp-slicked streets, and by sunset a great slimy vapor hung over the capital and the surrounding counties. McMurdo's suspicion of strangers had been in accord with the day's weather.

"I don't know none o' your friends," he'd explained to our guide, Thaddeus Sholto.

"Oh, yes you do, McMurdo," Holmes had replied. "I don't think you can have forgotten me. Don't you remember that amateur who fought three rounds with you at Alison's rooms on the night of your benefit four years back?"

"Not Mr. Sherlock Holmes!" exclaimed the big man, now clearly identified as a former prize-fighter, and apparently one of the bodyguards employed at Pondicherry Lodge. "God's truth! How could I have mistook you? If instead o' standin' there so quiet you had just stepped up and given me that cross-hit of yours under the jaw, I'd ha' known you without a question."

After he and Holmes exchanged a few further comments about the old days, we were admitted to the great house. My observations of McMurdo during that short period of time had led me to the conclusion that he was a good man, salt of the earth and a stalwart citizen, despite being on the sometimes-shady side of the law in terms of prize-fighting. And yet, now we found him under the orders of Professor Moriarty, by way of Robert Magellan.

"What happened?" repeated Sherlock Holmes.

McMurdo shook his head. "I can't say. It's . . . I have to stick to what I agreed."

Holmes was silent for a long moment, while McMurdo's eyes kept glancing at him, and then away, like a cowed dog who cannot directly meet one's gaze. Finally Holmes replied, his voice now almost too soft to hear.

"As I recall, you have a daughter. Is that not so?"

McMurdo's eyes widened then, almost in terror as if some secret had been exposed. He wasn't afraid to look at Holmes now, and he started to shake his head.

"Not to fear," whispered Holmes, his tone low but reassuring. "I understand. We'll speak to you soon, at Scotland Yard. No one will know. In the meantime, stay strong."

Then he backed away and raised his voice. "I should have known you'd come to such a sorry end, McMurdo. You always did scoff at the law." He turned toward Patterson. "Get this one to the Yard along with the rest of them."

He stepped away. McMurdo gave no sign of acknowledgement, instead allowing himself to be turned by a constable and shuffled into one of the prisoners' wagons.

Holmes stepped over to Patterson and whispered a word, and then walked five feet or so down the pavement, stopping to rub the bridge of his nose. I joined him and he said softly, "I'll apologize to Mrs. Watson tomorrow for extending your day even further. I'm afraid, if you're willing, that there's more work to be done – Now. Tonight. We need to get about disentangling McMurdo and his daughter from Moriarty's nets."

Chapter II

"A daughter," I said as Holmes and I walked down the Strand, the night still pressing around us, but now without the apparent threat of Magellan's troops slowly encircling us. "You believe that McMurdo has been forced into Moriarty's service by threats against his daughter – in the same way that the soldiers and train crew were manipulated into helping steal the naval gun."

"It seemed a logical leap," Holmes replied, "and if I'm not mistaken, McMurdo's reaction confirmed it. I've known him for a long time. He isn't the type to willingly involve himself in this type of work."

"Just how deep does Moriarty's influence extend?" I asked with angry exasperation, although after observing the Professor's pervasive influence for a number of years, the question was rather rhetorical.

"Deeper every day," was the weary answer. "Initially, he was a shadowy figure at the top of a large criminal pyramid, known only to the few lieutenants who have access to him – Moran, Magellan, Bassick, and a few others. You'll recall when I first became aware of him and would try to explain this arrangement to various inspectors – Lanner and MacDonald for instance – they would be skeptical. Thank Heavens Lestrade and Gregson and Bradstreet had more sense from the beginning, and were willing to work with us. MacDonald was convinced soon enough – he has a sharp mind – but I still have some questions about Lanner. Keep that in your thoughts, Watson, as we move forward."

"But my question stands," I answered. "How deep have Moriarty's tentacles twisted through society's fabric? We couldn't even be entirely certain of the loyalty of the constables on scene tonight."

Holmes nodded. "Tentacles is an apt image at this point. My initial description of Moriarty as a thin-legged spider sitting at the center of a web, feeling every vibration upon every strand, seems rather simplistic now. In those days, he was aware of everything, but rarely needed to involve himself – only when some complicated question arose. He mostly sat back, taking his financial cut that drifted upward to him from the many London's crimes, as inevitable as capillary action draws a liquid up a thread-like tube, defying gravity. But as his ambitions have grown, he's allowed his existence to become more widely known, using it as a force for intimidation, and increasing his influence.

"I believe that he changed – that he *wanted* people to be aware of him – after he fell from the Tower while trying to steal the Crown Jewels. [5] Before that, he'd treated his organization as an intellectual game – with me as the player on the other side of the chess board. After that affair, and his injuries, he could no longer pretend to be the innocent and persecuted mathematics professor, just trying to live a quiet life as an Army coach. He was known, and he realized the value of his reputation in coercing people to his will that hadn't already voluntarily joined him. And when he'd swelled his ranks all he could by that method, he became more aggressive still – using threats against family members."

He shook his head, and I asked, "Can he not be stopped?"

"You've asked me that before," Holmes replied, a tightness to his voice. "And what has been my answer? *You must give me time.* We have progressed quite far from five years ago, when this menace first became much more apparent. From his initial mistakes, I've been able – with the help of a number of good men such as yourselves and trustworthy policemen and Government officials, and a number of anonymous citizens whose aid will never be acknowledged – to slowly force Moriarty into a corner. But he will fight – like a rat, he'll fight harder now than ever. The next few months . . . things are going to become much more complicated. And dangerous – for all of us. There are so many pieces to watch. In many ways, the moves and counter-moves with Moriarty are even more complex than when we fought the Rippers." [6]

"But there were many of them," I said, "an abundance of killers, each with their own motives, working loosely in harness when it suited them to fulfill their various conspiracies. In the end, Moriarty is but one man. You've already removed Magellan, one of his lieutenants, and two others as well. His supporting base is being crumbled, one pillar at a time. Unlike the Rippers who hid in a dozen different rat-holes, you know where to find

393

Moriarty – his house in Russell Square, or the Limehouse tunnels. And every day, just as he intimidates someone into his unwilling service, you free two more of them – and they will see that. They'll see that he isn't invincible. That he can be beaten."

"Ah, but they'll also wonder and worry if it will be their own daughters whose throats are cut before I'm able to bring him down." He sighed. "Regardless, Watson, it's all coming to a head, and will be over in a few months. Moriarty is incommoded and inconvenienced and hampered, and with any luck, he'll be finished sooner rather than later."

Our conversation, not the first upon that topic, but rather a repetition of an oft-discussed subject meant to give us some comfort during the battle, had continued as we progressed down the Strand, turning left onto Wellington Street. Although offered a ride in a police vehicle, Holmes had wanted to walk, giving as his reason that he didn't want to arrive at Scotland Yard too quickly, forcing us to loiter while the prisoners were brought in and separated. I realized, however, that he also wanted time to think.

From Wellington we had emerged onto the Embankment, keeping up a steady pace until we reached the new Yard buildings, just across the road from Westminster Pier. Like everyone, I can never see various spots without associating them to memories of what occurred there, and I suppose that I'll never view that pier with recalling the night of 10 September, 1888, when Holmes and I boarded a police launch to follow Jonathan Small as he began his dash for freedom on the *Aurora*. Now, with the river fog rising to the level of the roadway, there was nothing to see but an undulating white blanket, shining with a faint luminescence in the darkness. If not for the gentle creakings of the moorings, the dock and the boats tied there might not have existed.

Scotland Yard is never truly quiet, even in the hours before dawn. Officers of all rank are always going here and there, quickly or with more leisured steps, all intent on their tasks. That night, a number of them were known to us, and they nodded in our direction – some more friendly than others – but none spoke as we moved deeper into the building, recognized and unhindered, toward the area where the inspector's offices are located.

Holmes has occasionally told me of his early days as a consulting detective, when interactions with the police were often frustrating at best. In his early twenties then, and fresh up to London from his abandoned university pursuits, I could imagine the impression he made, frequently, when bursting into the Yard, demanding to speak to someone with authority, either sharing information that wasn't requested or trusted, or demanding assistance or some fact toward completing his own investigation. (In truth, I had met him just a few years after this, first encountering him mere days before he turned twenty-seven years old, and he'd still displayed many of those traits.) There were some inspectors, back in those long-past days of the 1870's, who did listen to him and learned to trust him, and then to make use of his unique skills, realizing that his assistance would be invaluable toward clearing their own cases and obtaining justice – Inspectors Plummer and Nettings, for instance, and Lestrade and Gregson.

Patterson's office was empty – but that wasn't unusual, as he did not follow the typical inspector's way of doing things. Often out in the city, in disguise and amongst the lower elements to a great degree, he had made himself an expert on the subject of the underworld – a spider, in his own way, comparable to Moriarty at the center of a web. Initially Patterson hadn't fit in at the Yard at all, but it had made no difference to him as he set about his tasks, and as his successes steadily accumulated and his usefulness became apparent, he was left alone to carry on as he saw fit. He and Holmes had formed a good working relationship from Patterson's early days, especially after the matter of the Dicky Ferrin embezzlement scandal, and I always believed that Holmes had done much to help inculcate Patterson in the methods of the London criminal element, giving advice and instruction in many ways, including that of successful disguise.

Based on Holmes's whispered instructions in Fleet Street, Patterson had placed McMurdo into a separate interrogation room along a less-used hallway in the building's basement. It was there that we found him, after being admitted by Constable Wilkins, one of the officers that we most trusted. If Wilkins had been compromised by Moriarty, we were indeed in deep difficulties.

Wilkins shut the door behind us, leaving us alone with the prisoner.

McMurdo was no longer the defeated slump-shouldered man we'd encountered in Fleet Street. Instead, he was alert, tense, barely able to stay seated. His eyes were wide now, with the whites showing 'round the pupils as if he was on some sort of stimulant. I wondered what had come over him, and if we would soon be in a physical confrontation should he choose to make some move against us, but it was quickly apparent that his motivation was basic fear.

"My daughter," he said, his voice scraped hoarse with tension. "You mustn't – You can't cross these people, Mr. Holmes! Just let me take my punishment! It's the only way they'll let her be."

"So they don't have her yet," Holmes replied. "It's just the threat of harm that's been keeping you on the lead.

McMurdo nodded. "She's watched – all o' the time. I couldn't ha' taken her away if I'd tried. They're too many of them – everywhere. It was easier to do what they bid and then just hope . . . I'm always hoping.

Watching – for a way, you see. But I can trust no one, and have nowhere to go . . . ."

"You can trust me, McMurdo," replied Sherlock Holmes.

"Tell us about her," I interjected, hoping to calm him as he became more agitated at his intolerable situation.

McMurdo nodded and closed his eyes, perhaps sensing that relating his story was more productive. He licked his lips and locked the fingers of both hands together, large arthritic knuckles white underneath ancient scars.

"It was just over twenty years ago," he said. "I was but a lad in my twenties. Oh, I see your surprise, Doctor. I know I look to be sixty if I'm a day, but I've lived rough. Back then I wasn't so unpleasant to gaze upon, and I won the heart of a beautiful girl, my Lydia. We were both in service then, at a manor decorated with fine old copper beeches, not five miles on the far side of Winchester. It was a fine place back then. She worked as a maid, and I was in the stables. It's not great story one way or another – we were married and had a good life, and a year or so later we had a little girl, Jane. When our girl was but three, Lydia sickened and died. It was a tragedy, of course, but no different than what drops into other's lives. My heart wasn't in that place any longer, so I found another job closer to London, another manor south of the city doing the same work, and I settled in with my daughter.

"I married again, a good woman – a childless widow – who was already working there as the assistant cook. She helped raise Jane – as good a second mother as a girl could have. It was then that my size became of more interest – I became more broad as I aged and worked – and I became involved in the fancy – bare-knuckle boxing, and then prize-fighting. The owner of the manor had a fascination for it, and I was his fighter. It was just enjoyable, and nothing wrong, and I earned some extra money. You'll recall that's how you and I met, Mr. Holmes. My second wife died in '84, and you fought me at Alison's, at the benefit they arranged for me.

"I wasn't as broken up by Edith's death as I had been Lydia's. Edith was a good woman, but I'd never loved her like Lydia. Jane and I did fine and the next years passed. I continued to fight for a while, but I was getting too old and knew it. I was already worn out from the other work, too, truth be told, and when young Bartholomew Sholto put about that he was hiring bodyguards for the Lodge, not far from where Jane and I lived, it suited me down to the ground. He was an odd fellow, was Mister Bartholomew – though not as odd as his brother, Mister Thaddeus, I'll swear – but the work was easy beyond telling. I just had to be present, you see, in case some danger might show itself. None ever did – not until that terrible night.

396

Meanwhile, the two brothers tore up the grounds of the lodge like terriers digging for rats – never saying why, but we all knew they thought that their old dad had buried an Indian treasure.

"Then, after that night in '88 when you visited, everything changed. After Mr. Bartholomew was found dead, and that there had truly been a real treasure, there was no longer a place for me – for any of us. Mr. Thaddeus sold the lodge and went back to India. He'd always had a fascination with that place. The land developers knocked down the house and started cutting up the grounds into little streets and lanes, and building tiny cottages everywhere. I always half-suspected that Major Sholto really might have hidden some part of his treasure there on the grounds – he was ever a canny and suspicious sort – and that some house-builder maybe found it while scraping and digging and kept his mouth shut and is now living fine from the proceeds.

"In any case, Jane was of age then, and I found her a position with a seamstress off the Holborn, and moved us up to London. I've been working for a pub in Clerkenwell. The work is harder than I'd been used to for many a year with the Mr. Bartholomew, but I had to do something, and I was making do. Then, during the middle of this past year, a man who said he worked for Magellan came by, letting me know that my muscle would be working for them from now on."

His voice had grown dry, and I rose and opened the door, asking Wilkins to find some water. He nodded and departed, and I returned to my seat.

Holmes gave McMurdo a chance to pause, stating, "I've heard variations of this before. You were to keep your regular job, but be available when called upon for whatever little task was required. You might have initially resisted – " McMurdo nodded. " – but it was quickly explained to you that they knew where your daughter was. Who she was working for, her place of residence, her schedule, her routes to and from work and other errands – everything that they would need to know, should they choose that some harm would befall her. And the only way this might be prevented was if you capitulated to their requests."

McMurdo blinked while he followed Holmes's explanation, but seeming to decide that it was correct, he nodded again.

"Is she safe right now?" I asked.

McMurdo nodded, but a bit of the wildness came back to his eyes. He leaned forward. "I think so. She was as of last night. They don't call me very often, but when they do, I jump. I went to see her last night before joining Magellan's men – he'd heard of your meeting with Silas Haynor, and planned to put an end to you." He looked at Holmes, a pained expression twisting his face. "I've been with them before when a man has been beaten, or his shop ransacked. I was ashamed. But I've never . . . I was never in on a killing job. A few were like me – they had no choice. But some of the others were looking forward to it."

As Wilkins returned with the water and I poured him a glass, McMurdo looked back at me. As the constable departed, the old fighter continued. "My daughter was safe at home last night, in a small lodging house not far from where she works. But I fear, now, that since tonight has gone wrong, they'll punish us – all of us – by taking it out on those who are precious. You know how . . . You've heard how the Professor is." He whispered Moriarty's title, as if saying even that word aloud would attract the man's fiery gaze from whatever eyrie he was perched upon. "It wasn't our fault. We were just there to do as told. But he might think that one of us turned traitor, or got word to you ahead of time. Or he might just decide to teach a lesson to everyone – to show what a hard man he is."

He knotted his fingers tighter. "I'm being ground between two stones, Mr. Holmes. I did what they asked to save my daughter, to keep her safe, and still she may be punished. And what can I do? I'm in here, and there's no one who can protect her. No one!"

Holmes leaned forward, catching McMurdo's panicked eyes, and holding them until the big man had calmed himself.

"I will protect her, McMurdo. You can count on that. Now, I have many questions, and there is work to be done."

Chapter III

Although it was well after six a.m. when we walked out of the Yard, the November sky was still dark. Holmes frowned, muttered that, "It cannot be helped," and walked to the carriage that had just been arranged for our use. He'd already used the telephone inside to call and let his brother Mycroft know that we were on our way, though without providing a great deal of detail.

I've remarked elsewhere about the fixed rails upon which Mycroft Holmes carried out his day: From his lodgings at No. 48 Pall Mall to his unassuming office in Whitehall, and then back to Pall Mall, this time to No. 78, the Diogenes Club, just across the street from his rooms. [7] He had set times when he might be found at each and, like every normal man who wasn't out all night hunting criminals, he would be at home at this particular early hour.

Mycroft Holmes had cultivated a routine for himself that thoroughly suited his tastes, and especially the time spent at the Diogenes Club reflected the luxury-seeking aspect of his personality – but one ought never make the mistake from observing this aspect of his life that he was indolent or lazy. His heavy-set frame might prefer time spent seated in his specially made red-leather chair in the Diogenes Stranger's Room over movement, and he certainly appreciated the finer aspects of food and drink, but in no way was this to be taken for lethargic or shiftless loafing. His mind was always working, making connections and seeing patterns, wherever he was and at whatever time of day. Even as the clock over Parliament was chiming the seventh morning hour, we found Mycroft Holmes awake and alert, awaiting our report and the reason for our visit.

Once we were seated in Mycroft's study and had accepted strong black coffee and warm buttered scones, Mycroft gestured for his brother to speak. Holmes succinctly explained what had occurred during the previous night, leading to our interview with McMurdo.

"After we gained the basic points of how he was being pressured into assisting Magellan," Holmes stated, "it became apparent that three of the other men arrested tonight are in similar straits. Watson and I then spoke to each of them as well, although gaining their trust – all of them strangers to us who only know us by reputation – was initially difficult. We soon confirmed that in each case, however, that ongoing threats against their family members are what is keeping them in the Professor's servitude."

"What sort of threats? Death?"

"Or worse. McMurdo has a daughter. He was told that she would be taken and sold to an African brothel. The same for another man, Kildeane. The third, Belmont, has a sick wife that he adores and is terrified of losing – it was the simple threat of her particularly grim murder that keeps him in line. The fourth, Theobald, has a wife and small children. Their deaths, trapped in a house fire, were guaranteed if he doesn't cooperate."

Mycroft's eyes narrowed. I recalled discussions two years earlier, held during the months when we'd been attempting to catch the various Rippers, and how Mycroft and I had agreed that there was more suffering in the world – and the nation's capital – than could be helped. We'd each felt the same frustration, and Mycroft had commented, "It's as if one were trying to stop the incoming tide with a bucket." But in this instance, there were specific people that needed help – Holmes and I had met them and seen the anguish in their faces – and help could be provided, though it only be one small bucket's worth.

"What would you have me do?" Mycroft asked.

Holmes answered without hesitation. "I want you to take these men and their families away – in the same way you offered an alternative to the train crew and the soldiers and their families."

Holmes hadn't hinted to me his intentions, and I looked at him with some of the same surprise that Mycroft evinced.

"Take them?" I asked. "Where? Who is being taken?"

Holmes glanced at me, and then re-fixed his gaze upon his brother, who replied, "In the end, the only way that we could convince the soldiers and the crew to explain why they had helped Magellan carry out Moriarty's plan was to promise them safety – absolute safety – and the only safety that they believed possible was to completely leave England in secret to escape Moriarty's sphere of influence – at least for the foreseeable future – and take on new identities far away."

Holmes glanced at me. "They all felt – rightly so – that there is no safety on the Continent, and they instead insisted on relocation to America. They didn't realize that the Professor has reciprocal agreements with American criminals. We saw that in '88, when Moriarty provided assistance to the killer who came looking for Birdy Edwards."

I recalled the matter – and how Holmes had still ended up beating Moriarty in the end. [8]

Meanwhile, Mycroft and started to purse his lips, compressing them in and out while nearly closing his eyes as he considered Sherlock Holmes's new request. After a moment he took a massive deep breath and released it, almost with a sigh, before pulling himself straighter. His right finger was slowly inscribing a circle upon the arm of his chair, the only sign that he was somewhat perturbed.

"The plans to remove the fifteen men – soldiers and crew – and their entire families is already in place. In fact, tonight they'll be quietly taken by train to Liverpool, where they'll be discreetly placed on a ship bound for South Africa."

"Were there any problems extracting everyone?"

"Not at all. None of their families were actually being held hostage, only watched, and we were careful to spirit each person away at some moment yesterday when they were alone. The soldiers' families were easier than those of the railway men, obviously. There were a few unmarried soldiers whose parents were being threatened, but they have been approached and are willing to cooperate, with the understanding that when Moriarty and his organization have both been eliminated, they can return to England and resume their normal lives." He let a short silence fall into the conversation, as if reminding his brother that this immense task still needed completion, and the sooner the better.

A look of understanding passed between them, and then Mycroft asked, "How many more people are we talking about?"

"Not that many. The four men, two wives, two grown daughters, and two small children."

"Removing them may be a bit more difficult than the others," replied Mycroft, "as they are certainly being watched more closely, even as we speak. Yet it can be done, and adding ten more individuals to our plans isn't a burdensome problem. But the ship leaves *tonight*, Sherlock. It cannot be delayed. We used only our most trusted men to extract the families and transport them to Liverpool. You must do the same. They must be at the dock on time, and undetected. If any whiff of this is understood by Moriarty's agents – "

"I understand," said Holmes.

"And have you considered," added Mycroft, "that Moriarty may use this to his advantage? Once these people disappear, seemingly vanished without a trace, he can falsely spread the word that *he* was the one who removed them, making him seem even more omniscient and dangerous? And how can such a claim be countered without revealing the truth and possibly placing the families in new danger?"

"I believe that I've worked that out as well. We'll get out in front of Moriarty, leaking that each of the men has provided sworn statements of his involvement – not for the public press, but to be spread as gossip across London. After all, it's true that we'll have their statements in return for our help, and we can imply that they've been relocated to the Continent. Moriarty's attention will be misdirected, and it will undermine the notion that he's invincible. Once a few start to lose their fear of him, more will follow."

Mycroft nodded, but I could see he wasn't entirely convinced. "It won't fool Moriarty. I suspect hinting that everyone has headed east to the Continent will only serve to alert him that they are anywhere else *but* the Continent. Still, we can only try." He leaned forward, to emphasize, "But you must have them in Liverpool by *tonight*. The ship won't wait."

We returned to Scotland Yard by way of the waiting police vehicle. Holmes remained in quiet thought, his only comment being, "Patterson will not be pleased."

And he was correct. The inspector, living as he did with absolutely fanatical dedication toward stopping Moriarty to the point that he spent more time undercover than as himself, had an absolute black-and-white vision of justice and punishment. In his mind, the seven men arrested with Magellan were equally guilty, whether they had willingly joined Moriarty's cause or been coerced. He understood the pressure the men were under, forced to accompany Magellan on his various villainous outings, but that made no difference to him.

"They had a *choice!*" he whined irritably. I was reminded of some hint of gossip I'd once heard from Lestrade or Gregson that Patterson's father had been some low-level criminal. "And last night wasn't the first time they've assisted Magellan. We have confessions from all of them – the coerced and otherwise – as to numerous earlier beatings and other destructive mayhem. It isn't right to let some go free and for others to pay their debt!"

"Maybe not," agreed Lestrade, who along with Gregson and Bradstreet, were using their seniority to overrule Patterson. "But this is the way it's going to be."

"Think of it," added Gregson, "as tactically withdrawing from a skirmish to win the war."

"And rescuing these men and their families," Bradstreet contributed, "can be used as a tactical move against the Professor."

The six of us were crowded into Lestrade's small office, a secret meeting to explain what needed to be done. Patterson had erupted against the plan from the beginning, but when he realized that he had no choice in the matter, he shifted positions to add his practical knowledge toward safely extracting the various family members.

As the plans were developed for rescuing the families of each of the four men, Holmes indicated that his Irregulars, that band of street urchins who were pledged to being his eyes and ears, seeing everything, would be of great assistance. This time Lestrade disagreed.

"I'll admit their usefulness over the years," he stated. "But Mr. Holmes – Do you think it's wise to keep using them right now? A few of those lads, such as Wiggins and the Peake brothers, are your known associates. I'm not just speaking of involving them in these current events. If Moriarty decides to push back, he's going to use whatever leverage he can find – and him trapping and hurting those boys, no matter how canny they are, is a very real possibility that you must consider."

It isn't often that Sherlock Holmes has failed to take all the factors of a problem into consideration, but I believe that this was the first time this particular concern had surfaced for him. I knew that he'd taken precautions – both those I knew about and others that I didn't – to protect my wife and Mrs. Hudson, and likely me as well, but to him, the anonymity of the Irregulars was such a given that anything to the contrary had escaped notice. He'd always been proud that he'd recruited these lads (and lasses) who could so effortlessly vanish into the shadows – but Moriarty commanded creatures whose normal demesne was those same dark and lonesome places.

Holmes nodded. "You're right, Lestrade. I believe that for the next few months – until this matter is resolved – the Irregulars should maintain a very low profile. And there are a few who should specifically rusticate in the countryside for their own safety."

With information provided by the four prisoners who would be leaving, we soon had a clear idea of who to retrieve and where to find them. Without the use of his Irregulars to create distractions, Holmes pivoted to some of his older associates, including Porky Johnson and Burton Scott, two semi-criminals who both owed Holmes more than they could repay. They were not reformed, and they were not above recidivism in their day-to-day lives, but in their own ways, they were trustworthy, and neither had any love for Moriarty, nor were they under any obligation to him. Holmes had verified this on several occasions, and he was satisfied with their loyalty.

In each case, Holmes's agents were the first to quietly infiltrate the streets and alleys and passages around where the family members were to be extricated. When Moriarty's observers were located, word was passed back to waiting policemen, who just happened to walk by a moment later. Then, Lestrade or Gregson would initiate a conversation with the individual in question, phrasing questions offensively so that the matter quickly escalated to the point where the watcher was led away under arrest, allowing the family member to be approached.

McMurdo's daughter was the first. When informed that the coast was clear, the prize-fighter met her as she left home to walk to her place of employment. Without wasting any words, he told her to return inside immediately and gather what she needed to go away – clothing and valuable personal items – and to be back in five minutes.

"And be sure to bring your mother's photograph," he added.

"What? But Papa – I don't understand! Who are these men? Can you come inside too?"

McMurdo looked at Holmes, who was standing there with Bradstreet and me. Holmes shook his head.

"No," replied McMurdo. "No time. Things are in a hurry. I'll be waiting right here – and don't tell a soul inside what you're doing!"

She was back in ten minutes – understandable, given her confusion, and, as Bradstreet commented while we hurried away, impressive that she was able to quickly determine what was needed and what could be left behind.

"It wasn't so difficult," Jane McMurdo replied, nearly out of breath. She nodded to the carpetbag that Bradstreet was carrying for her. "We don't have very much, so packing what was needed was easy and obvious."

The procedure was completed successfully three other times, gathering in Thomas Kildeane's daughter from her job at an Aldgate pub, Michael Belmont's sick wife from their lodgings in Varden Street, not far south of the London Hospital in Whitechapel, and Andrew Theobald's wife and two young children from Rotherhithe.

It was only at the latter where any complications arose. Gregson had started conversing with Moriarty's watcher, heating the encounter to the

403

point where the suddenly angry young man would be temporarily taken into custody by the accompanying constables. But unlike the previous three instances, this young man, a lanky and greasy specimen in his early twenties who resembled a long-faced feral dog, instead chose to run. Fortunately for me, as I was feeling rather underused, he chose to escape by way of the street in which I was waiting with Holmes and Bradstreet.

Holmes, I'm certain, would have moved quickly and effectively in order to stop the fellow, but I stepped forward first, shoving my stick between the legs of the Professor's man, causing him to take a hard sprawl onto the pavement. After he was in custody, my quick examination showed no serious injuries. The sudden loss of his front teeth upon the roadway was only an improvement to his appearance. As we left, several children ran from the nearby shadows to collect them.

By noon, all four families were reunited and had been safely smuggled undetected into the cellar of the Royal Albert Hall. A special train car had been arranged for the 1:43 from Euston Station, and everyone was transported and safely placed aboard with time to spare. Having gone this far, Holmes and I agreed that we wished to see the matter through to the end – at least, the portion that was the end of how we could help. After the ship departed, the safety of all concerned would be in Mycroft's hands.

I sent a wire to Mary and rejoined Holmes on the platform, just minutes before we were to depart. We were both scanning surrounding crowd intently, as were the three police inspectors who had accompanied us. We observed nothing to concern us, and we were aboard and seated as the train left the station. Three hours later, our party had joined those already sent ahead by Mycroft, and not long after, the ship set sail.

"I don't know how to thank you, Mr. Holmes," said McMurdo before we took our leave of him. I could see that he was rather dazed at how quickly events had moved, but that was no different than the rest of the group. Anyone would have reacted the same way – going about one's business as normal in the morning, and then suddenly plucked out of routine and re-routed to the other side of the world. Around us, some of the families were just learning why such a move was necessary, having had no previous idea that Moriarty had gained a hold upon the men by so effectively threatening their family members.

I knew that for Holmes, no thanks were necessary, and that he was already considering the next move in this deadly game of chess where there would be only one winner.

Not long after, as we partook of a small meal in the station buffet, waiting for our return train to London, Gregson looked at Holmes, a frown darkening his light features.

"We can't rescue all of them, Mr. Holmes. This strategy worked this time, but what about the next? And the time after that? And this solution was only successful because these men were being forced into Moriarty's service. How do we stop those who join him willingly? What do we do about them?"

Holmes, who had only picked at his food in a distracted fashion, didn't answer for the longest time. But finally his gaze rose, and he looked at each of us in turn.

"We are restricted by laws, and decency, and doing the right thing. Moriarty is not. We're constrained by the fact that we are unwilling to cause damage and hurt. He is not. We're limited in our responses, lest we cross the line and use Moriarty's methods. He has no such limits.

"But what we can do," he added, "is to be *better* than Moriarty."

"How?" responded Lestrade. "How do we do that? We don't even know who we can trust. He has probably infiltrated the police. He probably has agents within high levels of government, and even some of the nobility may be under his sway. What advantage can we find?"

"We have the numbers," answered Holmes. "Do not forget that there are more good men than bad. When we find Moriarty's agents, we can convert them or prosecute and incarcerate them – or if necessary, legally execute them if warranted. That may not seem like much when they have no qualms at executing those who oppose them, but in the end, right will be victorious. But as we've seen, victories come with cost, and while victory will eventually be ours, there will a price to pay."

And victory was ours, but it required a terrible payment. Less than half-a-year later, Moriarty's organization was destroyed, and the Professor along with it, atop a remote Swiss waterfall. As Holmes wrote, just before he joined Moriarty in mortal and final combat, *"I am pleased to think that I shall be able to free society from any further effects of his presence, though I fear that it is at a cost which will give pain to my friends, and especially, my dear Watson, to you."*

The cost wasn't just the personal one suffered by Holmes and the friends who miss him. England, though free of Moriarty's pervasive evil, was left without one if its greatest champions. Still, as McMurdo and I were discussing the other day, following his recent return from Africa to his home now freed of threat, how the good accomplished by Holmes during his lifetime is a powerful and enduring testament not only to himself, but to all of those who suffer and sacrifice to protect what's good and decent in the world.

JHW
12 April, 1893

NOTES

1. In fact, Watson did change the name from "Mitre Court" to the fictionalized "Pope's Court". (See "The Red-Headed League", October 25, 1890.)
2. For more about Kirbishaw, the resident of No. 5A King's Bench Walk in the 1890's, see "The Curious Cardboard Boxes" in *The Collected Papers of Sherlock Holmes – Volume V: Chronicles*, and *The Strand Magazine*, Issue LIX, 2019. To learn how the later more-famous resident of No. 5A, Dr. John Thorndyke, came to inhabit those rooms, see "The Inner Temple Intruder", found in *The Collected Papers of Sherlock Holmes – Volume III: Accounts*, and also in *Sherlock Holmes and the Great Detectives*.
3. This map shows the area between the Three Bridges Station (top right) and the Crawley Station (bottom left). Though not specified in Watson's manuscript, it's possible that the temporary siding used to hide the train car was constructed in a wooded area about halfway between the stations, on the south side of the tracks. This area is still there to the present day.

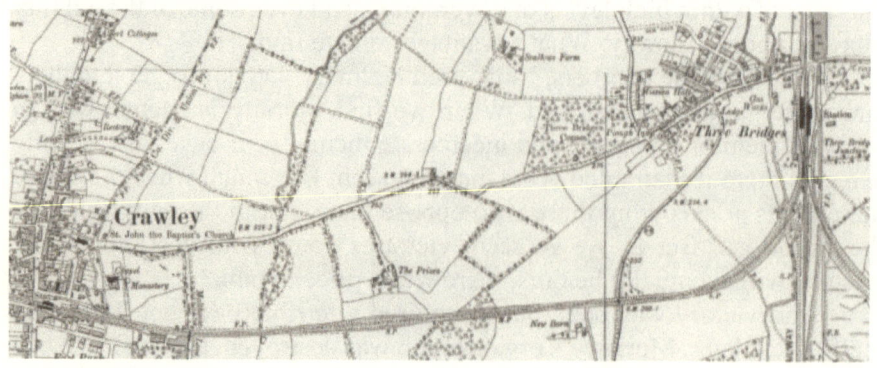

4. As related in *The Sign of the Four*, September 7-10, 1888.
5. These events, taking place from September 7-10, 1887 (one year exactly before *The Sign of the Four*) were recounted in the 1939 film, *The Adventures of Sherlock Holmes*.
6. A further examination of Holmes's overall investigation into the massive Rippers Conspiracy during the terrible Bloody Autumn of 1888 can be found in "November, 1888", published in *The Collected Papers of Sherlock Holmes – Volume III: Accounts*. It was originally published in *The Watsonian* (Fall 2015, Vol. 3, No.2) and in my online blog, *A Seventeen Step Program* at:
    https://17stepprogram.blogspot.com/2017/02/sherlock-holmes-versus-jack-ripper.html
7. An examination determining the exact location of Mycroft's rooms and the Diogenes Club can be found in my essay, "Pall Mall: Location the Diogenes Club", originally published in *The Baker Street Journal*, (Vol. 67, No. 2, Summer 2017).

8. For more about this affair, see "Some Notes Upon the Matter of John Douglas", available in *The Collected Papers of Sherlock Holmes – Volume III: Accounts*, and also *Beyond Holmes*.

A Meeting at the Lyons Café

"I'm getting too old for this," the man thought to himself, leaning back in his chair and stretching his long legs before him, aware that he was being watched, and carefully staying in character as he'd learned so long ago when, as a young man, he'd trod the boards for a year or so. He'd learned that even when he wasn't stage front, reciting his part, he was still expected to *be* the character, behaving as that character would, in every motion or pause, every turn or glance or scratching of his nose.

He really *wasn't* too old for this, and he mentally shook his head at the use of the cliché, even if it was only in the privacy of his own thoughts. Just a few weeks shy of his fifty-ninth birthday, he still felt that he was in his prime. His health was better than that of many others his own age, despite all the abuses he'd heaped upon himself as a younger man. He was very glad that he'd finally understood that his dark moods and restlessness could be distracted and eventually defeated by turning his mind in different directions – for if there were no problems to distract him along one line, he could do research down another, keeping himself occupied until the emptiness inside closed back up.

The café wasn't too crowded, as would be expected on a rainy Sunday night. The temperature was dropping, but he didn't think it would get cold enough to snow. Rather, the night would be miserable with that peculiar seaside dampness that slid under the collar and chilled the skin, and yet having the peculiar feeling that one's clothing was soaked with cold perspiration. In defense against it, he took a sip of whisky – *whiskey*, that is, he thought, smiling inward at the difference between the Scottish and Irish spellings of the word. After all, he was Irish – or had been for nearly a year now – and such little matters of pride and identity should now come natural. But they didn't, and it worried him, because he couldn't afford to slip. Not now that things were finally starting to get interesting. And dangerous.

"I really am getting too old for this," he thought to himself.

The patrons were what one would expect for that part of the city. He'd been to Liverpool many times before, but he'd never cared for it. He'd visited the rich houses, and the government buildings, and the Royal Albert Docks, but he'd never been here, Toxteth, just a couple-thousand feet east of the Royal Albert Dock. In truth, he'd never heard this place mentioned before until he was directed here to introduce himself to someone. He'd made his way to the Lyons Café, not far from the small boarding house in Mathew Street where he'd stayed since his arrival the previous night, directed by the little Irish widow, Mrs. O'Healy, who owned the place. She'd been anxious for news from America, somehow assuming that he would have certainly encountered at least one of her cousins who had long-ago emigrated there. Using tricks he'd learned long before from exposing fraudulent mediums – listening to her questions, seeing her reactions to his answers, and adjusting his next comment accordingly – had helped him to construct a series of vague-enough responses that she was pleased with what he told her, though thoroughly and completely fabricated, and anything that seemed a bit off in his answers was simply attributed to the fact that he was an Irish-American – or so he claimed – and she would expect such small differences from the statements of a true Irishman.

He shifted in his chair and wondered how long he'd need to wait before being able to converse with the man he'd come here to meet. He found that he was playing with his beard, even though he hadn't been aware of doing so, and, while he didn't abruptly stop, he frowned inwardly at himself. He hated the thing – it looked like a goat's tail on his otherwise clean-shaven face – but he'd begun growing it a full year before, in late 1911, on the very day that the Prime Minister had personally asked that he undertake this ill-defined but important mission.

The beard was a useful thing, a distraction on his lean face that helped prevent the need for more elaborate disguises, but he hated it nonetheless. Yet he realized that he was becoming a little too accustomed to it. Common sense told him that was a good thing – that he was sinking deeper into the safety of his role – but he didn't want to be too deep. After all, one day the beard would come off and he would return to his real life, and he didn't want to spend the next year after that reaching up to stroke his bare chin.

He tried to remember if he'd become someone else so deeply the last time he'd tried this, from 1891 to 1894, but he knew that he hadn't. Not really. He'd played so many roles during those three desperate years that when he'd returned to London in April of '94, settling back into his real life had been no worse than taking a long long-overdue bath to wash off too much accumulated grime.

There was some sort of commotion rising in the back room, whose plain closed door was straight across the café from where he sat, as if he were on the front row of a play as the play begins. He heard a woman's strident tones, and even though the words were unknowable, he knew that someone on the other side of the door was catching hell. He suspected that it was his the man he was here to see – a man named Alois.

He'd followed a long trail over the past year to this, the Lyons Café, in order to somehow convince Alois to introduce him to the German spy master. He'd started his pilgrimage in Chicago, graduated from an Irish secret society in Buffalo, and then crossed and ocean to give serious trouble to the constabulary at Skibbareen – all while making occasional hurried visits back to London to strategize with his brother, and then to Sussex in order to make appearances as himself before speedily returning to this, his other identity. It had taken a great deal of effort, and a bit of the luck that he'd always been able to make for himself, to create a completely new character and ease him into an existing society so that, just months after his initial appearance, it was hard to remember when he wasn't there.

When the Prime Minister had come to his Sussex home a year earlier to personally request his help, he'd agreed immediately, but it had taken a few more days to figure out exactly how he wanted to do it. There was a war coming, the Prime Minister had said, as if he were relating startling news that hadn't been considered before, which was ludicrous. The signs had been there since before the century's turn, and he and his brother, along with his best friend, had been working for years to prepare for, and also to delay, the inevitable for as long as possible. This had been done both in England and on the Continent, with a move here, a countermove there, the danger always ever-escalating. But now he was in much deeper than he'd ever anticipated, eleven months into a mission that could conceivably go on for many more years. As important as it was to delay the war, and get Britain on the best footing possible, he hoped that it wouldn't be for that long. "Christ," he muttered aloud to himself, his Irish-American accent flawless. He dropped his hand from his goat-tail beard, retrieved his *whiskey* (and not *whisky*) and took a sip as the plain door slammed open.

First out was Alois, the man he was here to meet. Alois was a German who had moved to England two or three years earlier, first settling in London, and then relocating to Liverpool. There was an angry frown on his pinched dark face. He was about thirty, had black hair – or so it appeared in the dim light of the café – oily-looking and brushed straight back, and a dark mustache. His lower lip was pulled up tight and thrust in forward what one might think was irritation, But he had also looked that way a few minutes earlier when he'd walked over to take the order for whiskey and a bowl of stew.

The plain door, which had drifted shut, opened again to reveal a dark-haired young woman of just twenty or so. It was to be assumed that she had been responsible for the rather shrill voice of a moment before. Her eyes went to Alois, who pointedly ignored her. Instead, he went to the small window leading back to the kitchen, where a couple of plates sat ready for delivery. He picked them up and carried them quickly – the long way around to avoid the woman – to a table along the back wall, near the

410

plain door, where he set them before a fat old man and his lady before pausing to converse with them for a moment.

The woman must have already been in the back room, because when the *faux* Irish-American had arrived a few minutes earlier, there had been no sign of her. Instead, he'd found his seat, placed his order with Alois, and within minutes received his food and drink. Then, seeing that everyone was taken care of for the moment, Alois had vanished through the plain door. It was only a minute or two later that the woman's voice had been raised, apparently causing Alois to flee back to his employment and responsibilities while the woman to followed, now watching him plaintively from the doorway.

The stew was good enough, and at least hot, and a couple more spoonfuls had been taken aboard when the plain door was pushed wider and another figure moved past the woman. He was a dark-haired fellow, his rather long hair parted on the right, and combed over his rather high forehead. He appeared to be around twenty-two, and he somewhat resembled Alois, although a bit shorter and heavier. His clothes were shabby, and his shirt, underneath his limp thin coat, had several colorful daubs, as if he had been painting – and not the walls of a room. No, the colors were more the shades one would find in amateur watercolors. A bit of closer observation showed that the backs of his fingers and knuckles had the same matching shades. Yes, definitely a painter, probably an amateur. There was something about his expression, however, already quite bitter for one so young, that indicated he would never be a true artist. He wouldn't have the soul for it. The *faux* Irish-American smiled to himself – that sounded like a description that his best friend might make, whereupon he would snap back to "Cut the poetry!"

Curiously, the younger man, who had been looking toward Alois, suddenly cut his eyes across the room, focusing with a dead contempt on the Irish-American, as if he'd heard his judgmental thoughts and was angered by them. It unnerving, jarring – like looking into a dark hole in the ground that has suddenly opened at one's feet, the cold breath of the deep earth and an accidental fall to terrifying death avoided by mere inches – but no outward response was given, other than to set down the spoon and take a sip of whiskey. And then the younger man looked away.

For just then, the woman made a small surprised jump and a tiny noise, and then turned to look behind her as yet one more person came through the plain door.

Alois, the younger man, and the woman, were all strangers. But not so the next to emerge from that back room. A familiar face – and one so unexpected in this grim place, and just at this moment, that the whiskey

411

caused a coughing fit as it went down the wrong way. It burned his throat while tears occluded his view of the newcomer.

The man was short – shorter than both the young man and the woman – but quite round. He had a round head as well, and he might have looked like a snowman if not for the black priest garb that adorned him. He carried a *cappello romano* in one hand, which when placed on his head out of doors would further ruin the snowman effect. In the other was a bundled black umbrella, usually never far from his grip. It had come in handy before on a number of occasions – and not just for protection from the rain.

The coughing caused by the whiskey's burn drew their attention, but Alois, the woman, and the younger man all looked right back at one another in some sort of *tableau*, a moment frozen in time that could go in any direction, any possibility. Then the woman threw back her shoulders and marched to the front door, throwing it open and stepping outside into the night. The younger man went to Alois and began to whisper harshly, his conversation punctuated with stabbing gestures. Meanwhile the priest, for that is what he was, glanced across the room and, seeing a subtle welcoming gesture of a couple of slightly moved fingers, crossed over and sat down.

"Mr. . . . ah . . . ?" asked the priest, looking at the man who was much changed from the last time they had met.

"Altamont," said the *faux* Irish-American in a flat mid-Western accent, with just a tinge of Irish lilt. He finished wiping his eyes. "From Chicago. You might recall when we met a few years ago."

The priest nodded. "I do. We've both traveled a bit since then."

"Would you care for something to drink?" asked Altamont, pushing back the remains of his stew. It had been more than decent, but he'd never been one to over-eat, and enough was enough.

"No thank you," said the priest. He looked Altamont up and down and said very softly, "You are much changed, sir. This is no short-term disguise. That beard – Well, it's been cultivated for a while."

"A year," said Altamont slowly, his voice just as low. He glanced from side to side, making sure that there was no one nearby who could overhear them. He'd been careful to choose this seat when he arrived, with his back to the wall facing the doorways in much the same way that an American gunfighter or Italian mobsman seats himself when in a public place so as to see approaching enemies. He'd also checked the table when he'd arrived for one of Edison's carbon-button microphones – there wasn't one, and he and the priest could converse freely – although this café could not be considered a safe space. Alois might simply work here as a waiter, or it could be the front for the German spy network working actively in Liverpool.

"I thought you were in Sussex," said the priest. "Clearly you have a different agenda."

Altamont nodded. "A year ago," he said, his voice very low and very un-Irish, "the Government asked me to help root out the German spies in England. The war we've feared for so long is now considered to be inevitable – it's not *if*, but *when*. I think that they pictured me moving back to London and setting up a room in some great stone ministry building, slowly filling it with cabinets of reports and diagrams pinned to the walls, and clerks running in and out with dispatches. That's what my brother went ahead and established. But I decided that the best plan would be to come at the situation from an oblique angle – to worm my way into their organization with established credentials that they can respect, and then stay embedded for as long as needed, gathering names and intelligence while feeding them crumbs to gain their trust before giving them a big lie at the very end, to choke them at just the right moment."

"And how does that get you here, in a dingy Liverpool café on a cold and rainy December night?"

"I considered the best way to approach the problem, and quite frankly, I didn't want to pretend to be German for as long as this might take. Then the idea of being Irish occurred to me. Quite frankly, I've borrowed a good bit of my plan from a brave American I met back in '88 – John Douglas, as I knew him then. He had gone by several other names before that. His real name was Birdie Edwards – a Pinkerton man – who had infiltrated a hive of Pennsylvania murderers called 'The Scowrers' under the name of 'John McMurdo' – a pleasant and winning Irishman from Chicago. He lived among the thieves and murderers for months, participating in their rituals, joining the crimes that couldn't be avoided and preventing those that he could, and gathering evidence until the lot of them – or at least almost all of them– were caught up in one great bag and brought to trial."

The priest nodded. "I understand. You went to Chicago and took on this new identity – *Altamont* – and you've been progressing since then."

Altamont nodded. "And gaining credibility as I went. I'm trying to attract the attention of the German spymaster, and I learned that one of his top agents is here – the waiter." He cut his eyes toward Alois. "I've arranged a meeting – but it seems that you were already here to meet with him first." He took a sip of whiskey, keeping his eyes locked across the glass upon the little priest. "Considering the importance of my mission, might I ask why?"

The smaller man smiled. "You may, and perhaps something I say may help you. Nothing that I've heard is secret under the sacred seal of confession." He glanced toward the counter, where the younger man was

413

now standing while Alois walked over to another of the tables, speaking with a man about something on his plate.

"A couple of years ago – in mid-1910, it was – I met Bridget – it was she whom you just saw leave. She is a good Catholic, but she'd had a falling out with her father over Alois. The two of them had met a few months earlier at a Dublin horse show and, in spite of the vociferous objections from her father, eloped to London, where they were married at the Marylebone Registry Office. Soon after, now feeling quite guilty for the events that led to her marriage, she came to the church where I was serving and spoke to me about it. As I said, this wasn't under the seal of confession, so sharing it with you is no violation.

"I counseled her and provided, I believe, some peace. Besides feeling guilt about her non-Catholic marriage, she was upset because her father disliked Alois so much – her husband is German, after all, and ten years older than Bridget. Soon after, the couple decided to move to Liverpool. I had no further thought of them until today, when I happened to be here on other business and ran into her. I'm on my way to Dublin with instructions regarding the planned response when the third Irish Home Rule Bill comes up in a few months. It's expected to fail, and it's uncertain what the reaction will be.

"I encountered Bridget in passing on the street, and she begged me to stop by their small apartment in Upper Stanhope Street. There, she told me what had happened in her life since her move to Liverpool, confiding that their marriage has been an unhappy one. She and her husband have a small son, born last year, and sadly Alois beats her when he drinks – which is far too often. She fears for their safety, and also that he will leave her and return to Germany, and she asked for me to speak with him – for all the good that it will do.

"Bridget asked a neighbor to watch her child, and then we set out for this café – a walk of about half-a-mile, I suppose. Not long after we left their apartment, we ran across Alois's half-brother, Adolf, who has been staying with them for the last month or so. He is . . . Well, perhaps I should keep that opinion to myself. But I gather that his presence is a further strain on both their marriage and their finances, as he refuses to find a job, instead, practicing to be a painter – an artist. If the works lying around their apartment are indication, he will not achieve his goal. They are dark things, and odd – the shadows, for instance, fall the wrong direction – *toward* the light source which causes them, instead of away.

"But in spite of the added strain that Adolf causes on the household, and the fact that the two brothers don't get along at all, Bridget felt that Adolf should come along with us and help to talk some sense into her husband – that he should ease his drinking, and perhaps start attending

414

church. We arrived at the café and she wheedled Alois into the back room. Between you and me, I knew it was a wasted effort – and it was – because he didn't have the time to talk with us now, and his heart is that of a hardened sinner, but I was compelled to try. Miracles do happen, after all. I have seen them – and so have you, although you might not name them as such."

Altamont nodded. "With age comes wisdom – and I'll admit that includes a realization that man's understanding of the overall world – Nay, the entire universe – around us, is really nothing at all. We understand the greater picture as well as an ant would if he were placed in the British Library and told to read and understand every book. You're right, Father – I have seen miracles, and I would not gainsay them, although man's power of reason, limited as it is – "

His thought was to remain unuttered, however. The front door suddenly opened and a plump well-dressed man in his fifties entered, paused, glanced around the room, and then walked with confidence toward and then behind the counter. The younger brother, Adolf, had by then slipped over to one side, now standing once more at the plain door. Alois glanced toward the counter, and then continued his conversation with the customer.

The well-dressed man moved as if he owned the place – and in fact, it would soon be known that he did. This was Mr. Herbert Creighton Vines, a fellow of great importance in his own mind, and in actuality, he did have some little influence in that immediate neighborhood, owning several other cafés, a number of downtrodden lodging houses, and a couple of brothels that catered to the sea trade. It was a rough neighborhood, quite close to the Mersey, but he had influence there.

He went to the till, pulling it open to retrieve the day's takings – although from the viewpoint of Altamont and the priest, it simply seemed as if he were opening a drawer. But it wasn't simple for very long, as he slammed it shut and cried, "Alois! Today's money – *It is gone!*"

The room, which had carried a low buzz of conversation throughout the last few minutes, fell silent as Lyons immediately became the center of attention.

Alois left the customer to whom he'd been talking and hurried over to Vines, where they began to carry on a fierce but whispered conversation, with much gesturing – first upon Vines' part, and then the German's. At one point, Alois raised his voice, saying in a thick German accent, "But Mr. Vines – !" Meanwhile, Altamont tapped a finger upon the table, thinking quickly.

"The half-brother stole the money," he said quietly.

"How do you know?" asked the priest.

415

"While we've been talking, I watched him slip open the drawer and load his pockets. I was trying to decide what to do about it – to ignore it, or inform Alois to somehow win his favor – when the door opened and that man came in – presumably the owner."

The priest glanced from the rising tensions between Vines and the waiter and back to Altamont, whose expression had grown quite dark.

"What is the difficulty?" he asked. "Surely it will be quickly sorted."

"But in what way?" hissed Altamont. "Up to this minute, the variables of the situation were only somewhat known to me. Now, regardless of whether Alois is accused, or his half-brother Adolf is exposed as the true thief, the situation will be turned upside down – at least for a while, and what I know may not matter. I need an introduction from Alois to the next spy up the chain, and I don't know enough about him to know how being fired from this job might affect him."

Before the priest could reply, Altamont continued. "I must do something bold – but I'll need your help. Can you distract Adolf – talk with him while I speak to Alois and the owner? I very much doubt if he would step forward and confess what he's done, but you must keep him from doing so."

The priest smiled. "It's an ethical dilemma, and that's for sure: Convince a thief to hold his tongue and hold onto his guilt, versus the greater good – "

"I assure you that it's for the greater good."

The priest nodded. "I'll worry about Adolf's soul in a few minutes, after your task is complete. But for now, what are you planning?"

"I recall that Birdie Edwards gained the trust of his foes by confronting the authorities. I'll do the same."

And by now the authorities were present – in the form of a weary-looking constable who had been summoned by the café owner regarding the emptying of his cash drawer. Altamont looked at the priest and nodded. "It was good to see you again, my friend. I look forward to doing so in the future."

"As they say across the Irish Sea," answered the priest, 'May the road rise to meet you.'"

They glanced toward the counter, where the owner was outlining for the policeman how he'd found the drawer empty and, with vicious jabs of an extended forefinger toward his waiter, how Alois must be the guilty party.

With a nod to the priest and a sighed comment – "I'm getting too old for this!" – Altamont rose and then began to move toward the door. When his movement caught the attention of the policeman, he broke into a run, seemingly slipping awkwardly on a slick spot as he reached the door, delaying him just enough to allow the constable to lurch into motion behind him and follow outside. Meanwhile, the priest rose and walked slowly to the younger brother, Adolf, by the plain door, moving as one would toward a skittish wild animal. He was soon beside the man an,d looking up into his face, he began to speak, rather amazed at what he saw and forcing himself to continue.

The constable returned with Altamont in tow, dragging him beside the owner and the waiter. With a rather vicious shake of his arm, Altamont explained how, must a few minutes earlier, he had seen that the waiter was in the back room and, when no one was paying any attention, he'd risen and crossed to the counter, where he'd opened the drawer and pulled out the daily takings. He then reached into his pocket, pulling out a roll of bills, which he handed to the owner.

Altamont suspected that his own funds, being used to fund this lie, were more than the owner was used to seeing on a typical day, let alone a rainy Sunday night, but he counted it and declared that he was satisfied and wouldn't press charges. It was likely that he didn't want any more association with the police than was necessary. The constable seemed relieved, but provided the typical warning that he'd best not see Altamont back in that neighborhood any more. Then he spun him toward the door and released him, causing the older man to stumble on his way outside. As he looked back before leaving, he observed Alois giving him a speculative glance. He knew that the German would now be willing to talk with him, if only because he was curious about Altamont's actions. And when Altamont explained it to him correctly, invoking the names of their common acquaintances, there would be enough of a connection for Alois to pass him upwards toward the German spymaster.

Finding a nearby alley, Altamont chose to wait for the priest. He was contemplating how best to re-approach Alois when he found that he was playing with the goat-tail beard – all without conscious thought. *This is intolerable!* he growled to himself, vowing to be more mindful of his every action. Someday he would leave Altamont behind, and he didn't want – at any time when that day came – to find himself still in any part of Altamont's skin.

The priest came out of the café and paused, looking at the ground. He stood there for almost a minute, a long and awkward time while Altamont waited to raise a hand and attract his attention. Finally, the priest gave what looked like a shudder, and then he threw back his shoulders as if tossing off something that was trying to climb upon him from behind.

Then he looked up and noticed Altamont in the shadows across the street. It almost looked as if he were deciding whether to cross over and speak one more time, or if he might turn and go in the other direction. Then, his decision made, he stepped forward toward the alley.

Altamont was shocked at his appearance. It was as if the little priest had aged ten years in ten minutes. Underneath his flat black hat, his face was pale and sunken, and his fingers clutched his umbrella so tightly that his knuckles were white. His lips were working as if repeating a catechism, and they were wet, as if he'd forgotten to swallow.

"Good God, man!" cried Altamont in a low voice when they were back in the alley, away from the street. "What has happened?"

The priest swallowed, and again. "I . . . barely know how to describe it. When . . . when we encountered Adolf on the street, while walking here, I gave him very little notice. The same when we spoke to Alois in the back room. But just now . . . when he turned his full attention onto me, curious as to why I seemed to know about his theft and what my motive might be in keeping him from becoming involved in your . . . intervention, he . . . he . . . ." He fell silent, searching for the words. Then he looked up. "When he turned his full gaze upon me, and then when I saw directly into his eyes, it . . . he . . . it . . . *It was as if I was seeing the fires of Hell!* I . . . ." His voice faded. There were no more words to explain.

The priest searched Altamont's face, seeing if he had conveyed what he had felt and seen, knowing that his words were inadequate – they could never explain what he'd perceived – and that he was talking to a man who prided himself on rational logical thought. "No ghosts need apply," Altamont had once said in another life, and surely that applied to . . . whatever it was that the priest had tried to express. His despair grew with the idea he'd never be able to adequately share what he'd seen, or how he could warn anyone. But then, the other man gripped his shoulder, forcing his attention back to the present.

"Father Brown," said Sherlock Holmes, all pretense of the Irish-American criminal Altamont gone for just that moment. "As I said, I have seen miracles – and as that word is defined, those are not just the product of the intervention of Divine Goodness. A miracle is, by definition, a surprising and inexplicable event, usually considered to be the work of a divine agency – and sometimes these interventions are terrible. The Bible tells of a flood that killed everyone on earth, save for one family. Entire cities were wiped from the earth for sinning against the Divine. The Egyptian Army died while pursuing the Israelites across the Red Sea during a miracle that only benefited them. The miraculous can also have a sinister side.

"I don't know what you have seen, but now that you have seen it, you can be an agent to oppose it. You have seen this for a reason, and there is no man I'd rather have on our side in the coming months and years."

"But – " said Father Brown, still shaken but rediscovering his usual resolve and moral certainty once again.

"You have been surprised," said Holmes. "Shocked by something beyond your immediate understanding. But you *will* understand. I am certain of it. And consider – now you *know*, and knowing is better than not knowing."

The priest nodded, at first hesitantly, and then more sure. He raised his hand to Holmes's, still gripping his shoulder, and squeezed in return.

Then, stepping apart, he said, "What is your plan now?"

Holmes – now Altamont once more – stroked his beard, saying, "Tomorrow I'll arrange an encounter with Alois Hitler and introduce myself, explaining that my own masters wouldn't have wanted to see him arrested. Then I expect things will move along as planned."

"And the half-brother?" asked Father Brown. "Adolf Hitler? Will you also – ?"

Altamont shook his head. "I think not. I am, of course, most curious whether I would also see what you observed, but I can think of no reason to involve him in my business with Alois. Perhaps I'll run across him another time." He started to add that for now, he would leave that to the priest, but he could see just how shaken the little man was at whatever he'd seen, and instead decided to end their renewed acquaintance then.

"Farewell, Father," he said, offering his hand. "Until we meet again."

"Go with God, Mr. Holmes."

They shook hands and then stepped back onto the rain-slicked pavement, lit only by the light from the café window across the street. Altamont turned north and the priest south, and then both were lost in the murky darkness.

NOTES

The question of whether Adolf Hitler, the most evil man to walk the earth until recently, lived in Liverpool from November 1912 to April 1913, has been debated for years. According to a manuscript written in 1930 by his sister-in-law, Bridget "Cissie" Dowling Hitler, Adolf moved there to avoid conscription in Austria-Hungary. She wrote that he spoke very little English, never obtained a job, and spent his time wandering the streets and drinking at a few local pubs.

Bridget Dowling had met Alois Hitler, Jr. in 1909 – some sources say at Dublin Horse Show, and others at Dublin's Shelborne Hotel. For a time, Alois convinced both Bridget and her father that he was a wealthy hotelier touring Europe. Bridget's father did not like the non-Catholic Alois, who was nine years older than his daughter, then just seventeen and fresh out of Convent School. In spite of the elder Dowling's feelings, Bridget and Alois traveled to London in June 1910 and eloped, moving back to Liverpool. Their son, William Hitler, was born nine months later in March 1911.

In Liverpool, Alois and Bridget lived at 102 Upper Stanhope Street, later destroyed by German bombings during World War II. During this time, Alois was employed at a cafe in Toxteth, a rough neighborhood to the east of the docks along the Mersey. Their uneasy relationship continued until May 1914, when Alois abandoned his wife and child, returning to Germany, where he bigamously married another wife.

In her 1930's manuscript, Bridget indicated that not only did Adolf Hitler stay with his half-brother's family for a while, but it was during that time she awakened his interest in astrology, and she also convinced him to shave the sides of his mustache, giving him that idiotic look that marks him as an irredeemable moron, along with being one of history's most evil pieces of filth.

Alois and Bridget's son, William, lived in Germany for much of the 1930's, working in a position that had been obtained for him by his half-uncle Adolf, but in 1938 he fled, not liking what he was seeing, and he and his mother ended up in the United States. At the start of the war, William was drafted into the US Navy, curiously retaining his name, "William Hitler". He was wounded, received the Purple Heart, and was discharged in 1947. Only at that point did he – and his mother – change their last names to "Stuart-Houston". They are buried side-by-side in Coram, New York.

Most historians discount the story of Adolf Hitler's visit to Liverpool as an urban legend. The only source is Bridget's manuscript, probably written in 1940-1941 during the early years of the war when there might have been an interest in its publication. In the 1970's, historian Robert Payne, writing his own biography of Hitler, found the manuscript, and a number of excerpts were published in newspapers. While historians general treat the idea as false, there is also no firm evidence that Adolf Hitler *wasn't* in England during those months.

I personally think that Hitler was in England. To paraphrase "The Second Stain":

"How did you know[he] was there?"
"Because I knew [he] was nowhere else."

More about the topic can be found at the BBC Website "Your Story: Adolf Hitler – Did He Visit Liverpool During 1912-13?"

https://www.bbc.co.uk/legacies/myths_legends/england/liverpool/user_1_article_1.shtml

The Curious Actions
of Captain Graves

Consulting hours were in session.

"The important thing to remember," Mrs. Finger was saying, her voice strained with emotion, "is that when Jeffrey – that's my son, you'll recall – when Jeffrey went back into the dining room after the wedding breakfast, the necklace was gone – and only Oswald – my other son, he's much younger – could have taken it, even though he claims he left fifteen minutes *after* we arrived home, staying just long enough to wish his sister the very best in her new marriage. Did I mention that they'd had a falling out last year?"

Holmes was staring at her with widely opened eyes. She seemed to appreciate his attentiveness, but I, who knew him, realized that he was much less engaged than if his eyes were shut. He was only allowing her to repeat herself because he held her in high esteem, having known her from his Montague Street days. I had been interested to meet her, but when it became apparent that no interesting tales of those years would be mentioned or discussed, and that she would instead immediately proceed to relate her account of a missing *cloisonné* necklace, a family heirloom, I settled in to listen and take notes. When the tale began to repeat itself, I set aside my notebook and took a sip of my cooling coffee.

When my own affairs were arranged accordingly, I always made a point of being in our sitting room, in my chair, while Holmes held his morning "consulting hours", as he sometimes phrased it. It was then, in those earlier days before his fame had spread so widely, that visitors from all walks of life journeyed from near and far to our rooms to seek his counsel.

As Holmes allowed Mrs. Finger to ramble, I recalled that from the earliest days that he and I had shared rooms, those in need had sought him out in this same way, although at first, I'd had no notion as to why. Wounded at Maiwand less than half-a-year before Holmes and I met, I was turned inward then, recovering both mentally and physically. Therefore, after the first week or so in Baker Street when Holmes began to ask to use the sitting room in the mornings "as a place of business" to meet with his various callers, I made no objection, instead withdrawing upstairs to my bedroom, or bundling myself up and setting forth in the January chill on a forced march to try and regain my strength.

Before absenting myself from our shared sitting room, I would often get a hurried chance to study one or another of these visitors. The first that I ever recall encountering was a rather obese railway porter in his velveteen uniform who, as I was shutting the door behind me, was facing Holmes in front of the fireplace, arm outstretched, and dramatically pouring a sizable number of coins upon the rug.

Over that first month or so, the great variety in Holmes's visitors was astounding. Rich and poor, city and country, young and old, official and furtive – they all seemed to find their way to that small nondescript house in Baker Street. Sometimes it would be men in plain clothes who, like Lestrade and Lanner, who were later introduced to me as Scotland Yard Inspectors. Once or twice constables paid a call, leaving me with especially strong curiosity as I shuffled out, and not a little worry that my fellow lodger was in some sort of trouble with the law. Several times, I would descend for a convalescent winter walk to discover someone tarrying just inside the front door, left there by the landlady to wait his or her turn, and on other occasions an intended visitor would be pacing outside upon the pavement, seemingly working up the nerve to ring the bell.

On a few instances, Holmes had provided what seemed to be an intentional opportunity for me to question him about his profession, but my own delicacy prevented me from forcing my fellow lodger into confiding in me when he wasn't willing to do so directly. Likewise, my own reticent nature, heightened at that time by ill health, prevented me from questioning Mrs. Hudson – for should she know anything about why the visitors were there, my efforts to winkle out the reasons would seem, in my mind, akin to gossip.

All of this began to change in early March of that year, when Holmes, having finally divulged that he was a "consulting detective", impulsively invited me to grab my hat and join him on a summons from the Yard to an empty house off the Brixton Road, where a man's body had been found under mysterious circumstances. After that, Holmes started to include me in more of his investigations – certainly not to the degree of participation that would follow in later years, but enough for me to begin to study his methods. My health still prevented me from joining him on all of his travels, when he had to get up from his armchair and "move around", as he called it, but I was no longer asked to vacate my seat by the fireplace during his morning consultations. Soon I was taking notes – initially for my own benefit, and to Holmes's amusement, but when I was later able to refer back to them in a helpful way, my usefulness became more apparent. (And in the back of my mind, I must admit, I nurtured the seed of one day publishing accounts of some of these investigations, if only to make the general public aware of Holmes's gifts, and to give him the credit he was due.)

Of course, I was certainly not privy to every one of Holmes's investigations, for he was far too busy, and I had my own affairs to conduct. In 1881, I had initially thought to return to the Army after my recuperation was complete, but when the Army had other ideas and that plan crumbled to ash, I had to find some way to pay my share of the rent. After painstakingly rebuilding my health, I began to find work, assisting at Barts and the London Hospital in Whitechapel, and then as a *locum* for private physicians. Additionally, I traveled a bit, once in relation to a distant family matter, but I was never gone from Baker Street for very long. And when I had the chance, I always observed Holmes's morning visitors with great interest.

Now, from the vantage of several decades later, and having related a couple-dozen of Holmes's cases to a gracious and interested public, I realize that I may have given several false impressions. One is that I was some sort of paid lackey, doing nothing but hanging around our sitting room like an overgrown page, answering the door for clients, fetching them a drink, taking notes, expressing pop-eyed and doltish amazement at some deduction, and regularly blurting foolish statements as a springboard for Holmes to leap in the correct direction. Nothing could be further from the truth. The other incorrect assumption on the reading public's part is that Holmes only had a few cases widely scattered amongst a vast wasteland of nothingness where he was continually mired in a series of dark depressions, curled on the sofa in a fit of sulky dumps and brown studies, unshaven and unwashed and drifting in a narcotic haze, and only barely functional or salvageable on the best days by way of my unceasing and unappreciated efforts. Perhaps in mentioning a few of his minor eccentricities I have given the impression that they made up the whole of the man, and in only publishing a few dozen narratives, I've made it seem as if he had no other cases than those I've chosen to illustrate his methods and personality – but this is wholeheartedly incorrect.

In fact, except for those early days before his fame began to spread, Holmes stayed quite busy, which suited him down to the ground. There were periods, certainly, when he despaired about the sameness of some of his cases, and the more *outrè* affairs were certainly the most satisfying to both of us, but he was first and foremost a *professional*, working very hard indeed to create the profession for which he was so long the sole member. He would not demean that by unprofessional behavior – even on such a morning in April 1886, when Mrs. Zelda Finger was repeating, now for the fifth tedious iteration, the story of her daughter's curious wedding and the vanishing necklace.

When she finally paused to take a breath, Holmes intervened.

"How long was Oswald alone in the dining room?"

Mrs. Finger was rattled, having intended to reiterate previously stated facts. "Not more than a minute. As I believe I mentioned, Reverend Greer – "

"Quite. I would advise, then, that when you return home, you should immediately look in the adjacent pantry and – How tall is Oswald? Not much over five feet, as I recall."

She nodded. "His father was short, too. He always – "

"Then look in the adjacent pantry, on a shelf about five feet from the floor – at Oswald's eye level. He will have pushed it back behind something. You say that he hasn't returned since the wedding?"

"That's right."

"And he has no key?"

"No, not after the row he had with his brothers last winter."

"Then he hasn't had a chance to retrieve it." Then he stood, indicating that the interview was complete. "You shall have the necklace back before he next comes to call, surely with some ruse to enter the pantry. Please let me know when you recover it."

Mrs. Finger seemed surprised that the consultation was seemingly at an end, but she nodded and stood as well. "Thank you, Mr. Holmes. I do appreciate it so."

I had stood as well, and after she was gone I went to call for downstairs for more coffee. Then, turning back to Holmes, I commented, "I noticed that there was no exchange of recompense – not even a few coins. What about your fees? Set upon a fixed scale – ?"

He waved a hand. "Except when I choose to remit them altogether. I've known Mrs. Finger for ten years, and she was once kind to me when I very much needed it. Besides, after Count Vevlo's generous reward last week, I can be charitable. As I recall, he made the same generous payment for your medical services as well, so you know of what I speak."

I nodded, about to reply, when he stepped to the mantel and retrieved a note that had been delivered the night before. "I didn't mind giving a few words of advice to Mrs. Finger – she and I have an old friendship, and I had an obligation. This, however, is an obligation of a different sort."

He handed me the short letter. It was simple request for an appointment at ten that morning – just a few minutes away – for someone named Charles Cruft. The author of the letter was apparently a friend or acquaintance of Cruft's named Major Henry Augustus Candy. The Major's handwriting was certain and straightforward, and the letter itself was on a plain heavy sheet, without monogram or address. It provided no other useful information.

"I once provided a service of some consequence to Major Candy, and as a result, he has sent two additional cases my way – both of which were quite useful in advancing my little practice, although each turned out to be rather unpleasant and seamy, involving military affairs and dishonorable conduct. One ended in the guilty party committing a very messy suicide. I don't recall either of them with fondness, and I wonder what this Charles Cruft will tell us.

We didn't have to wait long, for Cruft was prompt, knocking a few minutes later at the sitting room door. Mrs. Hudson followed him in almost immediately with a new pot of hot coffee and an extra cup, and our guest accepted the offer to partake with the enthusiasm of a long-time addict of the dark brew. While we settled, I had a chance to study him. He was in his mid-thirties, slightly taller than average and with a long rectangular face and hairline that receded rather broadly on each side, leaving a peninsula of dark hair lower down toward his eyes and combed flat. He had intelligent eyes and a beard and mustache covering a strong jaw. He was well-dressed and exuded an air of confidence and success in a modest way.

"Major Candy didn't indicate the nature of your visit," said Holmes after we'd settled, providing Cruft with an opening to state his case.

He nodded. "If you know the Major, then you're aware that he wouldn't waste time relating what I can tell you myself. Additionally, he's the soul of discretion, and I'm sure he left the story for me to relate in my own way." Then he seemed hesitant. "I fear that you will find this matter to be rather small – certainly below the sort of case in which you typically involve yourself. I heard, for instance, of your recent recovery of the hijacked bullion train outside of Portsmouth."

Holmes turned his head with interest. "As you say, Major Candy is discreet – and in any case, he didn't know about that, so it wasn't him that told you. It certainly wasn't in the newspapers. Someone else let that secret slip. I wonder who?"

Cruft shook his head. "It isn't for me to say, Mr. Holmes, but it will go no further from me, I assure you. In my position, I meet many individuals across all walks of life, and things are revealed in casual conversations that might not surface otherwise. This was one of those instances."

"And what is your position?"

"I am a manager, and a salesman of sorts, and in recent years, a promoter."

"No military connection then?"

"None."

Holmes nodded for him to continue, and Cruft took a sip. "You must understand my work to know about my concern. As a boy, my father arranged for me to follow in his profession, and he began training me to manufacture jewelry – it had successfully supported him for years – but it wasn't for me. I struck out in a different direction and became an office boy at Spratt's, the dog biscuit manufacturer."

I nodded. "I have seen the product. The biscuits are stamped with a Maltese cross."

"And I've noticed the company's shop in the Holborn," added Holmes.

"I've worked my way up, managing to get free of the office and travel about, soliciting orders for the biscuits from gamekeepers, dog fanciers, dog show promoters, and so on. It was through the growth in the business that I became the general manager, and additionally much associated with different purebreed dog shows. Earlier this year, Major Candy's daughter, Kathleen – she's only fourteen, but already quite influential, and destined for great things – personally asked me to take charge of Allied Terrier Club's show, held a few weeks ago at the Royal Aquarium in Westminster. The Major and his wife are good friends of ours, my wife and me, so it was really more of a favor for them than Kathleen that I took on the extra work. It should be noted, however, that Kathleen, despite her young age, has already been quite involved in the breeding and showing of terriers, as well as exhibiting and judging at shows. There were nearly six-hundred entries across fifty-seven classes. Lord Backwater and Lord Greystoke were among the patrons, and by all measures it was a huge success.

"The show – we called it 'The First Great Terrier Show' – ran for several days, and attracted terrier fanciers from all across England. As you can imagine, terriers generate interest from every walk of life. Some keep the purebreds as pets, while others find them indispensable as working dogs." He was leaning forward now, warming to his subject. Holmes, who had known a few terriers in his past, let the man speak.

"Originally there were only two recognized types – short legs and long legs, depending on the type of work that was required – but now there are several different divisions: The hunting types, used to kill small game and vermin, and the bull terriers, which are trained to go after bigger animals, and which are also used for fighting other dogs. The show was hectic and harried, as one would expect, and if Kathleen Candy hadn't called my attention to a certain attendee, I might not have noticed him – although he is certainly hard to ignore.

"By its nature, the tone of a dog show is geared toward the more successful members of society – those who can afford to keep the animals as pets, or dabble in breeding. But the shows are also very democratic, where those of the lower orders who have a daily interest in the working aspect of the dogs are also welcome. It's amazing to see the conversations that occur between the high- and low-born, those who would normally never meet or speak, when discussing different aspects of their dogs. There's quite an unexpected freemasonry across societal restrictions. And yet, the appearance and participation of Captain Graves, as he called himself, in last month's show was most unexpected and disruptive – and that has continued to the present. He's the reason that I've come to see you today, Mr. Holmes.

"Even among the rougher of the show's participants, Captain Graves would stand out. He's in his sixties, and very careworn. He's quite tall – closer to seven feet than six – although noticeably stooped, and thin as a rail. His skin is burned dark after years of being outdoors, and it's creased by deep grooves resembling ancient and worn leather. He walks with a rolling gait, as if a lifetime as sea has left him unprepared to be cast ashore. He has wild white hair, and his beard is just as long and tangled and unkempt. His knuckles are covered with blurred blue tattoos, and he wears clothes that are as shabby as the rest of him. They definitely look like those of a sailor – which fits with the short introduction he gave to me when I spoke with him.

"'Back from the sea, lad,'" he explained when I attempted to make conversation and find out more about him. 'Gone these forty years or more, with never any intention to return – but finally the call of London became too great. Especially when I heard of your terrier show. Always fancied the beasts, even when I was at sea, and never without one of my own. Gertrude here – ' He gestured to a rather scrofulous little Jack Russell squatting by his feet. ' – is just the latest of a long line. A fine ratter, she is. Never a shortage of rats on a ship, you understand.'

"Over the course of the show," continued Cruft, "Graves was quite the character, constantly on the move, conversing with anyone who would waste a few minutes with him. It was Kathleen who brought him to my attention, pointing out the Captain with some concern that he was negatively affecting the tone of the proceedings, and urging me to find out more about him. She didn't ask that he be removed – not then. It wasn't until his little escapade with the rats that he crossed the line."

I had followed Cruft's tale with interest, but this new aspect caused me to pay attention a bit further.

"In truth, gentlemen," said our visitor, "while I love all dogs, terriers are not necessarily my favorite breed. There is a cruelty about them. They aren't bred to be companions, or do work that's pleasant to watch, like the herding dogs who show such great intelligence. Rather, terriers seek out vermin and kill. That's what they do, what they're good at – killing as

428

many as they can, as fast as they can. Oh, they might be bred to look visually attractive, or to be small in order to sit in someone's lap, but even the pretty ones and the small ones are still killers inside, and they know it. Those instincts are never far below the surface."

Holmes nodded. "When I was at University, a particularly vicious example of the breed fastened upon my leg as I went down to chapel. I ended up becoming good friends with the animal's owner, but I never entirely relaxed when the dog was present."

I nodded. My experience with them was much the same. When Holmes and I first moved to Baker Street, Mrs. Hudson had owned an elderly terrier that, even in its diminished condition, had shown marked unfriendliness whenever our paths crossed. Soon, it became so feeble and ill that she asked me to euthanize it, but before I could do so, Holmes took on the task while testing whether or not a certain pill was poisonous. He gave some of the pill to the dog, dissolved in milk, and the creature died almost immediately. Learning of Holmes's own past experience with a vicious terrier, I wondered what his thoughts had been when that deed was done.

"It's an unavoidable fact," continued Cruft, "that a show highlighting terriers will have some aspects related to how successful they are as killers. Some of the dogs on display were clearly maimed from past violent encounters with cornered rats – or with other dogs. It was easy to believe their owners' boastful words about past ferocious victories, and descriptions of giant rats, and the incredible numbers of dead beasts that these dogs have eliminated in their short careers. But Captain Graves was more vocal than most, wandering the hall with his Gertrude, button-holing whomever he could corner, and relating many specific incidents in graphic detail that left a number of women, and even some of the more delicate men, in rather queasy discomfort.

"Still, we simply kept our eye on him, should the need arise to ask him to leave. And then I thought such a reason was provided to us on the third and final morning of the exhibition when he unexpectedly decided to give a practical demonstration.

"Soon after I arrived, I was called over by one of the attendants, quite urgent in his manner. He informed me that the Captain was going to show just how good Gertrude was. When I forced my way through the gathering throng, I found that Graves had upended a number of display tables, turning them on their sides and placing them end to end in order to create something of a closed pen. He stood in the middle of it, laughing and calling encouragement to his dog, an empty hessian sack on the ground beside him, and another in his hands, from which he was shaking out the last of a pack of big grimy sewer rats. On the ground around him were over

429

a dozen more, a few already dead, others wounded, and rest that were still alive running wildly around the closed area, trying to scrabble up the sides of the tables, and once or twice up the Captain's clothing, and always trying to avoid the dog, itself lost in a frenzy of killing. The squealing of the filthy beasts was terrible, and it was so shrill that it could be heard over the noises of the crowd – some expressing shocked dismay, while others – too many others – gave cheers every time another rat was violently slain.

"I was shocked into immobility, looking from the bloody spectacle being enacted around the old man to the surrounding crowd, surprised at how even those who I would have thought were too noble or refined to tolerate this had pushed to the front, with terrible lusty expressions upon their bright wide-eyed smiling faces. Sir Jason Bennis was there, a frightening leer on his face that I would never have imagined I'd see. Mrs. Witton of Curzon Street was crowded to the front, breathing heavily. Standing alongside was Lady Beatrice Falder. Adjacent was her brother, Sir Robert Norberton – both of them better known for their Shoscombe spaniels, the most exclusive breed in England, but with a strong interest in terriers as well. They too had a thrilled glint in their eyes that was most disconcerting.

"Back in the pen, Gertrude chased down each rat, one by one by one, grabbing one by its back with her powerful jaws and giving several mighty crushing shakes before casting it aside and moving on. Some rats were dead, and others still suffering. She would drop one animal and turn to another, and another. If she noticed one still alive, she'd rush back and give it another rough shake to finish it. The overhead light shined from the blood on her face and jaws, and on the damp faces of the cheering spectators. If I'd been just a minute later, I would have missed it all. She was that fast. And through it, Captain Graves danced from one foot to another, shaking off the occasional rat from his breeches and laughing and calling encouragement to the dog as if he were doing a sea jig.

"I must admit, I wasn't shocked at the dog's brutality. In my travels, I've seen terriers accomplish much more than that. There's a very credible story of one single terrier who killed over twenty-five-hundred rats in a single day, all in a rat-infested barn."

I nodded, interrupting. "I was once on a farm where the entire family, from the old and infirm to the smallest children, along with their pack of terriers, were clearing a field – a lowland where the rats had dug a maze of tunnels beneath the ground. Using pitch forks and shovels, the farmers and their wives and children would all turn over the ground, a foot at a time, foot after foot, exposing more and more of the tunnels. Each bit of earth laid bare spooked a dozen rats or more – and the dogs were upon them before they could run more than a yard or two. It went on for hours

430

– hundreds, if not thousands, of rats mounded around us – and at the end of the day, I suspect there were still that many again hiding underground, not yet revealed, and the dogs were no less enthusiastic than when they began."

Cruft nodded. "A vicious breed – in spite of how the owners try to domesticate them. And seeing the reactions of the people watching the Captain's demonstration, the humans are quite vicious as well. I overheard some conversations wishing that such displays had been a planned part of the show from the first day. And yet, these are some of the same people who campaign against the cruelty of dog fighting."

Holmes cleared his throat. I knew that he had been giving the visitor wide latitude because he'd been sent by Major Candy, to whom Holmes felt an obligation, but now he was ready to get back on track. "I take it that for young Kathleen, this was the final straw."

"It was. She is young, but already she has a great deal of authority. It was through her request and influence that I was given the chance to organize and run the show, and I didn't want to spoil the opportunity that it presented to me. While the Captain spoke with several enthusiastic admirers of his dog's ferocious exhibition, Kathleen whispered that he should be asked to leave immediately. As she turned and walked off, clearly sickened by the sight, I signaled to a few of the workers to replace the tables in their proper positions and then dispose of the carcasses and clean up the blood. Then, as the last of the man's well-wishers left him, I stepped forward, starting to tell him in no uncertain terms that he and his dog, now sitting calmly beside him and cleaning herself like a cat, would leave immediately. He gave me a belligerent look, rearing up to his full height and clearly intending to argue. I was prepared to escalate my position when we were interrupted by two people, both quite influential, who were most surprisingly there to take the Captain's side.

"I would have thought that they would be the last to involve themselves in such a matter, let alone take an active stance. It was Lord Crewe – Jonas Heanor – and his spinster sister, Lady Hilda Heanor. I've known them both for years, and in fact, we've become rather close friends. They are very active dog fanciers, particularly terriers, and they have never given any indication that they support the violent aspect of the species. And yet, they came to the defense, quite passionately, of this ragged man who is just one step above an East End vagrant. Well, Lady Hilda did. Her brother supported her, but with much less vigor and enthusiasm. In truth, he seemed rather embarrassed – but he held up her end nonetheless.

"I was quite shocked at the dressing-down she gave me. The employees cleaning up the mess were watching with undisguised interest, as was the crowd that was beginning to gather around us. But it seemed

431

that my surprise was only surpassed by that of Captain Graves himself, who was watching Lady Hilda with deep fascination, leaning forward as if he didn't want to miss a single syllable of her lecture to me on the proper treatment of the show's participants – *all* of them."

Holmes shifted in his chair, and I wondered, interesting as it had been to me, whether he was becoming impatient with Cruft's narrative. In truth, I had yet to hear anything that would explain why he would need to consult a detective. Perhaps it was true, as Cruft had initially intimated, that the affair wasn't up to the level of Holmes's more interesting cases. Cruft noticed Holmes's movement and intuitively sensed the same feeling.

"You wonder why I've asked for this appointment," Cruft said, "and what about this affair requires your help."

Holmes nodded. "While providing a few educational anecdotes about dog shows and the nature of terriers, I don't yet see where my involvement intersects with your experience. Has there been a death? A theft? You took pains to describe Lady Hilda's intervention in the affair. I suspect that she is the reason for your visit, but I don't understand where your interest lies. Do you have any connection with her that would necessitate your active involvement?"

"Not of a legal nature," Cruft replied. "But over the last few years, as my work at Spratt's has expanded to include participation in various dog shows as a way to make our product more relevant, the lady has provided considerable financial support. I've often worked closely with her in relation to various functions, and I have a fondness for her. She and her brother are both getting on in years, and I fear that her behavior in recent weeks, since the conclusion of the show, has been something of a concern to those of us who know her."

"And what behavior would that be?"

"She has taken up . . . *socially* with Captain Graves." He cleared his throat. "In fact, she is . . . *co-habitating* with him." His fingers curled into fists for a few seconds. Then, as he released them, he added, "This isn't known yet to the wider world, you understand, or her reputation would be ruined. I only know because her brother, Jonas, came to me, asking for help. He is at a loss – helpless. After their father died many years ago, it was Lady Hilda who took over the running of the family's assets. Jonas may have the title, but his sister has the intelligence and the responsibility. If she loses her credibility, then many people will be hurt, as the stain spreads across all their interests and connections."

"And why would Brother Jonas seek your assistance?" asked Holmes. I wondered the same thing myself.

"I have earned stature, in certain quarters – a reputation – as something of a 'fixer'. Being able to step in and do favors for certain people has returned great dividends – figuratively speaking, of course – in my business affairs. But in this case . . . ." He turned up his hands in surrender. "I am out of my depth, Mr. Holmes. I don't even know how to begin."

"What have you done so far?"

"Why, I attempted to see Lady Hilda – to speak with her – but she wouldn't allow me to enter! She must have known why I was there. I understand that since the Captain has moved into the house in Half Moon Street, she isn't seeing any visitors – although no one seems to question it yet, putting it down to some age-related infirmity."

"And the servants?" I asked. "Surely they know what's going on. They will have gossiped."

Cruft shook his head. "Over the last few years, Lady Hilda has reduced the household staff to the barest minimum, as she and Jonas require very little. All that's left is an elderly husband and wife, the Loughboroughs, and their middle-aged spinster daughter, who have all been there for decades. They're completely loyal – or so Jonas has explained to me when I asked the same question just the other day." He looked at Holmes. "I don't even know where to start, Mr. Holmes. Can you provide some answers – something that gives Jonas the leverage he needs to rescue his sister before it's too late?"

"I'll confess," said Holmes, "that I would prefer to deal with him directly. Why didn't he join you this morning?"

Cruft looked more uncomfortable than before. "He doesn't know that I made this appointment. I . . . I didn't want to worry him when I widened the number of people who are aware of the delicate situation."

Holmes started silently for a moment, pondering Cruft's answer to the point where the showman dropped his eyes. Then Holmes replied, "I'll look into it – but with no promise that anything I find will provide the kind of advantage you seek. I have found elderly ladies to be very set and willful."

Cruft nodded. "This is a basic truth. But anything that you can uncover will be more than I can find." He looked to me, as if I might have something to add, but I only nodded as well. Then he stood. "I appreciate your time, Mr. Holmes, and I look forward to hearing your report." He then reached into his waistcoat pocket, pulled forth two of his visiting cards, handed one to each of us, and then turned without any other words and departed, pulling the door shut behind him. We heard him descend, and a moment later, the front door opened and closed decisively.

Holmes glanced at Cruft's card. "Islington. Hmm. Apparently Mr. Cruft's ambition hasn't yet led him to move to Mayfair in order to be closer to his cohorts."

433

"Perhaps he likes that part of the city," I replied, before then asking, "What do you think you can discover?"

"Everything." That was typical of Holmes's confidence. In the old days, such a response would have had me muttering "Brag and bounce!" at his confidence, but I had learned over the past five years that if he said a thing, he meant it, and that in such a matter as this, he likely already had a clear idea of his path forward, and multiple sources where he could obtain information in an efficient manner. Those who had the impression that one of Holmes's investigations necessitated months of ineffective churning before a lone thin clue was uncovered did not understand his methods.

"How may I assist?" I asked, but he didn't answer, instead rising, crossing the room in a few steps, and retrieving one of his commonplace books. After a moment of study, he handed it to me and then vanished into his bedroom.

He'd left the book open to the entry for Jonas and Hilda Heanor. There wasn't much to see. They were both born in the early 1820's to the fifth Lord of that line, a man already in late middle-age when they came along, just a year apart. Their mother had died when both were small, and the father had passed in mid-1844, having amassed a fortune in shipping and textiles. Neither had ever married. Lady Hilda had remained in the family home in Half Moon Street, while Jonas Heanor had set up his own digs, over a quarter-century earlier, just 'round two corners in Queen Street. His undistinguished university degree was noted, as were a couple of the exclusive but uninteresting clubs that many of his level joined, but there was nothing else listed for either of them.

Holmes returned to the sitting room, dressed in one of his favorite reliable disguises, a down-at-luck sailor. "Any ideas?" he asked, apparently referring to my offer to help, and his subsequent conveyance of the limited information in the commonplace book.

By that time, I had been a part of Holmes's investigations for quite a while, and even though I would never rise to his level, I wasn't entirely helpless. "Perhaps," I ventured, "a discreet inquiry into the Heanor's backgrounds? Something to explain why she would fall sway to this stranger?"

Holmes nodded. "I had something like that in mind as well, after my visit to the docks. I would appreciate you carrying out an initial evaluation."

"Any suggestions?" I asked.

He smiled and shook his head. "Use your intelligence guided by experience." Then, with a nod and a statement that he would be back later in the day, he left.

434

Consulting hours were finished.

I sat for a few minutes, noting that I still had some time left in the morning before lunch. After considering that Holmes would be looking into the background and affairs of Captain Graves, I might find something useful from the other end at one of Lord Crewe's clubs. Accordingly, I informed Mrs. Hudson that neither Holmes nor I would home for lunch, and then set off for the Garrick Club, fittingly located in Garrick Street and founded a half-century earlier. The imposing building was much the same style as those around it, although the stone work was of an uninspiring gray that contrasted with the white buildings on either side. I was not a member, but Holmes and I had once found something very important for someone who was, a high-ranking fellow, and had partially paid the debt by making it clear we were always welcome.

I entered, immediately reminded from the interior decorations that the theme of the place centered on an interest in the arts, and specifically the theater. After my name was verified on the list at the front, I was allowed to continue onward to the inner sanctums. I wandered for a few minutes, as it had been a couple of years since my last visit. While it was a club, and catered to the members in the ways expected of such places, it also felt very much like a museum, having both an extensive theater-related library, and one of the finest collections of actor and actress portraits to be found anywhere. Pausing at any spot to examine one would then lead to the desire to see the one beside it, and then another and another, and before long a couple of hours would be gone. I had to stop myself earlier than I would have liked, instead looking around to make some sort of conversational engagement.

Not being an actual member was an advantage, as nearly everyone there was a stranger to me, but my presence seemed to confirm that I was one of them, and therefore worthy of acceptance and trust. My previous days of not wishing to engage in gossip were long-since vanished, and I had developed some small skill at drawing people out by little conversational nudges and cues. They universally wanted to talk about themselves, and it was easy to keep the conversations going, and then nudge them toward the topic that I desired. The basic facts that I'd read about Jonas Heanor were confirmed – that he'd inherited the title in his early twenties, and that his sister did the actual work of administering the estate. This information was conveyed in each case with a bit of innuendo, as if Lord Crewe had ceded some important part of himself by allowing his sister to take over that portion of his expected responsibilities. Everyone agreed, however, that Lord Crewe was a likeable-enough fellow, and an asset to the club.

His sister was more of a mystery. I spoke to a couple of older men, about the same age as the Heanors, who remembered when the lady had been quite the belle of society. But something happened in her early twenties, not long before the death of her father, that had caused her to withdraw from participation in the game of finding a spouse. This was rationalized by the old men that when she had to assume the running of the estate – as her brother wasn't really suited for it – she had no interest in sharing her life with a husband. At this point, more than forty years later, it was simply an accepted fact that the Heanors were who they were, and no one seemed to care very much otherwise. I wondered if bits of their dusty past would be dragged into the light as her relationship with Captain Graves became common knowledge.

I didn't feel that I'd learned very much, but I didn't know what other aspects to explore. I thought about questioning someone in the Mayfair neighborhood where they lived, but I realized that such tasks were better suited to Sherlock Holmes, who could disguise himself and work his way into the confidence of the staff at the Heanor's two homes, as well as those of the neighbors. My efforts would be awkward at best, and would only serve to arouse suspicion where none currently existed.

Having done all that I could do, and leaving with a fine lunch as well, I returned to Baker Street, whereupon I made a pretense of studying a medical journal until sleep overtook me a short time later.

I awoke as Holmes was passing through the sitting room to his bedroom, where he would remove his disguise. His step was light, and I perceived that he'd had some success. Looking at the mantel clock, I saw that it was mid-afternoon, and wondered what he had planned for the rest of the day. He soon informed me.

"Quite refreshed?" he asked, not bothering to return to his chair, but instead standing by the door in his normal clothing. "If so, perhaps you'd like to accompany me to Somerset House. I have a fact to confirm which I couldn't do in my sailor get-up."

I rose and nodded, and he pulled on his Inverness and fore-and-aft cap. I similarly donned my overcoat, and then we descended. On our way out, Mrs. Hudson handed Holmes a telegram, informing him that Mrs. Finger had found her missing *cloisonné* necklace where he'd specified. He passed it to me and, after reading it, I shoved it into my pocket.

Outside, we had to walk nearly to Baker Street Station to find a cab. We didn't speak until we were in motion, and then Holmes related where he'd been.

"I started at the West India Dock, intending to work my way south into the Isle of Dogs, seeking information on Captain Graves and his little companion, Gertrude. As I progressed, I recruited various men and women who have assisted in the past, along with a few Irregulars, and they spread out as well, asking questions about this unique individual. His great height was a lucky factor, and that was what eventually led me to *The Hilda*, docked in the Blackwall Basin for the last month, fresh from the Orient."

"*The Hilda!*" I cried softly.

Holmes nodded. "Owned lock, stock, and barrel by Captain Graves. He arrived, discharged a cargo of copra and coconut fibers, and then paid off and released the crew. Except for a few visits to check on the ship, the Captain has been living somewhere else – according to the boy he hired to keep watch. Luckily, the young fellow is more greedy than reliable, and a substantial payment – at least according to his standards – allowed me all the time I needed to search the boat."

Rather than question the ethics of such actions, for this was nothing new to me, I asked, "And what did you discover?"

"Everything." This was typical of Holmes's responses in such a situation. In some ways, he was an actor at heart, and he craved dramatic resolutions. In many cases, such wasn't possible – but that day, he had found an investigation that would let him reveal all in a way that pleased him . . . when one more fact was obtained.

He would tell me nothing further, and in any case we soon arrived at Somerset House. He knew the building far better than I, and a short time later we were entering the rooms set aside for marriage information. I began to have some small inkling of where this was headed. Ten minutes later, with the help of a friendly clerk who apparently – to hear him tell it – owed his very life to something Holmes had discovered in 1879, we were looking at a yellowed document from May 1844 that made clear, even to me, some of what was going on. The details of the painting were still incomplete, but the broad strokes were now in place.

"Now to Mayfair?" I asked, and Holmes nodded with a smile.

We were on our way to Half Moon Street, and I wanted to ask questions, but Holmes just shook his head, apparently preparing himself for our upcoming encounter with Lady Hilda and Captain Graves – as we supposed the latter would be with the former.

No. 4 was quite a bit smaller than I'd expected, narrow and seemingly just half-a-building wide. In fact, our modest residence in Baker Street was wider, although Lady Hilda's home was a full story taller. It was handsome red brick with ornate black wrought-ironwork of various curves and rectangles mounted outside the first-floor windows. Similar iron decorations surrounded the small stoop by the front door, and protected the areaway just to the right of it. There were three short black-painted steps that rose to the black door. Within moments of ringing the bell, we were admitted by an elderly man – surely the manservant, Loughbourough

– himself dressed in black. He gravely took our cards and asked us to wait. We took the opportunity to examine the narrow hall, admiring an ornate mirror over an old but excellently preserved table with a fine marble top, and a small dark portrait, something in the style of Rembrandt, of a young fellow with wild curly hair, his eyes in shadow.

In just a moment we were led through to a parlour, where we found an elderly heavy-set lady sitting on a solid chair, a sturdy cane leaning against the arm. Beside her stood a man, his hand resting possessively upon her shoulder, smiling toward us as if welcoming old friends. My first thought was that he was the brother, Jason Heanor, for he was well-dressed and groomed. But then I saw that I was surely mistaken. This man was tall – nearly seven feet I estimated – and his skin was brown like a nut, and deeply creased as one who has spent years facing the sea and the salt from the deck of a brigantine. His skin was a stark contrast to his white hair and beard, both cut short and well-barbered. A closer look showed that the knuckles and of his hands, extending out of expensive and rather new-looking clothing, were covered in old blurred tattoos.

Nearby, lying on the floor, its head raised and alert, body perfectly still, was a ragged Jack Russell terrier, watching Holmes and me with particular interest.

This, then, was Captain Graves, cleaned up and made as presentable as he could be.

"Mr. Holmes," said Lady Hilda. "I have heard of you – and Doctor Watson as well. I believe you were some assistance last year to the Wrexhams when they came down for the season. Their daughter owes a great deal to you both."

Holmes nodded in acknowledgement. "She made an unfortunate and impulsive choice. There was no need that her entire life be ruined as a consequence." He glanced at the captain. "May I take it, then, that you are both undoing a somewhat similar ruination?"

The captain laughed, a braying guffaw that startled me in such a refined room, but it only pleased Lady Hilda, who reached up and touched his hand, still upon her shoulder. "Very much like that," she said. "We have wasted the best parts of our lives."

"At least we can salvage the last of them," added Graves, his voice rough and loud, as if it had been damaged over the decades calling out commands loud enough for crews in the windy rigging to hear them.

"Are you taking the direct approach, Mr. Holmes?" asked Lady Hilda. "Come to ask me what's going on – or perhaps to reason with me about the dangers to my reputation?" When Holmes tilted his head in a questioning way, she added, "My brother cannot keep a secret – even one of his own. It was probably only a few hours after he asked Charles Cruft for help in reasoning with me about Claude – " She patted the captain's hand again. " – that he admitted to me what he'd done. I turned right around and summoned Charles here. He left not twenty minutes ago, having informed me that he'd approached you to carry the matter forward. I expect that you'll be hearing from him soon, releasing you from his request for help. So you've come to the horse's mouth to speak with me about my moral turpitude, have you?"

"Not at all. Simply to let you know that the tides of curiosity are rising, and that sooner or later, Captain Graves' presence here will be discovered. But," he added with a gesture to the tall grinning fellow, now much different from the description given to us that morning, "clearly you're prepared for that – to the point, I suspect, of finally acknowledging your long-ago and much neglected marriage."

Graves guffawed again, and Lady Hilda gave a surprised start before smiling as well. She gestured for us both to sit, and the captain – her husband – pulled a chair close to hers. Sitting down, he took her hand and asked us, "What do you know, then?"

"As I said: You are married, and have been since 1844, just before the death of the previous Lord Crewe. This much we've tracked down by various available clues. I must confess, Captain, that the lad watching your boat succumbed to my generous payment and allowed me to board *The Hilda* earlier today. The documents in your cabin – letters from the 1840's and other documents – "

"My journal, you mean," interrupted the man, a grin still on his face. "Oh, I'm not surprised you read it. I'd do the same if I'd been hired to find out the truth as you were, and had the opportunity to peruse such a document. Don't be embarrassed."

"I'm not. The journal was quite clear about what occurred. You were the second son of a wealthy northern family that owned a number of textile mills. Your family's business put you in contact with the Heanors, and a romance sprang up between you and Lady Hilda, then in your twenties. It apparently burned with great intensity – to the point where you were secretly married. Watson and I have just come from Somerset House, where we saw the official properly recorded document. After the marriage, you then had to reveal the truth to your families. And that's when the conflict arose."

Lady Hilda nodded sadly. "My father was furious! He had much different plans for me. I believe that the rage that filled him after I told him what Claude and I had done led to his early death, just a month or so later. Claude . . . Claude wanted me to come away with him. But I couldn't – Not then. First I had to make peace with my father. I tried! I tried so hard, but he wouldn't let me. And then he died – but by then, Claude had already left, angry that I seemingly chose my father over him." She looked at the weathered man beside her, who returned her gaze with great affection. "He's very proud, my Claude – too much, I suppose. And passionate. But so am I. We let the question grow so big and so fast that it drove us apart – for the better part of our lives. We missed so much! But now . . . now we're together again, and will make up for all we've lost."

Graves looked at us. "I saw the world – but I never forgot Hilda. When I earned enough to buy my own ship, that's what I named her. Finally, a man reaches the age where he acknowledges all of his stubborn foolishness. I felt the need to return to England, and the need to see my wife, if only to make amends for my wicked stubbornness. I came home.

"I looked around for a while, uncertain as to what I might find. I followed Hilda when she left home, and was there when she went to the dog show. Gertrude and I tarried there, watching. Finally, I got up my nerve to speak to her. Jonas was with her. Let's just say that the first meeting didn't go as I'd hoped – but not as badly as I'd feared!"

Lady Hilda smiled at him then, but didn't explain what he meant.

"Still, Hilda had responsibilities at the dog show, and I knew that's where I could continue to see her, so I stayed around. I'm afraid that over the years, I've lost whatever refinement might have once been trained into me. I'm a rough old cob now, as they say in America. I saw nothing wrong about letting Gertrude kill some rats at the show." At this, the dog raised her head, but seeing that nothing was required of her, she let it sink again upon her front paws while still watching all of us intently.

"That's when that Cruft fellow had enough, and started to order me away. I suppose that Hilda, despite being angry with me, decided to step in. Maybe she was afraid that after the way Cruft dressed me down, I'd leave again – this time for good."

Lady Hilda nodded and patted his hand.

"We talked again – this time just the two of us, without Jonas. This was much better. We found that we still loved one another, even after . . . even after everything. I moved back in, and the servants were all right with it. They love Hilda. But Jonas was so ugly about it – Hilda had never told him about our secret marriage, after seeing how her father took it, and we didn't tell him now. Maybe that was a mistake. He was angry that I was living here, and it pleased me in some way, knowing that we were married and his reaction was so foolish if only he'd known the truth. But then he asked for Cruft's help, and that led to your visit right now." He gestured up and down toward his fine clothing. "As you can see, I don't clean up as well as I should, but it's different than it was before, and Hilda and I always intended to reveal the truth. So you see, it all would have come out in a few days anyway."

Holmes nodded and abruptly stood, having learned what he wanted. I followed, and the seated couple looked up at us in surprise.

"Must you go so soon?" asked Lady Hilda. Before we could answer, her husband replied with a knowing look.

"I think they have what they needed. I suspect that's enough for a fellow like Mr. Holmes." He had a canny smile on his face. "This has all just been a question to be answered. A riddle to be solved, and we're just factors in the problem. Isn't that right?"

Holmes nodded. "You're correct, Captain. You have a wise understanding of people."

"Very kind of you, sir." Graves stood as well. "May I show you out?"

He beamed toward his wife and then let us proceed him to the front door. The dog had risen and followed. Slipping around us, the captain opened the door and let us outside. Then, to my surprise, he and the dog followed, and Graves pulled the door quietly shut behind him. The smile he'd carried through the house dropped like a fallen curtain, leaving a hard expression upon his creased visage.

"This turned out all right, Mr. Holmes," he said in a low voice. Gertrude, following his tone, bared her teeth and gave a low growl. "You found what you wanted. But be warned, sir: I don't like men going through my property, and reading my documents. Not at all. You've touched upon my business, but make sure it's the last time." He leaned forward, his hand still on the doorknob, his voice more quiet and sinister. There was none of the guffawing happy man we had just seen.

"I know men here in London that owe me – one in particular, very powerful – who are very dangerous. You don't want to cross me, and you don't want me to turn them loose in your direction. It wouldn't end well.

He straightened.

"Let this be the last I hear of you." He cut his eyes in my direction. "*Either of you.*"

Then he opened the door and let Gertrude cross the sill. He stepped back inside and shut us out.

The sudden shift from the cozy friendliness and long-time affection of the parlour to the implied threat on the stoop left me in something of a shock. "Holmes," I asked softly. "What have we stumbled into?"

My friend, didn't answer. He did, however, have a speculative smile upon his face.

"That was a serious mistake, Captain" he murmured. Then to me he added, "In truth, I didn't see anything on the Captain's boat to arouse my suspicions. Other than the typical paperwork related to the conveyance of cargo to a number of ports on several continents, there was nothing of interest. I stopped looking when I found the documentation of his long-standing love for his wife, and the circumstances of their parting."

"And now?" I asked, intrigued.

"And now I see the need to revisit *The Hilda* – Quickly. As soon as possible, before the Captain goes to check on what he thinks that I found." He took my arm and drew me hurriedly toward Piccadilly, where the chances of finding a cab were much more likely.

"Holmes," I said as we walked. "Lady Hilda – Is she safe? She's allowed this man back into her life. What should we do?"

"She will be protected. We'll report to Cruft later today. He'll know which of her friends that we'll need to speak to – with great discretion, of course. She'll be safe.

"I'll need your help," he added when our cab was in motion, with an offer from Holmes to pay double the fare if we reached our destination speedily. "I can't pay the boy guarding the ship twice. That would alert the Captain that I've returned for a second search. Instead, you must distract him – decoy him away so that I can enter the ship unseen." He took out his watch. "Ten minutes to Baker Street. Five to change back into my disguise. Another half-hour to the docks in a fast cab." He glanced forward. "We'll keep this one – I think that the horse can be goaded to a quicker pace. We should be able to pull it off, if the Captain doesn't leave for the docks immediately. It depends on how worried he is. And we'll only know what he has to worry about after I get back on board that ship." He glanced at me, adding, "He's is going to look down to find that I've frozen to his ankle like that vicious terrier of which he's so fond."

Then he allowed one of his rare fits of laughter, the sort that has always boded ill to somebody.

Gradually it subsided, and he turned to me with a smile. I found that I wore one as well. Yet I could simply wonder where this sudden shift in events might lead, only apparent to us by Captain Graves' foolish idea that he could warn us away from his mysterious business. Knowing how many of Holmes's other morning consultations had, one way or another, subsequently developed into satisfying and intriguing investigations from small beginnings, I expected that this one was also about to become most interesting.

We were passing Portman Square when a thought occurred to me. I turned to speak, but Holmes raised a hand and nodded. "It has occurred to you that involving the police might be of some use, and I agree. We can ill-afford the delay, but a stop by Scotland Yard on our way to the docks will likely prove useful."

In the end, they delay proved to be inconsequential. After slipping back into his disguise, we returned to the waiting cab. The driver, who had seen me enter Baker Street with Holmes and return with a shabby sailor, made no comment. He had the same lack of reaction when I instructed him to make his way to Scotland Yard with all possible speed. It occurred to me that after more than five years of Holmes being located there, it was quite possible that 221 Baker Street was gathering something of a reputation, and that cabbies were more and more aware that curious things happened there.

At the Yard, Holmes remained in the cab while I went inside to seek one of several inspectors who might be of assistance. For a moment, that's where our luck left us. The two most likely, Gregson and Lestrade, were busy with other matters. There were a couple of others that I knew would provide more complications than aid. Then I thought to ask about Inspector Alec MacDonald, the young but trusted member of the Force who Holmes had recently helped in a matter of importance, leading to the Scotchman's affection and respect for his amateur colleague. I was informed that MacDonald had gone for the day, but he could be found just around the corner, in the pub on the ground floor of the Northumberland Hotel, with a few of his cronies.

It was but a moment to 'round the block from No. 4 Whitehall Place and into Northumberland Avenue, and only moments after that for MacDonald to have tossed back the remains of his ale and joined us in the waiting growler. He looked with amusement at Holmes's disguise, his deep-set eyes twinkling beneath bushy eyebrows, set in a great cranium that spoke of keen intelligence. I had provided the barest of explanations inside the pub, and MacDonald's first words in the cab, spoken in his hard Aberdonian accent, were, "No time to obtain a warrant, then, Mr. Holmes?"

Holmes shook his head, elaborating on what I'd already told MacDonald – how we had been visited that morning by Cruft, who was concerned about his friend, Lady Hilda, the results of our separate afternoon investigations, and the resulting warning from Captain Graves. "He's now been alerted," concluded Holmes. "You can bet that whatever is hidden on that boat will be gone by morning. We have to find it before he returns."

MacDonald rubbed his jaw, considering. Finally he said, "It's a bit irregular, gentlemen, and I hate to play tricks with the law, but you're right. I just hope that you find what you're looking for, and it's worth whatever consequences might arise otherwise if we're wrong."

We arrived at *The Hilda* not long after. She was a double-masted schooner, likely quite useful for carrying small cargoes in and out of tight ports. Leaving Holmes and MacDonald in a nearby alley, I walked toward the ship, wondering if Captain Graves had already beaten us back. Calling

"Ahoy!" to the ship, I was relieved to see a young lad's head poke up in response.

"No," he replied, "Cap'n ain't back yet."

"Well, then you'll have to do," I said briskly, with authority. "I think he's forgotten the cargo he's supposed to retrieve by tonight. No one is there to pick it up. Come with me now so you can report back to him."

The boy argued for a minute, but my certainty and his sense of responsibility overcame any resistance. I led him away, noting from the corner of my eye that Holmes was already moving quickly toward the ship.

I took the boy through a warren of warehouses and alleyways, and my uncertainty as to where to turn next convinced him that I was lost – but he also lost any confidence in my story, and after a quarter-hour, try as I might, I could no longer hold his interest. He turned to return to the ship, and I could only hurry along behind him, afraid that I hadn't distracted him long enough and that my mission had failed.

My anxiety was in vain. Holmes had unearthed an investigative treasure.

Knowing that where he'd previously searched hadn't revealed anything suspicious, he searched elsewhere. It didn't take him long to find that the dimensions of the holds didn't quite add up. Graves and his men had been careless with the secret entrance of a hidden hold, not bothering to disguise various scratches when the hidden door had opened and closed. Inside that low chamber were guns and ammunition – a vast amount, along with documentation that they were intended for the disaffected residents of Belfast who were secretly arming themselves. The government's seizure of these weapons that day didn't prevent the riots that occurred two months later, but their removal from the equation certainly substantially reduced the losses of life that might have occurred otherwise.

By the time I returned, Holmes had already discovered the guns and alerted MacDonald, who had summoned a number of constables with the aid of his police whistle. They were swarming the boat when I saw someone approach from between two nearby alleys, taking a number of steps forward before quite realizing what was going on and faltering to a stop.

It was Captain Graves and, with a roar, he turned to flee.

But he was old, and a life at sea had not been kind to his joints. Holmes leaped to the dock, landing lightly, and took off in a flash of speed, tackling the captain before he'd covered a dozen feet along his abortive escape. I was there seconds later, the barrel of my service revolver alongside the villain's temple.

As many will recall, the arrest was something of a nine-days' wonder, but most of the details were kept out of the newspapers, both to avoid having any negative effect on Gladstone's recently introduced Government of Ireland Bill for Home Rule, and also to keep any undue embarrassment from settling upon Lady Hilda. She was shocked, of course, but not as much as many expected, for after all, she had lived most of her life without Graves, and his return hadn't been for long enough that she'd made many changes in her permanent habits. Her brother became more of a man than he had been, finally stepping up to take his responsibilities, and Charles Cruft deepened his friendship with the woman, which in turn was of great benefit to his career.

Graves was tried and convicted and the matter was mostly forgotten – but Holmes didn't forget the man's threat that day on the doorstep, when he'd bragged about knowing dangerous men – and one in particular. He kept worrying at it, and this became another thread in a very long and dangerous investigation. The encounter with the Captain turned out to be a chapter of a much longer and more complex tale, one that I am not yet prepared to fully relate, a story that ended five years later atop a Swiss waterfall . . . .

NOTE

Charles Cruft
(1852-1938)

Charles Cruft rose from office boy to general manager of Spratt's dog biscuit company, making important contacts both in England and on the Continent within the dog-owner community. As a way to grow the business, he was quite involved in dog shows, always seeking to raise their standards, and in 1886, he was asked by Kathleen Candy (later Kathleen Pehlam-Clinton, the Duchess of Newcastle) to run the national terrier show. The show was such a success that Cruft repeated it over the next few years, expanding it to include other breeds. In 1891, the show was rebranded as *Cruft's Greatest Dog Show* – the first of many that have continued to the present. Now known simply as *Crufts* – without the apostrophe – it was certified in 1991 by the Guinness Book of Records as the largest dog show in the world.

Gruner's Diary

"Ah, Watson," said Sherlock Holmes when I opened the door. "My strong right arm. Now we can continue."

I blinked as I sought to understand why I had been summoned. Holmes's wire had contained a note of urgency, and fortunately my practice was quiet enough, and it was late enough in the afternoon, that I was able to quickly divert the last of my medical responsibilities to a willing neighbor for whom I often did the same favor, explain to my wife that Holmes had requested my presence, and find a fast cab in Cavendish Square.

There was, however, some delay from that point. The distance between Queen Anne Street and Scotland Yard, could one traverse it in a straight leap, was just two or three miles, but at that time of day, the main thoroughfares were rather choked with vehicular traffic. My cabbie was seasoned enough to know the secondary routes – but there are many seasoned cabbies in London who know the same tricks, and they, too, had opted to avoid Regent Street, Haymarket, Trafalgar Square, and the other major paths. Nevertheless, despite delays and irregular turns that often seemed in the wrong direction to avoid congestion, I arrived at the Yard as quickly as I could and strode inside.

A small part of me, I suppose the remnants of that young boy who – if a fellow is lucky enough – is never entirely eradicated by the responsibilities of taking on adulthood, is always a bit secretly amazed that my path has led me to be so easily recognized, and even welcomed, by the officers of Scotland Yard. A quarter-century earlier, as I neared the completion of my medical studies, I never envisioned the life I would eventually lead. At some point I'd conceived the idea of joining the Army and, in the vague way that the young have of seeing the future, I pictured that type of life, based on the little I knew of soldiers. I would travel. There might be battles, but they would be successful, and then I'd return, having made lifelong comrades-in-arms, to great stretches of calm and orderly sameness in life.

But then came Maiwand, and injuries, and the unexpected severance of my Army association. I met Sherlock Holmes, thinking that ours would be nothing more than a temporary and expedient acquaintance while I husbanded my meagre funds and regained my shattered health. Then, on the fourth of March, 1881, he'd revealed to me his curious profession and, almost as an afterthought, asked me to join him when summoned by Scotland Yard to a murder investigation.

447

"We may as well go and have a look," he'd said, but I had no inclination that he actually meant for me to join him. "I shall work it out on my own hook. I may have a laugh at them, if I have nothing else. Come on!"

As he put on his coat, I still had no sense that he was truly inviting me to join him and observe his methods – about which I'd shown such skepticism only a moment before.

"Get your hat," he pointedly advised, this time making it clear that he expected me to join him.

"You wish me to come?" I considered what I'd planned for the day – perhaps a walk to some as-yet unexplored neighborhood as I labored to regain my strength. But Holmes really meant for me to come along.

"Yes, if you have nothing better to do."

At the lonesome and shabby house where the dead body had been discovered, we found two of the Yard's inspectors, Lestrade and Gregson. I'd met the former some weeks earlier on occasions when he stopped in to visit Holmes, but then I'd had no idea of his profession or the reason for his visits. In those early days, both Lestrade and Gregson had been great rivals – though perhaps not quite so much as Holmes liked to think, as it amused him to classify them as "a pair of professional beauties", jealous of one another and their successes. It was only as the years passed that I realized the two of them, while so different from one another in physical description, background, temperament, and method, actually had a grudging respect for one another that grew through time, and as Scotland Yard Professionals, they used their jealousy and one-upmanship to keep themselves sharp, honing themselves like knives, and working together toward doing the best job that they could.

My good opinion – and Holmes's too – had grown quite a bit toward both men in the nearly twenty-two years since that morning at No. 3 Lauriston Gardens, off the Brixton Road, where my life had unexpectedly pivoted away from being a young and aimless invalid, still mistakenly believing that I might return to Army life. I'd had no idea that Holmes's simple command to get my hat and join him, almost an afterthought which, to him, wouldn't have mattered one way or another, would be one of those moments where my life would change forever. That day, I'd simply thought Lestrade and Gregson to be a couple of strangers, met once in those terrible circumstance, and never to be re-encountered. As so many say when looking back at the twisting paths of their own lives, "*Little did I know . . . .*"

Now, on that afternoon in late 1902, I'd opened the door to Lestrade's office to find my three good friends – Holmes, Lestrade, and Gregson – with most-concerning looks of worry on their faces.

448

"Doctor," said Lestrade, while Gregson only nodded. The former was seated behind his small crowded desk, while Holmes and Gregson were in a couple of wooden chairs on the other side. I settled into a third and started to lay my hat upon some sort of wooden club resting on Lestrade's desk – a peg-leg, I realized, with some suspicious splintering around the lateral stabilizer and a dark stain at the end.

"I wouldn't," said Lestrade, raising a hand. "That's what Wooten used to kill his mistress. Her blood and brains are dried upon the end there. Your hat will stay cleaner if you just put it on that stack of papers."

I nodded, readjusted where I placed the hat, and looked expectantly at the trio, who looked back at me. Certainly they had been talking with one another before I arrived, but now they seemed to be at a loss for words.

The day outside was chill, as would be expected for that time of year, and the small coal fire in Lestrade's grate did little to counter it, even here, deep in the building. But it was better than nothing, and I trusted that I would soon feel warm enough.

In the short silence, I could see that both Lestrade and Gregson looked worried, while Holmes's mouth was tightened in irritation. Seeing that each party, the professionals and the consulting detective, were waiting for the other to begin, I chose the alternative and spoke first. "What has happened?"

Lestrade opened his mouth, but Holmes beat him. "Gruner's diary – it's been stolen."

With those few words, I immediately recalled the events of the previous September: A most illustrious visitor to Baker Street, representing the Crown itself. A noble old soldier's daughter in terrible deadly jeopardy. Holmes suffering a terrible beating, and the subsequent justice rendered upon the odious and wicked murderer behind it. And in the middle of it all, like some squatting cancerous toad, was a book – something like a journal or diary, but so much more vile and evil, and very much like the man who had written it.

Baron Adelbert Gruner was a killer. That should have been enough to outweigh any other factor about him. The Austrian nobleman had managed to murder his former wife without being caught, saved only by a legal technicality and the suspicious death of the only witness. Afterwards, he'd relocated to London and turned his sly attentions upon Violet de Merville, the only daughter of the famed hero who had made his name in the Khyber region. Before the general realized what was happening, Gruner had gained entrance into his daughter's life. The old soldier had been helpless against the reptilian fascination Gruner exerted upon the girl, and she would hear nothing against him. In fact, every delineated crime only made her cling to him more firmly. Marriage to Gruner, as everyone realized but the young lady, would lead to her complete and total ruin, both physically and spiritually, and she was racing toward that certain eventuality with a willing heart and open arms. For she loved the black-hearted sinner, and she would hear nothing against him.

Friends – both hers and her father's – tried to make her listen, but she believed that any stories against Gruner were either jealous exaggerations or total lies, and every effort that was expended to convince her otherwise only made her that much more stubborn. Even the testimony of one that he had cruelly wronged, a sad young woman named Kitty Winter, had no effect. From Kitty, Holmes learned of Gruner's diary – a dark chronicle of his perversions, written with cold and clinical precision and describing in graphic detail the defilement and destruction of every woman with whom he'd had substantial contact. Holmes realized that this book alone might be the only thing to convince Violet de Merville of the Baron's intent toward her – another page in his diary as she was systematically destroyed in every sense.

But before anything could be done, Gruner's men attacked Holmes, retribution for his efforts to dissuade the girl from the Baron. In desperation, as the Baron was leaving soon for America and would take the book with him, Holmes devised a rickety scheme in which I would distract the Baron, a noted collector of Chinese pottery – with a saucer from the Royal collection while Holmes searched for and retrieved the diary elsewhere in the Baron's house. But the plan nearly failed when he perceived my false position and then heard a faint sound from Holmes's search. All would have been lost if Kitty Winter had not rushed forward just then and flung vitriol into the Baron's snarling face, ruining his cruel handsome features forever.

My duty was clear: I had to stay and treat the patient, writhing in agony, no matter how justified his punishment. Holmes, meanwhile, escaped with the diary, and I saw it later in Baker Street. I did not wish to examine it, for Holmes explained that it was explicitly deranged in its exactly described details, with sketches and photographs tucked between the leaves. I was shocked to learn just how many notable women, many that I'd heard of and some that I knew, were in Gruner's collection – as if he were a butterfly collector who had pinned, corked, and carded them. At some point in our conversation, Holmes had looked at diary, the ugly brown book resting on the octagonal table by his chair, with distaste. "The Devil's pet bait," he'd murmured, although I hadn't understood his meaning then. It was only later, when Kitty Winter came to trial for throwing acid in her persecutor's face, that I followed his thought: There were secrets in that book to rock the nation, and if it fell into the wrong hands, the damage would be incalculable. That was one of the reasons that

Kitty's sentence was no more than a slap on the wrist – fear that her lawyer would introduce the book into evidence. (The other reason was that so many people were grateful for what she had done.)

After the trial, there was much discussion about what to do with the book.

It seemed to me that, after it was used to break Gruner's hold on Violet de Merville, the only answer was to destroy it, but more influential minds – that is to say, *scheming* minds – saw some value in preserving it, the way that the government builds bigger and more deadly bombs – *"Not to use them! No sir! We'd never do that! They're only here as a* deterrence *– in case some situation means that we* have *to use them. But we never will. But just in case there's no alternative, we'll have them . . . ."*

I was not privy to those conversations, and I had only heard about the decision to preserve the diary when Holmes described, with great disgust, how he had unsuccessfully taken the same position I held – that the book should be burned immediately. He was overruled.

I was unaware of what happened after that, and in truth had given the diary no further thought until that November day, in Lestrade's office, when I was told of its theft. The implications were immediately apparent.

"Has someone already made a blackmail attempt?" I asked.

Holmes shook his head. "If so, the chances that we would know about it this quickly would be nearly nil. The diary has only been gone for less than a few hours."

Still uncertain as to why I'd been summoned, I asked, "Where was it kept? How was it taken?"

Gregson sighed and replied. "The '*where*', Doctor, is *here*. In Lestrade's safe. The '*how*' has yet to be determined. That's why we asked for Mr. Holmes's help – and yours too."

I struggled to catch up, and to perceive the implications of such a theft occurring in the deep heart of Scotland Yard.

"Why . . . why was it kept here?" I finally chose as my first question. "Surely – "

"'Surely there were better places for it'?" interrupted Lestrade with disgust. "There's no denying that. But them that are smarter than the four of us thought that it would be safe here." He muttered a short curse under his breath. Then, "'*Safe*'," he repeated, shaking his head.

"It was felt that," explained Holmes, "for whatever reason, the book could not be simply destroyed. Without anyone actually making the statement aloud, it seems that Gruner was too good at describing . . . what he described, and those with devious and scheming minds saw that such information might be useful somewhere down the road – God knows how – to blackmail a minister into coming 'round to a certain opinion, perhaps,

451

by threatening that his wife's complete degradation might be revealed. Alternatively, they might force an industrialist to knuckle under to a government demand, lest his daughter's reputation be publicly destroyed by showing those pages in the diary devoted to her to a few influential and noisome individuals. My disgust knows no bounds in this affair. This is beyond any evil that was ever perpetrated by Milverton."

At that, the inspectors' gazes, previously unfocused and imagining the Government's dark intrigues, were both suddenly aimed rather sharply at Holmes, and I knew that they still had their suspicions about the true events on the night of Charles Augustus Milverton's murder, nearly four years before. Lestrade, who had investigated the brutal killing of the noted blackmailer, had hinted on more than one occasion that he'd still be looking for the middle-sized, strongly built man with a square jaw, thick neck, and moustache, nearly caught by the under-gardener as the fellow was escaping over Milverton's six-foot wall, if the blackmailer's death hadn't removed such a blight from the capital. I would probably tell him the truth someday over a couple of pints at The Ship in Wardour Street – but not yet.

Diverting attention from that topic, I stated, "Surely your brother wasn't involved in such a revolting scheme."

"Thankfully, he was not," Holmes replied. "Mycroft is devious, but honorable. However, even his influence was checked in this matter. All he could do, when it was apparent the diary would be preserved, was to insist that it be removed from the Halls of Power and deposited in a safer place – unknown to those who would use their influence to gain access to the book for their own purposes. When he achieved consent on that point – and such a compromise was no easy thing to wrest from those who are used to finding obsequious agreement with their every statement – Mycroft took the book and left it with Lestrade and Gregson."

"A most singular honor," growled the tall fair-haired inspector, while Lestrade fumed.

"Do you know how offensive it was," the smaller man asked, "to have that . . . *thing* in my safe? I buried it under papers and evidence so that I wouldn't have to look at it, but I still knew that it was there."

"And how long has it been here?" I asked.

"A month – or nearly so. After you and Mr. Holmes obtained it in mid-September, the politicians had to work through the great disagreement about what to do. Then Kitty Winter's attorney wanted to subpoena it for the trial – " He stopped abruptly and looked at Holmes. "And I have my suspicions as to how he got that idea."

"No need to wonder," replied Holmes. "Kitty deserved the best defense possible. I advised him to take that course."

452

Lestrade nodded, and Gregson said, "Would have done the same myself – as would Lestrade, if he doesn't mind me saying so."

"Wish I'd thought of it," Lestrade declared, and Gregson added, "He and I, as you might imagine, have discussed that filthy book a great deal."

"After Kitty's defense threatened to drag the diary into evidence, Higher Powers intervened." Lestrade's tone became rather bitter and somewhat sarcastic. "They argued for weeks before Mr. Mycroft Holmes, with his famed Solomon-like wisdom, dropped the whole mess onto the Yard – specifically the two of us."

"You should see it for the honor that it is," countered Holmes. "Mycroft knew that you were both above reproach, and that it would be safe here, of all places."

"And yet," growled Gregson, "it was *not* safe." He stood from his chair and walked to the side of the room, adding some coal the fire. "No reflection on Lestrade. If the two of us had instead decided to keep it in my office, it might have fared no better. He and I have the same type of locks upon the doors, and the same types of safes – brought with us from the old Yard when we moved here to the new building a dozen years ago." He gestured toward the old iron safe to the right of Lestrade's desk. "Mycroft Holmes asked us to keep the diary in a secure place, but where could we put it? Neither of us wanted that thing in our homes. There's no one we would have trusted to hide it for us except the two of you, and we didn't want to shift that burden onto your backs. Nor did we want to be seen putting it into a lock-box at a bank. Powerful men would give much to have that diary. It wouldn't take much influence for one of them to ask a favor of a bank president or director, and a way would be found to open the lock-box and remove it."

"And we didn't want to be checking on the lock-box once or twice a week," Lestrade, continuing Gregson's thought, "just to make sure it was still there while drawing attention to both us and the diary. It was much safer for it to simply disappear – and where better than deep in Scotland Yard? But even here, we had to be careful. We couldn't just bury it downstairs in the old evidence files, or jam it behind some loose brick in a little-used hallway. There was always the chance that it would be found. And the same as with the lock-box – We couldn't constantly check on it, which would draw too much attention. We finally thought that simply putting it in one of our safes and paying it no mind and attracting no interest, but able to verify regularly – and privately – that it was still there, was best."

"Who knew that you both had the diary?" I asked.

They looked at one another, and Gregson replied, "No one – but us and Mr. Mycroft Holmes." He looked at Sherlock Holmes. "I don't believe that you even knew what had become of it – or so I understood from your brother."

"That is correct," Holmes answered. "I was not told, and that was satisfactory. Now, for Watson's benefit, please repeat how you discovered that the diary was missing."

Lestrade pinched the bridge of his nose and, with eyes shut, related those events. "I know that the diary was in the safe last night. I had to put away the letters threatening Lord Rawchester's sister, and I took a moment – as I often do, to lift aside the other items resting on the diary and make sure that it's still there. It was. I re-covered it with the other files, put away the letters, and locked the safe. And I'm certain that I did so. I always make certain, but I'm also aware of just how often people *think* that they do something – a thing that has become an unthinking routine – and then actually forget to do it. But last night, I recall that when I spun the combination dial, it stopped exactly on the number *ten* – and as yesterday was November tenth, the moment stuck in my mind. Then, being finished for the day, I straightened my desk, extinguished the light, and left through the door. As is also my routine, I pulled the door shut and locked it – making sure several times that it was fully closed and locked. I don't have a corresponding fact to confirm it like the ten on the safe combination, but I absolutely recall closing the door. Wait – I do remember something. I had a newspaper in hand as I checked the door lock, folded open to yesterday's birthday honors. John Winthrop Hackett was knighted. You recall him, Mr. Holmes? The Australian newspaper proprietor who received that pair of horse eyes in the bloody box five years back?"

"So the doors to both the room and the safe were locked. I'm sure that it doesn't need to be confirmed that you were alone when this all occurred – checking the presence of the diary, re-covering it and locking the safe, and departing from the office?"

"That's correct. And the door was shut and the office empty when I verified that the diary was in the safe. This afternoon was the first time I needed to open the safe and retrieve a document. I unlocked it as usual, verified the fact that I needed, returned the document, and then made sure, as I nearly always do, that the diary was there. But it was *not*. I summoned Gregson."

"Lestrade and I looked at the safe," offered Gregson, "but we saw nothing. After much discussion, and before we notify Mr. Mycroft Holmes, we decided to consult with you, Mr. Holmes. Would you mind having a look?"

"I was about to suggest it."

As he rose and moved to the safe, Lestrade shifted his chair away to provide more room, while Gregson stepped back in the other direction.

How curious, I thought, to see how easily and willing the two seasoned inspectors were to seek Holmes's assistance. I was again reminded of that day in March 1881 when I first accompanied Holmes on an investigation. He had approached the body, lying in the ground-floor dining room of the empty house. The dead man's eyes has been open, and he was staring upward through the ceiling toward eternity. The corpse was twisted and rigid, and his expression bore a horrific and malignant rictus of agony, even in death.

After some discussion of the scene, and Lestrade's discovery of a telling word written in blood upon the wall, Holmes had finally begun his enthusiastic inspection of the room, moving here and there, making small noises and clicks and mutters, and entirely focused upon what he was observing – certainly so much more than the rest of us would ever see. Throughout, I looked away from whatever Holmes was accomplishing to glance at the two inspectors, seeing their expressions occasionally displaying curiosity, but more often a great deal of contempt. In later years, I was proud to note that I had recognized from that first encounter with Holmes's method that his ends were practical and directed, while it took some years for the official force to come around to that same way of thinking.

Now, with the same intensity he'd shown over twenty years earlier, Holmes examined Lestrade's old safe, its door open for his perusal. When he was done, he shut and locked the door, and then tried to open it this way and that without success. Afterwards, he examined the room around it, forcing us to shift aside when he needed to be where we were sitting or standing. Meanwhile, Lestrade and Gregson watched quietly and respectfully, as if – even at this late date – they might learn something useful.

After ten minutes, Holmes asked to see Gregson's office. Although he and Lestrade exchanged a look of confusion, and I could almost see the words, "*But Mr. Holmes, it was stolen from* my *safe!*" forming on the latter's lips, he bit his tongue. While they were out of the room, neither Lestrade nor I exchanged a word.

It wasn't long before Holmes and Gregson returned. I looked for any sign of encouragement, but even Sherlock Holmes's many skills were of no use just then, as he shook his head.

"There is nothing but coal ash in the fireplace, and not much of that – he didn't burn it. There are no footprints that one wouldn't expect – Lestrade, you keep your office far too clean. Not a speck of dust on the desk or safe, or even on the floor in the out-of-the-way corners, to retain a mark. Obviously there are no signs of forced entry to the room, or to the safe. As you say, it's an old model, and given enough time, there would be no difficulty using a physician's stethoscope to listen to the tumbler's falling into place, but there's nothing to indicate that occurred either."

He looked as if he wanted to pull out his pipe and think, but he restrained the impulse.

"Do you maintain that no one could get into the office or the safe except yourself?"

Lestrade shook his head. "I don't maintain that at all. The lock is nothing special, and there are other keys to the office. There's a duplicate in the Superintendent's safe, and Gregson has one as well."

"And Lestrade also has a key to my office," added Gregson. "It has saved a lot of time."

"And this has been your office since the Yard moved here from Whitehall Terrace," agreed Holmes, "so there wouldn't be a key in the hands of a former tenant. What about the safe?"

Lestrade's brow wrinkled. "You see how old it is. I inherited it from Dockery when he retired, back before I met you, Mr. Holmes. The old safes came with us from the old building when we moved here – it was determined that buying new ones would be too expensive." He had resumed his seat after Holmes's investigation, and he leaned forward, arms crossed upon his desk. "What are you thinking?"

"I'm thinking that this may not have been a planned theft, specifically targeted toward obtaining the diary. I'm satisfied that Mycroft didn't tell anyone that he was leaving the diary in your possession, and that neither of you have told anyone either."

Lestrade gave a firm shake of his head, and Gregson replied in a low tone, "Not a word."

"Then no one would know to look for it here," I said, rather obviously.

"I'm convinced," reiterated Holmes, "at least for the purposes of progressing forward, that only three people – Mycroft and you two, Gregson and Lestrade – knew that the diary was coming to Scotland Yard. And as you say, Mycroft didn't know where you intended to keep it once it was here. He trusted you –"

Lestrade snorted. "That turned out to be misplaced."

"He *trusted* you," Holmes repeated with emphasis, "and rightly so. But my point is this: No one but the two of you knew where the diary was hidden, so no one could come looking for it – intentionally and knowingly – here, in this office, and specifically in that safe. Therefore, it would be better to consider who has access to the office and might have discovered it accidentally and understood what he or she had found, rather than trying to determine who knew of the diary."

Gregson nodded. "Whoever found it realized what it was, and impulsively took it away."

"That is how I read it," agreed Holmes. "So the question becomes who has access to this office and your safe, Lestrade – which one would ideally hope might be impregnable. Who would have *reason* to enter your office and access your safe?"

Lestrade shook his head. "Not impregnable. You've seen that door lock, Mr. Holmes. Even if there are only three *known* keys, there's nothing there that would keep out a determined man or woman. And as I said, the safe is old, and the combination, as far as I know, is the same as it was when it was first installed in the old Yard."

Holmes nodded. "It's a fair assumption that someone went to this trouble for a reason, before unexpectedly finding the diary. Perhaps this person came here to see one of the other documents in your safe? What else of a sensitive nature in there, related to a current investigation? Have you looked to see if anything else is missing?"

Lestrade frowned, and I could see that he was both irritated and embarrassed with himself for not having made that examination earlier. But I could understand his thinking. If I'd been the keeper of such a dangerous object and noticed that it was gone, it would never occur to me that something of lesser value or importance was taken as well.

He rose and stepped to the safe. Holmes joined him, watching over his shoulder as Lestrade spun the combination without thought, and apparently with no hesitation at Holmes seeing and learning it. I considered the relations between the two of them when I first met both in early 1881 – the consulting detective holding the professional in contempt who, along with Gregson, was "the pick of a bad lot", while Lestrade would acknowledge Holmes's sometime assistance and usefulness to the Yard, but not much more than that.

Now, Holmes accepted Lestrade's limitations while admiring his many admirable traits – particularly his doggedness and his integrity – and Lestrade had said it best a couple of years before, while congratulating Holmes after a particularly neat piece of work, stating, "We're not jealous of you at Scotland Yard. No, sir, we are very proud of you, and if you come down tomorrow, there's not a man, from the oldest inspector to the youngest constable, who wouldn't be glad to shake you by the hand." If, as a young man of twenty-eight, I'd been swept forward nearly two decades in time and clapped down in front of Holmes and Lestrade and shown that scene, I wouldn't have believed it possible.

Lestrade had reopened the safe and lifted out a stack of papers, returning with them to his desk. There was a variety of envelopes, large and small and varying in shade, mixed in with a few worn manila folders.

The entire collection was no more than five or six inches high, and none of the packets were any thicker than the others. Lestrade began to go through each with great diligence, sheet by sheet, and, while one might have expected such a thorough inspection to become tedious, we three – Holmes, Gregson, and myself – remained fixated upon the inspector's secret files.

"The Whittaker forgery, and the true heir's identity," he explained with the first envelope opened. It was no more than five or six sheets, which he examined individually, replaced, and set aside. "The Russell Square Ripper," he said, opening a folder. This had a few clipped pages and one smaller envelope, containing a single sheet. "The confession," Lestrade said, holding it up with a grimace. "It wasn't accepted, as a 'better' solution was found implicating a dead man, and The Crown wanted to save one of their own." He closed that folder and set it aside with obvious disgust.

He continued to look through each set of papers – "The Templeton Plague. The Dutch Monkey Incident. The Stolen Greystoke Inheritance – you can bet we'll hear more about that one. That nasty business in the Dorset Street sewers. Milverton's shooting – " He paused to look toward Holmes and then me with a knowing expression and a raised eyebrow. "These are just the public facts, you understand. I haven't recorded my own theories – about the two men who escaped and were blamed by the servants, or the evidence I found of a lady in very expensive shoes who was on the scene. Bloody footprints, you understand – one of them on Milverton's face." Then he dropped his gaze back to the papers and resumed his examination. "The Siamese Quintuplets and their pet constrictor. The terrible business at the artificial knee-cap factory . . . ."

Five minutes later, he restacked all of the envelopes and folders and stated, "Every file is complete, to the last sheet and photograph and scrap. Only one is missing in its entirety: The Clissold suicide."

I recalled the terrible affair. Six weeks before, Floyd Clissold, a low-level agent of the British Government, suspected of taking payments from other interests, had been found dead in a Hackney room, which he'd apparently rented under an assumed name. He was supposed to be out of the country, and it was uncertain why he was back in London. If the body hadn't been recognized by one of the investigating sergeants who knew Clissold when he was a thieving lad roaming the streets, he might have been buried as an unknown in a pauper's grave. But when the dead man's name was revealed, someone within the Government who had dealings with him saw it in the newspaper and recognized it. There was some concern that he was in London without permission, and why Scotland Yard, escalating the investigation because of the Clissold's sudden

458

apparent importance, had Inspector Youghal approach Holmes for assistance. After he'd made some initial inquiries, Holmes was warned off the case by his brother Mycroft – "In the national interest" Mycroft had cryptically explained – and thus the matter stood, unsolved.

"It was clear," said Lestrade, "that – in spite of the obvious evidence – it was murder and not suicide. Even with the official position to step back and leave it be, I was asked to take over from Youghal and continue a low-level investigation, regardless of our efforts being quashed from higher up."

"And who asked you to do this?" asked Gregson, rightfully curious as to who within the police hierarchy would make such a command.

"Superintendent Blevins," Lestrade said, his eyes taking on a knowing look. Gregson nodded with understanding as well, and even Holmes seemed to comprehend the implications of Blevins' involvement. As usual, it was left to me to ask for help catching up, trying not to sound like an ignorant but curious child while the adults whispered above me about things that were none of my business.

"What is the significance of Superintendent Blevins?" I asked after all three had pondered for a silent moment.

Holmes deferred to the two inspectors. Gregson sighed. "He has been here forever, it seems. Not quite one of the original Peelers, but you'd be forgiven for thinking that he was. He was here when Lestrade and I arrived, and sometimes I wonder if he'll be here when we're gone. He's a big man, but not in an unhealthy way. His hair had gone gray when I met him, and it's slowly whitened. Likewise, his ruddy complexion has faded over the years, and now he moves through the hallways, slower than he once did, like some black-suited ghost."

"Understand," added Lestrade, "he's a good officer. He worked his way up, and he understands the . . . complications of being a policeman, from the lowest constable walking his set rounds to the inspectors being pulled between finding the truth and finding what the politicians want us to find. During the search for the Rippers, [1] he was our strong advocate against what the Masons were demanding from us more times than I can count."

"He was already a superintendent when I first started associating with the Yard," offered Holmes, looking in my direction, "and to his credit, he didn't discourage the first inspectors who sought my assistance – Plummer and Penner, for instance. A wrong word from him, and my opportunities would have been sharply limited." He turned his head back toward Lestrade. "Are you surprised to find that Blevins could have entered your office and opened your safe?"

Lestrade's arms had been resting on his desk, fingers intertwined. Now he unwound them, leaned back, and rubbed the heels of his palms on his eyes. "I suppose not. Nothing surprises me."

"The safe was the most secure place we could think of," Gregson said in Lestrade's defense. It was many years since their rivalry had defined their friendship. He felt the need to re-explain what they had already excused. "My office and safe would have been no more secure from such an . . . attack from within. Neither of us could have taken that . . . thing home with us. I wouldn't want it defiling where I live, and neither would Lestrade. And we couldn't tuck it away here in the building, for anyone to find. If a man can't trust the safe in his own office – "

"Peace," said Holmes, holding up a hand. "I am not faulting you – either of you. The question is, now that it seems likely to have been Blevins, does it make sense? That he was able to open your safe?"

"Yes," said Lestrade. "Yes to having a key to my office, and also to knowing the combination to the safe. Blevins was probably around when these safes were first purchased."

"Then it simply remains to confirm that he was the one who took the diary, and why. Will you take this matter to Sir Edward? Shall I now involve Mycroft?"

Lestrade and Gregson glanced at one another and silently reached immediate agreement. "Not your brother," said Gregson. "And not Sir Edward, either. He's approaching retirement, and not as . . . shall we say, *involved* in day-to-day affairs as we might wish."

I knew Colonel Sir Edward Bradford, the Metropolitan Police Commissioner, rather well, having encountered him a number of times by way of Holmes's investigations. He had taken the post in 1890, during that thankless period following the tenures of Sir Charles Warren and James Monro. Sir Charles had overseen the Yard during the Bloody Sunday riots, as well as the search for the Rippers, and when he resigned in late 1888, poor Monro had been left to pick up the pieces. Although popular with the Force, Monro's service had lasted just eighteen months, the shortest time of any commissioner. His replacement, Sir Edward, had served as a calming influence after the tumult of the previous years. The man's vast military experience – he'd gone out to India around the time I was born, and was still there after I was invalided home after Maiwand – had given him the administrative skills to manage the police force in a successful way. But Gregson's comment implied that, after a dozen years, Sir Edward might not be the man he once was.

"If we go to Sir Edward half-cocked," added Lestrade, "we may disrupt something we don't understand – some reason that Superintendent Blevins took the diary."

Holmes shifted in his seat, leaning back as if he were getting comfortable and about to watch a play. "Well, then, perhaps you might have him step in satisfy our curiosity."

"Mr. Holmes – " said Gregson, while Lestrade said, "It might be better if – "

Holmes shook his head. "Now that you see a possible solution, you're ready to send Watson and me away, so that we won't observe the Yard's dirty laundry. It won't do. We're involved now, and with – I believe – a legitimate interest in finding out what happened to Gruner's diary. Watson and I didn't work that hard to retrieve it, just to lose track of who has it next. And if you need another reason, consider me to be Mycroft's representative – officially undesignated just now, but that can be fixed with a quick telephone call, should you require it."

Lestrade and Gregson didn't need to confer, or even look at one another. They knew how stubborn Holmes could be. With a sigh, Lestrade pushed a button on the side of his desk, which was electrically wired to a bell in a nearby room. I knew that there were always a few constables there, and that one of them would answer momentarily. And within half-a-minute, a young officer – And they looked so young to me these days! – leaned in and was told by Gregson to please find Superintendent Blevins and ask him to step around to Lestrade's office.

Gregson, who had been standing for much of the time, reclaimed his own seat after setting another chair in place for Blevins, in a position where all of us could see him. None of us spoke, apparently agreeing that there was nothing left to say until we'd heard the superintendent's story. We only had to wait in silence for a couple of minutes before there was a slight knock upon the door, followed by the entrance of the elder policeman.

After he entered, I realized that I had seen him in the past – quite a few times, actually. I was rather surprised, after learning of the long occupancy of his position, that I hadn't actually met him during one or more of Holmes's investigations.

As described, he was a big man, but he moved with the carefulness that one acquires with age. I was then just turned fifty years old, and I had already noticed that I was more careful when going down stairs, or when crossing wet or icy pavement, having begun to realize that I was past those strong young and middle years when one feels indestructible.

Blevins shut the door behind him and took a moment to look around. He didn't exactly seem surprised to find four of us there, but an eyebrow did lift fractionally upon spotting Holmes and me. I didn't know if he would have recognized me in the street, but my being there along with Holmes probably gave him a good idea who I was.

"You asked to see me, Inspector Lestrade?" he asked, his voice soft, and rather rough with age. Lestrade only then decided it was a good idea to stand, and he did so, followed by Gregson. My long-ago military training urged me to do the same before I really gave it a thought, but I saw that Holmes remained seated, leaning back with one leg crossed over the other, and so I matched his response.

"I did, Superintendent. Umm, we did, actually. I . . . ."

It was only then that I – and I think Lestrade and Gregson as well – noticed that Blevins carried something in his hands, wrapped in a cloth. It was eight or nine inches long, five or so wide, and a couple of inches thick. I glanced at Holmes and saw that his eyes were also focused on the object. He had probably seen it as soon as Blevins entered. A small gleam was in his eyes.

Without being told, Blevins turned and seated himself in the empty chair like a witness in an interrogation, the object held in one hand and resting upon his lap. He gave a weary sigh, and he seemed to settle in upon himself, as if a bucket of stiff concrete was dumped upon the ground, slowly slumping from a cylindrical shape into a vague spreading mound.

The old man looked at Lestrade. "You wish to question me about the intrusion into your safe."

"Umm . . . ." Lestrade was clearly nervous – a condition which I've rarely seen him evince. I cut my eyes to see if his old rival was taking any pleasure in it. He was not.

Lestrade soldiered on. "In your position," he said, his voice becoming clearer as he spoke, "you have the right to enter any room here at the Yard, and to look into any safe. It's only that – "

Blevins raised his free hand. "A quick explanation is best, isn't it? We're all very experienced in this sort of thing. Any protestations upon my part are a waste of everyone's time." He turned his head toward Holmes, who was still sitting in a relaxed but interested manner.

"It's good to see you again, Mr. Holmes. I'm not surprised that Lestrade and Gregson sought your council. You have worked very well together over the years."

Holmes nodded. "I was honored to be asked by my friends to offer advice, but I really didn't have that much to give. An examination of the safe's papers revealed one set of missing case documents, and those were associated with you."

"Nevertheless," Blevins countered. He looked back at Lestrade. "That was my safe once, you know. When I was an inspector – years before you and Gregson came along – even before old Dockery. That old scratch on the front? That's where Darrell Finney tried to kill me with a wicked jack-knife as I interviewed him in my office. Just missed me and hit the safe door, before sliding off and giving my constable a terrible gash in the leg. I should have known better than to interview a killer like Finney in those circumstances without having him searched." He fell silent in the reminiscence, but then his fingers squeezed the object in his hand and he returned to us.

"The safe combination? Zero-seven, zero-two, thirty-five? That's my birthday, you see. When they bought the safes, the safe-maker let each of us pick a number that we could remember. That's how I was able to get into the safe this morning to retrieve the Clissold file." He shook his head. "You won't have heard yet, Lestrade, but it's being swept under the rug. Not a surprise, eh? I was ordered to retrieve all materials related to the matter and turn them over to the Commissioner. Apparently there are some Royals who might get burned if too much more about what Clissold was up to is discovered, and I'm rather on the hot seat for continuing to pursue it. I've made sure, however, that your name was kept out of it. They have no idea that you were keeping the file, or that it was you asking more questions."

Lestrade nodded, and the superintendent continued.

"I came down to your office to get the file, only to find your door locked. Quite right, of course, but I couldn't wait. Since the file was supposed to be in my keeping, and I was supposed to be retrieving it right then from my office to turn it over to Sir Edward and a palace representative waiting with him, I was forced to open your door with my master key. I knew that I could open the safe as well, so I did it. I was rooting around, looking for the Clissold file, when I unexpectedly found this . . . ."

And he held up the object in his hand, letting the cloth fall away.

It was a book.

I had only seen it once before, when Holmes showed it to me after he'd stolen it from Baron Gruner's private office while I distracted him in the adjacent room. I'd never seen inside it, and I didn't want to, but even without confirming the contents, I knew what it was. It was brown leather, with a lock on it. The cover was decorated with Gruner's Coat of Arms, a hideous red-and-yellow mess that appeared rather like something a sick animal would expel. There were feathers around the edges that looked more ichthian than bird-like, and some sort of knight's helmet in the top half which looked more like a low-headed eyeless chicken head. Below that was a red shield with a backward-facing Turkish crescent. I found it offensive, and would have done so even if I hadn't known anything about the book's original owner.

Holmes had described it as Gruner's "lust diary". He had first learned of the volume from the poor debauched girl, Kitty Winter, who told him that Gruner "collects women, and takes a pride in his collection, as some men collect moths or butterflies." She explained that it contained names, details, photographs – everything about the women he'd captured. *Souls I Have Ruined* was the title that Kitty suggested should be on the outside cover – but no such wording was there. Just that hideous Coat of Arms that seemed to illustrate so well with everything that I knew about Baron Adelbert Gruner.

Perhaps sensing that questioning their superior would be awkward, Holmes took the lead. "Once you found it, you had to read it?" He asked. "You'd heard of it and wanted to see just how bad it was?"

Blevins lips tightened in what might have been a gentle smile, or perhaps it was a grimace. The skin on his face was loose with age, and it was difficult to determine just what he meant to express. I saw that there might have been a tear in his eye – or perhaps it was just an old man's rheumy dampness.

"Correct, Mr. Holmes," Blevins replied. "I had to read it – and I had to know how bad it was."

He stopped, his voice having broken as he finished speaking. We were silent as well, sensing that some dark undercurrent was about to be exposed. Then Holmes said softly, "Someone you know is in that book."

Blevins' fingers tightened upon the volume, the old chalky knuckles turning even whiter. His lips tightened, and he just nodded – once in acknowledgement, and then again, with more decision. He looked up, now facing Holmes, as if my friend were to serve as the old man's confessor.

Blevins tried to speak, but his voice failed him. Then, with effort, he tried again, and as he talked, his voice became smoother, but the strain was not lessened.

"My wife," he rasped. "My dear, beautiful wife is in this book. Gruner took her and . . . My wife is in this book."

Once Blevins began his story, it seemed to pour out, for he had likely never had anyone with whom he could share it.

"I married late. Lestrade and Gregson may know – but then again, they might not." Both shook their heads. "I thought so. When I was an inspector, I could barely keep track of my work, let alone my own personal life. For so long, the work was enough – but then I met Elizabeth.

"She is Sir William Cress's youngest daughter – widowed in her forties. She was attending one of those social functions that occasionally require the presence of a police superintendent, and from the moment I saw her, it was as if I had awakened for the first time in my life – or as if my eyes had been covered and I was then just seeing sunshine.

"We talked that night, and I was thrilled that she was willing to entertain my presence. Having never held any interest in social functions,

I found myself making excuses to be at parties where she would be in attendance, and contriving further ways to have conversations with her. Long ago, such a one as me wouldn't have been welcome at some of these events, but times had changed, and I also began to understand that, because of my position, I'd gained more respect over the years than I'd realized, having limited myself before then by remaining focused solely upon my work, and not understanding how empty and lonely I was.

"One can't be a policeman and also be a coward, so I found the nerve to request her hand in marriage. At her age, there was no real objection, and I gave little thought to the difference in ages between us. And perhaps back then, it didn't seem as obvious. That was ten years ago, and I've had something of a steady collapse since then, while Elizabeth is still as beautiful as the day I first saw her. That's why, I fear, she soon became bored with our marriage.

"I was never under any illusion that she loved me as strongly as I loved her, but she did feel that it was a good match. I don't believe she came to fully regret it, but I did know that she didn't reciprocate my feelings. I didn't care. I still don't care. She has my heart, until the end.

"If she was having affairs, I didn't know. I didn't want to know. I was promised to her – My *lady*! – and that was the beginning and end of it. I had *promised*! But then . . . then Gruner set his sights upon her.

"I knew that she was different than she had been – at first, a bit happier, and then upset – but I didn't know why. And then she told me. It wasn't blackmail, and Gruner was through with her. She had nothing else that he wanted. But his . . . his true enjoyment didn't begin until he'd told her about his book . . . and that she was in it. It seems that he has a special type of cruelty that way. He doesn't demand money, or anything of value. He simply has to remind his victims, from time to time, what they did and how he has it recorded. He revels in their shame and pain. Finally, when she could stand it no more, she told me . . . ."

Blevins drifted in to silence, and Lestrade quietly asked him if he'd like some water. The old man shook his head, and his gaze drifted toward the fireplace, where the flames, ignorant and disinterested in the affairs of men, danced greedily upon the small mound of coal.

Then Blevins refocused on Holmes. "I understand that you've been to Gruner's house out in Kingston," he said. He cut his eyes in my direction. "And you too, Doctor Watson. You've seen what a beautiful place it is – the long drive, surrounded by shrubs, and the open space before the house dotted with statues. The architecture is peculiar, but I believe that it's what the former owner, Coetzee, wanted when he moved here from South Africa. In any case, there is a stateliness to the place, and one would never have suspected the cancer that dwelled within.

465

"Gruner welcomed me affably when I went to see him, and he offered no apologies that my wife was in his book. He told me . . . He shared specific details. Apparently my shame also pleased him. I demanded that he surrender the book. He refused, and gleefully told me specifics of other women that were also included – 'Of course, I shan't share names, Superintendent,' he murmured, his manner giving one the cold shivers, as if being too close to a serpent. 'It wouldn't be discreet, would it? But I can generally tell you about the M.P.'s wife, or the daughter of one of the Queen's cousins . . . .' He went on and on, and I was given to understand that any attempt on my part to retrieve the book would meet with failure, and prompt the very real chance that names and details would be made public.

"'Do not fear, Superintendent,' he said, clearly enjoying the power he held. 'I am neither a Milverton nor a Carruthers. I have no interest in blackmailing anyone. I derive my enjoyment from the fact that my ladies never forget that I *know* them, perhaps more than anyone else ever has or will, and that with my extensive notes, I shall never *forget* them. Now, the night is passing, and I have other appointments. Do give your lovely wife my best regards, and let her know that I think of her – quite often.'

"It seemed all that I could do to keep from killing him right then, but he knew me, too – he could see into me as easily as any of the women he ruined, and he understood that I wasn't a murderer. I hated myself as much as him as I slunk away, like some defeated lick-spittle cur.

"I returned home, and my wife knew before I spoke that I'd been beaten. I fear that she lost a great deal of respect for me that night – possibly whatever was left of any she'd had before. When you retrieved the diary, Mr. Holmes, and that girl threw acid in Gruner's face – Well, we knew then that others would read it, and our shame was increased exponentially, but no one has ever said a word, or approached me about it. We've gone on with our lives, and my love for my wife is still as certain as before. And yet . . . and yet . . . ."

"And yet," Holmes said softly, "you had to know. You didn't simply toss the diary into Lestrade's fireplace as soon as you found it."

"I did," whispered Blevins. "God help me, I had to know."

Then, as if hearing Holmes's words again, hearing the slight emphasis that Holmes had made, Blevins' mouth tightened, a decision made. He looked at Holmes, who nodded, almost imperceptibly – as if giving him permission.

Blevins stood, looked at Lestrade and Gregson, and me as well, to see if anyone would challenge him. When there was no response, he took two steps, leaned over, and laid the opened diary face-down upon the coal fire.

I think I expected Lestrade or Gregson to rise and make some protest, or to lurch forward to save the wicked thing from the flames. I was already tensed to rise and place myself in front of one or both of them, defending the old man and letting the thing burn. But neither inspector made a move, nor made a sound. They, like Holmes, were watching the hungry red-and-yellow tendrils first licking the book, and then hungrily consuming it. The leather cover curled quickly, throwing up a strong plume of black smoke, and then the pages that I could see browned and burst into flame. The room filled with hints of a terrible odor, as if some vile trapped spirit was being consumed.

Leaf by leaf, the sadness and grief that the book contained rose with the smoke. One might naively hope that such would erase the pain, but in truth, many in the book would never know that they were now free. Perhaps, somehow if there was any greater mercy, Gruner's victims could sense that their secrets were now burned, traveling in the air, never again to be discovered. But I doubted it.

Blevins had positioned the book in such a way that it settled deeper into the coal as it collapsed, insuring that it didn't fall out of the grate.

I don't know how long we watched – perhaps five minutes – before it was obvious that the volume was nearly gone. What was left was something made of ash that held the shape of a book. Only then did Lestrade rise and step quietly past Blevins. He reached for his small poker and prodded and flattened the remains, scattering them forever.

Replacing the poker, he turned to his superior and asked, "Did you find everything that you needed when you retrieved the Clissold file, sir?"

"I did, Inspector," replied the old man, still standing by the fireplace. "I did." And then he offered his hand, and Lestrade took it.

Nothing else was said as Blevins shook hands with Holmes, Gregson, and me before walking out of the office and pulling the door softly shut behind him.

No one said anything for several moments, until Holmes finally muttered, "Poor helpless worm. There, but for the grace of God . . . ."

Lestrade looked at him curiously. Holmes had said something similar to me long ago, when old John Turner had confessed how he'd killed his persecutor at Boscombe Pool. Lestrade had investigated the case at the time, but hadn't learned the truth until years later, when he and I had discussed it just before the narrative was published in *The Strand*. We both thought that Holmes was dead then, and I'd related to Lestrade how Holmes had chosen to show mercy to old Turner, as the old man was believed to be dying. [2] Lestrade had nodded then, confessing to me that he was often pulled between his sworn professional duty to catch and punish lawbreakers and his innate instinct see that actual justice took place, even if it meant turning a blind eye to the law.

That day, in Lestrade's office, both inspectors had wisely chosen the latter.

"I'll explain to Mycroft," Holmes added, and the inspectors nodded in gratitude. Then Holmes turned to me.

"Sorry it wasn't more of a chase, Watson," he said, his tone rather jovial after the gravity of what we'd just heard and seen.

I waved my hand, reluctant to simply close the subject. "The Superintendent – " I said. "Burning Gruner's diary hasn't really solved anything for him, has it?"

Gregson shook his head. "God help him. He loves her. You saw it. He's risked his career – even prison – if what he just did comes out, or if Mr. Mycroft Holmes takes a dim view of what has happened. He loves her – but to know what he knows now, having read it, and still – . The specifics and the details . . . ."

"Why did he have to look at it?" asked Lestrade. "He could have just burned it here, as soon as he pulled it from the safe. Why did he have to look – to *know*? It seems it would be the last nail in the coffin of his love."

"I can't pretend to know anything about love," said Holmes softly, "but I believe he had to set and pass one final test for himself. He said, 'God help me, I had to know.' I don't think he meant that he needed to see every explicit fact recorded in the diary about Gruner and his wife. He had to know if, after seeing that, he could still love her.

"He already knew that he loved her when she didn't quite love him back in the same way. He still loved her when she possibly had affairs, and even when the affair with Gruner was confirmed. He still loved her when the full shame of it became apparent. But with all of that, he had one more obstacle to overcome: To see just how great his love has to be. And I believe him when he said that, even after today, he still loves her. I believe that he will until his dying day – although I fear that this experience will hasten that event sooner than it might have been. I just hope the lady understands and appreciates what she has, instead of testing him even further before he's gone."

My friend often claims to lack an understanding of the human heart, but he's mistaken. Lestrade and Gregson nodded in agreement with Holmes's supposition. Then, with nothing left to say until next we met, hands were shaken, thanks were conveyed, and Holmes and I stepped outside, pulling Lestrade's office door shut behind us.

NOTES

1. For more information about Holmes's overall investigation into the massive Rippers Conspiracy during the terrible Bloody Autumn of 1888 can be found in "November, 1888", published in *The Collected Papers of Sherlock Holmes – Volume III: Accounts*. It was originally published in *The Watsonian* (Fall 2015, Vol. 3, No.2) and in my online blog, *A Seventeen Step Program* at:
   https://17stepprogram.blogspot.com/2017/02/sherlock-holmes-versus-jack-ripper.html

2. Further facts about John Turner's supposed death are revealed in "The True Account of the Bushell Street Killing", in *The Collected Papers of Sherlock Holmes: Volume V – Chronicles* and *Beyond the Adventures of Sherlock Holmes – Volume II*

The Seamy Circumstances
of the Imitation Ripper

"I thought that conditions were supposed to get better here." I looked around with both disappointment and disgust, but markedly more of the latter.

Holmes was also glancing from one side of the narrow street to another, but with a different purpose in mind: To see if someone was watching us from the shadows.

"It isn't glaringly obvious," he said softly, "especially on a dark autumn night such as this, but Whitechapel has, in fact, improved considerably after the glaring attention it received fifteen years ago."

I nodded, accepting his statement without seeing visible proof, as I was aware that through the years, he had been to this benighted district of London far more often than I. Intellectually, I knew that what he said was true: Efforts *had* been made to better the living conditions of those who spent their lives here, and to alleviate the terrible overcrowding, poverty, filth, and ignorance that had contributed to the events of 1888 – but standing there in the darkness on that brisk late-September night, one was hard pressed to believe it.

We had gradually allowed ourselves to separated somewhat from the crowd of two-dozen or so people with whom we had spent the last two hours, letting them get a bit ahead of us while trudging along one dark street after another. Things might have improved in this quarter, but it was still simply foolish to wander Whitechapel at night – especially along some of the routes and more remote spots that were part of the tour.

We had passed quite a few figures hurrying about their own business, ignoring us as they went by, anonymous in their dark hats and coats. Every few streets, with unfortunate regularity, our group encountered a sadly inebriated vagrant, each one staggering toward us and yelling obscenities, or the occasional prostitute, along with others of similar ilk, who would either watch in judgmental silence, or instead boldly call out with vulgar suggestions that would shock the innocent men and women who had no business being in that part of the city. Then, as our group would hurry along to the next site on our itinerary, we would hear the fading whoops of laughter, caused by the outraged reactions of our party.

Often we would pass through dark and narrow alleys that had never had a gaslight installed to make safe the night, or we would cross the opening of some black and baleful passage on one side or the other, suddenly finding ourselves filled with the same primitive feelings that our ancient ancestors must have experienced when passing the Stygian darkness of a cave, fully expecting a slavering and death-dealing monster to spring forth upon us. I knew that all of us – Holmes and myself included – placed some small faith that we had strength in numbers. And that might have been true, for we moved forward unaccosted except the occasional gibe or sneer, but I was glad nevertheless to feel the reassuring weight of my service revolver in my coat pocket. Holmes, as was typical, carried his sword cane, and additionally he was wearing the same weighted scarf that had accompanied him on those terrible nights of '88 when we'd roamed these same streets, actively seeking any kind of encounter that might save a life or advance our investigation.

"Mr. Holmes! Doctor!" called the man leading the group. He waved his hand, indicating that we should draw closer. "Please rejoin us! You'll be most interested in this next part. I'm going to discuss the *Juwes* message that was chalked on this doorway – Yes, that's right, ma'am. Right there." He pointed to a most unassuming entryway to a terribly plain and shabby building. "Mr. Holmes," he said again, either to get our attention or to remind the other members of the group that Sherlock Holmes was indeed among them. "I understand that you and Dr. Watson were both on hand on the night when the message was discovered. Any insights you have will be much appreciated."

I looked at Holmes and saw the same distaste reflected in his expression that was surely on mine. And yet, we had expected this when we arrived that night to participate in the tour. In any case, it seemed almost certain that whatever was certain to happen, the expected event that had brought us from our comfortable homes to this dangerous part of the city would occur in the next few minutes.

The previous weeks had been cold and unpleasant, but that hadn't stopped Amos Mann, our smiling and unctuous guide through Whitechapel, from carrying on, night after night, with his curiously off-putting venture. Events had progressed to the point that Holmes and I were now involved, although certainly not in the way that Mann had wished or foreseen. I was thankful that the terrible rains of the previous weeks had at last abated, and that in spite of standing in a dark Whitechapel street a few hours before midnight, we faced no other discomforts than a cold wind and nagging suspense.

We closed the distance between us and the small crowd that was circled around Mann, listening as he gave his lurid but nevertheless generally accurate account of what had occurred at that spot not-so-many years before. He was in his late fifties, fat in face and figure. He wore no hat, and his longish gray hair was somewhat wild in the night breeze.

471

Down each side of his red face were startlingly white Dundreary Weepers, themselves quite long, so that they peculiarly framed his face and made it stand out, highlighting his unhealthy color.

Mann had a lilt to his voice, and it suited the well-rehearsed script that he performed at each of our stops. I did not approve, as his tawdry showmanship made entertainment of tragedy. After watching him speak for moment, I turned to look upon the dark streets. The black night hid so much pain and tragedy. In some ways, it was hard to believe that we were only a decade-and-a-half past the horrific events that had occurred in these passages and alley-ways, but it also felt like a lifetime away.

Mann continued to drone on about the message that had been chalked in the doorway of that Ghoulson Street tenement, and I remembered how it had been when I saw it for myself – the thirtieth of September, 1888, the night when the Ripper had killed two women. "The Double Event", the newspapers had called it. As I looked at the doorway, standing in nearly the same spot I'd been on that night when I'd seen the chalk writing, I tried to gauge just how much I had changed.

Back then, I had just turned thirty-six a few weeks before – on 7 August, 1888, which was the same night that Martha Tabram was murdered, stabbed to death on a landing in the George Yard Buildings. Although another East End prostitute, Emma Smith, had also been murdered back in April, four months earlier, poor Martha's death was possibly the first victim of Jack the Ripper, although others thought that her death was a separate event. But putting all that happened during those terrible months underneath the plain umbrella of *"The Ripper"* was a vast oversimplification of what had actually occurred, as people later attempted to divide and sort the vast number of overlapping crimes into manageable and understandable pieces.

I had been a far different man then, at thirty-six, than I was now, nearly two months past my fifty-first birthday, and tentatively entering those days when a fellow starts to feel both his venerability and vulnerability. Back in those latter months of 1888, I was a relatively fresh widower who had just spent a very busy year assisting my friend Sherlock Holmes in his many investigations while I attempted to remake my life from the one I'd lost when my first wife died into something that was more tolerable. It was during one of these cases that fall that I met the woman who would heal my heart, the lovely Mary Morstan.

She was initially simply one of Holmes's clients, arriving at our Baker Street rooms in early September, just as the horrors of the Ripper investigation were beginning to intensify. Throughout that autumn, as my love for her grew quickly, so did my fear that somehow she might be pulled into the rising maelstrom of fear and death that was swirling around us. And inevitably she was, as the villains behind the Ripper conspiracy perceived that she had become my Achilles Heel, and through me, they could try and control Holmes. They took her, in an attempt to direct Holmes's actions when he came too close to the truth. But the Rippers didn't understand that Holmes was too smart for them, and that my rage, when ignited, was the last thing they wanted to find coming in their direction.

After Mary was rescued and hidden in a safe place, I completely understood just how much she meant to me – and that the societal convention I had worried about, wherein I was still too-recently widowed to remarry, was nonsense. I had learned yet again the fragile value of life's gifts. That's why it was so hard, after our marriage and several happy years, to lose her in 1893, after I already believed that my best friend, Holmes, had died in '91 at the Reichenbach Falls.

In the years that followed all of that, I'd seen Holmes unexpectedly return, and I'd been involved in many of his further investigations where I was able to help restore other people's happiness. The time flew by, as it does, and I had married once again, in the late summer of 1902, the previous year. At that time I was turning fifty – older, wiser, and sadly more wary about completely trusting in life's happiness. I regretted having been forced to learn that lesson, but I knew that one way or another, anyone who received the reward of additional days paid for them, somewhere along the line, in pain and caution. Since 1888, I had grown a tough and cautious skin – and that was likely the reason why Amos Mann and his distasteful enterprise – leading tours to the murder sites and principal locations of the Ripper murders – was so offensive to me. I well knew that others who had faced loss and heartbreak because of the Rippers' crimes had done their best to also grow tough skins over their own hurts, and Mann, through his purely greedy activities, was tearing it away, night after night and week after week, leaving raw and painful wounds reopened once more.

We had first heard of Amos Mann back in July. I had been reading the morning newspaper as I dawdled over my breakfast, and when I saw his advertisement, I dropped the paper in disgust.

"What tasteless twaddle!" I exclaimed.

My bride raised a brow in polite curiosity. "What's that, dear?"

"This fellow advertising in the newspaper!" I huffed. "Offering walking tours to see where the Ripper murders occurred! It's . . . it's *outrageous*!"

She nodded, certainly in full agreement, but without the emotional weight that had been reawakened for me, suddenly bearing me down in my seat. "You and Mr. Holmes were involved in that, weren't you?"

473

I nodded, suddenly overwhelmed once again by what had happened during those terrible months. In all the years that I had known Sherlock Holmes, I wasn't sure that there was any affair that was more complex than when he investigated the nearly impossible tangle of the Ripper Conspiracy, when so many killers roamed London, using the initial deaths brought about by a Freemason effort to preserve The Crown as an shield to hide their own bloody agendas. * I looked at my wife across the table and almost began to tell her just how involved we had been, but I stopped myself. It would be impossible to relate just one piece without touching upon two others, providing context for what had happened, and explaining how one event led to another, and then another and another. Even I didn't comprehend the entire tale, knowing that there were certain parts that had been kept from me for my own good, and having later discovered others on my own, making me realize I was only seeing small scenes that were part of a much larger drama.

So I kept my thoughts to myself, and simply confirmed to my wife that yes, Holmes and I had been very much involved. But Amos Mann continued to run through my mind for the rest of that day. I wasn't sure how long he'd been in business before I noticed his advertisement, but it couldn't have been more than a few weeks. The next morning, when one of the inspectors I'd known for years stopped by to have his recurring cough checked and receive his new prescription, I asked him what he knew.

He shook his head, his expression dark. "He's a carrion crow, Doctor," he said. "Feeding on the dead – that's what he's doing. It's no better than that. You remember what it was like back then – the . . . the *terror*." He shook his head, as if he couldn't think of any better word to relate what we both knew. "You could cut it with a knife. Every night when the sun went down, none of those poor women knew if they'd meet The Ripper 'round the next corner – and yet, they had no choice but to go about and live their sorry lives, such as they were. And now this Mann fellow strolls onto the scene, like some circus barker, giving tours of the different murder sites as if he's showing visitors around the Buckingham Gardens to look at the pinks and peonies."

I mentioned the shady affair a day or so later when I dropped by Baker Street, finding the advertisement in the newspaper and folding back the page so that Holmes could examine it:

Night falls! Long shadows reach forth!
Join us as we stalk Jack the Ripper!
Amos Mann's famous Jack the Ripper Tour!
Step by blood-curdling step – See where the murders occurred!
See the spots where The Ripper walked, and worshiped, and drank, and
KILLED!
And since he was never caught –
Maybe you'll even see The Ripper himself!

Holmes frowned and handed it back to me. "I have observed it. In fact . . . ." And he stood, crossed to the mantel, and unfixed the jack-knife which held his correspondence, sorting until he came to a plain sheet of cheap stationery. "I received this in the post several weeks ago."

I took it, noting that the handwriting was that of a man in the prime of life, with no overtly distinguishing features indicating notable character traits, for good or bad. The ink was black, and the nib was worn. The author was right-handed – none of which conveyed anything of importance. I glanced at Holmes. "The envelope was postmarked in Whitechapel," he said, "with no return address. Same type of paper as the letter."

I nodded and read the letter's text:

Mr. Holmes,

Permit me to introduce myself. My name is Amos Mann, and I have the good fortune to have created a walking tour that visits historic sites connected to the Ripper Murders of 1888.

As you are no doubt aware, the gruesome facts related to the case, as well as the lack of a solution, have only caused the affair to grow in the public's imagination over the last fifteen years. If you visit Whitechapel by day, you'll see any number of tourists – often American, but quite a few home-grown as well – visiting the sites of the crimes, as well as associated locations, like The Ten Bells pub, and Ghoulston Street, where the famed "Juwes" message was chalked onto the doorway.

Seeing a heretofore unseized opportunity, and knowing that tourism is always a certainty in the capital, I decided to form a business that leads tourists to these sites. Although some may feel that this is rather morbid, I believe that it's no different than when tourists stop at the former location of the

475

Tyburn Tree, or when lucky visitors to The Tower are able to see where the executions occurred. Mankind has always had a fascination for the dark stories, as shown by the ever-increasing curiosity about castles where famous deaths occurred, or tourism at battlefields such as Hastings and Culloden. These visitors certainly show a reverence for history, but there is also an unmistakable fascination with the idea of the vast numbers of deaths that took place there. It's no different in Whitechapel, where the lack of solution only adds an undeniable element of mystery.

It is my hope that you will agree to join one of my tours, gratis, *and on that night, my clients and I can question you regarding some of the facts that are unknown to the general public. In fact, I'll be happy to turn over the lecture to you entirely on such nights as you choose to honor us, for as much time as you wish to take. It would be an honor and privilege, and a particular treat for those who happen to be in attendance that night.*

I look forward to hearing from you, and I thank you for your time.

Amos Mann

I laid the letter upon the small table by my old chair, shaking my head. "Generous of him – offering to let you go on the tour for free and pontificate about the rest of the story. He doesn't offer to pay you a farthing, but at least he's polite."

"And well-reasoned," added Holmes. "He's correct – in spite of the unseemly idea of gawping at murder sites, he has identified an undeniable though unfortunate aspect of human nature. However much you and I might deny it, we were both guilty of wishing to see the never-fading bloodspot at Holyrood Palace during that investigation, despite everything else that was going on around us at the time. There's something about such violent events and where they occurred that titillates some primitive part of our minds. It may be as deeply seated in the brain as the ancient place which causes our hearts to beat."

I nodded, still disgusted with Mann's enterprise, and also amazed at his boldness in trying to involve Sherlock Holmes. "Did you respond to him?"

"Not at all. His unpleasant business shall fail or succeed without my help."

476

And thus we left it there. July moved into August, and on the seventh, a cool damp day typical of that abnormally cold summer, my wife had a small gathering to celebrate my fifty-first birthday, inviting a few close friends of both personal and professional acquaintance. Holmes attended, as did Mrs. Hudson, and a few Scotland Yarders as well. It was a pleasant evening, and I felt quite fortunate in all regards.

Within hours, I was to be reminded of dark events from the past.

In the newspaper the following morning, I read of a young woman who had been attacked in Whitechapel after being lured away from one of Amos Mann's expeditions. She was an unemployed governess, Deborah Waite, who had been curious about the tour after reading the newspaper advertisement and had decided on a lark to pay her shilling and join the dubious fun. The tour had met, as was typical, outside the entrance to the Tower Underground Station and set off to the north and east, following the usual route as led by Mann, and under the watchful eye of a retired constable, Josiah Fetterman, who was along to give assurances of safety. I remembered him – a solid-enough fellow, still big in spite of his age, but definitely not the clearest-thinking fellow, and unlikely to be much help in the dark alleyways.

The planned route wound through the streets to visit different sites in a generally chronological order, and with the amount of walking involved, it took several hours, finally ending at The Ten Bells, where participants would then be left to buy a drink and then find their own way home. Not long after Mann had led the group past the site of Martha Tabram's murder in George Yard, in the area boxed by Wentworth Street, Commercial Street, Whitechapel High Street, and Osborn Street, Miss Waite had somehow become separated from the group, although when later queried, no one remembered seeing her, or being aware that she was gone. She had been alone on the tour, stating that none of her friends wished to accompany her and, in any case, she'd always felt herself to be an adventurous soul, and she wasn't afraid of making the trip by herself.

Fortunately she was not killed, or even physically hurt. Rather, she had been rendered unconscious by the judicious use of chloroform (the scent of which was still on an unremarkable rag discovered lying nearby). She had been found when she awakened and her screams drew a passing workman and his wife. She was lying against a wall not far from the very spot where Martha Tabram had been stabbed to death, her clothing disarranged, and a number of red paint marks – no more than dots – had been applied to her upper chest and throat – thirty-nine of them. It didn't take Sherlock Holmes to realize that these marks were meant to represent the same number of stab wounds that had been found on Martha Tabram's body, likely from a bayonet, fifteen years earlier to the day. (It should be

477

noted, however, that these paint marks in no way matched the exact location of Tabram's wounds, which had been in much more intimate locations. The marks on Deborah Waite's body were a assuredly a violation, but much less so than if they had been applied to specifically simulate the manner of Martha Tabram's murder)

A further medical examination revealed that, except for the intrusion upon her dignity, she was otherwise physically unharmed. She indicated that she didn't remember how she lost contact with Mann's tour – only that the last thing she recalled was that he had been leading the group through the passage by George Yard from north to south toward Wentworth Street.

I read of the matter the next morning with great interest, for it was widely reported. Without mentioning the specific reasons why to my wife, I decided to abandon my practice and visit Baker Street instead. This wasn't the first time I had done such a thing, so she wasn't surprised, and it wasn't totally unexpected. Since shortly before my marriage in the late summer of 1902, I had been in residence at my new practice in Queen Anne Street – although at what point it was no longer "new" was debatable. Although I still found time to join Holmes on a number of investigations, it was not as often as before, nor as often as I might have liked. My wife was somewhat disconnected from Holmes, much more so than my previous two wives, and now that I was back in harness, she tended to see that aspect of my life as something in my past,. For the most part, this was all for the best, as 1903 had seen the nature of Holmes's investigations change quite a bit from earlier days, when he was most-often consulted by people from all walks of life – high and low, official and very unofficial – to gain his opinion. When something wasn't immediately obvious to him from his armchair, and would rise and "move around", as he sometimes put it.

But those later years saw a shift in the nature of Holmes's activities. Although still willing to involve himself in the aid of the downtrodden and helpless, many of Holmes's cases at that stage of his career were in service to the Government, wherein he used his unique skills and long-developed talents to provide options unavailable elsewhere. Just the previous fall, for instance, he had helped free a noble lady from the clutches of a vile simulacrum of a man, Baron Gruner, and in addition to salvaging her life from inevitable ruin, he had helped to remove the corrupt nobleman from the board in all sorts of other ways that would benefit England.

By the early 1900's, Holmes had something of an agency in place, constructed almost by accident by the use of various trusted associates. He still made use of his Irregulars, that band of street urchins who could go anywhere, unseen, and pick up facts that would be unobtainable for older agents. But in those latter days, Holmes also had several apprentices who carried out a lot of the tedious work that used to take so much of his time – watching a building for long periods, perhaps, through all hours and all manner of weather. They did the routine searches of records for facts that didn't require any sudden inspiration or interpretation. It wasn't unusual for them to travel to some distant village to verify when a person in question was in residence there. These apprentices – some of them now-adult Irregulars like Peake and Thorndyke, or Porter Jones, the sincere young man who wanted to learn the business, or the canny lad who I'll simply call "Siger", recently graduated from Oxford – all brought their own special skills while simultaneously learning Holmes's methods. And then there were those on the shadier side, such as Mercer and Shinwell Johnson, all quite able to fill in the less-than-legal pieces of any given puzzle. And I too had my own part to play in this "Agency".

I found upon my arrival in Baker Street that, of course, Holmes was well aware of the previous night's events in Whitechapel, and he was smoking a ruminative morning pipe and staring into the unlit fireplace while he considered it.

"It's indicative," he said, "that the victim was essentially uninjured, except for her pride and dignity, and also that such an obvious effort was made to link her assault with Martha Tabram's murder – the date, and the number of simulated wounds."

He leaned forward and handed me an envelope. "This arrived with the first post – it certainly didn't take him very long."

It was from Amos Mann, written by the same hand and on the same paper as before.

Dear Mr. Holmes,

By now, I'm sure that you've seen in the newspapers the unfortunate event that occurred last night when one of the members of the Whitechapel tour group was diverted and assaulted. Thank Heavens that there were no serious injuries!

I wish to re-extend my invitation that you join one or more of our excursions. We offer protection in the form of a retired police officer, but being able to say that our party is under your watchful eye as well will most certainly provide added comfort to the group as we traverse the East End.

We leave each evening from the Tower Underground Station, gathering near the section of old Roman wall. I look forward to seeing you there.

Sincerely,
Amos Mann

I handed it back to Holmes. "Still no mention of remuneration, but now he asks for your involvement in the name of public safety."

"Without," Holmes added, "realizing that it would be safer not to lead people into the East End at night at all."

Knowing that he would be doing something about it, I asked, "Will you join the group?"

He shook his head with a smile. "Not yet. I'm sure that there is a bit more of this situation that will escalate before I need to show my face there. The next Ripper victim, Mary Ann Nichols, was found in Buck's Row on August 31st – the anniversary of which will be three-and-a-half weeks from now. By then, I should know more about Mr. Mann and his tour."

"So you expect another attack on that night?"

"Don't you?" Holmes countered. "I'm curious to see just how ambitious this scheme is. I'll put some of the lads to work, and it shouldn't be long before I have a pretty complete picture of what's going on."

I rose, ready to return to my own daily duties. "Let me know when you need my help."

"As always," he agreed, and I departed.

I saw Holmes during the next few weeks, but I was careful not to pester him about what he had learned concerning the Whitechapel affair. I knew by that point in our friendship that he would tell me what he thought I should know when he was ready for me to know it. In any event, our time then was taken up by a number of other cases, including one of several where we encountered a trained cormorant, and another involving Graf Udo von Felseck and the missing German Envoy. (I have since learned, when preparing my notes, that there has been some recent confusion that this matter occurred in 1913, but in truth, those events took place in August 1903, while Holmes was still residing in Baker Street.)

I was irritated to see, on a regular basis, that Amos Mann had altered the advertisement of his tour to add an extra line: *The Case that Sherlock Holmes Could Not Solve!*

My initial reaction was to visit some of the newspapers where I was known, and where I was owed favors, to have this tripe quashed, but I knew that Holmes wouldn't be bothered by Mann's lies, and that I should simply let him continue with whatever steps he was taking to settle the matter.

August 31st arrived, and I waited to see what news would be reported the next day. When the papers arrived, it wasn't difficult to locate the story, for it was the leading item in most of them.

When Mary Ann Nichols was murdered on August 31st, 1888, the wider public was still largely indifferent to the crimes and conditions of Whitechapel. Any that were paying attention just then simply noted that another terrible murder of a prostitute had occurred. There has always been some public disagreement as to when the actual Ripper murders began, as opposed to general violent deaths in that part of the city, differentiating between earlier 1888 deaths, such as Emma Smith and Martha Tabram, and the later five women butchered in August, September, and November. The truth is that there were many more Ripper murders than the unfortunate women reported to have been killed that fall, including several men. If one widens the scope of related deaths to include the suicides resulting from Sherlock and Mycroft Holmes's relentless exposure of the guilty, then the count rises to a couple of dozen, at least.

Mary Ann Nichols had been found on the night of August 31st beside a stable entrance in Buck's Row, renamed Durward Street in 1892. Her throat had been cut and her clothing disrupted. Additionally, there were a number of terrible wounds to her body.

On the fifteenth anniversary of that event, a woman named Lydia Cate was found in the same location, unconscious, with a chloroform-soaked rag lying nearby. Red paint had been striped across her throat to simulate the same mortal wound found on Mary Ann Nichol's body. Unlike the attack on Deborah Waite earlier in the month, there was no attempt to duplicate the other wounds on the new victim's body. Her clothing, while unkempt, had not been disturbed in any major way.

Lydia Cate was found by a man who was passing while on his way to the nearby Whitechapel Station. He ran into the station and summoned a constable. The lady was removed to the adjacent London Hospital, where she told essentially the same story as Deborah Waite: She had been curious about Mann's tour and had journeyed to the East End to join it, unaccompanied by any family or friends. After visiting the spot where Mary Ann Nichols had died, the group had started to walk along to the next location, and that was the last she remembered. She had no recollection of anyone interfering with her, or applying the chloroform-soaked rag.

"I was among the group that interviewed her in the hospital," Holmes told me the next morning, September 1st, after I went around to Baker Street. "There were no signs of bruising or other injuries."

"Any indication on her mouth of chloroform burning?" I asked.

"None," he said with a smile. "But one wouldn't expect there to be."

481

I nodded. "The next murder occurred on September 8th," I said. "In Hanbury Street. Really, Holmes – how much rope are you going to allow?"

He shrugged. "Like you, I find it offensive, but I want to make sure that my investigation is complete. And besides – have you been reading the related newspaper articles? It's been fifteen years since the Ripper murders, long enough for many people to have forgotten. This, in spite of its unpleasant side, is reminding them of what occurred – the names of the poor victims, and the circumstances of their tragic lives. The awful conditions in which they lived, and in which so many people in Whitechapel still exist. This entire seamy affair appears to be reawakening strong feelings about the continuing poverty and unfair conditions, and that is a good thing. I'm inclined to let it percolate for a while longer – to shine a new light where it might have some benefit. As objectionable as this matter is, some good might come about before we end it."

Later that day, I was surprised and disgusted to receive my own invitation letter from Amos Mann, asking that I – either with Holmes or without him – join the tour to offer my own *"unique insights"*. I later confirmed that Holmes had received another similar missive as well. We both ignored them.

The morning of September 9th once again had a story related to a new assault the previous night on a female member of Amos Mann's tour group, also somehow spirited away from the group and left lying at the same spot in Hanbury Street where poor Annie Chapman had been discovered in 1888. I well recalled those grim events, as Holmes and I had been summoned there not long after to examine the unfortunate corpse. We were already quite weary, having spent the previous hours discovering the grotesquely murdered Bartholomew Sholto in Upper Norwood, and then unsuccessfully tracking his hideous killers across London with the assistance of a most-curious dog.

Like Lydia Cate, who had been attacked just a bit more than a week before, Susan Strickland was found by a passing workman with a chloroformed rag nearby, her clothing mildly disrupted, and a painted red slash across her throat to simulate the most obvious wound on Annie Chapman's body. Again, no effort was made to duplicate the terrible bodily mutilations that had marked the poor dead woman.

On the day before Susan Strickland's assault, on Tuesday the eighth, 1903, Holmes and I had returned from Camford, where we had traveled to make initial inquiries regarding the matter of Professor Presbury's curious medication. As we'd returned to London, we'd discussed what form that night's Whitechapel attack would take – for we were certain that such would occur. It was no surprise the next morning to read of it, but I was gratified to turn the page and see a scathing editorial upon the still-terrible living conditions in Whitechapel. I mentioned it to Holmes when I dropped in at Baker Street.

"I agree, Watson – I hate to let this affair continue any longer, but I'm steadily fixing my nets, and these newspaper reporters have their teeth in it now. They've turned improving Whitechapel into something of a new Crusade – and we should let that continue as long as possible.

"But surely you won't let it go another two months?" I said with some exasperation, thinking of the terrible murder of Mary Kelly in Miller's Court, in the early hours of November 9th, 1888."

Holmes nodded. "I agree. We will have wrested whatever good we can from these events by the end of this month, on the anniversary of the two murders. During October 1888, there were no deaths, although the public panic continued to escalate, particularly with the arrival of the letters sent '*From Hell*' by '*Jack the Ripper*'. While our current perpetrator may try to keep up the momentum by sending similar letters to the newspapers in mid-October, I can see no reason to let this go on for that long. No, I think that we'll be ready to put a stop to this on the thirtieth of September. Would you care to join me that night? It would be the perfect opportunity to finally accept Mr. Mann's invitation and offer some revelatory comments to the members of his tour."

And so the rest of the month passed quickly. We returned to Camford and freed Professor Presbury from the clutches of the drug which had ensnared him, and we cleared up several other cases as well. It was during these weeks that Holmes revealed some more specific details regarding his upcoming retirement and move to Sussex, and I began to have a sense of the part that I would play in helping maintain the illusion that he was removing himself there permanently to eke out a hermit's life, while forsaking all of his long-honed investigatory skills.

When recalling the crimes of the various Rippers, the early hours of September 30th came to be known as "The Double Event", for two women were killed that night: Elizabeth Stride in Dutfield's Yard, just off Berner Street, and then Catherine Eddowes in Mitre Square. The first murder, in which the body was much less violated, had been interrupted, causing the murderers to kill again less than an hour later. Each crime had inflicted terrible violations upon the poor women, but the second was much worse than the first, as they'd had more time, in spite of working in nearly black conditions. Holmes and I had been there that night, not long after both murders occurred, and had been part of the group that went on from Mitre Square to Ghoulston Street, where a message regarding the "Juwes" had been chalked (before it was ordered removed by Sir Charles Warren) on an otherwise unremarkable doorway, above a piece of bloody cloth torn from Catherine Eddowes' apron.

Now, on the last day of September in 1903, we were back in that same spot. I looked around, noting what was different, and what had stayed the same. Too much of the latter was still obvious, but there was hope for change and betterment. The recent news articles highlighting the still-terrible conditions of this neglected part of London were doing much to help, and I hoped that they would continue, even as the events related to Mann's morbid tours were brought to an end. Whatever happened with social reform, it was time to put a stop to the enthusiasm for the lurid aspects of these crimes. The victims deserved no less.

The group was alert, taking in every bit of an experience that was likely far beyond their normal lives. Not far away was the retired constable, Josiah Fetterman. He was less interested, standing weary and slumped and focused on the ground at his feet. It would be easy, if someone were culling out Mann's tourists, to go unnoticed.

Mann was speaking. "As you saw in Mitre Square, the spot where Catherine Eddowes was butchered would have been pitch black. There were no streetlights, and any light outside the two passages into the Square does not penetrate. It's still a mystery how the crimes, with such specific violations of the poor woman's body, were committed in such total darkness.

"Catherine Eddowes was killed about quarter-to-two in the morning. At around three a.m., Constable Alfred Long of the Metropolitan Police Force, in passing by this very spot, about a fifth-of-a-mile northeast of Mitre Square, noticed a piece of bloody rag lying on the ground – right here in this doorway. After examining it, he looked up and saw, written in chalk, something like '*The Juwes*' – spelled either *J-U-W-E-S* or *J-E-W-E-S* – '*are the men who will not be blamed for nothing.*' There is some disagreement as to the actual wording. The version I've just quoted was affirmed by Constable Long, and also Superintendent Arnold. Constable Daniel Halse thought it to be, '*The Juwes are not the men who will be blamed for nothing*', while Chief Inspector Swanson stated that it was '*The Juwes –* ' with an *E* – '*are not the men to be blamed for nothing*'. The City Surveyor, Frederick William Foster, agreed with this version, but stated that it was spelled *J-U-W-E-S*.

"In any case, before the writing could be photographed, Metropolitan Police Commissioner Sir Charles Warren visited this spot and then ordered that the writing be removed – ostensibly because he feared that it would generate violence against the Jewish community, who were already receiving threats because of rumors that the Ripper was Jewish – this in spite of the fact that the word '*Jews*' was misspelled. However, some believe that Sir Charles was actually protecting members of the Freemasons – Sir Charles being one of them! – whose rituals refer to the

'*Three Ruffians*' – *Jubela, Jubelo,* and *Jubelum* – also known as the '*Three Juwes*'. You'll note, of course, that their three names all begin with *J-U*."

Mann paused for breath and looked toward us. By now we had rejoined the group. "What do you think, Mr. Holmes? Which interpretation is correct? Was Sir Charles protecting the Jewish residents of Whitechapel from the rising fear overtaking these streets, or was he instead covering up for his fellow Masons?"

"I think," replied Holmes, "that this is the last stop of tonight's tour."

His comment left Mann at a loss for words, his mouth open and working up a response. In the meantime, the two-dozen members of the group looked at Holmes with the empty-eyed expression of a flock of sheep.

"Ladies and gentlemen," Holmes continued, his voice carrying far beyond the group, "there isn't much more to see. The murders which were just described occurred on September 30th, fifteen years ago tonight. Afterwards, fear continued to escalate, but thankfully no unfortunate street women were killed throughout the month of October. There were several letters to the press purporting to be from the killer. One of these, signed '*Jack the Ripper*', gave us the *sobriquet* under which the crimes are now classified. In the early hours of November 9th, a young woman named Mary Kelly was killed in Miller's Court, approximately one-sixth of a mile north of here." He gestured in that direction.

"It was the only Ripper murder to occur indoors, and having the protection of seclusion and a great deal more time free from disturbance, the killer perpetrated horrible mutilations to the body." I saw the women in the group, and many men as well, take on sick expressions as they contemplated the human cost of these crimes – which had generally remained unexamined by Amos Mann during his comments. I also noted that Holmes was careful to refer to the official line that this was the only Ripper murder to occur indoors, and that he used the word "killer" – singular – instead of giving any indication of the true scale of the deadly cabal that had terrorized London during those awful months.

Holmes raised his hand, which held a police whistle, and gave a short shrill blast. Instantly, from out of the alley leading to Middlesex Street, five men appeared, walking in our direction – three burly constables, a thin and penurious-looking fellow in a wool suit, and our old friend, Inspector Lestrade.

"All settled?" asked Holmes. The small policeman nodded, looking toward Mann with a satisfied expression.

"As Mr. Holmes indicated," said Lestrade to the surrounding crowd, "the venture has ended. Permanently. You will have the satisfaction of knowing that you were participants in the very last and final version of Mr. Mann's 'Jack the Ripper Tour'. It is now officially closed down."

At this, Mann finally started to speak, bluster really, but Lestrade spoke louder. "Ladies and gentlemen, we are just around the corner from the Aldgate Station, where you can enter the Underground. For those who wish, one of these officers will take you one street east into Commercial Street and then lead you north, past the entrance to Miller's Court, and then not much further to The Ten Bells at Fornier Street. From there, you may be able to get a cab. If not, he can take you on from there to the Bishopsgate Police Station."

Several of the group rendered a few feeble and unanswered questions, and one fellow who looked like a shopkeeper grumbled about getting his money back, but this seemed to be something of a pose to impress the woman who was with him. Within just a moment, all of Mann's group had all been led south to Whitechapel High Street. I have no idea where they went from there – into the Underground, or with the constable past the final murder location on the grotesque expedition.

Meanwhile, Holmes, Lestrade, and I, along with the remaining constables, were left surrounding Mann and old Josiah Fetterman, who looked confused. One of the officers stepped up and whispered something to him, taking his arm. "I'll get him home, Inspector."

Lestrade nodded, and Holmes asked, "Do you have all of them?"

"All of them," confirmed the inspector. "Even the accomplices who were supposed to 'find' the victims after tonight's supposed attacks."

"What are you talking about?" demanded Mann, now seemingly locating his irate courage after the unsettling interruption of a few minutes before.

Holmes looked at him as if deciding whether he deserved any explanation. Then he spoke. "Inspector Lestrade and his men were waiting near Berner Street and Mitre Square tonight for the two women to show up after the tour had moved along. He let them get settled – " He looked at Lestrade, who nodded in agreement. "He let them get settled onto the pavement, arranging themselves as if they had been attacked and placing the chloroformed-soaked rags to one side, and then he waited until their accomplices showed up to supposedly discover them and summon the police."

"We don't know specifics for this current bunch quite yet," added Lestrade, "names and such, but if they're like the rest of them – Deborah Waite and Lydia Cate and Susan Strickland, and the men and woman who found them and called for a constable – then they're all beholden to you somehow, and willing to act out these little farces to help build up your business."

486

"What — ?" said Mann, looking shifty from one of us to another. "What is the meaning of this? You can't shut me down! You have no right to — "

"You're correct," said Lestrade. "We can't technically shut you down. But I see it more as a *quid pro quo*: You willingly go out of business, and we refrain from pressing charges against you and all your helpers for wasting our time and resources in relation to the faked attacks — not to mention all of the fear you've generated as you created interest in your tours. Don't you agree, Mr. Yates?"

The thin man in the wool suit stepped forward. A reporter, he had been invited to reveal the full scope of Mann's scheme.

"That sounds more than right to me, Inspector." He said, pulling out a pad and pencil and looked at Mann. "George Yates of *The Times*. Now, Mr. Mann, as I understand it, from what Mr. Holmes and the Doctor told me earlier this evening, you have orchestrated each one of these fake attacks in order to build up interest in your tours, tying them to the anniversaries and locations of when the murders occurred, and even recreating the original fatal wounds to some small degree. Do you care to comment?"

Mann blustered and hawed, but didn't form any useful responses. Yates nodded as if he'd had an answer and continued.

"Before we set out tonight, I was able to interview the three women who feigned the earlier attacks, as well as the woman and three men who pretended to find them. All of them were rounded up and brought to Scotland Yard, and they've all made statements — which were made available to me. Each one has prior ties, one way or another, with you, Mr. Mann. Deborah Waite is your sister-in-law's niece. Lydia Cate is the daughter of your first-cousin. Susan Strickland is engaged to your wife's nephew. The others have similar connections. Do you have anything to say to our readers?"

During Yates' questioning, Mann's alternating expressions of outrage and offended innocence and harmless confusion all vanished, replaced by an angry scowl directed toward Sherlock Holmes, who looked complacently back at him as if indifferently studying a laboratory rat confined to a cage. Before Mann could speak again, Holmes said, "It really won't do. We established all of these facts long ago, beginning not long after the first attack. Did you really think that the supposed attacks would be accepted at face value without some sort of deeper investigation?

"It was simply too artificial," he continued. "Too contrived, having such events occur on the exact anniversary of the murders. After the second took place, when Lydia Cate was the apparent victim, we investigated both women to see if there was some aspect that might connect them. That connection – to you – was easily discovered, and that led us to check in greater depth upon the individuals who had seemingly discovered the women lying in the street and then summoned the police. By then it was obvious that you were orchestrating the entire thing, simply for the attention that your tours were receiving in the press.

"We only allowed it to continue as long as it did because – in spite of unfortunately giving you a measure of increased financial success – it also brought renewed attention to Whitechapel, and the reforms that are still needed here. This was something important that has decreased in the years since the Ripper murders, and anything that might somehow benefit these poor people is worthy – even if it meant that you were able to line your pocketbook for a bit longer. Isn't that correct, Mr. Yates?"

"It is indeed," replied the reporter, closing the notebook in which he had been making a series of urgent notes and returning it to his pocket. "And I can assure you that, in spite of the conclusion of this particular matter, I will make sure that the focus remains on these needful streets. But," he added, glancing toward Mann, "I don't think that we'll need to give you any more attention. Unless," he added, touching a finger to his hat, "I hear about you pulling something like this again. Then, Mr. Mann, it will be quite easy to inform people just what kind of person you truly are." Yates nodded and bid us all goodnight, turning away and walking back down the passage toward Middlesex Street.

Mann's face had gotten dangerously red, and he was flexing his fists as if he wanted to fight, or at least prove to himself that he'd made some effort to defend his reputation, but there was really nothing left for him to do. After looking around several times at the men surrounding him, he finally growled, "Am I free to go then?"

"You are," said Lestrade. "But that doesn't mean charges can't still be filed against you. We're watching you, Mr. Amos Mann. Straighten up, or you'll be hearing from us, I promise you!"

"And you will hear from me!" was the growled response, for he'd finally found something inside himself that made him think he could fight back. "My attorney will hear of this! You cannot – "

"Go!" Lestrade roared, taking a step toward the heavier man, stamping his foot as if he were running off a mangy dog. Mann's eyes went wide with shock. Then, as if finally realizing that he was beaten, he turned and hurried along Ghoulston Street, turning abruptly into one of the dark narrow passageways around Wentworth Street. If I had been him, I would have chosen a different route – south, for instance, to the better-lit and populated High Street. This was still a dangerous place, and his actions and behavior had roused dangerous feelings – and if one believed in such, possibly a few irate ghosts as well.

We stepped away from the remaining constables and Lestrade shook his head. "What a scoundrel!" he sighed. "Although, as was mentioned, perhaps some good will come of it."

Holmes nodded. "It already has. It's a new century, and one can only hope that we'll be better with each passing year." He looked around. "I don't know if these streets will ever feel truly safe, or be the people who abide here will be able to move past the suffering due to the lives that have been lost. Not just those taken by the Rippers," he added, and Lestrade glanced knowingly at his pluralization of the name, "but all the rest: Those who have died by other crimes, and hunger, and neglect. Still, one can but hope."

"That's true," agreed Lestrade.

"The work always continues," I added.

"Speaking of the work," said Holmes, changing the subject and smiling toward the inspector, "would you join Watson and me at The Ten Bells for a late pint, Lestrade? I have some news for you – details about my impending retirement. All is not as it seems, and I hope that I can count on you to help provide legitimacy for its forthcoming presentation."

Lestrade raised his eyebrows in surprise, but agreed to join us readily enough. Later, as we found a relatively quiet corner of the pub, he nodded as Holmes explained his plans and the inspector's purpose. I wasn't surprised that Lestrade agreed to provide assistance, for he had long been a man who could be counted upon. While the discussion continued, I sipped my beer and looked around at the crowded and noisy room, remembering past visits here, and seeing in my mind's eye other patrons – the poor victims who had drank here in life, not knowing that someday they would be infamously remembered for their horrible deaths, and also the men who had killed them, certainly patrons as well. Had the killers all stood at the bar, with those around them unaware of the darkness that they concealed? Or had they all instead been some of the quiet ones, sitting off to one side, possibly at the very table we now occupied, watching the women who came and went in the way that predators mark their next target.

"Jack" wasn't unique, I knew, and other like them might be in the pub right at that moment. Or somewhere on the streets, or residing in a comfortable neighborhood miles away.

As Holmes continued to describe aspects of his retirement, my thoughts turned grim. Mann's actions had reminded everyone of the past crimes, and some of us recalled just how much Holmes had done to stop them. What would happen, I wondered, the next time, when Sherlock Holmes was no longer in London to prevent them?

It was a worrisome thing. I had no easy answers, and my beer, as I continued to sip, became bitter like gall.

NOTE

* For more about 1888's "Autumn of Terror", and Holmes and Watson's battle against the various Rippers who carried out the crimes, see "November, 1888", published in *The Collected Papers of Sherlock Holmes – Volume III: Accounts*, and also *The Watsonian* (Fall 2015, Vol. 3, No.2) and in my online blog, A Seventeen Step Program at:
https://17stepprogram.blogspot.com/2017/02/sherlock-holmes-versus-jack-ripper.html

An Explanation:
Three Sherlockian Scripts

A word about these scripts . . . .

In Spring 2008, after being laid off from my civil engineering job, I wrote nine Sherlock Holmes pastiches – and then did nothing with them for several years. I was satisfied that I'd actually produced them, and I was very happy to simply print them in a binder and put them on the shelves of my Holmes collection.

But . . . eventually I had the notion to share one of them by email with a Sherlockian friend, and after receiving positive comments, I shared another and another, and then I let someone else read them, and before long, I wanted them to be a real book, and for lots of people to read them.

The only publisher I knew then was Dr. George Vanderburgh of the Battered Silicon Dispatch Box, and in 2011, he published the first edition of *The Papers of Sherlock Holmes.* And then I had that amazing sensation that authors and editors will understand – and it never gets old – of opening that box and seeing the real book – in my hands, and then on my shelves.

I had a whole box full of that first book, and besides putting one on the shelf and giving copies to family members, I decided to send several to some Sherlockians who had meant a lot to me – although they had absolutely no idea who I was.

I sent one to Roger Johnson, who was the editor of *The Sherlock Holmes Society of London Journal*, and he and his wife ended up being good friends who hosted me in their home during my second Holmes Pilgrimage to England in 2015. Additionally, Roger has written dozens of forewords for various books that I've since edited, and I've seen him on several other occasions on my other Holmes Pilgrimages to England.

I also sent a copy of *The Papers* to Lawrence "Larry" Albert, who, by way of Imagination Theater's Holmes broadcasts, has performed the part of "Watson" in more stories than any other actor.

I simply sent the book with words of admiration, and thanks for the enjoyment that Larry and the other cast members had brought to me over the years as they presented the True and Canonical Holmes. After that, we began to correspond, and Larry invited me to convert one of the original nine stories into a script.

Ah – Here was a new challenge!

I was thrilled with the idea. I truly love Sherlock Holmes on Radio. When I was just discovering Holmes, in 1975 at the age of ten, our public library had some old Holmes radio shows on phonograph records, starring Basil Rathbone and Nigel Bruce, and I checked them out and heard performances of both Canonical stories and pastiches. While Nigel Bruce was not – and has never been – my idea of Watson, Basil Rathbone was clearly born to play Holmes – both on screen and on radio. For years, to me he was *The Voice of Holmes.* To have a chance to contribute in some small way to The Great Holmes Radio Legacy was something that I wouldn't have missed.

Instead of adapting a full story from *The Papers*, I chose to use a piece of "The Haunting of Sutton House". In that story, Holmes and Watson explore an old historical house in the Hackney area of London – coincidentally, just before writing it, I'd recently seen an hour-long television documentary about the ghosts of Sutton House – and as they make their way through the various rooms of the building, and then settle in to wait for something to happen, Watson recalls the events of the previous few days, when he and Holmes had been involved in a tragic case at Lytton House. It was this latter tale-within-a-tale that I chose to pull out and adapt for the script, cutting out the entire Sutton House aspect entirely.

For three years when I was in college, I was a member of an audition-only acting troupe, the *Playmakers*, so I was familiar with script formatting. Also, over the years, I'd collected many Holmes scripts – for film and television and radio – so I knew what those particular scripts should look like. It only took a few days to prepare the script and send it to Larry Albert – with high hopes and fingers crossed.

It wasn't immediately accepted. Larry and I went back and forth over several iterations as he helped me to understand about avoiding long tedious speeches, and breaking up dialogue between actors. One of my greatest pet peeves is when someone adapts a literary work as a script and makes unnecessary changes – but after adapting my own work, I understood more why that sometimes has to happen. Pieces need to be cut, or explained in a quick line instead of a couple of obliquely approaching pages. Holmes's long explanatory speeches might work on paper to lead the reader along the path his thoughts followed to reach a solution, but when performed, they can seem to drone on and on. Breaking these speeches up between Holmes and Watson made things pop along – and it also gave Watson something to do.

Finally, on November 24th, 2013, the weekend before Thanksgiving, "The Terrible Tragedy of Lytton House" was performed on American Radio, and my family and I were glued to my computer – The show was broadcast online, which was almost like listening to it on old-time radio. Imagination Theater's Sherlockian theme music began – Saint-Saëns' *Danse Macabre* – and then John Patrick Lowery as Holmes and Larry

Albert as Watson began performing my script – *My words!* I truly felt like I was dreaming. Five years and some months earlier, I sat down to see if I could write a few Holmes stories, and now one of them was being performed by professional actors on a nationwide radio broadcast.

After that, I wanted to do it again.

I next set about dramatizing "The Singular Affair at Sissinghurst Castle", also from *The Papers of Sherlock Holmes* and, having learned a lot from Larry the first time, this was much more painless, and fewer iterations were required. I found that as I made the necessary revisions, I was punching up the dialogue to fit the actors. I was *hearing* John Patrick Lowery and Larry Albert saying the lines in my head. This second script was performed a couple of weeks before Thanksgiving the next year, November 23rd, 2014.

Just to show that scripts can have more than one life, each was later published in *Sherlock Holmes Mystery Magazine*, with "Sissinghurst Castle" in No. 20 and "Lytton House" in No. 23.

In the meantime, things became busier, both in real life, and also in terms of my Sherlockian writing and editing responsibilities. At some point, I adapted another story, "The London Wheel", from Part IV of *The MX Book of New Sherlock Holmes Stories*. Larry and I sent it back and forth, but it never quite got produced, and I filed it away and stayed busy elsewhere. Then . . . .

In August 2022, I was contacted by Mike Ranieri of The Bootmakers of Toronto, regarding their upcoming *Jubilee@221B* Conference to be held in Toronto. They wanted to present a 30-40 minutes Holmes play on the last day, and wondered if I had any suggestions – and I offered "The London Wheel". As I told Mike, when I wrote the original short story upon which the script was based, I wanted the feel of an old Rathbone and Bruce radio show. Originally some of the characters were named for individuals associated with the 1940's productions: Green (for Denis), Meiser (for Edith, instead of Meeser), Charteris (instead of Charters), and Boucher (instead of Bouchard). In the end, I altered the names because those were a little too distracting and on-the-nose.

The script was performed at the conference on September 25th, 2022, and even though I wasn't able to travel to Toronto, Mike Ranieri graciously sent me a video so I could watch it from home a few days later.

It was thrilling that the script was performed live, but imagine my gob-smacked surprise a few days before when I saw the promotion poster, announcing that "The London Wheel" was going to be directed by *Nicholas Meyer*! The man who started the current Sherlockian Golden Age in 1974 with *The Seven-Per-Cent Solution* – lighting a fire that's only burned hotter and hotter in the fifty years since. The man who saved *Star*

Trek with *The Wrath of Khan* – the movie that I've seen over and over again, more than any film in my whole life. Nicholas Meyer – truly one of my heroes . . . *was listed to direct my script.* Now, I wasn't there, and I don't know how much directing he actually did, but I have an advertisement that says he directed it (see page 547) – and how many people can show that Nicholas Meyer directed one of their scripts?

And now, Ladies and Gentlemen, I thank you for your patience and, without further ado, may I present . . . *Three Sherlockian Scripts*!

The Terrible Tragedy of Lytton House

CHARACTERS

- ☐ SHERLOCK HOLMES
- ☐ DR. JOHN H. WATSON
- ☐ INSPECTOR YOUGHAL
- ☐ LORD BRETTON
- ☐ EMILY – *His Daughter*
- ☐ JONAS – *The Caretaker*
- ☐ SIR SHEFFIELD FRYE

SOUND EFFECT: OPENING SEQUENCE, BIG BEN

ANNOUNCER: The *Further Adventures of Sherlock Holmes*, featuring John Patrick Lowrie as Holmes, and Lawrence Albert as Dr Watson.

SOUND EFFECT: *DANSE MACABRE* UP AND UNDER

MUSIC: OUT

SOUND EFFECT: A TRAIN STATION, BEFORE THE UPCOMING DEPARTURE OF A TRAIN: CROWD NOISES, CARRIAGE DOORS SLAMMING, WHISTLES

WATSON: *(To himself)* Where can he be? I rushed to the station without stopping for breakfast.

SOUND EFFECT: MORE WHISTLES AND SLAMMING DOORS – IMMINENT DEPARTURE

WATSON: *(To himself)* Holmes's note specifically said *this* train.

HOLMES: *(In the distance, running, out of breath, getting closer)* Watson! What compartment are you in? Watson!

WATSON: *(To himself, relieved)* There he is! *(Louder)* Holmes! Holmes! This way! Hurry man, you'll miss the train!

495

HOLMES: *(Out of breath)* Right on time, as usual.

WATSON: Good heavens, Holmes, you nearly missed your footing.

HOLMES: Not at all, Watson. What you perceived as a near miss was in fact a carefully calculated effort that resulted exactly as I had intended. I anticipated how much time I would need to arrive at the station, make my way in through the crowds, and to board the train without any time wasted. I –

WATSON: Holmes –

HOLMES: I was also aware of what I could expect in terms of my own athletic abilities in order to reach and board the train at the speed in which it was departing.

WATSON: *(Both exasperated and amused)* Norbury.

HOLMES: Hmm?

WATSON: Norbury, Holmes. *Norbury.* Surely you haven't already forgotten? It has only been two weeks since the matter of Mr. Grant Munro's mysterious neighbor. You might recall that you theorized a completely incorrect and rather grim solution to Mr. Munro's problem, and you asked me to –

HOLMES: – I asked you to whisper "Norbury" in my ear –

WATSON Exactly!

HOLMES – if I ever again seemed to be becoming over-confident in my powers, or not taking the proper amount of interest or care in a case. That does not apply in this situation.

WATSON: What? Certainly –

HOLMES: In this case, I was not over-confident, I was quite accurate in my comprehension of my ability to reach the train.

WATSON: Is that why you called out, trying to determine in which carriage I was riding?

HOLMES: What?

WATSON: You were calling as you ran in order to determine in which carriage I was riding. What would have happened if I had not heard you, or if I was sitting so far forward that you were unable to reach this compartment?

HOLMES: *(A beat)* I see that we shall have to agree to disagree upon this point.

SOUND EFFECT: RATTLE OF NEWSPAPER BEING RAISED

WATSON: *(After a short awkward silence)* Well, what *were* you doing that was so important that you arrived as the train was departing, exactly as you had apparently intended?

SOUND EFFECT: RATTLE OF NEWSPAPER QUICKLY BEING LOWERED

HOLMES: Research, Watson. This morning I received a wire from Inspector Youghal, requesting our presence in Surrey. Youghal's wire mentioned Lord Bretton, but did not provide any other information, except to state that the matter was urgent. I left a note for you in case you should wish to join me, and then I took a slight detour to ask some questions of that young up-and-coming gossip-monger named Langdale Pike.

WATSON: Oh-ho, Langdale Pike. Does he still fancy himself as a journalist?

HOLMES: He is my human book of reference upon all matters relating to society and social scandal.

WATSON: And what did that strange, languid creature tell you?

HOLMES: Some basic facts. Lord Bretton has an invalid wife and seven children. The family normally spends most of the year in London, but they recently returned to their Surrey home, a great run-down place called Lytton House.

WATSON: You risked missing the train and possibly a crippling or fatal injury in order to obtain those facts, which would doubtless have been supplied by Inspector Youghal?

HOLMES: Ah, Watson, I did learn a few other bits which might be of use.

WATSON: And those would be?

HOLMES: That Lord Bretton's finances are in a precarious position, following last year's scandal at the Netherland-Sumatra Company. He has recently been forced to sell his London property to a former business associate, and there are one or two unusual features associated with the sale. His household staff is reduced to a long-time housekeeper from the London house, and a caretaker at the country home. His family is very close-knit, and does not mix in society. In fact, his eldest daughter is nineteen years of age, and has not been presented. And his wife suffers a debilitating illness, which makes the family's move to Surrey something of a trial.

WATSON: All of that is very informative, but until we find out why Inspector Youghal has summoned us to Surrey, it is meaningless.

HOLMES: That is correct. As you know, I refuse to theorize without data. However, I can consider the facts that we do know in my mind, in case they turn out to be relevant at a later time. And now, Watson, I think I shall smoke a pipe or three and arrange my thoughts. I beg that you do not speak to me for fifty minutes.

MUSIC: SHORT BRIDGE

SOUND EFFECT: CARRIAGE SOUNDS (UNDER)

HOLMES: So, Inspector Youghal, please tell us why we are spending this beautiful morning winding our way through the Surrey countryside toward Lytton House?

YOUGHAL: Well, Mr. Holmes, it began simple enough. Last Wednesday, Lord Bretton's housekeeper – he only has the one servant down from London right now – noticed that an expensive painting was missing from its usual place in the dining room at the Surrey house. The painting has always been too unwieldy to move back and forth with the family when they live in London, and it is the only thing of real value in the Surrey house –

HOLMES: I'm told that Lord Bretton frequently describes it in private as the most valuable thing that he owns.

YOUGHAL: I've heard something of the sort as well. It may very well be the only thing of value that he owns right now at all, other than the two houses.

WATSON: Actually, Holmes has determined that Lord Bretton recently sold the London house, presumably because he needs the funds.

YOUGHAL: Hmm. In any case, the local police were called in on Wednesday regarding the missing painting, but no obvious clues were discovered. The next day, Thursday, Lord Bretton's youngest child, and his only son, Patrick, was last seen at breakfast by the housekeeper, Mrs. Jameson, who also serves now as the cook. No one else remembers seeing him for the rest of the day. That evening at dinner, it was finally realized that the boy was missing.

SOUND EFFECT: CARRIAGE SOUNDS SLOWING DOWN, HORSE BLOWING WEARILY (UNDER)

YOUGHAL: There it is, gentleman. Lytton House.

WATSON: A picturesque pile, isn't it? It certainly isn't very far from the station. Quite lovely, with all these wide fields and gently flowing hills. But the old farm buildings certainly give it a rather run-down feeling.

HOLMES: Already planning how you'll describe it in your journals, Watson? The fact that a child is missing seems to me to chill the setting, as if one is seeing it while suffering from an illness or fever.

YOUGHAL: That's the truth, Mr. Holmes. After the family searched high and low with no success on Thursday night, I was called in yesterday.

499

Once again, we systematically searched the house and grounds, and we have alerted the police in neighboring towns as well. I wasn't getting anywhere, and Lord Bretton, who has heard of you, insisted that you be brought in. Of course, I had no objections, and so this morning I sent you a wire.

HOLMES: *(Sharply)* And today is Saturday, Youghal. We are starting at quite a disadvantage. *(With a more level tone)* Well, it cannot be helped, I suppose.

WATSON: *(Grimly)* A missing child. This is a bad business.

YOUGHAL: I agree, doctor. I always hate a case with a missing child.

SOUND EFFECT: CARRIAGE SOUNDS END. MEN CLIMBING DOWN AS THE HORSE SHUFFLES

YOUGHAL: *(Undertone)* This is Lord Bretton, coming toward us now.

SOUND EFFECT: FOOTSTEPS APPROACH ACROSS GRAVEL

YOUGHAL: *(Louder)* Lord Bretton, may I introduce Mr. Sherlock Holmes and Dr. Watson?

BRETTON: Yes, of course. Thank you for coming, Mr. Holmes, Doctor. I have heard of your successes, and I insisted that Inspector Youghal obtain your assistance in this matter.

HOLMES: *(Impatient)* Yes, quite. May I see the location where the stolen painting hung?

BRETTON: *(Slightly taken aback)* Of course, Mr. Holmes. But . . . but what of my son? Perhaps it would be better –

HOLMES: I have certain questions in my mind that must be answered. To see the path toward finding your son, we must first clear away some of the brush regarding the missing painting, in order to determine if the events are related. If you please?

BRETTON: Certainly, certainly. Follow me to the house. The painting hung in the dining room.

SOUND EFFECT: FOOTSTEPS OF SEVERAL MEN ACROSS A
WOODEN FLOOR, DOOR OPENING

BRETTON: In here, Mr. Holmes. You can see that large, rather faded patch on the wall, where the painting has hung for more years than I can tell.

SOUND EFFECT: MENS' FOOTSTEPS END. MORE FOOTSTEPS FADE IN (LIGHTER, A WOMAN)

BRETTON: Ah, my dear. Gentlemen, may I introduce my oldest daughter, Emily. She is quite the lady of the house, due to my wife's unfortunate illness.

(AD-LIB GENERAL GREETINGS: *Nice to meet you, etc.*)

EMILY: Thank you for coming, gentlemen. We're most grateful.

BRETTON: Mr. Holmes wants to know about the missing painting, my dear.

EMILY: The painting? But surely . . . surely that is not why you are here. I thought that father summoned you regarding my brother, Patrick.

HOLMES: As I explained to your father, Miss, I must determine what the relationship is, if any, between the two incidents. What can you tell me about the painting?

EMILY: *(Confused)* Of course. Well, it is a rather obscure Constable. A landscape of the local area, I believe. Although it is not one of his better known works, it is considered to be somewhat valuable. It is quite large, and covered most of that wall, as you can see. The frame is rather solid, and is itself considered on its own to be something of a work of art –

HOLMES: Perhaps I should have been more specific. Do you have any facts which might throw light on how the painting came to disappear?

EMILY: Why, no, Mr. Holmes. The painting was discovered to be missing on Wednesday morning by Mrs. Jameson. *(With more emotion)* Why are you wasting time looking for the painting? It had already been found missing and investigated by the police a full day before Patrick vanished.

BRETTON: Now, now, Emily, Mr. Holmes knows his business. Dry your eyes, and run along and check on your sisters.

EMILY: Yes, Father. *(Sniffs)* It was good to meet you, gentlemen.

SOUND EFFECT: WOMAN'S FOOTSTEPS FADING

BRETTON: Poor girl. This has affected her terribly. I don't know what I would do without her. Since my poor wife has been ill, and since my unfortunate . . . financial reversals last year, it has been necessary for Emily to assume a great many additional responsibilities around the house. And she is like a second mother to the children. I assure you, gentlemen, that in a house filled with six daughters and a young son . . . . *(Stops, chokes with emotion)*

SOUND EFFECT: BOOT FOOTSTEPS QUICKLY ON WOODEN FLOOR

HOLMES: *(Briskly)* This window has been recently opened.

BRETTON: *(Composing himself)* Impossible, Mr. Holmes. We keep that window shut, even in summertime. The prevailing winds on this side of the house tend to cause terrible drafts in here. The drapes become tangled, the candles gutter terribly, and of course we want to protect the painting from the elements.

SOUND EFFECT: SOUND OF WINDOW OPENING

HOLMES: *(Softly, to himself)* The ground outside is gravel. No footprints. But what is this on the windowsill? *(Louder)* Nevertheless, this window has been opened, and recently. How often does this room get used?

SOUND EFFECT: SOUND OF WINDOW CLOSING

BRETTON: Rarely, Mr. Holmes. Our family tends to eat in the smaller, less-formal room, toward the rear of the house. The last time that we ate in here was a week ago, last Saturday, when we had a guest down from London.

502

HOLMES: A guest? And who might that have been, Lord Bretton?

BRETTON: Why, my former business partner, Sir Sheffield Frye. He is an old friend of mine and a frequent visitor at our London home, but this was the first time that he had joined us here in the wilds of Surrey. We had a bit of business to transact, and he accepted my invitation to visit and dine here. Sir Sheffield is a great favorite of all of us.

HOLMES: I see. And when did Sir Sheffield return to London?

BRETTON: On Sunday morning. I took him in the dogcart to the station myself. *(Quieter)* There was some difficulty at the time, you see, The caretaker was . . . unavailable, and I didn't mind driving, since we – since we no longer have a coachman.

HOLMES: Quite. And now, I believe I would like to question the staff.

BRETTON: Certainly. I'll send in Mrs. Jameson, the housekeeper, and then the caretaker. I have a list of instructions to pass along to Emily as well. Dr. Watson, I wonder – as long as you're here – if you wouldn't mind checking on my wife . . .

WATSON: Certainly. Lead the way, Lord Bretton

SOUND EFFECT: MEN'S FOOTSTEPS ON WOODEN FLOOR FADING

YOUGHAL: *(Softly)* That poor sad girl. Did you see the tears in her eyes? *(Louder)* What did you see at the window, Mr. Holmes?

HOLMES: *(Softly, almost to himself)* The sill has been rubbed, as if something – the painting, no doubt – was passed through. There are no marks upon the ground.

YOUGHAL: Do you see any light yet about the boy? Anything at all?

HOLMES: (Louder) Data, Youghal, data! I must have clay to make bricks!

MUSIC: SHORT BRIDGE

503

WATSON: Lady Bretton will be unable to tell us anything. Between her illness and her worry, she is just one short step away from brain fever.

YOUGHAL: Well, Mrs. Jameson certainly had nothing to add, either. She's more like a member of the family than a housekeeper. That one poor woman serves the needs of the entire family, dividing her time between the invalid lady of the house, the children, and the cooking duties as well.

HOLMES: We did learn a few relevant facts. Mrs. Jameson believes that the sale of the London house was somewhat sudden, and also understands that there will *not* be an increase of staff at this house, reflecting Lord Bretton's continued financial difficulties.

YOUGHAL: Also, she said that most of this building will continue to remain closed on a permanent basis, with only a few rooms reopened for use by the family, as it has been on those past occasions when they previously journeyed here from London in the spring and summer months. We searched the entire building yesterday, from top to bottom. There was no sign of Patrick, or the missing painting in any of those closed rooms. I'll swear to that.

HOLMES: Then far be it from me to have it searched again, Youghal.

SOUND EFFECT: DOOR OPENS, MAN'S FOOTSTEPS APPROACH

HOLMES: Ah, you must be Jonas, the caretaker. We were just discussing yesterday's search of the house. What can you tell me about the search of the grounds?

SOUND EFFECT: FOOTSTEPS END, CHAIR SCRAPING

JONAS: *(Somewhat surly)* Well, they were searched very well indeed. We went over the whole estate, including all of the old outbuildings and that small woodland to the south side. Took me away from my regular duties –

YOUGHAL: Here now, what regular duties might you have that are more important that searching for the master's missing son?

JONAS: *(Whining)* I'm the only man here, and I'm expected to take care of the whole place, and to keep things presentable without any assistance at all. And now the housekeeper tells me that the family has sold their London home and will be living here year round. Yet there has been no mention of getting any help for poor old Jonas, now has there?

WATSON: *(Trying to calm things down)* Jonas, we're simply trying to find out if you can provide any information that will help us locate young Patrick.

JONAS: I did what I could. I helped in the search. We looked everywhere, some places more than once. There was even some talk of dragging the mere . . . .

HOLMES: Yes, yes. Hopefully it won't come to that. Jonas, what can you tell us of Lord Bretton's family?

JONAS: Oh, no objections, I suppose.

YOUGHAL: What? You don't object to them!

JONAS: *(Snapping)* Well, I don't know a thing.

YOUGHAL: Watch your tongue, man!

JONAS: I've nothing to tell you, *sir*. They're a quiet family. They keep to themselves. When they *are* down from London, they all stay inside, all except Miss Emily.

WATSON: What do you mean?

JONAS: Miss Emily is the only one who ever really gets outside and walks over the grounds at any length and explores them. Between you and me, I think she wants some time to herself. She probably knows the place better than I do. It's been that way ever since Lord Bretton bought the place.

YOUGHAL: Bought the place? I thought this was his Lordship's family estate.

JONAS: Oh, no. No, *sir*. The previous owners all died out a few years ago, and Lord Bretton bought it at a bargain soon after. I hadn't been here

505

for very long myself, then, and Lord Bretton kept me around as caretaker when he let the rest of the staff go.

WATSON: How often do you see young Patrick? It strikes me that a young boy would want to get outside as often as possible.

JONAS: Well, he tries. I think that he would go out more, if his mother would allow it, but he's kept in as much as possible. *(Lowering his voice)* Can I tell you gentlemen what I think?

YOUGHAL: Certainly, certainly.

JONAS: It seems to me that if the family didn't have to live here, because of Lord Bretton's financial misfortunes, they wouldn't.

HOLMES: What do you know of the family finances?

JONAS: *(Softly)* Mrs. Jameson told me that the master's funds are limited, and getting worse. Nearly gone, as a matter of fact. That probably explains why he hasn't made any improvements here since he's owned the place. Some parts of the house are in desperate need of repairs, and some of the outbuildings and old barns are near falling down. Mrs. Jameson even said that he may be forced to sell this place soon, as well.

HOLMES: And what can you tell us of the missing painting?

JONAS: I've seen it, of course, when I've checked on the house while the family was in London.

WATSON: Do you have any idea where the painting might be, or how it was taken? We understand that it is rather large and cumbersome.

JONAS: No, I don't, and anybody that says different will answer to me. But I can tell you that it wouldn't be an easy thing to move, what with how big it is, and how it's in that great heavy frame.

HOLMES: Hmm . . . . How often does the family have visitors here at the Surrey home?

JONAS: Never, Mr. Holmes. I've heard from Mrs. Jameson that it's the same at the London house. They're a very close bunch, they are.

WATSON: Jonas, you said the family does not have visitors, yet we have been told that Sir Sheffield Frye was down just a week ago today.

JONAS: Oh, well, that is right. I forgot about him. He was just here for the one night. This was his first trip down to this house.

HOLMES: Why didn't you drive Sir Sheffield to the station last Sunday morning when it was time for his departure? Why was Lord Bretton forced to drive him in the dogcart?

JONAS: *(Suddenly hostile)* And why do you need to know about that? That doesn't have anything to do with anything!

YOUGHAL: Answer the question!

JONAS: Well, I . . . I suppose that I was unavailable then. I must have been out taking care of something on the estate.

YOUGHAL: *(Sarcastically)* Of course you were, early on a Sunday morning. *(More stern)* Jonas, do you have any knowledge concerning young Patrick's whereabouts?

JONAS: No. No, sir, but I can hardly blame the young scamp for running away.

WATSON: So you believe that he ran away, then?

JONAS: Well, it stands to reason, don't it? The only boy with six older sisters? That would have been enough to make me run away when I was a lad. I remember the time when the circus came to our village. There was this lady bareback rider. I thought that she —

WATSON: Really? I also —

HOLMES: *(Hastily)* Quite, quite. Thank you for your assistance, Jonas, and we'll let you know if we have any further questions.

SOUND EFFECT: CHAIR SCRAPING, FOOTSTEPS (FADING), DOOR CLOSING

WATSON: That certainly didn't add anything useful.

507

YOUGHAL: Well, I don't trust him. A man like that, having the run of an estate such as this for most of the year, suddenly finding out that he's going to be expected to work a full day again year round?

WATSON: And then he avoids the duties that he does have. From what I could judge of the man's appearance and character, I'm sure that he was unable to drive Sir Sheffield Frye to the station last Sunday morning because he was recovering from a trip to the local pub on Saturday night. Do you agree, Holmes? Did you learn anything from the conversation?

HOLMES: *(Distracted)* What? Oh, certainly Watson. He exhibited all the signs of a chronic drunkard. And yet, if I'm not mistaken, he's hiding something –

SOUND EFFECT: DOOR OPENS; MAN'S FOOTSTEPS ENTER AND STOP

HOLMES: Ah, Lord Bretton. Just the man I wanted to see. I have another question for you.

BRETTON: Yes, Mr. Holmes?

HOLMES: We have been given to understand that you have sold your London home. Is that correct?

BRETTON: *(Quiet, embarrassed)* Yes, that is true, Mr. Holmes. To my friend Sir Sheffield Frye. That was why he came down last Saturday, to deliver the proof of payment and the final copy of the papers.

HOLMES: May I see those documents, Lord Bretton?

BRETTON: Certainly. Although I don't see how – That is, I'll have them for you momentarily.

SOUND EFFECT: FOOTSTEPS (FADING)

WATSON: *(Softly)* Holmes, what do you make of this business? Do you see any hope?

HOLMES: *(Softly)* These are dark waters, Watson. I have a dim perception of what may have happened, but I hope I am wrong. Let us both hope that I am wrong!

MUSIC: SHORT BRIDGE

SOUND EFFECT: MEN'S FOOTSTEPS ON GRASS, BIRDS SINGING

WATSON: Did you learn anything from the documents, Holmes?

HOLMES: Hmm . . . They confirmed some of what Langdale Pike related to me this morning. Unfortunately, I believe that a conversation with Sir Sheffield in person in London is now unavoidable.

YOUGHAL: Mr. Holmes, I fail to see how traveling to London to interview Sir Sheffield Frye will get us any closer to finding the missing boy. If it was a question of ransom – But no ransom note has been received.

HOLMES: Nevertheless, everything indicates to me that we need to understand all that has happened here, starting a week ago, in order to get at the entire truth. We must run up to London immediately, and attempt to corner Sir Sheffield Frye.

MUSIC: SHORT BRIDGE

SOUND EFFECT: CAROUSING NOISES (GLASSES CLINKING, RANDOM CONVERSATION) UNDER

WATSON: *(Softly)* There he is, Holmes. Over there, at the card table.

YOUGHAL: We've only had to track him across half of London before finding him here, at the Nonpareil Club.

HOLMES: He appears to be somewhat inebriated. That may work to our advantage.

YOUGHAL: How, Mr. Holmes? I must admit that your theory, whatever it is, certainly seems to be correct. We found the painting, right where you said it would be. But I cannot see a connection between Sir Sheffield and the missing boy. And we cannot just walk up to a peer and imply that there is one.

HOLMES: *You* cannot, inspector. As you are now aware, Sir Sheffield is tied to the missing painting. And it appears more and more likely that the painting is related to the missing boy. *(Louder)* Sir Sheffield Frye? Perhaps you remember when we met last year, during the events of the Netherland-Sumatra affair? This is Dr. Watson, and Inspector Youghal of Scotland Yard. My name is –

FRYE: *(Somewhat intoxicated)* Of course I remember you. Mr. Sherlock Holmes. Holmes, the meddler. Well, what do you want? The cards are hot, man. Don't you understand what that means?

HOLMES: This may only take a few moments, Sir Sheffield, depending on your response. If we could just step over here, into this side room?

SOUND EFFECT: CHAIR SCRAPING, FOOTSTEPS. CAROUSING NOISES BECOMING MORE MUTED UNTIL DOOR CLOSES

FRYE: *(Impatient)* What is it, Holmes?

HOLMES We simply need for you to tell us, Sir Sheffield, what were the specific arrangements for stealing Lord Bretton's painting from the Surrey house?

YOUGHAL: *(Shocked, surprised)* Mr. Holmes? A moment . . . ?

WATSON: *(Softly)* Trust him, Youghal.

YOUGHAL: Mr. Holmes, you can't just –

FRYE: *(Sputters)* Steal his – Steal his painting? I have stolen *nothing*!

HOLMES: Sir Sheffield? Our time is precious, and your prevarication is wasted. The details, if you please.

FRYE: Inspector, I sense that you are not a willing participant in this slanderous behavior, but I assure you that your superiors will be made aware of this incident.

YOUGHAL: *(Urgent, quiet)* Mr. Holmes, could we converse outside?

HOLMES: *(Ignoring Youghal. Quiet, cold, completely in control)* Sir Sheffield, you will tell me the details of how you took possession of the painting, for I need to determine if my conclusions regarding its connection with Lord Bretton's missing son are correct. Only by clearing up the mystery surrounding the painting can we see about locating the boy.

YOUGHAL: *(Softly)* Doctor, do you know that Mr. Holmes is about?

WATSON: *(Softly)* I begin to have a dim perception. I hope that I'm wrong.

FRYE: *(More sober)* Bretton's son is missing? What has that to do with me? He was just fine when I . . . when I last saw him.

HOLMES: And when was that?

FRYE: Why, last Saturday, a week ago, of course. When I was at their Surrey home for dinner.

HOLMES: And if I tell you that you were seen when you returned to Surrey a few days later?

FRYE: Impossible! No one saw me –

HOLMES: Are you certain of that?

FRYE: *(Still a little drunk)* Why, I . . . I . . . No one saw me. You're bluffing!

WATSON: *(Quietly)* Holmes, it's almost unfair to take advantage of the man in his intoxicated state.

HOLMES: I have read the document that you prepared in order to purchase Lord Bretton's London house, Sir Sheffield. The odd clause that it contains helped me to understand what you intended.

YOUGHAL: Odd clause? I didn't notice anything unusual.

WATSON: I'm sure that we saw it, Youghal, but we did not *observe* it. It is a rather familiar experience for me.

511

HOLMES: The clause states that you were not only buying the London house, but whatever contents were contained within it at the time of purchase, without question. Those were the papers that you delivered when you visited the Surrey home last Saturday, one week ago today. Is that correct?

FRYE: Yes, yes. Of course. But that has nothing to do with the painting.

HOLMES: That isn't true, Sir Sheffield. You specifically included that particular and rather unusual clause so that you could claim ownership of the Constable painting, which had been accurately and repeatedly described to you by Lord Bretton as the most valuable thing that he owned. You intended to carry the painting back to London with you in secret when you left Surrey on Sunday morning, did you not, so it would be in the London house when the sale was finalized on Monday, thus making it your property?

YOUGHAL: Of course! As they say, possession *is* nine-tenths of the law.

WATSON: A fine way to treat your friend.

FRYE: *(Snarls)* Friend? What kind of a friend was he last year, during the Netherland-Sumatra affair? His idiocy nearly cost me everything that I had. He was too afraid to take the risks that were needed in order to save himself, and he nearly brought me down as well. I've had to work like the devil over the last year to recoup my losses. And then the fool comes to me and asks me to help him out of a hole for old time's sake by buying his London home, so that he'll have a little cash to live on for a while longer in Surrey.

HOLMES: That is *your* perception of the events of last year. You forget that I have some knowledge of the matter, as well. There is every indication that Lord Bretton's financial disaster was due to *you*, Sir Sheffield, and his foolish trust in *your* advice. Nevertheless, I'm certain that you have convinced yourself of your own innocence in the matter, and that you also convinced your accomplice in order to gain assistance in taking the painting.

YOUGHAL: Accomplice?

HOLMES: Of course. There had to be someone in the house who could inform Sir Sheffield that the painting would not immediately be missed. This person was also required to help make the arrangements with Jonas, in order to transport the painting to the train station on Sunday morning.

FRYE: *(To himself)* That drunken fool . . . .

HOLMES: No doubt the plan was for Sir Sheffield to leave with the painting early on Sunday, catching the milk train before the family was even awake. By the time Sir Sheffield and his co-conspirator realized that they would not have Jonas's help due to his inebriated state, and that it was too late to remove the painting that morning, Lord Bretton was up. Alternate plans were quickly made, and Sir Sheffield was forced to return later in the week to collect the painting.

FRYE: You devil! You don't know what you're talking about!

WATSON: We've seen the painting, Sir Sheffield. We've been to Lord Bretton's former London home, where it is hanging in the dining room as if it had always been there.

YOUGHAL: But Mr. Holmes, the family would have realized who took it, and how Sir Sheffield had swindled them with the wording of the contract. They would have been able to tell the authorities what had happened.

HOLMES: Not *all* of the family, Youghal.

WATSON: Of course. The accomplice would have lied for Sir Sheffield.

HOLMES: Very good, Watson. I see that you've caught up.

WATSON: It would have been their word against the rest of the family. What did you promise her, Sir Sheffield? Marriage?

FRYE: *(Grudgingly)* We had an arrangement. She said that she loved me. I . . . I suppose that I have feelings for her as well. She was going to leave her family to be with me.

YOUGHAL: She? It can't be the housekeeper? She was the one that reported the painting as being missing. And Lady Bretton is an invalid. Then the accomplice must be –

WATSON: Congratulations, Inspector. Now you are caught up as well.

HOLMES: *(Ignoring them)* According to my watch –

SOUND EFFECT: POCKET WATCH SNAPS OPEN

HOLMES: – we have unfortunately missed the last train back to Surrey.

SOUND EFFECT: POCKET WATCH SNAPS SHUT

HOLMES: However, Sir Sheffield, I am afraid that your card game is over. Inspector, have one of your men take him into custody. I must send a lengthy wire with instructions to the Surrey Constabulary, and then Sir Sheffield will provide us with additional information while we arrange for transportation back to Lytton House.

MUSIC: SHORT BRIDGE

SOUND EFFECT: FOOTSTEPS THROUGH GRASS

HOLMES: *(Angry)* Blast the trains! It would have been faster to have hired a carriage!

WATSON: We did what we could. We wired the local police. They were able to –

YOUGHAL: *(Out of breath, joining them)* The family is waiting at the house. I haven't told them anything. They all remained indoors while we were gone, much as we left them. After you sent your wire, Mr. Holmes, my men searched and found several abandoned barns and outbuildings on the south edge of the property. It took them a while to identify the right one, and to search it in order to find what they were looking for.

WATSON: And was it as we feared?

SOUND EFFECT: FOOTSTEPS THROUGH GRASS (OUT)

YOUGHAL: *(A pause, and then quietly somber)* I'm told that we'd better see for ourselves . . . .

YOUGHAL: *(Muffled from being inside the dusty barn)* Over here, gentlemen. My men said it was in the middle of the floor. Careful, watch your step . . . Down there.

WATSON: *(Softly)* Oh, my God.

HOLMES: *(Pause, then quietly)* Let us go back to the house.

MUSIC: SHORT BRIDGE

SOUND EFFECT: MAIN DOOR OPENING, MENS' FOOTSTEPS ENTER AND STOP

HOLMES: Where are they, Youghal?

YOUGHAL: Lord Bretton and Emily are in the dining room. The other children and Lady Bretton are upstairs.

WATSON: Well, let's get this over with.

SOUND EFFECT: DOOR OPENING, MEN'S FOOTSTEPS ENTER, STOP

HOLMES: *(Deep breath)* Lord Bretton, I am afraid that I have some terrible news.

BRETTON: *(With dread)* Patrick?

HOLMES: *(Very quiet)* I am sorry, sir. Your son is dead.

BRETTON: *(Anguished)* No! *(Softer)* No . . . .

EMILY: What? How – What has happened, Mr. Holmes?

BRETTON: *(Softly, gaining control of himself)* Yes, please, what has happened?

HOLMES: Last night, Inspector Youghal, Dr. Watson, and I located Sir Sheffield Frye in London –

515

BRETTON: *(Less emotional, puzzled)* Sir Sheffield Frye?

HOLMES: Yes, Lord Bretton. He has poorly repaid your trust in him as a guest. After we found Sir Sheffield at his club, it was a quick matter to get the complete story out of him. During his visits to your London home, he had been secretly romancing Emily. *(Tone changes, more harsh)* Not necessarily because he cared anything about her, of course. He was simply dallying with her, as he has with others before her, always on the lookout for an opportunity if one should present itself.

EMILY: *(Simply a statement of fact)* He loves me.

SOUND EFFECT: MAN'S FOOTSTEPS AS YOUGHAL STEPS BEHIND EMILY

BRETTON: Inspector, why are you gripping my daughter's shoulder?

WATSON: When you asked him to buy the London property, in order to save you financially, his initial response was to turn you down. He blames you for his reversals last year. However, it occurred to him that he could maneuver events so that he could gain ownership of the Constable painting. He could then sell it for more than he was paying you for the house, thus turning a profit, and still have the London house as well. He managed to get Emily to help him, believing that he could keep her quiet with further empty promises of love, and that the painting's theft wouldn't immediately be discovered. Later, with Emily under his thumb and backing up his version of events, the threat of scandal might silence the family if necessary.

BRETTON: I don't believe it. Emily . . . .

HOLMES: Emily removed the painting from the house and hid it in a root cellar in of the abandoned barns on the property. Unexpectedly, the painting was discovered missing on Wednesday. Emily, who volunteered to go to town to summon the police, also sent word to Sir Sheffield to stay away until the next day, Thursday, without telling him why. On Thursday morning she slipped away, intending to meet Frye at the barn and give him the painting.

BRETTON: *(Horrified)* Emily. Tell them it isn't true, Emily . . . .

WATSON: We learned this much from Sir Sheffield last night. He showed up on Thursday to receive the painting as planned. Of course, it had not been discovered the previous day by the police during their searches. They had paid scant attention to the abandoned building, and they hadn't even realized that there was a root cellar.

HOLMES: Sir Sheffield met Emily at the shed as arranged. As Frye took possession of the canvas, he was dismayed to hear Patrick, watching them through a crack in the building's wall.

MUSIC: SHORT BRIDGE

FRYE: *(Irritated)* What took you so long, girl? What if someone sees me or my wagon?

EMILY: *(Snappish, not like the Emily we've previously met at all)* I got here as quickly as I could. Jonas won't see you. He's drunk as usual, and asleep in his cottage. Everyone else is inside. They never come out, and we're well away from the house out here. Besides, I had to make sure that the police hadn't come back.

FRYE: *(Urgent)* The police? Do you mean to say they have already discovered that the painting is gone? You said the dining room where it hung goes unused for weeks!

EMILY: I thought that no one would notice that it was gone, but yesterday, the housekeeper saw that it was missing. Father insisted on calling in the police. It's the only thing of value that he still owns. I don't have to tell you how he's thrown everything else away. After you and I are married, perhaps we'll give him a little money. Maybe we'll make him beg for it. It will be nice to have him beholden to me for a change.

FRYE: Where is the root cellar?

EMILY: Over here. Help me . . . .

SOUND EFFECT: FOOTSTEPS ACROSS HOLLOW SOUNDING BOARDS. TRAP DOOR RAISING

517

EMILY: No, you don't have to climb down. It's not deep. Just reach in. I've turned the frame up on its side. It almost reaches the top of the cellar. Turn it, more, sideways, that's it . . . .

<u>SOUND EFFECT: SCRAMBLING SOUNDS, HEAVY BREATHING</u>

FRYE: Got it! Now – *(grunting)* – let's get it in the wagon –

<u>SOUND EFFECT: PAINTING BEING LIFTED OUT AND LOADED INTO THE WAGON</u>

FRYE: There!

<u>SOUND EFFECT: SOME LOGS SHIFT, MAKING A NOISE</u>

FRYE: What's that! Oh, dear lord, it's your brother!

EMILY: *(Urgent)* Run, Sheff! Run! I'll take care of Patrick!

FRYE: But –

EMILY: Run!

<u>SOUND EFFECT: RUNNING FOOTSTEPS CLIMBING INTO THE WAGON, HORSE AND WAGON DEPARTURE (FADING)</u>

EMILY: *(Softly, to herself)* I'll be with you soon, my love.

<u>MUSIC: SHORT BRIDGE</u>

HOLMES: *(Softly)* We went out to the abandoned barn a few moments ago. The trapdoor to the root cellar had been closed, and covered by straw so that it would not be found, except by someone who already knew that it was there. Were you aware that there was a root cellar in that building, Lord Bretton?

BRETTON: *(Whispers)* No. *(Clears his throat)* No, I had no idea.

HOLMES: We just spoke to Jonas, and he was unaware of it, as well. It is not much of a chamber, a mere five feet or so deep, and about the same area square. It is likely that unless you had plans to remove the building anytime soon, the whole thing would have continued its slow collapse on top of the chamber, and no one would have realized for many years, if ever, that it was there.

(Quietly) When we looked inside, we were dismayed to find the body of young Patrick.

BRETTON: *(Sobbing sound, softly)* Oh! Oh, my son!

WATSON: *(Softly)* Holmes . . . .

HOLMES: The boy had been wounded gravely on the head. A piece of bloodstained wood, cut for stove length, was tossed down beside the body.

YOUGHAL: *(Roughly, his voice cracking with emotion)* She had thrown lime over the boy. She didn't want him to be found. She covered up the trap door.

EMILY: *(Matter-of-fact)* Inspector, you are hurting my arm.

HOLMES: Sir Sheffield said that Emily believed that he was going to marry her. Of course, he never had any intention of that, since he is already married.

EMILY: *(Surprised)* What? You lie!

HOLMES: *(With an edge)* No doubt she feared if her perfidy were discovered too soon, her plans to be with Sir Sheffield would fall through. Perhaps she did not mean to kill Patrick, and only lashed out unthinkingly to stop him. However, once the deed was done, she deliberately hid the body, fixing it so that it would not be found. She threw lime liberally into the hole, in order to minimize the problems associated with decomposition. There was no lime stored in the abandoned building, so she would have had to get it from elsewhere on the grounds. This took intentional effort and planning. Then she covered the trap door with straw to make certain that the boy would not be found during the subsequent search which was sure to be made over the entire estate.

EMILY: *(Confused, and somewhat irritated, to herself)* Why did Sheff tell? No one would have ever known. He could have sold the painting, and then he would have come for me. Then I wouldn't have had to take care of the children any more. *(Softer)* I've never liked children.

BRETTON: *(In horror)* Emily –

YOUGHAL: *(Clearing his throat)* Constable. Constable!

SOUND EFFECT: MUFFLED FOOTSTEPS, DOOR OPENING, LOUDER FOOSTEPS

YOUGHAL: Take her in charge. And make sure that no one goes upstairs and tells the mother or children what's happened yet. The lady is in poor health, and I want to make sure she that she finds this out as mercifully as possible.

MUSIC: SHORT BRIDGE

SOUND EFFECT: OUTSIDE: BIRDS SINGING. FOOTSTEPS ON GRAVEL AND UNDER

YOUGHAL: Doctor, how is Lady Bretton?

WATSON: Not well, inspector. Not well.

YOUGHAL: *(Clears his throat)* Can I offer you gentlemen a ride back to the station? The carriage is waiting right over here.

WATSON: The one containing Emily and the constable? I don't fancy making the trip while staring at the mad, reddish wet gaze of that deluded young woman.

HOLMES: *(Quietly)* Very descriptive, Watson. *(Louder)* Thank you, Youghal, but I believe that we shall find our own way back to town.

MUSIC: SHORT BRIDGE

HOLMES: I believe that they will find her to be quite mad. I am afraid Lord Bretton's family is only at the beginning of their pain. Their only son and brother dead, and they have to live for years with the constant reminder of what happened in the form of Emily, who will no doubt be hospitalized for quite a long time. I do not see her condition improving.

520

WATSON: And Sir Sheffield Frye?

HOLMES: He will get a few years for the attempted theft of the painting, but he was clearly not involved in the murder. I hope that this will serve to break him, but a rogue like that will no doubt rise from all of this like some sort of phoenix.

SOUND EFFECT: HOLMES REACHES FOR THE VIOLIN, PLUCKING AND TUNING THE STRINGS. HE STOPS

HOLMES: Do you know, Watson, Lord Bretton had described that painting as his most valuable possession. How sad for him to realize only now that his most valuable possessions are his children.

SOUND EFFECT: HOLMES DRAGS THE BOW ACROSS THE STRINGS

HOLMES: Do you mind if I play for a while? Will it disturb you?

WATSON: No, Holmes. *(Pause)* Please play. *(Pause)* Good night.

HOLMES: Good night, Watson.

MUSIC: Mournful Notes, fade into . . . .

MUSIC: *DANSE MACABRE* UP AND UNDER

The Singular Affair at Sissinghurst Castle

CHARACTERS

- ☐ SHERLOCK HOLMES
- ☐ DR. JOHN H. WATSON
- ☐ DRIVER
- ☐ STANLEY CORNWALLIS
- ☐ PHILO T. BURKE
- ☐ CONSTABLE WAGNER
- ☐ REPORTERS No's 1, 2, and 3

SOUND EFFECT: OPENING SEQUENCE, BIG BEN

ANNOUNCER: *The Further Adventures of Sherlock Holmes,* starring John Patrick Lowrie as Sherlock Holmes, and Lawrence Albert as Dr. John H. Watson.

MUSIC: *DANSE MACABRE* (UP AND UNDER)

MUSIC: OUT

SOUND EFFECT: WAGON WHEELS AND HORSE WALKING STEADILY

WATSON: Holmes, I appreciate the chance to get out of London for the day, and Kent is certainly lovely in the spring, but you don't always have to be so mysterious. Why are we here?

HOLMES: We are going to Sissinghurst. Do you know of it?

WATSON: Not at all, I'm afraid.

HOLMES: I received a letter several days ago from the owner of Sissinghurst Castle and the surrounding farm, a Mr. Stanley Cornwallis.

WATSON: And what does Mr. Cornwallis require from Mr. Sherlock Holmes?

523

HOLMES: He is being bothered by a treasure hunter.

WATSON: Treasure? In Kent? I might believe that about some of the areas along the coast, with their centuries of smuggling and the occasional shipwreck. But deep in the heart of the county? Not likely.

HOLMES: There is more than one kind of treasure, Watson. It was only a few months ago that I told you about Reginald Musgrave at Hurlstone, and the recovery there of the lost crown of the former King of England.

WATSON: As I recall, King Charles's crown was hidden at Hurlstone during the reign of Cromwell during the Commonwealth. Does Cornwallis suspect something similar is at Sissinghurst?

HOLMES: No, he believes exactly the opposite. He is certain that there is *nothing* hidden at the house. The estate apparently has some connection with events relating to those muddled times of transition between Mary and Elizabeth. It is a common story in that area, but there has never been any hint of treasure.

WATSON: Then why is there a treasure hunter?

HOLMES: Several weeks ago, an American arrived in Sissinghurst who has repeatedly insisted on searching the buildings and grounds for something of value. So far, Mr. Cornwallis has denied him any access. However, it seems that, in spite of his initial disbelief, Mr. Cornwallis did become more interested in whether there is any truth to the American's claims.

WATSON: And so he communicated with you?

HOLMES: He wrote, asking if I would be interested in doing some research to determine if there was any possibility of truth in the matter. I replied, and then I devoted part of a day in the reading room at the British Museum. Although there is some local historical significance to Mr. Cornwallis's farm, I found no evidence of anything relevant to a treasure at Sissinghurst.

WATSON: They why have we traveled down here?

HOLMES: I was ready to relay my results to Mr. Cornwallis when this morning's wire arrived. Something seems to have happened that made our presence necessary. As you can see, the message is rather vague as to details.

WATSON: (*Reading*) "*Come at once. Situation becoming intolerable. Please wire details of arrival. Cornwallis*". (*Normal Voice*) Vague, indeed. It could be anything from an unpleasant encounter with the American, to murder.

HOLMES: Well, perhaps not murder. If it was that, Cornwallis might have used stronger language than to simply call the situation "*intolerable*". (*Louder*) Driver, what can you tell us about this area?

DRIVER: Not much to tell, sir. There's the village, and the main farm. It's well run, it is. The farmhouse is very nice. And then there's the old house beside it. Hundreds of years old, it is, but it's mostly fallen down now. Some calls it a castle, maybe because it has something of a tower, but it's really naught but an old house.

HOLMES: Did anything interesting ever happen there?

DRIVER: Not much. Of course there was "Bloody" Baker.

HOLMES: I learned something of the fellow during my researches. A fellow with the appellation "Bloody" certainly sounds somewhat interesting, eh, Watson? Driver. What can you tell us of this man?

DRIVER: Not much, sir. Baker were a Catholic man, back during the reign of Mary. He was the owner of Sissinghurst then, and he made it his business to make life hell for the Protestants living around here. That's about all I know for sure, but I've heard about him all my life.

SOUND EFFECT: WAGON WHEELS SLOW TO A STOP, THE HORSE NICKERS

DRIVER: There's Sissinghurst. We're nearly there now, sirs.

MUSIC: SHORT BRIDGE

CORNWALLIS: Mr. Holmes? I am Stanley Cornwallis. Thank you for coming. I apologize for not sending a carriage to the station. I have been too distracted by today's events.

HOLMES: It is quite all right, Mr. Cornwallis. We arranged for transportation. I have brought Dr. John Watson with me. He is an experienced investigator as well, and often accompanies me.

(AD-LIB GENERAL GREETINGS: *Nice to meet you, etc.*)

HOLMES: What are the events today to which you referred?

CORNWALLIS: Come this way, gentlemen, around to the back of the house.

SOUND EFFECT: FOOTSTEPS THROUGH GRASS OR ALONG WALKWAYS

CORNWALLIS: (*Slightly Winded*) Is Dr. Watson aware of the reason I originally wrote to you?

HOLMES: Somewhat. However, I have not revealed to him as yet the little bit of information that my researches revealed.

CORNWALLIS: (*Irate*) I have not received a report from you, either, Mr. Holmes. Did you find any indication whatsoever that there might be some sort of treasure at Sissinghurst?

HOLMES: None whatsoever. While there appears to be a long history to the place, there is nothing monumentally outstanding, and certainly nothing that makes this small byway any more interesting than countless other villages across Britain.

CORNWALLIS: (*Agitated*) Then why would that insane American do *that*?

SOUND EFFECT: FOOTSTEPS STOP

WATSON: Oh . . . my.

HOLMES: Is this what you meant, Mr. Cornwallis, when you wired that the situation was becoming "intolerable"?

CORNWALLIS: Of course that's what I meant. This situation! That American! It's all intolerable. And I want you to gather evidence to stop it. I will prosecute him, sir. I will! I wired for you as soon as we found this, and I have sent for the law as well. The man will pay!

WATSON: Your stone terrace, Mr. Cornwallis. It's . . . it's been nearly destroyed. Almost all of the stones are overturned –

HOLMES: What indication do you have that the American is responsible for this? Did you perhaps catch him in the act?

CORNWALLIS: No, no. It was this way when we came out this morning. He did it during the night. I'm sure he did it. He has been pestering me for weeks to dig on the grounds for his ridiculous treasure. When I said no, he obviously came back on his own and did this.

WATSON: And you say that you have called for the police?

CORNWALLIS: Actually, I did not notify them immediately. My first thought was to send for you, Mr. Holmes. I sent one of the farm hands into the village to send a wire. He waited for your reply, and then returned here. Later, I thought to send my man back for the constable, but I neglected to tell him to meet your train.

WATSON: (*To himself*) That explains why there was no one to meet us at the station.

HOLMES: Perhaps we could go inside while we wait for the constable to arrive, and you can tell us about this American. We can discuss the history of this estate and why there might – or might not – be any treasure at Sissinghurst.

MUSIC: SHORT BRIDGE

WATSON: Have you ever seen any indication of anything that might be considered treasure here?

CORNWALLIS: No, Dr. Watson. The property has been in my family for many generations, and there has never been anything like that here.

527

WATSON: Was there ever any evidence of visits here by royalty? Did anyone in your family ever travel or have adventures in foreign lands which might have given them an opportunity to obtain a treasure?

CORNWALLIS: There is a rumor that Edward I stayed here in the village in the early 1300's, but if so, he would certainly not have hidden a treasure here.

WATSON: No, that can't be it.

CORNWALLIS: And of course, there was Sir John Baker, who owned the house in the early 1500's, and was left two-hundred pounds by Henry VIII, in spite of Baker's noted pro-Catholic beliefs.

HOLMES: Ah, yes, "Bloody" Baker. He is the center of your American's treasure theories. What can you tell us of him?

CORNWALLIS: Why, that is Sir John, over there, in that painting over the fireplace.

WATSON: (*Muttering*) Grim looking fellow. (*Louder*) But overall he does not seem very threatening. Certainly not worth the name "Bloody" Baker.

HOLMES: Hmm. (*Reading*) "*Sir John Baker. 1488 to 1558*". (*Normal voice*) Long lived for his time. As I understand it, he was quite a successful man in this region.

CORNWALLIS: Yes, he was. Although he was fiercely pro-Catholic, Sir John enjoyed an excellent relationship with King Henry VIII, in spite of Henry's strong anti-Catholic beliefs.

HOLMES: In fact, I learned that during the time King Henry was taking so many estates, churches, and monasteries from pro-Catholic citizens and redistributing them to his friends and cronies, he actually gave many properties to Sir John, who ended up owning a number of manors and farms scattered around this area of Kent.

CORNWALLIS: Peacefully, I might add.

WATSON: But there was nothing bloody about any of that! Was there ever any indication of Baker showing excessive violence toward the local Protestants?

CORNWALLIS: None, Doctor. He questioned them, and often they had their property taken from them, but I have never heard anything that would lead to the name "Bloody" Baker.

HOLMES: As I understand it from your original letter, it is the claim of the American treasure hunter . . . I'm sorry, what was his name again, Mr. Cornwallis?

CORNWALLIS: Burke. Philo T. Burke.

HOLMES: Ah, yes. Peculiar name, isn't it, Watson? It is the claim of Mr. Burke that during this time Sir John Baker took something of great value from one of the local families and hid it here at Sissinghurst. During the confusion following Queen Mary's death, the item was never recovered. And soon after, Sir John died, and his secret with him.

CORNWALLIS: That is Burke's assertion, yes. However, there is no basis for such a fabrication. The local families have never mentioned any lost treasure, nor have they ever listed the theft of a treasure amongst their grievances against Sir John.

HOLMES: This location has spent the better part of the last thousand years in relative ease and peace. Even the tensions between Catholics and Protestants in the area never achieved any great level of bloodshed.

CORNWALLIS: Would you be willing to present your evidence to Burke? Excellent!

SOUND EFFECT: CARRIAGES ARRIVING OUTSIDE (MUTED)

CORNWALLIS: That will be the constable. Will you relate to him as well what you have told me?

HOLMES: Of course.

SOUND EFFECT: CURTAINS PULLING BACK AND WINDOW OPENING

529

CORNWALLS: Look out there! That's not the constable! It's Burke, with several carriages of rough-looking men with him!

MUSIC: SHORT BRIDGE

SOUND EFFECT: QUICK FOOTSTEPS ACROSS GRAVEL

CORNWALLIS: Burke! What is the meaning of this? I have told you that you are not allowed on my property!

BURKE: (*American accent*) Good morning to you, Mr. Cornwallis. I realize that we have had some disagreements in the past, but we cannot let something like that stand in the way of the historical find of the century! Just think, sir – When the truth is revealed, your little castle here will be the destination point of visitors from both Europe and America!

CORNWALLIS: Leave! Leave now! The law will be here soon, and then I will have you arrested! Do you think you can get away with vandalizing my property and trespassing? I will have you arrested and then deported!

BURKE: I don't think we've had the pleasure, gentleman. My name is Philo Burke, of Cleveland, Ohio. I'm sure Mr. Cornwallis has told you about me.

CORNWALLIS: Yes, I have. They are here because of *you*! They can debunk your whole treasure theory. This is –

HOLMES: (*Interrupting*) We have been doing been doing some research for Mr. Cornwallis in London. He is correct. There is no evidence of any historical event here that would indicate the presence of treasure.

BURKE: Of course that is what the official records would say. If there was a conspiracy to conceal the fact that "Bloody" Baker had hidden a treasure here, he would have covered his tracks well.

(AD-LIB: THE MEN OF THE PRESS MUTTERING TO THEMSELVES)

530

BURKE: (*Louder*) Boys, I've looked at the same papers in London that this gentleman is referring to, and I can tell you that there is more to it than he thinks. In fact, *(Lowering voice)* I was even able to find a coded message contained in the papers, which is what led me to search under the flagstone terrace behind the house!

CORNWALLIS: You destroyed that terrace! It has only been there for thirty years, since the current house was built. It wasn't even there when Sir John lived here!

BURKE: Mr. Cornwallis, I do not know if you are truly ignorant of the historical nature of what is hidden here, or if you yourself are part of the conspiracy to keep the truth hidden. But I tell you that the truth must come out, and you cannot stop it! I have brought these fine men of the press with me today, to assure that the truth will be told. For too long the secret has been kept! Come with me, boys!

SOUND EFFECT: MULTIPLE FOOTSTEPS ACROSS GRAVEL (FADING)

BURKE: (*Fading*) Follow me behind the house. Whatever it is, it's been buried for over three-hundred years. It's time to bring it out into the sunshine!

HOLMES: (*Low voice, but still near by*) What do you say to a day in Kent, Watson?

WATSON: (*Low voice*) Kent sounds wonderful. If we don't get killed in the crossfire. I assume you didn't want Burke to know you are a detective.

HOLMES: (*Low voice*) Exactly. Burke may or may not have heard of me, but I want to see what his game is for a while, and the best way to do that is to let him play it out. The terrace is already damaged. A little more destruction cannot hurt it too badly. Let us see what Mr. Burke has planned for us.

MUSIC: SHORT BRIDGE

HOLMES: Hurry, Watson, let us hear what Mr. Burke is saying to the press.

BURKE: (*Voice becoming louder – Speaking to the Press*) As you can see, I was unable to finish my search of the terrace last night. I was interrupted and forced to flee when I thought I was about to be discovered. Of course, I will recompense Mr. Cornwallis for the cost of repairs to his terrace.

CORNWALLIS: You certainly will!

BURKE: However, I feel that once the treasure is recovered, he will be so grateful that he will understand why this was necessary, and he may not even ask for any compensation.

REPORTER #1: And what is your deal in all this, Mr. Burke? If they find a treasure, you don't get to keep it.

BURKE: Certainly not. My only interest is in the advancement of historical knowledge.

REPORTER #2: How did you get onto it? Being from Ohio and all?

BURKE: I came across some old documents, which made references to other documents. I followed the trail, using the specialized knowledge I have acquired from a lifetime of study, until I found conclusive proof of the Sissinghurst Treasure.

SOUND EFFECT: FLAGSTONE STONE OVERTURNING (FADING)

REPORTER #3: (*Slightly off in the distance*) *Oi!* What's this?

HOLMES: (*Softly*) I believe we are about to see Mr. Burke's surprise, Watson.

REPORTER #2: It's a skeleton! Down in the hole underneath this terrace stone!

REPORTER #3: This stone wasn't flipped like all the others. I was just looking to see what was underneath. And – oh my God! The back of his bloody head's been knocked in!

REPORTER #1: Let me see!

REPORTER #2: Get out of the way, you!

BURKE: Well, I had not expected this. No, sir. Had you, Mr. Cornwallis? Did you perhaps know what we would find?

CORNWALLIS: (*Stunned*) No. No, of course not.

HOLMES: And what did you expect, Mr. Burke?

BURKE: Well, sir, to be honest, I did not rightly know. Treasure of some sort, of course, perhaps a chest, but I never expected to find a murder!

WAGNER: (*Fading in*) Murder? What's this about a murder? How was this found, sir?

CORNWALLIS: Constable Wagner! It's about time you arrived.

REPORTER #2: It's a skeleton. Underneath this paving stone.

WAGNER Any idea who this might be?

CORNWALLIS: None. This terrace is only thirty or so years old. There is no indication that there has ever been a treasure here, contrary to Mr. Burke's wild claims. Let alone a skeleton. This gentleman will tell you. He has researched the matter.

WAGNER: And your name sir? You look familiar to me. Wait, aren't you – ?

HOLMES: Might I speak with you in private for a moment?

WAGNER: Why, umm, certainly.

SOUND EFFECT: FOOTSTEPS ACROSS GRAVEL (FADING)

REPORTER #1: (*Yelling*) Mr. Cornwallis! Do you care to give a statement about this gruesome discovery?

REPORTER #2: (Abrasive) Mr. Cornwallis, sir! Do you know which member of your family killed this man and hid his body under the terrace?

533

REPORTER #3: (*Louder*) Do you feel that it is now the right time to reveal the location of the treasure?

CORNWALLIS: Burke! This is all your fault! I'll –

SOUND EFFECT: FOOTSTEPS APPROACHING ACROSS THE GRAVEL

WAGNER: (*Loud*) You people. I want your names and which paper you are with. Then I want you to clear off out of here. Return to the village, and don't leave until I tell you so. (NORMAL TONE) Mr. Cornwallis, I am going to leave the remains here under your responsibility until I can return. Mr. Burke, you will return to the village with me.

BURKE: (*Angry*) Wait! You cannot simply go off and leave this find unprotected. We don't know how it got here. His family may have had something to do with it. You may get back and the treasure may be gone! Or the bones!

WAGNER: Sir, there are a number of witnesses who have seen the skeleton, most of them reporters that you brought here yourself. Too many people have seen this. I do not think that anything will happen here while I'm gone, and I trust these men to watch over things until I get back. Gentlemen, until I return, good day.

SOUND EFFECT: FOOTSTEPS ACROSS GRAVEL (FADING)

CORNWALLIS: Mr. Holmes, what does it all mean? Is it possible that "Bloody" Baker was not the innocent man your researches showed?

HOLMES: Perhaps you should go inside and rest, Mr. Cornwallis. Dr. Watson and I will be responsible for the skeleton until the return of Constable Wagner.

CORNWALLIS: Yes, of course. Thank you, Mr. Holmes.

SOUND EFFECT: FOOTSTEPS ACROSS GRAVEL (FADING)

HOLMES: What do you make of it, Watson?

WATSON: This is certainly no murder, is it?

HOLMES: As I'm sure you can see, the bones are clean and white. More importantly, they were obviously once *wired together*. What does this suggest?

WATSON: This fellow has, until recently, been the resident of some sort of teaching facility, perhaps a hospital. I imagine, from his excellent condition, that he has not been dead and preserved for too many years, and that he certainly has not been in this hole for very long.

HOLMES: No, not for more than twelve hours or so, I would say. The bones are extremely clean, and there is no sign of discoloration from exposure to the soil or the groundwater. In addition, the sides of the hole are still quite vertical, and there has been no creep or collapse of the walls.

WATSON: But why was he placed here? I assume that Burke is behind this.

HOLMES: Oh, of course he is. Obviously, he came out here last night and buried the bones under a flagstone large enough to cover a skeleton before he replaced that stone and proceeded to disrupt a number of others. Then, as we saw a few minutes ago, he let someone else make the discovery, creating the shocking effect that he was attempting.

WATSON: But surely he realizes that a cursory examination would show that this skeleton is of very recent origin?

HOLMES: Possibly. It may be that he has such a low opinion of the country constabulary that he believed the skeleton's condition would not be noticed. Or more probably, he does not care. He intentionally made sure there were reporters here, and he seemed pleased that they were writing down everything they saw and heard.

WATSON: When you referred to this as Burke's surprise, did you know exactly what was going to be found?

HOLMES: Not at all. But when Burke arrived with the reporters, I realized that he had probably hidden something that he wanted to be found in front of witnesses. However, I did not know what form the item would take.

WATSON: But what about the hole in the skull?

HOLMES: It simply adds to the effect. I'm sure the hole was knocked there by Burke to give the initial impression that the fellow had been murdered. If you look, you can see that the exposed cracked edges around the hole are clean and white, even cleaner than the surface of the skull, indicating that the wound is of recent origin.

WATSON: So all this has been arranged for some reason as a show for those reporters brought down by Burke.

HOLMES: Exactly. Although I am not quite certain of his motive at this point, I believe that we shall have to give Mr. Burke a little more line in order to set the hook before we can reel him in.

WATSON: And the constable? Did you make him aware of all this?

HOLMES: I did. He appeared to recognize me, and was in fact about to identify me when I stopped him. I quickly explained to him what we have seen about the age and provenance of the skeleton, as well as Burke's apparent actions in the matter. He immediately picked up on what I was telling him, and he agreed that we should allow Mr. Burke to act out his little drama for a while.

WATSON: I see. In that way, we might have something more against him than a simple charge of terrace vandalism. As it stands now, Burke could simply claim it was a joke, make restitution or pay a small fine, and disappear without the real reasons behind this ever becoming known.

HOLMES: And now let us go inside, where you can check on Mr. Cornwallis, and I can smoke a pipe or two until Constable Wagner returns.

MUSIC: SHORT BRIDGE

WATSON: Cornwallis finally dropped off to sleep. The poor man is a nervous wreck. I'm afraid that if this continues, he'll suffer a case of brain fever.

HOLMES: And what news do you have for us, Constable Wagner?

WAGNER: The village doctor is outside, loading the skeleton. He has confirmed that is it is simply a medical exhibit, and not a murder victim.

HOLMES: And the laborers you brought with you? Can they be discreet?

WAGNER: I've sworn these men to secrecy. Burke is being watched by one of my men at the local inn. He's been holding court with those reporters, spinning one wild theory after another.

WATSON: I can just imagine.

WAGNER: By the time I left, he had one going where "Bloody" Baker had kidnapped half the countryside at one time or another during Queen Mary's reign, holding them for ransoms until the families gave him their valuables.

WATSON: Oh my Lord.

WAGNER: He's even saying that Mr. Cornwallis will be putting this place up for sale soon in order to get away from the horrible reputation that this place has acquired.

WATSON: You can't be serious.

WAGNER: He's hinting darkly that the place is haunted. The reporters are eating it up. They're already clogging up the local telegraph office, passing on these stories to their newspapers.

HOLMES: I am sorry that we must let Burke continue to play out this nonsense until we can discover his true motives. It is going to cause a certain amount of distress for Mr. Cornwallis before it's all over.

WATSON: (*Softly*) That is for certain.

HOLMES: However, as I told Watson, it will be better if we can arrest Burke for more than simple vandalism. Do you suppose that you could get a few wires off for me without alerting the reporters?

WAGNER: Of course. The telegraph agent is my brother-in-law.

HOLMES: Stress the urgency of these. The longer this goes on, the more mess Mr. Cornwallis will have to deal with.

WAGNER: Certainly, sir. I'll let you know if I hear anything. I'll be back out first thing in the morning.

SOUND EFFECT: FOOTSTEPS ACROSS ROOM (FADING). DOOR SHUTS

WATSON: What now, Holmes?

HOLMES: Now, old friend, we wait.

MUSIC: SHORT BRIDGE

WATSON: (*Narrating*) The next morning, the sun was quite high in the sky, and still there was no word from Constable Wagner, either of news regarding Burke's activities in the village the night before, or answers to Holmes's telegrams. And as for Holmes? He was becoming quite impatient.

HOLMES: Blast! Wagner seemed quite intelligent, Watson. I cannot understand why we have heard nothing!

WATSON: Perhaps he has nothing yet to tell. And if that gaggle of reporters is still in the village, he has no doubt had other matters to deal with.

HOLMES: Possibly, possibly. Ah, Mr. Cornwallis. How are you feeling this morning?

CORNWALLIS: Not well, Mr. Holmes. Not well at all. All night I tossed and turned, wondering what that man Burke will come up with next. What can be his purpose in all this?

HOLMES: I hope to have an answer for you soon. Ah, I perceive that Constable Wagner has arrived. Hopefully, he has some news.

SOUND EFFECT: FOOTSTEPS ENTERING THE ROOM

WAGNER: The story is in all the papers, I'm afraid, sir. Have a look at these, the latest editions down on the London train this morning.

538

SOUND EFFECT: NEWSPAPERS RUSTLING

HOLMES: What of the replies to my telegrams, Constable?

WAGNER: I have them right here, sir.

CORNWALLIS: (*Groans*) Treasure! They all have stories about the estate being filled with buried treasure. We shall be overrun!

WATSON: Secreted fortunes, bloody murders. There are speculations enough here to fire any boy's wildest dreams. This paper even hints that there are lost entrances to a vast underground cavern on the estate, filled with hoards of gold and jewels.

WAGNER: And what of this one? It speaks of the tower, which it says was designed with hidden passages and booby traps for the unwary.

WATSON: Look here! This reporter speculates that "*Mr. Cornwallis intends to sell the estate and leave the country, due to the fact that the* foully murdered victim *found under the* ancient flagstone terrace *is such an embarrassment to the family that he can no longer stand to remain in England.*"

CORNWALLIS: This states that I was aware of the murdered victim, as well as many others hidden around the estate, and that I will flee from the authorities before I can be questioned – or jailed!

WAGNER: Mr. Burke has spread it around that he will be exposing another surprise here today at eleven a.m. Mr. Cornwallis, I'm afraid that the reporters will be coming back here then. It appears that half the village will be joining them.

CORNWALLIS: Oh my.

WAGNER: My men and I will be here, but I'm afraid there aren't enough of us to stop them. We will arrest as many as we can, if you'd like, but I cannot do anything until they actually trespass on the property.

CORNWALLIS: Of course, of course. Thank you.

HOLMES: Based on the information in these wires from America, you *can* arrest Burke, however.

WAGNER: Yes, sir. Anytime you say. And a good thing, too. I simply wanted to speak with you about it first.

HOLMES: Excellent. Watson, will you hand me that *Bradshaw* from that shelf behind you? Thank you. Would you care to examine the telegrams while I ascertain today's train schedule?

SOUND EFFECT: BOOK PAGES RUSTLING

HOLMES: There is a train at eleven a.m, departing for London. An amazing coincidence, wouldn't you say? Exactly the time everyone will be gathering here at the Sissinghurst house.

WATSON: Perhaps we should be at the station then.

HOLMES: Quite.

CORNWALLIS: What? Won't you be here at eleven when Burke and the reporters come back? I don't understand.

HOLMES: I believe that the reporters will be here without Mr. Burke, and without him to provide any entertainment, I feel that they will soon become disinterested and leave. In the meantime, Mr. Burke will probably be attempting to slip out of town on the first train of the morning.

CORNWALLIS: What?

HOLMES: I am still not entirely certain as to Mr. Burke's reasons for creating this entire production, although certain aspects of the matter are becoming clear. However, yesterday, through the kindness of Constable Wagner and his brother-in-law, I cabled several acquaintances of mine in the United States, particularly a police officer in Cleveland, Ohio. What he replied about Mr. Philo T. Burke was of some interest indeed.

WATSON: These cables make interesting reading. Confidence man. Thief. Forger. Murderer. A very wanted man in America. It was

540

rather careless of Mr. Burke to reveal his true name and place of origin, wasn't it?

WAGNER: Once they found out where he was, the Americans then wired me as well as Mr. Holmes here to hold Burke until they can send someone after him. Should be here in about a week.

HOLMES: Do you have enough men to keep an eye on the reporters, as well as making sure that Burke cannot slip away?

WAGNER: As soon as I got this information, I quietly sent to surrounding areas, requesting some additional constables. Burke's under observation in the village by my men, but right now it's not a problem. He's still sitting around, feeding whatever crazy stories that he can think of to those reporters.

HOLMES: When the time comes to travel out here from the village, he will certainly arrange for the reporters to go on ahead of him. Then he will quietly slip away to the train station and head back to London.

WAGNER: That's the way I see it. Of course, we will prevent him.

HOLMES: Mr. Cornwallis, we must leave you now to stop Mr. Burke. Rest assured that this matter will soon be concluded.

MUSIC: SHORT BRIDGE

SOUND EFFECT: TRAIN STATION. A TRAIN IS PREPARING TO DEPART

WATSON: (*Softly*) There he is. On that bench on the up-side of the platform.

WAGNER: (*Softly*) I see him.

HOLMES: (*Normal tone*) Mr. Burke? A moment, if you please?

BURKE: (*Nervous*) Hmm? Is there a problem, gentlemen?

WAGNER: There doesn't need to be. Mr. Philo T. Burke, of Cleveland, Ohio, I place you under arrest.

BURKE: Oh, no, you don't!

(AD-LIB: SCUFFLE)

BURKE: (*Angrily, Out of breath*) What are you anyway? One of those Scotland Yarders?

HOLMES: I am Sherlock Holmes.

BURKE: (*A beat*) Heard about you. In fact, someone I met over here, never mind who, warned me not to get tangled up with you. I thought this far out in the country I would be safe. Never had a chance, did I?

WAGNER: Come on, get him to the station.

MUSIC: SHORT BRIDGE

BURKE: Search my bag all you like, gentlemen. There's nothing criminal in there.

HOLMES: Nothing but these newspapers and handwritten sheets, Burke.

BURKE: Those? They're nothing. Just some harmless scribbling. Certainly nothing illegal about them.

WATSON: What are they, Holmes?

HOLMES: See for yourself.

SOUND EFFECT: PAGES RUSTLING

WATSON: Why, each one of these is a handwritten draft, describing the upcoming sale of the Sissinghurst farm and castle.

WAGNER: Sale? How can he plan a sale of something that he does not own?

HOLMES: They are all very similar, having only slight variations from one another. Obviously the sheets were rough drafts of some sort of prospectus. Notice the numerous scratched out words, as if Mr. Burke had tried differing combinations before settling on phrasing that pleased him.

542

WAGNER: But what is the purpose, Mr. Holmes?

HOLMES: I am not completely certain, but I believe that I have a reasonable understanding of Burke's plan. It fits his background as a confidence man and trickster. Correct me if I'm incorrect, Mr. Burke.

BURKE: I've done nothing wrong here.

HOLMES: Burke had researched and found a likely spot in Sissinghurst. The place was old, but there never was any reason to think that treasure had been hidden there. However, there was enough history to the place that stories of treasure could be fabricated, at least long enough to serve Burke's purpose. And of course, there was the association with the fascinating "Bloody" Baker.

WAGNER: But where's the crime? If it hadn't been for those telegrams, we wouldn't have had reason to arrest him, except for a petty charge of vandalism. What did he gain from all of this?

HOLMES: After picking Sissinghurst, Burke showed up and began to make himself a nuisance to Mr. Cornwallis. His plan was to continue that for a few weeks until he could stage the incident with the reporters, the terrace, and the skeleton. I expect that when you got here, Mr. Burke, you did not know exactly where or how the incident would take place, but I'm sure you had the skeleton with you, as you looked for a likely spot. Did you buy the skeleton, Mr. Burke, or did you steal it from a medical school or hospital?

BURKE: This is your tale, Mr. Holmes. I'm simply an innocent victim.

WATSON: So it was his intent all along to create a story that would grab the imaginations of the reporters. He made it seem as mysterious and exciting as possible, throwing in hidden treasure, an unexpected dead man, and hints of hauntings and conspiracy.

HOLMES: What he was after, of course, was to have numerous stories about the incident in as many different newspapers as he could find. He never intended that the story should hold up to any kind of close scrutiny. He planned to be gone as soon as possible, and he didn't care if the exact origins of the skeleton were quickly discovered.

WATSON: Of course. As long as he had the newspapers containing the stories of treasure and a possible sale of the estate, he would be able to carry out the rest of his plan.

WAGNER: So after he left for London on this morning's train –

HOLMES: He would wait there for a few days, seeing if any other useful newspaper articles were printed that might add to the recently fabricated treasure legends of Sissinghurst Castle. He would buy up as many old copies of today's newspapers as he could reasonably carry, for future use.

WATSON: Then, after returning to America –

HOLMES: After returning, he would have printed a series of brochures, false deeds, and other bogus documents, each implying that he was the agent responsible for selling the Sissinghurst estate. He would let on that people in England were reluctant to buy the estate, possibly afraid of ghosts.

WATSON: By showing a number of legitimate British newspapers, each with stories verifying Burke's claim that the estate was for sale and why, he could sell the estate over and over again to gullible American investors.

HOLMES: Exactly.

WATSON: Each would think they were getting the place at a bargain, and not only acquiring an actual English estate with a castle, but also a property fairly loaded with hidden treasure and an interesting ghostly history.

HOLMES: Of course, after each false sale, he would simply move on and try the same thing in a different town. Is that substantially correct, Mr. Burke?

BURKE: You're the one telling it. I'm just listening. So far, all you can charge me with is vandalism of Cornwallis's terrace, and you'd have to prove that. What difference does it make if I decided to leave town? And maybe I just bought all those newspapers because I thought it was an interesting story.

BURKE: So unless you can do better than that, gentleman, I am going to depart.

HOLMES: I don't think so, Mr. Burke. You were a little careless in telling me that you were from Cleveland, Ohio. I wired to some professional acquaintances there about you. Your history is an interesting one. Apparently your violent attack on one of the city's most prominent citizens, which caused you to flee America late last year, is still the subject of much discussion there.

BURKE: It's a lie!

HOLMES: The man later died. The Cleveland Police were quite pleased to know that you are here, and they are sending someone to retrieve you, even as we speak.

(AD-LIB: SCUFFLE)

WAGNER: (*Winded*) Put him in a cell. He's the guest of Her Majesty now, until his own people come to fetch him.

MUSIC: SHORT BRIDGE

SOUND EFFECT: TRAIN TRAVELING AT A STEADY SPEED, OCCASIONAL WHISTLE

WATSON: Poor Mr. Cornwallis. I fear that he will be bothered by the aftermath of this affair for years to come.

HOLMES: Perhaps. He is certainly fearful that people will be trespassing on the estate, digging and looking for treasure, and then bringing suit against him if they somehow fall and hurt themselves in the process.

WATSON: Well, I hope it doesn't turn out that way. And after all, you were able to give the reporters most of the facts, and Constable Wagner will be telling them the rest of the story.

HOLMES: Hopefully the whole matter will die a quick death. (*A beat*) Watson, would you enjoy attending a concert tonight, when we arrive

545

back in London? They are playing German music, which I find especially appealing.

WATSON: Certainly.

HOLMES: Good. Then I believe we shall just have time for me to tell you of an investigation I conducted not long after I entered private practice in London. It was on an estate similar to Sissinghurst, in central Norfolk.

WATSON: Really?

HOLMES: Unlike Sissinghurst, however, this estate did indeed reveal a singular treasure, which we might, if you are interested and not too busy, go to see tomorrow at the British Museum.

MUSIC: *DANSE MACABRE*

WATSON: This is Dr. John H. Watson. I've had many more adventures with Sherlock Holmes, and I'll tell you another one . . . *when next we meet!*

MUSIC: (FADE OUT)

Poster for the live performance
of "The London Wheel"
at The Bootmaker's of Toronto
Jubilee@221B Conference
September 25th, 2022

The London Wheel

CHARACTERS

- ☐ SHERLOCK HOLMES
- ☐ DR. JOHN H. WATSON
- ☐ INSPECTOR LESTRADE
- ☐ BOUCHARD – *Circus co-owner, 50's*
- ☐ GREEN – *Circus co-owner, 50's*
- ☐ MEESER – *London Wheel Operator*
- ☐ CONSTABLE
- ☐ BARKER – *Detective*
- ☐ MAN IN CROWD

SOUND EFFECT: OPENING SEQUENCE, BIG BEN

SOUND EFFECT: *DANSE MACABRE* UP AND UNDER

MUSIC: OUT

SOUND EFFECT: (FADE IN) CARNIVAL NOISES (CALLIOPE MUSIC, BELLS, CROWDS, APPLAUSE) THROUGHOUT

HOLMES: *(Fading in, walking toward us)* Is something vexing you, Lestrade?

LESTRADE: *(Fading in, closer now)* It's that bloody wheel, Mr. Holmes. You've seen it, over here on the opposite shore, across from the Yard? Something like that has no business cluttering up the landscape.

WATSON: It's merely a Ferris Wheel. It seems harmless enough to me, Lestrade. What offends you so by its presence?

LESTRADE: It . . . well, it doesn't fit. Within sight of Parliament, for Heaven's sake. It just isn't right.

HOLMES: Surely it is far more pleasant, for instance, to see something devoted to recreation and pleasure than those buildings just to the south there. They, too, are within view from our government buildings, including Scotland Yard, and they stand as a silent accusation and a reminder of a great deal of unfortunate poverty, separated by only a waterway and a bridge from the wealth that rules them.

LESTRADE: I see your point, Mr. Holmes. Yet, I still cannot help but resent that my view is spoiled by that monstrosity.

HOLMES: And here we are, gentlemen. Bouchard and Green's Circus, and The London Wheel.

BOUCHARD: *(Fading in – Angry)* I won't stand for it, Green! I've suspected that you've been cheating me somehow, and the lease for this London Wheel which you have foisted upon us is simply the last straw!

LESTRADE: *(Hurrying forward)* Here, now! We'll have none of that.

BOUCHARD: *(Angrily)* Let me be! What right have you – ?

LESTRADE: I have *every* right. Inspector Lestrade of the Yard! Police! Now calm down, and let's see if this can't be discussed like gentlemen!

HOLMES: What is your name, sir?

BOUCHARD: *(Sullenly)* Bouchard. William White Bouchard.

LESTRADE: Well, Mr. Bouchard, I don't know what your disagreement is with Mr. Green, here, but violence is no way to settle it.

BOUCHARD: You're a policeman, you say? Then arrest this man. He has defrauded me, and I will not stand for it!

GREEN: Careful, my friend. That's slander, you know. That statement, in front of witnesses, might be enough for me to take everything you have.

HOLMES: I don't think it would be as cut-and-dried as all that.

GREEN: Sherlock Holmes, isn't it? You're just the man to settle this! I want to hire you!

HOLMES: *(Laughs)* For what, Mr. Green? I'm a consulting detective, not a solicitor or bookkeeper. I'm afraid a tedious case of possible fraud, or a defense against such a charge, is of little interest to me.

BOUCHARD: It's more than that, Mr. Holmes. I didn't mean what I said about Green, here. What you observed was the result of a great deal of stress creating friction between two old friends.

GREEN: He's right. Our circus may be small, but we've always been very successful. That is, until recently. There have been a series of accidents –

BOUCHARD: It's more than that. There have been deliberate attempts to drive us out of business!

WATSON: What sort of attempts?

GREEN: We had a fire a few weeks ago, not long after we set up here along the Thames. It destroyed a tent and also one of the supply wagons. Since then, equipment used in performances has been found broken in ways that could have only been intentional.

HOLMES: What else has happened?

BOUCHARD: Just last week, one of the animals in our menagerie, Walter the Lion, was poisoned to death in a most horrible and painful way.

GREEN: None of these things are enough in themselves to drive us out of business, but circus folk are a superstitious lot, and the word has spread quickly through our little family that we might be unlucky.

LESTRADE: *(Laughs)* You can't be serious.

HOLMES: That is a very real concern among circus people, Lestrade.

WATSON: One whiff that there is something wrong with the enterprise, and the performers will flee to a different operation that is considered more safe and acceptable.

BOUCHARD: Exactly. We've been quite successful until now, having recently completed a very profitable tour throughout northern

England. It was only after we arrived here, at *this* site, that our luck seemed to change.

GREEN: It's amazing how quickly the feelings amongst the performers can shift from a sense of safety and stability to one of unease. We were once like a family, but now my partner and I are being looked upon as enemies.

WATSON: If you're both concerned that the incidents are part of an attempt to drive you out of business, then what was the conversation that we interrupted, in which you, Mr. Bouchard, were accusing Mr. Green of cheating you? I believe that you mentioned that the lease for the London Wheel was "the last straw"?

BOUCHARD: *(Sheepish)* I was angry, and take back what I said about being cheated. But the fact is that the lease for this Ferris Wheel was negotiated without my knowledge. Following our last stop in Easingwold, I traveled down to Colchester for a few days to visit with my mother, who has been ill. During that time, the circus was packed up and moved here, as planned. We've negotiated an open-ended arrangement with the owners of this property, who had no objections to our setting up here, as it has been vacant land since a fire destroyed several buildings last year, or so I understand.

HOLMES: And then, something happened.

BOUCHARD: As you say. While I was away, Mr. Green was approached by the gentleman who built this wheel that you see behind us, offering to lease it at an exorbitant rate –

GREEN: It is *not* exorbitant! Our business has doubled – even tripled or quadrupled! – since we installed the wheel. Word of mouth alone, as people share the fact that one can obtain a new and different view of London, a bird's-eye view as it were, will only continue to increase our visitors.

BOUCHARD: Not true! I do not believe that we should be turning away from what has made our traditional circus so successful over the years, in favor of mechanical contraptions that cause a mere momentary sensation, only to quickly leave the patron jaded and expecting some other machine to provide and even bigger and better thrill. There is nothing wrong with traditional circus acts, thrilling

552

feats of skill and danger, and the possibility of something new and unexpected in each and every performance! You made the arrangements to lease the wheel from Charters without my knowledge or approval, because you knew I would never give it otherwise.

HOLMES: Charters?

GREEN: Lester Charters. He is the man from whom we leased the wheel. He built it.

WATSON: As partners, Mr. Bouchard, how was Mr. Green able to make such a deal without your approval?

GREEN: Our arrangement is one of trust, allowing us to make decisions without the other's approval. Granted, this has usually been in the form of hiring or firing performers as needed. When one or the other of us isn't available, we don't have to wait on the other to take care of something urgent. In this case, I was able to recognize the opportunity and seize it during the time when my friend was away.

BOUCHARD: You knew I wouldn't approve! And I've just returned from a meeting with our solicitor, who explained an interesting clause in the lease agreement that you seem to have missed, along with fact that Charters is about to be the subject of a lawsuit by the Ferris Wheel people, claiming that he stole their design!

MAN IN CROWD: *(Interrupting)* Oi! That fella there on the Wheel doesn't look well at all.

WATSON: What? Let me by.

SOUND EFFECT: CROWD NOISES, MUTTERING; METAL BAR OPENING AS THE FERRIS WHEEL CAR IS OPENED

WATSON: This man is dead.

MUSIC: SHORT BRIDGE

SOUND EFFECT: CARNIVAL NOISES (CALLIOPE MUSIC, BELLS, CROWDS, APPLAUSE) THROUGHOUT UNTIL *

LESTRADE: Dead? Are you sure, Doctor?

GREEN: Impossible! He was perfectly fine when he waved to me, not five minutes ago!

HOLMES: You know him then? Who is he?

BOUCHARD: That's Lester Charters – the man of whom we have been speaking. It was from him that we leased the wheel.

LESTRADE: You there, at the controls. What do you know about this?

MEESER: *(Whiny)* Nothing, sir. I stopped the wheel to let him off. I thought he might want to join in your discussion. But then I saw that he was . . . was . . . .

LESTRADE: Doctor, can you tell how he died?

WATSON: There are no obvious wounds. However, from the red coloring of the skin, the slight foam about the mouth, and the faint smell on his lips, I would venture that there is a possibility, in fact almost a certainty, that this man has been poisoned.

HOLMES: If I may, Doctor?

LESTRADE: Constable? Over here.

CONSTABLE: *(Huffing closer)* Yes, Inspector?

LESTRADE: Send for reinforcements. Double time. Good lad.

SOUND EFFECT: CROWD NOISES SURGE AS PEOPLE PRESS CLOSER

LESTRADE: Doctor! A bit of assistance with this crowd, if you don't mind!

WATSON: Right! Holmes, are you about finished? Holmes?

LESTRADE: Here come some additional constables. Thank goodness!

HOLMES: *(Calling over the crowd noise)* There is nothing more to be learned here. You may remove the body and release the other passengers.

WATSON: Is there somewhere where we can place him temporarily?

BOUCHARD: That tent. Over there.

SOUND EFFECT: * CARNIVAL NOISES (MUSIC, BELLS, CROWDS, APPLAUSE) END

MUSIC: SHORT BRIDGE

(INSIDE TENT)

HOLMES: These candy wrappers were in Charters' waistcoat pocket. Watson, what do you think?

SOUND EFFECT: PAPER CRINKLING

WATSON: *(Sniffs)* Cyanide. No doubt.

BOUCHARD: That is *your* favorite candy, Green. You eat them constantly.

GREEN: *(Sarcastically)* Thank you for that, my friend. That is not an unpopular type of candy, Inspector. Surely you don't believe that I had anything to do with this?

LESTRADE: Early days yet, Mr. Green. As you can see, we're only beginning to gather our facts.

WATSON: *(Softly)* Anything, Holmes?

HOLMES: Here, and . . . here. In his mouth. Do you see? Traces of chocolate still around the man's gums and in the crevices of his teeth. He must have eaten them very quickly.

SOUND EFFECT: SCUFFLE AS TWO MEN ENTER THE TENT

CONSTABLE: After this fellow let everyone off the wheel, I caught him trying to slip away.

LESTRADE: Here now! What is your name?

MEESER: *(Whiny)* Meeser. Edward Meeser.

LESTRADE: One of your employees, gentlemen?

BOUCHARD: Not exactly. We acquired him, so to speak, when we leased the wheel. He is an employee of Charters'.

HOLMES: Indeed. And what are your duties, Mr. Meeser?

MEESER: Well, as you saw, I run the wheel. I help load and unload the passengers, and keep track of how long each group has been on it, so as to make sure everyone gets a fair ride. There's a slow rotation where each car is loaded, and then I run it a spell before stopping it a few minutes later, running it slowly again to unload. I make certain there isn't any horsing around when the wheel is in motion. And I check the machinery and connections every day as well.

HOLMES: You do not look so well. Perhaps it is the shock of encountering Mr. Charters' body?

MEESER: That's the truth, sir. I never expected to see something like that come around.

HOLMES: I understand that Mr. Charters built the wheel. Can you tell me where his workshop is located?

MEESER: Down Stepney way, in Exmouth Street.

HOLMES: And what can you tell me about the accusation that Mr. Charters is about to be sued for building the wheel by using Ferris's plans without permission?

MEESER: *(Suddenly angry)* Nonsense! This wheel is much better than anything that Ferris ever came up with. There are a number of improvements with this design that are far more advanced than what

556

has been seen before. The mechanical works alone have many unique improvements that can be applied to a number of other machines.

HOLMES: You seem rather defensive of your employer's work. How long have you been associated with Mr. Charters?

MEESER: *(Whiny again)* Just a few months. But I know how much effort went into building this wheel. I can assure you that nothing was stolen or borrowed from any other inventor.

LESTRADE: *(Softly)* Except for the very idea of a giant wheel.

HOLMES: Why was Mr. Charters riding the wheel today? Surely he's ridden it before, probably many times.

GREEN: I believe I can answer that, Mr. Holmes. Mr. Charters stops by several times a week to check on the condition of his machinery, and part of that is to see how the wheel is operating.

MEESER: *(Softly)* He just liked to ride it.

LESTRADE: What's that?

MEESER: *(Louder)* He always wanted to have a go when he stopped by. No harm in it, was there?

GREEN: Be that as it may, he also visited us several times per week to go over the accounts and verify the number of people who ride on the wheel. Meeser here keeps track of that. Charters' agreement is to receive a certain percentage of the revenue, based on the number of riders.

BOUCHARD: Ridiculous. I would never have agreed to such an arrangement if I had been here.

GREEN: *(Escalating tone)* But I *did* agree to it!

BOUCHARD: You have no idea what you agreed to!

LESTRADE: *(Thundering, clearly fed up)* Gentlemen, please!

HOLMES: This agreement. I would like to see it, if possible.

GREEN: Certainly. Right this way. It's in our office.

BOUCHARD: It's here in my pocket. I took it to show the solicitor.

GREEN: *(Angry)* What! How dare you!

LESTRADE: Let's discuss it in your office.

MUSIC: SHORT BRIDGE

SOUND EFFECT: CARNIVAL NOISES (MUSIC, BELLS, CROWDS, APPLAUSE) UNTIL *

(OUTSIDE)

WATSON: *(Walking – Softly)* What did you just tell Lestrade?

HOLMES: *(Also walking – Softly)* Simply that he can release the other riders of the wheel, after making sure that we have their names and addresses. And also that he should make sure Mr. Meeser does not slip away from us too soon. *(Suddenly, louder, and with surprise)* Ha!

WATSON: Holmes?

LESTRADE: Where is he going? Who is that man with the dark glasses that he's talking with?

WATSON: That is Barker, the private enquiry agent that Holmes refers to as his "hated rival upon the Surrey shore".

LESTRADE: "Hated rival"? They don't seem unfriendly towards one another. Rather like they're friends.

WATSON: Oh, they are. In fact, it was just last month that they worked together on the little matter of the Rydberg Substitution, where we –

HOLMES: *(Returning a little breathlessly)* It was quite fortunate to notice our friend Barker. He is here on a completely unrelated matter, tracking a gang of pick-pockets. When I explained my preliminary conclusions, he immediately grasped what I needed, and has gone to follow up on a few questions.

LESTRADE: You have formed conclusions? Already? And might I ask what they are?

HOLMES: Ah, Lestrade, you know that I am loathe to reveal anything ahead of its time. Either I will be proven right, or not, and we shall move forward from there. For now, let us examine this contentious business agreement.

<u>SOUND EFFECT: * CARNIVAL NOISES (MUSIC, BELLS, CROWDS, APPLAUSE) END</u>

<u>MUSIC: SHORT BRIDGE</u>

(INSIDE WAGON)

BOUCHARD: As you can see, there is a clause here, buried within the legal mumbo-jumbo regarding payment, which our lawyer says will give a half-share of the circus to the owner of the wheel, should anything happen to one or the other of us. Or if something happens to both of us, he will get both shares.

GREEN: What?

BOUCHARD: It's true. You have a gift at running the day-to-day needs of a circus, but you have no skill whatsoever in matters of business, or contracts.

LESTRADE: Here now. How would something like that work?

BOUCHARD: As it was explained to me, the clause outlines that the owner of the wheel has a vested interest in the income from the thing, and therefore the success of the circus in general, as it helps attract business to the wheel. If for some reason either Green or I were to die, or become unable to manage the circus, then it would cause a negative and unplanned-for effect to the wheel owner's income.

GREEN: I never saw that.

BOUCHARD: Therefore, through this agreement, the wheel owner has the right to step in and take over the incapacitated owner's share of the circus, in order to keep things up and running, thus preventing any loss of his own income.

LESTRADE: Is that right? Can someone do that?

SOUND EFFECT: PASSING SHEET OF PAPER

HOLMES: Hmm, I believe that what the lawyer told you is correct, although I do not know if such an agreement would truly stand up in court. I assume this is not a normal clause in a document of this type.

BOUCHARD: Absolutely not. He had never seen the like of it before.

HOLMES: Do you also have a copy of your agreement for this property where the circus is currently located?

GREEN: Certainly. It is right here on my desk, under these papers – Wait! What's this, then?

SOUND EFFECT: PAPERS SHIFTING ON A DESK

GREEN: A box of chocolate-covered almonds – Now how did that get there?

HOLMES: *(Quiet but urgent)* Gentlemen, please do not move.

WATSON: *(Whispers, urgent)* What is it, Holmes? Is it a swamp adder? Should I summon one of the circus's snake handlers?

HOLMES: *(Smiling)* No, Watson, I don't believe that will be necessary. I only I wish to make a better examination before any of us move around more than we already have, possibly destroying any evidence.

GREEN: For goodness' sake.

HOLMES: There's a card. It says *'To my friend'*. And it's signed, *'Bouchard'*.

BOUCHARD: What! That isn't my handwriting! I did not provide that box of candy!

HOLMES: I have no doubt of that. You would not be that clumsy. I expect that after the contents of the box took care of Mr. Green, it was supposed to be found, thus implicating you in your business partner's murder. *(Sniffs)* Watson? Your opinion?

WATSON: *(Sniffs)* Yes.

HOLMES: There is the same faint bitter almond smell, indicating that other pieces, if not all, of the candy in the box are also poisoned with cyanide.

BOUCHARD: *(Sniffs)* I don't smell anything.

WATSON: You wouldn't necessarily. Only about four in ten people can actually smell cyanide in small doses. Holmes and I, and the inspector as well, have come across this before, and know what to expect.

LESTRADE: That's right. *(Sniffs loudly)* I smell it.

HOLMES: It would appear that you have an enemy, Mr. Green. And you, too, Mr. Bouchard, as someone is apparently trying to kill one and frame the other. Have either of you seen this box here before?

BOUCHARD: Certainly not!

HOLMES: Can you think of anyone who might have gained entrance to your caravan, in order to place the poisoned candy on the desk?

GREEN: No, The door is usually left unlocked, but this part of the circus is well away from the public, and the company knows to keep an eye on the wagon to make sure that strangers do not enter.

WATSON: Charters ate those poisoned candies. He must have been in here, seen the box, and taken some with him, eating them on the wheel and accidentally becoming the unintended victim.

HOLMES: Exactly, Watson. Is it unusual that Mr. Charters would enter the caravan?

GREEN: It is possible. He has done so before. He visits the circus a few times each week, and if one of us is not easily found on the grounds, he knows to check this caravan.

HOLMES: Did he come in here today?

GREEN: He may have, but I cannot know for sure.

BOUCHARD: He *must* have. After all, he ate some of the poisoned candy.

GREEN: I don't know. I suppose he came here first. I initially encountered him near the wheel. We talked for a few moments about the ongoing success of the enterprise, and then he took his ride. He said he never got tired of riding it. While I was standing there waiting, Bouchard returned from the solicitor's office and discovered me there, where you found us.

HOLMES: Mr. Bouchard, after you returned from seeing your solicitor, did you visit the caravan before proceeding to the wheel?

BOUCHARD: No. I was angry, and looking for Green, but I spotted him as soon as I entered the grounds and walked right up to him.

HOLMES: Stay still, gentlemen. This should only take a few moments.

SOUND EFFECT: RANDOM MOVEMENT AROUND THE WAGON AS HOLMES LOOKS FOR CLUES UNTIL *

GREEN: *(Softly)* What is he doing?

LESTRADE: Looking for clues. I've seen it before.

SOUND EFFECT: * RANDOM MOVEMENT ENDS

HOLMES: Now, may I examine the agreement for this location, Mr. Green?

SOUND EFFECT: PAPER BEING PASSED

HOLMES: Is this your standard agreement?

BOUCHARD: It is. We provide it whenever we set up at a site. The public has the idea that a circus randomly stops in some farmer's field or empty lot and performs until the urge arises to move on.

GREEN: It's much more complicated than that. Future sites are scouted, sometimes months in advance, and careful arrangements are made with property owners.

BOUCHARD: We never simply stop and set up where we do not have both permission and a signed agreement. I don't know how some smaller circuses work, but that's the way we do it here.

HOLMES: And this clause? Where you cannot be evicted while in operation?

BOUCHARD: For our own protection. It's set that way so that we cannot be forced to leave before we're ready, as packing and moving is quite complicated, as you might imagine. Additionally, the place where we are going next might not be ready for us.

HOLMES: Another interesting clause, then, especially in conjunction with the one contained in the wheel agreement. Has no one ever questioned it?

BOUCHARD: No. Why should they? It's always been a matter of straight-forward business.

HOLMES: Indeed.

SOUND EFFECT: FOLDING PAPER

HOLMES: There's nothing to be done, then, until Barker returns. Lestrade, are your men still holding the fort outside?

LESTRADE: Of course.

HOLMES: Excellent. Then might I suggest that we wait patiently until there are further developments. It shouldn't be too long.

MUSIC: SHORT BRIDGE

BOUCHARD: How much longer do we have to wait, Mr. Holmes?

HOLMES: Until Barker returns.

SOUND EFFECT: DRAWER OPENING. BOTTLE AND GLASSES CLINK AS THEY ARE REMOVED

GREEN: Well, nothing says that we should suffer while we wait. Whisky, gentlemen?

HOLMES: I wouldn't, Mr. Green. The same person who left you those candies might have added something to that bottle as well.

GREEN: *(Sickly)* Oh. Well, then . . . .

SOUND EFFECT: BOTTLE AND GLASSES BEING REPLACED IN DRAWER. DRAWER CLOSES

SOUND EFFECT: KNOCK AT THE DOOR

HOLMES: Ah. That will be Barker, I expect. Excuse me for just a moment.

SOUND EFFECT: FOOTSTEPS. DOOR OPENS AND CLOSES AS HOLMES LEAVES

BOUCHARD: *(A beat)* Surely something can be done instead of us simply waiting here.

WATSON: Never fear, Mr. Bouchard. Holmes has the situation well in hand.

SOUND EFFECT: DOOR OPENS AND CLOSES. HOLMES AND BARKER ENTER

HOLMES: Gentlemen, this is my fellow investigator, Mr. Barker.

BARKER: *(Gruffly)* Good afternoon.

HOLMES: Forgive me, Lestrade. I took the liberty of having one of your men bring the final player for today's drama.

SOUND EFFECT: DOOR OPENS. MEESER AND CONSTABLE ENTER

HOLMES: You all recall Mr. Meeser. Seat him in that chair over there, Constable.

CONSTABLE: Right, Mr. Holmes.

HOLMES: Now, I believe that I have enough amateur legal training that I can get a sense of the implications of the clauses in question in both of these documents.

SOUND EFFECT: PAPERS BEING PULLED FROM COAT AND UNFOLDED

LESTRADE: What about them?

HOLMES: As Mr. Bouchard explained, his attorney noted that there is an unacceptable clause in the agreement to lease the wheel, wherein the owner of said wheel obtains an ownership stake in the circus. The levels of this acquired ownership vary – if *both* owners are removed from the picture, then the wheel's owner takes over *all* of the shares. As I said, I don't know if it would stand up in court, and shows a certain optimistic ignorance on the part of the man who constructed it, but it was a bold effort nonetheless.

WATSON: Optimistic, indeed.

HOLMES: The other document, between the circus owners and the owner of the property where we are now located, also has an oddly phrased clause, essentially stating that the circus cannot be evicted as long as it is operating. I understand why this clause was included, but I'm surprised that no property owner has objected to it, as it is quite open-ended.

BOUCHARD: It was never a problem. It is the cycle of our business. Eventually attendance starts to dwindle, and we move to the next town. Overstaying our welcome has never been an issue.

HOLMES: I'm sure you're right, Mr. Bouchard. But these two documents together were a motivation for murder.

LESTRADE: I begin to see where you're going with this. But I'm still not sure why. You seem to be saying that it would be in the interest of the wheel's owner to somehow incapacitate one or both of the circus owners to get their shares. But you have stated that Mr. Bouchard did not leave the poison candy for Mr. Green. Therefore, it must have been the wheel's owner who left it. But if Charters did that, in an attempt to poison one and frame the other, then why would *he* turn right around and take some and eat it, thus killing himself?

HOLMES: Barker?

BARKER: Because Charters wasn't the owner of the wheel. This man is.

BOUCHARD: What? *Meeser*?

GREEN: Impossible. I've met with Charters multiple times over the last weeks. He was the owner and builder of the wheel, without a doubt.

BARKER: No, he wasn't. Based on what he observed, Mr. Holmes sent me to the workshop in Exmouth Street to ask a few questions. It didn't take long to winkle out that Meeser here was the true brains behind the operation.

MEESER: *(Hotly)* I deny it!

HOLMES: You'll have your chance, Mr. Meeser. Barker?

BARKER: Meeser owned the wheel. He's the one that designed it and built it, too. From some things he let slip to his neighbor, a widow named Mrs. Crabtree that he liked to brag in front of, he was worried that it was too close to Ferris's design, so he hid behind Charters, a man he hired to be the face of the business.

LESTRADE: Barker, you said "based on what he observed". Well, Mr. Holmes?

HOLMES: When I examined Charters' body, still reclining in one of the wheel's carriages, I found the candies and empty wrappers, as well as the evidence that Charters had recently eaten them. I could smell the poison on both his breath and later in the uneaten candies. But I also observed that Charters' hands were very soft and had no callosities whatsoever.

WATSON: Yes, his nails were quite clean, with no indications of dirt or grease that might be associated with one who builds and works with mechanical devices!

HOLMES: In short, his hands did not appear to be those of a working man. When I heard that he had supposedly designed and built the wheel, I did not believe it. What mechanical inventor would have such smooth hands?

LESTRADE: That isn't enough evidence to build a case.

HOLMES: I also noted that Mr. Charters' shoes were a notably large size of a very common style. At that point, it was only a fact to be docketed. Later, we were able to speak with Mr. Meeser. At that time, I already disbelieved the statement that Charters was the builder of the wheel. But here was a man who *did* have a workman's hands. Now, that is not unusual or unexpected, since he took care of the daily maintenance and operation of the wheel.

WATSON: He *was* rather defensive of the wheel, especially when a statement was made that the design had been copied from that of the Ferris Wheel.

HOLMES: But most important, his shoes, of a much smaller size, were very well made indeed, and though worn, quite expensive. A closer examination of his clothing revealed that, while it is well-used, it is of excellent quality, and quite likely tailored. I believe, in fact, that his garments were made by Tundell's, off the Strand. Again, a fact that by itself was only curious, but something to be retained for later.

LESTRADE: So you already had your eye on him, even then.

HOLMES: I had thus decided that Mr. Meeser might be the true designer and builder, and therefore the owner, of the wheel, although I had no idea why he would conceal the fact and hide behind the straw man, Charters, and it was not my business to reveal it at that time just for the satisfaction of confirming it.

WATSON: But knowing you –

HOLMES: Yes, I did want to learn the truth, since the supposed owner of the contraption had just been murdered, and perhaps there was a connection. When I luckily observed friend Barker here, I sent him to confirm or deny my hypothesis regarding Mr. Charters' status. As you've heard, he has done so.

WATSON: But the poisoned candies, Holmes. How does it all connect?

HOLMES: Surely it is obvious, Watson. The first clause gives ownership of the circus to the wheel's owner if something were to happen to either Mr. Green or Mr. Bouchard – or both, if one was dead and the other convicted of murder.

BOUCHARD: I understand. It's that second clause!

HOLMES: Yes. The second clause means that the circus could stay on this location indefinitely as long as some part of it were still functioning, since they could not be evicted while still in operation. It was a clear motivation for the wheel owner to try and gain control of the circus, thus giving him both ownership *and* a perpetual site in which to run his wheel.

GREEN: I had no idea –

BOUCHARD: No, old friend, you didn't.

HOLMES: After managing to get the agreement signed, with the naïve belief that it would hold up legally, our killer set about trying to sabotage the circus, hoping that one or the other of the owners would become dispirited and sell out to him, or forfeit his share per the agreement. Then, becoming impatient when that didn't seem to be working, he tried something more desperate, proving most certainly that his mechanical genius does *not* extend to planning a murder.

MEESER: *(Softly)* It's true that I am the wheel's owner. *(Louder)* But you have no proof that I poisoned any candy. I don't know why Charters killed himself that way, but you can't pin it on me.

HOLMES: My examination of the floor of this caravan confirmed that Mr. Charters was in here earlier today. I know that it was today because his large shoes were obviously damp from walking outside after the rains this morning.

WATSON: Ah. The importance of the shoes –

HOLMES: On the floor, his prints are underneath all of the other recent tracks that we have made since entering. He came in earlier, looking for either of the two owners, before leaving again and encountering Mr. Green by the wheel. While he was here, he noticed the big box of chocolate-covered almonds on the desk, and he couldn't resist taking some, probably thinking they wouldn't be missed. Even if he was one of the people who can smell cyanide in this form, he would have likely believed that it was part of the strong flavoring of the almonds.

MEESER: That means nothing. Charters was always eating something or other.

HOLMES: If Charters had eaten them as he walked from here to the wheel, or even while he stood at this desk, he would have died sooner. But he waited to enjoy them while taking his regular ride on the wheel.

MEESER: That still doesn't connect anything with me.

HOLMES: I believe you said that it would not be unusual for Mr. Charters to stop in here to look for either of you two gentlemen?

GREEN: That's right.

HOLMES: Would there have ever been any reason, *any reason at all*, for *Mr. Meeser* to have entered this caravan?

BOUCHARD: *(Definitely)* None whatsoever.

HOLMES: Not even to lean in the door?

BOUCHARD: No.

GREEN: Never.

HOLMES: And certainly he would not have been allowed or expected to walk up to Mr. Green's desk, for instance.

GREEN: Certainly not.

HOLMES: I did neglect to mention one important fact, Mr. Meeser. Along with the footprints of the deceased, Mr. Charters, on the floor, and those that came later from the owners, the Inspector, Dr. Watson, and myself, there was one other set. They were underneath and overlapped by those of Mr. Charters. They were your size, very good quality, and made by shoes carrying the distinctive design, also of Tundell's off the Strand. *You* left those prints, Mr. Meeser, when *you* brought in the box of poisoned candy, labeled with a false card to frame Mr. Bouchard, and deposited it here on Mr. Green's desk in order to kill him.

MEESER: No . . . .

HOLMES: Finally, it should be noted that there is a grease mark on the candy box that corresponds to that made by a left hand. The grease itself seems to be the type associated with machinery. And I note that, while the fact that the mark was made by a left hand is eventually inconclusive, as there are a great many left-handed people in the world, the only left-handed person in this room right now, who happens to have that same mechanical grease on his hands, is *you*, Mr. Meeser.

MEESER: *(A beat)* That idiot wasn't supposed to eat the candy. It was an accident. Granted I left it here, and you can try and prove why, but Charters' death was an accident. You can't charge me for an accident. It was his own fault for taking candy that didn't belong to him.

HOLMES: How did you know about the property clause that would allow the circus to stay on in perpetuity without being evicted?

MEESER: After I built the wheel, I couldn't find anywhere to set it up. I owed money for loans I'd acquired while constructing it, and I'd heard that Ferris was coming after me for stealing his design. *Which I didn't!* I went to the owners of this very property to see about putting the wheel here permanently. They weren't interested.

LESTRADE: Go on . . . .

MEESER: Something the property owners said made me curious about who *was* going to be leasing this property, and I broke into their offices to find out more about it. That's where I saw their copy of the lease that said the circus could stay here as long as it wanted. I recognized right off how powerful something like that could be. If I could somehow get my wheel in place at this circus, with that clause in the agreement, I would never have to leave.

BOUCHARD: Outrageous!

MEESER: Once I got it up and running, I wouldn't have to stop, as long as I could make the circus stay too. I could make enough money to pay off my debts, and I could use the mechanical ideas I've developed while building my wheel – other machines that the public will also want to ride. Bigger wheels, and vehicles that give the feeling of great speed or vertical drops.

HOLMES: A rather unique idea.

MEESER: After having identified this circus from the copy of the agreement in the owner's office, I traveled north for a few days to Easingwold and hung around, learning what I could. I found that Mr. Green was the one that would need to be approached. It worked out well that his partner was away for a few days. I schooled Charters in what to say, and got him to fix up the agreement. He'd been a salesman at some point, and a good one, too, and it worked well in convincing Mr. Green.

LESTRADE: Surely the document was non-binding, as it was signed as if Charters was the true owner.

MEESER: I had a separate arrangement giving him limited authorization to conduct such agreements in my stead.

HOLMES: But that was only the first part of the plan. The next was establishing that you would be a part-owner, should something happen to one of the real owners.

MEESER: Based on what I had read of the wording of the property agreement, I designed my own document so that I would end up with at least part ownership of the circus. Then, since we couldn't be evicted, I'd slowly switch from a traveling attraction to something permanent, a destination for people to visit who wanted to be thrilled with mechanical wonders, and not the same old trapeze acts and animal tamers.

WATSON: And so you began to create the accidents, giving the impression that the circus was now unlucky.

MEESER: *(Softly)* I thought if it became financially unsound, I could convince one or the other of the owners to sell out to me. I could open even more mechanical attractions to replace the lost income, as well as making sure that we wouldn't shut down or be evicted.

WATSON: But that didn't work.

HOLMES: An interesting vision, this mechanical carnival you planned. But surely it wasn't worth committing murder.

MEESER: *(Whining)* But this wasn't murder. Whatever might have been intended didn't happen. This is just an accident. *Charters killed himself*, you see. It's no different than if he'd been playing with a loaded gun and shot himself.

LESTRADE: An interesting defense. It might save you from the rope, but I doubt it. I'll be very interested indeed to hear how it plays at your trial, Mr. Meeser. Come with me.

MEESER: *(Calling back as he's pulled away)* I'll be sending someone else to keep track of my machine. The arrangement still stands, you know, whatever happens here. Whenever you run it, a part of the proceeds belongs to me. I suspect that I'll be needing them.

BOUCHARD: The wheel is closed. Effective immediately. *(Angrily)* There shall be no more proceeds!

MEESER: *(Stricken)* You . . . you can't! You can't do that! We have an agreement.

BOUCHARD: We have an agreement to give you a share from the operation of the wheel. We do not have to agree to keep running it. And I can assure you that the agreement will be dissolved altogether before the day is over, if I have my way! Good day, sir.

MUSIC: SHORT BRIDGE

SOUND EFFECT: CARNIVAL NOISES (CALLIOPE MUSIC, BELLS, CROWDS, APPLAUSE) THROUGHOUT

572

HOLMES: Lestrade?

LESTRADE: Yes, Mr. Holmes?

HOLMES: It seems as if you get your wish, and the wheel will be coming down, nearly immediately. But I've convinced these men to run it just one more time, so that you can have a ride on it, and conquer your apparent fears, before it's gone.

LESTRADE: *(Sudden panic)* Fears? I . . . well, I . . . umm, I would rather not.

HOLMES: Lestrade, how often will you have this opportunity? Don't pass it up. How else can you confront this aversion and defeat it? Shall Watson and I ride with you as well?

GREEN: That won't be necessary, Mr. Holmes. I believe that my partner, Mr. Bouchard, who has also never had a go on it, would benefit from a last spin of the London Wheel.

MUSIC: SHORT BRIDGE

SOUND EFFECT: CARNIVAL NOISES CONTINUE, ALONG WITH MECHANICAL FERRIS WHEEL NOISES

LESTRADE and BOUCHARD: *(Ad lib* childlike enjoyment, with whoops and delighted yelling.)

WATSON: *(Calling from the London Wheel)* Holmes! Holmes! Are you sure that you wouldn't like to ride as well? It's really rather amazing.

HOLMES: *(Calling from the ground)* No. Thank you, Watson. I believe that after using up most of my luck at the Reichenbach Falls, I will reserve whatever that I might have left without taking any foolhardy chances!

MUSIC: *DANSE MACABRE* UP AND UNDER

WATSON: This is Doctor John H. Watson. I had many more adventures during my long friendship with Sherlock Holmes, and I'll tell you another one . . . when next we meet!

About the Author

David Marcum plays *The Game* with deadly seriousness. He first discovered Sherlock Holmes in 1975 at the age of ten, and since that time, he has collected, read, and chronologicized literally thousands of traditional Holmes pastiches in the form of novels, short stories, radio and television episodes, movies and scripts, comics, fan-fiction, and unpublished manuscripts. He is the author of over one-hundred-thirty Sherlockian pastiches, some published in anthologies and magazines such as *The Best Mystery Stories of the Year 2021* and *The Strand*, and others collected in his own books, *The Papers of Sherlock Holmes*, *Sherlock Holmes and A Quantity of Debt*, *Sherlock Holmes – Tangled Skeins*, *Sherlock Holmes and The Eye of Heka*, and *The Collected Papers of Sherlock Holmes* – seven volumes and more to come.

He has won back-to-back first place fiction awards from *The Arthur Conan Doyle Society* (2023 and 2024) and the Nero Wolfe *Wolfe Pack*. He has edited over 1,200 Holmes adventures and nearly 100 books, including dozens of traditional Sherlockian anthologies, such as the ongoing series *The MX Book of New Sherlock Holmes Stories*, which he created in 2015 to promote traditional Canonical Holmes. This collection is now at forty-eight volumes, with more in preparation.

He was responsible for bringing back August Derleth's Solar Pons for a new generation with his collections of authorized Pons stories, *The Papers of Solar Pons* and *The Further Papers of Solar Pons*. Pons's return was further assisted by his editing of the reissued authorized versions of the original Pons books, and then several volumes of new Pons adventures. He has done the same for the adventures of Dr. Thorndyke, and has plans for similar projects in the future.

He has contributed numerous essays to various publications, and is a member of a number of Sherlockian groups and Scions, as well as *The Mystery Writers of America*. His irregular Sherlockian blog, *A Seventeen Step Program*, addresses various topics related to his favorite book friends (as his son used to call them when he was small), and can be found at *http://17stepprogram.blogspot.com/*

He is a licensed Civil Engineer, living in Tennessee with his wife and son. Since the age of nineteen, he has worn a deerstalker as his regular-and-only hat. In 2013, he and his deerstalker were finally able make his first trip-of-a-lifetime Holmes Pilgrimage to England, with return Pilgrimages in 2015, 2016, and 2024, where you may have spotted him. Another is planned in mid-2025. If you ever run into him and his deerstalker out and about, feel free to say hello!

576

Also by David Marcum
from MX Publishing

Traditional Canonical Holmes Adventures

The Collected Papers of Sherlock Holmes

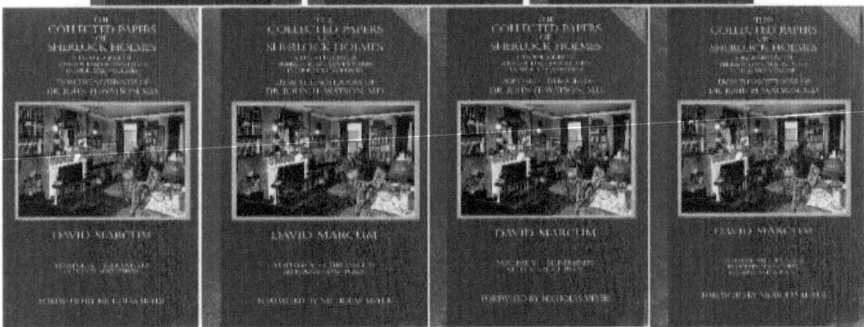

Volume I: Tales
Volume II: Records
Volume III: Accounts
Volume IV: Narratives
Volume V: Chronicles
Volume VI: Muniments
Volume VII: Annals

"Among the best I must number David Marcum, who, by this point has written more Holmes stories than Doyle himself. Characterized by unflagging imagination and ceaseless ingenuity, along with felicitous prose, these tales continue to provide what we all crave: more Sherlock."
– Nicholas Meyer - *New York Times* Bestselling Author

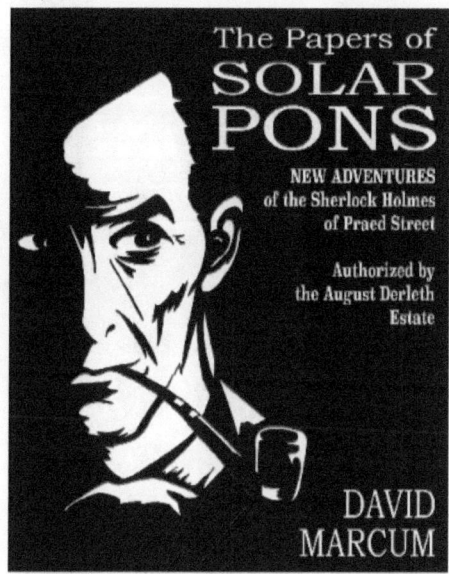

The MX Book of New Sherlock Holmes Stories
Edited by David Marcum
(MX Publishing, 2015-   )

The MX Book of New Sherlock Holmes Stories

Edited by David Marcum

(MX Publishing, 2015-   )

"This is the finest volume of Sherlockian fiction I have ever read, and I have read, literally, thousands." – Philip K. Jones

"Beyond Impressive . . . This is a splendid venture for a great cause!"
– Roger Johnson, Editor, *The Sherlock Holmes Journal,*
The Sherlock Holmes Society of London

Part I: 1881-1889; Part II: 1890-1895; Part III: 1896-1929

Part IV: 2016 Annual

Part V: Christmas Adventures

Part VI: 2017 Annual

Eliminate the Impossible
Part VII: (1880-1891); Part VIII: (1892-1905)

2018 Annual
Part IX: (1879-1895); Part X: (1896-1916)

Some Untold Cases
Part XI: (1880-1891); Part XII: (1894-1902)

2019 Annual
Part XIII: (1881-1890); Part XIV: (1891-1897); Part XV: (1898-1917)

Whatever Remains . . . Must be the Truth
Part XVI: (1881-1890); Part XVII: (1891-1898); Part XVIII: (1898-1925)

2020 Annual
Part XIX: (1882-1890); Part XX: (1891-1897); Part XXI: (1898-1923)·

Some More Untold Cases
Part XXII: (1877-1887); Part XXIII: (1888-1894); Part XXIV: (1895-1903)

2021 Annual
Part XXV: (1881-1888); Part XXVI: (1889-1897); Part XXVII: (1898-1928)

More Christmas Adventures
Part XXVIII: (1869-1888); Part XXIX: (1889-1896); Part XXX: (1897-1928)

2022 Annual
Part XXXI: (1875-1887); Part XXXII: (1888-1895); Part XXXIII: (1896-1919)

"However Improbable . . . ."
Part XXXIV: (1878-1888); Part XXXV: (1889-1896); Part XXXVI: (1897-1919)

2023 Annual
Parts XXXVII (1875-1889), XXXVIII (1889-1896), and XXXIX (1897-1923)

Further Untold Cases
Part XL: (1879-1886), Part XLI: (1887-1892) and Part XLII: (1894-1922)

2024 Annual
Parts XLIII (1874-1888), XLIV (1889-1897), and XLV (1898-1917)

Occupants of the Canonical Realm
Parts XLVI (1861-1889), XLVII (1890-1898), and XLVIII (1899-1924)

And in Preparation . . . The Final Volumes of
The MX Book of New Sherlock Holmes Stories: Parts XLIX and L

The MX Book of New Sherlock Holmes Stories

Edited by David Marcum

(MX Publishing, 2015-   )

Publishers Weekly says:

Part VI: *The traditional pastiche is alive and well . . . .*

Part VII: *Sherlockians eager for faithful-to-the-canon plots and characters will be delighted.*

Part VIII: *The imagination of the contributors in coming up with variations on the volume's theme is matched by their ingenious resolutions.*

Part IX: *The 18 stories . . . will satisfy fans of Conan Doyle's originals. Sherlockians will rejoice that more volumes are on the way.*

Part X: *. . . new Sherlock Holmes adventures of consistently high quality.*

Part XI: *. . . an essential volume for Sherlock Holmes fans.*

Part XII: *. . . continues to amaze with the number of high-quality pastiches.*

Part XIII: *. . . Amazingly, Marcum has found 22 superb pastiches . . . his is more catnip for fans of stories faithful to Conan Doyle's original*

Part XIV: *. . . this standout anthology of 21 short stories written in the spirit of Conan Doyle's originals.*

Part XV: *Stories pitting Sherlock Holmes against seemingly supernatural phenomena highlight Marcum's 15th anthology of superior short pastiches.*

Part XVI: *Marcum has once again done fans of Conan Doyle's originals a service.*

Part XVII: *This is yet another impressive array of new but traditional Holmes stories.*

Part XVIII: *Sherlockians will again be grateful to Marcum and MX for high-quality new Holmes tales.*

Part XIX: *Inventive plots and intriguing explorations of aspects of Dr. Watson's life and beliefs lift the 24 pastiches in Marcum's impressive 19th Sherlock Holmes anthology*

Part XX: *Marcum's reserve of high-quality new Holmes exploits seems endless.*

Part XXI: *This is another must-have for Sherlockians.*

Part XXII: *Marcum's superlative 22nd Sherlock Holmes pastiche anthology features 21 short stories that successfully emulate the spirit of Conan Doyle's originals while expanding on the canon's tantalizing references to mysteries Dr. Watson never got around to chronicling.*

Part XXIII: *Marcum's well of talented authors able to mimic the feel of The Canon seems bottomless.*

Part XXIV: *Marcum's expertise at selecting high-quality pastiches remains impressive.*

Part XXVIII: *All entries adhere to the spirit, language, and characterizations of Conan Doyle's originals, evincing the deep pool of talent Marcum has access to. Against the odds, this series remains strong, hundreds of stories in.*

Part XXXI: *. . . yet another stellar anthology of 21 short pastiches that effectively mimic the originals . . . Marcum's diligent searches for high-quality stories has again paid off for Sherlockians.*

Part XXXIV: *Mind-bending puzzles are the highlight of Marcum's fully satisfying 34th anthology, which again demonstrates that multiple authors are capable of giving Sherlock Holmes and Watson innovative mysteries to tackle while staying in character. Marcum's inventory of canonical pastiches shows no signs of being exhausted any time soon.*

An Investees' Anthology
Edited by David Marcum
(MX Publishing, 2022)

Selected Contributions to
The MX Book of New Sherlock Holmes Stories
by Members of
The Baker Street Irregulars

Edited by David Marcum
from MX Publishing

Imagination Theatre's Sherlock Holmes

The Further Adventures of Sherlock Holmes:
The Complete Jim French Imagination Theatre Scripts

Edited by David Marcum
from Belanger Books

Holmes Away From Home:
Adventures from The Great Hiatus
Volumes I and II

Sherlock Holmes:
Adventures Beyond the Canon
Volumes I, II, and III

Edited by David Marcum
from Belanger Books

Sherlock Holmes: Before Baker Street

Sherlock Holmes and Doctor Watson:
The Early Adventures
Volumes I, II, and III

Edited by David Marcum
from Belanger Books

After the East Wind Blows:
WWI and Roaring Twenties Adventures
of Sherlock Holmes
Volumes I, II, and III

The Nefarious Villains
of Sherlock Holmes
Volumes I and II

Edited by David Marcum
from Belanger Books

The Detective and the Clergyman
The Adventures of Sherlock Holmes and Father Brown

Edited by David Marcum
from Belanger Books

The Complete Solar Pons
by August Derleth

8-volume Paperback Edition

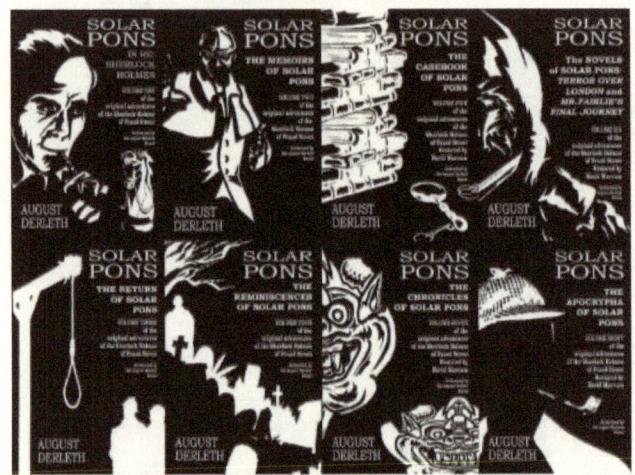

4-volume Hardcover Edition

Edited by David Marcum
from Belanger Books

The New Adventures of Solar Pons

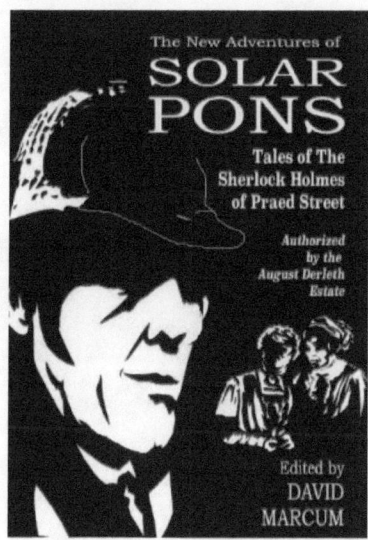

The Meeting of the Minds:
The Cases of Sherlock Holmes and Solar Pons

Edited by David Marcum
from Belanger Books

The American Adventures of Solar Pons

Edited by David Marcum
from MX Publishing

Sherlock Holmes in Montague Street
by Arthur Morrison
Sherlock Holmes's Early Investigations
Originally published as Martin Hewitt Adventures

Complete Hardcover Edition and Three-volume Paperback Edition

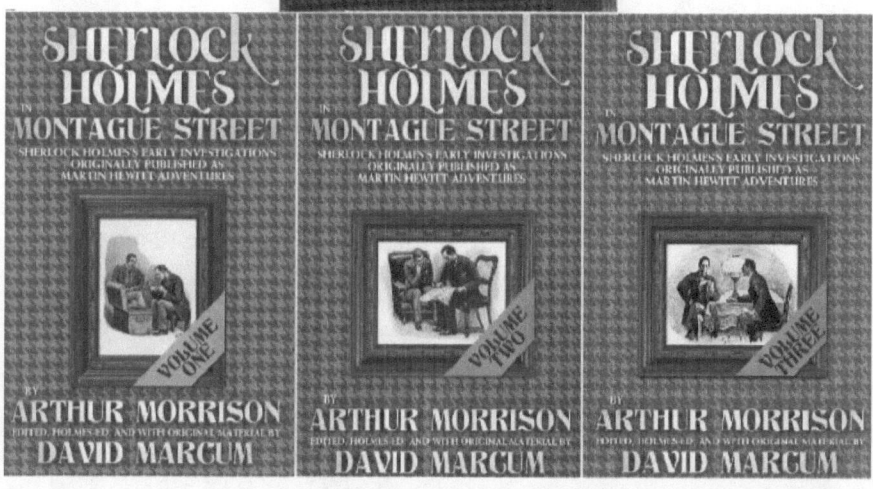

Edited by David Marcum
from MX Publishing

The Complete Dr. Thorndyke
by R. Austin Freeman
Volumes I-IX

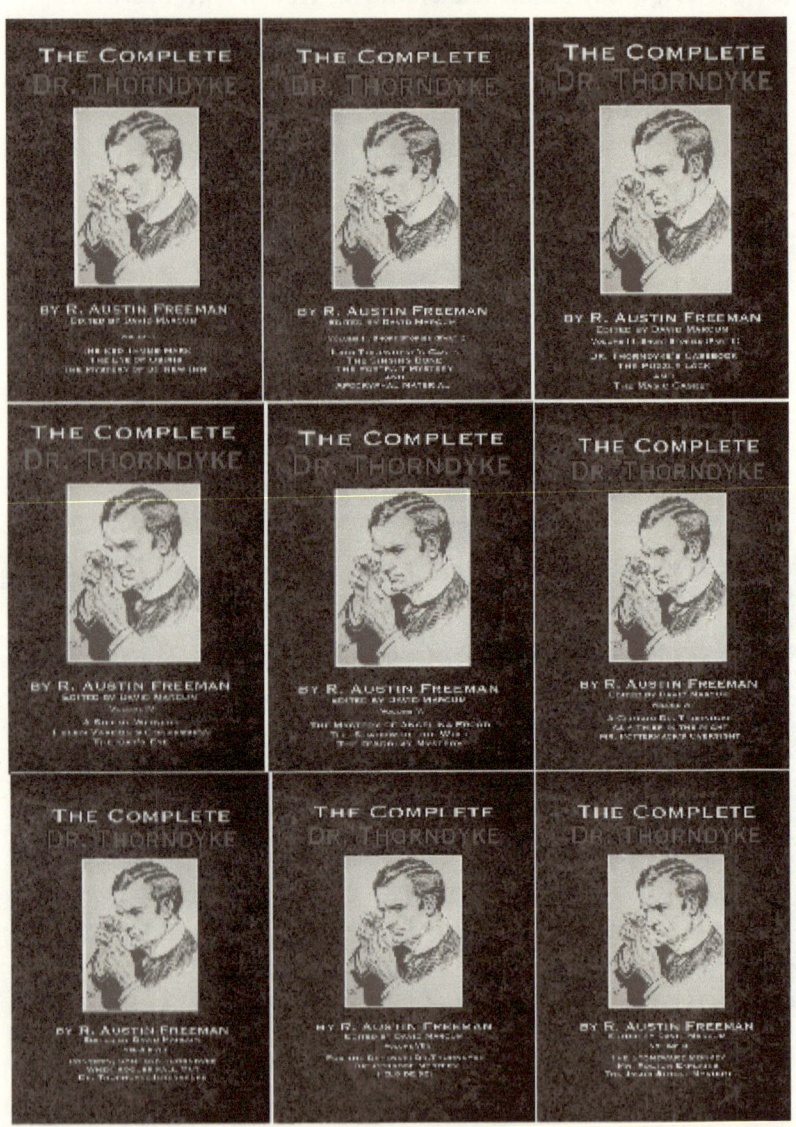

Edited by David Marcum
from MX Publishing

**A Proof Reader's Adventures of Sherlock Holmes
by Nick Dunn-Meynell**

**The Rediscovered Annals of Sherlock Holmes
Written by Terry Golledge
Curated by Niel Golledge**

Edited by David Marcum
from MX Publishing

Tales of Light, Shadow, and Darkness
by Tracy J. Revels

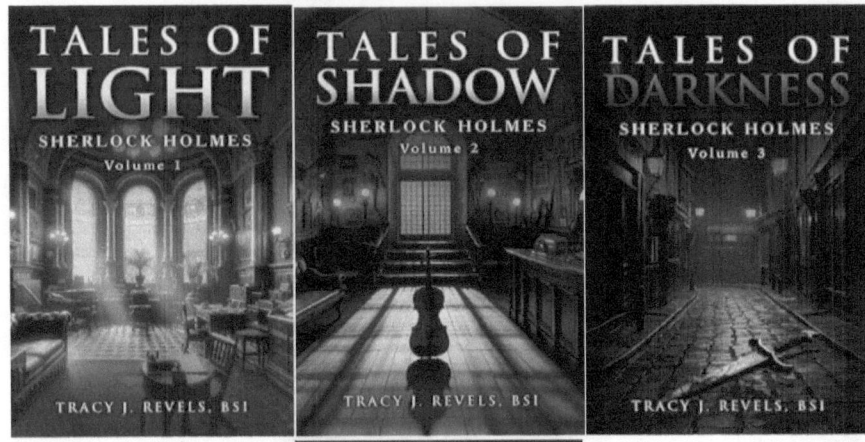

Edited by David Marcum,
Derrick Belanger, and Sonia Fetherston
from Belanger Books

Sherlock Holmes is Everywhere!

MX Publishing

MX Publishing is the world's largest specialist Sherlock Holmes publisher, with over six-hundred titles and over two-hundred authors creating the latest in Sherlock Holmes fiction and non-fiction

The catalogue includes several award winning books, and over four-hundred-and-fifty have been converted into audio.

MX Publishing also has one of the largest communities of Holmes fans on Facebook, with regular contributions from dozens of authors.

www.mxpublishing.com

@mxpublishing on Facebook, Twitter, and Instagram

9 781804 245842